BOB BLUNT, THE TRAVELLER.

"'HIP, HIP, HURRAH! I'M SOLE LORD OF TWENTY THOUSAND A YEAR,' CRIED BOB."

No. 1

Bob Blunt, the Traveller.

CHAPTER I.

THE LETTER—FAREWELL TO SCHOOL—BOB'S LITTLE JOKE—BLUNT CASTLE.

LETTER for you, sir, Mr. Blunt."

"Thank you, Fisher," said Mr. Bob Blunt, as the servant handed him an important-looking epistle in the schoolroom of Mr. Dashwood's Academy for the Sons of Gentlemen.

"May I read it, sir?" asked Bob of the principal, "for I think it looks as if it contained something important, or my prophetic soul is out in its reckoning."

Mr. Dashwood smiled assent, for Bob was a favourite and privileged pupil.

Bob broke open the letter.

He hastily read it.

It contained but a few lines, to the following purport :—

"Blunt Castle,
"Tuesday.

"MY DEAR SIR,—I regret to inform you of the death of the trustee to the property of Blunt Castle. Mr. Orm expired on Sunday, and the funeral obsequies are to take place Wednesday (to-morrow). You, my dear sir, as the heir to the property, are now your own master ; and therefore, no doubt, I may look for your speedy arrival here ; in the meantime believe me to be, my dear sir, your dutiful and obliged humble servant to command,

"JAMES SAWYER,
"Attorney and Agent to the Blunt
"Castle Estate.
"To Robert Blunt, Esquire,
"At Mr. Dashwood's,
"Gravesend."

Bob read this laconic epistle twice over, and then jumped up.

He handed the letter to Mr. Dashwood.

When that worthy gentleman had perused it, he said—

"Then we shall lose you, Blunt? I am sorry for it, for you have been a most promising and industrious pupil. I am proud of you. Now, my boy, I suppose you desire to depart at once?"

"I do, sir ; and thank you for all your kindness to me," replied Bob.

He left the room.

And Fisher, the man-servant, had soon packed a small hand valise with a few necessary articles.

The rest of the luggage Bob ordered to be forwarded to him to Blunt Castle.

Bob returned to the schoolroom—bade farewell to Mr. Dashwood and all the pupils, who wished him a hearty good-bye.

Then, accompanied by Fisher, he went to the office from whence the "Tantivy" coach started for Rochester.

Tipping the delighted Mr. Fisher with a piece of gold, Bob saw his name booked for Rochester, and at that moment the four horses were being harnessed to the coach.

Whilst our hero is waiting for his box seat let us take a peep at his appearance.

Bob Blunt was in his seventeenth year ; tall and muscular beyond his age—with a foot and hand that a dandy might envy.

His breadth across the chest was heightened by his slender waist ; added to this a face whose regular contour was expressive of good sense and intellect, and the reader has before him one of "Nature's noblemen."

When Bob looked at you with those clear grey-blue eyes of his straight in the face, and you noted the proud and decisive shape of his lips and chin you could but acknowledge that decision of character was closely knit with honesty of purpose.

Yet those eyes could laugh with irresistible humour, and Bob had a habit of running his hand through his crisp, curly brown hair when he was amused.

He had profited by his studies—had read extensively the works of ancient and modern authors, and his thoughtful mind had thus gleaned a fund of information which fitted him for the stern realities of life.

"Halloa, coachee! when are we going to start?" asked Bob, as a stout individual with a very red face, and his stumpy nether extremities encased in an abnormal pair of top boots, came up.

"'Mediately, sir; fine mornin', sir—fine a mornin' for a run with the 'Tantivy' as I seen this forty year."

"It is indeed—but halloa! who the dickens is this?" asked Bob.

A person somewhat of the same build as the coachman stepped forth from the hotel, and rolled—for it could not be called a walk—towards the coach.

His blue-bottle nose was filled with snuff, the refuse of the "pungent grains of titillating dust" depositing itself upon his ample shirt-front and silk-corded waistcoat.

"Who is it?" asked Bob again.

"Mr. Solomon Flint, tax collector," replied the coachman.

"Indeed! a very important personage, no doubt. I'll tackle him."

Mr. Flint now neared the coach.

A couple of waiters had brought a pair of steps to aid the unwieldy gentleman to mount the box.

Bob saluted him with mock politeness.

"Sir," he said, "may I ask if you are anybody particular?"

Mr. Flint's face assumed a deeper hue as he drew himself up.

He could hardly credit his ears.

He, Solomon Flint, to be asked whether he was anybody particular!

"Why all the world knows me, sir," he replied to our hero's question.

"Then pray, sir, will you inform a unit of the masses who and what you are, for I should very much like to know."

"My name is Solomon Flint."

"Indeed, I do not see much in it; in fact I don't like the name."

"Sir!" cried Mr. Flint, "you are very impertinent. John, help me up with the box."

Bob had preserved a gravity of demeanour that Mr. Flint could not understand.

Indeed, his understanding was not very clear, except to himself, for he was so wrapped up in his own dignity, that he did not see any shortcomings in himself.

The coachman, however, had very nearly choked himself with laughter, and it took a huge glass of brandy and water to preserve him from the consequences of his hearty merriment.

Bob seated himself by the side of the worthy Flint.

Away went the coach, rattling through the streets, and followed for some distance by a troop of shrieking boys.

Bob Blunt, as he passed the school he had so lately left, was greeted with a cheer from his fellow pupils, who lined the windows and road, eager to see the last of him.

"Belong there, sir?" asked the coachman.

"Yes, just left the place," said Bob, "and good luck to it."

And he began to declaim—

"Know ye that school, where the birch and the cane
  Are emblems much dreaded by mischievous boys?
For Dashwood delights in inflictions of pain,
  And considers a whacking the dearest of joys.
Where the hearts of the tutors are stony as flint;
  Where the tea is as weak as the water that's in it;
Where the beer is all sour, and life is a tomb,
  And mutton so tainted emits a perfume.
'Tis Dashwood's Academy, where I did dwell;
  But to-day I will bid it a lasting farewell."

"You're a poet, sir, I sees," said the coachman. "That's wery good, that is, 'ticlar that allusion to flint."

"Yes, I flatter myself it's neat, coachee. Halloa, sir, mind what you're up to."

These last words were addressed to Mr. Solomon Flint, who, in the act of applying a horn spoonful of snuff to his organ of smell, spilt it on his waistcoat, for our hero gave him a nudge on the elbow.

A slight wind blowing sent the snuff into Jehu's face and nearly blinded him.

"Now, then, sir, how am I to manage these 'ere cattle if you will—ashew !—send your—ashew !—confounded snuff into my—ashew !—heye ?" cried Jehu, in a rage.

Mr. Flint turned his bleared eyes upon our hero, and in a bass voice that sounded like distant thunder said solemnly—

"Look here, young man, you had better stow it. My name is Flint—don't forget, Flint."

"Indeed, what an awfully tough name, to be sure," said Bob ; "what a stony heart you must have."

"Well, sir, my name is Flint," cried the enraged tax-collector, "and snuff ——"

"Is my abomination," cried Bob, with a wink at the coachee.

"I tell you my name is Flint ; do you not know that name, sir ?"

"Why don't you say your name is Norval of the Grampian Hills, then I might be aware to whom I was speaking."

"He is a reg'lar grampus, puffing his snuff about—now, then, stow it," said the Jehu.

This last remark had reference to Mr. Flint, who, snuff box in hand, was diving into it with finger and thumb.

"Draw it mild, Norval," said Bob, giving Jehu a dig from behind Flint's back.

"Look here, young man, my aggrieved person will rebel against these constant attacks on my dignity," said Mr. Flint, drawing a deep breath, and inhaling the snuff.

A puff of wind came at that moment and sent the snuff again into Jehu's eyes.

"If you do that again, guv'nor, I'll drop you into the first horse-pond I come to, swop me if I don't," said the coachman, turning purple in the face ; and leaning towards the unhappy Mr. Flint, he spoke his words with a solemn gravity that made Bob roar again.

At this moment the "Tantivy" drew up at the first stage.

A commercial traveller got on to the roof with a good many packages.

Our hero ordered some brandy and water for the coachee, whose good-will he thus won, and refreshed himself with a glass of wine.

Away they went again through the fertile hills and dales of Kent.

The guard repeatedly made the echoes awaken with the cheery notes of the horn.

For a time Bob restrained his humorous inclinations, but at the foot of a hill one of the traces broke.

"Dash it all, that's unlucky. Bill, I'll have to get down. Look to the horses," said the coachman to the guard, and down he got.

So did Bob, and Mr. Flint.

The coachman took from a box beneath his seat a large packing needle, with some waxed twine.

He at once commenced to sew the broken trace, during which operation the portly Mr. Flint drew our hero aside.

"Sir," said Mr. Flint, thrusting his thumbs into the armpits of his waistcoat, "you asked me who I was ; I will inform you now."

"I shall be delighted to listen," said Bob.

"Well, then, sir, my name is Flint. I am churchwarden of two parishes, overseer of a third, a guardian of the poor, and one, sir—one, sir, whom all delight to honour."

"Lor'! now, who would have thought it? Well, you are a wonderful man!" cried Bob, with affected astonishment.

Mr. Flint, never dreaming how ridiculous he made himself, felt puffed up with his own importance, and continued—

"Yes, sir. Therefore it is fit that you should respect me. Being a guardian of the poor ——"

"The Lord have mercy on the poor!" ejaculated Bob, with sarcastic emotion.

"Exactly, sir. The Lord have mercy upon them. Now, sir, you see that you must pay me respect, for, as I surmise, you are in the mercantile line."

"You have hit it, sir. I am apprenticed to a linendraper," said Bob, with great gravity.

"Ah, young man, you must learn to pay homage to your betters. Life is made up of homage. I will receive yours."

"Thank you, my noble pal. Halloa, coachee, have you finished your job?"

"Yes, sir."

Whilst the coachman was fastening

the trace, Bob slyly possessed himself of the large needle.

Mounting the box, he raised the leather cushion and thrust the needle through it, so that it protruded the tenth part of an inch.

Mr. Flint mounted the box with the coachman, and, as he stood on the fly board, he began to extol the prospect that stretched out in green undulations before them.

"Wonderful!" ejaculated Flint. "This country of old England beats the world. Only a Tory and a churchwarden knows how to appreciate its beauties."

"Yes, it's very nice."

"Nice, sir ; nice is not the word—it's splendid! delightful!"

Down he sat.

But he quickly arose again.

"Oh! oh!" he roared.

"What's up now, guv'nor?" asked the innocent coachman.

"Oh, villain, it's you! Something has pricked me deeply here," cried Flint, clasping his hands behind him. "Oh! I bleed, I bleed!"

He hastily pulled up the seat.

There he discovered the packing-needle.

"Rascal! you have done this. I saw this needle last in your possession. As a tax-collector, churchwarden, overseer, and guardian, I resent this. Take that!"

And Mr. Flint launched out with his left, and struck the coachman full upon the nose, making the blood spurt out.

Bob Blunt was in ecstasies.

"Here, sir, hold the reins," shouted the coachman. "He swore that needle was in my possession last ; I defies him to prove it. Come down, you blackguard, come down, I say, or by the Lord Harry I'll spiflicate you. You won't? Take that!"

Mr. Flint, not being inclined to descend, received a blow on the os frontis that stretched him at his full length on the tail-board, where he lay snorting.

The coachman, thoroughly aroused, descended from the coach on perceiving our hero had possession of the reins, and that the horses were at a standstill, and then seeing that his fallen enemy had not descended, he seized him by the legs and brought him to the ground.

"You had that needle in your possession last, I swear it," cried Flint, now made desperate.

"You lie!" roared the coachman, taking off his coat and tucking up his sleeves. "Look at my nose. Come on, I'm ready for you."

"Go it, churchwarden," cried Bob.

"They're rum uns," said the traveller.

"They are. Now, fair play," shouted Bob, as he saw the coachman, with great energy, spar up to Flint.

"Coward! come on. Though I've seen three score, I'm not afeard on you, churchwarden though you be."

"I don't want to fight. You wounded me grievously in a tender part, and I shall have you locked up."

"Will you? How about my nose? Take that!"

The coachman sparred up to Mr. Flint, who, seeing his opponent meant mischief, stood on the defensive.

The bulky coachman could not recover his balance for a few seconds, so the churchwarden closed with him, and dealt him a stinging blow on the head.

It was a sight to see these two great men pommel each other.

Rage possessed them both.

One was up for the moment, then the other, until at last the coachman dealt the churchwarden so mighty a blow that the latter did not rise to time.

"It's all up," said Bob. "Now, then, have you had enough, or will you have a pinch of snuff and begin again?"

"I'll give him snuff if he wants it. I think I've settled him. Admit now that I didn't have the needle last," cried the triumphant coachman, kneeling down over his foe with raised fist.

"I don't know who it was, but perhaps it was the linendraper's apprentice," gasped the prostrate churchwarden.

"Oh! so you are about to saddle me with your iniquities, are you?" asked Bob from the top of the coach.

"I don't care who it was," replied the coachee ; "but it was you that punched my nose, so take that, churchwarden."

And the two stout pugilists went at it hammer and tongs again.

Bob, seeing they were fully engaged, winked at the commercial traveller and said—

"When gentlemen will quarrel, I, for one, think it best that they should be left to themselves. Guard! blow your horn, and gee-up, my beauties!"

The guard, who was seated behind above the rumble, blew his horn, and Bob started the horses with a gentle trot up the hill, being kept well informed of the movements of the two combatants by the commercial gentleman.

At first they did not notice the disappearance of the coach, but suddenly the fat coachee, looking up from beneath the churchwarden's arm, cried out—

"Halloa, they're off, by Jupiter!"

"Who are off?" gasped the churchwarden, wiping the dust from his face.

"The horses! That young gentleman has taken French leave on us. Stop, stop!"

But the more coachee cried "Stop," the faster did our hero drive.

"By Jove, he'll leave us behind; come on, churchwarden, let us run."

"What, up that hill!" cried Flint, aghast, vainly trying to open a damaged eye.

It was an edifying sight to see these two portly and elderly gentlemen training themselves to pedestrianism.

Our hero continued to turn round, whilst the commercial gent, highly elated, shouted out his encouragement.

Bob Blunt nearly fell off the seat, so greatly did he enjoy the fun; but when on the summit of the hill, he drew up his horses and awaited the arrival of the doughty champions.

"Well run, leathers, well done, churchwarden; that'll do your livers good," cried Bob, waving his whip to them.

"Let me get up, sir; I am regular blown. Oh, Lor'! I am busted," cried coachee.

"How is it with you, Flint? Ha, ha! when you were on the ground, Flint, you looked like a rolling stone," cried Bob.

That worthy could not reply; he could only gasp, and shake his fist at our hero.

"Well, I see you both want a little more exercise, so ta-ta for the present, my dear friends."

To the horror of the two stout gentlemen the coach started off once more.

There was no help for it.

The two fat men had to run after the coach, until, to their intense delight, it stopped at the second stage of the journey, a comfortable road-side inn, situated at the foot of the hill.

Bob and the commercial gentleman disappeared at once into the parlour.

"Here, waiter, bring us a couple of bottles of champagne, quick, and glasses for four; we must console those two, the churchwarden and the coachman," said Bob.

The commercial man grinned.

"When you get them on the box, offer them a cigar apiece," he said, handing our hero a couple of large regalias.

"I will. Halloa, here they are!"

The churchwarden and the coachman entered the room, steaming like racehorses.

"Welcome, gentlemen both. We were afraid we had lost you. Here, join us in champagne—here's your very good health," said Bob, filling their glasses.

The intense appreciation of fun that shone in our hero's eyes disarmed the storm of the coachman's wrath; but not so the churchwarden; he shook his fist at Bob, took a pinch of snuff to resuscitate himself, and dropped speechless into a chair.

Our hero, taking advantage of his helpless position, and filling a bumper of the wine, he poured it down the churchwarden's throat.

He gave a snort of satisfaction, and seeing this, Bob said—

"A joke, a joke! let us all be friends."

"I'm willin'," cried the good-natured coachman; "here's my fist, churchwarden."

"And here's mine."

They sat down quite amicably together, when the churchwarden suddenly whispered in a plethoric voice to the coachman—

"Don't you think the young man's been robbing his master's till?"

"Lor', now—why?" asked the coachee.

"I think so, and I'll tell him so. Young man, you have most cruelly used me, churchwarden Flint. I am wounded n a tender part, my eye is blackened, and I look an object for little boys to poke the finger of scorn at."

"You do look bad, poor thing," said Bob.

"But as you seem to be liberal with your money, may I ask whether it is honestly come by?"

Bob had overheard his remark to the coachee.

"I confess it is not," he said.

The three stared at him.

"There, didn't I say so?" cried Flint. "I am a great reader of human character."

Bob winked at the two, and they at once divined that he wished to deceive Flint.

"Come, gentlemen, drink up," said Bob; "see, the horses are ready."

They remounted, and were soon rattling along the road again.

"Have a cigar, gentlemen?" said our hero, handing the two to the coachman.

"Thank you, sir," he said, taking one.

"Have one, Norval?"

"No, young man; my conscience will not allow me to smoke a cigar procured dishonestly."

"But it's all right."

After much persuasion, however, the churchwarden was induced to accept it.

The two began puffing away to their heart's content, until they came in sight of a fine castle on the brow of a hill, some three miles the other side of Rochester.

"May I ask to whom that castle belongs, coachman?"

"Yes, sir, that's Blunt Castle, and it belongs to Robert Blunt, Esquire; I heard that he's just come into it."

"Lucky fellow," said Bob.

"Yes. A mile further on you will come to the lodge gates. It's a wonderful property, and I want to see the young squire myself; I understand he's a splendid fellow," said the churchwarden.

Bob was silent until he arrived at the aforesaid lodge, where he beheld a carriage and pair standing.

"Stop, coachman, I get down here."

"Wo, Nancy; you get down here, sir?" asked the astonished coachman.

"Yes—halloa, Buttons."

These words were addressed to a smart page boy, who was continually touching his hat.

"Knew you would come, sir; carriage is ready. Welcome, sir, Mr. Blunt, sir, welcome!" said Buttons.

"Good-bye, churchwarden," said Bob; "allow me to congratulate you upon the very wonderful way you discern character. Here, coachee, divide this five-shilling piece between you and the guard."

"Thank ye, your honour," said the coachee, touching his hat and looking astonished at Bob.

Bob got down from the box, and entered the carriage awaiting him.

The churchwarden never uttered a word, so completely taken aback was he.

With mouth wide open he stared after our hero.

"Why, that's Blunt of Castle Blunt. Oh, the idiot I am. What a very fascinating young gentleman to be sure," he cried.

"Wery, he's the right sort; look, he's looking at us. Halloa—murder!"

Bang!

Bang!

"Fire—fire!" roared the churchwarden. "What a very fascinating young gentleman, ha, ha!"

"I hope you like my cigars," cried Bob after them.

The commercial on the roof nearly choked himself with laughter, for he, being in the fancy goods line, knew the cigars to be explosive ones.

"What a very fascinating young gentleman, to be sure," said the reflective churchwarden, after he and the coachman had rid themselves of the sparks that covered them.

"He, he!" grinned Jehu. "Wot a great judge of character are you."

And with this, the coach rattled on to its destination.

CHAPTER II.

MR. SAWYER—THE WILL—PLANS FOR THE FUTURE.

IT was with feelings of delight that our hero drove through the park.

A drive of a mile brought him in sight of the castle.

It was built in the early Tudor style, with large towers and innumerable turrets.

As the carriage drew up at the marble vestibule, a little old gentleman, dressed in nankeens and a black dress coat, hurried down the steps to greet our hero.

"Welcome home, my dear sir : allow me to congratulate you," he said, extending his hand, which Bob shook heartily.

"Thanks, Mr. Sawyer."

Bob entered the hall.

A row of servants stood on each side of the hall.

Old suits of armour and swords with pictures of our hero's ancestors graced the walls, whilst the light, struggling through richly-stained glass windows, gave an air of proud solemnity to the scene.

Bob acknowledged the salutations of the servants, and then, followed by Mr. Sawyer and Buttons, he entered the dining hall of the castle.

This magnificent chamber somewhat resembled the vestibule.

Everywhere pictures, statues and armour were picturesquely placed.

"Welcome once more to the house of your ancestors, Mr. Blunt," said Mr. Sawyer. "You are now Blunt of Blunt Castle, and with your permission, sir, I'll produce your father's will, which we will read."

"That's it, my top Sawyer, you're a trump ; but when is the funeral of Mr. Orm to take place?"

"Mr. Orm died at his house, the Glen, and he will be buried to-morrow. He gave me this last will and testament of your late father, and his blessing for you."

"Poor old boy. Where is the will?"

"Here it is, sir."

He handed it to our hero.

"Shall I leave the room, sir?" asked Buttons.

"No, Buttons ; you may stay."

"Hurrah!" cried Buttons, who was possessed of an abundant flow of animal spirits, and devotedly attached to our hero.

Buttons was about fourteen years of age, slight in person, with a face that was always laughing, and a wonderful facility of standing on his head when anything made him particularly pleased.

He now watched our hero read the will with an anxious look.

Suddenly Bob gave a shout.

At this moment, the butler, the housekeeper, and several of the upper servants entered the room.

He jumped on a stool, and taking the will in his hand, he waved it over his head in triumph.

"Hip, hip, hurrah!" cried Bob ; "I'm sole lord of twenty thousand a year Buttons, you young dog, shout!"

"Hurrah!" cried the delighted Buttons. "Hurrah! I'm as happy as a king."

And at once his heels flew up in the air, and he stood on his head, clapping his feet together.

Mr. Sawyer could not help laughing to see the page boy standing on his head with joy.

Bob, when his excitement had somewhat cooled, jumped down from the stool, and taking Buttons by the heels, placed him panting in a chair.

"Yes, my dear sir." continued Mr. Sawyer, who was constantly putting a red silk handkerchief to his brow, "yes, you are now sole lord of yourself. By your father's will, he devises to you the whole of his property on the death of the trustee, Mr. Orm."

Bob shook the old man's hand.

"Thank you, my friend. You shall continue to manage my affairs as hitherto. I keep all the servants in my service. Now prepare me some luncheon."

The servants, with a loud shout of delight, withdrew.

"Buttons, my boy, you shall wait upon us. Now, sir, be seated."

The luncheon promptly made its appearance.

"My father," continued Bob, "dying when I was very young has, as you say, left me sole lord of myself at the age of seventeen. Now, sir, to be lord of oneself at this age is usually a heritage of woe. But that shall not be the case with me."

"I am very glad to hear it, sir. I know you possess a deal of good sense."

"Thanks for your good opinion. Buttons, fill our glasses again."

"Yes, sir."

"Here's to the memory of my dear father and mother," said Bob; "God bless them! I never knew my dear parents, but I have much to thank them for; and I will not betray the trust they reposed in me."

"What do you propose doing? A gentleman with such a fine fortune as you possess ought to be active," said Mr. Sawyer.

"Sir, I'll tell you what I intend to do."

"Go to college?"

"No. Listen. I will not participate in the senseless follies of the rich. In the great world I shall be courted for my wealth. If I go to college, I enter upon a career for which I have neither taste nor inclination. Besides, I can develop my education myself."

Mr. Sawyer was delighted with him.

"An ounce of practice is worth a pound of theory," continued Bob.

"True."

"And practice is only to be gleaned in the world at large."

"True, again," said Mr. Sawyer.

"Therefore, it stands to reason that I cannot become acquainted with the practical affairs of the world in a college."

"True, true."

"Listen, then. My mind is made up. I intend to travel. I will see the countries of the world. I will make a name for myself."

"Right and proper. You are a bold youth, and I agree with you," said Mr. Sawyer.

"I am glad you do. But to the point. You shall manage my affairs in my absence. I repose unlimited confidence in you, and from time to time you can inform me as to the property. But travel I will. Proud as I am of the name of Blunt of Blunt Castle, still I shall be prouder of another."

Bob charged his glass.

"What is the other?" asked the lawyer.

"I will ask you to drink success to the name I intend to win."

"With the greatest pleasure," said Mr. Sawyer, rising glass in hand.

Buttons gazed at them with open eyes.

"I will ask you to drink to the success——"

"Of who?" asked Mr. Sawyer, smiling.

"Bob Blunt, the traveller."

"Hip, hip, hurrah! Long life to Bob Blunt, the traveller."

The toast was drunk with three times three.

"Yes, my dear Mr. Sawyer," continued Bob, "I think it sounds well—Bob Blunt, the traveller; Blunt by name and Blunt by nature, that's me."

"And Blunt in pocket," said Mr. Sawyer, jocularly.

"Hear, hear!"

At this moment a deep sigh startled our hero. He looked round.

There was Buttons staring at him.

"Wake up, Buttons!" said Bob.

"Oh, master, won't you take me with you to foreign lands?" he moaned.

"Of course I will; you shall be one of my bodyguard," said Bob.

Buttons gave a shriek of delight.

So overjoyed was he that he danced

about the room, and in his usual way when pleased, stood on his head and clapped his feet together.

"Oh, I'm so happy, I'm to go with master, I'm to be a traveller, like Mr. Blunt, the traveller. Hip, hip, hurrah! I'm so happy."

"So am I," said Bob. "One more glass, Mr. Sawyer, to the success of Bob Blunt, the traveller."

CHAPTER III.

SEVERAL PERSONAGES ARE ADVERTISED FOR BY OUR HERO.

THE day after the funeral of the late Mr. Orm, which took place in a neighbouring parish, our hero returned with Mr. Sawyer to Blunt Castle.

"Look, my dear sir, what a splendid property this is," said the lawyer; "ten thousand acres of as fine land as any in England, bar none; and there is a castle. Look at the grey turrets, how fine and clear they stand out against the blue sky. 'Tis a paradise, and it seems a pity to leave so fine a place even to become a great traveller."

"True," said Bob, looking out of the carriage window, for they were driving through the park; "but my resolution is unalterable; some day I shall return to England and enjoy myself here, but for a few years I intend to be Bob Blunt, the Traveller."

Mr. Sawyer looked at the proud, resolute face of our hero, and saw unflinching determination written there.

"Yes," continued Bob, "and I shall want your advice as to my escort abroad. I have already thought over the sort of individuals I require, and you will be of material assistance to me in framing a suitable advertisement which I will have put in the papers at once."

"Good; I am ready," said the aged lawyer. "Ah, here we are."

The carriage drew up at the old hall door; the footman jumped down from the box, and our hero entered his house.

He did not, however, perceive two strange individuals lurking behind a laurel bush who intently watched his movements.

The one was a youth, who slouched his hat over his eyes, and held the cape of a long cloak over the lower part of his face.

The other was a burly man, with a thick bludgeon protruding from the pocket of his corduroy jacket, whilst a fur cap hung over his eyebrows.

"Is that the cove, guv'nor?" said this ruffian, pointing to our hero.

"That's him, Bill; mark him well, for you'll have to make his acquaintance some day or other," said the stranger with the slouched hat.

"I marks him, but halloa! we're hooked in the eye of that boy flunkey."

And in fact our young friend, Buttons, caught sight of them.

"We must not be observed," muttered the young stranger hastily. "Come on, Bill; I've a deep game to play, and discretion is the better part of valour."

"Course it are," said Bill.

And the two disappeared behind a splendid cypress tree that stood on one side of the lawn, and so into a shrubbery.

"Well, I'm blest," muttered Buttons; "those two chaps can't be up to much; I'll tell my master of this."

And Buttons reflectively entered his master's presence, and told him what he had seen.

"Hum!" said Bob Blunt, looking grave. "I noticed those two fellows at the park gates as I came through; I wonder who they are? And yet I thought the figure of one was familiar to me."

"Who did you suppose him to be?" asked Mr. Sawyer.

"Why, bad-tempered Dick Howard, my cousin."

"A bad fellow that, sir," said the lawyer.

"Yes, an evil-minded one; from his earliest years he was a brute. As a boy he delighted to torture poor dumb animals, and that alone shows an evil disposition. Of course, as I have not seen Howard for some years, I cannot be certain it was he."

"I should be wary of him, Mr. Blunt. As the next heir to this property, he will try to gain your position, and do you a mischief," said Mr. Sawyer.

"Pooh! sir, I don't fear him. Does the free eagle fear the serpent that crawls upon the ground? I love all the world; but if I see a reptile, sir, I put my foot on it and crush it."

And Bob ground his foot down on the carpet with a crash.

"That's it, sir," cried the elated Buttons, who, ever since our hero had promised to allow him to accompany him, was continually dancing a kind of polka, and changing the step by standing on his head, and clapping his feet. "That's it, sir, I am delighted with the idea. Going abroad. Oh! we shall cotch snakes there. Buttons is a made man. Hurrah! Who's afraid?"

"Quiet, Buttons; curb your exuberant spirits for a time," said Bob, good-naturedly, for Buttons was a privileged individual.

"Yes, master."

And Buttons stood on his head with joy.

"Now, Mr. Sawyer, we'll to business," continued our hero. "Buttons, bring writing materials."

Buttons obeyed, and placed them before the lawyer, who began to nibble a quill pen, whilst Bob, with his hands in his pockets, paced up and down the dining-hall.

At last he had made up his mind how to frame his advertisement, and pausing before Mr. Sawyer, he said, slowly—

"Write as follows, please."

"Ready," said Mr. Sawyer.

"Wanted by a gentleman of property about to travel—First—a gentleman of experience, well versed in languages, especially the native ones of Africa and America. medicine, natural philosophy and natural history. One with a diploma from an English or Scottish University preferred. He will be required to devote himself entirely to the advertiser, and most liberal terms will be given."

Bob paused.

"What do you think of that, sir?" he asked.

"Very wise of you. A doctor is a necessary companion to the traveller."

"And especially to Bob Blunt, the Traveller, to carry out his ideas. But to continue.

"'Secondly—Also wanted a gentleman amateur boxer, one capable of competing with a professional of acknowledged repute in the noble art of self-defence.'"

"Oh, my! ain't I glad just. First, there's the doctor to physic me if I'm ill, and the boxer to protect me if any big chap is going to whack me. I'll dance on my head with joy!" cried Buttons.

"Quiet, Buttons," said Bob, placing Buttons on his feet. "Now for the third.

"'Also a gentleman amateur runner, of a speed that can outlast the swiftest Indian.'"

"Hurrah, I shall get on his back if there's any row going on," muttered Buttons.

"Have you written that, Mr. Sawyer?" asked Bob, giving Buttons a gentle reminder to be quiet with a ruler.

"Yes, sir."

"Then fourthly——"

"What, any more?" cried the astonished lawyer. "Upon my word, you mean to have a very strong body-guard."

"I do, for I shall take all precautions against danger, for no doubt I shall meet with some amount during my travels. Now, fourthly—

"'Also a gentleman amateur wrestler, capable of throwing the strongest man. One who comprehends the Yorkshire fling preferred.'"

"Ha, ha! that's very good—Yorkshire fling. Any more?" laughed the lawyer.

"Yes. And fifthly—

"'Also a gentleman of powerful sight. He must be of an observant nature, and note everything in the country through which he travels. He will be required to compete with a practised scout, and be generally——"

"Up to the very knocker!" chimed in the irrepressible Buttons. "Hurrah!"

"Quiet," said Bob.

"I beg pardon, master."

"'Generally the advance guard of the party he accompanies. One used to Indian warfare and a good shot preferred,'" continued Bob, finishing the sentence that Buttons had interrupted.

"Any more?" asked Mr. Sawyer, when he had finished writing.

"No, I think that will do. Now I will conclude as follows—

"'None but those of acknowledged abilities need apply. All personal expenses will be allowed, as well as outfit, etc. Testimonials to be sent by the 16th of March to James Sawyer, Esq., solicitor, Rochester, and the applicants are requested to present themselves on the 18th of the same month, for a personal interview, to Robert Blunt, Esq., of Blunt Castle, by Rochester, Kent. N.B.—No agents need apply.' Now, that's the ticket, I think, sir," cried Bob, when he had concluded.

"Yes, if you are fortunate, your bodyguard will be a great protection to you. Now, my dear sir, I wish to ask you where you intend to go to," said the lawyer, leaning his arms on the table and looking at our hero.

"That's just what I was thinking about as you mentioned it," replied Bob.

"Well, have you made up your mind?"

"No, but I'll soon settle the point. Here, Buttons go and fetch your hat."

"Yes, master. Oh, I'm so happy."

And Buttons shot out of the room and soon returned with his hat.

"Now," said Bob, "I'll see to what part of the globe my destiny sends me—to any country save Europe, where I shall be bored out of my life by a lot of sycophants, who are ever ready to prey upon the youth born to wealth. I wish to keep my fine constitution unimpaired, and therefore London and all its enervating pleasures may go to the dogs for me."

"Oh master, I'm so glad! I'll follow you to the death. My father and mother died in your noble father's service, and

Buttons knows no other parent than the great traveller, R. Blunt, Esq."

Buttons drew up for want of breath.

Yet to display how very much he was delighted and gratified at Bob Blunt, Esquire's confidence in him, and also, perhaps, to prove his gratitude, he stood on his head once more, and finished by walking round the room on his hands.

When the laughter that Buttons caused had subsided Bob continued—

"Now, Buttons, give me your hat.

Our hero then took several pieces of paper, wrote on them the names of different countries, and placed them in the hat.

"Now, Buttons, my good boy, take the hat, shake it up, and whatever name Mr. Sawyer draws first, there will I steer my barque."

"Do you mind which way I shake the hat up, master?" asked Buttons.

"Not in the least."

"Then I will do it my own way. Up we go, and good luck to us. Hurrah for a traveller's life!"

And Buttons most dexterously stood on his head, took the hat up with his feet, and shook it well.

Mr. Sawyer then put his hand in the hat and drew out one of the papers.

Buttons turned a somersault and alighted on his feet.

"Open the paper sir," cried Bob.

Mr. Sawyer did so.

"What is the country?"

"Africa."

"Hum! Not the healthiest place in the world to be sure," said Bob, "but it will do; but there is plenty of sport to be found there."

"And you intend to go there?"

"I do, decidedly. Let me see."

And Bob took up the map.

"West coast of Africa—Cape Coast Castle; lately a Dutch settlement, now in possession of the English. That's the spot where I intend to land," he said, attentively examining the map before him.

"Then you will go to visit the Ashantees?" said Mr. Sawyer.

"Ashantees! Africa! Oh, my eye! I'm a-going to see furrin par'   .eality," cried Buttons. "I hope   .on't eat me ; but then there'll be the doctor, the boxer, the runner, the wrestler, and the man that can tell the time by the church clock at a mile, to protect me, not counting my brave and noble master."

"Quiet, Buttons ; you talk too much. Mr. Sawyer I will go to Ashanti. As the paper has turned up the name, so let it be."

And Bob closed the map-book with a bang, as if his mind were made up.

"And when do you propose to start ?"

"As soon as I have engaged my escort, and the necessary outfit can be prepared for all of us," said Bob.

"How shall I be dressed, master ?" asked Buttons, very anxiously.

"You shall not be dressed at all, but shall go in your natural clothes.

"What are they ?"

"Your skin shall be painted a bottle green, with bright intervening streaks of red and gold," said our hero, very seriously.

"Lor', master, what, no clothes on ? You don't mean that ?" cried the astonished Buttons, opening his eyes very wide.

"I do, though."

"Oh, why, I shall be a regular savage ; it ain't Christian. Oh, what'd my poor mother say ? But do all the people dress or undress like that there ?"

"All," said Bob.

"Then I'd rather stay at home, sir."

"What, are you afraid to follow my fortunes ? I thought better of you, Buttons, I did, indeed," said Bob.

"Oh, master, forgive me ; flay me alive, but don't leave your Buttons behind. I'll go with you to the world's end, wear anything that you like, or nothing at all," exclaimed Buttons.

"Now, sir, to Ashanti I will go first," continued Bob. "I will try to work my way into the heart of Africa, and if possible, discover the mystery of ages— I mean the source of the Nile. This much I will say : if energy, pluck, and endurance can accomplish it, Bob Blunt will explore the vast continent of Africa in the interests of mankind, and the progress of civilisation."

"And a noble object that is. Now, sir, what shall I do first ?" asked the lawyer.

"First, you will have that advertisement inserted in the columns of the daily newspapers ; next, when you receive the testimonials from the applicants, you will write to each of them and make it known to them that I shall not use their names," replied Bob.

"Not use their names ? How on earth will you distinguish them one from the other ?"

"Easily," responded Bob, "for I shall christen them myself."

"Ha, ha! I see," cried the old lawyer.

"Good ; you can write to one of the best outfitters in London and ask him to send a man down to take our orders," said Bob.

"I will do so. And from time to time I will keep you informed as to your affairs here whilst you are in——"

"Ashanti, my dear sir," said Bob, shaking the worthy man by the hand.

"In Ashanti then, where Robert Blunt, Esquire, will be found."

"No, not Esquire, but Bob Blunt, the Traveller," said Bob.

"Hurrah! I'm so happy," exclaimed Buttons, once more elevating his heels in the air. "I'm going to Ashanti. Lor', I'm the biggest chap in the world, for I'm going to Ashanti among tigers, monkeys, and oh, Lor', I don't know what."

And so delighted was he with this novel prospect, that during the remainder of the day he did nothing but wander about the mansion, walking on his hands, astounding the servants by muttering the word "Ashanti," until the old butler swore that the boy had Ashanti on the brain.

CHAPTER IV.

AN UNWELCOME VISITOR—THE ATTACK—BUTTONS TO THE RESCUE, IN WHICH HE

PROVES HIS PROWESS—PRIDE UNEXPECTEDLY HAS A FALL.

ON the afternoon of the following day, Robert Blunt, Esquire, had returned from a visit to his tenants, and was seated in the fine banqueting-room of the castle, reading a book of travels, when the door opened, and Buttons ushered in a visitor.

Bob started.

It was the same person he had seen at the park gates on the previous day.

Bob arose from his chair and faced his visitor, saying—

"Whom have I the pleasure of addressing?"

"Don't you recognise me, Robert Blunt?" replied the stranger, taking off the broad-brimmed hat he wore.

"Richard Howard!" cried our hero, starting back a pace.

"The same. And I call upon you as your kinsman, and the next heir to this property—providing you die childless—to ask you if you will allow me to live in want whilst you are living in the lap of luxury?"

Howard paused.

He eyed his young kinsman keenly, but if he had been a reader of character, he would have augured ill for his mission, for there was an ominous frown on our hero's face that was hardly to be mistaken.

Besides, the tone and manner that Howard assumed were absolutely repugnant.

"What do you want of me?" asked Bob, sternly.

"Money," was the laconic answer.

"Hum! a good many persons want that," replied Bob, drily.

"And they generally don't get it; but I intend to get it."

"Indeed?"

"I do. Allow me to help myself to a glass of wine?"

Howard coolly drew a chair up to the table and helped himself.

"Very good port, I know there is a goodly quantity in the cellars of the castle. My late uncle, your father, was a fine judge."

Bob was silent.

Yet, by his clenched hand and set teeth, passion was inwardly burning, and it wanted but a little to make the storm burst.

"I suppose now that you have come into this fine property, cousin, you will launch out a bit into life. I can put you up to a trick or two in town, and young fellows like you ought to see life and spend money," said Howard.

"Do you think that I will waste my patrimony like you, amongst card-sharpers, and other blacklegs? No, when you see that day call Bob Blunt a liar and a fool. I will none of you."

It was a noble sight to see the fine young lad's scorn as he spoke.

His whole soul revolted against the idea of becoming an associate of the men with whom his cousin was on intimate terms.

"Hoity toity! Why, we have here a version of Don Quixote. When will your worship set out on your tilting tour?" answered Howard.

But Bob kept his temper.

"Listen to me, Richard Howard. I know you thoroughly, as I said before; your career has been one of vice, even though you have not yet attained to years of manhood. You have squandered your substance amongst profligates, and now you come here asking me for money. I flatly refuse to give you any."

A dark scowl loomed on the brow of the schemer.

His eyes flashed fire.

He drew a deep breath, then asked in a voice husky with rage—

"Do you wish to insult me, cousin?"

"No; I wish to turn you from your evil courses."

"Look here, I did not come here to be preached at. If you don't want to see life I do. I ask you to advance me a sum of money; you have plenty and to spare."

"That is no reason why I should desire to see it thrown into the gutter."

"How?"

"Because it will only help to feed your vices. No, sir, there are thousands of more deserving persons in the world than you, and I think it will be more beneficial to give it to them than to you."

"You refuse me then?" hissed Howard.

"I do."

Howard could not see the fixed determination of Bob's manner, so he put on a hypocritical whine, which was even more repulsive than his bullying style.

"Look here, cousin, you won't leave me in the lurch. I'm really hard up now. Duns pestering me everywhere. I have only a paltry three hundred a year left; not enough, is it, to keep a dog alive?"

"Many worthy and deserving persons have to live on less, and I don't see why you should not," said Bob.

"Hark you, Robert Blunt, I am a desperate man; give me a cheque, or it will be the worse for you."

"To squander? No."

Howard rushed to the door.

"Bill!" he cried.

In another second the burly ruffian entered the room.

He was a man of prodigious strength.

His broad chest, bull neck, and long, muscular arms seemed out of all proportion with his low stature, which was balanced on a pair of bow legs, that won him the appellation of Bow-legged Bill.

To this ruffian Howard beckoned.

"Muzzle this young cub," he said, pointing to Bob, who had sprung to his feet.

Our hero stood on the defensive, although he did not dream that Howard would dare attack him in his own house.

"Right yer are, guv'nor," cried Bill.

"Now, Mr. Blunt, you shall repeat your words."

Howard advanced towards Bob.

He rushed at him, but was met with a blow on the nose that made the blood spurt out freely.

Howard recoiled from the blow Bob had given him.

Bow-legged Bill, however, advanced to the front, and doubling up his fists, rushed at our hero, who met this fresh attack by felling the bully with a chair.

Down went Bow-legged Bill.

"Come on, ye curs," cried Bob, now thoroughly aroused; "come on! You shall see what a boy fresh from school can do."

"I will show you what I can do; take that," cried Howard.

And he again aimed a blow at Bob, which would have decided the fight, had not our hero dexterously stepped back and thus made Howard fight the air, lose his balance, and fall forward.

As he fell forward, Bob struck him a tremendous blow in the mouth.

Howard fell back on the carpet.

At this moment, Bow-legged Bill managed to scramble to his feet.

Half-dazed by the blow he had received from the chair, he was collecting his scattered senses, when he beheld his patron lying at his length on the floor, and our hero standing over him in the act of repeating the dose he had already given.

"Halloa! I'm a-coming, master," he shouted.

He was about to rush forward, when the door was thrown open and Buttons made an appearance, breathless.

The page at once saw the state of affairs.

In the corner of the room stood a large bass-viol.

Buttons, before he well knew what he was doing, seized it by the upper part with his two hands, swung it round in a semicircle, and brought the body of the instrument with a crash upon Bow-legged Bill's head, thus effectually impeding that worthy's further progress.

With such force did the bass-viol crash down, that the bow-legged gentle-

"'I'VE GOT YOU NOW, AND I MEAN TO KEEP YOU,' CRIED THE VICTORIOUS BUTTONS."

man's closely-cropped head protruded through it.

"I have got you now, my beauty, and by the soul of the fiddler's cat, I mean to keep you," cried the victorious Buttons. "Hurrah! how do you like it, old boy?"

With that, he began to pull the captured bully about, and the broken edges of the viol gave excruciating pain to the throat of the captive, who could not effect his release.

In the meantime, Bob Blunt had not been idle.

Howard had sprung up, and Bob again rained a shower of blows upon him till that worthy was compelled to cry for quarter.

"Get up, you cur," cried Bob, giving his prostrate foe a kick.

With a groan, Howard obeyed.

Then our hero, despite his anger, could not control his laughter at the very ridiculous position of Bow-legged Bill.

"What shall I do with him, master?" asked Buttons, swinging him round.

"Drag him into the hall."

"Right, sir. Come along, my beauty."

"Now, sir, go," said Bob to Howard, pointing to the door; "and beware how you cross my path again."

Without a word, the crestfallen and vanquished schemer quitted the hall.

When at the head of the marble steps, he raised his clenched fist, and with a look of savage rage, heightened by the deadly glare of hatred that gleamed in his eyes, he cried out, huskily—

"Robert Blunt, beware; from this day we are sworn foes. I will have my revenge. I can wait for it, but have it I will. Curse you. I will have my revenge, if I follow you to the end of the world."

Then, with a howl like to a wild beast's, he rushed down the steps, and disappeared down the avenue, not waiting for his ally, who still remained a prisoner in the bass-viol.

"Let that fellow go," said Bob, turning to Buttons.

"The villain; he was going to kill you, sir, and injure me for life," said Buttons.

"How injure you?"

"Why, he was going to kill you, sir,

and then I should not go to Ashanti land. Oh! how miserable I should have been."

And Buttons gave the bully another swing round.

Bob laughed.

His good humour was quickly restored to him now that he had foiled the machinations of his villainous cousin.

"Let the fellow go, Buttons."

"It's all very well, sir, to say let him go, but his head is as securely fixed in this here musical instrument as in a dog's collar. A very musical noise he's making, isn't he? Play up a little louder, bully. Go it, my beauty."

In truth, Bow-legged Bill was howling dismally, and pleading to be set at liberty.

"A nice musical instrument, isn't he, sir? I think I'll take out a patent for it. It'll beat the barrel-organs into fits, and I might realise a comfortable fortune by it, only I'm going to Ashanti," said Buttons, who continued to swerve the viol on Bill's neck.

"Let me go; you're cutting my head off, you are," cried Bill.

"Let him go," said Bob.

"As you managed to get your head through, I suppose you can manage to get it out again, unless it's twice the size which it ought to be."

With much pulling, Bow-legged Bill's bullet head was at last extricated from the viol.

But not without causing severe pain on the face of the bully did Buttons succeed in liberating him.

He presented a most abject appearance to the lookers-on, for a dozen servants had crowded into the hall.

"Now, look here, fellow; I let you off this time in consideration of him who employed you," said Bob; "but I doubt whether I am not acting wrongly in not handing you over into the hands of the police."

"Oh, sir, let me off; I'll never come here again if I knows it. I have had enough of it to last me a life time," said Bow-legged Bill with a whine, and wiping the blood from his lacerated neck and head.

"And serve you right too. Now, go."

"Go!" shouted Buttons, taking up the bass-viol again.

With a bound Bow-legged Bill made for the steps, followed by Buttons

So terrified was the ruffian, for fear of coming within reach of the terrified instrument again, that he took the steps two at a time, and looking back, he saw Buttons following close upon his heels, so he quickened his pace, lost his footing, and rolled precipitately down the steps.

At that moment a very portly and dignified gentleman was about to ascend to the hall.

So wrapt up was he in his own importance that he held his head aloft, saw not the figure of Bow-legged Bill before him, and lo! the magnificent gentleman measured his length upon the steps.

With a howl Bow-legged Bill extricated himself from the heap of flesh above, and fled as fast as his bow legs could carry him, glad to get away so cheap.

Meanwhile the important personage's arrival had not been quite unobserved by Bob Blunt.

But when Mr. Churchwarden Flint—for it was he—suddenly was prostrated on the steps, Bob could scarcely contain his laughter.

He, however, contrived to bottle it up, and ran to Mr. Flint's assistance.

"Mr. Flint, this is an unlucky affair," he said ; "but the ruffian who was the cause of it has already been sufficiently punished. Come in, my dear sir."

Mr. Flint arose with a groan.

The knees of his trousers were split, his shins bruised, his shirt rumpled, and his shiny hat bulged in.

"Sir—Mr. Blunt, excuse me, I did not count upon this. I, Solomon Flint, am not now in a state to enter an English gentleman's princely mansion. Oh, dear ! I think I am hurt," said the churchwarden.

"Pooh ! you take matters too seriously. Come in and have a glass of wine."

Mr. Flint was soon seated in a comfortable armchair.

"Mr. Blunt," he began, "since the day I had the great honour of meeting you, my feeling soul," here the churchwarden placed a huge red hand over his heart, "my feeling soul has been lacerated with the idea that I was guilty of the most rude behaviour to you. Therefore I have come to apologise in person."

Here the churchwarden arose and made a bow, the dignity of which was not enhanced by the rents in the knees of his trousers, and a slight contusion near the corner of the right eye.

"Don't mention it, sir."

"Sir," continued Flint, "you are a great landed proprietor. I would therefore beg of you to recommend me to the honour of a seat amongst the unpaid magistracy of the said county."

Mr. Flint paused.

Bob's ire was great.

"Mr. Flint, you make a great mistake. I possess no influence at all with the lord-lieutenant."

"Pardon me, sir, but you will see the great gift of natural eloquence I possess fits me for that position. Ahem !"

Here Mr. Flint looked hard at Bob.

"Sir, I do not know the lord-lieutenant, neither do I desire to know him. If you feel yourself fitted for the post, which I do not profess to doubt, your own individual merits will raise you to the post."

"Sir, will you not give me a letter of recommendation to the lord——"

"No, sir ; in a few days I shall sail for Africa, and perhaps not return for years," replied Bob.

"Africa ! What, with your wealth ?" And Mr. Flint raised his two hands as if Bob had committed sacrilege."

"Yes, I hate to be toadied ; good morning, sir. Buttons, show Mr. Flint the door."

Mr. Flint arose, bowed, and walked out of the room as in a dream, ejaculating—

"Africa ; oh Lor' ; the world is mad. Had I his money ! Africa, Africa ; oh, Lor', if I had his money !"

And he continued muttering this all the way home.

"Buttons, whenever any one like the churchwarden seeks an interview with me, refuse him. I will not favour a lot of fellows who seek to crawl into power on other people's shoulders, for I hate all toadies."

And bravely did Bob Blunt keep his word, resolving to fly from Europe quickly, and seek knowledge and adventure as a traveller.

He knew full well that he would have to endure privations and encounter dangers, but that knowledge did not cause him to hésitate one moment.

For what true Boy of England was ever deterred by fear?

CHAPTER V.

THE PERSONAGES ADVERTISED FOR ARRIVE, AS WELL AS ONE NOT ADVERTISED FOR.

ON the morning of the 18th March, Mr. Sawyer entered the dining-hall of Blunt Castle.

The young heir was seated in a chair poring over the books on Africa with which he had supplied himself.

He looked up as Mr. Sawyer entered.

"News, Mr. Blunt. I have the testimonials from the gentlemen you wish to engage for your travelling companions."

"I am glad to hear it, for I am anxious to start on my travels. I trust they are all brave and good men."

"Yes, I think you will find them all you can wish for your body-guard. They will arrive to-day at twelve o'clock."

"Let me see ; it wants ten minutes to the time,"said Bob, looking at a large bronze time-piece on the mantel.

"Look here sir," replied Mr. Sawyer ; "we will have them in one at the time, the learned gentleman first. Halloa! they're here."

"Well, Buttons?" said Bob, as the youth entered.

That hero, for since his treatment of Bow-legged Bill he had justly considered himself one, entered the room with a grin on his facile physiognomy.

"There are six gentlemen a-waiting to see you, sir," he said.

"Six!" cried Bob, "Why, I thought five were the requisite number."

"There are six, sir, although the sixth is but half a man," replied Buttons.

"You had better go and interview them, Mr. Sawyer. Mind you, the doctor first."

Mr. Sawyer left the room.

He found six gentlemen sitting in the ante-room looking at each other, each wondering who and what the other was.

He soon found out the learned man, and at once ushered him into our hero's presence.

When the door opened, Bob beheld a little man of about five feet five making his bow to him.

"Sir," said Bob, "I suppose you are a gentleman well acquainted with the languages and sciences that I require ?"

"My testimonials," said the doctor, for such he was, "are——"

"Enough, sir ; I am satisfied with them," said Mr. Sawyer.

The little man bowed.

"My name, sir," continued the doctor, "is——"

"Pardon me," said Bob ; "one of my stipulations is that I do not require to use your real name."

The doctor bowed.

He was bordering on fifty.

In person he was slight, and, as we have said, of medium height.

His countenance was of a mild, almost child-like expression.

After consulting with Mr. Sawyer, Bob approached him.

"Doctor, I am satisfied with your testimonials ; you will suit me to a T, and no doubt we shall get on well together. All affairs of cash will be arranged by Mr. Sawyer."

An expression of intense relief came over the doctor's face.

A heavy weight had been taken off his mind, for be it known that the doctor was very poor.

So when Bob shook him by the hand, he arose and stammered——

"You accept my services, sir ?"

"Yes."

"Oh, I am so happy. Rely upon my best powers, for they shall be dedicated to your service."

"I believe you; for the present take a seat and help yourself to wine."

The learned man took the chair proffered him, drew his knees up, and helped himself to an abstemious glass of wine and water.

"Now, Buttons, show in the gentleman professor of the noble art of self-defence at once," said Bob.

"Yes, sir."

Presently Buttons introduced a man of about twenty-five years of age, dressed in a rough pilot coat.

The boxer, for such he was, had a red face, clean shaved, clear merry blue eyes, short hair, and a pair of fists that would have done honour to a blacksmith, so large and sinewy were they,

"Mr. Blunt, sir," cried Buttons, ushering in this formidable person. "Sir, the gentleman who knocks 'em down, and doesn't pick 'em up again. The gentleman who plays at skittles with mankind in general."

Bob smiled.

"My young friend here has exactly described my character, sir. I have been in the army for seven years, but owing to my having once fought the drum-major, two corporals, and a sergeant-at-arms before breakfast in the barrack-square, and having politely left them to be carried home on a shutter, I am now free to roam the wide world, the authorities having ill-naturedly requested me to send in my papers. I should have like to have had it out man to man with the War Office, but they would not fight."

"That is no drawback with me," said Bob; "I think you suit me. Mr. Sawyer, this gentleman's testimonials, are they correct and good?"

"Satisfactory. What the gentleman says is true. One of the papers tells me that he is the greatest amateur boxer in England."

The gentleman was asked to take a chair and have some wine.

"Excuse me, but if you have such a thing as a pot of porter in the place it would be more acceptable. I always make a practice of breakfasting upon a semi-broiled beefsteak and a pot of porter."

Bob laughed, and ordered the porter, whilst Buttons was sent to introduce the wrestler.

"This gentleman is up to the Yorkshire fling, being a high-falutin way of coming down a cropper on your back," cried Buttons.

The gentleman introduced was a short, thick-set person, with remarkably broad shoulders, a face expressive of dogged determination, whiskerless, and as smooth as a girl's.

He stood like Hercules, firm as a rock, upon his well-shapen legs.

"I am a wrestler, sir," he said. "In the whole of the North country I have held my own, which my papers will prove. Recently I have been an attorney-at-law; but that profession is disgustingly mean, and not alive to anything but shifty tricks."

"That's not complimentary to your profession, Mr. Sawyer," said Bob, smiling.

"I pardon the noble wrestler; this not being a personal allusion but a professional one. I have a professional duck's back from which it will run," replied Mr. Sawyer with a smile.

"Most of your brethren have the same, sir; but I will continue. I had a case of disputed possession to a house. My brother attorney on the opposite side floored me. I then told the judge that, with his permission, I would wrestle the aforesaid attorney for possession of the premises. But the judge rebuked me, as I placed the aforesaid attorney on his back in open court."

Mr. Sawyer laughed heartily.

"Well, every man to his trade. I think you will be suited now as one of my body guard," said Bob.

"I hope so, sir."

"Take a chair."

The wrestler sat down, the doctor making room for him and gazing at him with awe.

"Now show in the next gentleman," said Bob.

Presently Buttons introduced a tall, thin man, with a very lean face, dressed in very tightly fitting frock coat.

He had a pair of very long legs.

His face was elongated, whilst a heavy brown mustache covered his mouth.

"The gentleman who can beat the 'Flying Dutchman' hollow," said Buttons.

"Not quite, sir, but very nearly," said the runner. "Sir, I'm a Cambridge man, took my degree, sir, M.A. Became an usher in a school; drat it, not active enough; gave it up, and desire a situation."

"I have one for you, then. I think by your build you are a good runner."

"Sir, I may nearly say I was born running, drew in swiftness with my mother's milk, sir; run twenty mile with anyone."

"That will do; take a seat, sir."

The runner sat himself down by the side of the wrestler.

"Now, Buttons, bring the next gentleman that wishes to serve me in my travels."

Buttons soon ushered in an extraordinary-looking personage with the announcement—

"The gentleman who can see through a mile stone, or behind the moon on a foggy night."

"That is a long distance; now, sir, I have looked through your papers, and they are satisfactory in the extreme," said Mr. Sawyer.

"I am glad to hear it, sir," replied the gentleman, seating himself.

He was a man of thirty, with eyes of a sleepy black, not speaking of the "melting soul," but rather of a cool penetration, whilst his countenance was of that colour which Europeans have in tropical climes.

"Now," said Bob, when he had assured himself that all the testimonials were satisfactory. "Now, gentlemen, I am going to put you on a trial of skill; come."

"Sir, there is the half of a man with a big head still waiting to see you," said Buttons.

"Fetch him, Buttons," said Bob.

"Yes, sir."

And presently Buttons ushered in a dwarf of such a very diminutive stature that Bob was astonished.

Save for his head, which would have suited a giant, there was nothing abnormally ugly about him, yet the muscular thickness of his neck denoted great strength, and his arms were long and sinewy.

His face was refined and pleasing, whilst his eyes brimmed over with laughing mischief which was irresistibly comic.

Bob was attracted at once.

The little man made a bow to our hero, and said—

"Sir, I know you did not advertise for one of my stature, but I am without friends, and possessing a musical talent, I thought you might desire one of my qualities as a faithful companion."

Bob determined to engage the dwarf.

"My friend," he said, "I think I can find room for you in my body guard; in the meantime you can accompany me."

The delight of the dwarf was extreme.

He cut such capers as Bob shook him by the hand that our hero laughed till the tears ran down his eyes.

After which the dwarf brought forth a large trombone from the ante-room and began to play first a wild, melancholy air, and then he broke into a "louder and a longer strain," a burst of merry music that charmed every one.

"Bravo! Now, gentlemen, follow me."

Bob led the way through several passages until they reached a meadow at the back of the house, where there were three men awaiting them, who were a professional runner, boxer, and wrestler.

Bob had ordered them to attend in order to test the powers of the candidates.

"Now, gentlemen, you will be pleased to try your powers. Mr. Boxer, you first."

"Eh!" said the ex-army man, "I'm ready; this is a treat."

The boxer stripped.

Gloves were produced, and a set-to began between the amateur and the professional.

The professional boxer was a stout-built man; but the amateur was a match for him in every point.

At the eighth round Bob was satisfied with his boxer.

"You will do, my boy; now then, for a wrestle," he said to the man who wished to serve Bob.

The two wrestlers commenced.

Bob Blunt's man soon overcame his opponent, for he gave him that dexterous North country fling that very few can stand against.

Then Bob's runner tried, and out-distanced his opponent.

Our hero was satisfied.

"Now, sir, see whether you can discern the church clock yonder," said Bob to the gentleman with the long sight.

That worthy scout did so.

"It is a quarter to two."

Bob looked at his watch.

"It is so."

No one else could discern the hands of the clock at that distance.

With a smile of satisfaction at his success in meeting with the persons he required to serve him in his dangerous travels, he said cheerily—

"Now, gentlemen, it is time for luncheon; come, and I will give you all the names you will be known by, and I hope you will like them."

He led the way into the dining hall, after dismissing the professionals with a handsome gratuity for their services.

The dwarf followed his new employer with eager eyes.

"He is a good and kind master. I will follow him to the death," he muttered.

"You will have to share that service with me, then, for Buttons allows no one to interfere with his master."

"We will together, then, serve him true to the death," said the dwarf.

"Right," replied Buttons; "you are a trump, my boy."

CHAPTER VI.

IN WHICH OUR HERO CHRISTENS HIS BODY GUARD OF BRAVE MEN, AT WHICH BUTTONS ASSISTS WITH MUSICAL HONOURS.

THE luncheon was partaken of with great gusto by Bob's men.

"Now, gentlemen," cried Bob, when the cloth was removed, "fill your glasses."

Each one, when his glass was well filled, turned towards Bob.

"Gentlemen, I have now to inform you that I purpose an expedition to wild and savage Africa, in which all of you are to accompany me, and share my dangers. Now, in the first place, all of you must desire to be known to the natives of that wild country by some name, and that name I will give you."

"Hear, hear!" came from all sides of the room.

"You, doctor, are the first; please advance," said Bob.

The doctor, who was exceedingly short-sighted, approached the head of the table where Bob was seated in a sort of zig-zag fashion, highly amusing to witness.

"Doctor," said Bob, "kneel down, please."

The doctor knelt.

"Now listen. As my expedition is something new, I desire all those who follow me to conform to my rule, and bear the name that I give them."

Bob paused.

The doctor looked up in his face, and said in his mild voice—

"I am ready."

"Good; now, doctor, as I know you to be a very learned man, and acquainted with all the native languages of Africa, your name for the future shall be, Dr. Know-all. Three cheers for Dr. Know-all."

Three cheers were given, so heartily that the roof rang again, and the clamour was further heightened by Buttons vigorously rattling on a teaboard, on which he played with the drumstick of the dinner gong.

"That will do, Buttons, for the present," cried Bob.

When silence was restored, he took up a glass of champagne, and said—

"Now, Dr. Know-all, arise."

With that he dashed the glass of wine over the doctor's head, who took it very good-humouredly.

"You are christened; arise. Now, Mr. Boxer," said Bob, dismissing the doctor.

The gentleman of the noble art advanced, and came down in one stride.

"Sir," said Bob, "you are a man of strength, the Sampson of our party; your health is magnificent, and your bodily stature of vast power. But there is one thing for which you are especially noted, and that is your fist. Give us it."

The boxer placed his great hand in Bob's.

"This hand is the emblem of your strength, and for that reason you shall be called Ironfist. Gentlemen, the health of Ironfist, the boxer."

Bob christened him with the champagne in the same way he had done the doctor, and then the plaudits again rang out.

Buttons this time began to bang the tea-tray violently against his knees.

"Now, gentlemen," continued Bob, "I will ask our friend the wrestler to come forward."

The wrestler advanced.

"You," said Bob, "are one who excels in the art of putting a man on his back; therefore, you shall be called Strongback, in token of your own strong back. Arise, Strongback."

His health was drunk, and such was Buttons' delight, that this time he began to beat the tea-tray on his head.

"Thank you, Buttons, that will do. now," continued Bob, "I will require our friend the runner to advance."

That gentleman obeyed.

"You have a pair of very agile legs," said Bob. "They have served you well, and I hope they will never force you to fly an enemy. Having those appendages of swiftness, you shall be called Swiftfoot. Good speed to Swiftfoot, the runner."

Again the health was drunk, the cheers were given, and this time, to vary the proceedings, Buttons stood on his head with the tea-tray on his feet, on which he continued to beat a tattoo with his heels.

Then Bob beckoned for the gentleman who could see behind the moon on a foggy night.

"You, sir," he said, "have a genius given to you by nature."

"Which gift I cultivate by wearing the colours that nature wears," said the gentleman, pointing to his green coat, cap and umbrella.

"Exactly; and being able to distinguish any object, as well as to note all the minor details of road, river, or landscape in general, I shall christen you Longsight."

Bob poured another glass of wine over the long-sighted gentleman's head and then proposed his health.

Again the merry company responded.

Buttons this time had enticed the dwarf into the centre of the room.

Seizing him round the waist, he danced with him round the room, deposited him in a corner, and asked him to play "Rule Britannia" on his trombone, whilst he accompanied him on the tea-tray, which harmonious concert the two continued until they were silenced by our hero.

But as soon as silence once more assumed its sway, Bob spoke.

"Now, Mr. Dwarf, come here."

The little musical fellow approached our hero, with his trombone about him, and knelt down.

"You are here to accompany me, and therefore you must have a name."

"I have a name; it is——"

"I do not desire to guess it," said Bob, interrupting him. "I will give you a name; yea, a better one than your godfathers and godmothers gave you, I warrant. Kneel down."

The dwarf knelt down.

"Let me see, what are your peculiar powers?" said Bob, looking kindly pwn on the little man.

"Master," replied the dwarf, "my stature may be small, but few know my strength; none but those who have experienced it. Look at my head. I could burst open a door with it."

"Oh Lor! I hope you won't come and burst me open with it. I shall get out of your way, my friend," cried Buttons, retreating.

"Do not be afraid. I say I could burst open a door with it; and look at my arms."

And the dwarf drew up the sleeves of his coat, and disclosed two long wiry arms, with sinews like knotted cords, which ran down to his hands.

These hands were long and of massive grasp.

Bob Blunt had not previously noticed these muscular appendages.

Now he was struck with them.

"Upon my word," he said, "you are a giant in all but the body; however, you must have a name. "Now, what shall I call you—Long Hands? No; that will not do. Ah, I know; your name shall be Stumps."

"Thanks, master; I am satisfied."

The dwarf received this new name without further parley, and when Bob gave him the last glass of champagne over his tawny hair, he ejaculated—

"Now, I am happy. I have found a master, and I will be faithful to death. I am stumps by nature, and Stumps by the will of my master. He gave me that name; anyone who dares to vilify it, shall feel the strength of my arm. I am Stumps."

He folded his arms across his chest, and stood proudly in an attitude of defiance.

"Bravo, Stumps. Play your cards well and you'll do for trumps," cried Buttons.

"Master, I must show you a taste of my quality. Hah! I have you."

Stumps rushed at Buttons.

He seized him in his arms and held him up on high, so that his head and legs were parallel.

"Oh, ain't I a sweet cherub? I'll forgive you, Stumps; please let me down. I'll never do it again."

"Never?"

"Never," replied Buttons.

"Then I'll let you go."

Stumps put him down.

"Hurrah, Stumps! Oh, I'm so happy; we're going to Africa. Hurrah, Stumps, my boy!"

And Buttons stood on his head in a corner of the room, and in his usual manner clapped his heels together as if he was satisfied with himself, and deserved applause.

"That reminds me, gentlemen. I purpose going to Ashanti first," said Bob.

"I have been there," said Dr. Know-all.

"And so have I. Know the country well. Talk about alligators and elephants, why, the whole country swarms with them," said Longsight.

"Does it? Oh, Lor'! are there many of them?" asked Buttons.

"Yes; I should think so. I once remember meeting with an alligator," continued Longsight. "At the moment I was having my *siesta* beneath a large palm-tree. Suddenly I awoke and saw the brute within an inch of my nose."

"Awful," muttered the astonished Buttons. "He might have bit your nose off."

"Yes; but he didn't. It was awful. Well, there I lay, and the brute was opening his huge jaws so wide that I could nearly see into the pit of his stomach," said Longsight, winking at Bob Blunt, who enjoyed the yarn.

"In fact, Longsight, you saw what the brute had had for dinner the previous day," said Bob.

"Of course I did, sir."

"What had he?" asked the awe-struck Buttons.

"Why, three babies and a boy about your size. I declare I saw them as large as life."

"Not chawed up?" asked Buttons, with his hair standing on end.

"No, swallowed whole."

"Oh, master, don't go to Ashanti," cried Buttons, turning very pale.

"Stay, don't be afraid. I'll tell you how I got rid of him," continued Longsight. "Well, I had this identical green umbrella over my head, so when I beheld the brute, I clapped it between us in a trice."

"Did he go away then?" asked the simple Buttons.

"No. What did he do, but poke his nose beneath my best gingham, and make up to my face ready to devour me? I was in an awful fix. At that moment, I bethought myself of my snuff box. I drew it out of my pocket, opened it, and threw the contents into the brute's nose. It drew back."

"What did it do next?" asked Buttons, with open mouth.

"It gave one loud sneeze, that blew me up in the air, and decamped."

"Lor'!" cried the astonished Buttons, who believed the story. "Lor', master, before we go to Ashanti, just buy a hundredweight of the best Lundyfoot snuff, and I'll never go without my pockets full whilst I'm in Ashanti."

At this the company laughed.

"Gentlemen all, are your glasses charged?"

"Yes," cried they all.

"Then drink the health of my friend and manager, James Sawyer, Esq.," said Bob, rising.

The toast was drunk with musical honours, for Buttons drew forth the tea-tray, whilst Stumps played a deep bass on his trombone.

After this, Dr. Know-all arose "Gentlemen," he said, "I have to propose the health of one who has but lately become our friend and patron—I mean our host. Long life to Robert Blunt, Esq., of Blunt Castle. May happiness attend him in his travels."

"I thank you all, gentlemen," said Bob. "But there is one thing I will beg you to note—namely, that I am not to be known as Robert Blunt, Esq., of Blunt Castle, but as Bob Blunt, the Traveller. Don't forget this."

"Long life to Bob Blunt, the Traveller," they cried, "our master, our friend, and our guide. May he travel through the whole world, and we'll stick to him in all danger to a man," cried Ironfist.

"To a man," cried all.

And thus ended the christening of Bob Blunt's body-guard, who were to accompany him to Africa, where danger and death would surround him by day and night.

CHAPTER VII.

STUMPS PROVES HIS PROWESS WITH A VENGEANCE.

ON the evening of the day of the christening, Bob Blunt, knowing he should soon leave the country, resolved to visit some of the scenes of his boyhood.

He therefore sallied forth into the park alone.

Bob enjoyed the lovely prospect before him, and when he turned back and beheld the stately towers of his ancestral home gleam in the light of the setting sun, his heart swelled within him with varying emotions of pleasure and pain.

Pleasure that he could see them in their grandeur and their glory ; pain that he was about to leave the home of his boyhood, perhaps never to return.

"Old towers, your owner shall be worthy of you, and some day he will return never more to leave you," said Bob, looking fondly at the stately pile.

Then, turning his back upon them, he sauntered leisurely through the park.

He soon gained the high road.

Turning aside from his own lodge-gates, he walked along the road until he reached a lane, on each side of which was a great hedge of may and honeysuckle.

"Well do I remember this place. Love Lane they call it, because the village girls usually meet their lovers here, I suppose. Ah, old Buttons, I remember, took a bird's nest up that tree, and in his descent he got fixed by the seat of his trousers, as if he were hung out to dry."

Bob smiled at the recollection of Buttons' strange position. He passed on.

So wrapt up in his own thoughts was he, that he did not notice the faces of two men peering at him from behind the hedge.

They followed him with stealthy caution.

At last, when a gap admitted of their egress into the lane, they crept close up behind him, and before he was aware of it, a heavy bludgeon struck our hero on the head.

He sank to the ground bleeding.

"Help!" he cried.

"You may shout; no one will help you here," hissed Dick Howard, for it was he, and the bully Bow-legged Bill.

"Ha, ha!" laughed Howard, "we can make our own terms here. I'm glad we did not leave the neighbourhood, Bill."

"So'm I, guv'nor."

"What do you want?" asked Bob, raising himself on one arm.

"Want! It's our turn now; we want money and intend to have it, or you do not leave this place alive," said Howard.

"Would you murder me?" asked Bob.

"Yes; like a shot," replied Bow-legged Bill. "Let him give me the word, and, now we got you down, I do it."

"You would, would you? Well, I believe you both capable of it. But just listen to me. I will not beg my life at the hands of any ruffian, and it shall never be said that Bob Blunt is a coward."

"He will not give in; I know his stubborn nature too well. Hit him on the head, Bill," cried Howard, furiously.

"I'll settle him, guv'nor. This club of mine shan't miss its mark."

And Bill advanced towards our hero with uplifted stick.

Bob Blunt saw his peril, for the blow he had received made him almost helpless.

With a last despairing effort he shouted for help, and seizing a stone, he hurled it at Bow-legged Bill.

It happened to catch him on the knee.

Again Bob shouted for help, for Howard stood near him with a bludgeon, ready to strike if he were to move.

"Curse him, I'll settle him for that!" said Bow-legged Bill, when the pain of his knee had subsided a little.

He was in the act of raising his bludgeon and rushing at our hero, when there was a loud thud on the turf, and before Howard could speak, he found himself lying on his back in a stagnant cattle pond.

Bow-legged Bill got a blow in the stomach that appeared to come from a battering-ram, then two strong arms raised him from the ground and threw him into the hedge, where he yelled frightfully, for he alighted upon a thorny part of the hedge, which pierced his flesh, whilst a cluster of stinging nettles did not improve his complexion.

Meanwhile, the deliverer of Bob stood proudly contemplating the work of his hands.

"Why, Stumps, you're a champion!" cried Bob, leaning faintly against a tree.

"There, look whether Stumps cannot prove himself to be generally useful. There is a specimen of my handiwork," cried the dwarf.

"A pretty good specimen, too," cried Buttons, coming up just then. "The curs! I'll kill them! Hurrah, master's all right."

Then, to vary the proceedings, he stood on his head on a milestone, and clapped his heels in token of his joy.

"The chap wot give me the music on my skull," cried Bow-legged Bill, on seeing Buttons. "Guv'nor, cut's the word. Quick, let's be off."

With that, Bow-legged Bill managed to scramble out of the hedge and make a speedy exit, followed by his employer, whose curses at his mishap were loud and deep.

"Thank you for this timely service," said Bob, shaking the dwarf by the hand. "The rascals, they nearly had me."

"Oh, I'm so happy," cried Buttons, walking round his young master on his hands, with his feet in the air.

"Come here, stupid," cried Bob, "and stand upon your feet."

"Oh, master, I'm so happy Stumps came in time to save you," cried Buttons.

Bob did not reply to Buttons, for his mind was full of Howard's villainy.

"He is a villain, and I fear will yet work me a mischief. He is my cousin—the descendant of a noble house—yet what can ennoble fools, or slaves, or cowards? Alas! not all the blood of all the Howards."

"No, master ; but if he plays treacherously towards you, there is one will watch him like the eagle does the kite."

"Who is that?" asked Bob.

"Stumps, master ; Stumps, your faithful servant for life."

Bob pressed Stump's hand in silence.

On reaching the hall, Bob said, turning to his followers suddenly—

"Stumps, and you, Buttons, get ready, for I will leave this country and start for Africa at once. There I shall find sport and adventure to suit the mind of an English lad."

CHAPTER VIII.

THE EMBARKATION—NEARLY DROWNED—BUTTONS' SNUFF.

BOB BLUNT continued to entertain his friends at Blunt Castle until the vessel by which he intended to sail was ready to leave the dock where she had been lying.

He had ordered the outfit for the whole of the party.

Guns, revolvers, rifles, daggers, waterproofs, presents for the chiefs of the African tribes, and all the thousand and one necessaries suitable for the traveller in the tropics.

Buttons continually urged his master to purchase the hundredweight of Lundyfoot's snuff, but our hero only laughed at him.

Longsight's anecdote had made a great impression upon Buttons.

He had dreamt that he had been swallowed up by alligators, torn to bits by tigers, trampled to death by elephants, on several nights, and he resolved, on the first opportunity, to procure enough snuff to guard himself against all the alligators of Africa.

"Blest if I'm going to be done brown by an alligator, or any other wild beast ; if snuff will do them, why, then it shall not be my fault if I'm not up to snuff," soliloquised Buttons, on the morning of their departure for the docks.

We will draw a veil over our hero's parting with his tenants and servants.

Enough that the most fervent good wishes followed him.

In due time the party arrived at the East India Docks.

The luggage, and plenty of all sorts there were, had been sent on before them, and was now being lowered into the hold of the good ship "Busy Bee."

She was a fine schooner, and noted for her sailing powers.

The "Busy Bee" was moored alongside of the quay.

"Now, then, are we all here?" cried Bob Blunt, reviewing his body-guard.

"All," said Stumps.

"Where is Buttons?" asked Bob.

"That's more than I can tell," replied the dwarf, with a grin. "I last saw him on deck with a large box on his back."

"Well, he must look sharp. Halloa, here is the captain," said Bob.

A stout little man with a very red face approached them.

This was none other than Captain Jones the commander of the "Busy Bee."

"How do, sir? I hope we shall have a nice trip together ; Mr. Blunt, I'm right glad to see one of your mettle. You look born a traveller, sir."

"Thank you, captain, for the compliment ; now, are you all on board?" cried Bob.

"All," said the dwarf.

"We can't wait any longer, sir. Everything's ready, and we must take the tide," said the captain.

"Of course we must. Now, Mr. Sawyer, on board with you—we will take you with us a little way ; Gravesend is your destination.''

The lawyer smiled in reply at Bob's words and went on board.

At this moment, there was a loud cry in the rear of the party.

"Oh, Mr. Captain, Mr. Captain, don't leave a poor woman behind, much as you despise the sex. Pray stop a bit ; I've no one to protect me.''

Bob turned round.

"Halloa ! whom have we here ?" cried the captain. "What, it looks like Sarah Gamp !''

Well might the gallant sailor think of the renowned nurse.

A stout lady, yet so tall that her stoutness was not so observable, rushed towards the vessel in frantic haste.

She wore a poke bonnet, with great frills all round it, a large shawl fastened by a carved imitation of an elephant's tooth set in silver, whilst in her right hand she waved a huge blue umbrella, in her left a pair of pattens, and beneath her arm a brown earthenware teapot.

"This is the ship I booked for. Am I right for Africa ?" she asked, in a shrill treble.

"Right, marm ; we're going to start directly," said the captain.

"Now then, Dr. Know-all, help the lady on board," said Bob, "or she'll tumble over.''

"With pleasure, sir. Allow me, madam," replied Dr. Know-all, advancing towards the lady, who drew herself up to her full height.

"Paws off, Pompey," cried the amiable lady, raising her umbrella aloft. "I allows no man to touch me.''

Now the doctor did not hear this remark, so he advanced to the lady, took her by the arm, and was about to hand her down the gangway leading to the ship, when the irritable lady brought her umbrella down with a bang on the unfortunate Dr. Know-all's head.

So astonished was he, that he fell right into the arms of the good lady, and she, little expecting this embrace, fell back, catching her foot in the rope that ran through a sliding pulley.

She made a desperate clutch at Dr. Know-all to save herself.

She succeeded in throwing her arm around his neck, and before the doctor knew well what was about to occur he found himself struggling in the green water in the dock, with the lady's arm nearly choking him.

"Help, help, Mr. Blunt ! This lady is choking me !" he cried.

A dozen grinning sailors who were leaning over the bulwarks at once threw a rope out to the couple.

One sailor with a long boat hook managed to place the point in the seat of the doctor's loose inexpressibles, and began to haul him up.

The rope fortunately got under the lady's armpits, and so with much puffing, wheezing, and blowing the pair were safely hauled on to the deck of the " Busy Bee.''

"So much for gallantry," cried the doctor, when he could recover his breath. "I will never have anything to do with women again.''

"Oh, the monster !" shrieked the lady, "to dare place his arm round me.''

"On board, gentlemen all, if you please," cried Captain Jones. "Time's up.''

Bob Blunt and his friends put foot upon the " Busy Bee's " deck.

The lady arose with awful dignity when she beheld our hero and his friends shaking their sides with laughter at the mishap that had befallen her.

"Wretched men !" she said. "Do you know who I am ?''

"I have not the pleasure," replied Bob, with a bow of mock solemnity.

"Oh, where is my umbrella, my teapot, my pattens ? Wretch, give them to me !''

These last words were addressed to poor Stumps, who had collected the aforesaid articles, and the lady snatched them out of his hands.

With the pair of pattens in her left, her umbrella in her right hand, and the teapot under her arm, the lady drew herself up, and despite her wet dress and shawl, she strode up and down the deck, and then with majestic mien, paused before our hero.

"Sir," she began, "sir, have you never heard the name of Elizabeth Ann Stinger?"

Our hero confessed his ignorance of that celebrity in a quiet voice.

"Not heard of Elizabeth Ann Stinger! Lives there a boy or a man that does not tremble at that name?"

Here Miss Stinger flourished her umbrella with such determination that the doctor, who was gazing at her with all eyes, received a blow on the side of the head that made him reel again.

"Assault and battery!" cried the doctor. "Oh, why was woman born to torment simple man?"

"Bah! go to the police-court, I fear them not, much as my sex is ill-treated by that base biped, man. But I am a champion of my sex. Sir, I despise all animals that wear breeches."

"I think you have a good stout pair of your own at any rate," muttered Bob.

"Sir," continued Miss Stinger, "I leave this benighted land of England; I leave it, sir, with a terrible obtusity of my sex; but I scorn them all. They are poor creatures. Women have no rights in England. Why, I always refuse to pay my taxes for the simple reason that I have no voice in the management of affairs in this country."

"A lucky thing it is for the country that you have not," said Bob to the doctor.

"Women have no rights, therefore I leave my own, my native land in disgust. Sir, I go to Africa; sooner will I dwell amongst the untutored savages, and become a leader in the march of civilisation than to drag out an enervating existence where the breeched biped aforesaid reigns and rules supreme. I have done; to Africa I go, and I fight with man for supremacy to the death."

With that, Elizabeth Ann Stinger gave a farewell flourish with her umbrella that scattered all the men near her, and disappeared down into the cabin, a roar of laughter following her departure.

"Well, if that is not a strong-minded lady, I'm done brown," said Bob.

"Lord have mercy upon us," ejaculated Dr. Know-all, with upraised eyes. "If that woman is to accompany us, I'll pray to Heaven every night to deliver us from her society."

"Come, now, gentlemen, here is the tug; we're off," cried the captain.

And indeed the steam-tug was already fastened to the "Busy Bee."

As soon as they were out of the dock, and in the act of leaving the Black wall Pier, Bob suddenly cried out—

"Why, where is my boy Buttons gone?"

In truth that youthful adventurer was not to be seen.

At that moment there was a loud shout heard on the quay, and then elbowing his way through the crowd of people who usually throng on the pier to witness the coming and going of the ships, Buttons was seen to struggle.

"Hi, Mr. Blunt, stop a bit; don't go to Ashanti with out your Buttons," he gasped.

"Jump, Buttons," cried Bob.

"Oh, it's too much; I shall lose my snuff," he replied.

"Throw your box in first."

Buttons did so, then as the vessel was moving rapidly away from him, Buttons had no alternative but to jump.

Which he did.

But alas!

He alighted full upon the deck, right in front of the cabin stairs, and as ill-luck would have it, into the wide embrace of Elizabeth Ann Stinger, who was in the act of coming on deck to fill her teapot with water, no doubt to refresh herself after her recent bath.

There was a loud scream from Stinger; then both of them rolled down the cabin stairs together, and did not pause until they arrived on the mat at the foot of them.

"I'm murdered!" exclaimed the Stinger. "Drat that boy! Oh, my back; drat that boy!"

This last exclamation was followed by a violent fit of sneezing.

A packet of snuff that Buttons had in his pocket had burst, and some of it had titillated the olfactory organs of both Stinger and Buttons.

There they stood gazing and sneezing at each other, with looks that spoke more than words.

"Oh, Lor', I shall sneeze my head off," shrieked Stinger.

Buttons, when the sneezing fit was somewhat subsided, said—

"What do you mean, ma'am, by getting in my way?—you ain't an alligator. You don't want my snuff."

"Snuff—mean," gasped the Stinger; "mean, you boy, drat you! Oh, I could kill you outright. Sniff—achew—achew! Oh, I shall be blown to bits."

"Well, Buttons, you're well off for snuff?" said Bob, who had come with the others to see the end of the fall.

"Here is some, sir; thank Heaven it is not all spilt. I have a large box full on deck, and then I went on shore to buy another pound or two, when the ship went off. Will you have a little more ma'am?"

"Oh, drat the boy," cried Stinger. "He'll be as evil as the rest of the men when he grows up."

"Never mind, I'm so happy; I haven't missed the train—I mean the ship that's going to Ashanti."

And Buttons, to express his joy, stood on his head, clapped approval with his heels, then turned a somersault, and, alighting on his feet, he came to within an inch of the red nose of Miss Stinger.

"Lor', drat the boy," cried the astonished virago. "Is he going with us?"

"Yes, ma'am; your obedient Buttons is going to Ashanti land," replied Buttons, with a very low bow. "Happy to look after your little comforts."

"Then I protest, in the outraged name of my sex. I protest, captain, that infants should not be allowed to travel to Africa with their pockets full of snuff."

The captain was not below at the time, but the Stinger addressed herself to Longsight.

She was evidently smitten with his green umbrella, being somewhat similar to her own, only about a fourth the size.

"Infants!" cried Buttons, highly incensed at this remark. "You shall see, marm, whether I'm an infant. Buttons is a man, every inch of him, and, you must confess, up to snuff."

"Oh, indeed; well, if you'll be kind enough to clear out, I'll have my tea."

And Elizabeth Ann seated herself at the table, and began to busy herself with sundry packages which formed the staple of her luggage.

Buttons managed to sprinkle a little more snuff round Stinger's tea-tray, and then retired on deck, with our hero and the others.

"Now, Mr. Longsight, can you see that clock over Woolwich?" said Bob.

"See it; yes, it is ten minutes past two o'clock."

"Then I'll set my watch by it, and we shall know the right time when we are in the forests of Africa."

Bob set his gold repeater, and then sat down in the midst of his body-guard on the deck, watching the panorama of the river, and taking a last glance at familiar spots.

At last Gravesend came in view.

Here Mr. Sawyer took leave of our hero and his friends.

"Good-bye, and may you return from your adventures in Africa safe and well," said the lawyer. "Let me hear from you soon, my dear sir, and depend upon it all your affairs shall be well looked after."

"Good-bye, and God bless you; three cheers for Mr. Sawyer."

The three cheers were given, and then Mr. Sawyer stepped into the boat that was to take him ashore, leaving Bob on board bound for Ashanti.

"MISS STINGER MADE A DESPERATE CLUTCH AT DR. KNOW-ALL TO SAVE HERSELF."

CHAPTER IX.

THE TWO STRANGERS—A FIRST NIGHT AT SEA—BUTTONS' DISTRESS AND STUMPS'
CONSOLATIONS.

WHILST Bob Blunt was looking over the gunwale, waving his adieux to Mr. Sawyer, a boat hailed the " Busy Bee."

This boat contained, besides the boatman, two men who at once attracted our hero's attention, for there was something peculiar about them.

The one, the taller of the two, was dressed in a tight-fitting shooting coat, with shooting boots that fitted him tightly above the knee.

A large felt hat and a loose, flowing comforter nearly hid his face ; but Bob saw enough of it to judge that the owner had very black eyes, a heavy black moustache and beard, and deep olive complexion.

This man's companion was of a shorter build, his huge bulk was enveloped in a large blue pea-jacket, his face covered with a huge brown beard, and he looked very much like a settler from the backwoods.

"Two more passengers?" said Bob, inquiringly to the captain.

" Yes ; I had a telegram that they would meet the ship at Gravesend. Now, then, gentlemen, look alive ; it's time you were on board," cried Captain Jones.

"All right," cried the tall stranger, mounting the ladder, and quickly followed by his companion.

Then the dark man gave our hero a deep, penetrating glance, and hurried down to the cabin.

"Strange," muttered Bob ; " I seem to remember those eyes ; but no, I must be deceived, or I could have sworn that those eyes belonged to Dick Howard."

Yet he threw off this idea at once.

Howard would never dare to follow him to Africa.

This settled all doubt in Bob's mind.

He at once forgot all about the stranger.

He remained on deck with the captain until evening was closing in.

The vessel was now scudding before a favourable breeze in the Downs.

It was a magnificent sight to see the red sun setting on the waste of the wide waters, deluging the waves with long floods of light, and making the white cliffs of England gleam through a purple mist.

Bob watched this magnificent scene with eager eyes.

" Fine sight to look at the cliffs of Old England, sir," said an old sailor to our hero.

" Yes, my man."

" I have seen those old cliffs many a time ; these forty years, man and boy, the ocean has been my home, and I'm never happy unless when I'm afloat on the briny. Old Tom Bunting knows every inch of the sea, from Wapping Old Stairs to the Ganges."

Bob began to feel interested in the old tar, for he was full of yarns.

" Now, look ye here, sir ; I see you be a affable young gent, so old Tom will put you up to a move or two."

" I'm all attention, Bunting," said Bob.

" Don't call me Bunting, please, sir ; I don't care for it, although it's my name. My mates of the ' Jolly Tar,' at Wapping, allus calls me old Tom—two penn'orth of old Tom, they say sometimes—but I'm up to their larks, and I can take my own part."

" I believe you can, old Tom," said Bob.

" Never fear that ; but look, take your last glance of Old England ; the sun's gone, every streak of it."

Bob looked up.

He could just see the last gleam of the sun on the cliff.

Then old Tom broke out into a song racy of the sea.

His voice had that roll usual to the sailor—loud, deep, and sonorous as the waves.

After the first line, the entire ship's company, passengers and crew, joined in.

> "A wet sheet and a flowing sail,
>   A wind that follows fast,
> And fills the rustling sail,
>   And bends the gallant mast,
> And bends the gallant mast, my boys,
>   While, like the eagle, free,
> Away the good ship flies, and leaves
>   Old England on the lee."

When the last strain had subsided, Bob and his friends went below.

Here Buttons and Stumps were waiting whilst the steward prepared the tea.

The table was spread with all kinds of eatables, and Buttons' eyes were eagerly devouring them in anticipation.

"Oh, my! won't we have a feed, just!" said Buttons. "Oh, this sea air does make me feel awfully peckish. How do you feel, Stumps?"

"As if I could eat something," replied Stumps, "more tender than you, Buttons, my boy."

"Then fall to, gentlemen," said the captain, taking his seat at the head of the table. "Mr. Blunt, sir, will you oblige me by taking the vice-chair?"

"With pleasure; ah, room for the ladies," cried Bob.

Miss Stinger and two lady passengers who do not call for particular description entered the cabin at this moment.

The Stinger had robed herself in a puce-coloured velvet dress, with a low body, a set of feathers that drooped down on her neck, and freely mingled with the few stray ringlets which she was pleased to call her curls.

With a haughty air, the lady took her seat at the table, and to the surprise of all she produced her brown earthenware teapot, put some tea into it, and then in sonorous accents—

"Stew-ard, some hot water."

That functionary at once obeyed the awful command with trembling alacrity.

"Ma'am, there is tea in the urn on the table," he said.

"Man, how dare you? I prefer my own tea in my own pot, so no words about it."

The steward gave the lady a jug of hot water, and she made her own tea.

"Now, Stumps, my boy, we shall have a feed," said Buttons, who was seated at a side table with the dwarf.

Stumps nodded a reply.

"My eye! what a pie!" cried Buttons, when the steward placed a large meat pie before them.

Both of them began to eat most ravenously.

"Wait a bit," whispered Longsight, to our hero. "The wind is freshening, and the good ship 'Busy Bee' will soon pitch and roll."

Bob laughed.

"Give me a nice roll. I can do without the pitch."

Longsight said nothing, but watched Buttons very anxiously for a time.

When the meal was concluded, the cabin-boy summoned the captain on deck.

"Make all right and tight, steward, for I expect we shall have a bit of a blow. I hope it won't inconvenience you, ladies and gentlemen," said the captain, before leaving them.

"All right, sir. We'll look after the ladies," said Longsight.

"Indeed, young man. Perhaps you'll take care of yourself. Miss Stinger is equal to the occasion," replied Stinger.

"Now, Buttons, have the goodness to open the piano. I think we'll have a little music. Miss Stinger, may I ask you to oblige the company with a song?" said Bob.

"Sir, I consider singing a frivolous amusement. Thank the Lord I have no vanity in my nature—all sound common sense, sir."

Here Miss Stinger cast a glance of superlative contempt at two lady passengers who volunteered a duet.

The music was duly applauded, and then, on its conclusion, Buttons began to open his mouth very wide and yawn tremendously.

"Are you tired, Buttons?" asked Bob.

"No, sir, but I think I have taken rather too much pork-pie, and, oh, I say, don't I feel queer! Oh my! Oh my! Oh my!"

Here Buttons yawned louder than before in the face of the Stinger.

"Is the boy mad, drat him?" said that strong-minded lady, with a frown, and a shake at Buttons' collar.

"I ain't off my nut, marm," said Buttons. "Here, I say, Miss Stinger, that'll do; you are shaking up the porkpie."

Presently he seemed to grow very pale.

"Why don't you stand on your head and clap your feet with joy, Buttons, my boy?" said Stumps, with a grin.

"Oh, don't, please. I feel—I feel such a rumpus down here; ugh! Oh, Stumps, something is the matter with me."

And Buttons began to rub the region of his stomach with both hands.

"Have a little more pie, Buttons, my boy; perhaps that will do you good—a nice little piece of fat now," said Stumps. "Do try a piece of fat."

"Oh, don't, Stumps, don't, my boy. I do feel a rumpus; ugh! I'm getting so bad."

"Come, now, what do you say? Shall I tell the steward to bring you a nice fat piece of bacon, nicely fried—frizzly fat, you know, nice and glossy?" said Stumps.

"Ugh! you beast," gasped Buttons.

He was gradually growing paler.

"Don't, don't, dear Stumps, don't talk of fat bacon. Oh, that pie, that pie! It disagrees with me so. Ugh!" implored Buttons, beseechingly, "come and hold me up."

"What, Buttons, you are not about to be sea-sick?" said Bob.

"No, no, sir; but that pie—it do rummage my in'ards about. I'm not going to be ill. Look at me; ain't I all right? Where's old Stinger?"

Buttons drew himself up as if to appear very well.

But the effort was a dismal failure, for, as he sat very erect, he began to open his mouth very wide.

Then he arose to his feet.

"Ugh! the rummages are commencing again. Oh Lor', oh Lor', ask Miss Stinger to give me a drop of brandy out of her teapot. Oh, it's coming!"

He gave one gasp, and then rushed blindly forward.

He fell into the arms of Miss Stinger.

Before that strong-minded lady could effect a retreat, Buttons had deposited the pie laying so heavy on his chest into her lap.

"Oh, drat that boy! Help, help, I'm smothered. Take him away. Oh, you little monster! you have spoilt my new dress."

Miss Stinger arose, and giving Buttons a push, she sent him back into the arms of the grinning Stumps.

"What, Buttons, you're not so bad as all that; hold up. Why, man alive, I thought you had a better stomach."

"Oh, Stumps, my dear Stumps, don't abuse me. I tell you it's the rummages. I feel going up—then going down—then going up mountains high—something awful. Lead me to my bunk and let me die! Oh, it's coming on again."

"Poor, poor, Buttons. Have a little more fat bacon—fat."

"No. Oh, my poor, poor head; oh, Stumps, lead me to my bunk and let me die in peace. Say prayers over me, and deposit the remains of poor Buttons in the vasty deep—uncuddled, uncoffined, but not unwept. You, dear Stumps will weep for your Buttons; tell my dear master how——"

"How the vessel rocks," said Stumps.

There suddenly came a change over the features of Stumps.

The vessel rocked fearfully.

Up and down, up and down.

Stumps grew very pale.

"Buttons," he said.

"What?"

"Buttons, my boy, the pie is beginning to disagree with me; my friend, we will die together. Oh, this up and down is dreadful."

"Bravo, Stumps; I shall soon be dead, death has got hold of me. Oh, I'm bad again. Oh, oh!"

"So am I!" gasped Stumps.

The ladies also began to experience the qualms of sea sickness.

Miss Stinger was the last to withdraw, but she did so with great dignity.

With her teapot under her arm, she bowed to the company, her feathers nodding like the plumes of a hearse.

She had proceeded as far as the cabin

stairs when the vessel gave a greater lurch than before.

Miss Stinger could not withstand this last shock at all.

She measured her length upon the floor at the feet of Doctor Know-all.

"Where is my lancet?" cried the doctor; "I will bleed her."

"Bleed me, you leech; help me to my feet. Elizabeth Ann is herself again."

Miss Stinger arose.

She grasped her teapot, shook it in the face of wicked man, and disappeared from view.

In the meantime Stumps and Buttons had been rolling over each other.

The dwarf was very ill.

He now found that it was no joke.

The poor dwarf was fearfully taken aback when the burly Ironfist came and put a piece of fat pork right under his nose so that he had a good sniff at it.

"The rummages; oh, don't Mr. Ironfist. I am so queer, so very, very queer. My friend Buttons will take the pork; he likes it. I am not up to it just at present."

"Oh, Mr. Blunt, sir," groaned Buttons, "are we going to the bottom of the sea? When the vessel pitches down, I think we shall never get up again. Oh, if we were only in Ashanti, I don't mind the alligators. I have got some snuff for them, but for the rummages; ugh!"

"Be quiet, you stupid," said Bob; "you're only sea-sick; it will do you good,

take away the superfluous bile. Come, look up."

"I can't."

"Neither can I," moaned Stumps.

"What, my brave Stumps floored by sea-sickness? I could hardly believe it. Come look up, man."

"I can't, sir. Buttons will look up for me."

"Then we will have to carry you to your bunks. Ironfist, Strongback, Swiftfoot, and Longsight, take them below," cried Bob.

The four at once arose.

Stumps and Buttons were carried neck and crop into their bunks.

When they found themselves on their backs they grew worse.

"I must sit up," cried Buttons. "How do you feel now, Stumps?"

"Ugh! very bad."

"Let us leave them," said Bob; "when they are in the dark they will go to sleep. Here, boys, I leave you a tumbler of brandy and water; no doubt you will want it by-and-by."

Bob then returned to the cabin with his friends.

Grog was brewed, and they passed a pleasant evening together; but one thing surprised Bob.

This was that neither of the two strangers who had come on board the "Busy Bee" at Gravesend put in an appearance in the cabin during the entire evening.

CHAPTER X.

THE SCHEMERS—MISS STINGER'S FRIGHT—HOW BUTTONS UNKNOWINGLY THWARTED A MURDER.

IT was midnight.

The passengers of the "Busy Bee" were in a deep sleep.

The chief cabin of the "Busy Bee" was semi-circular, with a partition in the centre, dividing the gentlemen's from the ladies' saloon, so that the sleeping compartments were all round it.

At the one nearest the door Buttons and Stump were located.

Next to him were Ironfist and Longsight, and the next was occupied by Bob Blunt.

The next cabin, a large one, was tenanted by the two strangers.

Their door was locked and bolted on the inside, but we will take a peep behind it.

The two worthies were seated each on a camp stool, smoking.

They were none others than the villains Dick Howard and Bow-legged Bill, but admirably disguised.

"Well, guv'nor, I think we have done the trick this time," said Bow-legged Bill, blowing out huge volumes of tobacco smoke. "Why the cove didn't know no more than the blessed babe unborn. Blow me, it's stunnin'."

"It won't be for long if you continue to open those confounded gills of yours in that way. Will you never learn discretion?" said Howard, with a scowl on his brow.

"All right, guv'nor, I'll soon come to the gen'lman ; talk the lingo of the swells like one o'clock."

"Now listen to me, Mr. Willliam Walker."

"Yes ; that's my name, Dicky How ——"

"Hush ! not that name ; the partitions of the cabin are not built like the walls of Newgate."

"Right again, Muster Chawles Delorme ; but what did you wish to say ?"

"I say that the fellow I hate like poison, Bob Blunt, does not recognise me. I mean to get rid of him by fair means or foul."

"Beautiful ! I owe him a grudge, and don't forget that terrible Buttons. Lor', I shall never forget that bass wiol kivering my head, nor the tupenny of that cussed dwarf. I think he was made with a mill-stone in his skull."

"All in good time, my dear fellow ; we must rid ourselves of the master mind first. Bob Blunt must be settled."

"Bravo ! How shall we do it ?"

"Look at this."

Howard drew a small bottle from his pocket and held it up to the light."

"What's that ?"

"Poison that shall take the life of Bob Blunt the Traveller."

"Whew ! I see," said Bill.

"You don't yet."

"Why, give him a dose, and settle him at once," said Bill.

"That's were you are mistaken, my friend. This little vial contains arsenic ; a great dose would betray us. No, we must go very cautiously to work. We will give it by degrees ; a grain at the time, and when Mr. Bob Blunt arrives in Africa he will be food for the worms, and then his death will be put down to jungle fever. Don't you see, my hearty ?" said Howard, or rather Mr. Charles Delorme, to call him at present by the name he had assumed.

"I see. Why don't you give him a dollop at once, then ?" asked Bill.

"That's what I intended to do. Now, Bill, you go and see whether there's anybody about."

"Right."

Bill silently opened the door.

"There's a light in the saloon, but it only burns dimly. The coast is clear, for I can hear the captain on deck."

"Right again. Now, then, take your boots off ; we will creep into the cub's cabin, and put a slight dose of the mixture into his glass. He will be sure to drink it the first thing in the morning."

"Come, then."

The two crept into the saloon.

The faint light the swinging lamp gave afforded them sufficient light to see their way into the saloon.

The two crept with noiseless steps towards the cabin which they presumed our hero occupied.

"This is it," said Bill.

"Try the handle, then," replied Howard.

"Right."

Bill turned the handle and entered the cabin.

"This is it," he whispered.

"Where is the glass ?"

"Here."

Howard took up the glass and was in the act of putting some of the arsenic into it when his eyes lighted upon a heap of female attire, and above all a blue gingham umbrella that lay astride of the occupant of the bunk as if ready for defence or attack.

"Why, Bill, this isn't the cabin. Man alive ! we're in a woman's berth."

"Blessed if we ain't," muttered Bill. "By Jove! let us slope. Slope's the word."

At this moment the occupant of the bunk, evidently aroused by the noise the intruders made, started up in bed.

Beneath a frilled nightcap peered the face of Elizabeth Ann Stinger.

"Dowse the glim," muttered Bill.

Howard had taken that precaution, but not soon enough.

The Stinger saw distinctly the figures of the two men, but she could not discern their features.

"What, two men in my bedroom?" she cried. "Murder, thieves, fire! I, Elizabeth Ann Stinger, my room is defiled by base mankind. Murder!"

"Hush, ma'am," said Howard, hastily; "we have mistaken your cabin for our own. Pray accept our apologies."

"No, I won't accept of anything. Out with you, base men. Do you think that Elizabeth Ann Stinger cannot take care of herself? Go; and tremble, for my arm is strong. Begone!"

And with these words the Stinger raised her umbrella, and caught the retreating head of Bow-legged Bill a blow that made him reel again.

Then jumping from her couch she securely bolted the door against all further intruders.

Being a strong-minded woman she did not trouble herself much about the men, but went to sleep vowing she would knock the next man's head off that dared to enter her room.

Howard and Bill returned to the saloon.

"You fool," hissed the former, "why did you not make sure of the cabin?"

"All serene, guv'nor. I'll tell you what it is; I swear I saw Blunt's name on that cabin this afternoon. They must have removed it; but this is it."

He pointed to a door that stood ajar and bore the name of Robert Blunt, Esq., on the exterior.

"That's it. Why, I can see the infernal bloke sleeping there," said Bill.

"Let us in, then. Keep silent."

Silently the two, now sure of the cabin, pushed the door open and entered.

But they soon retreated.

There before them was the figure of Buttons, seated on a chest, and with nothing on but his night-gown.

Buttons' eyes were wide open.

The two villains gazed at him for a moment, but he did not move.

Only one word issued from his lips.

This word, spoken with awe, was one that the intruders could not comprehend.

It was, however, uppermost in the brain of the redoubtable Buttons, for it had been the cause of much suffering to him.

"Rummages inside!"

That was all.

Buttons did not move.

Howard then thought him to be asleep and advanced into the cabin.

"Rummages inside, oh!"

"What does he mean?" asked Howard.

"He's fast asleep," replied Bill.

"So much the better. Now, then, stand in front of him," whispered Howard.

"I am."

"Then I'll leave a dose of physic in Blunt's glass. Keep watch, but be silent as the grave."

Howard made a movement to empty a part of the arsenic in the glass, when Buttons arose from the chest still in his sleep.

He advanced noiselessly towards the pair.

His eyes were firmly fixed upon Howard, so firmly that the latter quailed before them and hesitated to carry out his evil purpose.

"He is awake!" said Bill; "if so, let us begone."

"Oh, rummages inside! Oh," moaned Buttons in his sleep, "don't the beastly ship rock about?"

"By Jove! he talks as if he were wide awake enough now," whispered Bill. "Shall I let him have one?"

And Bill raised his clenched hand.

"No violence, fool; you will spoil all. He is talking in his sleep. Come," said Howard.

He saw that Buttons did not move an inch further than the entrance of the door, so that he could not reach the glass, for it stood behind Buttons.

The two worthies, therefore, quietly returned to their own cabin.

Soon after they had gone Bob Blunt awoke.

His surprise on seeing Buttons was great.

The latter still stood in the attitude that had foiled Howard.

Bob knew not that Buttons was walking in his sleep.

"Buttons!" he cried.

"Yes, master."

With a cry that sounded very much like the word "Rummages," Buttons awoke.

"Buttons, what is the matter?"

"Oh, master, I have had such a dream, oh, so horrible! I thought two men were about to murder you."

"Murder me? Pooh! no doubt about your dreaming; who should murder me?" asked Bob.

"Why, master, I thought it was Howard and that bow-legged bully Bill."

"Ha, ha! Why, they are in Old England, which they have not left as yet for their country's good. Go to bed, again, Buttons; it was only a dream. Your nerves are rather excited; no doubt your brain was too active after the discharge of the rummages."

But Buttons did not answer to Bob's smile.

His face was drawn up with portentous gravity that would have been funny had not Buttons been so thoroughly in earnest.

"Go to bed, my boy," said Bob, kindly. "I thank you for the solicitude you have shown on my behalf. I shall not forget it."

Buttons left the cabin.

Then Bob got up and doubly locked the door, nor did he sleep one night without taking that precaution during the rest of the voyage.

Buttons' dream had evidently made an impression, although he did not care to let his faithful tiger see how much he was moved by the recital of that dream.

"But I will be on the alert," muttered Bob, before he went to sleep again. "I fear no open enemy, but who can guard against a secret foe? However, courage, Bob Blunt; woe to him who seeks to spoil your travels!"

And with this resolution he fell asleep.

CHAPTER XI.

MAN OVERBOARD—A NARROW ESCAPE—THE STINGER'S SYMPATHY—WHO IS THE BRAVE MAN?

BOB BLUNT had become a great favourite with the sailors, for he had been liberal to them by the occasional bestowal of a jorum of grog.

If you desire to make Jack Tar your friend give him grog when at sea; it will find its way to his heart better than anything.

Bob was pacing the captain's little quarter-deck with the gallant commander towards night.

The sea was high.

"Where are we now?" asked Bob.

"Well, as near as I can guess, about forty miles off Cape Finisterre northwest-by-west," replied the captain.

"Shall you put into port anywhere, captain?"

"Yes; we touch at Lisbon."

"That'll be jolly; I long to have a peep at the Portuguese ladies."

"I should have thought there was sufficient fascination on board the 'Busy Bee,'" said the captain.

"How?"

"Look at the fairest of the fair."

"Angels and ministers of grace defend us!" cried Bob.

He pointed to the strong-minded lady—Miss Stinger.

That virgin had her hair tied up in curl papers, her shawl tied over her head, her body enveloped in a stout reefing jacket, her pattens on her feet, and to crown all, her huge blue gingham protected that delicate face from the spray of the salt sea waves.

She also held a telescope in her hand and occasionally scanned the horizon with a majestic and confident flourish of the glass.

One of the lady passengers was asking her how far she thought they were from the nearest point of land.

"I don't know, ma'am, but I will inquire. Captain Frobisher Jones will inform me."

A marked stress for the "me," as if to imply that any information the captain had to impart would be given by reason of her superior intelligence.

She accordingly advanced to the quarter-deck.

"Captain," she said, in her masculine voice.

"Marm," said the captain, touching his hat with due deference to the superior intelligence.

"Captain, where are we now?"

The captain put his two hands to the side of his mouth, and replied in a voice that sounded like the growl of distant thunder—

"Where are we now? Why, where should we be? Can't you tell?"

"No, captain; I desire to know."

"Well, marm, we are on board the 'Busy Bee,' marm."

"And where is the 'Busy Bee,' captain?" queried the lady.

"On the mighty deep, marm."

The laughter that followed this sally of the captain's only raised a frown on the brow of Elizabeth Ann.

And the Stinger walked aft in all the dignity of umbrella, pattens, and telescope, and as if her nerves were not sufficiently braced, she took a long draught from her brown earthenware teapot which stood near at hand.

Bob continued his conversation with the captain, and was informed that the ship was now breasting the broad swell of the Atlantic.

This was apparent by the vessel pitching with greater force than before.

The sailors were in the yards.

Old Tom was astride the main-brace, busily employed in mending the sail, and trolling out a foc'sle ditty the burden of which was—

"Oh, the rolling deep, the rolling deep,
    I leave my Wapping Poll
  For the rolling deep."

"Halloa, old Tom," cried Bob, "how are you getting on here?"

"Tight as a rum puncheon ere it's tapped. Muster Blunt, sir, you should come up here and listen to the music of the wind; it's piping a tune that would make the cockles of your heart dance."

"Thank you. I'll give you a look-up."

"Hold on tight, Mr. Blunt," said the captain. "I tell you it's no joke clinging to the tarry ropes if you're not used to it."

"All right, captain; I'll hold on like grim death," replied Bob.

"I wish he would slip and get dashed to bits on the deck, or get drowned," muttered Mr. Charles Delorme to his crony Mr. William Walker.

The two were watching our hero from the gunwale of the ship.

Bob mounted into the rigging.

He had nearly reached the main yards when the ship gave a lurch to starboard.

"Hold on, sir," cried old Tom, on seeing our hero rather shaky.

He stooped down to give our hero a helping hand, but the vessel pitched heavily, and as the rain came down pretty fast, Bob did not see the old sailor's outstretched hand before him.

"Steady, sir, steady," cried old Tom to our hero.

At that moment the ship lurched to larboard, and a heavy wave to starboard prevented her righting immediately.

Bob heard the old sailor cry—

"Darn me, if I ain't gone!"

He felt something slip by him, and on looking up, the place where old Tom had sat astride was vacant.

In an instant he divined what had happened.

Old Tom had fallen into the sea.

"Man overboard!" cried Bob—"man overboard!"

Down he went, and soon reached the deck, quicker than he had ascended.

"Old Tom's overboard," said Bob to the captain, "and it's my fault."

"Port the helm! slacken sail! and lower a boat."

The captain's orders were instantly obeyed, and the ship swung round in answer to her helm.

All persons on deck now crowded to the bulwarks, to witness the exciting scene.

But Bob Blunt was fearfully excited.

"He shan't drown, if I can help it. Clear the way there. I save him or die!"

He threw off his coat and boots, and before anyone could prevent him, he leapt overboard into the sea.

"He's a gone coon, Walker, my boy," muttered Delorme. "The fool has gone to his death."

"Out with the boat!" cried the captain.

"Oh, my master, my noble master, he will be drowned," cried Buttons and Stumps with anguish.

In the meantime Bob was seen to rise to the surface.

He was a capital swimmer, but poor old Tom was a very bad one, as is frequently the case with sailors.

Bob saw the object of his search some twenty yards ahead of him.

"Keep up, old Tom, keep up, man!"

His voice was drowned on the wind.

He, however, with strong and rapid strokes, managed to reach the old tar.

"Halloa, Tom!"

"Here, your honour."

"Can you keep up?"

"A little longer. Darn me, I've lost my sea legs. But why did you come? You'll be drowned, sir."

"Never mind, I am here. Can't you swim?" cried Bob.

"Like a stone, darn me!"

"Stiffen your legs, put your arms close to your sides, and I think the mighty Atlantic has buoyancy enough to keep you afloat like a feather."

"Right, your honour!"

"Now, then, off we go!"

Bob grasped with one hand tightly the sailor's shirt at the nape of the neck, and then propelled him towards the vessel.

But the waves rolled very high.

Occasionally when they breasted the summit of the waves they could see the ship as through a haze.

Then, when engulfed in the trough of the sea, she was lost to sight, and it appeared to Bob as if they never should see her again, so vast was the feeling of intense solitude in that living tomb.

But the boat was nearing them.

They saw the welcome forms of the men in her.

"Hurrah! We shall be saved. Courage, old Tom, they near us. Hurrah!"

The boat was now close upon them.

"Here, lads!" shouted Bob.

"Darn you, here! Come on, you lubbers; old Tom has got enough salt water in him to mix his grog for the rest of his life. Pull away, pull away, boys."

"Hurrah!"

The boat was alongside of them.

The welcome faces of Buttons and Stumps peered at them.

"Hurrah! Saved, saved!"

And Buttons, despite the rocking of the boat, made abortive attempts to stand on his head, and only desisted when Stumps held him down by main force.

* * * * *

In the meantime, the excitement on board the ship had increased after the boat had left to the rescue.

The Stinger's nature was entirely at war with her feelings.

"Shall England's brave sailors die in the mighty deep? If you are men, show it; if not, I will show you that I am very much a man. Come on."

"No, thank you, ma'am," replied Delorme, to whom the Stinger's heroic words were addressed; "we value our lives; besides, it is no use trying to help them, they are drowned."

"Is that a reason why we should not exert ourselves on behalf of a fellow creature? Away, I am boiling over with sympathy!"

She rushed up and down, now and then gazing out at sea.

Presently the boat came in sight.

The "Busy Bee" tacked so as to come alongside of it.

When those on board beheld Bob and old Tom safe in the boat, their delight was expressed in repeated volleys of cheering.

"My sympathy is at boiling point. Hurrah! I wish I was a man."

At that moment the boat was within a couple of lengths from the ship.

"Lend a hand," cried the Stinger, seizing a rope to throw it to old Tom.

The doctor, who was nearest to her, made a movement to do so, when the ship gave a lurch.

The Stinger was hurled against the doctor, who clutched a rope to save himself, and before anyone could grasp her, she fell backwards through the open port-hole into the sea.

Old Tom, who had hold of the rope, was hauled from the boat.

The Stinger seized him.

Down they fell.

The two were floating in the water.

"Oh, my pattens! I shall lose them!" cried the Stinger, throwing her arms around old Tom's neck.

"Darn your pattens, ma'am; am I then going to the bottom arter all?"

"Help! help!" screamed the Stinger.

Old Tom struggled hard to free himself from the Stinger's grasp, and they would inevitably have been drowned had not the boat come to their rescue.

Bob Blunt took a boat hook, and the hook fortunately caught the Stinger's garments.

He pulled her into the boat.

Old Tom followed.

"Well, by Davy Jones's locker, if that isn't a squeak. The old cat nearly did for me. I am darned!" he cried.

"Oh, you brute! Call yourself a man? Pretty man indeed. Didn't I, brimming over with sympathy, try to throw you a rope? Ugh! I am the brave man, not you. Who is the brave man, sirs? Why, Elizabeth Ann Stinger—where's my pattens? Ah, all right!"

When Bob Blunt mounted the deck, three ringing cheers were given for him.

In the meantime, the Stinger rushed about in a state of great excitement.

She waved her umbrella over his head, and cheered lustily, and then danced a tattoo with her pattens.

CHAPTER XII.

THE VOYAGE CONTINUED—THE STINGER'S SCORN OF OLD TOM—OVERBOARD AGAIN—A CRY OF "SHARK!"—BOB AND HIS ESCORT TO THE RESCUE—HURRAH FOR THE STINGER!—A NOVEL RIDE IN THE ATLANTIC—"WHERE'S MY HAT?"—SHARK PIE, AND GENERAL TRIUMPH OF ALL.

THE next morning, the sun rose brightly, and the sea was comparatively smooth.

We may be sure that the mishap of the previous day had been greatly discussed by all on board.

The Stinger began to conceive herself the heroine of the day, or rather the hero, she preferring the masculine appellation.

All the passengers were assembled on board the " Busy Bee."

"What a lovely morning," cried the Stinger, throwing out her arms and chest as if inhaling the fresh sea-breeze.

"Lovely, marm."

She turned round and beheld old Tom.

"Is it you, you dog? How dare you call me lovely? You were nearly drowned yesterday."

"I was, marm; all through you."

"Through me? Ungrateful man!"

"Yes, marm."

"It is a base invention. Out of the way, man. Make room for me. My name is Stinger."

With that, the Stinger raised her umbrella and began to belabour old Tom with all the strength of her sinewy arms.

Old Tom retreated backwards.

"I say," cried the old tar, "leave off, or you'll knock me into little bits. Leave off, and I'll try to make love to you, my lovely rosebud."

The Stinger continued her blows, and

Tom put his arm over his face to protect himself, half in jest, half in earnest, for the Stinger was now furious.

"I'll give it you for lying and saying you will make love to me, you wretch, you old salt-water junk," she cried, greatly to the amusement of Bob and his friends, who followed her up.

But the jest was not to end in a jest.

Old Tom, as he went backwards, stumbled over a coil of rope.

He fell and disappeared out of sight.

"He's gone again," gasped the Stinger, who had measured her length on the deck in an abortive attempt to grasp old Tom by the legs.

"By Jove! old Tom's overboard again," cried Bob, jumping on to the bulwarks with the rest of his friends. "Look! the old fellow is being carried out to sea, and will be lost."

"I've been the cause of his death!" groaned the Stinger; "the hand of fate is in this. Oh, dear! why was I born a woman?"

She put up her umbrella, the rain coming down, and mounted the bulwarks.

"Oh, I was in the sea with him yesterday. Both of us were nearly drowned, and now I am the unhappy cause of this fresh disaster; verily, I shall have all my sympathy washed out of me soon."

A rope had been thrown to old Tom who grasped it.

But at this moment a thrill of horror ran through all on board.

A large shark was seen to swim towards old Tom.

"Oh, I am the cause of his death. Look at the shark!" shrieked the Stinger. "Somebody save him; and——"

What the Stinger might have continued to say was never known, for she lost her balance and fell overboard, the umbrella still raised in her hand.

"Another one over!" cried Bob, rushing forward with a long dagger in his hand, "another one to fill the maws of the monster of the deep. Not if I know it. I'll fight it out with the shark!"

And before anyone could prevent him, he leapt overboard, dagger in hand.

"Oh, my master, my good, brave master, he will be drowned or swallowed up," cried Buttons, leaning over the bulwarks.

"Not alone," cried Ironfist, who in the meantime had stripped himself to the waist, and mounted the bulwarks. "I'm after him," and down he dived into the deep sea.

Strongback was climbing down the bowsprit ready to jump and risk his life for gallant Bob.

"Stay back," cried Bob; "we don't want too many. Leave me alone to fight this monster."

Bob was swimming hard towards the shark.

Ironfist swam towards old Tom, whom he managed to grasp, just as the shark passed over his head with his jaws downwards.

The shark made a dive and came up to the surface on his back in close proximity to Bob Blunt, who swam out of his reach, and then, the shark making a dash at him, our hero dived under his belly, planting the dagger up to the hilt in the back of its neck.

When Bob arose to the surface, the shark swam away, dyeing the water around with his blood.

"Stay on board, Strongback; I can manage this beast by myself; and you, Swiftfoot and Longsight, we don't want any more down here. Keep back."

"Here he comes again; look out, Mr. Blunt," cried Longsight.

"I'm ready for him," replied Bob.

"Oh, to think that Elizabeth Ann is to be food for sharks! Oh, thank Heaven, I've got my cork belt on, and I can't sink. Oh, Mr. Blunt, there he comes; keep him from me, for I'm a useful member of society. Ugh! you brute, I'll shut you out from looking at me."

Elizabeth Ann put her umbrella before her, for the shark was swimming towards her, with his fins in the air.

Bob saw that he had had nearly enough of it.

He swam towards the monster, dived again, and this time sent his dagger into its throat.

Down went the shark.

Bob, panting with the exertion, waited warily for the finny enemy to rise again to the surface.

The excitement of those on board was intense during the combat.

"There, take that!" shouted Bob, plunging his dagger into the shark as he again came to the surface.

But his race was nearly run.

He gave a great plunge with his tail, and as Bob again drove his dagger into the monster, he had the satisfaction of seeing it turn over on its back, dead.

"Hurrah! Hip, hip, hurrah!" cried those on board.

"What's hurrah?" asked the floating Stinger, glaring behind the umbrella.

"The shark," said Bob.

"Is he dead?"

"As a door-nail."

"Hurrah! Elizabeth Ann's herself again. Mind my cork belt, and give me a lift, Mr. Blunt."

"What for?"

"I'm going to mount the shark—ride on him in delight."

"All right. Up you go."

A line was now thrown from the ship, and Bob fastened it round the body of the shark.

In the meantime Ironfist and old Tom, with his help, had gained the spot where Bob and the Stinger were now busy.

When the rope was fastened round the shark, the Stinger waved her umbrella.

But not keeping her balance, the body lurched over, and Elizabeth Ann went over the other side.

The corks that she wore would not allow her to sink.

She soon came to the surface.

"Hold on, ma'am; I'm with you. Look here: clap your legs round him like this, and you'll keep on," said old Tom, mounting the shark.

"I forgive you all your wickedness for trying to make love to me. Old Tom, give us your hand," said the Stinger, floating alongside of the shark.

With the assistance of Bob and Ironfist, the Stinger was placed on the shark. One arm she threw lovingly around old Tom's waist, the other held her umbrella over the two.

"Now, are you right?"

"Right!" replied the Stinger. "Oh, I ought to have been born a man."

"Pull away," cried Bob.

Ironfist took hold of the tail of the shark, whilst Bob mounted the head, and thus they were dragged towards the "Busy Bee."

As soon as they came within hail of the vessel, three ringing cheers greeted them.

"Bravo, Stinger! Hurrah for the Stinger! She's a Briton!" cried Buttons, waving his hat frantically aloft. "Stinger, you shall be my mother. Hurrah!"

"Drat that boy! He's always making fun of me," said the Stinger.

"Never mind, ma'am, you'll have the laugh of him this time," said old Tom.

"Three cheers for Bob Blunt, the traveller, and Ironfist, the brave, and the lovely young Stinger!" cried Buttons, waving his hat as they came alongside of the ship, and a rope-ladder was lowered for them to reach the deck.

The cheers were given with all that spontaneous heartiness peculiar to the inhabitants of the British Isles.

"Now, then, Miss Stinger. Ladies first."

"Oh, but the gentlemen always ascend the stairs first. Betsy Stinger is not over fond of showing her ankles; they are her own private property, and no one has a right to see them."

"Very well, we'll go first. Up with you, old Tom."

"Aye, aye, sir."

Old Tom soon reached the deck.

Ironfist and the others followed.

Buttons danced with joy, and then stood on his head, and clapped his feet just under the nose of Miss Stinger.

"Drat that boy!" she cried, bringing down her umbrella with a downward stroke on the back of Buttons.

"Oh, my! I've got it," shouted Buttons.

The shark was hauled on board.

"Man, is it good to eat?" asked the Stinger of old Tom.

"Of course it is, ma'am; it's like cod fish."

"Then I vote, as an unprotected female, that we will have some."

"So we will," said Buttons, coming up again to the Stinger. "There's the axe; and now you will have to sever its tail, for the ladies always do that."

"I'm ready. Stand aside, men."

With that Miss Stinger seized the axe, and with a few vigorous strokes she severed the shark's tail from its body.

"You are a brave un," said Buttons to her; "I'll not have you for my mother any longer; 'pon my word, I'm in love with you. Give us a kiss."

And before the Stinger knew what was about to happen, Buttons threw his arms around her neck, and gave the Stinger a sounding kiss.

"There!" he cried, "I've been and gone and done it that time."

"Oh, that boy; to think that the virgin lips of Elizabeth Ann are to be defiled by a boy's lips. Drat the boy!"

And Stinger, with a firm grip on her umbrella, and a step as though she had the seven-leagued boots on, went after Buttons.

"Oh, she's coming to make love to me now," grinned Buttons. "I say, Elizabeth Ann, do drop your bottle sunshade; it's too much for your faithful Buttons."

"I've got you now," cried the Stinger, making a dash at poor Buttons, and holding him firmly by the nape of the neck.

"Oh, what d'ye mean by catchin' hold of a man like that?" cried Buttons.

"Man!" cried the Stinger, "you're only a buttons, a hop-o'-my-thumb. Get out, you urchin."

With that she picked up her umbrella, and made a blow at Buttons.

But that youngster twisted himself out of the reach of the terrible gingham; he beat a hasty retreat down into the cabin, leaving the Stinger on deck to bear the laughter of Bob and his friends, which she did with a good grace, and joining in heartily herself.

But during this time of merriment, the Stinger found that she still had her damp clothes on.

She departed to change them.

Bob went down to change his clothes, preparatory to joining Captain Frobisher Jones at dinner.

But there were two persons on board who had built greatly on the death of our hero and were much disappointed that on the two several occasions Bob Blunt, the Traveller, had not found his death in a watery grave.

But it was not to be.

When Bob Blunt was seen to step on board the "Busy Bee," safe and well, and the hero of the day after slaying the shark, the disappointment marked on the countenance of the two ruffians was great.

So plain was it that Longsight noticed it at once.

"Those are rum uns; I'll keep my eye upon them, for I begin to think they are a couple of swindlers, who have eloped with the coin of the realm," muttered Longsight.

But Bob did not notice them.

He was too much engaged in answering the congratulations of his friends.

"Well," muttered Bow-legged Bill, "this is a killer; that chap is not born to be drowned, cuss him!"

"No; I was in hopes that the sea would make me the owner of thirty thousand a year, but luck's against me."

"Never mind, Delorme, my boy, better luck next time, say I."

"I hope so. Look how the chap is being toadied upon. The idiots, they know he has thirty thousand a year."

With a curse, the two worthies descended into the cabin, where Bob was already enjoying himself.

He noticed the two attentively, and then turned aside.

Howard met his glance unflinchingly.

He assumed an easy, nonchalant manner, with a slight swagger.

It would not do for him to show his teeth at present, although in his present angry mood he felt very much inclined to pick a quarrel with Bob.

"Never mind, I can wait. I heard the captain say that we should stop at Lisbon for a day, to unload and take in cargo; that will give me an opportunity, and, perhaps, speed my return to Old England, not as a penniless adventurer, but a rich man."

These thoughts possessed him as he sat at the table.

He then entered into a gay conversation with the company in general.

But Bow-legged Bill held his tongue, only dropping a word now and then.

He sat stroking his false beard, and helping himself to all the dainties on the table, but watching, with a lynx eye, the countenance of our hero.

CHAPTER XIII.

AFTER DINNER—THE STINGER HAS THE TOOTHACHE—THE LOVE PAIN—BUTTONS' OWN PILL—THE DOCTOR CATCHES IT HOT—BUTTONS' MANŒUVRE, WHICH ENDS BY THE WRONG PARTY GETTING IN THE WAY.

NOW, I wonder what that fellow Delorme is so very bland and polite to me for?" asked Bob Blunt of the doctor.

"I can't tell; but I fancy he may have some ulterior views upon the hand of that strong-minded female, the Stinger."

"I should think that hardly probable."

"Nothing is impossible, nor improbable, where money is concerned," remarked the doctor.

"True, that is a motive," said Bob. "Holloa! what is the matter with the Stinger?"

In truth that lady had given signs of derangement.

She first of all began to pick her teeth with a fork, then gulp down several glasses of wine, then hold her hand to her cheek, rock her head on one side, open her mouth, insert her forefinger into it, and then, all of these remedies failing, she gave vent to a very loud groan.

"What is it, ma'am?" asked the captain, very politely. "Anything the matter?"

"Toothache."

"Indeed; that is very bad. Let me recommend a little hot grog; about a pint, hot and strong."

"No."

"Well, lie down for a little time."

"I can't. Oh, my back tooth, oh!"

"It's the love pain you have got, Miss Stinger; all for the love of me," said Buttons.

"You! Drat you, I'm born to misery. Oh, this dreadful tooth."

"Well, if the pain does not subside soon, send for me," said the ship doctor, rising and going on deck.

"I am sure to do that," moaned the Stinger. "Oh! I have got my death through tumbling into the beastly sea after that wretched old salt. I am born to bad luck."

"Sweet child, rest your weary head on my faithful bosom," said Buttons, with a comical expression in his face.

"Oh, it pains awfully," cried Stinger, jumping up and coming down on her feet, like a young elephant.

"Come, my pet lamb; come to its own Buttons."

And that lively youth made a motion with his arms.

The Stinger gave another big jump.

"Away, you imp. Oh, my tooth. Am I never to have any peace?" she cried.

"Yes; when you become the beautiful Mrs. Buttons."

"Drat that boy! Get out of the cabin."

And the Stinger arose, driving the redoubtable Buttons before her, until he was forced to evacuate the cabin.

But the pain increased on his departure, and she was compelled to throw herself at length upon a couch.

Here she lay, groaning and moaning to an alarming extent.

So excruciating was the pain, that the Stinger's legs played a tattoo upon the

"SHE SEIZED HER UMBRELLA, AND GAVE CHASE TO BUTTONS."

sofa, as she lay, and at that moment, Buttons reappeared.

"Well, how is the love pain, my love?" he asked, demurely. "Is not the young and lovely Stinger any better?"

"Better! no. Oh it hurts terribly," groaned the Stinger.

"Indeed; well, the doctor has given me a pill for you. It is an infallible cure for the toothache, and as you won't accept my love, I will tell you it is a cure for the heartache as well; here, allow me to place it in the corner of that beautiful hollow tooth."

The Stinger, by this time, was open to any remedy that was likely to effect a cure.

"Does the doctor say it will do me good?"

"Certainly, at once. Open your mouth and shut your eyes," said Buttons.

The Stinger complied.

"Which is the tooth?"

"Here; right at the back."

"Now, then, this is one of Buttons' own pills, sure to cure. I'm going to take a patent out for them, and I know that I shall drive a roaring trade with them amongst the natives of Africa. Now then—hey presto! the pain's gone."

Buttons inserted the pill into the Stinger's hollow tooth, and then discreetly withdrew to a safe distance, to see the effect of his infallible remedy.

At first the Stinger sat bolt upright.

"Has the pain ceased?" asked Buttons, from a distance.

"Yes; I think it has a little."

"I told you so; now you ought to reward me with a medal for curing you of the terrible love pain."

"Oh! I believe the pill is melting in my mouth," said the Stinger.

"Why, that's the way it acts; don't you see?" replied Buttons.

"Oh! how nasty it tastes—achew! Why—why, you scamp, it's—achew!—it's snuff, you rascal."

And the Stinger began to shake her head and sneeze to an alarming extent.

"Oh, oh, Lor'; fetch me something to wash my mouth out. Achew—achew!"

When she had recovered herself a little, she said sternly—

"Buttons, who gave you that pill?"

"My godfathers and godmothers at my baptism; I mean the learned Doctor Know-all," replied Buttons.

"He gave it to you, did he?"

"He did; hasn't it cured you?"

"Cured me! An abominable snuff pill cure me—achew! Ha, here is the doctor," said the Stinger.

In fact the innocent doctor had at that moment returned to the cabin.

As soon as the Stinger caught sight of him she rushed upon him.

"You sent me that pill!" she cried. "That horrid snuff pill!"

"Really, madam, you are labouring under a mistake," cried the astonished doctor.

"Mistake or not, you sent it; I'll teach you to play your pranks off upon Elizabeth Ann Stinger—take that, it's better than snuff pills."

Her umbrella was close at hand, she seized it, and began to belabour the doctor with it as hard as she could.

The doctor beat a hasty retreat up the cabin stairs.

Stinger followed him.

So did Buttons, who was delighted with the turn affairs had taken.

But once on deck the doctor soon got out of reach.

The enraged Stinger, baffled in vengeance, leaned against the mast to draw breath, and then she caught sight of the grinning Buttons.

"Has Buttons' Nervine cured the tic-dolereux, may I ask the charming Stinger?" he said.

"Oh, drat that boy! It was you, was it?"

"It was, my love; my lovely Stinger," grinned Buttons.

"Drat you! I'll be even with you," growled the Stinger. "Oh, my tooth, my poor, poor tooth! It's coming on again."

The doctor at this moment approached the Stinger very warily.

"I beg your pardon, doctor," said the Stinger. "I do, indeed; it was that confounded boy Buttons who gave me a snuff pill, and told me it came from you."

"I accept the apology; but I must

beg of you not to be so hasty for the future."

" I will not."

" Let there be peace between us, then. Is your tooth better ?"

" No ; it's worse. There, it's going it ; oh, dear, oh, Lor'."

" Let me recommend you to have it out, then," said the doctor.

" Out, oh ! I cannot bear to lose my teeth ; they are my principal adornment," said the Stinger showing them.

" That may be so ; but that one particular tooth will always annoy you. It is a hollow one, and in time will affect the others."

" Then I'll venture to have it out. But, doctor, dear doctor, don't hurt me too much. I'm a poor unprotected female, you know."

" I'll do it very gently. Buttons, go and fetch me my instruments."

" Yes, sir."

Buttons soon appeared with a large case of instruments.

" Now I would recommend you to kneel down," said the doctor.

" Had we not better go below ?" said Miss Stinger, looking with terror at the dreaded instruments the doctor held in his hand.

" No ; the light is better on deck. Here, Buttons, come and hold the lady's head."

" Oh, with pleasure. I'll hold her head for an hour if you like," said Buttons.

" Hark at him ! he glories in my anguish. I'll punch you with pleasure presently," cried the Stinger, shaking her fists at Buttons. " Oh, my poor tooth !"

" Hold still, now ; we won't be long before it's out."

Buttons held the Stinger by the head with both hands, with a happy grin on his face, whilst the doctor inserted the tooth-drawer into her mouth.

He fixed the instrument.

" Now, hold tight, Buttons."

" Right, sir. I've got her."

The doctor gave a tremendous pull.

But the Stinger's tooth was stubborn.

" Oh, you brute !" she groaned ; " you will pull my head off."

" Hold, hard, ma'am."

The doctor gave another pull.

This time with a result.

The Stinger's tooth came out so suddenly that the doctor fell on his back, whilst Buttons, who was holding the lady, found himself on the deck with the Stinger on the top of him.

" Oh, murder ! Look ; the blood—my tooth !" cried the Stinger.

" You're a-smothering me ; get up. I can't breathe !" cried Buttons.

Old Tom, coming up at that moment, raised the Stinger to her feet, and then said—

" Well, you're all right, ma'am ; the pain has gone."

" Gone ; no. I believe he has drawn the wrong tooth."

" That I'll swear I have not ; this is the one—and a stunner it is."

He held it up.

"Why, it's a pig's tooth," cried Buttons.

" You brat ! Why, I have always been famed for my teeth."

" Oh, well, that tooth's big enough for an elephant's."

And Buttons held it aloft.

" But I'm happy it's out. Bravo ! we've been saved from the sharks, and now my sweetheart's got rid of her little tooth."

" Hurrah ! Buttons," cried old Tom.

Buttons looked round to see where he could find a convenient place to practise his usual trick whenever he was excited or moved.

At last, seeing a water-cask, the bottom of which offered a convenient opportunity for the display of his propensity, he placed his head on it, and elevating his heels high in the air, he expressed the joy he felt with energetic applause with his feet.

But a sudden roll of the ship precipitated him on to the deck.

Coming in contact with the Stinger's legs, that worthy lady was sent prone on her hands and knees over him.

" Oh, Lor' ! I've done it again. Madam Bluebottle, I beg your pardon."

" You wretch !" she screamed, and scrambling to her feet, she seized her umbrella, and gave chase to Buttons, who dodged her around the water-cask, taking a sight at the same time.

"Now, then, mind who you are hitting. I won't marry you, Stinger, if you don't drop that little umbrella," cried Buttons.

Stinger drove him towards the cabin steps, and as she raised her umbrella to strike him, he fell down.

He had placed himself close to Dr. Know-all.

Down came the umbrella upon the skull of the learned doctor.

Buttons crept away.

"Madam, what means this outrage? My head, madam, I beg leave to say, was not made for you to practise your stump speeches upon. Action and attitude are everything in oratory, but I must request you to restrain your ardour, and reserve your umbrella for the next time you address the benighted inhabitants of Africa."

With that the doctor donned his crumpled beaver, and stalked majestically away.

The Stinger espied the face of the grinning Buttons on the top of the cabin stairs.

She shook her fist at him.

"You shall have it!" she cried.

"Thank you; not to-day, baker. Any other day you may oblige by calling; hot and crummy one, nice and doughy, but for the present, I'd rather not."

"Drat that boy! He worries me more than the wrongs of my sex. Well, I'll console my wounded spirit with a cup of tea."

"Go it, old un. I've got the tooth," cried Buttons.

"Oh! I must have my tooth. Give me the tooth, Buttons, and I'll forgive you."

"Oh! come and fetch it," said Buttons, running up the rigging.

The Stinger caught him on the posterior with her umbrella as he was mounting.

"Oh!" cried Buttons.

"Come down!"

"I will, if you don't hit me."

"Will you give me my tooth?"

"Yes."

"Then come down!"

Buttons slowly descended the rigging, and then gave the Stinger what she supposed to be her tooth, for it was wrapped up in a handkerchief.

"Come, Mr. Blunt," she said to our hero, who had been an amused spectator of what had passed; "come, you shall see me burn my tooth for luck."

Without taking the least notice of Buttons, she descended into the cabin.

But when she untied the handkerchief, she found, instead of her tooth, a bone of a sheep's foot.

"Lor,' what a tooth!" cried Buttons, who was close behind her. "Ain't it a pretty one, Stinger?"

"You villain, give me my tooth."

"Why, you've got it. Call that a small tooth. Bah! why, a horse has got a smaller one than that."

"Oh, I shall throw myself overboard. My life is becoming unbearable; that brat of a boy is the worry of my life. Give me my tooth."

"Kiss me, then, and swear to be mine on the hymeneal haltar."

"A halter to hang yourself with, I'll give you. Now, my tooth."

"Ha, ha! what a tooth!"

"Give it up, Buttons," said Bob.

"Well, sir, as you command me, of course I'll do it; but I wanted to have it mounted on a gold pin as a memento from my lovely sweetheart, Elizabeth Ann Stinger."

Miss Stinger deigned no reply.

She burnt her tooth with some salt, and vowed she should be lucky from that hour.

CHAPTER XIV.

LISBON—THE CAFE—THE STINGER COMES OUT STRONG—SHE HARANGUES THE
NATIVES—ON THE ROAD TO CINTRA—THE RETURN—THE ASSASSINS—ONE UP, ONE
DOWN—THE DEVIL TAKE THE HINDMOST—HURRAH FOR MESSIEURS IRONFIST AND
STUMPS!—SWIFTFOOT PROVES THAT HE IS SWIFT OF FOOT—"AIN'T THIS JOLLY?"

OWING to contrary winds, the good
ship "Busy Bee" did not reach
Lisbon until two days after the
rescue of old Tom and the Stinger
from the maws of the shark.

On the morning of the third day they
sighted the city, and the hearts of all
were elated.

"Now, attention, Buttons. Summon
my body guard, for I intend to go on
shore."

"Yes, sir."

Buttons here called out their names.

"Mr. Doctor Know-all-about-it."

"Here."

"Mr. Strongback."

"Here!"

"Mr. Longsight."

"Here!"

"Mr. Swiftfoot."

"Here!"

"Mr. Ironfist."

"Here!"

"Mr. Stumpy Stumps."

"Here!"

"Now, gentlemen, I shall require your
company. We will explore the city of
Lisbon. The ship is in the harbour, and
will not sail until the morning, so we
shall have plenty of time to look about
us," said Bob.

"Hurrah! ain't this prime, just!"
cried Buttons.

"If you have no objection, Mr. Blunt,
I would be thankful for your escort."

It was Miss Stinger.

Now Bob was fully alive to the ridiculous appearance of the Stinger.

Her huge poke bonnet, pattens, and
umbrella, as well as a bundle of pamphlets on "Woman's Rights," with which
she was about to convert the Lisbon
ladies, were sure to attract the attention
of the crowd.

He hesitated.

"Am I not nicely clad for the occasion,
sir?" she asked.

"Oh, yes, we shall be glad of your
society," replied Bob, at length, much to
Dr. Know-all's chagrin, for he repeatedly
nudged our hero not to grant the Stinger's
request.

But Bob resolved she should go.

"Come along, Miss Stinger. I'll
stand by you, for I believe you are a
trump."

"Sir, I have a mission to fulfil," said
the Stinger.

Bob handed her into the boat and they
were soon on the quay.

Old Tom was requested to accompany
the party, which he did with great
glee.

Since the moment of his rescue by our
hero, he had been assiduous in his at-
tentions to his rescuer.

A crowd of idlers were looking on, and
Elizabeth Ann at once attracted their
attention.

"What are they staring at? Don't
you think they are impressed with the
dignity of my appearance, Mr. Blunt?"
asked the Stinger.

"It looks very much like it," replied
Bob.

"Well, I'll address them. I will
arouse them to their wrongs. Weak off-
spring of degenerate man!"

Elizabeth Ann here raised her umbrella, and this action seemed to terrify
the beholders, for they one and all gave
the Stinger a wide berth.

"Well, now, this is strange. I call
that giving in. The march of intellect
drives ignorance before it. On!"

With that the Stinger flourished her
umbrella with a determined air, and,
linking her arm in that of the doctor's,

much to his disgust, she marched on through the streets.

Nothing could express the doctor's horror as the Stinger dragged him along.

"Ma'am, ma'am, let me go."

"Be not afraid," replied the lady in a protecting manner. "I'll take care of you; no one shall interfere with me."

"I don't think they will," muttered Bob.

He saw the principal sights of Lisbon, and then the party, feeling tired, they entered a large café in the main street.

A grove of orange and lemon trees skirted the outside of the café, beneath which little tables were placed, so that the numerous customers could sit outside and enjoy the fresh air and their refreshments simultaneously.

The arrival of Bob Blunt and his friends created a stir amongst the *habitués* of the café.

They took seats outside.

All eyes were fixed upon the Stinger.

She, very little disconcerted, returned stare for stare.

Whilst the refreshments were being consumed, Bob ordered Longsight to procure mules and a guide for a visit to Cintra, the spot where Sir H. Dalrymple signed a convention with Marshal Junot, in the year 1808.

Buttons had discreetly retired to a considerable distance from the Stinger.

The doctor had imitated his example, and the two were enjoying the profound astonishment that the Stinger caused to the natives.

She had produced her teapot.

"Drat the people! What are they looking at?" cried the indignant spinster.

These words were addressed to an elderly gentleman and two ladies, who were clad in the becoming mantilla of the country, and who were staring in mute astonishment.

"You had better ask them the question," suggested Bob, in a whisper.

"I will."

With that the Stinger strode up to the astonished Portuguese gentleman—for such she presumed him to be—and putting one foot foremost with great determination, said—

"Sir, my name is Stinger—Elizabeth Ann. I hail from London. But perhaps you may not have heard the name of Stinger in these benighted regions where women are slaves. I am the lady with a mission—ask that man there, for whose sake I ventured into the briny deep, and who nearly was the cause of washing human sympathy out of me."

This last allusion was to old Tom, who had come in dangerous proximity to the manly spinster.

"Talk about men," continued she; "men! Why, I'm a better man than all of them. I am a lady with a mission to obtain justice all over the world for women. I am the pioneer of liberty. No longer shall man usurp our rights. Know, then, at the very first opportunity I shall discard the dress of my sex. I will wear leather and corduroys. It shall not be said that Elizabeth Ann Stinger refused to assert the privileges of a freeborn Briton in order to vindicate her sex against the tyranny of man."

The Stinger was forced to pause for want of breath.

A crowd had by this time assembled round them.

"They don't understand your lingo, marm," said old Tom; "you know you're a furriner over here."

"Me a foreigner! Me that was born within the chimes of Bow bells; me, man? Do you know that I shall bring an action at law against you for slander?"

Her excitement increased with her volubility of expression.

"Benighted foreigners, I come to rescue you from heathendom. Here, here read this, and be converted to my creed."

With this she produced her bundle of pamphlets, and distributed them amongst the crowd.

As she thrust one into the hands of the strange gentleman, whom she thought a Portuguese, he replied to her evident astonishment—

"Ma'am, I have been thinking you're a rum un, but good for trade. Now, if you'll give me your horder for the corduroys and leathers I'll let you have 'em cheap. I'm in the tally line, No. 16, Saveloy Alley, close to Aldgate pump.

Name over the door, Isaacs. N.B.—Weekly payments taken."

"Lor'!"

"True, marm."

"You idiot, why didn't you say you were not a foreigner?" cried the exasperated Miss Stinger. "I have long since given up all hopes of converting my fellow-cockneys. Man, you're a deceiver."

By this time our hero thought it best to decamp, for the crowd had increased, and several men in uniform were seen to push through the crowd towards them.

He beheld Longsight in the distance with the mules and the guides.

But as he was in the act of drawing the Stinger away, two policemen placed themselves on each side of the lady.

"What does this mean? Man, do you know who I am?" she cried.

The men muttered something, and then Dr. Know-all interpreted their acts to our hero, who at once saw that the Stinger was likely to get them into a scrape.

"You are arrested, Miss Stinger, for causing an assemblage of the populace, which is against the laws of the country. Further, with distributing, so they suppose, political tracts, inciting to sedition."

"Lor'! drat them, ain't I a Briton? Let me go. I appeal to the outraged laws of my country—justice I'll have. Keep your hands off."

Miss Stinger by a vigorous thrust freed herself from the hands of the two men, but two more came to their assistance, and Miss Stinger was deprived of her umbrella, teapot, and bundle of pamphlets.

This last indignity rose the lady to fury, but her tongue made up for it.

She continued to vociferate loudly, when a gentleman stepped forward, and politely addressed himself to our hero.

He proved to be none other than the British consul.

Bob, in a few words, explained the matter to him, and then the consul, after a consultation with the officer, asked Miss Stinger for her passport, which she gave him.

"If I'm going to be a martyr, let me be a martyr. My blood shall go up to Heaven, and vengeance, dread vengeance fall upon base man!"

"No, you will not be a martyr yet, ma'am," said the consul, laughingly; "but I have promised to be responsible for your good behaviour during the remainder of your stay in Lisbon."

"My umbrella! my teapot! My pattens! My papers! Betsy is herself again! Doctor, your arm," said the Stinger.

There was no time for the doctor to get away, for the Stinger took his arm, and marched him off to the road.

"Will you go with us?" asked Bob of her, when away from the cafe.

"Go with you? Of course. I never mean to leave you," she replied.

"Then be kind enough to mount."

"What! that there donkey?"

"It is not a donkey, it is a mule," said Bob.

"Well, it is all the same; but how am I ever to get across that animal?" asked Miss Stinger, pointing to the mule.

"You see we have improvised a side-saddle for you," said Bob.

"It shall never be said that Elizabeth Ann Stinger was afraid to cross a foreign donkey; so I mount. Heigho!"

And the Stinger swung, with Bob's assistance, on to the back of the mule.

Seeing that the lady was mounted, our hero and his friends followed suit, and the whole party were now beyond the dirty bye streets of Lisbon.

The road then greatly increased in undulations.

"Oh! master. I'm a traveller now, in real earnest. I wonder what they'd say to me in old England, if they could see me now in all my glory," exclaimed the delighted Buttons.

"They'd take you for the King of the Cannibal Islands," said Bob.

"Would they, now? Halloa! look at them there hills."

"Yes; that is Cintra," said the doctor.

"'And Cintra's mountains greet them on their way,'" quoted Bob, from Byron. "Yes, this land is truly described as an Eden, peopled by slaves, on whom nature wastes her wonders."

They saw the palace where the convention was signed. "The horrid crags by toppling convent crowned," and all the beauties of that favoured land.

Well did they mark such favoured spots, until the sun gave them warning it was time to return to Lisbon.

They accordingly made haste to retrace their steps.

Miss Elizabeth Ann Stinger had become very merry.

The numerous bottles of wine that had been tapped, and of which the Stinger had freely partaken, had an exhilarating effect upon the lady with a mission.

She rode her mule very carelessly, or rather unsteadily.

Occasionally she slid on one side, and then the gallant Buttons would support her.

The whole party paused on the decline of a hill to catch the last gleams of the setting sun on Cintra's woody height.

"Beautiful, beautiful!" cried the Stinger. "I could be happy here."

"Halloa! a spill."

A loud scream from the Stinger proclaimed the news that something had happened.

"Oh!" she groaned, "that horrid donkey has kicked me off. Oh! I suffer. Help!"

Bob assisted her to rise.

It was then found that the pommel at the saddle had broken off, most probably with the weight that was brought to bear against it by the Stinger.

"What is to be done?" asked Bob.

"Do you think I am a woman to be baulked by trifles? Give me a hand, Mr. Blunt," replied the Stinger.

Bob did so.

She was on the left side of the mule.

Placing her right foot in the stirrup, she swung herself into the saddle, and to her surprise found herself with her face to the tail, which latter appendage was offered to her by Buttons.

"Why, I believe I'm the wrong side," cried the astonished Stinger.

"All right, ma'am; take the reins," replied Buttons, holding up the donkey's tail.

"Drat that boy! I've got up the wrong side, Mr. Blunt. I must get down again."

The Stinger got down accordingly, amidst much laughter, and she mounted left foot first, this time with her face to the head of the animal, and astride of it like a man.

"Now, then, put up my umbrella. Give me my pattens. Where's my papers? Off we go. March!"

Gradually the sun went down, and then a clear twilight stole over the landscape.

Our friends were very merry.

Old Tom occasionally awoke the echoes with his lively ditties, and then the Stinger followed suit with her usual lamentations on women's wrongs.

Thus they passed on until they reached the outskirts of Lisbon.

Darkness had now set in.

Suddenly, when they were passing through a narrow lane, a peculiar kind of cry startled them.

"What was that?" asked Bob.

"Nothing. The hoot of an owl I think," replied the doctor.

Then Bob's mule stumbled.

He knew something must be in the way to impede their progress.

"Halt!" he cried.

He was stooping down to examine the ground before them, when he thought he beheld several men glide along, and he at once thought that they were beset by robbers.

"Draw your revolvers," cried Bob.

"Oh, I feel so funky," moaned Buttons.

"Silence!" shouted Bob. "One at the time, single file."

He advanced very cautiously, concealing his revolver by his side.

Before he had passed a yard further, three men confronted him.

"Stand!" cried one.

"What do you want?" asked Bob.

A thrust from a dagger was the answer he received; but before the blow could reach him, Bob raised his revolver and fired.

The man fell dead.

"That is Number One. Back, or you are dead men," cried Bob.

Then a howl rent the lane.

A howl of rage from the robbers on seeing their leader fall.

A dozen men rushed forward.

"Keep back, or you're dead men," shouted Bob.

He fired right and left.

Several men fell to the shots from his seven-shooter.

The robbers fell back.

"Now, lads, all in a body—charge!" cried Bob, leading the way.

The affrighted mules turned back their ears and ran hard, but the road was narrow and dark, and the Stinger could not retain her balance on the mule.

She came to the ground.

The cry arrested the flight of our hero, who commanded a halt.

The Stinger was put upon her mule.

"Hold on, marm," said old Tom; "I'll splice you to the back of Mr. Moke in a jiffy."

With that, he produced a stout coil of tarred twine, and before the lady well knew what he was about, old Tom had tied her securely to the mule.

"A gale of wind won't blow you off now, marm," said old Tom.

In the meantime the assassins had not been slow to perceive that the fugitives had been compelled to pause.

They rushed up to the narrow lane in a body.

Their numbers had been augmented to some twenty.

Bob saw that he was outnumbered.

"We must face them. Who shall be in the front?" he cried.

"Ironfist is here," cried the brave fellow, stepping forward.

"And Stumps."

"And Strongback,"

"Hurrah for Ironfist! Hurrah for Strongback! Hurrah for Stumps! Go it, little one. I'll back you up," cried Buttons.

And he patted the colossal back of Ironfist approvingly.

The giant smiled grimly as he took off his coat.

"Let them come; I'm quite ready for about a dozen."

It was a very narrow lane here—three could impede the progress of a dozen.

Ironfist stood like a gladiator, Strongback and Stumps by the side of him.

As the foremost assassins came face to face with them, with uplifted stilettoes,

Ironfist lunged out with his terrible fist at the foe.

The blow crashed into his face.

He lay as if dead.

Stumps had not been inactive.

As one of them advanced towards him, Stumps crouched down.

The man did not perceive him, but he soon felt the hardness of his head.

Crash!

Stumps had quickly sent him flying into the air.

He had placed his neck between the man's legs and hurled him over his shoulder with terrific force.

The crash that struck the ears of all was the man's skull as it came in contact with the stone flags.

"That's Number Two," cried Buttons.

"Number Three follows," cried Strongback, throwing a burly robber in the centre of the band, where he fell with a broken neck.

Numbers Four, Five and Six were treated in the same way.

The robbers paused.

They were consulting together.

But Bob Blunt knew better than to allow them breathing time.

He stood up in the stirrups of his saddle, and fired.

The doctor did the same.

They could not stand this long.

With a wild cry, they turned and fled up the lane.

"Now, the devil take the hindmost!" cried Tom. "On to them."

"Hurrah!" cried the Stinger, waving her umbrella, frantically.

"Hurrah!" repeated Buttons.

"Hurrah!" cried Swiftfoot, running with incredible speed after the robbers.

"Stop!" cried Bob.

But Swiftfoot did not reply.

He was out of sight and hearing.

They waited for his return with great anxiety, and Longsight stood up in the saddle, peering into the darkness.

"Can you see him?" asked Bob.

"No."

They waited a little longer.

Lights were gleaming in many of the houses, but the inhabitants were evidently too much accustomed to brawls to take much notice of what was going on.

At length Longsight cried out—

"He comes."

"That is fortunate."

Presently Swiftfoot came in sight of the others.

He bore a burden on his back.

This was a man.

He threw the fellow on the ground, where he lay the picture of terror.

"There is one of them. Now we shall have the truth of the assassins."

"Bravo, Swiftfoot! you have done well," cried Bob, delighted at the keen foresight that Swiftfoot had displayed.

"This black-looking rascal belongs to me," said Strongback.

With that he swung the captive up, and tied him on his mule.

"Well, we are the victors. Hurrah! my friends, I think we can hold our own against any number," said Bob.

"I never thought I should take part in a real live battle," cried Buttons. "Hurrah, Buttons, my boy, you are a hero."

"You are indeed, Buttons," said Bob, winking at the doctor. "Now let us on to the café!"

The entire company of nine, with the two guides, soon drew up in front of the café.

The British consul was smoking his cigar in front of the café as our hero dismounted from his mule.

"Unfasten my legs quick!" cried Miss Stinger. "You man, do you think one of my sex can gallop astride of a donkey for miles and miles, and be attacked by savages without a little refreshment?"

Old Tom soon liberated the lady.

"You are safe once more," cried Buttons. "Oh! I feel so jolly proud. I say, Stinger, ain't you proud of your brave Buttons?"

"Drat the boy! Get away," cried Miss Stinger.

Bob briefly narrated to the consul what had occurred to him.

"Bring up the prisoner," he said.

Strongback took the man in his arms as he would a kitten.

"Stand there, you craven cur!" cried Strongback.

The man was severely cross-questioned as to the cause of the attack upon Bob and his friends.

But all they could elicit was that two Englishmen had engaged their chief to assassinate our hero and his friends.

Who they were he knew not.

He had not seen them.

His chief had.

The man was handed over to the care of the police, who promised to investigate the affair.

But the man's confession set Bob thinking seriously.

What enemy had he?

None but his cousin Howard

But the latter was in England.

He began to think it was an attack merely for the sake of plunder.

But again and again the idea that Howard had instigated it came uppermost.

However, Bob soon forgot all about the night attack.

Buttons was reclining at his ease on three chairs, fanning himself with his hat, as if to cool himself.

"Ain't this jolly! There is rest for a tired warrior; I'm one. Hurrah! I'm Buttons, the traveller."

Our friends enjoyed themselves till midnight, when it was time to return to the good ship "Busy Bee."

As Bob was mounting the gangway, he saw the two strange passengers leaning over the bulwarks of the ship.

"Hope you enjoyed yourself on shore, Mr. Blunt," said Delorme.

"Thank you—yes, very much."

"Glad to hear it. Fine night."

"It is. Good night, sir; I'm sleepy," replied Bob.

"Good night."

Bob and his friends disappeared into their respective cabins.

"Curse him! He has escaped again. Our money is thrown away. Those villains we engaged to kill them must have played us false!" hissed Howard.

CHAPTER XV.

CAPE COAST CASTLE—THE LANDING—A CHOPPING SEA—THE STINGER'S BATH—JINGO
JOHNSON—THE STINGER MAKES A CONQUEST.

NO further incident interrupted the harmony of our friends during the remainder of the voyage.

One fine morning they were pacing the deck together, when old Tom at the masthead cried out—

"Land ho!"

"Hurrah! Africa, by the powers!"

Soon a long line of coast appeared in sight, and then the white light-house, which was the most prominent object at Cape Coast Castle.

"Land at last!" cried Bob. "Now then, our baggage. I have enough to fill a waggon; look it up."

All was bustle and hurry in looking up Bob's goods.

Cloaks, waterproofs, swords, guns, pistols, large cases of cloth, rum, tobacco, and other goods that Bob intended to present to the African chiefs to gain their help and good wishes; in fact, Bob's cargo consisted of all that was necessary for a traveller in African forests.

"Where's my pattens—my umbrella— my teapot?" cried the Stinger, bustling about with a huge bonnet-box in her hand.

"All right, marm," said old Tom; "here yer are. Dont hurry yourself, for you won't be able to land yet."

The "Busy Bee" now swung at anchor in the roads.

And as soon as this was the case, a dozen boats, crowded with natives, approached her.

"How shall we get ashore, captain?" asked Bob.

"You see, Mr. Blunt, it's rather awkward landing here. There is always a cross-current, and no boat can reach the shore very well; but if you wish to land now, you can hire the niggers to carry you through the surf."

"That'll do! Are you game, Miss Stinger?" asked Bob.

"Elizabeth Ann is always ready to do her duty, sir."

With that she flourished her umbrella, and prepared to descend into the boat.

"Good-bye, captain," said Bob. "I shall see you on shore. Some of my people will see my luggage delivered safe."

"Yes, sir. You have plenty of it."

"Now then, Buttons, jump into the boat. Go on, Stumps; are you ready?"

"All ready, sir."

"Then down with you."

"Here, sir; I wants to speak to you," said old Tom, drawing our hero aside.

"Well?"

"Ever since you saved me from that there narrow squeak from drownin', I'm your devoted sarvint. Now, I axed Captain Frobisher Jones' permission to cancel my agreement to sail with him. He consents, and I'm no longer on the ship's books."

"How! What do you intend to do then, my friend?" asked Bob.

"Ship with your honour, if you'll take an honest old salt."

"But I have not a ship."

"No matter. I daresay there'll be plenty of breeze where you're a-going to, quite enough to swell my sails."

"Well, old Tom, you may enter my service."

"In 'arnest, now?"

"Yes."

"Then I'm the fortunatest tar in the world. I'm your'n for life."

"Jump into the boat, old Tom."

"Like a shot, your honour."

"You're not going to take the man that washed all the sympathy out of me, and nearly got me eat up by a shark, Mr. Blunt?" asked the Stinger.

"Yes, ma'am."

"Oh, the brute. I'll never forgive or forget that he was the cause of my weak emotion getting the better of me."

"He goes with us. Now, are you ready, Miss Stinger?"

"I am ready. I do not intend to leave you."

"Then get into the boat."

"What, with all those grinning niggers? oh, no, not for Betsy!"

"Pooh! they won't hurt you."

"Hurt me! ha, ha, ha! Elizabeth Ann does not fear men; she is well able to protect herself against black and white."

"If that is so, jump in."

The Stinger fastened her clothing tightly round her, and very gingerly descended into the boat, where she seated herself in the stern-sheets, close to the doctor.

Bob was the last to enter the boat.

Then the blacks began to row, singing a drowsy song.

When within fifty yards of the shore, the boat grated on the bottom.

But the waves were still flowing inland, although the boat could not reach the landing-place.

"There is no help for it; we shall have to mount on the backs of the niggers," said Bob.

"What, me!" cried the Stinger.

"Yes; there is no harm in that. They will carry you safe ashore," said Bob.

"Oh, me carry you, missie; me carry you well, 'brella, boxie, missie, and all, on um shoulders. Jingo Johnson werry strong, strong arm, missie."

These words were delivered by a large and ugly grinning negro, who stood upright in the boat.

"That's the ticket, Jingo Johnson; you carry the lady," said Bob.

"Oh, horrid creature, keep away, or dread the arm of E. A. Stinger."

"Lubly missie, Jingo carry um like unborn babe," said the nigger, grinning.

"Avaunt! I want no babies about me, you black dog. Know I am Elizabeth Ann Stinger, come to convert the heathens. Keep off, horrid man."

By this time Swiftfoot, Strongback, Longsight, Ironfist, Stumps, and our hero had mounted on the back of a nigger apiece.

Miss Stinger saw that she would be left behind, so she beckoned to the willing Jingo Johnson, who seized her in his brawny arms, and stepped into the water with his not too light burden on his back.

"Be careful, nigger," said Elizabeth Ann, severely, and clutching her bonnet box; "be very careful."

"Me berry careful, missie," replied Jingo.

"That's right. Don't hold me so tight, you horrible creature."

Jingo followed in the wake of the other niggers, who had enough to do, for their burdens laughed so immoderately at their novel situations that a spill nearly took place.

Buttons was delightedly riding on the back of a nigger.

Suddenly, a loud scream made Bob and his friends, who were on shore, look round.

The Stinger and Jingo were floundering in the sea.

The frightened nigger soon got upon his legs.

"Oh, golly, missie; me berry, berry sad too," he cried, seizing the Stinger by the petticoats, and placing her on her feet.

Then a huge wave came completely over her, knocking her over, but the next moment she was up again, shouting—

"My bonnet box."

She had fallen upon her bonnet box, and smashed as it was it floated away upon the strong tide.

"Oh, my best Sunday bonnet, in which I always look so beautiful. Oh, nigger —black devil, you shall pay for my best Sunday bonnet," cried the Stinger.

"Oh, golly, golly, missie, dar now; Jingo Johnson am a fool—him punch him own head. Take that, nigger."

And the astute Jingo began to belabour his own head with one of the Stinger's pattens.

At this moment the Stinger beheld her bonnet box rise again to the surface and float away upon the strong tide.

"There it is, nigger. Fetch it; fetch it, and E. A. Stinger will forgive you."

"Oh, golly!" cried Jingo, as Miss Stinger brought her umbrella repeatedly down on his strong head. "Oh, golly, missie; you am bery lubly woman; I fetch your boxie."

Away went Jingo back into the sea.

Miss Stinger stood gazing at him, then she turned round, at last aroused to the repeated peals of laughter that came from the shore, where the others were enjoying the fun.

The doctor and Buttons, mounted upon the backs of the niggers, were amused spectators of the Stinger's mishap.

But as they were still laughing there came a larger wave than usual, and lo! their laughter ceased on the instant, for they found themselves in the water.

"Save me!" cried Buttons, clutching frantically at his nigger.

"And me!" roared the doctor, who, being particularly short-sighted, mistook Buttons' leg for a boat.

He grasped it with such energy that Buttons was dragged under water.

There would have been an end to the unlucky Buttons had not Miss Stinger rushed towards him, and laying a vigorous hand upon the seat of his trousers, placed him upon his feet on the beach.

"Oh, lovely Stinger, I thank you," gasped Buttons.

The negroes were too well inured to a ducking to heed it.

"It is all the fault of that grinning black demon there," cried the Stinger, shaking her umbrella at Jingo Johnson.

"Oh, missie, lubly missie, I lub you," said Jingo, dropping Stinger suddenly on the beach.

"Love me?" cried the Stinger, falling back upon the doctor in her astonishment.

"Yes; lub your booful nose."

"My nose?"

"Yes; a booful nose dat bloom like de lubly flower of the forest. Which it am a booful nose. I lub dat nose; it am nice and red."

The roar of laughter that greeted Jingo's sally utterly disconcerted the Stinger.

But Jingo said the words in all earnestness, for he rolled his black eyes so high up into his head that nothing but the whites were to be seen.

The Stinger when she had somewhat recovered from her astonishment turned her wrathful gaze upon Jingo, who still looked at her with the white of his eyes.

She raised her umbrella.

"You black nigger; how dare you make love to me? To me, E. A. Stinger, who scorns all men. Yes, scorns man from the bottom of her heart, although England's proudest aristocracy have knelt at her feet and humbly sued her hand. But Elizabeth Ann refused them all; and now, a nigger, and oh, Lord! such a nigger, dares to pester her with his vile tongue. Take that from, never yours, E. A. Stinger."

And down came the umbrella on the head of Jingo, who during her oration had gradually lowered his vision until he brought it to bear upon the Stinger.

"Oh, missie, hit nigger again; he lub to be hit. He lub you for it; he will follow you through the world, and ven he die he will bless your nose."

"Oh, my dignity! to be made love to by a nigger. On, or I shall have the ague before the night is out. Oh, where's my teapot?"

And Miss Stinger clutching hold of her favourite teapot retired to some little distance.

Bob and his friends were soon joined by Mr. Delorme and William Walker, who had already landed.

"Now, then," said Bob, "I hope our luggage will arrive safe; there is one trunk I wish particularly to guard. I think, Ironfist, you will be the very one to protect it."

"I will, sir."

"Keep a strict watch upon it."

"Right. What does it contain?"

"Our arms and ammunition; and without these we shall be up a tree."

"I think so; I'll guard it with my life."

"And so will I," muttered Delorme to Walker, as he walked away. "If we can gain possession of that, Bill, I think we shall win the day."

"Then we will have it; for I don't half care for Africa," replied Bow-legged Bill.

CHAPTER XVI.

THE AMMUNITION BOX—"DAT LUBLY NOSE"—START FOR THE INTERIOR.

NOW Bob had his suspicions of the two worthies, and he eyed them carefully as they walked towards the town.

"Ironfist, just spot those two fellows moving off there," said Bob.

"I do."

"Mark them well, for I do not like the look of them. Now we will make for our quarters," said Bob.

"Mr. Blunt, sir, your arm."

It was the Stinger's voice.

Bob turned round.

"Here, Jingo Johnson," he cried.

"Yes, massa, here him am."

"Carry this lady's box, and see that no arm befalls her."

"Yes, massa, Jingo look after lubly lady."

"Oh, Mr. Blunt, I asked you to protect me, not a nigger—and such a nigger," replied Elizabeth Ann, majestically.

"I have not time to attend to you, Miss Stinger. I shall have all my work to do to look after my people."

"Very well, Mr. Blunt; this is your gallantry to the sex. Doctor, I'll put myself under your protection."

"No, thank you," cried the doctor, beating a precipitate retreat, as the amiable spinster was about to take his arm.

"Here, missie, here am your own nigger; lub you bery much. Him always go with you, neber leave you. Dis nigger lub you."

"Out, you nigger; Elizabeth Ann will protect herself. Get away."

And the Stinger with all her dripping garments about her went ahead of the party with majestic strides.

They soon reached the hotel where Bob intended to reside until he had made his arrangements.

Here also Howard and Bow-legged Bill had taken up their quarters.

The entire party went to change their wet clothes, and then reassembled in the private room that Bob had ordered.

When a substantial meal had been discussed Bob arose.

"Gentlemen," he said, "you know what is before us. We shall have to rough it. Now you are all prepared to follow me, I trust."

"To a man," was the cry of all.

"Old Tom is ready," cried the sailor.

"And your faithful Buttons."

"And Elizabeth Ann Stinger, not caring where she goes to do good to her fellow-creatures, will not be behindhand."

"What, you too?" cried Bob. "I think, Miss Stinger, you will be rather in the way. The forests of Africa are not intended for ladies."

"But I am a man; at least in courage. I intend to go, even if I have to go by myself."

"Very well, you shall come."

"Heave oh, there," cried several voices out in the corridor.

"What is that?" asked Bob.

Old Tom opened the door.

"It is the luggage, sir; my eyes, what a lot," he said.

Four sailors from the "Busy Bee" here entered, carrying some of the luggage.

One of the boxes was a large iron-bound one.

It was as much as they could do to carry it, so heavy was it.

"Ah! here is our ammunition case, Ironfist; I commit that to your custody."

"And I will take care of it, watch day and night."

Ironfist then jumped upon the case, and doubling his brawny fists, said—

"I should like to see the man who could rob me of it."

"You will do," said Bob. "Now, doctor, have you all your medicines and chemicals in your possession?"

"All, sir."

"That is well. Now we must make some arrangements with the natives. We must have at least two dozen to carry our luggage. Where is Jingo Johnson?"

"Here, massa."

"Where?"

"Here."

The voice proceeded from under the table, and Bob, searching there, found the redoubtable Jingo beneath it.

"What are you doing there?" asked Bob. "Come out at once."

"Oh, massa, Jingo berry much in lub with lady with um lubly nose. Jingo want to go with you, massa."

"And so you shall, Jingo. Stand up, man."

Jingo raised himself up.

When in a line with Miss Stinger, he lifted his hands to his head, rolled his eyes, and ejaculated—

"Oh, golly, you am lubly; boofullest woman ever nigger sawed."

"Saw me?—I will chop you up first. Oh, nigger, nigger! you and I shall quarrel."

"Here, Jingo Johnson, I'm going to make you leader of the carriers. You must engage two dozen stout fellows for me," said Bob.

"Yes, massa."

"Then off with you. Now, gentlemen, I am resolved to leave for the interior in two days' time. I hope all preparations will be completed by then," said Bob.

"We will do all we can," replied the doctor.

"That is settled. Halloa! back again?"

These last words were addressed to Jingo Johnson, who put his woolly head into the room.

"Yes, massa. Here am my frien's—brave, big, fine frien's; but me not let em lub dat lubly lady."

Behind Jingo peered some dozen or two other niggers, all eager to be engaged.

Bob had them marshalled before him, and finding they suited him, he engaged them on the spot.

"Oh, I am berry happy. Jingo am going where dat lubly nosie am going."

"You brute!" cried the exasperated Stinger. "I shall drown you in the very first river we come to."

"My fetiche am lucky, missie; here it am."

And Jingo, much to the Stinger's horror, produced a human skull.

"Oh, the cannibal!" shrieked the Stinger.

"My good Jingo, just hide your charm, or fetiche, as you call it; for I do not wish my digestion to be spoiled by the sight of your ugly trophy," said Bob.

"Bery good, massa; you see plenty fetiche in Ashanti land. King Koff, great king, hab many, many fetiche."

"That may be; but I have no particular liking for them," replied Bob.

"Oh, white massa hab better fetiche."

"How?"

"He hab um lubly nose. Make nice fetiche," cried Jingo, pointing to the Stinger.

The idea of making a fetiche of Miss Stinger's nose was sublime.

But the spinster did not altogether see the fun of it.

She uttered an indignant protest, raised her umbrella, and rushed at Jingo.

"Drat him!" cried the Stinger. "To think the wretch wants my nose for charm, or fetiche, as he calls it. My nose, E. A. Stinger. Oh, it's horrible."

*   *   *   *   *

When Bob Blunt inquired for the two passengers who had been seen in Cape Coast, he was told that they had started for the interior, on a shooting expedition.

This news puzzled our hero.

"Delorme and Walker mean me some mischief, perhaps murder," said Bob.

"A GLITTERING ARRAY OF BEADS AND CHAINS FASCINATED THE KING'S EYES."

CHAPTER XVII.

FIRST SIGHT OF THE NATIVES—BUTTONS' DELIGHT—BOB'S FIRST LION.

THREE days after, Bob Blunt started from Cape Coast into the interior. They were soon in the midst of Prah, or jungle.

It was early morning.

There is no intermediate twilight in tropical regions.

Darkness changes rapidly to light.

An African forest, when the sun first darts its radiance amidst the deep woods, is delicious.

Bob travelled on till noon.

Then he ordered a halt at the entrance of the deep wood.

Provisions were produced, and the party sat down to their first meal in the wilds of Africa.

Whilst they were lazily stretched on the grass, a strange noise was heard in the distance.

"What is that, Jingo?" asked Bob.

"Niggers."

"Niggers, yes, they am going to village," said Jingo, with great indifference.

Soon the natives came in sight.

At first some twenty women loaded with packages, their children strapped on to the weights they carried, or on to their backs, whilst those who could walk rambled by their side.

"What, are those women?" asked the Stinger.

"Yes, missie, wives of the chiefs."

"Wives of the chiefs," cried Stinger. "What, do they do all the work then?"

"Yes, missie."

At this instant some dozen blacks armed with clubs and spears brought up the rear.

The men took it very easily.

"Verily, this land is worse than England. They make the women do all the work. I will protest against this indignity, this base cruelty towards the weaker sex."

"Halt!"

The Stinger placed herself in front of the natives, who regarded her with intense astonishment, as well they might, some of the blacks even showing their weapons, as if to defend themselves.

E. A. Stinger took little notice of their fierce looks, but taking forth her bundle of pamphlets, she gave each of them one.

"Be free," she cried. "Are you men, that allow the women to do all the work? For shame! liberty for all and justice. Elizabeth Ann will see you righted. Man, take that burden, will you?"

The Stinger took one of the bundles from the women, and placed it in the arms of one of the chiefs.

"There now, carry that, you black rascal."

The black did not know what to make of it.

He looked at the pamphlet, then at the bundle in his arms.

"Take up your burden and walk," cried Elizabeth Ann, with a flourish of her gingham.

"He does not understand you," said Bob Blunt.

"He does ; look !"

The African hurled the bundle at his terrified wife, knocking her down with it, thrust the pamphlet in the white calico that covered his loins, and giving a shriek, darted away through the forest, followed by his companions.

"Well, I never !" gasped Elizabeth Ann. "What does the black wretch mean?"

"You have scared them," said Bob Blunt, laughing.

"I think I have, but I have a mission. Elizabeth Ann will spread the truth throughout this benighted heathen land, and I may be happy yet."

No more was said.

The travellers continued their journey. Towards evening they entered another wide range of forest.

The grass was like velvet beneath their feet, the trees hung like a panoply about, them.

"Hark!" said Buttons to E. A. Stinger. "What a strange sound!"

Stinger listened.

As they passed on, a loud, chattering noise attracted Bob's attention.

The sound came from an innumerable tribe of monkeys.

They literally swarmed amongst the boughs of the trees.

"I must have a shot at them," said Bob. "Clear the way, lads."

Bang!

A young monkey fell wounded at his feet.

Bob stooped to pick it up.

He was in the act of doing so when a shriek like that of a child made him turn round.

The mother of the wounded one was behind him.

Her eyes seemed filled with tears.

Bob took up the young one and raised it in his arms.

The old one watched his movements with eager eyes.

"Poor little thing," said Bob. "I wish I had not fired the shot. Here, doctor, come and see whether you can cure it. I don't think the wound is mortal."

The doctor came up and very carefully bandaged up the wound.

The old one all this time stood looking on, whilst Bob held the young one very tenderly in his arms.

Bob now thought that if he carried the young one the old one would follow him.

He accordingly walked on with it.

The old monkey followed them, occasionally giving vent to a plaintive moan.

In the meantime Buttons had lagged behind the rest of the party.

"I don't feel up to this sort of thing," he muttered to himself. "Africa is a fine place, but it's awfully hard work to get along; yet I'm Buttons, the traveller, and what won't they think of me when I'm once more in Old England? Hurrah, then, Buttons is himself again. On you go, old boy."

He put his hands in his pockets and began to whistle "Pop goes the Weasel" with great energy.

All of a sudden his attention was aroused by a very large monkey who stood jabbering at him.

"Oh, my, you're a fine fellow. I should like to take you to London," cried Buttons, stopping to look at him.

The monkey began to chatter at him with great volubility.

"Get out of the way," said Buttons, taking up a stone and throwing it at him.

The monkey retorted by flinging a large cocoa nut in return, knocking Buttons' hat off.

"I say, you beast, mind my hat; I can't get a new one in this country. But here goes. Three shies a penny, old fellow. As many as you like."

He threw another stone.

The monkey and his companions threw down such a heap of cocoa nuts that Buttons stooped down to pick them up saying—

"Oh, ain't this jolly! But I must not lose master."

He had his arms full of cocoa nuts.

Suddenly he felt something heavy jump on to his back.

It was the large monkey.

"Oh, Lor'!" cried Buttons, so terrified at this that he could not move for some seconds.

The monkey grinned with delight, and as Buttons at length managed to gain his feet, the animal seized his hat, placed it on his own head, and with incredible swiftness clambered up a tree.

"Oh, you thief, you've got my hat, have you?" cried Buttons. "I'll soon make you give it up."

With that Buttons began to climb the tree in pursuit of the monkey.

He soon reached the topmost bough, but the monkey retreated to another tree. grinning and chattering with delight, with the trophy firmly planted on his cranium.

Buttons began to despair.

"The beggar, I shall have to call for master to bring him down with a gun

I'll go in search of Mr. Blunt, my fine fellow."

With that he began to descend the tree, bough by bough.

He was hanging by a bough, when he was startled by a loud roar beneath him.

"Holloa! Gemini! what's that?" he cried, nearly losing his hold.

Oh, horror!

He looked down.

Beneath him was a lion, who, with open mouth, was contemplating Buttons with great eagerness.

"Oh, it's all up with me. I shall never see Old England again. It's a lion, and a big one too, waiting for me. Oh, this is too much for Buttons. I'm done for."

The lion gave another roar, louder than before.

"Oh, dear, oh, Lor'! the monkey's got my hat, and now that beastly wild beast is waiting with open mouth for me. Help, help!"

He roared out with all the strength of his lungs.

The monkeys, on the appearance of the lion, had retreated, but they continued to hurl down cocoa nuts on the brute.

Buttons sat himself down on a bough, shaking all over with fright.

"You can't climb, old fellow, and I can, so that is one in my favour. I'm up to a trick or two, and what do you say to a cocoa nut?"

With that Buttons began to pelt the lion with as many nuts as he could find within reach.

The monkeys too added their quantum, and the lion received several blows on the head and face, which only increased his rage.

"Go away, you beast!" cried Buttons, with chattering teeth; "here, there's one, for your nob."

Buttons at last hit the lion on the nose.

The lion could not stand this; he gave a great roar, and began to tear up the ground with his paws.

Buttons now had used all the cocoa nuts within his reach, and after calling loudly for his master, he made a movement from the bough on which he was seated to another where there was a further supply.

He hurled down an immense one that struck the lion on the head.

The brute howled horribly.

"Ha! I let you have one that time."

Buttons now made a movement to grasp a bough that seemed within his reach, but he fell several feet, and nearly came to the ground and into the maws of the lion.

"Oh, Lor," groaned Buttons; "that was a near squeak; you haven't got me yet, old fellow. Buttons is worth half-a-dozen dead ones yet. Oh there it goes!"

This last exclamation was occasioned by the sudden cracking of the bough.

Buttons' weight had caused it to crack, but luckily it did not entirely give way.

He groaned in agony and shouted again for help.

Buttons knew the slightest movement would cause the bough to break, and he would be precipitated into the mouth of the furious beast, who was lashing his tail and tearing up the earth with his talons.

Buttons hung on to the bough with all his might with one leg and his hands.

He dared not move, or try to get astride of the tree.

His strength was fast leaving him.

"I shall be eaten by the lion. I cannot hold on much longer. Oh, that I ever became a traveller. Help, help!" he cried. "Buttons is going to be eaten up alive, oh, by a lion."

Suddenly he heard a shout, and beheld Bob Blunt and the doctor advancing through the forest, rifle in hand.

He uttered a cry of joy on seeing them advance.

Bob, who had missed his comical attendant, had sent back two niggers, and then returned himself to ascertain what had become of him.

To his intense surprise he beheld Buttons up a tree—a lion waiting for a savoury morsel, a monkey grinning and chattering above him, with a livery hat on his head.

The two niggers had come upon the lion unexpectedly, and one of them had fallen down overcome by fright, while the other was running away. But the lion was too intent on Buttons to notice them.

Bob took in the whole state of affairs at once.

He crept cautiously from tree to tree until within gun-shot of the lion.

But it was difficult for him to aim.

The lion continually shifted about, walking round the tree, and giving vent to loud roars at being baulked of his prey.

Bob Blunt, however, fixed him.

He took careful aim.

Bang!

The lion sprang fully four yards in the air, and fell apparently dead.

"Hurrah!" cried Bob, rushing forward. "Come down, Buttons, I have saved you. Come down, it's all right."

"Oh, master, the bough is rotten, but I'll come. Heads below!"

And Buttons dropped from the bough, and fell on to the lion.

The brute was not dead.

As Buttons fell on to the body with a thud, the lion raised his head, and opened his big jaws, showing his teeth close to poor Buttons' head.

Buttons was on his side.

The thud on the ribs the lion had received aroused his dying fury.

He roared loudly.

Buttons immediately scrambled off the body of the lion.

"Oh, oh! he's alive and kicking. I shall be devoured; but I'll not die without a stroke. Here, take that."

And Buttons drew a long knife from his side, and plunged it into the lion's throat.

"Ha, ha! do you think, master, that I didn't provide myself with a weapon of defence? Look here; I made a case for this knife, and it fits firmly in the inside of my trousers. Buttons the brave is the conqueror now. Old fellow"— addressing the defunct lion—"how do you feel? I'll make a coat of your hide, you beast!"

"Bravo, Buttons!" said Bob, delighted. "You have shown yourself plucky. Holloa! what are you doing now?" asked Bob, for Buttons was busy at the lion's nose.

"Doing, sir? I'm giving him a pinch of snuff."

And Buttons continued to rub the lion's nose with the snuff.

When he had done so, he suddenly bethought himself of his hat.

"Oh, my valuable hat; that cursed monkey has got it. There it is, master. Oh, the varmint! he's laughing at me."

The monkey, in fact, was grinning and showing his teeth at them, and pressing the hat on his head.

"He'll spoil it, my best hat. Why, I shall make no show when we meet the kings of the country, if I don't recover my hat."

"Well, look out, Buttons."

Buttons opened his arms.

Bob raised his breechloader.

"Fire!" cried Buttons.

And Bob did fire.

The ape fell dead.

"Get out, you brute, and let me have my hat. Oh, my poor hat; he's been and gone and bulged it in the crown— ugh!"

Buttons put his hat on.

"Now I don't care a dump for anyone. Hurrah! master, you've got your lion, and I've got my hat."

"Oh, golly, massa! you hab kill um big lion; you am mighty hunter," cried a big nigger, running up at that moment.

It was Jingo Johnson.

"Give us a lift, Jingo, old boy," cried Bob. "Here, take hold of his feet and turn him on his back.

"Oh, he fine lion," cried the nigger, "me go to fetch Lady Nosie to look at um."

And away rushed Jingo through the forest as hard as he could, soon returning with the others of the party.

"Lor', is the monster alive?" gasped the Stinger, on seeing the lion.

"Alive! no, you don't usually see a live lion on his back, with Buttons sitting on him," replied Bob. "Doctor, you will prepare the skin for me?"

"With pleasure. I never saw a finer lion in my life; he is full grown," said the doctor, examining the animal's teeth.

"So much the better; now then, we will skin him."

"I'm your man, then, for that," said Ironfist, tucking up his sleeves.

"You?" cried Bob.

"Yes, I understand the work; I'll skin him in a jiffey."

And Ironfist, seizing a knife, began to operate on the beast.

When the skin had been separated from the belly, and laid open down to the spine, the lion was turned over.

All our friends stood round the body in a circle, watching with attentive eyes the swift movements of Ironfist's knife.

Suddenly the Stinger gave a scream.

"What is the matter?" asked Bob.

"Look, look!" she cried, "there, at those terrible eyes. It is a wild beast."

Bob looked in the direction to which the lady pointed with her umbrella.

Two eyes, that gleamed like live coals, peered at him from the brushwood.

"Come forth," cried Bob, "or I fire."

The eyes blinked a reply, and then a tall black bounded boldly into the open.

"What do you here in the hunting grounds of King Pluto?" he asked. "The lion is his prey, not that of the white man, who sells rum and linen, and works like a woman. The hunting grounds are sacred to the children of the gods."

CHAPTER XVIII

THE UNKNOWN—NIGHT IN AN AFRICAN FOREST—BUTTONS AND THE STINGER HAVE A FRIGHT—CATCHING A SNAKE.

BEFORE our hero replied to the words of the unknown, he took stock of him.

The black was a man of gigantic height—his limbs massive and muscular.

He was dressed in a long robe of scarlet cloth, the borders of which were trimmed with his fetiche, consisting of human bones, and heads of coloured glass and several shells.

On his head he wore a number of eagles' plumes, fastened in a band of gold, that fitted his head like a coronet.

A large spear was in his hand, whilst a bow, and arrows in a quiver, was slung at his back.

This formidable personage caused some commotion amongst our travellers.

The Stinger kept to the side of Ironfist, whilst Buttons discreetly hid himself behind her skirts.

"Are you the dreaded King Pluto?" said Bob.

The doctor interpreted.

"No," replied the black; "I am not worthy to bend the bow of the mighty king. He is great as the sun himself, and this is his realm on which you dare to tread."

The savage pointed with a fierce look to the ground.

"It is better to conciliate this mighty king," said Bob, slowly. "Not that I am frightened of him, but we will try peaceable means first."

"Right," replied the doctor. "Let us put a bold front upon it."

Then said Bob—

"Know, stranger, I am prepared to meet your king to-morrow, three miles from the place where we now stand. I will then confer with him. In the meantime take this as a present from me."

And Bob took three rows of large vari-coloured glass beads from the baggage, and gave them to the savage, whose eyes glistened as he grasped them, and eagerly handled them.

But to the astonishment of all, the savage placed the beads round his neck, and seemed delighted.

But as if a sudden thought came into his brain, he took them off again, and dashed them to the ground at our hero's feet.

"No," he cried, passionately; "the great King Pluto cannot accept the present of the strangers; to-morrow he will be there."

And, pointing to the spot indicated, he disappeared into the depths of the forest.

"There is something behind this," said

the doctor to Bob. "I never knew a savage refuse a present before."

"What can it be?" asked Bob.

"That I cannot tell, but that King Pluto does not wish us well is certain. However, these tribes are all jealous of each other, and we can easily make friends of his enemies."

"That's well," cried the Stinger, brandishing her umbrella.

"Now, then, let us finish the lion's skin quick, Ironfist," said Bob.

The lion was soon skinned, and then the entire party pursued their journey towards the spot appointed by our hero to meet the mighty chief.

When they reached it, darkness had nearly set in.

The tents were pitched, and the evening meal was cooked.

Before it was ready, the night had set in.

The fires burnt brightly.

The Stinger was in high spirits.

At last it was time to go to rest.

The fires were left burning, and Longsight was left to act as sentinel.

It might have been two hours after, when the wary Longsight was startled by a prolonged groan.

It came from the tent where the Stinger and Buttons were, up till then, snoring like a couple of Bengal tigers.

Longsight was not very quick at hearing, so he peered into the darkness of the forest.

But it was impenetrable to even his keen sight, so thick was the mist that drifted between the trees.

He then thought the groan must have proceeded from a hungry hyæna or a leopard, for he had been repeatedly startled by their wild cries in the night.

But again the groan came.

This time, he caught the direction whence the sound came.

He crept on his hands and knees towards the tent, and peered into it.

The light from the fire allowed him to see Buttons indistinctly, but he beheld that worthy lying on his back, with his mouth wide open, his hair standing erect, and his hands clenched in the agony of a strong nightmare.

Longsight crept close to the couch, and

gave Buttons a shake which caused him to sit up in bed, and howl as hard as the hungry hyæna.

"Save me, save me!" cried Buttons. "Oh! it will eat me!"

"Wake up," cried Longsight. "What do you think will eat you, stupid?"

"Oh! I'm frightened. I had such an orful dream. I dreamt I was being devoured by a great big creeping thing."

"Pooh, you have had the nightmare," cried Longsight.

"Have I?" replied Buttons. "Well, I should have done better without it."

"Go to sleep again."

"I will, but I don't like to sleep alone."

"You're not alone; why, there's Miss Stinger there snoring; she'll protect you."

"All right."

He turned himself round, and wrapped the blankets round him; but no sooner had he done so than he gave a bound like a Red Indian at the war dance.

"What's the matter now?" asked Longsight, astonished at this move on the part of Buttons.

"Oh, oh! it's there. It wasn't the nightmare, it's true—there's something in my bed creeping; go and look."

Longsight was suspicious, and now very cautious how he proceeded.

"Buttons, old boy, what is it you felt?" he asked.

"Oh, something horrible—a great living thing, cold and gluey," said Buttons. "Put your hand down and feel."

Longsight cautiously went to the edge of the bed.

With two fingers he raised the blanket.

As he did so, there was a loud, hissing noise, and the head of a large snake looked him in the face.

"Oh, Lor', didn't I say so? It's a snake, and in my bed; keep it away. Oh, Lor'! it's looking at me."

The snake reared its head up and darted its fangs at Buttons, who, whilst retreating backwards, fell over a camp stool, and came with a thud upon the head of E. A. Stinger.

"Oh, it's all over with me," shouted Buttons.

" Get up, you brute, whoever you are," screamed Stinger.

" Oh! it's coming, Stinger; it's a snake!" cried Buttons.

" A snake! where's my pattens?" cried the Stinger, jumping up.

" Here it comes; save me, Stinger!"

And Buttons, with a bound, jumped into the Stinger's bed.

He buried his head under the clothes, but no sooner had he done so than he felt something cold touch him on the hand.

In an instant the clothes were thrown off, and he jumped out with a loud yell.

" Oh, murder! here's another! he's got me! I believe he's stung me to death."

" What, another?" asked Longsight.

The Stinger uttered a loud scream and retreated into a corner of the tent.

In the meantime, the two snakes had been hissing terribly.

Buttons clung behind the Stinger, whilst Longsight took a large wooden log and struck the snake such a blow on the head that he killed it.

The other one, in the meantime, had advanced towards Buttons, who tremblingly awaited his doom.

" It's going to have me. Look! it sees my livery buttons—take 'em, swallow the lot, but don't kill me."

And Buttons threw his jacket at the snake.

But whilst the snake was making abortive efforts to swallow Buttons' jacket, Longsight came behind it, and with one blow from an axe, severed its head from its body.

" Hurrah! Stinger, we're all right again," cried Buttons.

And Buttons began to dance a hornpipe, as he dragged his jacket from the fangs of the snake.

" Go to bed," growled Longsight; " you're always in mischief, and you're keeping the lady up."

" Yes, drat the boy, he's always bringing me into trouble," said the Stinger.

" Hurrah! Longsight, I'm very much obliged to you. Look out for snakes."

" It's all very well to talk, but keeping guard over such fel'ows as you, Buttons, isn't amusing," said Longsight, as he resumed his watch.

CHAPTER XIX

THE MEETING OF THE KINGS—BOB BLUNT SHOWS THAT HE IS A MIGHTY WARRIOR —AND OTHER INCIDENTS.

THE sun rose brightly on the morning of the day when Bob Blunt, the traveller, expected the different chieftains to assemble in the forest.

Our hero resolved to make as dignified an appearance as possible.

" Up with you all," he cried. " This is no time for lying in bed. Buttons, bring me my rifle, and polish it well. Up, up! Where's Stumps, my gallant trumpeter? Buttons is too sleepy. Arouse him with a mighty crash from the trombone."

" Here, master," cried Stumps, rushing forward with his huge trombone under his arm, and his face bearing its usually anxious look.

" Stumps, sound the morning call," said Bob, putting on his white helmet.

" Yes, master."

Stumps placed the trombone to his lips, and blew a deep blast, so that in one instant the Stinger and Buttons appeared in the entrance of their tent.

" What is the matter, now? Any more snakes about?" asked the Stinger.

" Snakes! no; but you must remember that to-day will decide our future in Africa, for if we can conciliate, by an imposing presence, the several native tribes, our future progress will be so much the easier," said Bob.

"Then I'll astonish the entire tribes. Elizabeth Ann has brought some fine ribbon with her, a new Paisley shawl of sixteen different colours, a bonnet—ah ! Jingo Johnson rather put it out of shape —but no matter, it will do for this occasion—and I will show to these barbarian tribes that a British female can appear with becoming dignity when she is required to do so."

"Bravo, Miss Stinger ; my own lovely Stinger, and I'll back you up," said Buttons.

Bob commanded silence, for there was no time for jesting now.

In front of his tent he arranged all his luggage, and placed the several negroes, amongst them Jingo Johnson, who was to hold a large umbrella over his head.

This umbrella Bob had procured in England, knowing it was the principal emblem of royalty in Africa.

It was one mass of gold, on a blue background, and it presented a very imposing appearance, and no doubt would tend to put the natives in great awe.

Everyone carried a rifle, a dagger, and a sword.

About three hours after sunrise, Swiftfoot came rushing into the little camp with the announcement that the chiefs were advancing in several directions.

"Oh, the cannibals !" cried the Stinger. "Will they expect us to worship them ?"

"No, no ; only keep quiet," said Bob.

"Very good ; I'll prepare myself, however, in case I should faint."

With that she hastened into the tent, and soon reappeared with a bottle of rum, which she tried to force into her pocket.

This action did not escape the keen eyes of an observant nigger, who resolved to steal it, on the very first occasion that allowed him to use his dexterous fingers.

The loud blowing of horns now resounded from the forest.

"Gather up close to me, all of you," cried Bob. "In a circle round me, and up with your gingham, Stinger. Stumps this side of me, and on the first approach

of the kings, when within a few yards of me, blow your trombone as if you were going to burst it. Buttons, kneel down in front of me, and open the boxes of presents when I command you. Dr. Know-all, stand at my left, please, and be ready with your advice at the moment."

These commands were rapidly obeyed, and when three different bodies of blacks were seen to issue from three different directions, and line the open circle that lay around Bob Blunt's encampment, the eyes of all were fixed upon the newcomers.

Bob had wisely chosen the situation for the reception of the chiefs.

His tents were pitched close to the back of a rock ; whilst an open space in front of him permitted a full view of the different natives.

As the three kings met in the front of the camp, each waved his followers to stand back, which they did, filing round the circle, and completely closing in our friends.

"Hum !" muttered Bob, "this looks dickey. If these gentry were to turn against us, we should have enough to do to beat them."

"Whatever you do now, keep cool, sir," said the doctor ; "don't move a muscle."

"I won't so much as raise an individual hair of my eyebrows," replied Bob. "Halloa ! here they come. Stumps, blow your trombone and split their ears."

Three chiefs, attended by their followers, now advanced towards our hero, but when within a dozen yards, Stumps blew such a blast on his trombone that the sound somewhat disturbed their equanimity, which pleased our hero very much, for it gave him an advantage.

The chiefs placed their hands up to their ears, but when the sound ceased, they advanced timidly.

In the first, our friends recognised the native who had surprised them in the forest, when Buttons had met with the lion.

"This must be no other than King Pluto himself," said Bob. "The artful rascal ; I don't like the look of him. Are all your rifles ready ?"

"Every barrel!" responded each member of the determined little band.

The three kings now came close to our hero, and placed their hands on their breasts, bowing low.

They were three fine men.

King Pluto was the tallest and the strongest.

Their arms and legs and feet bare, white cloths round their loins, and gold anklets, and bracelets on their arms, rings in their ears, and a plume of feathers on their heads, fastened in a massive crown of gold and ivory.

Bob Blunt took in their personal appearance at a glance.

The first king advanced, and thrusting his spear in the ground he began with a dignified mien to address the white men.

"Chief of the white men—peace."

"To thee, peace," replied Bob, returning the king's salutation.

"Why art thou come to the country of King Kalu, of King Pluto, and King Aga? Come ye in peace, to trade with us; to barter the white cloth for the teeth of the elephants?" said King Kalu, at which each of the others bowed humbly.

"We come not to trade, but to hunt the wild elephant, the lion, and the leopard; to see the wide forests and the beautiful land of the great kings. We come in peace to all," said Bob.

"Hum, hum!" grunted King Kalu. "'Tis well, very well; but what guarantee have we, O chief of the white men, that you do not intend to work us mischief?"

"Mischief! Why, O king, can we, a few men, compete against a mighty host like yourselves? The white men are your brothers, and wish you well. They bring you presents and wish to live in amity with you."

At the word presents, King Kalu's eyes began to sparkle.

"Hum! my white friend speaks well. 'Tis peace. King Kalu wishes you well. White chief is a great man, his umbrella is of gold and the blue sky colour. King Kalu and all his tribe are your friends."

There was an ominous frown on the face of King Pluto when Kalu had concluded his speech and shaken hands with our hero.

"Open the box, Buttons."

"Yes, sir," said Buttons, looking up at the dreaded chiefs in fear.

Buttons opened the box.

A glittering array of beads, daggers, chains and charms, fascinated the eyes of the king when he beheld them.

Bob gave him a quantity of beads, cloth, and a few pistols—that would shoot any way but straight—and daggers.

As the king received them, Stumps took up his trombone and blew a loud triumphant blast that made the king jump again.

His eyes alighted this time, not on the trombone, but upon the dwarf.

First astonishment took possession of him at sight of the little man, then a superstitious dread, for dwarfs inspire a great reverence in the breasts of the natives of Africa.

The king trembled all over.

He looked up into the sky.

He clasped his hands, and then with a low moan fell upon his face and kissed the ground before Stumps.

"Hush!" whispered Bob. "Don't make an observation, Stumps; he evidently thinks you a god; let him. Look very dignified, for these people venerate dwarfs."

Stumps folded his mighty arms across his chest.

"Oh, crikey! he's in love with Stumps. Oh, you're out of it altogether, Stinger, my lovely angel. If the king had fallen in love with you, I should have challenged him to fight; but I will spare his life," cried Buttons.

"Chief, I accept your presents," cried King Kalu, rising. "You have a mighty man with you, and the spear of King Kalu shall rest its point in the air, his arrows shall stay your enemies, and his tribe protect you."

"I thank you," replied Bob. "King Kalu, go in peace."

"Mighty chief, may your fetiche prove to be fortunate; King Kalu wishes you well."

With that the king retired, his attendants taking up the presents with low bows.

Bob Blunt seated himself again.

The Stinger gazed with all eyes upon the king.

At this moment the nigger nearest to her saw his opportunity to possess himself of her rum bottle.

With a stealthy movement he inserted his hand into the Stinger's pocket.

In an instant she caught sight of him.

"You black thief," she cried, closing her umbrella. "You rascal, leave go my bottle. Ah! I have your wool."

She brought her umbrella to bear upon the nigger's skull, and then fastening her hand in his wool she pulled it with all her might and main.

"Oh, missie, golly, missie, me hab not got it," cried the nigger, rolling his eyes about and shouting with agony depicted on every line of his sable countenance.

"No, you have not got it ; but I have you," cried the Stinger continuing to shake him.

"Silence!" cried Bob. "We shall imperil all our lives if we do not keep up a dignified appearance."

"Oh, Elizabeth Ann, keep up your dignity," said Buttons.

And the Stinger at once brought herself to the attitude of attention.

"Oh, golly, her nose—booful, like my fetiche," cried Jingo.

"See, here comes the second king."

In the meantime there had been a fierce argument between King Pluto and King Aga, which did not escape the observant eyes of Bob Blunt and his friends.

"What are they up to now?" asked Bob of the doctor.

"They are having it out. I think King Pluto is trying to persuade King Aga to something he will not agree to. King Kalu is satisfied ; see how he harangues his warlike tribe," replied the doctor.

"Never mind ; if we can cause a split in the camp we will do so. Now, King Aga, I will speak with you."

King Aga advanced.

Aga was a man of lighter colour than the others, and of a mild cast of countenance.

But his person had a distinguished and commanding mien.

"Aga is a great king," began Bob ; "his fame has travelled beyond his own land."

"What thou sayest, O mighty chief, is pleasant to the soul of Aga. But comest thou in peace with thy chiefs to the great hunting grounds of our country ?"

"I come in peace, and wish to be your brother, O king. To hunt the wild lion and the wild elephant, to give presents to King Aga, and to be his friend until I reach the territory of the great King Koff."

"And you go to Coomassie ?" queried King Aga, with a sly look.

"Yes."

"Hum !" he grunted ; "King Koff is no friend to the white man."

"Do you think we are in danger if we enter his territory ?"

"Yes ; great danger."

"That is, if we go by ourselves."

"True," grunted Aga.

"But not if we have an ally," said Bob, very quietly.

"Not if you have an ally," said the king, repeating the words very slowly. "But, perhaps, O white chief, you might find an ally."

"Where ?"

"Hum !" grunted the king. "The tribe of King Aga amounts to three hundred bold warriors, and their fetiche is good."

"Listen, King Aga," said Bob. "Be my ally. I will reward you, and——"

"Listen not to the smooth tongue of King Pluto," said Aga, interrupting.

Bob saw his chance.

He knew there was enmity between the two kings, and resolved to do all in his power to make wider the breach between King Pluto and King Aga.

"King, I will help you to the death. But King Kalu, is he your friend ?"

"He is my brother."

"Good, very good. Buttons, give the king some of the finest pistols, beads, and bracelets in our possession, and also twenty yards of coloured cloth."

Buttons did so, and laid them at the king's feet, who took them up with a low salaam.

"Now, we are friends," said Bob extending his hand.

"Friends for life."

" Retire, then, my brave ally, and let me meet King Pluto."

Aga bowed and withdrew.

As soon as he had done so, King Pluto advanced with quick, hasty steps, and struck his spear point fiercely into the ground, in token of his animosity.

" What does the white chief in the territory of King Pluto, who is a king of kings ?" he asked, with fierce eloquence in voice and action. " Am I a child? Am I like the white antelope before the spotted leopard ? King Pluto is mighty. His gods have told him of the white men. They come to conquer, and shed the blood of the children of the sun."

" Who told you that, King Pluto ?" asked Bob, with a frown.

" My gods."

" Your gods have deceived you."

" Never : I have scouts all over the world, and two scouts, who are the best of scouts ; they have told me all concerning the white chief and his men. You are an enemy."

" And you will not accept my presents, in token of peace ?" asked Bob.

" King Pluto takes no presents from his foes ; he will take their lives," he replied, haughtily.

" Enough ; do as you list."

Bob drew his sword, and stuck the point of it in the ground.

King Pluto did the same, and withdrew.

" Now, I know you," muttered Bob. " Did you notice his allusion to two scouts ?"

" I did," said the doctor, " and it strikes me they do not belong to his tribe."

" So do I ; especially when he alluded to having scouts all over the world."

" That makes me believe they are white men," replied the doctor.

" The same idea struck me ; but look, King Pluto is moving away with his warriors, and they are blowing their warhorns, with a vengeance."

This was the case, but the two friendly kings marched towards our hero.

" Let the devil go," cried King Aga. " The white chief has friends in this country who will not see him wronged."

" Hip-hip-hurrah !" came from Bob and his friends, in response to this hearty cry of adherence.

" I do not fear them, now I have such brave friends as King Aga and King Kalu," said Bob, grasping a hand of each.

" And so you shall find us both. Now, you must come with me to my encampment, eight miles from here, to the west, and I will send out my scouts, who shall inform you of all that King Pluto designs. You can go hunting in safety, for no one will wish to do you an injury but King Pluto, and he has not mashalled all his warriors yet."

" Then, to-morrow, I will be with you," replied Bob, as King Aga concluded.

" Yes ; and now I will tell you why I hate King Pluto."

" I am all attention, and thank you for your confidence, King Aga," said Bob.

" Listen, then. I have a daughter, Nahita by name ; she is the light of her father's eyes, and Nahita is beautiful as rose of the forest when it opens its eyes to the sun. She is as graceful as the antelope that leaps on the hills, there in the great valleys beyond the mountains of the moon (Æthiopia), and many chiefs have sought her hand, but to all her father has refused to give the child of his home, for he loves her and would not let her be the bondswoman of any of the rude chiefs."

" Here, Stinger, listen to what the king says," cried Bob. " Here you have woman's rights and no mistake."

" I hear him ; here, great and mighty ruler, read that and you will respect our sex for ever after."

And Elizabeth Ann handed him a tract, which the king took with graceful dignity, and thrust it on his sword hilt, thinking it a charm.

" Well," continued the king, " amongst the suitors for the hand of my daughter is King Pluto. I refused him, and we are enemies, and he has tried everything in his power to get my daughter into his hands, and if he once succeeds, I know what her fate will be."

" What, marriage ?" asked Bob.

" Yes, and death ; for he hates me as he does poison. I must hasten back now, or he will steal a march upon me."

"We will conquer him. To-morrow, by sunrise, we shall be with you at your village, brave king," said Bob.

"Good!" grunted the pleased Aga.

Then, placing himself at the head of his fighting men, he marched away.

"Now, King Kalu, you are a friend of Aga's."

"I am; his village is close to mine, and my wife is his sister."

"That is a bond of friendship between you. Let me see you here, while I visit King Aga's camp," said Bob.

"Yes; I will see you, but—but is that your god?"

"Who?"

"There."

And King Kalu pointed to Stumps.

"Yes."

"Ah, white chief conquer all his enemies; great god! my fetiche say he is great. Farewell."

And King Kalu dived into the forest, followed by his entire tribe.

The entire party, after the departure of the natives, sat down to their meal, whilst Bob Blunt was musing deeply over the desperate life before him.

CHAPTER XX.

DEEPER INTO THE FOREST—CROSSING THE FIRST RIVER—ALLIGATORS—JINGO'S FETICHE TO CHARM THE LUBLY NOSE—A HALT—SWIFTFOOT'S CHASE—THE ALARM.

DURING the heat of the day our friends continued in the shelter of their encampment, and here they found enough to do to keep themselves cool, for the sun poured his tropical heat down upon the canvas which the blacks constantly deluged with water, in order to cool the air within.

"Well, Miss Stinger, I hope you like Africa?" said Bob, to the lady, who was fanning herself with the back of a small tea-tray, in a corner of the tent.

"It's awful, the heat I mean. Rotten Row in the dog-days is a flea-bite to it. But our lot is to suffer in this world, and so I will go on to the end, until I drop. Africa for ever, say I, and light to the natives."

Buttons determined to get what he called a "rise out of the old lady," so he seized Jingo Johnson by the arm, and thrust him forward, saying—

"Will you marry the nigger? He is dying in love with you, Miss Stinger."

"Me! E. A. Stinger marry! Never; I love my liberty too well to be at the mercy of man. I follow Bob Blunt, the Traveller, through the forests of Africa, to spread civilisation, and gain the name of the first woman who ever crossed the continent of Africa."

"Bravo! Stinger, you stick to me, and no harm will come to you," said Bob.

"I will; and in due time you will see Elizabeth Ann in the full costume of man. This leg was made for jack-boots," cried the Stinger, thrusting forth one foot encased in a stout boot, and an ankle that was anything but tapering; and it left no doubt in the mind of the beholder of its capabilities in filling out the aforesaid jack-boots.

Thus the conversation continued until the heat of the day had passed, and then Bob ordered the tents to be struck.

This was soon accomplished, the tents were placed upon the waggon, which was drawn by oxen, guided by Jingo and his comrades.

As they progressed, the forests deepened around them; huge groves of mango trees, planted as if by art, interspersed with long, waving grapes, and the loveliest flowers, through which butterflies and birds of the most resplendent colours sported.

It was like a scene in fairyland.

The wonder and delight of all knew no bounds.

Bob was enchanted.

And when the doctor brought forth his net and added a number of butterflies to his collection, he cried out enthusiastically—

"Now, my friends, is not this better than staying in old England, amongst smoky chimneys and money-grubbers? This is paradise and freedom if you like. What do you say, my trusty companions?"

"It is wonderful," ejaculated the doctor, "wonderful! Why, I shall enrich the cabinets of Blunt Castle with the most rare and gorgeous specimens of plants, butterflies, and birds, and make it the altar to which every naturalist in the world will gladly pilgrimage to and worship."

"First rate," cried Buttons. "I wouldn't mind it at all if there were no alligators and lions about, not forgetting monkeys."

"Pooh! you are afraid," cried Stumps. "Look at me; I never was so happy in all my life; it's glorious!"

And the dwarf moved his long arms over his head.

"It's delightful! positively delightful!" echoed the Stinger. "Look at the sky! Oh, man! the beauties of nature are revealed to you in all bounty—oh, man; base man!"

How much further the rhapsodies of Elizabeth Ann might have continued we cannot say, but they were brought to an abrupt conclusion, for the Stinger, with uplifted eyes, had not noticed a morass covered with beautiful green moss, so she, supposing it to be solid ground, walked on to it, but to her consternation she discovered that the treacherous surface gave way beneath her, and she was now up to the waist in the swamp.

"This is delightful! positively delightful," roared Buttons, as he saw the Stinger sink into the swamp.

"Oh, help me out! I'm sinking fast. Help, Mr. Blunt, help!"

"Oh, my lubly nosie, me help you quick—quick," cried Jingo.

And seizing a rope in one hand, he gave the other to a comrade, and they threw it across the bog, which proved not to be wide in circumference.

The Stinger had now sunk down nearly to her armpits.

"Hold fast, missie, to the rope, or your lubly nose will get all over mud," cried Jingo.

Jingo had by this time brought the rope beneath the Stinger's arms.

She threw a coil of the rope round her body, and then with a vigorous tug they hauled her safe on to dry land, the bog closing up with a loud flop, filling up the space of the Stinger's body in an instant.

"By Jove! that's a narrow squeak," cried the doctor, aghast.

"Squeak!" retorted the gasping Stinger. "Look at me!"

They might well look.

The Stinger was one mass of green fœtid slime from head to foot.

Jingo Johnson busied himself to wipe the poor Stinger down with some grass.

"On my word I have met with nothing but misfortune since I have been in this benighted land. But Elizabeth Ann has some philosophy in her composition. Face danger, sir! Why, I'll face the evil one himself."

"Bravo, Stinger!" cried Buttons.

"Bravo, old girl!" muttered Ironfist.

"Stunnerer!" cried Strongback.

"Grand!" cried Swiftfoot.

"Regular cock-o'-the-walk," growled Longsight.

"Beautiful self-denial," said Stumps.

"Angelic creature," growled the doctor, with a half-sneer on his lips.

"Lubly red nosie," said Jingo Johnson, rubbing his hands.

"Look here, Miss Stinger, I'll protect your bonnet, gingham, pattens, teapot and all," said Bob; "there shall be no tricks, before high heaven, whilst Bob Blunt is in the way."

"Oh, thank you, Mr. Blunt. You black beast, you've got my teapot,"

These words were to Jingo Johnson.

He had the teapot to his mouth, and was imbibing its contents.

"Oh, golly, it um fine;"

"How does it taste?" asked Buttons.

"Oh, booful—very booful; make nigger hab deli'ful burn in um troat."

"Tea burn?" muttered Stumps.

"Yes; um burn," replied Jingo,

"Let me taste," said Buttons, seizing the teapot and tasting it, first carefully wiping the spout, in fear of being contaminated by Jingo's mouth, as he said.

Buttons tasted it.

He drew the spout from his lips after taking a hearty drink.

"Oh!" he gasped, "ain't it nice."

Elizabeth Ann made a rush at him, but Buttons dodged her.

"Not if I know it," he cried. "Oh, this is very delightful. Oh, you artful sweet thing; you're found out. I am not at all surprised that you carry a teapot. Say now, speak the truth, were you ever in Jamaica?"

"What do you mean?" replied the Stinger, growing very red in the face.

"Mean, Betsy; which you know Jamaica is an island where the niggers thrive, like my friend Jingo, and where they make nice rum."

"Boy, you try my patience," said the Stinger, gathering her skirts about her and trying to look dignified. "I know nothing of Jamaica."

"Why, within this teapot is a concoction—we'll call it so because it's a fine word— is a concoction which is usually called rum—Jamaica rum. Ah, we've found you out at last. Oh, Betsy, you're a deep one. No wonder you're fond of your teapot."

The Stinger looked nonplussed.

"I admit it, boy, but my excuse is that I am troubled wlth a chronic cold, and therefore I take the beverage medicinally, you know, by order of the doctor; but I hate rum."

"We are wasting time; let us advance," said Bob.

Our travellers continued their way through the forest till night.

Fortunately the moon arose, and they could see to continue their journey.

At length they came to the river that glided white between two dark lines of trees.

"How the deuce are we to cross this?" asked Bob, of Jingo."

"Wait, massa."

Jingo began to whistle softly.

Presently an answering whistle came from the opposite side, and then a negro was seen to paddle a frail canoe towards them.

"Who is that?" asked Bob.

"Negro ferryman; always here, him friend to eberyone."

"Oh, indeed; a philanthropist, I presume. Does he transport people to the other side for nothing?"

"He, he!" grinned Jingo, "he hab not fool enub in him."

"Oh! I see; he carries on this trade for a consideration."

"Yes, sar; for piece cloth or drop ob rum, carry ober de riber," said Jingo.

By this time the sable Charon's frail bark touched the shore.

"Booful boat," cried Jingo; "carry massa and lots ob friends."

"Well, I'll try it. Jump in, Buttons and Ironfist," said Bob.

The three got in.

Buttons had his large case of snuff in the boat, and also a box in his hand.

He stood at the prow of the boat, looking eagerly into the river.

"What are you looking for?" asked Bob.

"Alligators."

"Why, are there some here?"

"I think so, but I'm ready for them. I'll give them a pinch of snuff."

Buttons was really in earnest, so Bob forbore to laugh at him.

The black paddled them slowly along.

At that moment the canoe struck the trunk of a tree.

"Oh, Lor', here's a go!" cried Buttons, as the shock sent him over into the water.

"By Jove, he is gone," cried Ironfist.

At that moment a large alligator was seen swimming towards him.

"Look!" shouted Bob; "the beast! He'll have him."

"Not if I know it; out of the way, sir; I know how to manage these creatures, so here goes to save Buttons."

With that Ironfist drew a long dagger, and plunged into the water.

He swam towards the alligator.

Buttons turned round, and beheld the animal, with extended jaws, making direct towards him.

"THREE TIMES DID THEIR VOLLEYS POUR INTO THE MIDST OF THE ENEMY."

" Oh, my snuff! It's wet. I'm done for. Oh, somebody throw a handful of snuff at him. Oh, here he comes."

Just then, Ironfist swam between Buttons and the alligator.

With desperate force, Ironfist plunged his knife up to the hilt into his throat.

The alligator turned on its new foe.

Coolly and deliberately Ironfist awaited the return of the furious animal as it came on to the attack.

As it arrived within reach, Ironfist dived, and plunged his knife repeatedly into its belly.

Then he arose to the surface.

The alligator lashed the water into a foam with its tail.

But Ironfist knew that its only vulnerable part was its eye, for then he could reach the animal's brain.

The alligator swam away.

In the meantime, Buttons had been hauled, half dead with fright, into the canoe by Bob.

As soon as he beheld himself safe, he seized a handful of snuff, and held it out to Ironfist.

" Here, give him a pinch," he cried, " settle him at once."

But Ironfist was otherwise engaged, and heeded him not.

The alligator, smarting under his defeat, darted at his foe with wide-extended jaws.

Ironfist allowed it to come within reach of him, then darting suddenly outside, he plunged his unerring knife into the animal's eye.

The blow was fatal.

The alligator uttered a piercing shriek, then turned over on its side, pierced to the brain, dead.

A loud shout of triumph greeted Ironfist, as he hauled his prey triumphantly to shore, and looked at him.

" Well, he's a whopper," said Buttons, jumping on the body. " Here, take a pinch of snuff. My eye, Mr. Ironfist, you are a stunner," patting the strong man on the back. " You have saved poor old Buttons from death. I am very thankful."

" All right, Buttons; don't thank me, only the next time you will know how to kill alligators," said Ironfist, with apparent nonchalance.

" Well, as long as I can count such brave followers as yourself amongst my friends, I don't fear all the natives of Africa put together," said Bob, shaking Ironfist by the hand.

" Don't praise me ; I only did my duty. Besides I knew while I was battling with that brute, you had covered him with your rifle, ready to fire if I was worsted," said Ironfist.

" Truly, we will mark this deed in our log-book," said Bob.

By this time the others had been ferried over.

Jingo Johnson had brought the bullock waggon safely across.

As soon as he beheld the alligator, he ran towards it.

Seizing his knife, he cut off one of the animal's scales, and immediately tied it as a gory fetiche around his waist.

" What is that for ?" asked Bob.

" Fetiche, massa ; me now make lubly nose in lub with me. Great devil help Jingo to make missie like me."

Jingo went to the head of his oxen, elated with his fetiche, and dreaming of the day when he should become the sole possessor of the Stinger's lovely nose for a fetiche.

The entire party now continued their route until they reached a long ridge of rocks, before which stretched an open plain for some distance, and then again a line of hills covered with forest and interspersed with valleys.

" I think we will encamp here," said Bob. " If we pitch our tents against these rocks we need not fear an attack in our rear, whilst we can pretty well see the advance of an enemy in the valley before us, although there are several pieces of cover under which an enemy might lie concealed."

" Yes, but we can defend ourselves against a thousand here," said the doctor.

" I think so too ; so let us choose a place to encamp."

On approaching the rocks they discovered the entrance to a cave.

Bob thought they might venture into it, so he ordered a torch to be ignited, and when this was done they explored it.

It proved to be a cave of wide dimensions.

The roof was high, and as the torch was raised, they beheld that it was studded with the most beautiful stalactites, that shone like diamonds in the flare of the torch.

There were several entrances from this cave, but Bob resolved to leave their exploration until the morning.

"This is the very place for us," said Bob. "Now, Jingo, unyoke your bullocks and kindle a fire."

"Yes, massa."

This was soon accomplished.

Then supper was got ready, and they all sat down to it.

After supper each one retired to his couch in the cave, the floor of which was very dry.

"By Jingo Johnson!" said Buttons, "we are at last under a roof again. I declare it's as good as Blunt Castle."

"Now, whose turn is it to keep watch?" asked Bob.

"Mine," said Swiftfoot.

"And mine," said Stumps.

"Then to your duty."

"Yes, sir."

The two sat down in front of the cave, Stumps with his trombone to sound the alarm in case of an attack during the night.

Soon all was quiet within the cave, and Bob Blunt and his band of brave followers little dreamed how soon they would be in deadly conflict with the savage natives."

The silence was unbroken for a time, except by the occasional shriek of a nightbird, or the howl of a hyæna.

Suddenly a dusky object might have been seen to glide like a snake along the ground.

So silently did it steal towards the cavern where the watch-fire blazed, that Swiftfoot did not notice it.

On it came.

It neared the sides of the rock.

Here it stood upright in the shade, erect and motionless.

It was a black man.

For the space of five minutes the native did not move.

At last, seeing all was quiet, he advanced close to the cavern.

Swiftfoot's rifle was lying at his feet, where he had placed it.

The African crouched down and possessed himself of the rifle.

Then starting up, he retreated within the shadow of the rock.

At that instant Swiftfoot awoke with a start.

The native saw him move, and glided away along the rocks.

Swiftfoot looked for his rifle, and he found it gone.

"Halloa! Stumps, where's my rifle?" asked Swiftfoot.

The dwarf started.

"What, is it not there?"

"No."

"Who could have taken it?"

"That's just what I desire to know. Ah! someone has been here."

"How?"

"Look."

And Swiftfoot pointed to a footprint in the sand.

"Well?" asked Stumps.

"That's a naked nigger's foot, and he's not far off, for I did not doze but a short time."

Swiftfoot, with his experience of Indian warfare, divined at once that the thief who stole his rifle would avail himself of the shadow of the rocks to escape with his spoil.

He accordingly started off in that direction, and the native, seeing his movements, darted off into the open country, with the rifle in hand.

The negro had fully fifty yards start.

Swiftfoot had all his work to do to catch the nigger.

"He must fly in the air, or I shall catch him," cried Swiftfoot, as he sped along like the wind.

And catch him he did.

The negro heard the rapid breathing of his pursuer, and then turned to discharge the rifle at Swiftfoot, but it happened to be a breech-loader, and he did not know the trick of working the triggers, and Swiftfoot was upon him.

"You black thief!" he cried. "Give me my rifle, or I'll have your life."

He seized his weapon in one hand, and

with the other caught the nigger in the hape of the neck, nearly shaking the life out of him.

The nigger began to howl.

"Speak," cried Swiftfoot; "who sent you to spy on our movements?"

Before he could reply, a shower of arrows fell around Swiftfoot.

"Oh, I see how it is; your friends are there—take that."

He gave the nigger a heavy kick, which sent him flying a dozen paces, and then firing his rifle twice in the direction from whence the arrows came, he started back for the cave.

A howl told Swiftfoot that his shots had told.

The shots were heard by Stumps, who began at once to blow his trombone.

"Arm, arm! the enemy are upon us," cried Swiftfoot, rushing towards the cave.

In an instant the sleepers were aroused, and Bob Blunt jumped up, ready and armed for the fray.

Swiftfoot hastily narrated what had occurred, and then preparations were made to defend the place.

"Where's my boots?"

It was the Stinger's voice in the cave.

"Stay where you are," replied Buttons; "you'll only get a bullet through you. I'm going to stand and fight by my master; I don't like wild beasts, yet I'm not afraid of a nigger."

Buttons was very brave now.

"Give me a rifle," he said to Ironfist, who had charge of the ammunition box.

"Will you use it?"

"Like a Briton."

"There is one."

"And give me one," said the Stinger, advancing, with one bootless foot.

"You?"

"Yes, me. Elizabeth Ann."

At this moment Bob Blunt's voice was heard.

"Stand close, lads, and don't waste a shot. Let the enemy advance, let each pick his man, for it is with us life or death."

CHAPTER XXI.

THE NIGHT ATTACK ON THE CAVE—THE RETREAT.

THE cave being in the shade, and the valley bathed in moonlight, our friends could see the advance of the enemy.

But a few trees afforded them a cover, and thus they could see the enemy advancing.

"If we are worsted," said Bob to Ironfist, "whatever you do, don't leave the ammunition chest behind you."

"I'll leave my body first," replied Ironfist.

"I hope none of us shall leave our bodies, but that the enemy may leave a good many of theirs, never to rise again," murmured Bob.

"I am trembling like a mouse," said Buttons. "Now then, sweetheart, take care of yours truly."

"E. A. S. is here."

"E, A, S, Y, easy then. Halloa, murder! they are going to fire. There they've been and gone and done it."

A loud report was heard, and a bullet struck the rock and fell at their feet.

Bob picked it up.

"This is a cartridge bullet, fired from a breechloader," he said, examining it.

"And the natives are not in possession of that kind of arm," said the doctor.

"No; and that tells me we have Europeans to deal with. Ha!" a sudden thought striking him, "do you think that our late fellow passengers have any finger in this pie ?"

" You mean Delorme and Walker ?" said Ironfist.

" Yes."

" And they are enemies, I swear," said Ironfist, " for I shall never forget that fellow Delorme's evil look when he saw that you escaped the clutches of the shark."

" I remember it well," said Bob. " Halloa !"

The last word was addressed to the enemy, who had sent several bullets and arrows at our friends, all of which missed their mark.

Finding no answer to their shots, the enemy became bolder and began to creep forth in several directions.

" Down flat, all of you. They can't see you," cried Bob.

The watch fire had been extinguished.

All complied with the command.

Several dusky forms were now seen to glide towards them, creeping first behind a stone, or the trunk of a tree.

" Now, the next time they rise we will fire. Each one take his man, and don't waste a shot," said Bob.

Even the Stinger fell flat to the ground.

" Now, fire," cried Bob, as he saw several of the enemy rise.

Simultaneous to the command, nine shots rang out on the silence of the night, and nine blacks were seen to jump into the air, and then fall with a loud cry.

This terrible reply to the enemy proved to them that Bob and his friends were wide awake, and ready to defend themselves.

The enemy retired.

" They are consulting together for a fresh attack, but we will be even with them. Where is Jingo ?"

" Here, massa."

" Now, Jingo, you know the country," said Bob.

" Berry well, massa."

" That is good ; now listen, Jingo, and don't lose a word of that which I am about to tell you."

" No, massa," said Jingo, extending his jaws to their fullest extent, as though the words were to go down his throat.

" Then mark well this ; you and your men must make your way to King Aga's camp, and inform him that we are beset, and most probably by King Pluto's tribe. Tell him to keep a sharp look-out for us," said Bob.

" Yes, massa."

" And, listen further, Jingo ; I entrust the whole of our luggage to your care."

" The ammunition box, and all ?" asked Ironfist, who was seated upon it.

" Yes ; we must be without encumbrances. Let us supply ourselves with sufficient ammunition, and let Jingo and his men take care of the box with our other goods. He will escape, for we shall take up all the attention of the enemy."

" Not a bad idea ; but Miss Stinger had better go with the waggon," said Swiftfoot.

" Me ! E. A. Stinger ; allow me to tell you I intend to follow Bob Blunt to the death. Hurrah ! for Blunt, the Traveller."

And the Stinger swung the musket over her head.

" Quiet, now ; the enemy have withdrawn to consult together. Jingo, yoke your oxen, and leave us to fight our way. You, Strongback, provide yourself with a coil of rope, in case we have to lower ourselves down the rocks. You, Stumps, carry an extra supply of cartridges, for it is well to provide against any contingencies that may happen to us. Thus, with only ourselves to look to, we can manage to defend ourselves against a thousand of these savages."

Thus spoke Bob Blunt.

The oxen were yoked to the waggon, and Jingo managed to drive it into the shade without being perceived, and was soon out of sight.

" Now, Longsight, you go and explore the caves."

" Yes. Here, Buttons, give me a piece of rope for a torch."

When this was provided, Longsight at once disappeared into the recesses of the cavern.

" Now," said Bob, " keep a sharp lookout ; lay flat, and when I give the word, fire."

" Yes, sir," came from Bob's band.

They had not long to wait.

Presently the tall form of a black arose in the moonlight.

"Don't fire," said Bob; "let us see their game first."

A sudden discordant noise of the war-drums, the blowing of horns announced to our anxious and expectant friends that the consultations of the enemy had come to a definite result.

There was a sudden pause, then the enemy were seen to separate into three parties.

The first body of savage men advanced in close and serried ranks in front.

The two others branched off on each side, and thus it was evident they were going to drive the little band into the cave, and there exterminate them.

With the centre party were two men in European costume.

On they came with a rush.

"Ready. Now fire," cried Bob; "both barrels, and reload quick."

Three times did the volleys pour into the midst of the enemy, and again brought them to a standstill.

"Bravo, all of us!" cried Buttons. "I never thought to be in a battle; it's very stunning, as long as you don't get a stunning hit."

"Hush!" muttered Bob; "get ready again, men; the devils are up to something."

In truth they had retired some distance off, carrying their dead and wounded with them.

At this moment Longsight returned from his inspection of the cave.

"Well, what is the news of the caves?" asked Bob.

"Marvellous!" replied Longsight.

"Did you explore them all?"

"No; that would take a week to do, but I went far enough, and saw enough to convince me that we can effect our escape by means of them. To all appearances they are interminable."

"If that should prove to be the case, how can we escape through them?"

"How? Why, I am certain there is an outlet somewhere."

"What makes you think so?"

"Because on suddenly entering the cave, I felt a current of air."

Bob was lost in a train of thought for some moments.

Then suddenly bringing his hand down on his thigh, he cried—

"I have it. Hurrah! we will give these devils another peppering. Then we will show them that with all their cunning we can match them. Come, listen, gentlemen, to my plans."

The whole of our hero's friends now gathered round him.

"Now, gentlemen, you see we are outnumbered by the enemy. Therefore, I have a plan in case they renew the attack, which I doubt not they will do as soon as they have matured their plans. We will then give a double volley, and retreat into the cave."

Bob paused.

"Speak up, doctor."

"Why cannot they follow us?"

"Ha, ha! you have not foresight enough, doctor. We must secure our retreat by blocking up the entrance to the cave."

"And how is that to be done?" asked the doctor.

"Listen, doctor. Where is your supply of dynamite?"

"Ah! I begin to understand."

"Stumps has charge of all the doctor's stuff, master," said Buttons.

"Very good," said Bob. "Then all you have to do is to place the dynamite in the crevices of the rock. The opening is but small. The rock, when the explosion takes place, will completely block up the entrance."

"A good idea. We'll trick the savages yet."

The dynamite was produced, and they all set to work to undermine the rock.

Then six trains of gunpowder were laid from the mined parts into the inner cavern.

When this had been accomplished, our friends again directed their attention to the doings of the enemy.

They, in the meantime, evidently had come to the conclusion that the foe was not to be taken in open battle.

Accordingly, after a time, our friends beheld something rise in the moonlight that looked like the wall of a house.

"Oh, master, what is it coming this way?" asked Buttons.

"They have made a kind of shield on a large scale, to keep them from our bullets. Thus they hope to come to close quarters with us," said Bob. "I see it is made of bamboos strung together; but let the black devils come on; they will get more than they bargained for."

The huge rampart advanced.

"Now, men," said Bob; "when they are within reach, fire a last volley straight into them, just by way of an adieu."

"We are ready," came the deep voices of the men.

When within twenty yards of the cave, Bob gave the word to fire at the enemy.

Bang! bang! bang!

The balls struck the moving rampart, and several of the blacks were seen to fall.

"That's it, my boys," cried Bob; "give them another volley, and then into the cave and await them."

This was done.

The blacks still advanced steadily, and paused within a few yards of the cave, as if in doubt what to do.

Bob sent his friends into the cave, whilst he himself awaited the advance of the enemy.

The doctor stood ready to fire the train, and Bob also held a lighted match in his hand.

The foe, seeing its advance guard come unmolested to the cave, came up with them with a rush.

"We have them safe. On to the cave and block them in," cried an English voice in the centre of the blacks.

Bob heard the voice, but could not recognise it.

"Let them come on, I do not fear them," thought Bob. "Let them block us in. I think they will stagger when they find out what's in store for them."

And no doubt they did.

Soon the blacks reached the mouth of the cave, blocking up the entrance with the bamboo ramparts.

"Now is our time," cried Bob; "fire away, doctor, and let us have a scientific result."

"Quick—take care!" the doctor cried. "Now, ready."

Simultaneously the three trains of gunpowder were fired, then there resulted a rumbling sound like distant thunder, and huge masses of rock came tumbling down, completely blocking up the entrance.

One piece fell amongst the niggers, maiming several of them, and causing the others to beat a hasty retreat.

"Curse them! they have escaped," said Delorme, *alias* Howard, for it was he who had joined the tribe of King Pluto, whom he had bribed, and sworn to be his ally against all enemies.

"They have; but they must be inside of that 'ere cave," responded Bow-legged Bill, in his husky voice.

"True."

"True," cried Snika, King Pluto's executioner, for the king himself was not present. "They must be in the cave, and we will have them yet."

"Come on then," said Howard. "I am ready to strike the blow."

"Hold, master, the night is not lucky. The hunter seeks not his prey when the owls are hooting. No, we will wait until daybreak; then death to the white foe."

"Yes, 'tis as well; let us wait, for I'm tired as a dog, and we must have lost already near upon thirty men," said Howard.

"True, master, true; but the Great Spirit has received them."

"Now come; we cannot do better than to sleep."

With this resolution, the whole band slunk off to the neighbouring forest.

CHAPTER XXII.

THE CAVES—A NEW DISCOVERY—THE FORESIGHT OF THE RENOWNED STUMPS—THE
WONDERFUL CAVES OF THE SEVEN PILLARS.

SAFE for the present," cried Bob Blunt when he beheld the rocks falling and blocking up the entrance.

"Hurrah!" cried Buttons. "By Jove! when I get back to England, I'll write my life, for the boys of England to read."

"But suppose you never were to return to England?" said the Stinger.

"How?"

"Why if the savages were to eat you."

"Oh, I never thought of that. Well, my master will write my life then, and tell how heroically I died for the cause. Weep, my Stinger, weep for your Buttons at his tomb, and declare how he died for a noble cause—the cause of——"

"Silence, you two," cried Bob; "we are going to explore the caves."

His order was instantly obeyed.

They now issued into a long passage through which they could only pass one at the time, until at last they entered a wider cave.

The torches were here ignited, and by their light they could see that the cave was of a vast extent.

It was semi-circular in form.

The sides were as smooth as marble chiselled by the mason, whilst the roof was twisted into jagged and fantastic shapes, that appeared to our explorers like so many mummified heads.

The floor was of a fine sand, very dry, and proved to our hero that no water was near this cavern.

"I think we will sojourn here till daylight," said Bob, after they had explored the cave.

Each one then refreshed himself with the provisions they had secured in the knapsacks.

Stumps sat beside Bob.

He was lost in thought.

"I was thinking, master, of the pro-found impression my appearance made in the superstitious breast of that villain, King Pluto."

"True."

"The reverence he paid to my dwarfed stature inspired me with an idea at the time," continued Stumps.

"What is the idea, Stumps, my boy? Out with it," said Bob.

"Well, King Pluto's fear and admiration of myself—very flattering, isn't it?—inspired me with an idea which may prove of vast advantage to all of us in our future adventures. I thought of giving myself out to the natives as a wise man, who could prophesy—in fact, a walking oracle, whose words are the words of the wise, and I think I shall succeed."

"Now, Stumps, tell us how you intend to do this little bit of mystification," said Bob.

"Master, all in good time. I shall have to work hard; but I shall succeed by means of this."

And Stumps, to the surprise of all present, produced a solid piece of white rock from behind him.

"From that you will succeed?" asked the doctor. "Pooh! you had better avail yourself of some of my chemicals."

"I may want them too; but from this piece of rock I intend to astonish all the natives," replied Stumps.

"Very well, Stumps. What you say is strange, but I leave it to you," said Bob. "Now, I'm going to sleep, and I advise all of you to do the same."

"All but myself; I will keep watch in case of danger," said Stumps.

"Very well," replied Bob.

And before the words were well out of his mouth his loud breathing betokened that he was asleep, and his companions were not long in following his example.

As soon as Stumps beheld them all asleep, he drew a small chisel out of his pocket and by means of a stone he began to work on the soft piece of rock.

What the dwarf was to fashion from it will be seen in due course.

Bob Blunt awoke in a few hours.

"Time to be moving ; up, boys."

All of them jumped up.

"Now, Longsight, my boy, lead the way," said Bob.

They passed out from the cave, through many windings and turnings, until they reached an immense cave that appeared like a large hall.

There were seven pillars in it, arched as if formed by hand, but really by nature.

"This is the sort of place for a store-house," said Bob. "Let us see how it looks by torchlight."

A number of extra torches were ignited, and then the effect was perfectly dazzling in its splendour.

The walls of the cave seemed studded with gold, which glittered and sparkled in the flare of the torches.

"Lor', is it gold?" asked the Stinger ; "let's have a bit."

"It is," said the doctor ; "every bit of it, and it seems to me as if this cavern has been used some time or the other by the worshippers of whom Ptolemy and Herodotus speak."

"It's a heathen temple, sure enough," said Bob. "Look, there is a kind of altar, and from here are several lesser caverns."

"That's where the mysteries were performed. Look, there are seven steps leading up to the altar ; and those were the mystical seven, a sacred number in the religion of the East," continued the doctor.

"I say, master, mightn't we carry a lot of this gold home with us?" said Buttons. "Oh, I should look fine with big gold buttons all down my jacket."

"No," said Bob. "Let us rather turn all our attention to discoveries that may open a path for civilisation. If you wish for gold, barter with the natives. They will give you plenty for beads and cloth."

"Hum! thank you, sir. I think it would look very fine to see on a red board, in blue letters—'Buttons, Stumps, Stinger and Co., dealers in bullion. Gold dust taken in exchange for old clothes.' Eh, how we would thrive, and astonish the Londoners, where in time I might become Lord Mayor, the Stinger alderman, and Stumps turnkey of New-gate."

All laughed at Buttons' description.

But Bob soon put an end to it.

"Come on ; we will make our exit from this place, and see whether or not we can join King Aga, and so contrive to get rid of our enemies."

Bob led the way.

At length they beheld a faint streak of light in the distance.

Soon the caves widened above them, and at last they saw the welcome daylight in the full glory of sunshine.

CHAPTER XXIII.

THE ALARM—SWIFTFOOT'S AND STRONGBACK'S ESCAPE—HOWARD'S PERIL—BOB'S
GENEROSITY—VICTORY.

A SCENE of marvellous beauty dazzled the eyes of our hero and his friends as they emerged into the light.

Before them stretched a chain of blue mountains, a deep ravine running be-tween them, whilst nearer lay a lovely valley, through which a rapid river poured its waters.

When they had reached the opening of the caves, Bob, to his astonishment, found that there were four different openings, some twenty feet from the ground.

"It's lucky we have got a rope to let ourselves down by," said Bob. "Here, Ironfist, give me the rope."

"What shall we fasten it to?" asked Ironfist.

"What?—why——"

"Oh, Lord! I see a nigger!" suddenly cried Buttons, starting back.

"Where?"

"There—look! Don't you see him move amongst that grove of trees?"

"No."

"Pooh! you're dreaming, boy," said the Stinger. "Come, let us descend."

"Am I! Well, Stinger, I'll show you that Buttons is right. I'll prove to you that it is a nigger."

With that Buttons drew his rifle to his shoulder, and fired at the spot where he thought he beheld the nigger.

Whiz went the bullet.

A shriek!

An exclamation of astonishment from all.

A black bounded from the spot, holding his two hands on his posterior, where Buttons' bullet had evidently taken effect.

"By Jupiter! you're right, Buttons. You have unearthed a nigger this time," said Bob.

"That's one for you, Buttons, my boy," cried Stumps, slapping him on the back.

"Gentlemen, you do me proud. I am Buttons the brave now," he replied.

"But hold," cried Bob; "there are a number of men coming on to the rescue of that wounded nigger. They have discovered our place of retreat."

A number of savages were seen advancing through the brushwood.

"Down with you into the other cave below me; you, doctor, Ironfist, and Longsight, can fire better from thence, for we are too crowded up here. Away with you, for this will be sharp work."

"Like a shot, I'm off. Come on, you fellows, come on."

And Ironfist bolted down into the lower cave, whilst Bob, the Stinger, Stumps, Buttons, Swiftfoot, and Strongback remained in the upper cave.

Soon a number of men were seen in ambuscade below them.

"Are you all ready?" then cried Bob.

"Ready, sir," they all cried.

"Fire!" said Bob; "fire all of you, and do not miss your man."

"Right, sir."

"One."

"Two!" cried the Stinger.

"Three!" roared Buttons.

And the shots one after the other sped home amidst the savage men.

At that moment Bob beheld a number of men coming through the ravine, and he made sure that they were some of King Aga's men, coming to reinforce them.

"Look, Longsight," he said. "Do you not see that body of men defiling down the mountain pass?"

"Yes."

"They are King Aga's men come to our rescue."

"Yes."

"How shall we let them know that we are here, for Jingo Johnson will guide them to the mouth of the cave?"

"True; but we'll soon remedy that. Strongback, will you follow me? We'll make for the blacks," said Longsight.

"I am ready."

"Come on, then."

Before Bob could prevent them, both of them dropped down from the cave on to the ground.

A swarm of blacks at once gave chase; although one or two were shot down by Bob, the rest started in pursuit.

Swiftfoot was soon beyond reach of them, but Strongback was not so fleet.

He paused.

He faced his pursuers.

Three of them he shot down with his revolver.

The fourth he struck to the earth with his fist.

They came up in a body, but were driven back with a perfect fusilade of bullets.

Three more with savage yells rushed at him, but he fired the remaining barrels of his revolver at them, and before any more could reach him, he turned, and soon disappeared in the windings of the forest.

"Bravo, Strongback! you did for them that time. Now we must defend ourselves until help arrives," said Bob. "See that your weapons are well charged, friends, for the savage wretches look as though they would eat us. Look, they are upon us."

The blacks were now determined to surround our friends, for they advanced boldly and in great numbers.

"That's it, Buttons, my boy; fire away. Go it, Stinger, my beloved. How fine you fire," said Bob.

Cheering them on with words like these, our hero managed to make the blacks withdraw from beneath the caves to the security of the dense forests.

"That's the sort," cried Bob. "Now we shall have a chance for our lives. I only hope Swiftfoot and Strongback will escape, and bring up the reinforcements."

"Yes, I think they have escaped," said the Stinger.

"Halloa! who is this coming?" said Stumps, pointing to the forest.

Two white men were seen to come forth, followed by two or three blacks, with a flag of truce.

"Down with your guns, and let us hear what they have got to say for themselves," said Bob.

But when the white men came closer, Bob, to his supreme astonishment recognised in them Howard and Bow-legged Bill.

"What, is it to you that I owe this attack?" he cried. "You double-faced villain, I've a good mind to end your career."

And Bob pointed his revolver at Howard, with every disposition to put a stop to his villainous relative's life.

"Put down your pistol and listen, Bob Blunt," said Howard, coolly. "You and I are mortal enemies. But I will be lenient with you, though I will have part of your wealth. Yield yourself our prisoner, agree to give me half of your property, and your companions may go their way in peace."

"How very kind, to be sure," sneered Bob. "I think we are the victors at present, and it is with us to dictate terms."

"You will be forced to surrender, for we will starve you out," replied Howard.

"Wait till your bellies begin to grumble," said Bill.

"Eh, you curs? I'll warrant yours shall grumble first. Begone, or I fire upon you, and thus your death be on your own heads," cried Bob.

"Oh, we are very plucky now, ain't we?" laughed Howard.

"We can fight," retorted Bob.

"Then you won't accept our terms?" said Howard again.

"Never, villain!"

"Never is a long day," said Howard. "We can afford to wait, my boy."

He stood leaning on his rifle, looking stedfastly at the cave.

Suddenly Bob gave vent to a cry.

Above Howard's head, twining its huge length along a branch of a tree, was a boa constrictor.

None of Howard's followers beheld it, so silently did the serpent glide along.

"Listen, Howard. Villain as you are, I do not wish for your death, and I will save your life. It lies in my power," said Bob.

"You lie; you have no power over my life, but I will have yours."

"Look up; death is there," cried Bob.

Howard looked up, dropped his gun, and stood spellbound before the eyes of the serpent, who was protruding his deadly fangs over Howard.

"Oh, horrible! look at the beast!" cried Bow-legged Bill, rushing away, and overturning a couple of niggers in his flight.

Howard could not move.

He stood trembling with his eyes fixed on the serpent that was about to coil around him.

Bang!

It was the report of Bob's revolver.

The boa constrictor was pierced to the brain, and it fell full upon Howard.

Bob saw that his enemy had swooned.

He had been struck down by the force of the serpent's fall.

Bob beckoned to Howard's followers to come and relieve him.

One by one they came in fear and trembling, and Bow-legged Bill was more afraid than the others.

Timidly did the niggers approach, until they beheld the boa with shattered head lying motionless on the ground.

They dragged Howard from beneath it, and he gradually revived.

But when he beheld the serpent lying dead at his feet, he groaned out—

"Heaven! what an escape! horrible monster; and I owe my life to my enemy."

This last thought seemed to pain him more than anything.

He looked up at Bob.

A scowl was on his brow, but he spoke up.

"I'd rather you had shot me dead than to owe you my life; but that shall not spare you from my vengeance. I hate you fifty times the more."

"Oh, noble soul! How the coward speaks in you, without one spark of generosity. Go, and beware how you cross my path for the future, for the next time you may not escape so easily, nor I be forgiving enough to spare your life. You are black at heart."

"Shoot the blackguard," cried the Stinger, exasperated at Howard's hardness of heart.

"Give it him, sir," said Buttons "shooting is best for him. Let me have a shot at him, sir."

"No, it's too good for him. Hanging is the only thing that will do for him," cried Bob.

"Bah! I hate you all, and will yet have your lives. Yours, Blunt, shall be the first. Here is my rifle, and the shot is for you."

And before our friends knew what he was about to do, he raised the weapon to his shoulder and fired it at our hero.

Bob saw the movement in time.

He accordingly threw himself upon the ground.

The bullet whizzed above him, and struck the rocks.

Before, however, the doctor and the others could return the shot, Howard disappeared into the depth of the forest.

There was no thought of mercy now.

Bang, bang! went the rifles after him, but he escaped.

"The scoundrel!" cried Bob, enraged at this piece of treachery.

At this moment there was a loud shout from the forest.

"Hurrah! our friends," cried Buttons. "Hurrah! we shall lick them now."

And before any one could prevent him, he dropped from the cave on the ground, at the moment when Swiftfoot and Strongback appeared with half a hundred blacks at their backs.

Bob at once followed Buttons' example, and joined Swiftfoot and Strongback.

"Where is King Aga?" he asked of the new arrivals.

"He is in the camp, massa," said Jingo Johnson.

"Why did he not come to our assistance in person?"

"Becos he am busy with 'im fetiche," said Jingo.

"Oh; and these are his men, I presume?" said Bob, scanning the swarthy group.

"Ebery one on 'em, massa; fighting men, massa."

"Come, then, we'll go in pursuit of these rogues. I think we're all in a fighting humour now."

And Bob started off, followed by the blacks.

But before they had gone many yards, there was a cry—

"Help! help!"

The cry came from the Stinger.

The good lady had not been able to make her descent from the caves.

"Help!" she cried. "Are you going to leave a poor lone woman to be devoured by monsters? What becomes of woman's rights?"

"What! my Stinger in distress?" cried Buttons, rushing forward.

"Missie Nosie. Oh, I will save her. I lub her."

And both Buttons and Jingo rushed forward to rescue the unfortunate Stinger from her predicament.

"How shall I get down, you wretched men?" she cried despairingly.

"Why, jump, missie. Me catch you in my arms. Me lub you."

"You!"

"Yes, missie; me lub you. Me catch you."

"Go on, Stinger. Jump into Jingo's

arms. I will hold him up. It's all right."

"Is there no other way?"

"None."

"Then I suppose I must. But it's an awful jump."

She first threw down her umbrella, then her pattens, and lastly gathered up her skirts about her, then craned over and looked down.

"Oh, it's awful. It's like jumping from the monument. What must not E. A. Stinger suffer for the cause? But virtue is its own reward. I will dare the terrific leap."

"Come on," cried Jingo.

"Are you ready?" shrieked E. A. S., at the top of her voice.

"Yes."

Jingo planted his legs astride, whilst Buttons went behind him, placing his two hands in the small of Jingo's back, in order to support him.

"Now, then," said Elizabeth Ann.

"Ready, Betsy."

"When I have counted three, then I am ready to jump."

"Right."

"One—two, and——"

"Three!" cried Buttons.

"Three!" reiterated the Stinger.

And with that she took the leap.

But her weight was none of the lightest.

She jumped into Jingo's arms, but the shock threw that redoubtable nigger back.

He fell upon Buttons, nearly smothering him.

"Well, I fall soft," cried the Stinger, picking herself up.

"You do, and you did. Oh, get up, Jingo. Let me breathe."

Poor Buttons did not calculate upon this mishap.

When at last Jingo arose from him, Buttons could hardly breathe for a moment.

"That'll do, thank you," said Buttons. "Come on. Mr. Blunt is waiting for us."

Stinger and the others started off in pursuit of Bob, who was making his way through the brushwood.

The Stinger soon joined him.

"I have lost my rifle, Mr. Blunt. How am I to do battle against the savages?" she asked.

"Use your claws."

"I will."

They now issued into the open country.

They came up with Howard and his men.

Our hero gave chase.

But he soon saw that he might be led into an ambuscade, there to meet their death, so he desisted in his pursuit of the natives.

"Halt!" he cried. "I see that we have numberless difficulties before us. Therefore, I shall adjourn to King Aga's camp, and await further action on the part of our enemies. Do you agree with me?"

"We do," was the unanimous reply of all his followers.

"Then march, Jingo, and guide us to King Aga."

"Right, massa. Me walk by the side of my lubly nosie, Missie Stinger. Peace is in King Aga's camp."

CHAPTER XXIV.

THE ARRIVAL AT KING AGA'S CAMP—SAD NEWS—THE STINGER'S INDIGNATION AT KING PLUTO'S VILLAINY—A HANDFUL OF WOOL.

BOB BLUNT felt elated with the victory which he had had over Dick Howard.

But he marvelled that he had not known of his arrival before, and that he had not recognised him on board the "Busy Bee."

Still, now that he had come face to

face with his enemies, our bold young hero did not fear their machinations for the future.

He accordingly led the van of the negroes that had been sent to his assistance.

Buttons and the Stinger trudged on together.

"Oh, my eyes, Stinger, ain't we been in danger—and ain't we just escaped? Oh, you are as plucky as I am."

The Stinger looked down.

"You are, Buttons, my boy; but in this sad vale of tears "—here the Stinger sought to wipe her eyes with the corner of her dress—"but in this vale of tears, bravery is naught unless it's accompanied by discretion, and discretion is the better part of valour. You remember the lines of the author of Hudibras—

> "'He that is in battle slain,
> Can never rise to fight again;
> But he that fights and runs away,
> May live to fight another day.'"

"Why, Stinger, you're quite an authority on literary matters," said Bob Blunt, who had overheard the foregoing conversation. "I didn't think you knew so much about the poets. But those lines are not from Hudibras, Miss Stinger."

"Mr. Blunt, sir," replied the Stinger, looking with awful solemnity at our hero, "do you think that E. A. S., the champion of woman's rights, would venture out into the wilds of Africa without making herself thoroughly acquainted with polite learning? What would the benighted inhabitants of Africa think of her if she did not know everything, eh?"

Bob now commanded Stinger and Buttons to keep silent, as he wanted them to make a dignified entrance into King Aga's town.

This request was at once complied with.

So they tramped on through the glorious forest, until the advance guard began to blow their horns, and with loud shouts announced that they were in sight of King Aga's village.

Bob was greatly interested to see what kind of a place it was.

Soon, through an opening in the forest, they beheld on the declivity of a gentle hill a number of huts, that appeared like so many beehives to our travellers, for the houses were all thatched with broad palm leaves, and were of a conical shape.

The town was built in a circle.

The entrances ran one into the other through the town.

As they came within fifty yards of the town, they commenced chanting a monotonous song.

But there was no reply from the town, and it seemed apparently deserted when they reached the strong palisade which formed the entrance.

"Why, Jingo, there is no one to be seen here. What does it mean?" inquired Bob, astonished that the king did not appear to give him welcome.

"Know not, massa? King Aga am sick; perhaps he dead."

"Dead? Nonsense, we should have heard all about it," said Bob.

"Um, massa; let white fetiche man make noise," replied Jingo.

"And who is my fetiche?"

"Why, little mannie wid um big dunder drum," replied Jingo, pointing to Stumps.

"Yes, a good idea. Stumps, out with your trombone and wake the echoes."

Stumps unstrapped the instrument which he had on his back, and putting it to his lips struck up the martial air of "Rule Britannia."

At the first notes a number of women and children ran from the houses in a great state of alarm.

They shrank back timidly behind the matting that formed the doors, and gazed in open-eyed wonder at the white men.

Bob wanted to know where the king's residence was, and was informed that it was right in the centre of the town.

It was a building somewhat larger than the others, and apparently built of wood and a kind of clay.

As Bob came in sight of it a loud wailing noise was heard.

"What is that?" asked Bob.

"King dead. Mourners lamenting," replied Jingo Johnson, with awe.

"I hope not, Jingo, but it looks very much like it," said Bob, for he caught sight of a number of women and men with their faces to the earth and strewing dust upon their heads. "Some great calamity has evidently befallen King Aga," said Bob. "Stumps, just blow with all your might."

Stumps complied.

The noise aroused the mourners.

When they beheld our friends they rushed away with a shriek, but the sound brought the king's chief officer from the house.

Without saying a word he motioned Bob to enter the house.

He entered a large room.

On every side were women and men with the utmost dejection pictured on every feature of their swarthy countenances.

At the foot of his chair of state lay King Aga.

Every now and then he uttered a deep groan, then beat his head on the floor in his excessive grief.

"What is the cause of all this lamentation?" asked Bob.

But no one answered.

Then our hero went up to King Aga, and laying his hand upon his shoulder, he said in a solemn tone—

"Will not the king tell his white friend the cause of his sorrow?"

The king looked up.

"Ah, the great white chief. Oh, ye gods! ye have sent him to assist a bereaved father. I thank you."

"Arise and tell me what has occurred," said our hero, gently.

The king arose.

Gradually his grief took a milder form, he sighed deeply, and thus began—

"Know, great chief, the cause of my sorrow. Last night your messenger came and reported to me that you were in danger. I at once sent my warriors to your assistance, and shortly after I followed myself. But I had not gone far ere one of my men overtook me, and compelled my return. I did return, and found, oh, cruel fate! the light of my house, the star of my existence, my lovely daughter, Nahita, had been forcibly abducted during my absence."

The king's grief burst out afresh.

For some time Bob Blunt allowed it to have way; then, when the king was somewhat recovered, he said—

"And by whom has your daughter been abducted, my friend?"

"By my fierce enemy, King Pluto."

"Indeed! that is the reason I did not see him amongst his tribe."

"No."

"And have you not followed him?"

"Not yet."

"It may not be too late to overtake him, and wrest his prey from him."

The king shook his head.

"It shall not be too late," cried the Stinger, who had attentively listened to this recital, "it shall not be too late, if E. A. S. can help it. What! am I not here to avenge the wrongs of my sex? Come on, then, to the rescue of the maiden."

And the Stinger gave a flourish with her umbrella, as if she meant it.

"Right again, Betsy!" said Buttons.

"Not so fast, not so fast," cried Bob.

"But you are right, Stinger, we will go; we will help this good king."

"Stinger is ready for the fight. Woman's rights is my motto."

And another flourish with her umbrella increased the astonishment of the natives present, whose curiosity was so great that one of them was examining her pocket.

As he was in the act of doing so, the Stinger's umbrella came with a thud upon his scalp.

Seeing he was about to commit a theft from her person, the Stinger, before the nigger could rise from the blow, caught him by his woolly head.

"I'll teach you to steal my scent bottle, you villain," she cried; "now I've got you; ba, ba! black sheep, I mean to gather wool."

And she did, with such effect, that before the black could free himself, the Stinger had possessed herself of a handful of his wool.

He roared with rage and pain.

But when he was free, he jumped away a dozen yards and stood rubbing his head, and staring at his foe with horror and astonishment depicted upon his countenance.

"I'll show them that women are not to be treated like cattle," she cried. "I'll

"HOWARD DROPPED HIS GUN, AND STOOD SPELLBOUND BEFORE THE SERPENT."

get up an army of my own sex, to fight you all."

"That's the ticket, my Betsy. I'll back you against all Africa," cried Buttons.

The Stinger walked majestically away, and as the niggers shrank away from her as she passed them, she took her seat upon a bench, pulled out her flask from her pocket, and took a long pull, with evident satisfaction, and totally ignoring her company.

Bob Blunt, during this pantomimic performance by the Stinger, had fired King Aga to give immediate chase to King Pluto.

The king, now that his grief had somewhat subsided, was bent upon revenge.

He gave immediate orders to his chiefs, and in an incredibly short space of time, some two hundred warriors were arranged in front of the king's palace.

Bob saw that they were a very fine body of warriors, although most of them were hideously painted in green and red, whilst the chiefs wore such a quantity of massive gold bracelets and necklets, that it was a wonder they could walk.

King Aga himself soon appeared, ten times more gorgeously attired than the rest, and at his appearance the drums beat, the horns were sounded, until the noise was deafening.

Bob Blunt summoned his own escort to attend him personally.

"Now, Swiftfoot, show these fellows how you can scout."

"I will; but first we must find the trail," he replied.

"Good. Now then, attention, all of you, and listen to what King Aga says."

Bob then made known to the king his wishes.

The king divined that Pluto would not return to his own village but would go up the country with his prize.

"Then lead the way. I'm ready now to revenge your loss, and am eager for the fray. Stumps, old man, sound the advance."

Stumps sounded a war note, and the little army marched away from King Aga's camp, followed by the lamentations of the women and children.

CHAPTER XXV.

THE PURSUIT—KING PLUTO SIGHTED—THE WATERFALL—FOILED.

KING PLUTO had effected the abduction of the pretty Nahita during his enemy's absence, and had it not been that one of her slaves had seen him leave the tent, her disappearance would have been unaccounted for.

But as it was, Aga knew the man who had done him this grievous injury, and the feeling of revenge was great within him.

Bob and King Aga walked side by side through the forest.

Swiftfoot had been sent in advance, and whilst he was gone they awaited his return in a deep hollow.

King Aga's impatience was great.

But Bob contrived to calm him until at length Swiftfoot returned.

He came up panting and breathless.

"Well?" asked Bob.

"Six miles away," he gasped. "I came up with King Pluto. He has only a dozen warriors with him, and they were resting close to a mighty river, near which there is a waterfall. They did not see me."

"Did you see Nahita?"

"No; but there was a small tent erected on one side of them, and several of the warriors lay around it. I have no hesitation in saying that it contains the daughter of the king."

"That is well. Now, we had better start. But I don't think it is necessary for us all to go in pursuit. King Aga, myself, Stumps, Strongback, Swiftfoot, and a dozen others will do."

"And I," cried the Stinger. "Mr. Blunt, you will never think of leaving me behind. Look, I am ready to help save the king's daughter."

"Take me," cried Buttons.

"You may come, both of you, but mind you manage to hold your tongues, or you will spoil all," said Bob.

"Now, Buttons," said the Stinger, "if I catch you playing any of your tricks, it will be the worse for you, so look out."

"All serene, my trump! I won't give much for King Pluto if our Stinger happens to get hold of his wool."

"Now, then, away we go," cried Bob.

Strict orders were given for the warriors not to move from the spot, and then Bob, King Aga, Stumps, Swiftfoot, and Strongback, with the Stinger and Buttons, and a dozen natives started away in pursuit of King Pluto.

Swiftfoot, with wonderful sagacity, trod his way through the forest, although their progress was naturally slow, for the dense brushwood on every side of them impeded them.

The stronger members of the party gradually forged ahead.

Their strong arms and sharp axes could make a path through which they could stumble.

So Bob and most of his male associates got some distance in front of Miss Stinger.

Suddenly Jingo Johnson, who had kept well in front, exclaimed—

"Look! Lookee dere, massa."

"What's up?" demanded Bob.

"Dere, black man."

Bob looked in the direction indicated by Jingo Johnson's finger, which was right ahead, and saw—or fancied he saw—a black man, if not two, rushing off through the jungle.

"Yoicks! tallyho!" he shouted. "Forward, friends; there are are the villains!"

And away he darted, followed by Strongback and outstripped by Swiftfoot, who crashed through the bamboo canes at a most surprising rate.

King Aga and his best warriors were not far behind.

Presently the bamboo jungle ceased, and they came to a kind of open grove.

"Now, look out," exclaimed Bob. "The country is a trifle clearer, and we may perhaps see them."

"Dere 'im am," shouted Jingo Johnson, again pointing forward.

Bob looked, and saw some black figures dodging from tree to tree.

Two or three times he raised his rifle, but could get no aim, but at length one of them paused a second, and then fell forward dead as our hero's breechloader belched forth its load of smoke and death.

"There's one down; now forward for the others."

They rushed up to the place where the dead man had fallen, and there, to their intense disgust, beheld a dead monkey.

A monkey of large size and covered with black hair.

"We must return to the old trail," said Bob, after ruefully contemplating his victim.

So they gradually retraced their steps to the spot where they had left Buttons and the Stinger, who was beginning to get rather alarmed at being alone in the African wilds.

Then they resumed their difficult track through the jungle.

But the exertion was too much for the poor Stinger.

"I—why, my strength is nearly gone. I must rest my weary bones on this stump of a tree, and take a refresher," she exclaimed.

The bottle came to her mouth, and she took a long pull.

"There, now, I'm myself again. Lend me your arm, Buttons."

"Here, get the niggers to carry you," said Buttons.

"A good idea, a splendid idea. Tell the beasts of burden, Buttons."

"Here, you niggers, come and carry my sweetheart," he said.

Two of the blacks at once proffered their services.

"One at the time. Lend me the loan of your back."

She placed her arms around the nigger's neck, and in another moment she was being carried along at a jog trot.

This was satisfactory.

They soon got over the ground in this way, until at length Swiftfoot whispered to Bob, who at once commanded a halt.

They had by that time reached a slight eminence.

Swiftfoot separated the long grass, and pointing through it, he said—

"There they are."

Bob looked.

He beheld several blacks, lying at their full length around a fire.

King Aga looked.

"Ah, they are worshipping fetiche; look, they have a monkey to sacrifice. Oh, ye gods," continued Aga, lifting up his hands to the heavens, and devotedly touching several human bones that hung at his girdle, "grant that ye will not accept their sacrifice. Grant that Aga may overcome his enemies."

"I hope your prayer will be granted," said Bob. "But the first thing we had better do, is to surround them."

"Come," said Swiftfoot; "I will lead you near to them."

"Single file," cried Bob.

"Yes."

"Then on with you; now, silence all."

Swiftfoot led the way.

They came to within twenty yards of King Pluto, when the Stinger gave a loud scream. A small snake had twisted itself round her legs.

"That has spoilt all," whispered Bob.

He peered through the long grass.

At the first note of the Stinger's voice, King Pluto and his warriors leaped to their feet and listened.

The cry was not repeated.

Yet their suspicions were aroused.

They stood for a few moments, when unfortunately, they heard a slight rustle in the grass.

It was the unfortunate Stinger again, for in her eagerness to see, she had pushed Buttons forward.

This time there was no doubt at all about it.

King Pluto's men formed themselves into a compact body, whilst he himself rushed into the tent.

He did not reappear, but his followers gave a loud shout, turned tail, and rushed off in a body.

Bob raised his rifle, and sent a couple of bullets after them.

A cry of agony told him that the shots had taken effect.

All further concealment was now useless, as he cried—

"Away! Give chase, boys."

King Aga and Bob were neck by neck, and first in the open.

The king uttered a cry of rage.

He beheld his daughter Nahita the beautiful, in the arms of Pluto.

"Tallyho!" roared Stumps, then sounding his trombone.

The sound only gave wings to King Pluto's terrified followers.

Away they went, never pausing to look behind.

Aga's rage was so great he could hardly contain himself.

"Courage," cried Bob, "my English lads will catch hold of him yet. There goes King Pluto."

The chase was now up hill, and at that moment Pluto disappeared.

When our friends came again in view of him, he was in the act of crossing deep and dangerous waterfalls.

Two huge trunks of trees were thrown over a narrow part of the cataract, forming a rather perilous bridge.

King Pluto chose the highest one.

"I dare not fire," cried Bob; "I might hit Nahita. Ah, the scoundrel knows he is perfectly safe. Look how he shakes his fist at us."

By this time they had gained the banks of the waterfall.

Bob and King Aga rushed at the lower bridge, and as he was crossing, our hero brought one of King Pluto's men down with his revolver.

The fellow fell into the water, and rapidly disappeared, carried away by the strong current.

The Stinger, with marvellous courage, was crossing the bridge that King Pluto was crossing.

Buttons held determinedly on to the end of her skirts.

The tree was firmly fixed, yet as soon as King Pluto had crossed, he beheld the

Stinger and Buttons on the tree, and with fiendish malice he tried to loosen it with his foot.

Bob saw what he was about to do, and cried out to the Stinger and Buttons to return at once.

"Stand back a moment ; I will bring that fellow down."

Bang !

The next moment, one of King Pluto's men tumbled headfirst into the raging torrent, brought down by a shot from Bob.

"Now for King Pluto," he cried, and taking steady aim, he fired.

But for once Bob Blunt missed his mark, and King Pluto was unhurt.

Miss Stinger and Buttons, however, had heard our hero's warning shout and had managed to get back on *terra firma*, seeing which King Pluto ceased his endeavours to hurl the log over into the stream, and stood erect on it, holding his captive in his arms.

"This way, Miss Stinger. Buttons, come here," shouted our hero.

And obedient to his call, they both hurried down to the lower of the two trees.

"There's another of the villains !" exclaimed Bob, as one of King Pluto's men ran out on the tree to aid his master. "I can pot him, at all events."

Bang! went the third chamber of Bob's revolver, and the third nigger went tumbling into the stream.

But that nigger was not the only person who fell.

Buttons, who had managed to gain a place close by King Aga, was startled by the sudden report, and slipped.

To save himself from falling into the raging cataract, he clutched at Miss Stinger with one hand, while the other hand grasped a broken branch.

Miss Stinger was compelled to sit down suddenly.

They both hung for a moment, and then were swept down the roaring cataract.

Both shrieked for help.

But Bob did not see the mishap in time to render them any assistance.

"What is to be done ?" cried Bob. "Poor Buttons, and poor old Stinger ; they will be drowned. Who can give help ? I am powerless."

He stood on the tree trunk with King Aga, the picture of despair.

They beheld the Stinger and Buttons rise to the surface, catch hold of a floating log, and then disappear round a curve in the stream.

"Poor Buttons, I will avenge you," cried Bob, " or die."

In the meantime, King Pluto remained grinning in triumph from above.

Bob dared not fire at him, for the villain held the beautiful Nahita in his arms, and he would inevitably kill her.

But when King Pluto beheld his enemy, King Aga, rush up to the bank in pursuit of him, he threw a spear at him, uttered a loud shout of triumph, and immediately afterwards disappeared.

Bob followed King Aga, but on reaching the bank, they saw that all pursuit was worse than useless.

King Pluto was beyond reach.

"Let us search, and see whether we can find any trace of poor Buttons and the Stinger. If they are dead, I will follow King Pluto to the world's end, and revenge that poor boy Buttons."

Bob's grief was intense, for he felt a great liking for his humble friend ; and King Aga shared in his grief as they returned again across the river, and joined Swiftfoot, Stumps, and the others.

CHAPTER XXVI.

BOB'S DESPAIR—RESOLVES TO RETURN TO KING AGA'S CAMP—NEWS OF THE STINGER—THE SEARCH—THE MYSTERIOUS UMBRELLA—THE FOOT PRINTS IN THE SAND—THE MYSTERY STILL UNEXPLAINED.

WITH sorrowful face and bowed head, Bob Blunt and King Aga left the bridge behind them, and travelling through the forest, they soon gained the sides of the torrent.

Bob cast an anxious glance on the rapid river.

"There is hope still, King Aga," he said to his friend, "for Buttons and poor Miss Stinger may yet be saved."

"My daughter—oh, my beautiful Nahita !" moaned King Aga.

"Pardon me, that I have for a moment forgotten your grief, in my anxiety to know the fate of those in whom I feel interested," said Bob. "I did not know until now how much I liked poor Buttons and Stinger ; their harmless natures were a source of endless amusement, and everyone will regret their untimely end."

Bob Blunt did not expect a reply from King Aga, for he walked on, unable to conceal his emotion.

Swiftfoot and Stumps were likewise very downhearted at what had occurred.

They continued their way along the river side.

But no trace of Buttons or the Stinger did they find.

Bob despaired of ever seeing them again.

"Let us return to the camp," he said, at length ; "perhaps we may find a means of renewing our search for our friends after calm reflection."

Accordingly, they sat down and had some refreshment.

Then they consulted as to their future action.

After this they continued their journey until they came up with several natives who were fishing in the river.

Of these, Jingo Johnson inquired whether they had seen anything of the Stinger and Buttons, describing them and their perilous position with great exactitude.

The natives replied that they had seen the tree bridge float past with two persons clinging to it, but had been unable to render them any assistance.

This news was encouraging.

Bob now resolved to prosecute his search, in case he might come up with the unlucky ones in the hour of their need, when they might possibly have been cast upon the shore.

He accordingly made known his intentions to King Aga, who assented.

They followed the windings of the stream until their course was abruptly brought to a standstill by a huge ravine, through which the cataract foamed with great speed.

"We can go no further," exclaimed Bob, sadly.

"No, and we don't want to. Look ; if that is not the Stinger's umbrella, I'm not Stumps, the dwarf."

All eyes were directed towards the object mentioned by Stumps.

Bob rushed towards it.

Firmly imbedded in the golden sand was an umbrella exactly like the Stinger's.

The handle was thrust into the sand.

The little group gathered around it, and examined in mute wonder.

At length Bob spoke.

"The Stinger must have come safe to shore, or how should this be imbedded here ?"

"She never would leave her gingham behind her. I know her too well for that ; why she would sooner leave her rum bottle," said the dwarf.

"True," muttered Bob, "but I see no signs of Buttons."

"But I do," exclaimed Stumps. "Look, sir,"

And Stumps pointed to several footprints in the sand.

Bob examined them carefully.

"Yes; that's the Stinger's, and there is Buttons' hoof, hurrah! They are saved; they must have floated to shore."

"Exactly," said Stumps. "Let us follow the trail."

"Right you are, Stumps, my boy. Now, Swiftfoot, do you think you can trace the footsteps?"

"Yes."

"Good; then go ahead. Here, Jingo, take care of the umbrella."

"Right, massa! My lubly missie miss her 'brella. Jingo am the man to gib um her, 'cause she lub me and me lub her."

"Now push along, for it will soon be dark," said Bob.

They traced the footprints for a long way on the sands, but at last they came over a wide stretch of hard rock, and here all trace was lost.

"We can go no further," said Swiftfoot. "This rocky soil has no impression of their footprints."

"Then we will return to the camp.

Perhaps they have made their way towards it, for the Stinger is no fool, and can easily guide herself in that direction by the sun," said Bob. "But it is terrible to think that they must be exposed to all the dangers of an African forest by night."

"Come, then; but remember revenge upon the cause of all our wrongs," cried the Ashanti king. "I will never rest till the robber of my daughter falls beneath my hand. Vengeance on King Pluto, or my death."

"I will aid you to the death; fear not," said Bob.

"Master, fear not. Only let Stumps once have a chance, and he will soon return King Aga's daughter to her father's arms."

"How Stumps?"

"Ask me not at present, but wait, master; little men may have but puny bodies, but they have often quick and inventive brains. God Almighty seems to have atoned to them mentally what they lack bodily, and you will see in due time that I am right in my words."

"I believe you. Now let us hasten on, or darkness will soon overtake us, and danger from man and beast lay before us."

CHAPTER XXVII.

THE ADVENTURES THAT BEFELL THE GALLANT BUTTONS AND THE BRAVE STINGER.

IT was a moment of awful feeling when E. A. Stinger found herself going into the waterfalls below.

Poor Betsy could not cry out, for fear took possession of her.

"Hold tight to me, my dear Buttons," she whispered, "for we are going to kingdom come."

"Where?" queried Buttons.

"We are going—oh!—down we go."

And, as aforesaid, down they went, providentially rising near the floating log before mentioned.

The tree glided down the river with incredible swiftness.

The Stinger's horror and Buttons' terror were fearful, but the Stinger plucked up courage.

"Are you there, Buttons?" she asked.

"Yes," stammered Buttons. "I hardly know where I am, but I'm holding tight to this old trunk of a tree."

"Keep up your courage, boy; we may be saved yet; while there is life there is hope," said the Stinger.

"I'm getting used to it now, like the eels that are skinned every day. Lor'! we go down the river as quick as a steam engine. I wonder where we shall come to a full stop?"

"That's the way to take it, my boy—halloa, down we go—hold on !"

The tree fell a considerable height down one of the waterfalls, but soon floated along in the wake of the stream.

Thus they continued their progress for a considerable while in great peril, but hoping that as long as the torrent did not increase, they might yet be enabled to save themselves from death.

And the Stinger was also able to recover her umbrella, which floated not far from them.

At last they came in sight of a gloomy ravine.

The rocks arose jagged and vast on each side, whilst the torrent swelled to a river as it dashed into the opening.

"It's all up with us, Buttons, unless we can manage to stop the tree."

"Oh !" groaned Buttons, "this is having a bath with a vengeance."

"Look, I see a number of rocks rising out of the water. We must cling to one of them, if possible ; keep your eyes open, Buttons, Stinger is near you."

There was no need for Buttons to open his eyes, for they were nearly starting from his head, as he looked at the seething waters rushing into the ravine.

They nearly reached it.

When within fifty yards of it, the tree suddenly turned sideways.

The tree began to turn round and round, a sure proof that the terrific force of the current was drawing them into the vortex of waters.

On they still went.

The tree struck one of the islets.

As it did so the Stinger turned round, clutched Buttons by the hair, and literally rolled on to *terra firma*.

The next instant the current bore the tree along, and it disappeared with great velocity into the ravine.

Hardly breathing, the two horrified travellers saw with what violence the tree was borne into the raging waters.

"What an escape," said the Stinger. "Oh, Buttons, we are saved."

"We are, Stinger, and you have not lost a Buttons."

And the two, whose nerves had been strung to the utmost tension, found relief in tears.

When their emotions had somewhat subsided, they both gave thanks to God for their marvellous deliverance from a frightful death.

But they were not yet out of danger.

The Stinger looked round, but there was no place near enough for them to climb to, no dry land.

They were in the centre of the river, whilst the waters hastened into the ravine with such force that it was impossible for even a strong swimmer to breast them.

The Stinger brought forth her rum bottle and handing it to Buttons, said—

"Here, take a drink at the consoler."

Buttons was nothing loath.

He took a hearty pull.

"Oh, that gives me courage," he cried, handing it back. "What a good thing you didn't let the cork come out."

"Yes, Buttons, I know when to let the cork come out. Your health, Buttons."

The Stinger's eyes were elevated to the heavens for at least six seconds.

With a loud groan of intense relief she put the bottle back into her pocket, crying—

"Now I'm a woman again ; there's life in E. A. Stinger yet."

"There is ; never say die. Come on, Betsy ; let us see whether we can reach the shore."

"No ; that we can't."

"We shall—hurrah ! Buttons' eyes are wide open. I'm not to be beaten."

"Is the boy daft ?" cried the Stinger, as she beheld Buttons gazing with all his might into the water. "What do you see ?"

"See," he rejoined. "My lovely Betsy, can't you see a lot of green below the surface ?"

"Yes."

"Well, those are rocks ; a chain of them beneath the water. We may walk ashore."

The Stinger saw the green mass.

"Yes, they are rocks. Oh, Buttons, my dear, we are saved by a merciful Providence. Try the rocks."

"I will, like a bird."

Buttons slowly descended the sides of the islet, putting one foot into the water first, and finding he touched on solid matter he drew the other after him.

The rocks were about a foot below the surface of the water, and this was the cause of the river rushing with greater rapidity towards the ravine, the rocky impediment diverting its channel to one outlet.

"Now take the arm of a Buttons, and he'll take you safely on land."

The Stinger, seeing Buttons safe, at once followed him.

Fortunately the chain of rocks reached within a yard of the banks of the river.

This yard Buttons and the Stinger jumped.

"Saved! Hurrah! Betsy—hurrah! we're saved."

"We are," gasped the Stinger; "so far, at any rate. Oh, Buttons, how are your poor, poor feet? Mine are a little bruised."

"So are mine. But, there, what does that matter?

"With Betsy! with Betsy!
To live and die in Africa
With my beloved Betsy,
Heigho! heigho!
To live and die with Betsy."

And Buttons danced on the yellow sands in joy at his escape.

"We are not saved yet, Buttons. And how are we to find Mr. Blunt in this awful wilderness, where there are no turnpike roads, no signposts to guide us?"

"True, Betsy," said Buttons, rather crestfallen. "But I've my revolver, and some dry cartridges in my tin case, and you your umbrella, so we can manage to fight our way through the heart of Africa."

"We will!" cried the Stinger.

"Done! Who's afraid?"

"Not E. A. Stinger."

"Not Buttons."

The two shook hands upon it.

Buttons put his hand to his forehead as if in great thought.

"I have it, Betsy."

"Don't call me Betsy any more, Buttons. My name is Elizabeth Ann Stinger. Familiarity breeds contempt; but I pardon you."

"Look here, I was going to remark before you had the cheek to interrupt me—which was very rude of you, Betsy —I was going to remark that my master would never forsake his Buttons either dead or alive. I know he would see the end of me, so I am certain he will go in search of us."

"Right, Buttons."

"Now, we must make some landmarks, and find something conspicuous like, and also something familiar to him."

"Your hat, Buttons," suggested the Stinger, pointing to his somewhat bulged, gold-laced head covering.

"My hat!" cried Buttous, taking it off and regarding it with great affection. "My hat! Betsy, I would not take millions for it; it reminds me of Old England."

"Oh!" cried the Stinger.

"Yes, oh! you may laugh, but I value that hat as much as my life; it was a beauty once."

"Well, leave your jacket behind us as a token of our escape."

"Jacket, Betsy," said Buttons. looking with pride at it. "No, that's as dear to me as my hat; but I tell you what I was about to suggest; you shall stick up your umbrella in the sand! My master knows that well enough."

"My umbrella!" shrieked the Stinger. "Never, never, never. I'll die first."

"Well, then, we'll have to die."

"Won't the empty rum bottle do as well?" asked the Stinger.

"Won't do."

"Or my shawl?"

"Never."

"Oh, my umbrella!"

"Will you leave it?"

"Oh, Buttons, if it will help to save our lives, I will."

And the Stinger thrust the handle of her umbrella with vindictive force into the sands.

"Farewell," she cried; "now I am like a teapot without a handle, a glass without a bottom, a lamp without a wick, a candle without a pair of snuffers, a body without a heart. Betsy Stinger is alone, alone without her umbrella."

Her emotions were so powerful that she rushed away, leaving Buttons contemplating the umbrella with a grin. He hastened after the Stinger.

"Betsy, stay, you have me to protect you. Halt, heigho, stay! Oh, Betsy, stay!"

He found her at the back of a small rock, draining the bottle to console her wounded feelings.

The Stinger disconsolately contemplated the empty bottle, and then putting it in her pocket, she said—

"Come on, Buttons. We will rove through the forest, and track to their lair the lion and tiger, and the big——"

"Roosian bear," chimed in Buttons, who saw that the Stinger was rather elevated.

"No, no, no; and track to his lair Pluto, who stole the fair."

"Bravo, Stinger, you're a trump; we will let him have it hot. Come on, now we are free."

"Oh, my umbrella!"

"Never mind that, we'll soon find another. Come on, my Betsy."

He took her by the hand, and the two struck off across a wide, sweeping valley that lay before them.

As they were about to enter the precincts of the forest they heard a wild chant issue therefrom.

"What is that?" asked Buttons.

"Don't know," ejaculated Stinger.

"Oh, Lor', something the matter."

"It is—halloa! look, Buttons, here comes a troop of niggers."

Five long files of natives were seen to issue from the forest.

About a dozen white men were walking on either side of them.

"Look, there are a lot of Europeans; they will direct us to Mr. Blunt."

"Hurrah for them, then. Come on, my Buttons, we're in luck's way."

"We are."

The two hastened towards the troop advancing towards them.

To Buttons' and Stinger's surprise they discovered that the blacks were chained together in a long row of a dozen; there were five rows of them.

"Gentlemen," said Buttons, "we are travelling in Africa. Have you seen some Englishmen here? We wish to find Mr. Blunt and his friends? Can you direct us?"

"Yes, zar, we Portuguese, you Inglese. Senor Blunt is this way, will you walk vid us? We are merchants."

The speaker whom Buttons had addressed was a swarthy Portuguese.

Buttons did not like the look of him.

The man wore a broad sombrero, and carried a large whip, the thong being knotted with lead.

"You are merchants, are you?" said the Stinger, who did not like the looks of the party. "You are merchants, are you? Pray what do you deal in?"

"All sorts ov dings," said the man with a grin.

"What?"

"Dere!" and he pointed to the niggers, who were still chanting their dismal dirge amidst wringing of hands.

"Oh, you are merchants in human flesh. Come on, Buttons, we will have no dealings with them."

"We won't."

They made a movement as if to retreat, but the slave-dealer, for such undoubtedly he was, placed himself in their path.

"Hold!" he cried, "you go not to Cape Coast, you go vid us."

"We won't," said the Stinger.

"You shall."

"You dare not stop us," cried Buttons, placing himself beside Stinger.

"Ha, ha! we dare. You come with us."

Before they could make a movement some of the slave-dealers seized them, and although they resisted they were soon securely chained together.

The Stinger groaned under this indignity.

"Oh, Buttons, Buttons, all luck has left me with my umbrella. Oh, we shall never know peace again. All through you, Buttons; the gingham was the staff of my fortunes."

And the poor Stinger, now chained as a slave, wept.

Buttons was too much alarmed to answer her complaint.

"Slaves! oh, fancy, Stinger, they are going to make slaves of us."

"Slaves? Never! Britons never shall be slaves. You ruffians, let us go, let us go, or you shall suffer for this. Do you know that I am Elizabeth Ann Stinger, the apostle of women's rights, and do you think that I am going to stand this ?"

"Nor I ?" cried Buttons.

They tore at their chains, but the Portuguese slave-driver uttered an oath and brought his broad lash to bear upon poor Stinger's back, and Buttons also received a smart cut on the legs.

"It's no use, Betsy ; they have got us, and we must bide our time."

"Fancy, who ever thought E. A. S. would be a slave ? It's awful. Oh, where is woman's right ?"

"There's no right, it's all wrong, it is," said poor Buttons.

The slave-drivers now urged on their human cattle.

The Stinger and Buttons were forced to keep up with them.

To be sold into slavery was a fate they did not contemplate.

The Stinger bemoaned her hard fate, and it was Buttons who now exerted all his youthful energy to cheer his companion up.

"Oh, Buttons, it's the gingham that's done it," exclaimed the Stinger ; "my luck has forsaken me, and not even a drop in the bottle. Oh, what misery !"

"Cheer up, Betsy, and we'll escape yet. Don't be down in the mouth, old lady ; all's well that ends well, and it's a long lane that hasn't a turning."

"What's the use of proverbs ? What's the earthly use of them now ? Oh, that I were a bird."

Thus she continued to groan her very heart out, for the chains were most galling to her, and the Stinger had a spirit that scorned control, but as the night was coming on, the slave-drivers resolved to camp, which they did, under the shade of some rocks.

Utterly weary, the Stinger and Buttons laid down to rest, but not to sleep, for their busy brains were weaving plans of escape from the power of the slave-dealers.

CHAPTER XXVIII.

THE ADVENTURES OF BUTTONS CONTINUES.

NEVER had the stars appeared so bright to Buttons and Stinger as on the night when they both were stretched beneath the open sky, in the power of the slave-owners.

To be driven away as slaves was an awful thing for them both.

They could hardly realise it.

"We shall be taken into the interior of the country, and never more shall we see the faces of our dear friends again," whispered the Stinger.

Buttons groaned in reply.

"Stinger," he whispered at length, "I think I can manage to free myself from this chain."

"How ?" she asked.

"By squeezing my hand as small as possible. Look, I have done it," exclaimed Buttons.

"And what do you intend to do ?"

"Cut it."

"Without me ?"

"Yes, because you would not be able to run as fast as I can."

"Oh, Buttons, I didn't think you would behave so unkindly towards your Stinger that's taken such care of you. Not only have you robbed me of my umbrella, but now you're going to forsake me, and leave me to the tender mercies of these savages."

"Now," began Buttons, "you don't see my drift. If I escape I shall find my master, and he will soon return to liberate you and punish these chaps."

"But if you should not happen to find him?"

"Hum!" said Buttons, taken aback by this direct query; "hum! then you would have to remain. But I'll take my chance and ten to one I shall succeed."

"But, Buttons, think when I'm here without you. What shall I do?"

"The best you can."

"You won't stay or take me?" asked the Stinger.

"No."

"You are determined?"

"Of course. I think they are all asleep now. So good-bye, Stinger; give us a kiss. Keep up your pecker and hope for the best. Here goes; for he who hesitates is lost, as the proverb says."

And he glided away on all fours, and was soon beyond the reach of pursuit.

"You don't catch Buttons again, my slave-driver friends; and if I don't bring a hornets' nest about you, in the person of Bob Blunt, the Traveller, and his friends, my name is not Buttons."

He shook his fist in the direction of the camp, then hastened on.

He entered the forest.

The roar of the beasts of prey was terribly hideous to Buttons' ears.

There were heard the shriek of the jackals, the roar of the hyæna, and countless sounds of discord from the throats of the night birds.

"I don't like this at all, at all, as Joe said when he felt the copper becoming rather warm," muttered Buttons, "and therefore, I think I shall climb up a tree, and remain there till daylight."

No sooner said than done.

He mounted a palm tree.

But he could not sleep.

Until the sun arose above the tops of the trees did Buttons have to stand holding on to the bough of the tree.

At last, when the welcome light appeared, Buttons descended from the tree.

He looked to his revolver, that, in his fright at being taken for a slave, he had forgotten, and saw that cartridges were in the six chambers of the weapon.

"Now, I shall find my master or die," he cried. "Hurrah! I'm off to bring help for poor Stinger."

As well as he was able, he followed the windings of the forest, crushing occasionally through long grass, and then appearing again in the open.

At last he reached a quiet glade.

Here he rested for a time.

Then, continuing his way, he at last reached the banks of a small rivulet, which he crossed, and then, to his terror, he heard a violent stamping in a jungle of dry grass.

What was it?

It seemed as if an army was in full retreat.

Buttons stood still, and listened.

He heard sounds proceed as of the blowing of horns.

"I dare not go further," he muttered, "so I will now go backwards. I know what it is; they are the savages."

He was about to turn tail, when the crushing through the grass and reeds became more and more perceptible, and then, to his horror, he beheld the huge bulks of several elephants approaching through the grass.

To fly was the work of an instant.

Pressing his hat tightly over his eyes, Buttons took to his heels.

Some thirty elephants now rushed from the jungle, their trunks elevated in the air, and trumpeting loudly.

A general stampede.

Evidently they were being pursued, for their terror was great.

On they came.

Buttons ran as hard as he possibly could to get out of their way.

He looked over his shoulders.

He had passed the herd and thought he was safe.

"What an escape!" he cried, wiping the perspiration from his brow. "I should have been trodden as flat as a pancake beneath the feet of those brutes in another moment. Ugh! what monsters; look at them, Halloa!"

This last exclamation was caused by a crashing sound, and, before he could move a step, a large elephant rushed out of the jungle.

Buttons could not move.

The animal was close upon him.

There was no time for action.

Buttons uttered a cry for help, clapped his hat on his head, and, before he knew what was being done to him, the huge beast twined his trunk round poor Buttons, and lifted him high in the air.

"Help!" shrieked Buttons. "Oh, murder! Buttons is packed up in a trunk. Oh Stinger, oh Mr. Blunt! Somebody come and help me."

The elephant did not let him fall, but rushed away through the forest for some distance.

Presently it slackened its pace, then there was a loud report, a wreath of white smoke curling from the muzzle of a rifle, and while trying to move forward, the elephant rolled over dead.

A bullet had struck it in the ear, and pierced its brain.

Buttons lay insensible on the ground, the elephant beside him,

At that moment, several persons issued from the jungle.

It was Bob Blunt and his white friends, with two or three of King Aga's negroes.

Bob rushed towards Buttons.

"Poor Buttons is dead," said Bob.

"No, I ain't."

It was Buttons' voice.

"Hurrah!" cried Bob, "he is saved. How is it with you, Buttons? Speak. How on earth do I find you here?"

Bob gave him a drink of brandy from his flask.

This revived him.

Buttons burst into tears.

"Oh, master, is that you?"

"Yes, Buttons. You're safe now. Speak up," said Bob kindly.

"Safe! Oh, I have had an awful nightmare. I thought I was being devoured by an elephant."

And Buttons shuddered.

"You had a narrow escape, Buttons; but you are safe now."

"Am I?"

"Yes; can you rise?"

"I'll try."

"Up, then."

Buttons got up.

When he beheld the elephant, his astonishment was great.

"Dead!" he exclaimed.

"As a doornail," said the doctor.

"This beats the cataract and the lion."

"How did you escape from that peril, Buttons, and where is the Stinger?" asked Bob, wondering greatly.

"The Stinger!" said Buttons. "Oh, my poor Stinger. She is done for."

"How—dead?" asked Bob.

"Dead! Not that I know of."

"What then?"

Buttons rolled his eyes in his head, and said in a sepulchral voice—

"She's worse than dead; she's going to be sold into slavery, and perhaps eaten up alive. Oh, Stinger!"

This news astonished Bob.

Our hero and his friends marvelled greatly as they listened to Buttons' recital of the events that had happened to him and the Stinger since they had lost sight of him.

"It's all true," said Buttons.

"We do not doubt your assertion," said Bob. "But we must go in immediate pursuit of the slavers, and rescue the Stinger. Poor old girl, she will be in a fine way."

"We must wait for King Aga," said Swiftfoot.

"Yes; but we must resume our hunting expedition. We can combine the two. The war path and the hunting path is our motto now."

"Right," said the doctor. "There is as fine an elephant as I have ever seen. It's a lucky one, too, I must say."

"Lucky, yes; it's lucky I thought of tracking these beasts, or it would have been all up with poor Buttons by this time; the brute was aroused and savage."

"Look, here are King Aga and the rest of his men," cried Swiftfoot.

"It is well. We will at once in pursuit of these slavers."

"Hurrah! I told them my master would exact a great revenge," said Buttons.

"Then let us start in immediate chase," said Bob, going forth to meet the king.

CHAPTER XXIX.

THE SLAVE MERCHANTS OVERTAKEN—THE STINGER'S JOY—"OH, MY UMBRELLA! MY LUCK'S RETURNING!"—BOB'S JUDGMENT ON THE SLAVERS.

KING AGA'S astonishment on seeing Buttons was great.

He thought it impossible for him to escape the danger of the waterfalls.

Buttons was as proud as a peacock.

Never had a page passed through such peril before.

Bob Blunt had organised a great hunting expedition, which should extend over a wide tract of country.

In this he hoped to be successful in rescuing Nahita from King Pluto.

Accordingly when King Aga came up with him he made known his intentions to him, and it was resolved that they should start in immediate pursuit.

Bob now at the head of his own immediate followers marched on ahead of the natives.

They were on the right track, as was proved by finding Miss Stinger's umbrella.

Buttons to the best of his ability directed them towards the spot where the slavers had encamped for the night.

But, as they expected, the slavers had long since departed.

Then it was resolved that their track should be followed, and as usual Swiftfoot was sent on ahead to scout.

Bob Blunt resolved to rescue the Stinger from her degrading position, even if he had to search for the slavers through the whole continent of Africa.

During the mid-day halt Swiftfoot returned and announced that he had overtaken the slavers.

They were distant some five miles, and encamped in a hollow.

This news spurred all to overtake them, and exact summary vengeance on the slavers.

Away they went.

Bob Blunt first, his rifle in hand, and eager for the fray.

In two hours' time they came in sight of the slavers.

They were marching ahead of their slaves, so Bob commanded a detour in order to face them.

Two parties branched off at once, and as the slavers defiled into a long valley, on each side of which were mighty trees, Bob Blunt and his friends suddenly stood in their way.

"That's the chap," cried Buttons, pointing out the Portuguese who had so roughly put him in chains.

"Stand!" cried Bob.

"What want you, senor?" asked the slaver, turning pale when he beheld our hero, with gun in hand, ready to fire.

"You are a slave-dealer; do you know that under the British flag no one can be a slave?" said Bob.

"No."

"Then you shall learn."

"How, senor?"

"Where is the lady whom you have captured?" asked Bob.

"Vat ladie?" replied the slave-dealer, with profuse gesticulations.

"What lady, you black brute? Why, my Stinger," cried Buttons, "my dear Betsy."

"My lubly red, white, and blue nosie," echoed Jingo.

"Here I am."

It was the Stinger's voice.

"Where are you, Betsy?" cried Buttons.

"Here, my dear boy."

"I'm coming."

With that, Buttons rushed through the band of niggers between whom he beheld the Stinger.

He saw she was chained.

He dragged her forth.

"That's it, my love. Come on. I've found my master. I'm here, all serene. Oh you are saved!"

"Betsy's a slave no longer. Here I am, Mr. Blunt. Hurrah for women's rights!"

"Hurrah!" cried the English.

The natives, too, joined in with a loud clapping of hands.

"Miss Stinger, you are safe," said Bob. "Now I am going to exact a summary vengeance on these fellows."

The slave-drivers were consulting together in evident fear.

At this moment the Stinger caught sight of Jingo Johnson.

"What's that I see?" she cried.

"Missie Nosie," replied Jingo, showing his white teeth, "I found it for you."

"My umbrella! No—yes—no. It is, it is, my luck has returned."

With that she made a start at Jingo, seized him by the wool, and wrenched her umbrella from his grasp.

"I have it—I have it! My luck, my dear luck."

And she hugged the umbrella to her bosom, although her hands were not yet freed from the chains that the slavers had put upon her.

She was, however, at once released.

Her joy was great.

She now shook hands with Jingo Johnson, hugged Buttons afresh, kissed Bob Blunt, and shook her fist in the faces of the slave-owners.

"British females are not slaves; never will be, although E. A. S. must suffer for the cause of humanity. Now you shall suffer, you black-hearted brutes."

"They shall," cried Bob.

"Torture and kill them," said King Aga.

He beckoned to his executioner, a terrible person, dressed in a red cloak, and painted all over.

As soon as the slave-owners beheld this man, they fell on their knees, imploring for mercy in the most abject manner.

Bob regarded them with contempt.

"What a set of curs these brutal fellows are. Get up."

The slave-dealers did not move, whilst the slaves stood gazing at the white men in open-eyed wonder.

Bob resolved to make an example of the slave-dealers.

"Seize all of them," he cried.

"Right. Oh, what a happy day is this," exclaimed the Stinger, holding one hand heavenwards, whilst with the other she smoothed Buttons' hair into his eyes.

"Now, Stinger, don't, there is a good girl. Come, leave off; I am not a lap dog."

"Silence, you two," said Bob, as Jingo Johnson, Strongback and the others had seized the slave-owners; "silence. Now, then, take off the chains from the slaves; let them be free."

This command was instantly obeyed.

The slaves were greatly astonished when they saw their new captors, as they deemed them to be, take off the hated fetters.

Bob then ordered the slave-dealers to be linked together.

They set up a howl of terror.

"Tell the liberated slaves that they are free to go where they like, Jingo," said Bob, when the slave-dealers had been closely linked together, and the slaves stood in a wondering row.

Jingo did so.

A look of astonishment, a cry of joy followed Jingo's announcement.

Then one by one they came and knelt at our hero's feet, and kissed them, and wept and uttered little cries of gratitude that went to the hearts of all the white men present.

King Aga alone stood aloof.

He looked at Bob for a moment, then said—

"Know, my brother, that if you let these slaves free, their owners will seek a dire revenge. Through all the tribes the news will spread, and you will have the future enmity of the kings to contend with. They will be your bitter enemies, for they have sold these slaves."

"What care I? Do you think, King Aga, that I fear for myself, and that any black king should prohibit me from doing a virtuous action? No; and these slave-owners are not yet free. I will send them to Cape Coast and let them be tried there by the authorities for capturing a free-born British subject."

"That's me!" cried the Stinger.

"A good plan," said the doctor.

"THERE WAS A REPORT—A WREATH OF SMOKE CAME FROM THE MUZZLE OF THE RIFLE."

" These poor people may now depart in peace."

" Yes."

Jingo informed them that they might depart.

In an instant there was a great scrimmage amongst them ; men, women, and children seized their baggage, and then one of the eldest advanced towards Bob.

" Great chief," he said, " if we return to our native villages we shall be sold again into slavery. Grant that we may stay with you ; we will work for you, fight for you, die for you."

Bob was greatly moved.

" Do as you please," he said. " If you like you can follow me, but mind, you will have plenty of fighting to do."

When this was announced to them their joy knew no bounds.

They were accordingly enrolled in the tribe of King Aga, and it was there and then resolved to send them back to the king's village with the slave-dealers as prisoners.

Bob and his friends grinned heartily when they saw the slave-dealers driven along into a captivity they had not expected, Bob telling a strong black fellow that if they objected to move quickly he was to use the whip about them.

When they were gone, Bob turned to his friends.

" Now we will prosecute our search for King Pluto, and continue our great hunting expedition. What say you ?"

" Fine, Mr. Blunt. Hurrah ! I'm ready to hunt whatever comes in my way, even if it is King Pluto, a tiger, or an old cow," said the Stinger.

" Your wish may be gratified," said Bob. " Now come on, boys ; let us push on, for I long to be at them. Sport always makes me hungry, and as I have already killed an elephant I should like to follow up the game."

" To think that I should ever be cradled in the trunk of an elephant. Me, that's born in England. Oh, Africa, what a fine place you are. I'll return yet a millionaire, or a———"

" Milliner, you mean," interrupted the Stinger, softly.

" Exactly, either one or the other. What's the odds as long as you're happy, eh, Betsy the beautiful ?"

" Stuff !" cried the Stinger. " Look, Mr. Blunt is going the pace. Come on, Buttons."

" Lead on, MacStinger ; your Buttons follows."

CHAPTER XXX.

THE GREAT HUNT—THE PERIL OF THE CHASE—STRONGBACK MEETS HIS FATE BY TREACHERY—WHO FIRED THE SHOT ?—BOB'S GRIEF.

BOB BLUNT now entered fully into the excitement of his nomad existence in Africa, and as yet he did not regret leaving luxury behind him.

He was happy, and so were all his companions.

When the natives had spread themselves over a vast tract of ground, and beaten the grass for the game, Bob divided his party into separate bodies.

Himself, Buttons, Stumps, and the Stinger went in one body, whilst the others took any direction they pleased.

Accordingly Bob and his three companions soon found themselves separated from the rest of the party.

They stationed themselves against a tree, in a small opening in the forest, so that they could command an uninterrupted view of a long stretch of jungle.

Soon the shrieks of monkeys and birds proclaimed that they had been disturbed in their solitude by the beaters.

"Look out; we shall soon have some wild animals upon us," said Bob.

"I'm ready," cried the Stinger, opening out her umbrella.

"And I," said Buttons. "Here, Jingo, give me my snuff. Never no more do I go without it; never, never, never!"

And he pulled out a large horn of snuff.

"That's it, Buttons, my boy; let them have it hot; there's nothing like it. I've got my umbrella, whilst you have your snuff, and so I think we shall be a match for all the natives and wild beasteses. Never say die, my boy."

"Not I. Halloa! here comes a monster. Mr. Blunt, look, look! it's a man in a monkey's skin. Oh, Lor', he's coming."

"By Jove! it's a gorilla, and a mighty one too," said Bob.

"A gorilla! Oh, Lor'! Why he's bigger and more ugly than a man," cried the Stinger, flourishing her umbrella.

"He is," said Bob. "Keep quiet and see what he will be up to."

The huge brute opened its enormous jaws, and stood looking at the four hunters who barred his progress.

He knew the beaters were behind him, and so he beheld—

"Death in the front, destruction in the rear."

Evidently he resolved to charge them, for with a deep and loud growl he came down on all fours.

Buttons held his snuff-box out.

The gorilla stood for a moment, then made a furious bound to within a few yards.

Then Buttons saw his opportunity.

"Now to try the power of snuff," he cried, throwing a boxful in the gorilla's face.

The animal uttered a howl of agony and rubbed its mighty paws over his face.

"Hurrah! I've done it this time," said Buttons; "if we had a rope we would try and capture him."

"Splendid idea!" cried the Stinger. "Run, Buttons, and find Strongback; he has a rope."

"I'm off; take care and let him have

plenty more snuff if he comes near you."

Buttons ran as hard as he could in the direction he thought Strongback would be.

Bob Blunt, after watching the raging gorilla for a few seconds, found it necessary to despatch the brute with a well-aimed shot.

Pushing his way through the tangled brakes he at last reached a dense part of the forest.

Here he suddenly heard a cry for help.

He paused to listen.

Again the cry was repeated.

"There is some one in distress," cried Buttons. "I'm a good mind to return to seek master."

He was debating in his mind whether he should do so or not when again the cry was repeated with terrible distinctness this time.

"Dash it all, old boy, you ain't quite a coward," muttered Buttons; "so here goes."

With that he dashed on.

A turn in the trees made him recoil.

He saw a man lying on the ground, evidently in agony, and, in the act to spring, a furious male leopard.

The beautiful animal lashed its tail, and then with a growl of rage it took a magnificent leap upon the fallen man, and fastened its deadly grip upon his throat.

Buttons stood for a moment horrified.

Then, acting on the impulse of the moment, he rushed forward, revolver in hand.

He fired at the brute, and wounded it, but not mortally.

"Oh, Lor'! I've done it now," cried Buttons, retreating. "He'll be after me now."

The leopard relaxed its grip of the fallen man, whom Buttons did not recognise through the blood.

The brute turned his fury upon his fresh foe.

Before Buttons had time to retreat, the leopard darted forward.

Buttons fired again.

The bullet struck the animal in the thigh, causing it to utter a howl of mingled rage and pain.

Buttons plucked up courage with his success.

But when he was in the act of firing again the revolver missed fire, and to his horror he saw that all the cartridges were spent.

"Oh, Lor'! I'm done for," he groaned. "I'm done for; no snuff, no bullets. Buttons must run for it."

The leopard had paused to lick its wounds, but still keeping his glowing eyes upon poor Buttons with a terrible fascination, from which he could not withdraw his gaze.

The brute in great pain slowly arose to its feet.

Then crouching down on its belly, it stretched itself out, with tail erect, to take its last spring.

Then Buttons turned and ran.

But the leopard was upon him.

He felt its terrible claws fix themselves in his back.

He uttered a shriek for help, and fell on his face.

But his shriek was heard.

Bang!

The brute fell dead, bespattering poor Buttons with its brains.

"Good Lord! what an escape for Buttons," cried Bob Blunt, standing over the now dead brute, revolver in hand.

Buttons had fainted.

The Stinger tenderly raised his head on her lap, and applied some of the inexhaustible contents of her bottle to his lips, and bathed his temples with the cordial.

Soon Buttons opened his eyes.

"Where is the man I saw?" said Buttons.

"What man?" asked Bob.

"A man whom I did not recognise was attacked by the leopard a little way from here," said Buttons.

"Where?" asked the doctor, who had arrived.

"I'll show you."

Buttons arose and led the way through the long grass until they came to where the body of a man lay at length upon the grass, his face covered with blood.

Bob recognised him in a moment.

It was Strongback.

"How did this happen?" cried Bob, horrified at the sight.

"Is he dead?" asked the Stinger.

"Out of the way. Let me see," said the doctor, pushing all aside.

He knelt down by the side of Strongback, and carefully examined him.

All awaited his verdict with bated breath, and then he said—

The man is wounded mortally."

"How—by the leopard?" asked Bob.

"Does this look like a leopard's bite?" said the doctor, pointing to a stream of blood slowly oozing from a deep wound in Strongback's chest.

"No," said Bob.

"He has been shot," said the doctor.

"By whom?"

"That I cannot say. Here, give me some brandy; I must bring him to."

The brandy was administered, and then the doctor managed to stop the bleeding.

In due time Strongback opened his eyes.

The Stinger had washed the blood from his face, but it was fearfully lacerated by the leopard's claws.

Strongback's position was still a mystery to his friends.

Bob took one of his hands, and said—

"How are you now, Strongback, old friend?"

"Better," he replied, faintly. "Water."

The water was given him.

"Do you feel pain?" asked the doctor.

"No; only a sort of numbness here."

And he laid his hand on his brawny chest.

"Ah, I thought so. Hæmorrhage has set in; the man's bleeding to death inwardly, and it is hopeless to try and extract the bullet; it has lodged in the spine," muttered the doctor to our hero.

This was sad news, to lose by death, so early, one of their best and bravest.

"Are you strong enough to tell us how you came to this plight, my brave friend?" said Bob, sorrowfully.

A gleam of light shone in the strong man's eyes, previously dull and filmy.

He raised himself half up.

The effort was but momentary, weakness compelling him to fall back again.

But the light in his eyes gleamed with intense ferocity.

He gasped between his set teeth, then he calmed himself with an effort.

" You know me well enough, my noble and generous friend," he began, pressing our hero's hand with great affection. " You know me well enough to vouch for my bravery—without boasting, I never feared to meet mortal man in a fair field, and in fair play—but even the bravest cannot guard against treachery."

" Whose treachery, dear Strongback ?"

" Listen ; in the ardour of the chase, I followed a female leopard into her lair. I had fired both barrels of my rifle at her, but unfortunately missed her. Well, I was in the act of reloading, when there was a sudden report amongst the trees ; I felt a pain in my breast, and sank to the ground. I knew that I was wounded."

" By whom ?" asked Bob, whose stern-set face bespoke the agony of mind he endured during Strongback's recital of this dastardly act of villainy.

" By whom, I can tell you but by guesswork. As I fell, I turned my gaze in the direction from whence the shot had proceeded, and distinctly saw two white men and a black beating a precipitate retreat."

" Did you recognise them ?"

" No ; but I heard one of them cry— ' Thus perish all the friends of Bob Blunt. This is the first ; the others shall follow. ' "

" It was Howard, Bow-legged Bill, and King Pluto, on my life," cried Bob, springing up, and seizing his rifle. " Oh, that I was near them now."

" Stay ; it is useless to pursue them," cried Swiftfoot and Ironfist, seizing our hero and holding him back.

" I will hunt them to death, the cowardly assassins ! Poor, dear Strongback !" he cried.

" I know you will, my friend ; but let me conclude, for I have not over long to live, and I can die like an Englishman. Well, no sooner had the human beasts of prey escaped, than the unreasoning animal turned upon me, no doubt scenting the blood. With a bound the leopard was upon me, but I drew my knife ; as it fell upon me, I buried it up to the hilt in its belly, and flung it with all my might over my head. I think you will find it dead."

Bob motioned to Stumps to search for the animal, and he soon returned, dragging a dead leopard behind him, of larger size than the one that attacked Buttons.

Strongback smiled grimly as he viewed the animal.

" You are the last who will feel the force of my arm," he said.

" Can't you save him, doctor ?" cried Bob, as Strongback's impending dissolution evidently drew nearer.

The doctor sadly shook his head.

That negative was enough for all, and it did not escape Strongback.

" Don't worry, Mr. Blunt," he said ; " a man can die but once, although it's hard he should be shot down like a dog, and not return the debt in their own coin. Well, to continue ; I thought to die in peace, having settled the brute, when, lo, and behold ! another leopard suddenly appeared creeping through the grass. I thought all was up with me now ; but I gave three vigorous shouts for help as a last resource. Then the leopard was upon me, and I have an indistinct recollection of some one firing, and that is all."

" It was me," moaned Buttons.

" You !" cried Strongback.

" Yes, me."

" Well done, my boy ; give me your hand. You have begun well. Give me your hand."

He shook Buttons by the hand.

" Now, Mr. Blunt, I die easy. All my friends about me, and all I ask you to do is to bury me decently, and do not forget Strongback too soon, for I have been true to all."

All were deeply affected.

Even King Aga stood moodily looking upon Strongback, although he could hardly comprehend the grief of his white friends, when they ought to know that their friend was travelling to the regions of the sun.

To him death was a deliverance, and in his strange belief in fatalism, he could not but think that their grief ought to be joy.

"We won't forget you, Strongback," said Bob, with tears in his eyes; "have you any message to deliver to any friends in England?"

"Friends in England! No; they are all dead. I should not have left England had I any. Bury me decently, Mr. Blunt, that is all, and read the prayers of the Church I was bred and born in over me. There is no finer service for the dead, in my opinion, than the dear old Church of England."

"I will," said Bob.

"Blunt, dear friend, my mind travels far away now. Back to the peaceful green fields and dales of my native Kent. I see the old church where I worshipped as a boy; where my father and mother rest, and where I shall never sleep. You will find some papers amongst my luggage; they will tell you who I am. But on my grave plant a simple cross, and carve on it the name you have given me with the addition of the country of my birth. Write—

"Here lies Strongback, a man of England."

"I will do all you require, my dear, dear Strongback. Oh, this is hard to bear—hard to part with so brave a friend."

Strongback's utterance became more and more incoherent.

The bleeding of his wounds had long since ceased, and now his death was only a question of time.

Gradually he sank calm as an infant, and just before the last throes of death were apparent to all, Strongback opened his eyes.

"Oh, Lord, forgive me my sins!" he gasped. "Blunt, dear friend, pray remember Strongback."

And with these words on his lips, his brave spirit passed to Him who had given it.

CHAPTER XXXI.

THE RETURN TO KING AGA'S CAMP.

IS he dead?" gasped Bob, hardly crediting the fact.

"He is," said the doctor.

"God rest him; he was a noble and brave man!"

This eulogy on the dead was just, and every one fervently said—

"Amen!"

It was a solemn scene to see that little band of white men standing around their dead comrade in the dense African forest.

Bob was greatly affected.

He wept bitterly when he beheld that fine figure stretched out in the solemnity of death, and thought how a little while back poor Strongback was full of life and activity.

But there was no time for hesitation.

"We must return to the camp, my friend," he said to King Aga.

"My daughter," replied the king, laconically.

"I promise you I will do my best to bring her abductors to justice, but first I must pay befitting respects to my dead friend," said Bob.

The king acquiesced,

A rude litter of boughs was hastily made, and on it the body of Strongback was laid, and carried by his mourning friends, Longsight, Swiftfoot, Ironfist, and Bob Blunt.

Silently the sad *cortege* passed through the dense forests.

At length they came to the spot where Buttons had blinded the gorilla with the infallible shot the snuff.

Buttons stared when he beheld the huge brute with a bullet in his brain.

"He's dead!" he cried.

"Yes; I had to shoot him," said Bob. "He could not get rid of the snuff, though."

"I thought not," said Buttons. "That dose was enough for him."

"And this dose is nearly enough for me," chimed in the Stinger; "I begin to think it is not so safe to travel about in the wilds of Africa as it is in the Zoological Gardens in London."

Bob could hardly repress a smile.

But the Stinger did not smile.

She wore a very serious look on her jolly countenance.

By easy stages our travellers at last reached King Aga's village.

Loud tones of sorrow greeted Bob and his friends.

They put their burden down in the principal room of King Aga's palace, and prepared to perform the last obsequies to the dead.

A rude kind of coffin was put together, and brave little Stumps spent the hours before the funeral in carving out the cross—which Strongback desired— with his name on it.

Our friends recruited their exhausted strength, and then dressed themselves in their best clothes.

They took one last glance at Strongback, who lay calm as in life, in his narrow coffin, and then they put the lid on.

A grave had been dug on the summit of a gentle hill, surrounded by waving palm trees.

It was situated behind King Aga's town, and thither the sorrowful *cortége* marched, bearing their dead to its last resting place.

With reversed arms, they proceeded along, the doctor, Swiftfoot, Ironfist, and Longsight carrying the coffin, whilst Bob headed the bier as chief mourner, which, in fact, he was, for he had lost a trusty and brave follower and friend.

The natives, with King Aga at their head, brought up the rear.

Soon they reached the open grave, and the body was lowered into it.

Then Bob read the solemn service for the dead, his voice husky with emotion, after which, everyone present fired a volley over the dead man's grave.

The red sun was rapidly sinking in the west, as the third and last volley was fired, and his dying beams shone between the trees, and added to the solemnity of the scene.

The earth was piled upon the coffin.

A green mound was formed over the grave, and they placed his cross at its head.

Slowly the Englishmen left the spot.

Again and again they turned, and Bob Blunt saw that one gleam of sunshine illuminated the cross and the inscription on it—

"Here rests Strongback, an Englishman."

"He has found the peace of the blessed, for there shines upon his grave a halo of immortality," said Bob, with a sob, as he turned away.

*　　*　　●　　*　　●

They returned to the camp.

Bob Blunt and his friends would not hear of proceeding in search of King Pluto on the following day.

That day was given up to mourning for their lost friend, brave Strongback.

But on the evening of that day King Aga summoned them to a council.

Bob and the others attended.

"Friends," said Bob, as they proceeded to see King Aga, "friends, we must not mourn for our friend openly any longer; whatever we may feel, let us disguise it; our duty now is to act, and act we will. Let us be up and doing. What say you?"

"Right, sir," said Ironfist.

"So say I," said Swiftfoot, brandishing a long lance he had made.

"And I," said Longsight.

"And I. And I," cried the Stinger and Buttons, in great excitement.

"And I," growled the doctor; "for if you don't keep quiet, you two, I shall have to bleed you. If it had not been for your row, we should have captured this Pluto and his associates."

Buttons and the Stinger were silent.

"True. The Stinger and Buttons nearly paid with their lives for the fault they committed, for if we had captured Pluto they would not have been precipitated into the river, so no wrangling now. Up, let us act," said Bob.

"I mean to," said Stumps. "I mean to astonish you all before long with my secret work."

"I hope you will, Stumps. But now let us on to the council chamber, for King Aga awaits us."

When they reached the king's dwelling, a loud droning noise was heard within.

"What demon's noise is this?" inquired Bob of Jingo Johnson.

"Me not know, massa," replied Jingo.

"Well let us go and see. Stumps, my boy, sound your trombone to announce our arrival to the king."

Stumps blew a loud blast.

Immediate silence followed.

"Now then, in we go."

He entered the chamber.

The king was seated in his chair of state, and a number of warriors had encompassed him about.

When Bob entered the room, a most strange spectacle met his view.

In the centre of the chamber was a man who presented a most hideous appearance.

His face was one mass of paint, his body was clad in the painted skins of animals, whilst a number of human skulls and bones hung about his apparel as so many bells on a maypole.

The man was making a most hideous noise upon a huge bullock's horn, and dancing a kind of double-shuffle.

"Who is this?" asked Bob.

"Hush, massa!" said Jingo; "he bunder of bunder, he berry great fetiche man, and he am feared by all de dribes, from King Koff to de little Nizo on de Congo."

Stumps pricked up his ears at this.

"Oh, he is one of the mystery men, is he?" said Stumps.

"Yes," replied Jingo, "he am. All fear um, for he berry, berry great fetiche. Nobody knows where he come from, massa."

"Discoorse him, Stumps, as Paddy would say," said Bob, "whilst I go to the king."

"Yes, sir."

Bob saw that King Aga was very uneasy.

He shunned our hero's steadfast look, as if he were troubled in his mind.

"Well, my great friend," said Bob, "are we to decide what steps we are to take against King Pluto?"

"Great chief, let us wait until to-morrow. The mighty fetiche man will aid us in our enterprise; he knows the will of the gods; what he says is right."

Bob saw at once that King Aga was under the spell of his juggler.

He resolved to open King Aga's eyes by the aid of the doughty Stumps.

"Well, O king," he replied to King Aga, at length, "thou knowest best; but be assured I am ready to take the war-path at once. I have lost one of my best warriors already, and it may still happen that I may lose others. I fear not; but if you will be advised by me, let us go and attack King Pluto in his own territory, exact summary justice from him for the abduction of your daughter by burning his town about his ears."

The king's eyes sparkled.

Bob's fiery words aroused him.

But then his glance fell upon the fetiche man, and his courage was again lost in a maze of superstition.

"Wait, O white chief," he said. "Wait till the sun rises to-morrow over the grave of thy friend. The fetiche man has advised me; he is all powerful."

Bob, knowing the power this wily man of charms swayed over the king, did not wish to undeceive him but by apparently open means.

He therefore bowed in assent.

"So be it then, but I thought you were in a hurry to recover your daughter awhile since, and now——"

"Wait," interrupted the king, hastily; "I will consult with him."

In the meantime Stumps had diligently studied the mental calibre of the great fetiche man, and he found it consisted of an immense amount of cunning.

As soon as the fetiche man beheld the dwarf, he gave a convulsive shudder, paused in his gyrations around the room, and then putting his bullock's horn to his lips, he blew a discordant note, then gave a howl, and looked at Stumps with all the fierceness he could assume.

But to his astonishment Stumps was not at all afraid.

On the contrary, he was quite calm.

"Booh!" said the fetiche man, shaking the ghastly trophies on his dress.

"Booh!" replied Stumps.

"Booh, booh!" said the other.

"Booh, booh, booh, oh!" retorted Stumps.

These tactics appeared to puzzle the fetiche man extremely.

Therefore he sounded his horn again, and uttered a piercing shriek.

Stumps, as before, wore his usual placid smile, and then deliberately unslinging his trombone from his back, he sounded the loudest notes he could command, so that the very rafters rang again.

"I think they fear him the most who can kick up the greatest noise, sir," said Stumps to the doctor, who was bursting his sides with laughter.

The effect of Stumps' music had not the charm upon the senses of the man of magic that music is supposed to have.

On the contrary, he uttered a piteous howl, and started back with astonishment and terror depicted upon his ill-looking visage, which Stumps styled a makeshift for a face.

"That fetched his *fetiche*-ship," said Buttons, delightedly, walking round the fetiche man on his hands, and clapping his feet under his nose.

"It did," said Bob, who, unobserved, had been an amused witness of Stumps' marvellous victory.

The fetiche man saw that he was not able to cope with the great medicine man of the white king, and did not understand the strange movements of Buttons, so he slunk off behind King Aga's chair of state.

But the surrounding warriors began to regard Stumps with greater awe than before, which Bob was slow to notice.

He thought it time to be off, now that Stumps had made an impression on all present.

"So far so good, sir," said Stumps. "Now I have a plan by which we can even charm the brutal King Pluto."

"How, Stumps?"

"I will tell you, sir."

And Stumps unfolded to Bob a plan of such intense adroitness, that our hero was charmed with the idea.

"It will do," he cried.

"What?" asked the doctor.

"I will tell you, learned sir, for I shall require your chemical knowledge in order to carry out my plans."

"You shall have it."

Then Stumps told the doctor his design.

CHAPTER XXXII.

THE FETICHE MAN'S POWER PROVOKES THE KING TO COMMIT A TERRIBLE CRIME.

NO sooner had Bob Blunt and his friends left the king's council chamber, than the fetiche man's manner changed in a moment.

With a bound, he jumped into the centre of the room, and with the most diabolical gestures he addressed the king.

"Great king, if thou wouldst recover thy daughter, the god of the maidens desires blood; and the white man's blood "

King Aga started.

"What meanest thou, O terrible fetiche?"

"The white man's blood must pour as a sacrifice, or you will never see your daughter more."

King Aga groaned.

"The white man's blood shall flow," he at length said.

The fetiche man could not repress a cry of triumph.

"When, O mighty king, shall the white men die?"

"When you will it."

"I will it now."

"Then it shall be done."

"I will return then to pray for thy daughter, in the silence of the woods."

The fetiche man left the chamber.

Now King Aga was greatly troubled.

He dared not disobey the commands of the fetiche man, for even his own warriors would revolt if he did.

Yet the gods desired blood, and blood of the white men.

Was he therefore to sacrifice his friends in order to regain his daughter?

No; he could not do that.

Still when the fetiche man desired white men's blood, he resolved to grant his request.

His native cunning came to his aid.

He resolved that white blood should flow in order to regain his daughter, and, as the great fetiche man did not say whose life was to be taken, so long as it was the blood of the white man, a sudden thought struck him.

He remembered that he still held captive the Portuguese slave-dealers.

He resolved to sacrifice them instead of Bob Blunt, as he supposed the fetiche man desired, for he knew that the latter was not aware that he had any white prisoners in his power.

No sooner had the fetiche man left the place than he commanded that the Portuguese should be brought before him.

His warriors were now like wolves when they scent blood.

They rushed out, and soon returned with the prisoners.

They were tied in couples.

The king made a motion to a man who stood behind his chair.

This was his chief executioner, an important attendant on all the kings of Africa.

He was stripped to the waist, the better to perform his duties.

In his hand was a sharp, heavy, curved sword.

When the Portuguese beheld him they at once divined their fate.

Falling upon their knees they piteously implored for mercy.

The king was inexorable.

He motioned to the executioner, whose assistants at once placed the first Portuguese upon his knees, with his neck on a tree stump, and before the man had hardly time to cry out, the terrible sword was raised high in the air, and in another second the man's head was severed from his body.

His companions shrieked with terror when they saw the gory head roll towards them.

But the utmost apathy was shown by the native warriors.

One, two, three, four, and five of the Portuguese met with the same fate, and the shrieks were terrible.

Again five more were executed, and there were placed in a ghastly row eleven gory heads.

The warriors dipped their hands in the streams of blood that gushed down the floor and besmeared their faces, arms, and bodies with it, all the time uttering loud cries as if thanking the gods for granting the king's wishes.

The executioner had just placed the last victim before the block in the centre of the chamber, when the matting of the door was suddenly thrown back, and the faces of Bob Blunt, Buttons, and the Stinger were seen.

All started back with horror at the dreadful sight that presented itself to their eyes.

Alarmed by the repeated cries, Bob had rushed to the palace.

Bob saw the executioner with his sword raised to kill the last victim.

"Murderers, hold!" cried Bob; "what does this mean? Release the captive."

The king stared.

"He must die," he replied.

"No, he shall not."

"The fetiche wills it."

"I care not for the fetiche; if he were here he should die by my hand. King Aga, tell me why should this white man be killed?"

"For me to regain my daughter."

"Bah!"

"The great fetiche told me that the blood of a white man was necessary.

"And did he know that there were any other white men but ourselves in your town, King Aga ?" asked Bob, looking keenly at him.

" No."

A sudden thought entered Bob's mind.

This fetiche man had been sent by Pluto and Howard to work upon the superstitious fears of the king, and by saying that the gods would give him back his daughter if he sacrificed Bob and his friends ; thus Howard's evil wishes would be fulfilled.

He resolved to thwart this scheme.

" Listen, King Aga. This fetiche man has been sent by your enemy, King Pluto, in order to advise you to your destruction."

The king signed to the executioner to pause in his occupation.

" You were to kill us. Was not that the advice that the fetiche man gave you, he not knowing that there were any other white men present ?"

The king bowed his head in assent.

" Then I will prove to you that the fetiche man is an enemy."

" When ?"

" To-morrow."

" Good."

" And for the present I intend to take this captive under my own charge," said Bob.

And he cut the bonds of the trembling Portuguese with his knife and drew him to his side.

The youth gave him a look of deep gratitude.

" Now, King Aga, you must detain this fetiche man."

" He is gone."

" Ah ! thinking you would kill us he has gone back to King Pluto."

King Aga stared.

" How know you that this great fetiche is an emissary of King Pluto ?" he asked, doubtfully. " His calling is sacred."

" That may be ; but I have my own fetiche man, who is one hundred million times greater and wiser than the devil who cunningly inveigled you to slay those poor wretches."

" Who is that ?"

" Why, my great medicine man and magician, Stumps ; he will prove to you that you were betrayed."

These words had the desired effect upon the king.

" Now," said Bob, " you will at once consign the bodies of those poor murdered wretches to the earth and give immediate chase to this false fetiche man."

" I will."

" Hurrah ! Ready all," cried Bob. " We'll give immediate chase to this rascal."

CHAPTER XXXIII.

HUNTING A FETICHE MAN.

IN the wide open space that lay in front of the houses, King Aga already had his warriors assembled for the chase.

All were now as eager to capture the false fetiche man as previously they had been ready to fulfil his commands.

Bob tried to persuade the Stinger to remain behind, but the fair lady said " she would die first," and as she usually meant what she said, Bob let her come.

The fetiche man would evidently lay close within the neighbourhood until the news reached him that the white men had been sacrificed by King Aga.

This Bob divined at once, for he had become fully alive to the subtle cunning of the African.

The whole of the natives now spread themselves over the plain, and then began to beat the bushes with long sticks.

Bob had several large dogs with him,

and these began to sniff into every waving clump of grass, and occasionally gave vent to short, sharp cries.

"Now, gentlemen," said Bob to his immediate followers, "the one who first catches this artful knave, a reward of ten pounds and the best dinner."

"Hurrah! I'm off," cried Buttons; "come on, my lovely Betsy."

"I'm with you, old Butt; we'll catch him first," she cried.

"Me catch fetiche too," said Jingo, showing his teeth. "Me follow missie."

Away went the three as hard as they could run.

Bob spread his men over a wide tract of country, resolving to meet at a certain spot where the fetiche man would most likely be caught.

The Stinger, Buttons, and Jingo kept very close together.

They soon lost sight of the others.

For a long time they continued their journey until at length they reached the river where Strongback had slain the crocodile.

Keeping the banks of the stream in view for some distance, they branched off, and after a time they reached the entrance to the cave where Bob had been first attacked by Howard.

To their surprise, the rock which had blocked up the entrance in consequence of the explosion of dynamite had been forcibly removed.

"Someone has entered here, I suppose," cried Buttons.

"Oh, de debbel hab done it, he bery strong—strong as de fire-water lubly missie keep in her pocket."

"You black rogue, what do you mean? Do you suppose that I have any dealings with the devil?" cried the indignant Stinger, threatening Jingo with her umbrella.

"Beg pardon, me nebber do it again."

And the repentant nigger fell on his knees and groaned terribly.

The Stinger thought it was through fear of her wrath, but she was greatly mistaken.

The cause of Jingo's terror was that he had seen a terrible face scowling at him from the interior of the cave.

The Stinger followed his glance, and she too beheld it.

"Halloa! What's that?" she cried.

"What?" asked Buttons.

"Look!"

But the face had disappeared.

"Now, what is it?" gasped the Stinger.

"Oh, it am de great fetiche man. He am the bery debbel."

"The fetiche man, did you say?" exclaimed the Stinger.

"Him bery self or him shadow."

"Hurrah! then, we've got him! I'm with you, Buttons. Come on, Jingo, we'll catch him, and gain the prize."

"Nebber, nebber, nebber!"

"Why, what have you to be afraid of?" muttered the Stinger.

"He kill me—he bery great."

"Great be bothered! Come on, my Butt, we'll have him."

"I don't half like it," said Buttons. "He looks awful."

"Shall E. A. S. go by herself, then? Come on, I say—victory or death!"

And without more to do, the brave Stinger rushed into the cave.

It was empty.

Jingo, in the meantime, had provided himself with a torch.

Buttons saw nothing left for him to do but to follow the Stinger.

"You had better come with us, Jingo," he said.

"Nebber! de fetiche man am de debbel."

"You won't come?" said Buttons. "Then, by the powers, I'll make you. Look here, Jingo, you'll either go alive or dead; now which do you prefer?"

And Buttons drew forth his revolver, and presented it at Jingo.

"Me go, massa; but oh! de fetiche man kill us all."

"Come on, then."

Buttons made Jingo Johnson precede him, and he cried out—

"Where are you, Betsy?"

"Here, Buttons."

The Stinger's voice sounded hollow in the distance.

Buttons and Jingo made their way through intricate passages until they reached the Stinger, who was about to enter the hall of the seven pillars already described.

"Here you are, Stinger ; have you seen any signs of him ?"

"No ; but I believe he has gone in that place."

And the Stinger pointed to the cave.

"Then we will nab him."

Slowly and very cautiously the three proceeded, Buttons bringing up the rear, in order to keep Jingo up to the mark, for the negro's teeth chattered like castanets.

"Oh, golly, golly !" he groaned. "What will he do to me ?"

Buttons gave him a gentle reminder to be quiet, by kicking his shins.

No sooner had the Stinger turned the entrance to the hall, than either a man or an animal butted her.

She fell back upon Jingo.

That affrighted nigger gave a howl and tumbled upon Buttons.

The three went to the ground.

In the meantime, the Stinger saw the fetiche man running down the passage.

As soon as she could recover her breath, she cried out—

"There he goes ! After him ; tally ho, tally ho ! my boys."

Her excitement was great, and Buttons, as soon as he could compel the groaning Jingo to rise, urged him on and followed as fast as he could.

They soon came in view of the Stinger again, and then the welcome daylight appeared once more.

They saw the fetiche man flying towards the opening.

But the Stinger was close upon his heels, and shouting with all her might.

The fetiche man's terror was evidently great, for he had never seen a specimen of a strong-minded British female before.

Elizabeth had caught him by his long hair, but by a dexterous movement he eluded her grasp, and jumped through the opening of the cave on to the ground.

"He's gone. Ah, but I'll have him yet," she cried.

Her eyes had fallen on the rifle she had forgotten to take with her when last in the cave.

She seized it, and cocking it, she pulled the trigger at the moment when the fetiche man was disappearing through the trees.

Bang !

A howl from the fetiche man told her that he had been wounded by the bullet.

"Come on ; let us have him now. Hurrah for E. A. S. and women's rights !"

She threw her umbrella and the rifle to the ground, and before Jingo knew what she was about to do, the brave Stinger jumped from the cave.

She was no light weight, and the shock was terrific.

It knocked all the wind out of her for a time, but as soon as she could draw breath, she cried out—

"Come on, my Butt, we'll have him. Now up with me."

But this was no easy task.

"Give me a hand, Butt."

"Jump, Jingo, jump."

"Right, massa ; me bery glad de fetiche man not got me in de cave."

And Jingo, delighted to see daylight once more, jumped from the cave, quickly followed by Buttons.

The Stinger was soon on her feet, and the three ran in the direction the fugitive had taken.

They soon sighted him.

He was running hard, but encumbered by his charms and skins, they clung to the sides of the bushes through which he rushed.

The Stinger was mad with the excitement of the chase.

"I'll have the black brute," she gasped.

"So will I," cried Buttons.

"And me, massa," said Jingo, who, now that the supernatural danger of the cave had passed, did not fear to follow in pursuit.

Never heeding the obstacles in their path, they rushed on neck to neck like so many racehorses.

But the poor Stinger was becoming dead beat, when the fetiche man suddenly fell upon his face in the long grass.

The Stinger was upon him.

Determined to lay the first hand upon him, she fell upon the top of the fetiche man, nearly knocking the breath out of his body, and twining her fingers in the tow-like locks of his hair.

"Got you at last," she cried, and then fell senseless, but never relaxing her hold upon his hair. Jingo Johnson raised her up.

Buttons at once searched her pockets, and found the seldom-empty bottle.

He took a good pull of the contents himself, smacking his lips after.

He then rubbed her temples with it and gave her some to drink.

She opened her eyes.

"Have I got him?" she gasped.

"Right, Betsy, as tight as wax."

"Where?"

"In your hand."

"Ha! I've got you."

And she gave the fetiche man such a pull by his locks that he howled with pain.

"Turn him over, Buttons, and see whether I have wounded him."

Buttons and Jingo did so.

The fetiche man had received a slight scalp wound, the bullet having evidently glanced off from one of the human bones with which he was adorned, and thus saved his life.

But his terror was great.

"Now, Buttons, we must bind his hands and carry him to Mr. Blunt."

"We will. Here, Jingo, tear the skins off his back into strips; "we'll soon fasten his lovely limbs together."

Jingo complied with alacrity.

When the fetiche man was bound, the Stinger shouldered her rifle, and taking another good sip at the bottle, she offered it to Buttons and Jingo, and then opening out her beloved umbrella, she gave the word of command in stentorian tones.

"March to our quarters, my brave army. Now, then, prisoner, quick march."

And away they tramped in the direction of King Aga's town.

After travelling for some time, a loud noise was heard at some distance from them, and the Stinger at once thought that it must be Bob Blunt.

The noise increased, and then at last they beheld a herd of wild antelopes break through the long grass, and astride on the foremost one was the doctor, his hair streaming in the wind, his eyes glaring through his spectacles, and his arms tightly clasped round the animal's neck.*

CHAPTER XXXIV.

FURTHER ADVENTURES IN SEARCH OF THE FETICHE—WHERE ARE BUTTONS, THE STINGER AND JINGO.

BOB BLUNT arrived at the spot he had appointed to meet his friends. King Aga and his warriors made their appearance first, and ultimately the doctor, Swiftfoot, Ironfist, and Longsight.

"Well, no luck?" asked Bob.

"None," was the answer he received.

"This fellow must be found. A good deal depends upon his capture. Where are Buttons, the Stinger, and Jingo? In danger again I expect."

They waited some time, and the gallant Stinger and Buttons not putting in an appearance, Bob said—

"I think, great king, you had better beat the forest in the direction opposite to that which we will take, and we will meet at your camp."

"As my white friend wills it," said the king, in his quiet manner.

And beckoning to his warriors, they soon disappeared in the wilds of the forest.

Bob Blunt now proposed that they should go in search of the Stinger.

---

*The Koodoo (A. Strepsiceros) is one of the largest African antelopes, frequently measuring four feet in height at the shoulder, and eight feet in length from nose to tail. Such an animal would carry a man easily.

"We should not have left them; they are always in danger. However, on with us, before it is too late."

They had not proceeded far on their way when a deep growl was heard.

"Be ready, friends," said Bob, as he halted and cocked his rifle.

The others instantly followed the example of their leader, and stood prepared for any danger.

In an instant the animal that had alarmed our friends became visible.

It was a fine female leopard, and had in its mouth a small antelope.

The animal bounded into the path just in front of Bob, paused a moment as if meditating an attack, but then probably remembering that its young ones at home were waiting for their dinner, turned and hurried off.

Bob sent a bullet after her, but missed, and the animal disappeared in the jungle.

At evening they reached a village, where they resolved to rest for the night, or perhaps longer, for King Aga had sent out scouts who might perhaps be gone a day or two before they could find the direction taken by King Pluto.

For that astute chieftain had so cleverly hidden his trail that for some hours they had been simply going by guess work.

CHAPTER XXXV.

AN EXCURSION—DANGER AHEAD—THE HIPPOPOTAMI—STUMPS'S STRATAGEM—"OH! MY UMBRELLA!"—BOB BLUNT'S MIRACULOUS FIND—THE STINGER'S JOY.

NEXT day, in order to kill time till the scouts returned, Bob granted Buttons and Stumps permission to go on a fishing excursion, and Jingo Johnson undertook to show them the likeliest places to catch fish.

Buttons and Stumps accordingly provided themselves with rods and tackle, and were about to start when Bob met them.

"Hold!" he said, "you shall not go by yourselves. Take a few of our niggers with you, Stumps, for I think it is rather dangerous to go by yourselves."

"Very well, sir," replied Stumps. "But do you think the niggers would be any protection to us?"

"Certainly, because on the least sign of danger, you can send them back to me, and I will be close at hand."

Stumps bowed.

He accordingly selected a dozen niggers, and thus accompanied, he proceeded with Buttons and Jingo towards the river, where two canoes were awaiting them.

As they were trudging along they came across the Stinger.

"Halloa! where are you going to?" asked the brave lady.

"Going fishing," said Buttons.

"I'll go with you."

"All right; come on."

The Stinger was delighted, and at once shouldered her umbrella.

Buttons, Stumps, the Stinger, and Jingo entered the one canoe, whilst the niggers entered the other.

The river ran very rapidly, and it required very little effort on the part of the rowers to propel the boat along.

The Stinger drew the attention of Buttons to the wonderful scenery on the river.

"That's what I call paradise," said the Stinger. "Now, I haven't seen a prettier bit of scenery since I went on an excursion up the Thames with a host of my noble adorers, waiting to gain a smile from my sweet lips."

She looked round and caught Buttons grinning.

"Don't mind my smile, Betsy, but I thought it so funny you should have such

"BOB SAW THE EXECUTIONER WITH HIS SWORD RAISED."

a lot of noble adorers whilst you ware such an old poke bonnet as that."

"No doubt you may think it funny, Butt ; still, when you hear the history of that bonnet, you will not wonder at my evident partiality for it. I was travelling in the Alps once, and in order to rid myself of my adorers, I ascended the mighty mountains in a Sedan chair. I was in the highest state of joy and pride in showing my bravery to my adorers, wh——"

What Miss Stinger's fate might have been Buttons was not told, for the narrative was interrupted, for at that moment the water was violently agitated some thirty yards in front of them.

"Halloa! what's that?" asked Miss Stinger.

"Oh, crikey! Crocodiles," shouted Buttons.

"Hush!" said Stumps ; "let the niggers go on ahead ; we will try to back water as much as possible, for I begin to think there is something larger than a crocodile beneath the water."

All stood up in the canoe.

The niggers went on heedlessly.

Suddenly there arose on the surface the huge bulk of a hippopotamus.

The Stinger shrieked with alarm.

Buttons pressed his hat on his head, whilst Jingo's teeth began to chatter.

"Oh, golly, golly ! he'll make bellyful ob de bery lot on us," moaned Jingo.

"Quiet," commanded Stumps, whose coolness and energy did not forsake him in the hour of peril ; "quiet, I say, we will manage to elude him."

The huge beast lay with his mighty jaws extended on the surface of the river.

The niggers in the other canoe were discharging arrows at the brute in quick succession, much to the danger of Buttons and Stinger, for one or two arrows and spears came unpleasantly close to them.

Stumps saw the danger was imminent, and no time was to be lost if they wished to escape.

At this moment another hippopotamus appeared behind the other also extending its terrible jaws.

This increased the general terror.

They were rapidly drifting towards the two brutes, when Stumps suddenly divested himself of his coat, boots, and hat, and before anyone could prevent him he dived into the river.

"Where's he gone to?" shrieked the Stinger, rising in the canoe.

Stumps arose to the surface.

"Back the canoe," he cried. "I intend to upset the niggers' boat and so divert the attention of those hungry brutes. Never mind me, I'm all right."

With that he dived again.

Suddenly the Stinger beheld the canoe which contained the niggers capsize.

A wild cry arose from them.

Stumps re-appeared on the surface, and climbed upon the overturned canoe before the hippopotamus could dart after him.

"Hold back !" he cried to the others.

The hippopotami as soon as they espied the niggers in the water, dived, but came quickly to the surface again, whilst the niggers swam away in all directions.

The canoe in which the Stinger was, at this moment glided with great rapidity past the hippopotamus.

The Stinger thought they were going to be engulfed, and such was her terror, that she raised her beloved umbrella to strike, and it fell right into the brute's jaws.

"He has it," she cried. "Oh, save—oh, save my umbrella."

The hippopotami fortunately were in search of a stray nigger, as the canoe glided safely past the brutes.

Stumps saw that the niggers had swum safely ashore, and then, with a few strokes rejoined the Stinger.

"If I had not upset their canoe it would have been all up with us. Look at the monsters how they are floundering about."

"It's gone, gone for ever. I shall never see it any more, never."

"What's up now?" asked Buttons, who had been on his knees all the time.

"The venerable companion of my wanderings has departed down into the regions of a 'potamus. Oh, I'd rather have gone down there myself; the big brute swallowed it at one mouthful."

"Well, I never. Did you ever hear the like, Stumps? She's not thankful for her miraculous preservation. Oh, Miss Stinger, how can you set all your affections upon that umbrella?."

"I'd rather have been swallowed up by those hippopotamusses than have lost my my umbrella—I would rather—oh Lor'! my favourite umbrella; here he comes; he'll have us now."

This last cry came from the Stinger on the sudden reappearance of the hippopotami.

"Paddle for your lives!" cried Stumps.

"Oh Lor'—oh Lor'! whenever will these adventures come to an end?"

"Paddle away; we are going with the stream, so go ahead, my boys," shouted Stumps.

Jingo and Buttons obeyed, and the light canoe literally flew over the water, the hippopotami following in their track.

At last they came to a narrow part of the stream, and they made for this.

To push the canoe to the shore was the work of a moment.

When once more on terra firma, they took to their heels.

The hippopotami quickly followed them up the bank.

Buttons, the Stinger, Jingo, and Stumps, ran away as fast as they could.

They came up with several niggers, and at last met Bob Blunt.

"Hurrah!" cried Buttons, "come on, sir—here's plenty of sport to be had. Look at those little dears after us."

"What, are you all safe?" said Bob. "Why, a pretty spill you have given those poor devils of niggers."

Bob at once collected his party, and with their rifles and revolvers they went forward.

When within ten yards of the river, a loud snorting told them that the animals were returning to the water.

Bob hastened on in order to intercept them if possible.

Coming suddenly through a break in the jungle, they espied them.

"Now, men, ready. Fire!" he cried.

Bang—bang.

One of the animals fell dead, having been pierced in the eye by a bullet from Bob's rifle.

"That's number one—now for the other—quick, fire."

A dozen shots were sent at the other brute, but none wounded him mortally, and snorting with rage and pain, the hippopotamus charged our adventurous friends.

The Stinger fled aghast, followed by Buttons and Jingo.

Bob dodged behind some trees, and taking careful aim he fired two shots in succession.

The hippopotamus rolled heavily over on his side.

When the Stinger beheld this she stayed her flight.

"That's my enemy," she cried; "I know him by his jaws. He swallowed my umbrella. He's got it inside."

"Got what inside?"

Stumps explained to our hero the mishap that had befallen the lady.

"You shall have your umbrella again, Miss Stinger. Ho! Buttons, summon all the natives. Ah! he's not dead yet."

In truth the hippopotamus was not quite dead, and tried to rise.

Another bullet, however, gave it its *quietus*, and then Miss Stinger's joy was beyond all bounds.

The native, seeing their terrible foes dead before them, came in a body.

Bob ordered Jingo to open one of the animals, the one that was supposed to have made a meal of the Stinger's umbrella.

This was no easy task.

But the niggers worked with a will, and then in the stomach a blue-striped article appeared, that caused the Stinger to utter a cry of joy.

"It is, it is! Oh, my beloved gingham. Gently, Jingo, gently, old boy."

With great care the resuscitated gingham was brought to light again and washed.

"Well, I never thought I should be the cause of such a miraculous find," said Bob, as he handed Miss Stinger the somewhat crushed umbrella.

"Oh, thank you, thank you a thousand

times; luck's mine, yet. I'm so happy I've got it again."

And the Stinger danced about to the great amusement of all present.

The niggers had brought long ropes and tied them to the animals.

Thus they were dragged in triumph to the village, and were met with a chorus of yells, shouts, and screams from the excited population, who thus saw their dreaded enemies slain.

But the Stinger retired to her own sanctum, where she was busy during the rest of the day in repairing whatever damage had been done to her gingham by the ponderous jaws of the hippopotamus.

"Never will I take you on a fishing excursion again," she mentally vowed. "Never will I trust you out of my sight, for if I lose you, all luck has gone for ever from E. A. S."

We will see how she kept her word.

CHAPTER XXXVI.

AN OLD FRIEND COMES AGAIN ON THE SCENE—THE STINGER'S LOVERS—BUTTONS' TRICKS—'POSSUM UP A GUM TREE.

THE next morning, at the first welcome appearance of the sun, there was heard in close proximity to our hero's quarters, a cheery voice trolling out the following song, in notes as clear and fresh as the morning air—

> "Is not the sea
> Made for the free!
> Land for courts and chains alone!
> There we are slaves,
> But on the waves,
> Love and liberty's all our own."

The Stinger, Buttons, Stumps, and all the sleepers heard these jovial strains.

They jumped up from their repose wondering who the singer could be, as the voice did not belong to either of their party.

The Stinger was out first.

"Halloa, there!" she cried.

"Below, there! avast. Bless my sea-pipers, it's roused a mermaid."

"What, old Tom, jolly old Tom— are you up again?" cried the Stinger, shaking him by the hand.

"Yes, marm; Doctor Knowall kept me in my bunk long enough. Don't be afeard; it ain't 'tagious," said old Tom, for it was the brave old tar of the "Busy Bee."

"I'm not afraid if it is contagious, Tom. I am so glad to see you up again."

"Yes, it were unlucky to be boxed up in bunk while you were rushing into all kinds o' scrapes."

"Well, the fever's left you?"

"Of course it has, marm. Do you suppose it would chuck old Tom into Davy Jones' locker? Why, I've had yellar Jack a score of times, and now jungle fever ain't worse to me than the scrumatics."

By this conversation it will be seen that old Tom had been very ill.

In fact, he had caught a very bad fever on the very day of Bob's entry into King Aga's salubrious city.

He was the only white man who had been attacked by the malignant disease, and had been ordered by Dr. Knowall to keep quite close in a small cabin, where an old negro woman had attended upon him during the time of the doctor's absence, and administered the proper remedies.

Bob now came out and welcomed the old salt.

"How are you, Tom?"

"Your honour, I'm all right—like a fish put back in the sea; and there's Buttons. How are you, Buttons, my boy? Give me your fin. I'm mighty glad to see you. Ah, Stumps, and Mr. Longsight, Mr. Swiftfoot, Mr. Ironfist, how are you all, gentlemen? Let me see, I miss someone."

"There is a vacancy in the ranks, old Tom," said Bob, with deep emotion.

"Ah! what?"

"Don't you miss anyone, Tom?" asked Bob.

"Yes; let me see. Where is Mr. Strongback?"

"Ah, Tom, he is——"

"Dead?" said Tom.

"Yes; he died bravely and like a man. But he was murdered."

"Murdered!" said old Tom, speaking as in a dream.

Bob briefly told him what had occurred during his illness.

"Lord save him!" said the old sailor, reverentially folding his hands, after taking his hat off. "What a death!"

Then in a burst of passion—

"If ever I gets larboard or starboard of any of them 'ere land sharks, I'll whip my jack-knife into them, swop my Poll if I don't."

And old Tom's action was so energetic that all felt he would act up to what he said.

"Never mind, old Tom, about your jack-knife; we'll revenge brave Strongback's death together. I've a good plan ready, and in due time it will be carried out," said Bob.

Yet the words of old Tom had, however, made a deep impression upon all.

It confirmed the resolution in the breast of Bob's followers, namely, that it was clearly their duty to act unanimously in attacking King Pluto and Howard.

After the entire party had broken their fast, they severally strolled about the native village near which they had passed the night.

The Stinger was elated.

She flaunted about in all her dignity, her umbrella over her head, her bottle in pocket, and a bundle of woman's rights pamphlets in her hand.

As she peeped into the houses of the natives, the women and children ran away and hid themselves, for the Stinger's commanding look had a marked effect upon them.

"What are they afraid of? Lor'!

what timid things these women are. No doubt centuries of beatings from vile men have entirely broken their spirits. Come here, you little dear, here's a sweetie for you."

The Stinger put on a very amiable expression to a little black child, and held out a lump of sugar to it.

But the little one drew back and hid itself behind its mother.

The Stinger was at a loss what to do to conciliate the infant African, when Jingo Johnson suddenly made his appearance with another nigger.

"He, general, dere she am—he, he! yah! Dere, did you eber see more lubly nosie?"

"Golly! Jing, you am right," said the other nigger, who was not quite as tall as Jingo, but he made up for it in dignity.

His dignity was something awful to contemplate.

He was naked save across the loins, where he had the usual white linen covering, but on his head was a general's cocked hat, and fastened to a belt, trailed an old cavalry sabre in a battered sheath.

This nigger, who had been an officer's servant at Cape Coast Castle, was known to all as General Bombast.

Not that his godfathers or godmothers had given him that name, but he had assumed it by virtue of his cocked hat and sabre, of which he was very proud.

His bombastic manner had earned him the soubriquet from the officers stationed at Cape Coast.

He wore around his neck, by a string, the frame of a large magnifying glass.

He was wont to use it as an eyeglass, but finding he could not see through the glass, he had thrown it aside as superfluous, but used the frame, it answering the same purpose, in the most affected manner.

When Jingo Johnson drew the general's attention to the Stinger, the general put one foot forward, and bending his body to an angle of ten degrees to the right, he placed the glassless frame in his eyes and scrutinised the Stinger with the air of a connoisseur.

"She am; golly, she am proper Miss, bery good day, fine weader—yah!"

The Stinger turned round.

"Who are you?" she asked.

"Me! oh, Majar-general Bombast," replied the nigger, drawling out his words, and gallantly raising his cocked hat.

"Lor'!" cried the Stinger, amazed.

"Yes, dat's I; bery fond ob de ladies, me ladies' man, majar-general, up to all tricks—dance can-can; fust foot up, den down—so."

And the general began to dance the gay Parisian quadrille with all the grace imaginable.

When his terpsichorean evolutions had concluded, the general opened his very wide mouth, and spoke—

"Oh, you bery booful, missie; me lub you already. Majar-general Bombast am your'n for eber and eber. Amen."

The general bowed again, with his glass in his eye.

"What do you put that thing in your eye for?" asked the Stinger.

"To see you de better, missie," replied the general, winking through the eye-glass.

"See me? Why, you fool, there's no glass in the thing?"

"No matter, missie; it am de fashion."

"Oh, jiminy, hear him; a nigger talking about the fashion."

The Stinger burst into such a peal of laughter that it could be heard by Buttons and old Tom, who were chatting together in front of Bob's quarters.

They ran to see what was the matter.

When they beheld the general, their mirth was as boisterous as the Stinger's.

"Halloa! here's another guy. Who is this? Why—no—is it a hossifer?" cried Buttons, eyeing the general up and down.

"No, page-boy. Me am Majar-general Orlando Bombast," replied that gallant officer with great dignity.

"How dare you call me page-boy?" cried Buttons, in a rage.

"Lots like you at Cape Coast. Ha, ha! you may be walley-de-shamble," said the general, with dignity.

"I may be, but you don't call me either if I can help it," said Buttons.

"That's it, young un; don't you be bullied," exclaimed old Tom.

"Look here; where did you steal that hat and sword?" asked Buttons.

"Me not a tief," said the general, proudly, raising himself to his full height.

"Oh, Lor'! look at the swell. He is trying to make three eyes. Well, three-eyes, you're about the funniest customer I've seen for many a long day. Are you another of the Stinger's lovers, eh?"

"Me am."

"You are?" shrieked the Stinger.

"To de deaf."

"Oh, what jealousy there will be amongst the lot of you," exclaimed Buttons.

The Stinger walked away in a very dignified manner, scorning the general and his proffered love.

The others did not follow her, for it was the hour when all usually went to enjoy their repose during the heat of the day.

The Stinger walked into a grove of wide-spreading palm-trees, where the beams of the sun could not penetrate.

Selecting a nice shady spot, she stretched herself at length at the foot of a large palm tree, and placing her inseparable gingham by her side, she drew forth her bottle, took a sip, and then, spreading her handkerchief over her face, resigned herself to repose.

The two niggers, as soon as they saw the Stinger asleep, looked at each other.

Jingo winked knowingly, jerked his thumb over his shoulder in the Stinger's direction and grinned, and the general as knowingly returned the wink.

"Well?" said Jingo.

"Yah!" said the general. "Jing, 'blige me with the lean of your arm. Yah!"

And the general cocked his hat on the corner of the eye that held his glass, took Jingo's arm, and walked on towards the grove of palm trees, his cavalry sabre beating against his bare legs as he went.

This pantomimic action had not been lost upon Buttons and old Tom.

They followed close upon the heels of the two niggers, but taking care to keep out of sight.

The general and Jingo reached the

Stinger, whose stertorous breathing raised the handkerchief from her face at every respiration.

"Dere she am. de lubliest crittur in de wide world. Oh, general, me am bery much in lub."

"So am I, Jing."

"What wouldn't me guv for a kiss! Oh, to kiss de angel's nose! Dat nose, dat am de wision ob me dreams!"

And Jingo sighed like a pair of bellows, rolled his eyes in his head, and groaned.

The general did the same.

"Jing," he said, at last, "what hab Nosie dere in de pocket?"

"Where, gen?"

"Dere."

"Oh, golly, it am—it am de fire-water bottle," said Jingo, who beheld the bottle peeping from the Stinger's pocket.

"Rum, Jingo; not fire-water—rum, to warm the belly of genum."

"I say, gen, like drop? asked Jingo, his eyes wandering from the "lubly nosie" to the "b'u'ful bottle."

"Yos."

"Me get it den."

Jingo crept slyly to the Stinger's pocket, but at the moment he was about to lay his dusky fingers upon the coveted flask, the Stinger's hand closed over it, as if her dreams had revealed to her the close proximity of a possible thief.

"Oh!" groaned Jingo, "she am awake."

"What?"

"She am awake. It's my 'pinion, gen, she hab eyes in her nose; dere is so many liddle holes in it, just like a thimble what old Sal sews shirts with."

"Ah, den better not offend her; but if we can't hab drop rum, nobody else shall, for sartin," said the general.

"Neber!"

"We'll watch her."

"Yes."

The two niggers lay down a little way off, and shut their eyes, rather a new way to keep watch.

As soon as they were asleep, Buttons and old Tom crept slyly up.

Buttons had decided in his own mind that the general was legitimate game, and had determined to have a lark with him.

Buttons had procured a large bag of sand tied to a long cord.

"Now, Tom, I'll show you some fun. Wait until I get up this tree."

Buttons was soon up the tree amongst the leafy foliage.

He then lowered his bag.

Old Tom tied a piece of string to the rope in order to regulate its movements, as Buttons swung it about like the pendulum of a clock.

Tom hid himself behind a tree, and then signalled to Buttons that he was ready.

Buttons first attacked the general.

He dropped the bag heavily on the general's nose, and old Tom quickly drew it aside before it could be seen.

"Golly! what was dat?" asked the general.

He rubbed the injured organ, and then his eyes fell upon Jingo, who lay with his mouth wide open.

"Ah! he's gwine to make a fool ob me, but I'm gwine to make a gollopshus 'possum ob him."

With that the general lay quietly down again, and then raising his arm, he brought it down sideways upon the pit of Jingo Johnson's stomach.

Then the general lay perfectly still.

"Oh!" roared Jingo.

He looked round and could see no one, whilst the general lay peacefully snoring by his side, to all intents and purposes entirely innocent of giving the blow.

"Bery strange," muttered Jingo. "I could swear that was the general. No matter, de time will come whe——"

"Is dat you a-talking, Jing?" asked the general, yawning almost wide enough to swallow his companion.

"It be."

"What de matter?"

"Did you wollop me?"

"Me?"

"Yes, you, gen."

"Oh, golly, me wollop you," cried the general, highly indignant.

"Beg pardon, I thought it was."

"Bosh!"

The two niggers turned face to face, and both pretended to be asleep, but both were watching each other.

Buttons saw their drift.

He motioned to Tom, and then let the

sand bag fall with force upon the kerchief over the Stinger's face.

Tom quickly withdrew it.

The Stinger started up with a snort.

She saw the niggers upon the ground close by.

She seized her umbrella.

Whack—whack!

Right and left did she batter into the two niggers, screaming out—

"You black thieves, to dare to—to dare to play your tricks on E. A. S."

"Oh, missie, missie, it was not me," cried Jingo; "it was him."

Pointing to the general.

"You lie, Jing," replied Major-general Bombast.

"I don't care who it was; but know this—paws off E. A. S."

The Stinger laid down again, and after awhile the niggers did the same.

The Stinger had, however, thrown her handkerchief over her fair face this time in order to watch.

Buttons motioned to Tom, and the bag was drawn to the tree.

Then Buttons pierced a number of small holes in the sand bag, guiding it first over Miss Stinger, and then over the niggers, as the sand very gently began to run out.

They did not heed the falling sand any further, for all three shut their eyes, and the sand came down so gradually that they did not notice it.

At last their faces were covered with it.

At last the general jumped up.

He found his face covered with sand, which had got into his wool, mouth, nose, and ears.

Sputtering and shaking himself, he cried—

"Oh, golly, Jingo, de hebens is raining de earth down on us. Oh, de bery end ob de world hab come at last."

Jingo started up in great alarm.

"Oh!" he yelped, "my—phew!—my eyes, gen. Oh, de dust—de dust ob heben hab got into de lubly Nosie's nosie."

He aroused the Stinger.

She awoke with a start, and began to sputter as much as the niggers had done.

Buttons, when he saw that the sand had answered its purpose, crept slyly down the tree and rejoined old Tom.

They were heartily enjoying the joke when the Stinger, having rid herself of the sand, turned her fury upon the two niggers.

"Take that, you black rascals, take that," said the Stinger, belabouring the two with her umbrella.

"Oh, missie, it was not me, missie; neber do such um ting," cried Jingo, sheltering himself behind the general.

But the Stinger continued to beat the pair of them until she heard a loud explosion of laughter behind her.

This caused her to turn round in time to see old Tom and Buttons, who were dodging behind a tree.

"Ah!" she cried, there the villains are, Jingo, Bombast. After them, boys, they are the rascals. We must nab 'em."

Away the Stinger tore after Buttons round the tree, followed by Jingo and the general, who were both red-hot for revenge.

Buttons dodged her once, then suddenly putting forth his leg, the Stinger fell, and Jingo, with the general, being close behind her, they too came to a sudden stop, the general's cocked hat flying off, and his sword-hilt digging the unlucky Jingo in the ribs.

There they lay in a heap, groaning and moaning, whilst the delighted Buttons and the jolly sailor danced a war-dance around them, that only irritated the the Stinger more.

"Now then, general, get up, and lead your army to the field," said Buttons.

The general arose.

Jingo also got up, his face grey with rage.

"You pig, you dig your sword in my belly, you 'fernal cuss. Take that—dar."

And he caught the astonished general a blow on the head that made him reel again.

"What you do dat for, Jingo?" demanded Major-general Bombast, as he slowly rose to his feet.

"You dug dat sword in my belly, you debbil, you."

"Me, Jingo."

"Yas."

"Oh, Heben!"

And the indignant general, in assertion of his innocence, rolled his white eyeballs towards the firmament.

Meanwhile, the Stinger had got on to her legs again.

Her wrath was so great that she could not give utterance to it.

Buttons wisely kept out of her reach, but she this time pounced upon the general, belabouring him hard.

"It is all your fault, Jing ; me'll hab it out with you," he cried, freeing himself with an effort from the lady's grasp.

"Berry well, when you like, sar. I'm your man. I fight," said Jingo, defiantly.

"And I'll be your second," said Buttons.

"And I yours, general," echoed old Tom.

"Good ; me'll hab you," said Jingo.

"And me you," said the general.

"I'll be even with the lot of you," shrieked the Stinger, shaking her umbrella at them, and rushing away.

Buttons and old Tom laughed.

"You shall have it out with each other before long, Jingo and Bombast, but for the present we must postpone the battle, for I see a messenger from Mr. Blunt coming.

This proved to be the case, and so the whole party returned to the native village.

*   *   *   *   *

And now we must give a few words of deferred explanation about the doctor and his antelope ride.

When Miss Stinger and Buttons saw the worthy medico, as related in Chapter XXXIII., bestriding the animal on which he had fallen by accident, while climbing a tree after a rare flower, the first impulse of the strong-minded female was to raise her rifle and fire.

But before she could do so, the animal put its foot in the chasm of the ground, and rolled over with a broken leg, while the doctor, with the exception of a few bruises, was uninjured.

Buttons and the Stinger helped him up, and they soon fell in with Bob Blunt.

Our hero, however, cordially welcomed them, and the captive fetiche man was ordered to be kept in close custody, till Bob had time to expose the tricks which had terrified King Aga.

The place they selected for their residence that night was one of the outlying villages of King Aga's kingdom, and after a good supper, they sought their couches.

CHAPTER XXXVII.

THE HAUNT OF THE WILD BEASTS—"I'M A ROVER!"—A NEW-FASHIONED SOMERSAULT—JINGO'S PRESENCE OF MIND—ALL RIGHT AGAIN.

UP, up with the lark, you English drones."

It was Bob Blunt's cheery voice that sang out to his sleeping comrades, who were still in their several hammocks.

"Rouse up, Buttons ; what are you blowing so hard for ? What's the matter with you ? Up, up with you."

Buttons was asleep with his mouth wide open, and was blowing a blast through his nostrils that made the place echo again.

But on our hero following up his summons with twitching his nose, Buttons started up at once.

"Oh, crikey, sir," he said ; "I had such an orful dream. Old nick was pitching me into a mighty abyss, where there was a lot of wild beasts, and one of them swallowed me."

"Bosh !" replied Bob ; "you had too much supper, that's all. Get up and clean my rifle, for I'm anxious to be off."

One by one Bob's trusty followers arose, and each having had his morning's cold bath, they sallied forth.

"Well, Betsy," said Buttons to Miss Stinger, "how are you after yesterday's lively performance, eh?"

"Well, Butt, well. E. A. S. is satisfied; that is only the beginning of what I intend to do to astonish the niggers."

"Here, Buttons," said Bob, "give me my gun."

Buttons took our hero's rifle, and handed him his small shot gun.

A covey of red-legged African partridges had flown up a short distance ahead of the party, and settled down again.

Bob followed them up closely.

The ground on which he stood was a piece of rich herbage, but on all sides arose the mighty trees, and long, trailing plants and creepers obscured the view through the avenues.

He was in the act of aiming at the partridges that were whizzing from their covert, when he caught sight of a scene that made him pause in his resolve to fire.

"Hush!" he whispered.

"What is it, sir?" asked Stumps.

"Look, there is one of the most wonderful sights I have ever seen."

All crowded around our hero, silently, and looked through the intertwining tendrils that dropped from the trees.

A vast scene of grandeur presented itself to their view.

In the centre of a chain of rocks, covered with the most lovely flowers, a number of rushing springs met in a clear, limpid pool.

Through a wide avenue came a large herd of elephants.

Some were already drinking from the river, or bathing in it; and a few hippopotami were swimming about.

The trees branched over the river, their dense foliage shutting out the sky.

Monkeys and birds innumerable swarmed amidst the branches, and created an endless chattering noise.

Bob and his friends stood entranced, when they beheld this wondrous spectacle.

"Oh—let us creep nearer to them," said Stumps, "and if possible, without attracting their attention, for it is something to behold these wonderful creatures disporting themselves in their native state."

"I agree with you, Stumps; come on, single file, and quietly as mice," said our hero, delighted with the scene before him.

Bob led the way.

He made a *detour*.

By these means he managed to reach a broad ledge of rock in close proximity to the beasts—and without disturbing them.

One by one Bob's followers stood beside him, viewing the playful gambols of the huge animals.

"I can't see them well," said Buttons.

"Come along, Buttons; climb up the tree with Jing," said the black.

"Right," replied Buttons, "but have you got any means of climbing these trees?—for I'm blest if I can span them."

"Soon done, massa."

Here Jingo uncoiled a long rope, and throwing it over a branch with great dexterity, he pulled himself up.

Buttons followed him.

Then Jingo uncoiled the rope again and made a slip knot.

"Me catch monkey for Missie Rednose," he said, grinningly, making his way along the trees, followed by Buttons.

"All right, go ahead, my trump," said Buttons, looking down upon the huge hippopotami in the water beneath him with great dread. "My eyes, I never did see the like—why, there's dozens of them about; but when I return to England, I shall say there were millions—it's a traveller's trick to exaggerate, you know, Jing."

"Cos, massa, it is," said Jingo, turning to follow a monkey. "Mind you don't fall in de water, or you be swallowed up."

"Oh, what jaws, my eye!"

Buttons looked down.

"They can't catch me, though—he, he! I'm up a tree—ha, ha! Mr. Blunt should come up here, and my beloved Betsy; oh, Buttons, you are the hero of the age. I shall call myself Buttons the Rover in future."

And he sang—

"I'm a rover, I'm a rover!
 I'm always free.
In England or in Africa
 A rover and up a tree.
 I'm a rover——"

The last word died in a cry, for swinging on the bough, it suddenly snapped, and Buttons, in an abortive attempt to grasp at another branch, turned a complete somersault, and then came with a plump into the water in the middle of a dozen elephants, and more than one hippopotamus.

Jingo had made an attempt to catch Buttons with his lasso, as he was in the act of falling, but the page-boy slipped through before the noose could be drawn tight.

"Oh, golly! he am gone," cried Jingo. "Help, massa, help! Buttons be swallowed up."

Jingo ran quickly from bough to bough.

The noise Buttons made in falling caused the elephants to trumpet loudly and look about them.

But the hippopotami were some distance apart as Buttons appeared on the surface of the water, his hat crushed over his ears, and calling for help.

Bob Blunt and the Stinger, petrified for a moment at Buttons' mishap, ran now towards the banks of the river.

One of the hippopotami was swimming towards Buttons, when Bob Blunt commanded a volley to be fired at it.

A dozen balls struck the animal, and it sank beneath the water.

Buttons' terror was extreme.

He beheld two more of the monsters swimming towards him.

"Oh, I'm in for it again. Somebody come and help Buttons. Oh, here comes a beauty with his ugly mouth open! Oh, Lor', he'll have me!"

By this time Jingo had come within reach of him, and with a sudden swing, the powerful negro again threw his lasso out from the tree, this time with better success.

The noose passed over Buttons and caught him under the arms.

Another moment it would have been too late, for one of the monsters was within a few feet of him as Buttons was being rapidly hoisted into the air by the delighted Jingo.

Bob Blunt and the others cheered lustily when they beheld this exploit.

"I got you now," cried Jingo. "Hippopotamus go without Buttons in him belly dis morning."

Buttons could not reply.

He fainted in Jingo's arms.

The negro lowered him down to Bob, who received him.

"Poor old Buttons," groaned the Stinger, putting his head in her lap and bathing it with some water.

After a time Buttons recovered.

"My dream, my dream, has come true," he said, with a mournful shake of the head.

The shock had been too great for him to bear, so Jingo Johnson carried him to King Aga's village in his arms.

In consequence of Buttons' mishap, Bob had to postpone the unmasking of the fetiche man until the following day.

Bob continued in close companionship with King Aga, in order to guard against the possibility of another fetiche man playing upon the credulity of his superstitious nature.

But Stumps was very busy.

"To-morrow, sir, I'll make the hair of all the natives stand on end with terror," he said.

"That's the ticket, my boy, and success to you, for everything depends upon it. I want to move from here in search of Pluto and Howard, but without King Aga I cannot act."

"He shall follow you to the death. I'll make him."

CHAPTER XXXVIII.

THE MYSTERY OF THE MAGIC HEAD.

IN front of Bob's quarters stood next day an eager and curious mob of natives.

They had assembled there at an early hour the morning after the conversation just related.

Presently the blowing horns and drums announced that the king and his principal warriors had arrived.

The fetiche man walked behind the king with a proudly confidential air.

He was clad in all the hideous paraphernalia of his calling, having been released from confinement for a short time that he might decorate himself for the trial of skill he was to engage in with Stumps.

"Welcome, King Aga," said Bob; "my great medicine man is ready to decide any doubts concerning the truth of my assertions with regard to the fetiche of King Pluto, and of his intentions towards you and myself."

The king bowed.

Bob ordered the mattings of the door to be thrown open, and then the entire company marched into a long tent.

Bob and the king seated themselves in a chair of state each.

Their umbrellas were held over them, and then Bob and their followers ranged themselves on each side.

A silence fell upon all present.

The native mystery man did not appear at all at his ease.

There was a large canopy in the centre of the room, which looked like another tent.

"Now, fetiche, say whether you are an emissary of King Pluto's or not," said the doctor, who acted as interpreter.

"No, I am not."

"Good; then we will disprove your assertion. Lift up the canopy."

In a moment, Bob pulled a long rope, which was fastened to the head of the canopy, and ran over a pulley in the roof.

The canopy was dragged up to the roof, Bob fastening the rope so that he could let it fall at will.

As it arose, there came to view the person of Stumps, dressed in the garb of an astrologer.

His robes were painted with symbolic representations of the sun, moon, and stars, and the forms of animals indigenous to Africa, and usually held in awe by the natives.

On his head he wore a pointed cap, crowned with a skull.

In manner he was grave and discreet, and stood silently scanning the warriors present, whose faces bespoke the agitation they felt.

Stumps was satisfied.

By his side was a round table, supported upon a single massive pillar.

On the table stood a head.

It was of a pure white, like marble, and chiselled so as to look like a demon.

Its eyebrows were painted a bright red, and likewise the lips, which were parted wide enough for the tongue to be seen.

In all other respects it was like a statue whose body and bust were imbedded in the pillar on which the table rested.

Stumps advanced before the chiefs.

"Great chiefs," he began, "after long watching and studying of the stars, the Great Spirit has vouchsafed to grant my prayer. I have here a head to which is given the power of answering any questions that may be put to it. Above all things, it speaks the truth, and nothing but the truth, for, if it did not, its power would be lost for ever."

Stumps paused while the doctor translated his speech to the warriors of King Aga.

His words had a great effect upon the audience.

Bob turned to the king.

"My friend and powerful ally, have you any question to ask of my fetiche man?"

"Yes."

"Then come."

King Aga, with evident fear in his every action, advanced towards the head.

Stumps motioned to him to kneel.

The king obeyed.

"Now, great king, what is your wish?"

"I demand to know whether the fetiche man was sent by my enemy King Pluto to assassinate me?"

"You shall learn the truth."

Stumps drew forth a piece of paper and a pencil, and writing the message upon it, he twisted up the note in as small a compass as possible, put it in the mouth of the head, and blew it down its throat.

He then repeated the words aloud.

"You will have an answer in one minute," said Stumps to the king.

All crowded around.

The king trembled visibly.

Presently there issued a hollow groan from the head, which was re-echoed by the trembling warriors present.

Then there issued from the mouth of the head the following words, uttered in a deep, hollow tone—

"The fetiche man is an emissary of King Pluto. He came here in order to assassinate Bob Blunt the Traveller, the great chief of the white men. King Pluto promised to make him the chief fetiche man of all his tribe as a reward, if he encompassed the death of the white men and King Aga."

"There," said Stumps, when this had been interpreted to the terror-stricken gree-gree, or fetiche man; "there, that is the truth, and nothing but the truth."

King Aga turned towards the fetiche man.

"Thou art an impostor," cried he fiercely, rising, and turning with fury upon the gree-gree, "and no mercy shalt thou have from me."

"I am not. Oh, great king, hear me before you condemn me."

"Speak."

"I am innocent."

"He lies!" cried the head.

"Do you hear? You lie," cried Bob.

"Come, confess, and your life may yet be spared. Down on your knees."

"On your blessed marrow bones," cried the head again.

Bob and his friends could hardly repress their laughter at this exclamation.

The gree-gree fell on his knees.

"I am guilty. I confess all; only keep me from the wrath of the mighty spirit that speaks from the stone."

"Speak on then," said the head.

"I was sent by King Pluto to persuade you to kill the white men, and to arouse a feeling of hatred against you, great and powerful King Aga, amongst the tribe. But the Great Spirit wills it that you should be spared. I am powerless, and all the gods are against us."

When these words had been interpreted by the doctor, Bob said—

"Now, O king, are you satisfied this man is a villain and an impostor on his own admission? King Pluto has stolen your daughter, and you cannot believe anything but evil will emanate from him. Ask the head, and it will tell you of the future in store for you. Ask as you will, and the spirit will answer you."

"I desire to know what has become of my daughter, Nahita; and whether she is alive?" said the king.

"Good," replied Stumps.

With the same action as before he awaited the reply from the head.

"Nahita is well. She awaits anxiously her father's arrival. She mourns for him, and rejects the overtures of Pluto."

A smile stole over the king's face.

"I shall see her then, but how?"

"If you carry war into the very country of the king, you will see her," replied the head.

"I will! Chiefs and warriors, the oracle has spoken; we will follow this King Pluto to his home, and punish him for his treachery."

A loud cry of approval came from all the dusky warriors.

"Have you anything else to ask of the oracle?" said Stumps.

"Yes."

"Name it."

"What shall be the fate of the gree-gree?"

"He shall be kept as a hostage until

it suits King Pluto to return your daughter to you," replied the head, after Stumps had sent the message as before.

"I am content," said King Aga, retiring.

"Are there any more questions you have to ask?" said Stumps.

But none of the niggers ventured to even approach it.

They were all silent.

Such were the marvellous effects of superstition.

At last Stumps saw that none of them ventured to come forth, and was about to have the canopy lowered again, when Jingo Johnson and the general were seen to nudge each other, and push each other forward, and then retreat again as if in fear.

Stumps saw them.

"Come on," he cried. "Any question you may ask will be answered."

"He, he! You go first gin'ral. You got sword, cock-hat, and wonderful presence um mind; me, poor nig, hab not."

"I'm frightened, Jing. De head be bery artful. Me not ask."

"Oh, gin'ral, you am coward."

"So am you."

"Neber! but you go first.'"

"Neber!"

"Look here, den; we boff go togeder?"

"Yes."

"Come, then; but you lead the vay, and I valk in your tracks," said Jingo.

"Do you call dat togeder?" said the general, drawing back.

"Go on, both of you," said the Stinger. "You've only to ask, and you will be answered."

"Come on, den."

The two niggers, with much trepidation, advanced towards the head, and paused in front of the terrible magician.

"What do you desire to know?" asked Stumps.

"Noting," they replied.

"Then what the deuce do you come here for?" he said majestically.

"Oh, massa, bery sorry, but it am dat gin'ral's cussed cur'osity," said Jingo.

"No, it am not; but Jingo wants to know de state ob his heart."

"The state of his heart!" cried Stumps. "Has he got heart disease?"

"Yes, massa."

"He had better go to the doctor, then. The oracle does not give medical advice gratis. The ills of the flesh are not administered to here, but the ills of the mind. If you are *non compos mentis*, we may advise you."

"Yes, me am," said Jingo; "me am 'mense pain ob de head and de heart."

"What do you require?" said Stumps.

"Me am in lub," said Jingo, placing his hands on his stomach, and fetching a deep sigh from the lower regions with a gulp.

"So am me," said the general, imitating him in everything.

"The fact of it is, you are in love, and you want to know whether your affection is returned or not," said Stumps.

"Ees, massa, dat am it," they replied.

"Well, then, we'll put this question for you at once."

And Stumps did so.

Presently the answer came from the head.

"Who are you in love with?"

"Do you hear?" said Stumps. "The oracle wishes to know the object of your affections."

"Me am in lub with a nose," said Jingo Johnson, very gravely.

"So am me," continued the general.

"What nose?" was the answer.

"De lubly nose of the lubly Missie Stinger," said Jingo, in reply.

"Dat's it," echoed the general. "But we want to know which nigger the lubly Nosie lub the best."

"So you shall."

"The nose loves that one the best who can fight the best," was the answer.

"And who am dat?" asked the general.

"You must fight to decide that question," was the answer.

"Me got to fight you, Jing—he, he!"

"Me am ready; but I wants to be made 'cute. If I lick you, will de lubly Nosie be mine for ever and ever, eh?" said Jingo.

The Stinger had listened to what had passed and discreetly kept silent.

"Say, sar, that if I am the conqueror in the battle, I shall win de nose?" asked the general.

"And I, sar?" echoed Jingo.

"Here the oracle is silent, but you'd

better place your ears close to the mouth of the head, and it will tell you."

"Neber!" cried the niggers, aghast.

"What! are you afraid?"

"Bery much 'fraid," they replied.

"Very well; then you can't have an answer," said Stumps, decisively.

The niggers were nonplussed on receiving this reply; but after much hesitation, and pushing each other forward, they at last placed their ears close to the mouth of the head, holding each other by the hand.

"Now then for the answer," said Stumps.

"Keep close watch over the fetiche man, and see that he does not escape you two darkies," said the head.

"We will."

"And then when you have done your duty, you will win."

"What shall we win?" gasped the two darkies, looking intently into the mouth.

Before they received a second answer, a long stream of fire suddenly darted from the mouth of the head—which at last emitted a loud bang as if from a cracker.

Jingo and Bombast fell back with a cry of terror.

As soon as King Aga and his warriors beheld it, they rushed to the door.

"Oh, golly! it am de debel!" cried the niggers, and away they went, leaving Bob and his friends the sole occupants of the tent, and laughing heartily.

Bob followed the general stampede into the open, and then beheld the gree-gree rushing off in hot haste.

"Jingo, general," he cried, "catch the fetiche; remember your promise."

The terrified niggers turned.

They saw the gree-gree and captured him.

"Ah! we will not let you go; we hab you for eber and eber," cried the niggers, bringing the unlucky gree-gree back.

Bob was satisfied.

But no inducement on his part could compel King Aga and his chief to return to the great magician Stumps.

Bob carefully closed the mattings of the shanty, and then returned to the interior.

Stumps was divesting himself of his gorgeous robes as he entered.

"Now then, release the oracle, Stumps, my boy, for I must say it has been a great success, and answered all our purposes," said Bob, patting Stumps on the back.

"Right, sir, I agree with you. We have agreed together to settle the gree-gree, and have done it well," replied Stumps.

"Let me out!" cried the head. "I'm nearly choking down here."

Stumps took up the head, unscrewed the top of the table, removed the pillar, and there, in a cavity underground, was the renowned and redoubtable Buttons, with a face as red as a turkey-cock's.

Stumps assisted him out of the hole.

"Blow me if I don't deserve a gold medal for this," said Buttons, creeping forth. "Cruelty to animals! Was there ever an animal more cruelly used than I have been?—to be pent up in that blessed den all that time; it's awful!"

"Never mind, Buttons. You have done your work well. It was a capital idea," said Bob again bursting out in peals of laughter.

"The approval of my master is enough for me. But I wish Stumps had done his own conjuring," he replied.

"So I have. Did I not think of the stone in the cave? Did I not fashion it, and did I not work the true-born necromancer of the olden time?" said Stumps with dignity.

"Enough you both did, and now have done your best. We have succeeded in our object, and there is an end of it. To-morrow we shall leave this place, for King Aga's scouts have returned with important news, and I am certain we shall find plenty of war and sport, which will soon make us merry."

"But, for all that, I mean to keep my head, for who knows but it will be of great service to us yet?" said Stumps.

"Do so, but for the present keep dark. Our course is clear, but all we have to do is to fight and conquer."

So said Bob, and all the others agreed with him in this, but during the remainder of the day nothing was seen of King Aga and his warriors, so completely had the mysterious head subdued them, and impressed them with the power of the great white chief, Bob Blunt, the traveller.

"THE STINGER RAISED HER UMBRELLA TO STRIKE."

CHAPTER XXXIX.

ON THE TRAIL—THE FOREST ON FIRE.

KING AGA was thoroughly aroused for action after Bob Blunt had confirmed him in his opinion of the gree-gree, and also when his spies had reported the direction taken by King Pluto.

On the morrow Bob arose, and all his followers were fully prepared for the expedition, having arranged their guns and apparel to the best advantage.

In fact nothing to ensure their protection was neglected by our friends.

When they sallied forth, King Aga was ready to receive them.

Fully armed and equipped, his warriors presented a very martial appearance.

"King Aga," said Bob, greeting the king with all kindness, "we are sworn friends now, so let us follow in pursuit of the villains who have robbed you of your daughter, and flinch not from the risk."

"The Great Spirit has spoken, through the mighty magician, the white gree-gree, and I will obey," replied the king.

"True, O king! then let us away at once."

Buttons had a restive companion with him on this day.

This was none other than the monkey that Bob had wounded on his first arrival in the African forest.

The monkey had, after a time, become very fond of our hero, for he petted and humoured it very much, and allowed it to follow him about after the death of its young one.

Away they went.

The forest opened occasionally into little valleys, radiant with flowers and with vernal grass, between slopes that seemed like a scene in some grand old park in England.

Later in the day, however, the vegetation became thicker, and it was occasionally necessary to make the negroes cut a path through the jungle.

When night came on, they selected a spot where the ground rose a little higher than usual, and having cleared away some of the undergrowth, resolved to rest there till daybreak.

They made a hearty meal, and then laid down to sleep, some of the niggers being appointed to keep guard against the attack of enemies and wild beasts.

Now it so happened that those particular black men had rendered Miss Stinger a good deal of help during the day, and she had rewarded them with a drink from her bottle.

The unaccustomed liquor had affected their heads, and as soon as the camp was quiet, they dropped off to sleep.

Buttons, who had taken up a position not far from Miss Stinger, did not feel sleepy, neither did that lady.

"Do you see that light, Betsy?" said he, pointing to a flickering point of flame that seemed to be moving about in the jungle. "It's a will-o'-the-wisp, I suppose."

"Yes; there's four or five of them."

"Betsy Stinger, what have you been doing with that bottle? You not only see double, but quadruple."

"Don't bother, Buttons; I am trying to go to sleep."

Buttons sat quietly for some time, when he became aware of a strange light that was gradually illuminating the forest.

It was not the light of either sun or moon, and not knowing what to make of it, he aroused his master.

Bob Blunt jumped up, and in an instant saw what was the matter.

In stentorian tones, he shouted—

"Up, all of you! Up for your lives! The forest is on fire!"

"The forest is on fire!"

These fearful and startling words brought all the sleepers to their feet.

"Where is the fire?"

"Who has done this?"

"What shall we do?"

Such were the hurried exclamations that met our hero's ear as his friends and companions became aware of the terrible danger by which they were threatened.

"Some clumsy lubber has made a nice mess of it," remarked old Tom, as he surveyed the scene.

"Say, rather, that some malignant enemy has taken us at a disadvantage," replied our hero. "Watch those points of fire darting from place to place; they are torches carried by human beings, and wherever they pass, the jungle is instantly in a blaze."

"Then here goes to douse their glims," said the sailor, catching up his rifle and firing in the direction of one of the torch bearers.

There was a scream of agony, and then from the darkness of the surrounding forest came a series of horrible yells.

"Massa!" exclaimed Jingo Johnson, "dem niggers belong to that waggabone King Pluto."

"How do you know?"

"I know dere talkee, massa, speak dere langwidge all proper."

"Now then for the fire!" shouted our hero; "cut down the bushes, and clear away as much space as possible."

"Why not try the American dodge?" said Doctor Know-all; "fight fire with fire by burning a clear space before us."

This suggestion was translated to King Aga, and met with the immediate and unqualified approval of that sagacious warrior.

The dusky monarch immediately caused his warriors to cut down a quantity of the brushwood between the camp and the body of flames that seemed to be advancing most rapidly.

Then they set fire to the jungle in such a manner that the flames were blown away from the camp, and as the fire died out, they took possession of the space thus cleared.

It was a grand and terrible sight.

Trees that had a resinous sap would blaze in full brilliancy for some minutes and then die out, leaving nothing but a glowing skeleton.

Other trees that were full of sap would appear for a time to defy the raging element, and stand aloft in gloomy magnificence. But then some vine or creeping plant would ignite, flames would swiftly run up among the branches, and then the head of the monarch of the forest would glow with a crown of fire.

There was fire on the right hand and upon the left; flames were darting overhead, and scorching embers lay under their feet.

They kept on, however, and were soon in comparative safety—the great danger being from the sparks that descended in showers upon their ammunition boxes.

However, there was no explosion, and they soon reached a clearing where they could rest in safety.

But there were few of the party who had not received one or more burns on the face or hands.

"Thank Heaven!" exclaimed the Stinger, fervently, when safety was assured. "I don't want such a trial as that again."

"Well, Betsy, you can say with truth now that you have been through fire and water with your own Buttons."

"Get out!" replied the strong-minded female, making a blow at the page with her dilapidated umbrella.

And Buttons deemed it best to keep beyond her reach.

Another camp was formed, and they lay down to rest—not to sleep—while for miles round the blazing forest cast a wild, unearthly radiance upon the scene.

By the next morning, however, the flames had died out, and they were able to continue their journey.

The little army soon after this passed the boundary of King Aga's territory and entered that of King Pluto.

Every step of the way was a scene for wonderment to our friends.

Bob, when they halted, discovered such magnificent scenes that he transferred them to his sketch-book; but all the powers of pen or pencil would not do justice to the sublime and lovely grandeur of many of the scenes through which they passed.

Two days did they travel thus when Swiftfoot and Longsight, who had been sent out to scout, returned to the camp.

Bob thought the intelligence they brought worthy of notice.

They had not come across any of King Pluto's tribe since the burning of the forest, but in passing a mighty river they saw a small canoe shoot out from a fissure of the rocks, containing a black, paddle rapidly up the stream, and disappear again into a wide ravine.

They had marked the spot well.

This was enough for Bob.

He resolved to go in pursuit at once.

He only took his own immediate followers and King Aga with him.

It was late in the day when they went on their expedition.

Bob left the monkey behind him, for he could not well be encumbered with Molly, although she cried bitterly on seeing our hero depart.

Four natives brought a large canoe with them on their shoulders.

Into this Bob, King Aga, Buttons, Stumps, Longsight, and the Stinger entered when it was launched.

Two natives paddled them to the ravine, and they were to return for the others.

The ravine was a wide one, and on each side rose mighty rocks sloping down to the waterfalls, and covered with some green grass and shrubs.

But there were no signs of an opening on either side of the ravine.

But the keen eyes of Longsight at length espied a small pathway where the grass had been trodden down as if by the passage of many feet, and here the canoe was at once brought up.

Bob jumped out.

They followed the track to the summit of the rocks, and when Bob looked over the declivity into a hollow through which the waters surged, and the rocks circled around, there was but an extremely narrow path around the hollow.

On a lower shelf of rocks two mighty vultures sat, brooding and making the solitude greater by their presence.

Bob lay looking at this scene for a moment, when he suddenly caught sight of a black sitting in the entrance of a cave.

He looked again, and was certain.

" Oh, that's where the fellows have hidden themselves ; the spot is discovered. Now for it ; we'll have them."

Stumps peered over his shoulder.

" How are we to avoid attracting that fellow's attention ?" he asked.

" True ; he is a sentinel. We cannot advance unless we settle him, for he would immediately raise an alarm," said Bob.

" He would ; but we have a remedy."

" What ?"

" You forget, sir, the air gun."

" Ah, yes ; give it to me," cried Bob, suddenly recollecting it.

Stumps brought it forth.

Bob arranged the weapon, and taking careful aim he discharged it at the negro.

The loud whirr startled the vultures, who rose above the waters, and circling around with a hoarse shriek, they alighted again upon the lower shelf of rocks.

The black fell dead within the cave, the half of his body protruding and hanging over the edge of it.

Bob now resolved to proceed.

" I will go and reconnoitre this way, whilst the rest of you make the best of your way round the hollow and you can meet me on the other side," said Bob, pointing to the place where the nigger lay.

The others at once started off.

Bob made the best of his way around the rocks until he stood beneath the cave where the negro had fallen.

Here he paused.

A sharp angle of the rocks most probably led to another part of the ravine, so he turned round here.

No sooner had he done so than he came face to face with two gigantic negroes.

Bob started back.

The one was King Pluto, the other his executioner, and both were in all the grandeur of their trappings.

Pluto wore, as an ornament on his side, a large human skull.

As soon as King Pluto beheld Bob he started back.

But the next moment with a shout of rage he rushed upon Bob.

Bob drew his sword.

He did not reckon upon two to one, but he resolved to fight.

Pluto attacked him with his sword, a thick, double-edged weapon.

Bob parried the first blow, but the executioner made a side attack upon him.

"I must hold my ground," muttered Bob, "or these devils will force me back to the precipice. Ha! King Pluto, thou art foiled, yes."

Bob had parried a blow of the executioner's, and, that worthy falling back, Bob cut him across the leg.

This blow was so effectual in its aim that all Bob had to do was to parry the thrusts of the king.

The combat lasted for some time when Bob suddenly drew back, and in retreating he turned the angle of the rocks, and found the mighty vultures hovering below the rock where the dead black lay.

King Pluto followed up Bob with heavy blows from his sword, shouting—

"White boy, I will kill you!"

"Villain!" cried Bob; "it shall be your life or mine!"

Bob placed himself with his back to the cave, and still defended himself bravely.

The king's executioner had recovered somewhat, and now rushed up to renew his attack on Bob.

Bob in avoiding his blows had to fall farther back again, and then the executioner with a sharp blow knocked Bob's sword from his grasp.

Bob now seemed at their mercy, and would have been cut down by Pluto but at that moment he caught sight of a heavy club lying at his feet. He snatched it up and brought it round with great force on King Pluto's legs.

A few seconds later he regained his sword, and with a desperate effort he suddenly struck with all his might at King Pluto, but the blow missing its aim he was brought on to his knees.

The king's executioner, seeing this, rushed forward.

Bob saw him coming, but did not see on the opposite side of the waterfall a nigger with a gun ready to fire.

Bob with a desperate effort struck at the king and then fell back again when he had delivered the blow.

The king received the blow on his hand.

He dropped his sword with a loud cry of agony.

Bob saw two of Pluto's fingers lying on the ground, and therefore he knew that his aim had been true, and that he had succeeded in disarming his enemy.

But he could not rise.

King Pluto, despite his intense pain, seized his sword in the left hand and rushed again at Bob.

At that moment the black figure on the opposite side of the ravine fired.

Bang!

A shot rang out.

King Pluto felt a stinging sensation in the side, and the skull that he wore as a fetiche dropped on to the ground at his feet.

This saved Bob.

The king seized the skull with a cry of joy.

"Saved! saved! by the Great Spirit!" he cried, looking at the skull with delight.

Bob, during this providential interruption, found time to rise to his feet, though he was still on the edge of the rock.

King Pluto did not attack him.

He stood looking intently at our hero for some time, when Bob saw that all thoughts of battle had left him.

The wound in his hand hurt him terribly, for he bound it up with all the linen he could tear away from his cloak, but still it bled terribly.

The vultures swept around the spot, smelling the blood.

But at that moment Jingo Johnson and all Bob's friends were making their way around the ravine.

King Pluto caught sight of them.

"We must escape. Listen, white chief; Pluto is thine enemy. Beware of him, he will hunt thee to the death!"

Before Bob could reply, for he had received a grievous shock in the fight, King Pluto, with the shot rattling in his skull, he looked upon as a charm, rushed with lightning-like speed round the angle of the rocks, and disappeared from sight.

"Go," said Bob, "you have left a part of yourself behind you, and before long you shall leave more, or my name is not Bob Blunt. Come on, Jingo; come on; we will follow them up."

Bob left the spot.

The moment he had done so, the two vultures swooped overhead and settled upon the spot.

They at once devoured the two fingers which Bob had so dexterously knocked from off King Pluto's hand.

"Ha, ha!" said Bob. "For the future I shall call you three-fingered Pluto, that is if I have the chance of catching you again."

Bob saw that it was useless to search for the king.

So as soon as his followers came up he said—

"Now, boys, we will explore these caves and see whether there is any trace of Howard to be found here."

"Right you are, sir, I'm always ready," said Buttons, "and I know that Jingo Johnson is. Halloa! here's a dead darkey."

Bob climbed up into the cave.

One by one his followers came up with him, and they followed the windings of the cave, but could find no further traces of the enemy.

Bob saw no outlet before him.

Yet he resolved to continue the search, and, if possible, end the pursuit.

At last they came to the end of the caves, and then a wider stretch of country was revealed to them.

"Look!" said Bob, there are the villains. "They have scented us and are off. It is Howard and King Pluto as I live. We must rescue the girl now they have her; tally ho!"

Bob jumped from the cavern and started in pursuit, followed by Buttons.

But they were seen by the fugitives, and night coming on Bob was compelled to desist from the chase, and with great reluctance he returned to the camp where King Aga had left his warriors.

CHAPTER XL.

THE FETICHE MAN—JINGO'S CHASE—HIS AIM IS TRUE—BOB'S ILLNESS—THE SEARCH POSTPONED.

BOB passed a restless night. Wild dreams in which many personages appeared in great confusion did not tend to improve his spirits in the morning.

When he awoke he felt feverish and exhausted, and half inclined to go to sleep again.

But the king came to him and said—

"White chief, we must be up and after the thieves who have robbed me of my daughter."

"We will," said Bob; "but I have much to think of first, and therefore I shall postpone the expedition until mid-day."

The king shrugged his shoulders in reply and went away.

Bob felt too ill to move, and put himself under the doctor's hands.

Doctor Know-all pronounced him to be suffering from a slight attack of fever, and treated him accordingly.

In the meantime Jingo Johnson and the general had kept strict watch and ward over the fetiche man.

They had bound him to a tree with cords, but still feeling a kind of superstitious awe for his calling, they had not fastened his bonds very tightly.

"We got um, general," said Jingo, lying at a safe distance from the gree-gree; "we got um, only don't let um touch you on de face or he kill us. He bery dangerous."

"Right, Jingo; "but we must sleep, or massa Blunt will find us lazy."

"True—dat's enuf, I'm off."

And Jingo closed his eyes.

The general followed suit, and the two were soon fast asleep.

The gree-gree watched them intently.

He looked around.

The camp was some distance off, and not a soul in sight.

The cunning gree-gree soon discovered that, and seeing his guards were apparently fast asleep, he slowly began to loosen his bonds with his teeth and hands.

He soon succeeded in standing a free man, and giving a hasty glance in the direction of his guards, he at once took to his heels.

He had hardly succeeded in going a dozen yards before Jingo awoke.

His first glance was for the gree-gree.

Of course he did not see him, so he opened his eyes very wide, and then started up with a loud cry.

"Golly, gen'ral, de fetiche hab 'scaped."

Up jumped the general.

"Oh, golly, where?"

"De Lord only knows. He am dreadful man; gone to kingdom come, perhaps. Oh, general, we shall be killed if we don't find him."

"What for?" asked Buttons, who, at the moment coming up, overheard the last remark.

"What for? Oh, massa, de gree-gree am clean gone," said Jingo.

"Gone!"

"He am; ebery blessed bone of um body am gone."

"Where?"

"To de—no—what—dere he am."

Jingo just caught sight of the gree-gree rushing down the path.

"After him," roared Buttons.

"Bery well—here am fire gun; come on, gen'ral," said Jingo.

Jingo seized an old musket, and followed by the general and Buttons, he rushed after the gree-gree with incredible swiftness, and soon came in sight of the fugitive, who showed a pretty clean pair of heels to his pursuers.

"Dere he am," cried Jingo; "away after him; we catch him."

"Go it, you cripples," cried Buttons; "go it. We'll have him and skin him alive, and make a drum of his hide."

Jingo grinned.

He was swiftest of foot.

The general was impeded by his cavalry sword, and would not on any account leave it behind him.

Buttons could not run very fast, but Jingo continued to run for at least half-an-hour, now and again losing sight of the gree-gree, who disappeared occasionally in the denser parts of the forest.

At last Jingo spied him flying with incredible speed along an avenue that afforded a clear ground for a chase.

Jingo uttered a wild whoop and put forth all his strength.

The gree-gree heard Jingo's loud panting behind him.

He felt that he would be captured, so he suddenly made up his mind to a course of action that he would very probably be the means of saving him.

Jingo was rushing on, now followed by the general and Buttons, when the gree-gree suddenly stopped, and lifting both hands in the air, he faced Jingo and uttered a loud shout.

The affrighted Jingo drew up.

"Oh, golly! he am going to fetiche me, he am. General, where am you? Oh, de fetiche man kill me. General, where am you?"

"Here, Jingo," said the general, who had taken shelter behind a tree, "here me am, ebery inch of me; but don't let him touch me, he am going to bewitch me. Yah, keep away."

And the general peered out at the fetiche man, for he was in as great a dread of him as the redoubtable Jingo himself.

"What shall I do, gen'ral?" asked the perplexed Jingo, shaking all over.

"Ask him to come with us."

"Will you come with us?" said Jingo to the gree-gree.

That cunning man, feeling that he had a certain amount of power over the two niggers, shook his head and frowned.

"What's to do, gen'ral?" asked Jingo, again of his fellow.

Whilst they were consulting as to the best means, the gree-gree set off again at a smart pace.

Jingo plucked up his courage now the fetiche man's back was towards him.

Away he went again.

The chase was renewed, and Buttons was nearly beaten, when the gree-gree, finding it would be impossible for him to escape, turned again with uplifted hands, and uttered a loud horrid shout.

"Fire at him!" cried Buttons. "Bring him down if he won't surrender."

"Oh, me not go near him!" groaned the general, placing one of his arms before his eyes and slinking again behind a tree.

"Look here, massa fetiche, if you do not come down on your marrowbones, me fire you dead," said Jingo, raising his musket and cocking it.

The fetiche replied with such an awful groan that Jingo shivered.

Buttons was within a few yards of him, but was compelled to pause for want of breath.

Jingo still pointed the musket at the gree-gree, and every time the latter uttered a groan, Jingo shivered and trembled in every limb, so great was his agitation and fright.

Not only was he afraid of the fetiche, but also of the musket, for not being in the habit of handling fire-arms, he felt afraid it would go off without his knowledge, so he shut his eyes as he aimed it at the fetiche man, whilst his knees knocked together.

The fetiche, however, stood with his hands raised, making the most hideous grimaces, trying to frighten them.

"Will you give in?" said Jingo.

A loud groan came from the fetiche man.

"Give in," echoed the general from behind a tree.

"Knock him over," cried Buttons.

"Oh!" groaned Jingo.

Bang!

The musket was discharged, and with a terrible cry the fetiche jumped into the air a foot, then measured his length upon the sward.

"Oh, massa, what hab I done?"

Jingo did not open his eyes.

"Settled him, by jingo!" cried Buttons, rushing forward.

The general fell on his back when the report took took place.

Jingo still stood with the musket in his hand and his eyes closed, when Buttons touched him on the shoulder.

"Wake up, Jingo," said Buttons.

"Oh, murder! what has poor old Jingo been done to?" he asked, without opening his eyes.

"Been done to? Why, you are all right," said Buttons, giving him a slap on the back.

"Oh! I'm killed—I'm dead; I feel I'm dead. Oh, oh!" groaned Jingo.

"Why, you are all right! open your eyes."

"I can't."

"Why not?"

"It am gone into de top of me head."

"Fetch um down then."

"De fetiche hab got um up dere."

"No; I think it is you who have the fetiche down there," said Buttons, looking towards the gree-gree. "So open your eyes, old man."

"Neber."

"You shall, though. Now then."

Buttons gave him a tremendous punch in the stomach.

This doubled Jingo up.

He opened his eyes.

He caught sight of the gree-gree, who was lying quietly upon his back.

"What's matter wid him, sar?" he asked, in a hoarse whisper.

"That's your latest victim."

"Am he dead?"

"You had better go and see."

Jingo beckoned to the general.

"Gen'ral," he gasped, "we hab been gone and done it this time; de blood of de fetiche am on our heads."

"Not mine, Jingo; you fired the dunder at him," said the general, receding from Jingo as if he feared to come in contact with him.

"Me! Oh! me didn't mean to do it. Let me see um."

Jingo crawled slowly up.

He was as pale as a nigger could well be, namely, a kind of steel grey.

The gree-gree was quite dead.

The bullet had penetrated the heart, causing almost instant death.

"Oh, me be haunted, me killed sacred fetiche man," cried Jingo, throwing himself upon his knees before the corpse, and performing sundry mysterious rites, which he thought necessary to preserve him from the evil the fetiche might put upon him from the other world.

"It's no use crying over spilled milk," said Buttons. "The fellow brought his death upon himself; you summoned him to surrender, he would not, so there's an end to it."

"Neber; me am haunted for the berry rest of my blessed life!" cried Jingo, in accents of despair.

"Bah! you're a fool. Dig a hole in one of the hollows, and pitch him in, and say no more about it," suggested Buttons, coolly.

"Me touch him!" cried Jingo, aghast. "Neber, neber, neber; he make me dead on de instant and bury me in the grave me make for him."

"Well, then, the general and I must do it," said Buttons.

"Neber," cried the general.

"Oh, very well, we will leave him where he is; the wild beasts will soon make a meal of him. There is no cause to be alarmed," said Buttons, putting his hands in his pockets and coolly walking away in the direction of the camp.

Jingo and the general followed him, both shaking with fear.

When they reached the camp, Buttons at once told his master what had taken place.

"I'm sorry the fellow is killed, for I'm always against taking life carelessly; but what is done can't be helped. Where is Jingo?"

"Bring him in, shall I, sir?"

"Yes, Buttons."

Bob fell back upon his pillow, for he was very unwell.

Stumps and the doctor attended upon him.

"You had better console poor Jingo, Stumps, for if he believes the fetiche man has bewitched him, he will take it very much to heart," said Bob.

"That is true," said the doctor; "I have known cases where a man has died from merely believing he has been bewitched by a gree-gree."

"Then exert your influence, Stumps, to quiet Jingo's conscience; for we cannot afford to lose even one man at the present juncture," said Bob.

Stumps promised.

At this moment Buttons introduced the general and Jingo.

The two came in with great diffidence.

"Come here, my great gree-gree," said Bob to Stumps.

"Yes, sir."

"Was Jingo right in killing the gree-gree, whom we have unmasked as a liar, and no true fetiche?"

"Yes."

"And he is not bewitched?"

"No."

"Oh, golly, gen'ral, I'm so glad, so bery glad; de 'witchment am not true, and de debel is dead."

"All right. Come, Jingo, we'll seek Missie Nosie for a drop of rum. It do us good."

And the general, seizing Jingo by the arm, marched him out.

CHAPTER XLI.

TAKING A BATH—A FEARFUL PERIL—OLD TOM HARBORD—IRONFIST TO THE RESCUE —WHERE IS LONGSIGHT?

IN consequence of Bob's illness the attempt to follow up the pursuit of King Pluto was abandoned for the time.

A stout palisade was built round the camp, for the wild beasts were so numerous in this part of the country that the natives stood in constant dread of an attack, mostly at night.

None of the white men were to go away from the camp unarmed, by Bob's especial orders.

So when old Tom proposed that they should go and have a bath, all of them went fully armed in case of an attack.

"Come on, Buttons, you look as if you wanted a wash," said old Tom.

"So do you, old sea-horse. How do you feel now?"

"Crumby, Buttons, crumby; and all the better when I have had a cooler."

"Then I'm your man. Who'll go with us? Don't all speak at once."

"I'll go," said Ironfist.

Old Tom, Ironfist, Buttons, Jingo, and the general accordingly made their way to the river alone.

"Above all things," said Ironfist, "let us choose a clear spot of water beyond the reach of hippopotami and alligators, for I don't fancy meeting any more of those gentry."

"Right," said Tom. "You find us a clear place for a dive, Jingo."

"Yes, massa."

Jingo accordingly took the lead.

Soon they arrived at the river, and they selected a place that was remarkably clear.

In fact they could see the sandy bottom and so felt satisfied that here at least no alligators could be in hiding.

The entire party soon undressed and deposited their clothes at the foot of a large tree.

Old Tom, who could not swim continued to disport himself close within shore, whilst the others had a good swim more in the centre of the river.

Suddenly, from out of the depths of the forest there appeared the form of Longsight.

He was walking leisurely along with his green umbrella over his head, and apparently immersed in deep thought.

"Holloa!" cried Tom, "come on, sir, and have a swim. I'm goin' it like an old millstone myself; down to the bottom, then up we comes again."

Longsight came and had a look at them, and after exchanging a few words with them, he continued his way along the river side until he disappeared in the thick of the forest.

No sooner had he gone than the bathers heard a loud cry for help.

"Hark!" said Buttons; "Longsight is calling for help."

Once more the cry was repeated.

"He is in danger," cried Ironfist. "Up boys, and to the rescue."

They at once left the river and landed.

When in the act of going to the tree where they had left their clothes, they beheld three large alligators lying directly in their path, and basking in the sun.

This staggered them.

"What's to be done now?" asked Buttons, aghast. "Oh, that I had my snuff with me; what a dose I would give them."

"Hush! Try to creep round them, so that we can get our clothes," said Tom.

"Hark! there is another cry for help," said Ironfist.

"Then take your guns," said old Tom, in a tone of authority.

Fortunately they had left their guns and knives close to shore.

"When they advance, and should they attack us, follow my example," said Ironfist.

"What's that?" asked Buttons.

"You keep quiet, Buttons; only keep a knife in your hand. Now we who are the strongest—Jingo, old Tom, and myself—stand on guard with the stocks of our guns, and when they advance, let them swallow the bait; for the rest, wait till I give you instructions."

The three stood ready prepared.

"We must get our clothes, or we cannot go to the help of Longsight. Stir them up," said Tom.

"Quiet!" cried Ironfist; "you do not know the extent of our danger, or you would not take it quite so easy, master Buttons."

"Hush!" whispered Ironfist, as he saw the alligators move.

"Now, stand to your guns, my lads, and give them a dose."

Jingo and Tom obeyed his command.

Though very frightened, Jingo knew it was a matter of life, so he watched Ironfist attentively in all his movements.

The alligators came on, and, when within a yard of them, they extended their hideous jaws, and at the same moment the three thrust their guns down the throats of the creatures.

They bit at the guns with a ferocious snap.

"Whack," cried Ironfist. "Now, boys, stand steady ; we shall have to jump upon their backs, and mind that you don't get within reach of their tails, or it will be all over with you—'ware them, then."

With a bound, the three leapt upon the backs of the alligators.

"Now then, all together."

Ironfist raised his knife and plunged it into the creature's eye.

The others did the same.

Ironfist felt the animal shiver beneath him, and knew that it was stone dead.

Jingo had been as successful as Ironfist, but poor old Tom was not so lucky in despatching his foe.

He rolled over to larboard.

The alligator, half blinded with the blood flowing from its wounds, nearly rolled upon old Tom, who cried loudly for help.

Ironfist heard him. He rushed to the rescue.

Throwing himself with a bound upon the alligator's back, he plunged his knife into its eye with great force.

The blow was fatal.

The alligator was as stone dead as his late comrades.

Buttons seeing that all danger was past, rushed for the clothes.

"Hurrah !" he cried, "we are safe—safe as houses—thanks to Ironfist."

"All right. But, now on with your clothes—never mind taking off your bathing trousers—for we must go and see what has become of Longsight since he called for help."

They all dressed quickly.

Then, hurrying to the thicket from whence Longsight's cry had proceeded, they began to search for him.

But they could find no trace of him, although they searched high and low.

"What could have become of him ?" they asked each other.

"He may have gone back to the camp," suggested Buttons.

"True," said Ironfist. "Let us proceed there at once."

Away they went.

"But we must take our alligators with us," said Jingo.

"What for?"

"Make booful fetiche."

"Bah !" said Ironfist. "But you can bring them along if you like."

Accordingly, the alligators were pulled along by willing niggers, one at the time, and so anxious were they to secure them, that they returned with a body of niggers who dragged the remaining alligators in triumph to the camp.

But when Ironfist came to make inquiries for Longsight, he was not to be found in the camp.

This news alarmed our hero greatly, and he ordered scouts to be sent out in all directions.

But Longsight was not to be found.

All this increased our hero's illness, and he was forced to keep his bed.

CHAPTER XLII.

AWAY TO KING PLUTO'S LAND AND WHAT THEY FOUND THERE.

WHEN we headed the above with these words we did not mean to imply that our hero and his trusty companions were about to journey to the regions of his Satanic Majesty but to follow out that scheme of Bob's in which he had set himself to recover King Aga's daughter from the bloodthirsty and cruel King Pluto.

Bob gradually recovered from his illness, and awoke much refreshed.

"Now away to King Pluto's land,"

said Bob. "Up, my boys, all! I think we shall not fail this time."

Again were the arms furbished up, the tents packed, waggons and horses got ready, and all the arrangements made to complete and perfect the expedition.

They started early in the morning in order to have the whole day before them.

Bob did not feel too sanguine.

He doubted the courage of his warriors, not his friends but the natives.

There was a good deal of talking amongst them as to what they would do, but Bob found that when they really were in action, there was very little "do," and a good deal of hesitation.

But still he hoped King Aga's example would fire the craven natives to meet the fiercer and more daring troops of King Pluto.

"At any rate," he said, in confidence to the doctor, "we will make this last attempt, and we must make it the more so now that Longsight has so mysteriously disappeared."

"It's my opinion that he has been kidnapped by some of Howard's followers," said the doctor.

"Then you think he is carried up the country?" asked Bob.

"Yes, I do; and what is more, they intend to keep him as a hostage."

"Perhaps so," said Bob. "But now let us away."

Buttons, the Stinger, and Stumps went together, each fully equipped.

Each had a rifle and a revolver, and E. A. S. was still as fond as usual of her blue cotton umbrella, bearing it along with all triumph, for she believed it brought her luck.

The little army pursued its way through the dense tropical forests steadily.

Not an inch of ground was unexplored.

It was not till late in the day that Bob commanded a halt.

They had not come up with any stragglers from Pluto's camp, but still there was hope.

They knew Pluto would not venture within the territory of a rival chief, and thus they hoped gradually to surround him in his own demesne.

Towards evening they again encamped for a time, the scouts having brought intelligence of the enemy.

Bob resolved after the evening meal to set out, and if possible to effect a capture of King Pluto, in order to hold him as a hostage.

Accordingly, after they had partaken of the evening meal, Bob, with some followers, started on the perilous undertaking.

The Stinger and Buttons persisted in their resolve to go with him.

Bob consented.

They at once made for the place that the scouts had indicated to them.

From the summit of a hill they looked down into a dark glen.

In the centre, arising from some trees, they beheld a faint smoke wreath issuing, and a scout indicated that spot as the last refuge of King Pluto.

"There, then, we will try and effect the capture," said Bob.

"I'm on," muttered Buttons.

"Let me only just come within reach of him, and I'll warm his head with my little parasol," cried the Stinger, swinging her huge umbrella about.

"All right, E. A. S.; you shall take your part, but be careful," said Bob. "Mind, I take the lead."

Bob glided away into the thicket, whilst all of his comrades separated, so as to gradually encompass the spot from where the smoke proceeded.

Bob hastened ahead.

He found the place to be farther than he had at first conjectured.

The ground beneath his feet sloped down deeper and deeper.

At last he came to a hollow from whence he could scan the entire hills around.

He at once thought that King Pluto had chosen this spot in order not to be taken by surprise.

He wondered whether he had been observed by the enemy.

"I'll take my chance," muttered Bob. "At any rate, we can fight for it, and that will just suit me."

He continued to proceed very cautiously, until his progress was suddenly arrested by a plaintive voice singing.

Bob paused and listened.

It was a girl's voice.

The tones were so sweet and familiar that Bob thought the air sounded like "Home, sweet home."

"Can it be Nahita?" he asked himself over and over again.

His prayer was that it might be.

"I must see."

He accordingly crept in.

Closer and closer did he approach the sweet singer, until at last he beheld through the dense brushwood the form of a young girl.

She was seated in front of a tent made of the leaves of the palm.

Her attitude was one of deep dejection.

Her arms folded, her eyes raised whilst she was singing, her hair falling over her face.

A slight noise caused by Bob made her turn her eyes and brush the hair from her face.

Then to our hero's delight and astonishment he beheld that her eyes were deeply, darkly, beautifully blue, and her complexion nearly as fair as that of a European.

"This surely can never be King Aga's daughter," muttered Bob.

Then his eyes alighted on the form of a huge negro, who was evidently set there to watch her.

But the black was fast asleep.

Bob saw at once that King Pluto and his followers had departed for the hunt to procure their evening meal.

They might soon return.

He at once made up his mind how to act, for he should never have such another opportunity again.

He did not fear the negro, who was lying there with his eyes closed, so drawing his revolver he slipped softly from the thicket.

When Nahita beheld him she could hardly suppress a cry, but Bob placed his finger on his lips in order for her to keep silence.

She understood him.

"Hush!" he whispered. "Nahita, I have come to save you."

"My father!" she gasped in very good English.

"Is close at hand," said Bob.

She sighed deeply, and made a motion as if to seek him.

Bob pointed to the sleeping negro.

"Watch," she whispered.

"Where is King Pluto?"

"Gone; will return soon. Hunting the wild antelope," she whispered.

"Come, Nahita," said Bob, taking her hand.

She at once agreed, but looked fearfully at the sentinel.

"Never fear him," said Bob. "I will keep guard over you."

He was about to lead her through the thicket when the black opened his eyes.

He saw them.

Starting up with a bound, he seized his spear and was about to hurl it at the audacious intruder.

Bob did not flinch.

He slowly raised his revolver in a line with the negro's heart and fired.

The black fell dead.

But the report resounded like five hundred, for the echoes repeated it again and again.

"We shall have a hornet's nest about our ears now," muttered Bob. "Let us make haste, Nahita."

He took her in his arms, and she reclined half fainting over his shoulder, when at that moment a huge form stood before them.

It was King Pluto.

His face was convulsed with rage, and he hardly knew how to control his passion.

He threw down a large antelope which he bore across his shoulders.

Before he could begin the attack, Bob struck him over his javelin arm with the butt end of his revolver.

King Pluto uttered a cry of rage.

His hand hung powerless by his side.

Bob did not give him breathing time, he seized King Pluto by the throat with an iron grip.

"Now, you black devil, I'll shake the life out of you!" hissed Bob.

King Pluto evidently thought so too, for he showed the whites of his eyes very much, and gasped for breath.

But his followers were close behind him, and it would have gone hard with

Bob had not Buttons, the Stinger, and several others arrived upon the spot at the moment.

Bang, bang !

Crack—crack ! the shots went.

Several niggers fell dead.

"Hurrah !" cried the Stinger, felling a nigger with her revolver, and then standing over him with her umbrella.

"I'm at you, you nigger," said Buttons, falling upon a nigger and pummelling him with his fists, until the black roared for mercy.

The rest of the niggers beheld more white men coming, and they beat a hasty retreat.

Bob being encumbered by the weight of the beautiful Nahita, was compelled to relax his hold of King Pluto.

Half choked, breathing dire vengeance, the king staggered back, then seeing Bob's revolver pointed at his head, he turned tail and fled.

"Ha, ha, ha ! three-fingered Pluto, you may go, but I have your prize, and by Heaven ! no one shall rob me of her again. Wake up my little queen."

Bob laid the beautiful girl on the grass, and used every means to restore her to consciousness.

At last she opened her eyes.

"My father ?" she murmured.

"Will be here soon—is here," cried Bob, as he beheld King Aga advancing through the forest with a rapid step.

Nahita started up.

The king opened his arms to his daughter and she rushed into them.

Bob stood a little aloof.

Presently he heard his name called.

He turned and beheld the king standing by his side with his daughter.

"Well, my friend?" said Bob, quietly.

"Your fetiche is a great fetiche, and a true one. He told me he would bring me my daughter, and he has done so, through you, O white king of the white men."

"I told you it would be so, my great friend," said Bob. "Your fetiche was false, sent by Pluto. Mine is always faithful and friendly towards my friends."

Bob said this very coolly.

But the large, expressive eyes of Nahita looked pleadingly at him.

"My preserver," she murmured, falling impulsively at his feet, and clasping his hand, she pressed it to her forehead.

"Rise, Nahita ; you are safe now, and have nothing to fear. For the future, both your father and myself will watch over you."

Bob gave her his hand, and Nahita, with deep gratitude marked on every feature of her fine countenance, arose, but continued to keep her eyes upon our hero.

"Now we have accomplished the first step towards our object," said Bob.

"We have. Hurrah ! I've killed a nigger," said Buttons, pointing to his prostrate foe, who lay without motion.

"No, you don't say so," said the Stinger, advancing towards him.

"Dead as a door nail, Betsy, my bloomin' summer cabbage ; look at him. 'Give his nose a tweak. Now, then I will. Look, he's done for."

Buttons gave the nigger such a tweak on the nose that it appeared as if he were dead indeed.

But on pulling it harder still, the nigger—who was only shamming—could not bear the pain, and suddenly jumped up.

His head happened to catch Buttons in the stomach as he arose.

Down went Buttons.

The black jumped to his feet, gave a terrified look around, and then took to his heels with great swiftness.

"Don't fire at him. Let the poor fellow go," said Bob.

Poor Buttons could hardly speak.

"Gone !" he gasped, "not dead ! I would as soon have touched a live lion as to put my fingers near a nigger's jaws. But I'll have him yet."

Buttons arose, seized his rifle, and before anyone could prevent him, he fired at the retreating nigger without taking aim.

The black uttered a cry of pain, and fell on his face.

"You've killed him this time," said Bob. "Buttons, never fire again without my permission."

Bob said the words with severe asperity

He did not care for a useless sacrifice of life.

"I didn't mean to hit him, sir, but he did rile me so," replied Buttons.

They went up to the black.

He still lay upon his face.

Bob turned him over.

"The man's dead!"

"Let me see," said the doctor.

He turned him on his face again, and then discovered that the ball had struck one of the fetiche bones that the black wore across his back.

But the force of the bullet had sent the bone into the poor fellow's back.

The doctor extricated it, and then the man rallied again.

After some more restoratives had been applied, Bob gave the man to understand that he was free to depart.

His astonishment was great.

He went away as if in a dream.

"Now, Buttons, you'll obey orders for the future, and not fire unless by my command," said Bob.

"No, sir," said Buttons, slinking off behind Stinger.

"Look here, Betsy," he said, "if ever you wish me to pull a nigger's nose again, do it yourself, for I'll not attempt to give ocular demonstration of any nigger as long as I live; there!"

CHAPTER XLIII.

LONGSIGHT.

LET us return for a time to Longsight.

When he had left the bathers, he wandered along, smoking his cheroot and enjoying the quiet of the forest.

Feeling fatigued, he sat down beneath the shade of a mighty tree.

Here, at his ease, he sat, watching the numerous butterflies that sported around.

Gradually his eyelids closed, and he sank into a slumber.

How long he slept he knew not.

But he was suddenly awakened by being seized tightly by both arms.

He awoke with a cry.

As soon as he gained his feet, a rope was thrown around his body, and his arms pinioned to his side.

"Help, help!" roared Longsight.

But a heavy hand was placed over his mouth, and he was dragged forcibly and hurriedly away, until he found himself beyond the reach of his friends.

Four gigantic negroes were his captors.

Longsight, the first surprise over, kept cool, collected, and quiet.

"It's no use resisting now; I'm a prisoner, therefore I'll make the best of it, but woe betide any of these black chaps when I once get free. Blow you, you nigger, don't you tear my umbrella."

One of Longsight's captors here made rather free with his umbrella.

He turned it inside out.

"Now, if you do that again I'll do for you, as sure as my name is Longsight—which it isn't, but it will do."

Longsight ground his teeth.

His captors took no notice of him.

Longsight from this time forth preserved a solemn silence.

"Bah! what's the use of talking to these brutes?" he thought.

He walked doggedly on.

The blacks dragged him on without saying a word during the whole of the night until Longsight nearly dropped with fatigue of the terrible tracks they took.

"THE BRANCH SNAPPED, AND BUTTONS TURNED A COMPLETE SOMERSAULT IN FALLING."

"I won't give in," he muttered; "but if I only had my arms free I'd make them pay for it in a way they would not like at all."

Poor Longsight went resignedly along.

His captors never paused until they reached a large village with palisades all round it.

This they did on the evening of the second day after Longsight's capture.

It was night.

As Longsight entered the village there was a mighty hubbub.

The captors of Longsight paused.

"What the deuce is up now?" muttered the brave Longsight.

It was soon apparent what was up.

King Pluto with a few of his followers was entering the village.

"Halloa! I'm in for it," muttered Longsight. "I'm in for it, but I'll stand it like a Briton. I'm game yet for Bob Blunt's sake."

Longsight kept his eyes open.

He saw King Pluto entering the village, and at its entrance he met Longsight with the natives.

"Now I'm in for it."

Longsight muttered these words as he beheld two Englishmen, for such he took them to be, advancing to meet King Pluto.

They met, and had a hurried conversation together.

"I'm done for," muttered Longsight.

The Englishmen he recognised as Howard and Bow-legged Bill.

They saw him.

"Ah!" cried Howard, "a captive. We want them; ah, we want them; and where is Nahita?"

King Pluto frowned, and laid his fingers upon his lips.

Howard nodded.

"They have lost her," thought Longsight. "Brave, true-hearted Bob Blunt has foiled them in this. He has recovered Nahita, and given King Pluto a confounded licking. Ha, ha!"

In fact, King Pluto continually grasped his throat as if he felt it had been hurt.

Longsight stood perfectly still, whilst Howard and King Pluto conversed together.

"I'm in for it now; for these scoundrels will wreak their vengeance upon me. It appears that some of them have had a tussle with Bob Blunt; and I'm glad of it."

After conferring for some time together King Pluto left Howard, and the latter with great rage addressed himself to Longsight.

"You shall be kept in close confinement for the present," he said; "and if your master persists in braving us he may find you some fine day comfortably suspended in a noose," he said, with a sneer.

"Very good, my friend; you are easily recognisable now, for you have rid yourself of that superfluity of hair that adorned your face. I must say it is an improvement. We can now see the full map of villainy enrolled in the lines of your countenance."

Howard frowned.

He knew not how to retort.

His face worked with passion, which seemed to please Longsight immensely.

Longsight had seemed entirely to ignore Howard's mute expressions of rage.

The latter foamed at the mouth.

"Curse you!" he gasped. "Take him away."

"Much obliged; very glad to have such a nice view of your amiable face. How much did you say it was worth?"

This last retort was too much for Howard.

He rushed away.

Longsight was taken to a shanty.

Here, in an underground cellar, he was placed.

He looked around.

It was not the most enticing place.

The sides were nothing but soft clay, from which the water oozed in drops.

"If I'm to stay here long i'ts a case of rheumatic fever for me; but I'll hope on to the last."

With this resolution he threw himself down on the leaves which were to serve him for a bed.

He heard the trap-door cover up the hole through which he had passed.

He was thus in total darkness.

CHAPTER XLIV.

CONSCIENCE MAKES COWARDS OF US ALL.

BOB BLUNT and King Aga returned to the camp with great joy.

Something had at last been gained by them—the recovery of Nahita.

The king's confidence in our hero was now without doubt.

He regarded him as all-powerful, and his attention to Stumps was great.

But the little dwarf preserved the same cool and quiet demeanour he always had had during his sojourn in Africa.

But this only served to raise him in the estimation of his dusky friends, and gave to his character an air of deeper mystery and solemnity.

The general and Jingo had built themselves a shelter for the night.

Buttons saw the full effect he might cause if he—as he styled it—stirred the two niggers up with a long pole that should cause them to remember him for many a long day.

"Fun, I will have, if I die for it," he said to himself; "but how? Let me see, I must work in the dark."

He stood gazing at the two darkeys with all attention.

They were busy making up their beds for the night.

"I have it," suddenly cried Buttons. "My plans are laid, and I'll pay them out for the sins of their kind."

He retired to the privacy of his own domicile where he made all the arrangements necessary for his purpose.

*   *   *   *   *

It was night when Jingo and the general retired to rest.

"I say, jin'ral," said Jingo, placing himself in a position to command a view of the entrance to the hut, "I'm goin' to bed bery happy. I've drunk well and my dinner hab filled my eyes wid de gravy ob itself. Oh, it am bery nice to be satisfied."

"It am, Jingo; it am; but let us go to de arms of Morpus."

"Who am he?"

"Fetiche of sleep; de officers at Cape Coast call him Morpus."

"Oh! me neber see him."

They composed themselves to rest, and were soon, in fact, in the arms of Morpheus.

*   *   *   *   *

They had hardly slept an hour when there was a slight rustling noise in the neighbouring tent, where the Stinger slept.

Presently a hideous form was seen to present itself in front of Jingo's tent.

It was Buttons.

As he passed the Stinger's tent the noise he made startled the good lady.

She accordingly arose and peeped through the folds of the tent.

She did not recognise Buttons, but thought him like the gree-gree.

His face was quite white save round the eyes, which were black as ink.

On his head he wore a skull and a pair of cow's horns, and all the appurtenances of the fetiche man.

"Good Heaven!" cried the Stinger. "What can this horrible thing be?"

She crept slowly and tremblingly behind the supposed gree-gree and stood watching him.

Presently Buttons disappeared in Jingo's tent, and the Stinger lost sight of him.

Buttons saw that Jingo and the general were fast asleep.

It was sufficiently light for him to see them both.

Jingo lay with his mouth wide open, as fast asleep as a church.

Buttons eyed him with a grin of satisfaction, and taking a pea-shooter from his pocket, he took careful aim and fired a pea into Jingo's gullet.

The darkey awoke with a loud spluttering, and sat up in his bed.

As soon as he was awake, he felt the pea in his mouth.

"Good Heben! Wat's this?" he cried. "It am—oh, murder! De Lord hab mercy upon a poor nig!"

He caught sight of the gree-gree standing at the foot of his bed.

Struck with horror at the sight, the nigger remained silent for a time, with the pea nearly choking him.

"Oh, de gree-gree!" he gasped at length, with chattering teeth.

"Jingo," said the spectre.

"Dat's me."

"Jingo, you wretched nigger."

"Yes, dat's me."

"You killed me."

"Oh! Lord hab mercy! Me didn't go to do it. Oh!"

Another groan that had the effect of arousing the general.

"Jingo," continued the spectre; "your time's up. I've come to fetch you."

"Oh, golly, Jingo, you old nigger, what am it?" cried the terrified general.

"It am de gree-gree!" responded Jingo, with another groan. "Oh, Lor'! de ghost come for me."

"Oh!" groaned the general, "does he want me? His face am white."

"Oh, de black man's face get white cos him a ghost," groaned Jingo.

"Jingo, you wicked nigger!" said the spectre again, "Jingo, you put a bullet into me; I've come to fetch you now, and make fetiche of you."

"Oh! me am lost for ever, general; he want me—I must go; look at de fire coming out of him mouth, him nose, him eyes, him ears, him hair—him every part of him blessed boddies. Oh, I must go wid de ghost!"

In fact, Buttons had so besmeared himself with phosporous, that he presented a most ghastly spectacle.

The terror of the two niggers was extreme, and Buttons began to think he had gone far enough with the joke.

"You want me, fetiche," began Jingo in trembling tones; "I'm comin'. Good-bye, gin'ral, good-bye; you neber see poor Jingo no more. He kill de child ob de great spirit—great spirit want

him, so Jingo him time hab come. Oh, Lor'! he going, like me, into de other world."

Buttons began to be alarmed.

Jingo rose in his bed.

He jumped out.

"Stop!" cried Buttons; "do not move, or you will go where—hem!—you wouldn't like to go to; stay, murderer!"

Jingo paused.

"De debel, jin'ral, he won't hab me now; he want you," said Jingo.

"Oh, let him hab you, Jingo, den I'll be safe. You go way wid him, me go to sleep."

And the general disappeared under the straw and left Jingo to his fate.

"I think they have had enough of it," thought Buttons now. "Well, I'll try a different move. Jingo Johnson, go back and lie down."

Jingo, with teeth chattering and dismal countenance, was too frightened to understand.

"Yes, I come forth, great spirit; cos I kill you in de wood. I'm here. Take me, wool and all. Yah! here me am. Yah, yah! Jingo going to t'other world, long wid de gree-gree."

He jumped out of bed.

Buttons drew aside to let him pass, when Jingo, with his head down, rushed forward to the entrance of the tent.

But here an unexpected obstacle presented itself to Jingo which he little expected.

The Stinger, whose curiosity had been greatly excited by the movements of the strange figure, had crept gradually towards the entrance of the tent, and at the moment when Jingo was rushing forth, head downwards, the Stinger incautiously placed herself in his way.

The result was that head met head with terrific force, and, as a natural consequence, then came the tug of war.

The Stinger was brought to the ground, and Jingo was thrown on his back.

"Hullo! where are you going to after nearly knocking my head off?" shrieked the Stinger, at the top of her voice.

"To the debel," replied Jingo. "Oh, let me go; he am after me. I shall neber get rid ob him. Ask him take you instead of me, or let me go."

"Let you go? Not if I know it," cried the Stinger.

And seizing him by the hair, she began to tug him about right and left.

In the meantime the general kept under his bed, and Buttons saw his opportunity to escape from Jingo's tent.

He rushed forward in hopes of passing Miss Stinger without further observation, but in his hurry some of the fetiche ornaments he wore fell off.

"Here's a pretty go. Well, I'll have to give in now!" he muttered.

The Stinger caught sight of him.

"Now we'll explore this mystery. I'm at you," she cried, rushing at Buttons.

"Don't, Nosie, don't. He am the debel from the other side of de water. Where de gen'ral? Oh, he hab already taken him."

In spite of these warnings on Jingo's part the Stinger grasped Buttons by the hair of his head, and made the ghastly charms ring again.

"Now then, no nonsense. Come, look alive, who and what are you?" said the Stinger, giving the spectre a shake.

"Booh!" said Buttons, "you'll shake my head off."

This remark made the general writhe beneath his bedclothes and Jingo jump a foot from the ground.

"I'm not to be played with, hark you," said the Stinger, again.

"Oh, don't, you'll shake me all to bits. I'm Buttons—your Buttons, Stinger."

Jingo opened his mouth.

"Who?" he gasped.

"Why, it is Buttons," said the Stinger. "He has been having a game with you, and I have got him now. Come here, you young rascal."

Jingo stood with mouth wide open for a moment.

"Oh, Lor', he am not de gree-gree. Yah, yah, me gib him something."

With that, Jingo Johnson's face changed considerably, and going up to Buttons, he shook his fist in his face.

"Dere now, you do dat 'gain, Massa Buttons, you dare do dat again, and I punch you. De gree-gree—he, he! I

don't care for de gree-gree; dat for de gree-gree!"

And Jingo snapped his fingers with great scorn. The Stinger let Buttons go.

"Hold him—hold him, missie. Here, you 'fernal cuss—wake up, you gen'ral, wot hab not got spirit ob mouse; me hab you out, gen'ral."

He rushed at him, and pulled him forcibly from under the bed.

"Oh!" groaned the general, "he hab me now, he hab me by de collar-bone of de middle of my foot."

"Me got you; wake up, you nigger!" cried Jingo.

"De debel! Oh, where am me now?"

"Here, me got de gree-gree. Open your eyes. De debel am alive oh! like a monkey, and he am Buttons."

The general opened his eyes.

"Look," said Jingo, "dere him am."

"Who am he, Jing?"

"Buttons."

"Den, by the soul ob the boots ob General Orlando, me will settle him. Where is my sword? Me am afraid ob nothing; me scorn to tell a lie."

The general, without more to-do, put on his cocked hat, and seizing his sword, he drew it from its battered sheath and rushed at poor Buttons, shouting—

"Me cut him head off."

"Oh, Elizabeth Ann, save me from their vengeance, save me," cried Buttons. "The brutes will kill me."

"Hold!" cried the Stinger, standing before them. "Hold! you must not hurt him."

"But he was gree-gree, and he hab de debel in him. He am bewitched to 'witch us," said Jingo, savagely.

"Eh, he wanted de bravest warrior in de world," said the general, flourishing his sword vigorously, close to Jingo's head. "He wanted to take us off where dere was much smoke and no air"

"Where was that?" asked Buttons.

"To de oder world," replied the general, hoarsely.

"I didn't mean to hurt you."

"Come up, no palaver, gen'ral. We'll hab ourselves back out of him. He hab boned our mortal souls; him got um in him own body."

"I haven't. You don't wear boots, do you?" said Buttons, with a grin.

"We don't mean dat dere, we mean the souls in our bussums, not the soles ob our feets. You'se got 'em, massa, and we means to hab 'em back again."

"Right you are, and so you shall take them in the name of the gree-gree. I give them back to you."

With that, Buttons, with a vigorous thrust, knocked Jingo over, and then butting his head down, he planted it comfortably in the very pit of the general's stomach.

"So much for you two niggers. I don't think you will want any more, for you have got back your immortal souls, and I hope you will be able to digest them."

With a loud laugh he rushed away to his own tent.

"Golly, gen'ral, hab you got your soul back in de middle of your body?" asked Jingo.

"Me hab," replied that doughty warrior, as soon as he could recover his lost breath. "Me hab got it here."

"So hab me. Now den, I'm not 'fraid of any more debels. Me 'fraid nebber. Me knew it was 'fernal Buttons all de time up to him debel's tricks."

"Oh, Jingo," said the Stinger, laughing at him.

"True, missie, me always speak truff."

"Fact," said the general, "me scorn to tell a lie."

"Now, both of you know it is a fib; but no matter, you have got back what you wanted."

"What's dat, missie?"

"Your immortal souls."

"We hab—we hab indeed; we feel it, but we want something more, don't we, general?" said Jingo, with a cunning leer.

"What is that?" asked the Stinger.

"De lub ob de lubly Stinger, eh, gen'ral?"

"Dat's it."

"Then look here, you two darkeys," said the Stinger, solemnly. If ever you trouble me with that nonsense again, I'll pay you both out. Me, E. A. S., to be insulted by the proposals of a couple of darkeys, when I have had offers of marriage from some of the noblest in the land, in fact from a member of the royal family? Faugh!"

The Stinger was rather prone to stretch the long bow, when descanting upon her aristocratic lovers.

In fact, it was an amiable weakness of hers, and as we all have our failings, we must make allowance for this one in the Stinger's otherwise truthful character.

The two niggers looked at each other as the Stinger walked proudly away.

"Do you hear dat, gen'ral?"

"Me do, and me knows she scorns to tell a lie."

"She won't have nufin to do wid us. Bless my soul, de ladies that hab such bery lubly nosie, am de proudest of de proud; but now to bed; me am sleepy, but if any more gree-gree come, me smash him."

"So will I," cried the general, "for I scorn to tell a lie."

The two niggers were not disturbed during the remainder of the night.

CHAPTER XLV.

BOB MEETS WITH SOME FURTHER ADVENTURES, IN WHICH HIS FRIENDS AND ALLIES HELP TO MAKE BOTH ENDS MEET.

BOB arose from his couch with a light heart.

"I have captured pretty Nahita," he said, "and now I am determined to rout out the whole of that villanous band. First, Howard, and then King Pluto, for I am certain they have entrapped my friend Longsight."

These words he addressed to his usual confidants, the doctor and Stumps.

" When shall we be off then ?" asked Stumps.

"This morning. I feel a new man. We must beat them ; I say we must, because we have the will."

Bob walked up and down the front of his tent, arranging his plans.

Presently King Aga came up to him.

The king was clad in a long, flowing white robe, which suited him admirably.

His tall and robust figure was erect now, for he had his daughter by his side, who blushingly acknowledged our hero's gay salute, and then ran up to him and kissed his hand.

"The ladies don't do that in my country, Nahita ; the gentlemen always kiss the hands of the ladies."

And Bob kissed her hand, at which action Nahita opened her beautiful eyes in great surprise.

"That's how we do it," said Bob.

"How nice," she replied, naively.

Bob laughed.

"You will see more of that kind of thing when you come to Cape Coast."

"I have been there. I was born there. My mother was the sister of the white men."

"I thought so," said Bob, delightedly. "You are very beautiful."

This unexpected remark made Nahita blush again, although Bob was perfectly sincere, for it was the truth without a particle of flattery.

"Now, King Aga, are we ready to start ? Halloa, there, Tom ! Pipe all hands together."

"Right, your honor, right. Now, then, clear out, all of you."

Old Tom blew his whistle, which the darkeys knew well, and quickly the tents were struck, the baggage packed, and every man belonging to the baggage carriers took up his burden.

"Now, Ironfist, if we can only get these fellows to fight well, we shall gain a victory. Do you answer for the bravery of your chiefs and men, King Aga ?"

"Yes, they will fight when I lead them, but not without."

"Then you shall be present to encourage them ; but let them stick to the baggage, whilst we advance with a few followers to scour the forest."

King Aga agreed to this.

"But Nahita ?" said Bob to the king.

"She never leaves my side again, or she would fall into the clutches of that villain ; but I knew he did not dare to hurt a hair of her, or——"

"You would have roasted him over a slow fire," said Bob.

"I would ; but let us get on."

"Hurrah ! Come my brave followers, away for more adventures."

And Bob set the example by going on ahead with Ironfist.

They had, during the past few days, made considerable progress into the interior of the country.

Bob now made a *detour*, so as to come round towards King Aga's village— although they were some thirty miles away from it—and thus he hoped to encompass King Pluto, and catch him in a net, if possible.

Bob stalked on ahead with Ironfist, whilst Swiftfoot was sent to scout as usual, and Buttons, Stumps, the Stinger, Jingo, and the general formed another separate body, the others bringing up the rear.

Owing to the narrow, and often tortuous progress they made, Buttons and the others were compelled to make their way through the forest as best they could.

"I'm jolly happy, Stinger," cried Buttons, when several thorny plants had thrice deprived him of his well-beloved head gear.

"So you ought to be," said the Stinger, "for you have given two mortals their two immortal souls, and that is more than many can say."

"Dat's it, missie, dat's it. But look up, there comes Massa Blunt ; me run meet him."

"Hurrah !" cried Buttons joyfully ; "see who gets first to our noble master."

Away went Buttons and the niggers.

So excited were they to reach our hero that they did not notice anything in their way.

But suddenly they were brought to a standstill.

"Hold !" cried Buttons, beneath his breath. "What was that ?"

" Don't know," replied Jingo. " What am it ?"

They stood still and listened.

A terrific noise proceeded from behind the rock, on which another part of a thick jungle bordered.

In turning a point they had taken the wrong road, and had lost sight of Bob.

" Oh, Lor'," said Buttons, " what a dreadful noise. We had better return ; there is something I don't like going on behind that rock."

" What ?" gasped Jingo.

" It may be the dead fetiche," said Buttons.

This was enough.

The two darkeys vented their fear in a hollow groan, and trembled all over.

" Oh, here comes the Stinger ; let's get behind her."

The roaring continued, so they did not venture to come forth.

In the meantime Bob Blunt and Ironfist had also come upon the plain, but on the opposite side of the rock to which the Stinger and Buttons were.

They too heard the sound proceeding from the depths of the forest.

" What is it, Ironfist ?" asked Bob, pausing with his rifle ready to be brought to his shoulder in a moment.

" It's a fight between some wild beasts ; you stay here, Mr. Blunt, and I'll make a *détour*, and see whether I can get a shot at them."

Ironfist accordingly plunged into the depths of the forest.

Bob crouched down and waited patiently to see the result of the noise.

He had not long to wait.

The roaring noise he knew could only proceed from a lion.

Presently there rushed from the forest a huge rhinoceros, covered with blood, pursued by an immense lion.

Bob saw that they were engaged upon a mortal combat and therefore watched the battle with great interest.

The lion, as soon as the rhinoceros had its back turned, leaped at it, and placed its fangs in the fleshy part of the huge beast's belly.

It uttered a piercing cry of agony, and turned again.

The lion sprang back.

The rhinoceros lowered its head, and rushed at his enemy with intense rage, tearing up the ground, and trying to gore the lion with his huge horn.

" Now," thought Bob, " comes the tug of war. Lion against rhinoceros."

The immense bulk of the rhinoceros could not vie with the graceful agility of the king of the forest.

His tusk was buried deep into the ground, and before it could recover itself, the lion sprang at its vulnerable part beneath the throat.

The roars of both animals were now terrible to hear.

The combat continued for some time, until the rhinoceros lay quite still, only the froth and smoke from its nostrils proclaiming that it was yet alive.

The lion stood lashing its tail and glaring at it, and then with a loud roar of triumph, he leaped upon the back of his foe with the proud consciousness of victory, and shaking his tawny mane, he raised his head erect in the air.

Bob thought he had never seen a grander scene than this.

But suddenly the lion ceased his motion, and stood perfectly quiet on the back of the rhinoceros as if in the attitude of listening.

Bob saw that he scented danger.

" He is conscious of somebody's presence, perhaps Ironfist's," thought Bob.

But of a sudden he caught sight of Buttons, the general, and Jingo creeping along, all unconscious of their near proximity to the king of the forest.

They, thinking now that all was quiet, the danger was past, were approaching within reach of the wild beasts.

The Stinger had remained hiding behind a large rock, and the low rocks hid the lion from the others' view, as they continued to advance.

Bob saw that they would walk right into the lion's mouth if they were not warned of their danger.

So he arose and crept up toward the lion, and then when he knew that his friends could see him he waved his hand to them to go back.

But in vain.

Buttons thought he beckoned them on, and not seeing the lion did not pause.

He came in a line with the rock, and then his terrified look proclaimed that he had caught sight of the lion standing proudly on the body of his now prostrate enemy.

"Oh, Lord, a lion, a lion!" gasped Buttons.

"Where am it, massa?" asked Jingo.

"Oh, he'll have some of us. Look," groaned Buttons again, his knees knocking together.

A look was enough.

No sooner had the general and Jingo caught sight of the brute than they turned tail and fled, the general falling over his sword and losing his cocked hat.

Poor Buttons went sprawling into a prickly bush, shouting—

"Save me, master, save me! The lion looks dreadfully hungry ; fire, fire, at the beast."

The lion was now evidently aware of the presence of a human foe.

He gave a loud roar and so did Buttons.

Bob saw Ironfist looking through the brushwood, and he raised his hand to fire.

Bang!

The ball struck the lion, breaking his leg, and he rolled over in agony.

But his roars proclaimed that he was not dead, so Bob crept up further, and then taking careful aim, he fired, and his shot crashed close to the lion's skull.

"Hurrah!" cried Bob, rushing forward. "Victory! We've got him. Up with you, brave Buttons."

Ironfist came from his ambush.

"A good shot, sir."

"All right ; it was a narrow squeak for poor Buttons. Halloa! Come on—all safe now—he's dead."

Buttons rose up out of the bush, and the others when they heard Bob's call at once came and joined him.

"Oh, Buttons, what a fine meal this chap would have had off you," said Bob, pointing to the lion.

"Yes ; but if he had swallowed me, he might not have found the pride of my life —I mean my fine hat—so easy of digestion—halloa!"

This last cry was called forth by the lion suddenly rising to his feet.

Away went the niggers again with Stinger, who had just ventured out of her hiding place.

The general again fell flat upon his face, for his sword was the cause of this mishap.

Bob saw the lion was not dead.

He raised his revolver and fired.

"This time there is no mistake," he said, as the lion fell back.

"And neither shall there be with the other," responded Ironfist, shooting the rhinoceros in the ear, for he saw that the brute was not dead.

"Is all safe?" asked Buttons, after he had heard the two shots fired.

"Safe as houses," said Bob ; "now come on ; we have have had a glorious triumph, and here we will camp till the rest of our chums come up."

Bob sat down.

It was not long ere the doctor, who had as usual been in pursuit of butterflies and beetles, came up, and presently King Aga and the rest of his warriors.

"Now then, we have got a feast in store for us. Look, O king, this is a token that we shall be victorious."

The astonishment of the natives was great when they saw this new feat of Bob's, done as it appeared miraculously.

They looked at the dead lion, then at the rhinoceros, and raised their hands in wonder and delight.

Bob resolved now to encamp during the mid-day meal—on the spot, and so afford time for the doctor to skin the lion —for our hero was bent upon bearing these trophies to England with him.

The camp was soon formed, and then the little army sat down to repose.

All save Swiftfoot.

He alone had gone off to see whether he could glean any intelligence of the enemy or Longsight, and Bob resolved to await his return before he again ventured upon the track.

CHAPTER XLVI.

AT LAST.

IT was sunset before Swiftfoot returned from his expedition.

He was heated and tired.

Bob let him rest and refresh himself before asking him any questions.

When Swiftfoot felt somewhat restored all gathered round him.

"Well," said Bob, "what news?"

"Pretty good, and pretty bad."

"That is very dubious," replied Bob; "but out with it."

"Well, I went to King Pluto's town, fortress, or village, whatever he may call it, and I saw——"

"Pluto?" asked Buttons, hastily.

"Don't interrupt," said Bob.

"And I saw that this was only an outlying post of King Pluto's domains, and a queer looking place it is. It lies in a hole and is strongly fortified with palisades. As for Pluto, he was not to be seen, but I watched Howard and his factotum, Bow-legged-Bill, away from the village; they went shooting."

"In what direction?" inquired Bob, very eagerly.

"East from this point."

"Why, they must come this way."

"Perhaps so, but very possibly not," replied Swiftfoot; "but you have not heard all yet. They went away from King Pluto's camp because there is some devilry breeding there."

"How?"

"Listen, I slunk up close to the town, and lay concealed as Howard and Bill passed me. From the few words that I could glean of their conversation, I divined that they desired to be out of the way whilst certain proceedings of King Pluto were about to be perpetrated."

"Their words, man; speak!" cried Bob, looking troubled.

These were the words—

"Let him do it, never mind how; we will be out of the way; his death is nothing to us, and I only hope they will serve Bob Blunt the infernal the same. It would put me into a good many thousand a year. The young scoundrel has thwarted me long enough.'"

"Were those his words?"

"To a letter."

"Enough—go on, go on."

"I then took full stock of what was going on in the town, and I saw that the dusky warriors were painting their bodies, sharpening their weapons, and the women were singing songs of triumph."

"What does it mean?"

"That they are going to torture and kill some one," replied Swiftfoot slowly.

"Who?" asked Bob, with trembling lips.

"That I can't say."

"Ah, do you think it is Longsight?" cried Bob suddenly.

"Yes, it may be."

"May be," cried Bob, "it must be, I tell you; there is no time to be lost, we must be off. Oh, up, men, up, and let's away at once to the rescue of our friend."

"The preparations will take until to-morrow. I heard Howard say so."

"Thank God for that; we thus gain time to mature our plans. We will, however, haste on towards Pluto's village at once, for we must be in the immediate neighbourhood, but silently and secretly, or all will be in vain."

The news that Swiftfoot had brought electrified all present.

Every one vowed vengeance against the dastardly King Pluto.

Arms were furbished up, and every preparation made for a battle.

And Bob saw that a battle was imminent, and he was determined to risk all to save his faithful servant Longsight.

* * * * *

It was evening before his camp broke up, and silently, under the guidance of

Swiftfoot, proceeded in the direction of King Pluto's village.

Night in an African forest is not particularly pleasant, for the roar of the jackals and wild beasts far and near is not conducive to sleep.

But on this particular occasion the mellow moon lighted them on their way, and the glare of the torches the natives carried served to keep the wild beasts at a pretty respectable distance.

"I think we do look a weird and fantastic procession," said Bob to the doctor, looking back upon the long line of natives stalking darkly through the forest.

"Yes, I should like to make a sketch of it," said the doctor, "and send it to the Boys of England."

They had now been gone some hours on the journey till at last Swiftfoot, who had been much in advance, returned.

"Well?" asked Bob.

"Good news; we are within half a mile of the camp—all is still there," said Swiftfoot.

"Then we will pitch our tents for the night," said Bob.

A suitable spot was selected, sentinels were posted, and the tired warriors retired to rest for the night.

All save Bob.

He alone was awake.

He could not sleep, so he sat in front of his tent for a time, and the night being very beautiful he resolved to go and explore the ground around King Pluto's village in order to expedite the attack for the morrow.

Slinging his rifle over his shoulder he wandered on through the forest, nor did he observe a slight figure, so absorbed was he in his own thoughts, gliding after him.

At last the grandeur of the scenery attracted his attention.

The ground suddenly arose to an altitude of fifty feet, until he reached the summit of a chain of rocks.

Here he stood for a moment entranced, his finely-built form standing out clear against the moonlight.

But he swiftly knelt down in case he might be perceived.

The view that he beheld was sublime.

It was like a scene in fairyland.

Bob watched it for a time, then continued his way down a rocky path that led from the side of a chasm.

He had not gone far before a scream struck upon his ears.

He stood and listened.

Again it was repeated.

Bob saw no one in sight, but he instantly rushed in the direction from whence the sound came.

He had not gone far when at an angle of a rock he beheld a young girl struggling with two men.

He recognised them.

It was Howard and Bow-legged Bill.

The girl was Nahita.

Bob rushed forward and confronted them with fierce determination.

"Villains!" he cried, "unhand the girl. It is I, Bob Blunt, who command you, your foe to the death. Unhand the girl, I say!"

And Bob Blunt rushed towards them, sword in hand.

CHAPTER XLVII.

THE FIGHT.

THE astonishment betrayed by the two arch villains as Bob Blunt so suddenly confronted them, deprived them for the time of all power of action.

They released Nahita.

"Now—come on," cried Bob. "I will protect this girl with my life."

And without more to-do he rushed at Howard and dealt him a violent blow in the face.

Howard rolled back.

The blood streamed from his face.

"All right, guv'nor, don't you be afeard. I worn't called Boxing Billy for nothin'—not I. However, look out for squalls, for you shall have 'em. Pepper's the order of the day, and I'll give it you, Bob Blunt."

"Oh, very well, come on; you'll find me ready for fighting," said Bob, coolly, for his rage had somewhat subsided.

Bow-legged Bill came on in all the full consciousness of his burly strength.

Bob saw that if he allowed the brute to close with him it would be pretty well all up with him.

So he resolved to keep him off as long as he could.

Howard was not able to rise from the ground.

Nahita watched the fight with great anxiety behind a rock.

Bow-legged Bill came on to the attack with confidence.

He presumed his would be an easy victory, so he did not take much care; but he reckoned without his host.

Bob saw him come and lunged at him jeeringly, and before he could well say how it happened, Bow-legged Bill was upon the ground by the side of Howard.

"Number one," said Bob "Number two; take it and may it agree with you."

Bow-legged Bill again fell back.

"Now, my young baccy-stopper, you shall have it as hot as ginger."

And Bill rose from the ground.

He gathered himself together for a last grand effort.

Crash, crash!

Bob rained a shower of blows upon him that made him roar again.

Bill's face was covered with blood, which he vainly tried to staunch.

He reeled like a drunken man.

"Have you had enough?"

"Nearly; but the bulldog's in me yet."

"Then you'll want a little more taken out of you."

Bob did not give him time to rally.

He rushed at him, and with two vigorous blows he stretched Bow-legged Bill at his length upon the ground.

"I've got it now!" he cried, shielding his face with his arm, yet with all the dogged stolidity peculiar to his country and especially to the genus London rough.

Bob turned away from him without saying a word, but before he could pick up his rifle Howard rushed at him and dealt him a vindictive blow in the chest that made him stagger back.

"Ha! I have you now; you shall not escape this time. I'll have your life."

Bob did not reply.

He drew a deep breath, and then with a bound like a young tiger, he sprang at Howard and seized him by the throat.

"Now, you rascal, I have you," said Bob, shaking him by the throat until he could hardly breathe.

Howard struggled desperately, but Bob held him hard, until Howard, by a sudden writhe, released himself and then grappled with our hero.

Bob did not despair of victory.

He remembered Strongback.

"Yes; I think I know the trick he taught me," he muttered.

Then, suddenly exerting all his strength, Bob gave his foe a back throw over his leg with great skill.

Howard came to the ground with such force, that he lay quite still for some few seconds after.

"Now I have done it," said Bob, gazing at his prostrate foe.

"No, not yet," cried Howard, suddenly rising, and drawing his knife, he rushed again at our hero, who avoided the blow by springing aside with great agility, so that Howard, missing his aim, rolled over on to his face.

"Curse it!" he exclaimed. "Why did we leave our fire-arms at the fire? 'Twas the girl's fault—Bill, help!"

But Bow-legged Bill was slinking off as hard as he could.

Bob saw him in time, and knowing he had gone in search of the fire-arms, our hero drew his revolver, and taking careful aim, fired at Bill.

A cry was the result.

Bow-legged Bill placed his two hands down on his left knee, and sank to the ground.

"I've hit him!" cried Bob. "Now

for the future you shall not only be known as Bow-legged Bill, but also as Lame-legged Bill. I think I shall know my work again."

Howard had seen the effect of the shot, and as Bob turned, he made a sudden rush over the side of the hill, and disappeared with incredible swiftness into the dark recesses of the forest.

Bob looked after him for a moment, then he laughed to himself—

"Well, I have given them pepper this time, at any rate. I have the satisfaction of making them cut it. Two of them—ha, ha! licked by one, but—"

A sudden thought struck him.

"But if I had only made them prisoners. They will inform King Pluto of our arrival here, and then——"

He rushed away in the direction that Bow-legged or Lame-legged Bill had taken, and when he came to the spot, that worthy was nowhere to be seen.

"Gone!" cried Bob; "but I will be even with their cunning—I will place my sentinels all round King Pluto's village, so as to prevent the possibility of their having any communication with the king, and informing him that we are here."

With this resolve, he retraced his steps, and was hastening back to his own camp when a soft and gentle hand was placed upon his shoulder.

Bob started.

"Nahita!" he exclaimed. "Ah! I had forgotten you for a moment."

"You have saved my life—you have been my protector once more."

"Why, what on earth made you come out this time of the night?" said Bob.

"To see you."

"Why?"

"Because—because——"

She did not complete the sentence, for she burst into a flood of tears and hid her face in her hands.

"Why, Nahita, what is it? Have I offended you?" said Bob, tenderly, for he could not account for this outburst on Nahita's part.

"You offended me?" she cried, looking at him reproachfully.

"Then, what is it?"

"Nothing. Come, we will return to the camp; my father may miss me."

Bob said no more.

He did not care to fathom her secret at the present time.

They reached the camp in safety.

Bob at once sent off a detachment of men under Ironfist's guidance, to see that Howard and Bow-legged Bill did not enter King Pluto's village.

He briefly narrated what had occurred, and thus making sure that no communication could pass between the enemy, he retired to rest.

But over and over again he thought of the strange emotion Nahita had displayed when he had addressed her.

"Pshaw!" muttered Bob, as he threw himself down on his bed, "it is only gratitude and nothing more. She is grateful for my saving her from Pluto, that is all; it cannot be love."

Little did Bob dream that it was love for himself that had caused Nahita's emotion.

CHAPTER XLVIII.

AN ATTACK OF BILE—ANTS ALIVE OH!—"I'M NOT IN A GOOD TEMPER!—MIND YOUR HEAD"—THE STINGER, PUT OUT, RESOLVES TO PUT ALL OUT WHO COME IN HER WAY.

NEXT morning the lively Buttons strolled down the temporary encampment whistling "Rule Britannia" with all his strength of lungs.

A deep mist arose all around and shrouded the tents as in a deep veil.

"I wonder how the lovely Betsy is this morning," thought Buttons; "this place is not half so lively as I thought. Now a little musical entertainment would do the Stinger good."

Buttons crept up to the Stinger's tent and began to sing—

"Oh, my Buffalo gal, are you coming out to-night?"

"Drat you! I hear you," cried Miss Stinger from within.

"Do you? Oh, very well, I'll sing away, and gladden your poor little heart shall I?"

And Buttons continued to sing away until his attention was suddenly called to Bob Blunt's monkey, Molly Bawn.

"Now, then, for it, come here, Molly."

The ape grinned, and came as soon as Buttons held out a biscuit to her.

He then took her and thrust her into the Stinger's tent.

Peeping through the entrance, he beheld the Stinger taking her hair out of curl papers before a small looking-glass.

The monkey with a bound jumped on to her shoulders and began to scratch her head with his claws.

"Go it, Molly," cried Buttons.

"Oh, the brute," yelled the Stinger.

The monkey held on.

At last the Stinger knocked the animal off, which at once leaped into her hammock, and stood chattering at her.

"I'll give it you, you brute," cried the Stinger, now foaming with rage.

Seizing her umbrella, she dashed it down with great force on the hammock, and the ape, seeing this, leaped down on the other side—and made her escape through the folds of the tent.

"I've got the old girl's pecker up now," thought Buttons, "she won't be long before she is out, and I'll make her dance."

The Stinger finished her toilet with great haste, breathing vengeance dire.

Buttons saw her sit down on a camp stool and search for her never failing consoler—the bottle.

She drew it forth.

It was empty.

"Oh, I'm so unwell, and not a drain. I'm sure I left some in the bottle last night, but no doubt some of those niggers have been at it."

The Stinger arose, and taking her umbrella, she left the tent, determined to procure a stimulant in order to correct the acidity under which she laboured.

But as she passed out a leg was suddenly thrust out in front of her.

She did not perceive it, and in consequence came to the ground with a thud.

Up she got again, but with the leg clutched tightly which brought Buttons to the ground.

No mercy did he receive.

The Stinger banged him until he roared for pardon.

"I'll teach you to taunt me when I'm bilious," she cried.

"Oh, Jingo—general, come and help me!" shrieked Buttons, catching sight of the two darkies, who were laughing heartily at him.

"You do if you dare," said the Stinger. "I'm not in a good temper this morning —I'm bilious. It rises; and woe betide anyone that interferes with E. A. Stinger."

Buttons struggled desperately to free himself.

But in vain.

The darkies seeing the state of affairs grinned at each other.

"De rum, Jingo, out of de old gal's pocket."

"Yes, jin'ral."

Jingo, with a desperate movement possessed himself of the Stinger's bottle only to find it empty.

"You black pickpockets," shrieked the Stinger, now perfectly furious; "you villains, to do that before my very nose! Drop it at once."

Taking her umbrella she floored the general with it, and then followed up Jingo, whose chagrin was so great on finding the bottle empty that he stood with it in his hand—the picture of woe.

"Mind your head," cried Buttons to Jingo.

The warning was too late.

A back-handed blow from the Stinger fell with no light weight on the nigger's skull.

"Oh, my poor head!" cried Jingo.

"Oh, I am killed," moaned the general.

"Oh, my poor head, how it aches and throbs," cried the Stinger. "I'm ill,

I'm bilious ; I shall be very ill if—if you don't instantly run and fetch me a drop of brandy."

"Look here, E. A. S.," cried Buttons, "you don't love us ; but we'll return good for evil. Run, Bombast, and procure a drop of cratur for our poor, dear old Betsy ; she's got the hiccups."

Away went the general.

He was not long before he returned with a bottle, but very little brandy in it.

"You rascal," shouted Stinger, "you have been drinking nearly all my medicine."

"Well, I call that too bad of you, Stinger, to put the bottle away in your pocket."

"It ain't good for little boys and niggers," she added.

"No, only good for niggers and lubly ladies," said Jingo.

The Stinger grinned.

She continued to rub her chest with her hand, when she suddenly started up with a loud scream.

"Holloa! what's up now?" asked Buttons.

The Stinger did not reply, but danced about and shook her petticoats.

"What is it?" continued Buttons, wondering whether the Stinger made these fantastic dances for their amusement or not.

"Where did I sit?" she gasped. "I'm alive—they're creeping about me, I'm sure of it ; there they go."

"What is it?"

"They creep—creep—creep, oh! they bite, bite, bite."

The Stinger danced about with greater energy than before.

"Oh, me know," cried Jingo ; "de lubly missie hab been a sitting down on a ants' nest."

"What ?" yelled the Stinger.

"Ants."

She looked at her feet, and there sure enough were thousands of ants, in fact completely hiding the whiteness of poor Stinger's stockings.

"Oh, Betsy, you have got them now ; I hope you like them," said Buttons, walking round her on his hands with his feet in the air.

"Take 'm off me," yelled Stinger ; "they're biting me to death. Oh! they're up my back. Help !"

"All alive, alive oh !" laughed Buttons ; "we'll cure her. Here, run Jingo ; fetch a pail of water."

Away went the niggers.

They soon returned with the water.

"Now, Elizabeth, my dear, stand still."

Buttons took a drinking cup, whilst Jingo held the pail, and poured the water down the Stinger's back.

"She stands it like a lamb," said Buttons.

In truth the Stinger was so irritated, that the water was a welcome relief.

But when the irritation the ants caused her had subsided, she felt the chill.

She cuffed Buttons right and left, sent Jingo and the general flying from her, then cried out—

"Now, I'm put out. I'm off for a walk ; I'll circulate my blood, and impart fresh vigour to my impaired liver. May you all have the bile as bad as I have, and get covered all over with ants. Begone !"

With this parting anathema, the Stinger clutched her umbrella, took a good pull at the bottle, and disappeared at a rapid pace into the neighbouring forest.

"HE CAUGHT UP A HEAVY CLUB, AND BROUGHT IT ROUND WITH GREAT FORCE."

CHAPTER XLIX.

THE STINGER'S NEW LOVER—HER TERROR AND ABDUCTION—HER LOVER'S LOVE, AND HER LOVER'S FOE—UP A TREE—A TIMELY INTERFERENCE—"HOW ARE YOU NOW?"—BUTTONS FORGIVES AND FORGETS—THE BILE IS SETTLED.

"WELL, I'm blest; I never saw the lovely Betsy in a greater tiff before in my life—shall we go after her?" asked Buttons.

Jingo shook his head.

He rubbed his cheek-bone.

"Had enough of it, Jingo? Halloa, here's Mr. Blunt."

"Well, Buttons, what's up this morning?" asked Bob.

"Oh, the very deuce, sir. The Stinger's got the bile."

"Indeed!"

"And then she took some brandy neat."

"Of course."

"And I gave her some cold water down her back."

"You did? I don't think she would thank you for that."

"She did, though."

"How was that?"

"Why, she took it into her head——"

"The water?"

"No, sir. She took it into her head to sit down on an ants' nest."

"Oh, Jupiter!"

"And they swarmed over her. I cured her by pouring the water down her back to drown the ants. She took it very kindly, and now she's gone to hang herself out to dry," said Buttons.

"I expect, Master Buttons, you have been playing your tricks upon the poor Stinger. Where's she gone to now?"

"Into the forest, sir."

"What, alone?"

"Yes, sir."

"She must not go," said Bob. "The enemies' scouts may be out, and then it may happen to her like it did to poor Longsight. Lead the way, Buttons, in the direction she went."

Accordingly our hero and his friend, with the two darkies followed the footsteps of the Stinger.

For a long time they could see or hear nothing of her.

But they had not proceeded a mile before a loud scream startled them all.

But they could not see the Stinger.

"Some one has got hold of her," cried Bob. "Come on; we must save her."

Away they went.

As soon as they came to a bend in the forest, they beheld the Stinger some thirty yards ahead of them, and facing her an enormous gorilla, chattering and gesticulating with his arms, that swung round like the huge sails of a windmill.

The Stinger screamed again lustily, and tried to ward the gorilla off by shaking her umbrella at him.

"By Heaven! he will kill her," cried Bob, clutching his rifle.

"No," said the doctor. "Look, he is coaxing her to him."

They paused to watch the proceedings of the gorilla.

"Let us creep close up to the brute; we shall manage to get a shot at him, perhaps," said Bob, "and save the Stinger."

As cautiously and silently as they advanced towards the gorilla, still he heard them.

He stood in a listening attitude, and then caught sight of them.

With a savage cry he grasped the terrified Stinger in his arms, and rushed away through the forest with her.

"The brute has got her. On, men; let us rescue poor Stinger from that monster."

Bob rushed forward.

"Who would have dreamed of a gorilla taking a fancy to poor old Stinger?" said Bob, to the doctor.

"She has one lover the more," replied the doctor, with a grin.

"And one whose affection may be

dearly purchased," said Bob. " But we will protect her with our lives."

They accordingly continued their way through the forest.

But the gorilla and his prey were long since out of sight.

Elizabeth Ann in the meantime retained her presence of mind enough not to swoon away, although her position was one of extreme danger.

The gorilla carried her with the greatest imaginable ease, and as tenderly as a child.

At length he paused.

He looked round.

No pursuers were in sight.

This satisfied him.

He bore the Stinger to the foot of a large tree, whose massive trunk had grown so that it formed a regular arch, and it was easy of ascent.

The Stinger, finding herself at liberty, stood looking at the gorilla, expecting every moment to be attacked by him.

But to her surprise the immense brute did not harm her.

On the contrary he forced her down and then sat down beside her.

His huge arm was round her waist, and he rubbed his hairy face against her own with great gentleness.

"Oh, Lor'! my nerves. Where's woman's rights now?" she groaned.

"B-r-r!" jabbered the gorilla, very coaxingly to her.

"The beast is making love to me, I declare," muttered the Stinger. "Oh, I should like to knock his head off with my umbrella."

Seeing she did not return his affectionate attention the gorilla ran rapidly up a tree and brought her down a large water-melon which he offered to her.

The Stinger took it with trembling hands.

This appeared to please him.

But poor Stinger was anxiously looking round for a place of escape.

No opening, however, presented itself to her confounded senses.

The gorilla, seeing she did not eat the melon, as he presumed she would, became impatient.

He ran away again and returned with a handful of nuts.

During his absence this time the Stinger took to her heels and ran.

When the gorilla returned and found her gone his rage knew no bounds, and he looked everywhere for her.

At last he espied her and with a bound of great agility he was soon by her side, and seized her in his powerful arms and bore her back to the tree.

"Oh, Lor'! I'm lost—I'm run away with by a gorilla! Oh, it's dreadfully awful! Oh, farewell to woman's rights!"

Thus the poor Stinger lamented her hard fate, whilst the gorilla tried everything to persuade her to eat.

But the Stinger was past eating.

She rejected all his offers.

Then the gorilla appeared to be at his wits' ends.

Suddenly he caught hold of a long, tough creeping plant, and before the Stinger well knew what he was about to do she found herself fastened to the tree.

Then the gorilla grinned a ghastly grin and sped rapidly away.

In about three minutes' time he returned with two very large cocoa-nuts.

He stripped the outer fibres off.

Then taking the nut, he cracked it close to the Stinger's head.

When the cocoa-nut was divided he placed half of it with the milk in it close to the Stinger's lips.

This she drank greedily.

It appeared to please him.

He gave her the other nut to drink from, breaking it in the same way, and when she had drunk the milk he rushed away again.

At this moment the Stinger caught sight of Bob Blunt's white helmet gleaming in the distance.

The sight nerved her to action.

With a desperate effort she broke the rope that held her, and before the gorilla had time to return she mounted the tree and crawled along the thickest branches and hid herself amongst the foliage as well as she could.

When the gorilla returned and found his prey gone his rage knew no bounds for the moment.

He tore up the ground.

He gnashed his teeth, and uttered the

most horrible cries it was possible to imagine.

The Stinger, in fear and trembling, hid amidst the boughs in hopes that he would not perceive her.

But alas, his keen instinct made him examine the tree.

He espied her.

With a great cry he followed her, and as she lay at length on the bough of the tree, he could reach up to her easily, which he did.

He seized her by the wrist.

The Stinger seized her umbrella, frantically shouting—

"Help, help! E. A. S. is in great trouble. Help!" for she had seen Bob Blunt and her other friends not far away.

The gorilla when he had her once more in his grasp grinned up in her face, and did not relax his hold on her hand.

Bob Blunt had seen all that had passed between the Stinger and the gorilla.

When he saw that the Stinger had climbed the tree in safety, and the gorilla was alone beneath it, he raised his rifle.

"Now, I've got a clean shot at the beast, and I think I can manage him."

Bob was about to fire when the doctor held his arms.

"Stop! don't fire. What do you see there facing the gorilla?" he asked.

Bob paused.

"See?" he cried. "Why, good Heaven, it's a boa-constrictor!"

"Oh, golly, golly!" cried Jingo, dancing about in great excitement. "We all better run away."

"Look, look! the gorilla's foe is at his throat. It's a case of death for him," cried the doctor.

This was, in fact, the case.

The gorilla was about to pull the Stinger down into his arms, when from a rocky hollow the flat head and gleaming eyes of a boa appeared.

The boa happened to be very hungry, and therefore unwound his coils with great rapidity.

Its folds went round the gorilla's body, and its deadly fangs were pointed at its throat.

The Stinger received this new arrival with dread, but felt somewhat relieved when the gorilla released her wrist to grapple with his foe.

With his long and sinewy hands he seized the boa round the neck, uttering at first quick short sobs, and then piercing cries of rage, which ended in a ferocious growl of intense rage and fear.

The boa, although it felt the pressure of the gorilla's muscular hands, continued to wind its coils round the body of its foe.

But it was easy to see who would be the victor.

The gorilla held on vigorously, and then the Stinger could see that its grasp was losing its terrific power.

In the meantime Bob Blunt had crept on to watch the result of this very strange combat.

They kept perfectly quiet.

Suddenly, when the boa had nearly twined its full length round the gorilla's body, the latter relaxed his hold with a cry.

All could hear his bones crack as the boa squeezed him tightly.

Then the boa stuck his teeth into the gorilla's throat.

He was dead.

The Stinger breathed a sigh of relief when she saw the end of her strange and importunate lover.

"Dead! hurrah! the Stinger's free, and I wish all mankind that pesters me was served the same way as the gorilla," she exclaimed.

Then the boa slowly unwound its coils, and opening its huge maw began to devour the gorilla head first.

It was a curious sight to see the huge gorilla disappear into the boa's maw, and then when it had devoured him, lie down to digest its meal.

"All right now," cried the Stinger. "My ugly lover has disappeared for ever. Hurrah!"

"Hurrah!" cried a voice, in close proximity to her. "Hurrah! your Buttons is here."

The Stinger easily retraced her steps along the bough of the tree.

"Well, how are you? How is the bile, eh? All gone?" cried Buttons.

"All," gasped the Stinger; "all. Take

the bottle out of my pocket, Buttons, and hold it to my lips for a few moments."

Buttons complied.

"Oh, I'm dear, now, am I? All right, I'll forget and forgive; give your own Buttons a regular, downright, smacking whopper of a kiss, that's a tramp."

Buttons gave her a good hug.

"Oh, Mr. Blunt, here you are, sir; I'm nearly done for; it's awful. I'm not to have any peace it seems."

"Yes, you are, Stinger; you're a brave one, and deserve—why ninety-nine women out of a hundred would have gone into hysterics—you deserve a medal," said Bob.

"She does," they all cried.

"Hysterics!" said Betsy. "I scorn the idea; it's first rate, A 1 fun; I'll put it down in my diary. 'This day E. A. S. made a new conquest, and, thank God, saw the end of him,' which is more than I can always truthfully say."

"Right; now look here, you leave the Stinger alone for the future, do you, Buttons, Jingo, and Bombast," said Bob.

"Yes, sir," replied Buttons, winking knowingly at the Stinger and the darkies.

"Yes, massa, we'll neber, no—no more, will we, Jingo?" said the general.

"Neber no more," echoed Jingo.

"Till the next time," chimed in Buttons.

"Well, that's decided then; now I'm going to kill the boa."

Bob took a hatchet from Stumps.

The boa lay perfectly still.

It was in fact incapable.

The huge bulk of the gorilla could be distinctly seen in its belly.

Bob took a hatchet, and going up to its head, whilst Ironfist went to its tail, he gave the word—

"Strike!"

Simultaneously two strokes severed the head and the tail.

The boa was dead.

But the headless and tailless part writhed and reared as much as in life.

The natives skinned the boa, and brought it to the camp, where it was cooked, although none of the white men could be brought to partake of it.

The Stinger was completely cured of the bile.

She was highly elated.

"I am the only one of our company who has ever been loved and carried away by a gorilla, so drink to the health of Betsy Stinger, three times three, altogether."

The reader may be sure that her health was drunk with enthusiasm by all, and the Stinger retired to rest happy.

CHAPTER L.

TORTURE—TWO IN ONE TO THE RESCUE.

IN the meantime poor Longsight had been pining in his fetid underground dungeon.

He could hear repeated noises about him that told him that there was some unwonted stir in the camp of his enemies.

The cords with which he was bound chafed his wrists and ankles, and not once had they been removed since his capture.

In consequence his limbs were so stiff with constantly being kept in one place that poor Longsight nearly fainted with agony.

On the morning of the third day after his confinement, Longsight was aroused by an unusual scuffling of feet above him.

The trap was removed, several niggers descended, and with little ceremony,

Longsight was hauled into broad day-light.

Twelve strong niggers, all hideously painted, stood before him.

One of them had possessed himself of Longsight's green umbrella, his green hat, spectacles, and coat.

"The black devil," he muttered. "I should like to have my hands at liberty for half an hour; I'd soon make him drop my umbrella."

The niggers now untied Longsight.

As soon as the chords were loosened, Longsight tried to move his arms and legs.

But all power had left them.

The niggers tried to make him walk, but all his efforts were fruitless.

They were then compelled to allow him to lie down and chafe his limbs.

In a short time circulation returned, and then Longsight was able to walk.

They led him out into the open.

Here an extraordinary sight met him, for all round the open circle of the shanties stood ranged about one hundred and fifty men, and more than two hundred women and children.

When Longsight appeared, a cry of triumph arose from all.

The tom-toms beat, horns were blown, and the hubbub grew deafening.

What did it all mean?

Longsight wondered greatly, when suddenly his eyes met those of King Pluto.

The fierce chief was gorgeously clad and seated upon a throne, around which were crowded his principal warriors.

"Bring up the white prisoner!" cried the king in stentorian tones.

His command was instantly obeyed.

Longsight continued as calm as before.

He stood with folded arms, and returned the fierce looks that met him on all sides with one of haughty disdain.

"Know, thou serpent of the white face," began Pluto, "thou reptile slave of the white king, thy days are numbered? Dost see yon stake?"

Longsight turned, and saw a long stake planted in the ground.

It was very sharp at the top, and well he knew the death he was about to suffer.

Impalement!

Horrible torture; slow and agonising did Longsight know it to be.

Yet he flinched not.

He knew all eyes were upon him.

King Pluto watched him, and seeing no sign of emotion upon the implacable face of his destined victim, he could not repress a glance of admiration at his courage.

"Dost thou not fear?" he asked.

"No; a man can but die once."

"Yes; but if that death is long and protracted?"

"Then it is very difficult to die; but a brave man will make up his mind to it."

"We shall see," replied the king with a sinister smile.

Longsight was taken some dozen yards from him, and then a score of niggers, stripped, and hideously painted, began to approach him.

They were armed with long bamboos, the points of which had spears fine as pointed nails.

Longsight shuddered.

Longsight knew that these spears meant preliminary tortures to him, and he looked in vain for any sign of a rescue.

He breathed a prayer, and then he was commanded to mount the trunk of a tree, some four feet in height, and over twenty in diameter.

When on the summit, he could look over the palisades on to the country beyond.

But no signs of his friends could he see.

Then the negroes began to walk around him.

At first slowly, uttering low and discordant sounds, until gradually their pace increased, their voices were raised louder and louder, the spears were hurled in the air and caught in the crowd, hurled back again, and then pointed at the prisoner.

Longsight stood on the trunk of the tree, his arms folded, his head sunk upon his breast, and his attitude that of a man completely resigned to his fate.

He heeded not the motions of the demons before him, till suddenly he felt something prick him in the side, and this made him tremble violently.

It was the point of a spear, and blood dropped from the wound.

The air was now rent with the ferocious shouts of the men and women assembled.

Their cries were deafening, but Longsight relapsed into the same attitude of stolid indifference to all around.

Suddenly a silence fell upon the assembly.

The torturers paused in their frantic dance, and then all were as silent as previously they were noisy.

Longsight looked down.

The king and his warriors stood spellbound, glancing towards the entrance of the town, where a strange sight arrested their attention.

A gleam of intelligence shot into Longsight's eyes, as he beheld a figure, ten feet in height, slowly and solemnly approaching in the direction of the king's throne.

The face of this huge person disclosed to Longsight the familiar countenance of the renowned dwarf Stumps.

He was hideously painted, and wore around his brow a number of little bells fastened to a golden ring, and from the centre of which arose a human skull, the eyes of which were of red glass, and emitted a ghastly glare in the sunshine.

He was clad in a loosely flowing robe, that nearly reached to the ground.

In one hand he held a long, hollow rod, and in the other his trombone.

Without looking at Longsight, he advanced towards the king.

He blew his trombone, and then the women and children fled into their houses.

King Pluto had gazed at this terrible apparition with mixed awe and wonder.

"What is it?" he gasped at length, falling back upon his chair of state, and capsizing the sturdy warrior who held his umbrella over him.

"I am the great medicine man and all-powerful gree-gree of the mighty white king," said Stumps, again blowing another tremendous blast.

"What would you?" asked the king.

"Listen, and I will tell you. Be not afraid, for I shall not harm you if you take my advice ; but if you do not hear-ken to me, I can speak words of fire to consume you and your warriors."

These bold words awed the king.

He looked at the gigantic figure before him, and trembled.

"He must, indeed, be a powerful magician who can so suddenly raise his stature six feet," thought the king.

Then aloud—

"Great gree-gree, I am attentive. What would you of me ?"

"You must deliver up to me your captive," said Stumps.

A gleam of mistrust passed over the king's face, but quickly suppressing his emotion, he said—"And why ?"

"Because he is my victim ; he has bewitched the great white king's friend."

"Is that true ?"

"The feticheer of the whites never lies," replied Stumps proudly.

"Show me your power first."

"Easily ; what would you have ?"

Stumps looked around, and saw that a number of the frightened warriors had gained courage, and were looking at him.

"Look, O king !" he continued. "I will strike fire from the earth if you will it, but beware of the result."

The king trembled.

"Show me," he cried, his curiosity getting the better of his discretion.

Stumps walked away for some distance, and then waved his rod.

All the warriors made room for him.

Then Stumps drew from his wide sleeve what appeared to be a round ball.

He took care that none of the blacks perceived him.

Then suddenly launching out his arm, he cast the ball some distance from him.

In an instant there was a loud explosion, and a stream of fire leaped up from the ground.

"There is my power," cried Stumps, as he beheld not only the warriors running away, but also King Pluto, whose throne was overturned in the scuffle, and whose gorgeous umbrella was flying before the wind ; for all the savages were too frightened to look behind.

"I have done it now," cried Stumps, looking after the retreating darkies ; "Longsight, my boy, you are safe—safe as houses !"

Longsight jumped from the tree trunk, and ran towards Stumps.

"You're a Briton ; you're my saviour. Who the deuce is underneath you ?" cried Longsight.

"Hush ! it's me—Ironfist," whispered that stalwart giant from beneath the robe.

"Yes, it's Ironfist ; he's made a giant of me," cried Stumps. "Halloa, they're coming back again ! Hold tight, old man."

In truth King Pluto, having got over his first alarm, was returning towards the great white feticheer.

"Run, Longsight, for your life, to the entrance, and tell Mr. Blunt the state of affairs. He is without. Leave me to settle with three-fingered Pluto."

Longsight took the hint.

Away he went.

As soon as King Pluto saw him running, his suspicions were aroused.

Seizing a spear, he rushed forward.

Stumps faced him.

King Pluto came on, and was in the act of hurling his spear at the gigantic dwarf, when Stumps let him have another fire ball right in front of him.

The explosion caused the king to retreat, and then Ironfist set off at a gallop in Longsight's wake.

King Pluto, calling to his warriors, started in pursuit.

He was furious at losing his intended victim, and heedless of all, rushed forward, burning with revenge.

He reached the palisade.

In another moment he would be within reach of the fugitives.

He was in the act of passing through the palisade, when he looked up on each side of the entrance, and beheld the two sentinels he had posted there lying stiff and stark at their posts.

He recoiled when he beheld this.

When he lifted his eyes again in the direction, the mighty feticheer had disappeared, and he beheld in his stead the proud and dauntless form of Bob Blunt.

CHAPTER LI.

THE BATTLE.

KING PLUTO recoiled.

"We meet at last again," said Bob Blunt ; "and now we will decide our differences !"

King Pluto still stood spellbound as Bob uttered these words.

Then suddenly seeing Bob about to attack him, and realising his position, he rushed back into his town, uttering a wild cry of alarm.

In an instant Bob followed.

He gave a view hallo, and then there appeared behind a crowd of dusky faces.

King Pluto turned and saw them.

"Betrayed !" he cried. "Up, arm, arm— the accursed white chief is upon us !"

This cry was immediately responded to by his followers, for the women and children sought shelter, whilst the men crowded together round the king's house, ready to meet the foe.

In the meantime Bob Blunt collected his followers, and set sentinels to watch the movements of the enemy.

When this was done, he assembled his own followers around him.

Longsight had had his wounds dressed by the doctor, and now came forth with King Pluto's state umbrella over him.

"They stole my clothes," he said ; "but that is nothing. I have a prize over me that will answer my purpose."

"Aye, Longsight, but you had a narrow squeak for it. If we had not kept Howard and his chum Lame-legged Bill away from the town, I don't think we should have been able to rescue you alive

They would have seen through the trick, and then, old fellow——"

"Exactly—a bullet would have been my speedy end; but bless you, Stumps, my boy. Give us your fin."

The robes were taken from Stumps, and then he leaped from Ironfist's shoulders to receive the thanks of the grateful Longsight, and then he subsided into the background to escape further thanks.

Bob now directed his attention to the town, and saw that King Pluto had encamped at the further end of it.

"We must smoke them out," he cried, "and now for it.

"How?" asked the doctor.

"We will fire the town at this end, and I reckon it will not be long before the fire spreads round."

"At once, then."

A lighted torch of the palm-oil tree soon set alight to the thatch of the shanties on each side of the entrance.

African villages being mostly built in a circle, with a stout palisading running round them, the fire at once spread from house to house.

King Pluto saw that he would be encircled by the flames if he did not escape at once.

Accordingly he broke down the palisade, and beat a retreat towards the rear of the burning town.

Bob saw his drift.

He marshalled his little army and prepared them to fight.

"Now, my king," said Bob to Aga, "we must fight these fierce warriors, for depend upon it, they will give us battle. We are outnumbered, and it will be a tough job."

"We shall conquer them by the aid of the Great Spirit," replied King Aga, solemnly raising his hands above.

A sudden idea struck Bob.

"What if Stumps again mounts on Ironfist's shoulders? It will intimidate the enemy more that anything else."

Ironfist objected.

"Think, sir; I shall be powerless to fight if you smother me up again in that robe. I don't like it; besides, I will fight any six niggers, but I must be free."

"So you shall be; here you, general and Jingo, come on—one of you will do as well—you shall carry Stumps," said Bob.

The niggers cut wry faces.

They evidently did not like the ordeal.

"What, you will not?" cried Bob.

"No, massa," said the general.

"Why, what are you afraid of?"

"Ob de debil."

"You fool!" said Bob; "and you, Jingo?"

"Ob de same gen'man; me 'fraid of de debil same as dat nigger."

"Well, you are a couple of noodles."

"We am," they replied.

"Now, look here; if you don't obey me," said Bob, sternly, "I will have you put in irons. Which of you will volunteer to carry Stumps? One of you must."

The niggers were silent.

Each looked at the other, as much as to say—

"You go; there's a good chap."

"Well, I will decide the matter at once. Here, Buttons, give me two of those rushes, and he who draws the longest one of the two shall carry Stumps."

Button handed the rushes to his master, and then Bob shortened one, and held them in his closed hand.

"Now, general, draw first."

Seeing there was no help for it, the general advanced and tried to look up Bob's sleeve where the ends of the rushes were hid.

He hesitated for a time, and then put his two fingers upon the rushes very much as if he were handling the fangs of a deadly serpent.

"Is it right?" said Bob.

"No, massa, me not like dat one; no, de oder."

"Very well, take it."

The general took hold of it and pulled it slowly forth.

It was not a very long one, so he cried—

"Oh, golly, it am me!"

"Here, Jingo, take yours."

Jingo, with a disconsolate face, drew the remaining rush.

"Now, who is the man?"

The darkies now measured the lengths of their respective rushes.

"Oh, golly, Jingo, it am you dat go to de debil!"

Jingo looked despairingly at our hero, but Bob ordered him to take Stumps upon his shoulders at once.

With great reluctance on Jingo's part, he obeyed, and Stumps was soon elevated again to his proud position.

Bob ordered him to the rear, where he could yet be seen by the foe.

"Now, we are prepared. The ladies to the rear, and then on."

"Indeed, I won't," said the Stinger, stoutly. "It isn't fair, Mr. Blunt, to wish to have all the glory. Elizabeth Ann is quite as capable of taking care of herself—aye, and of fighting too—as any of those greasy niggers."

"No doubt; but you will take care of the king's daughter in the rear, won't you?" said Bob, coaxingly.

To this the Stinger consented.

"But remember, if you require help, E. A. S. is ready to 'Present—Fire!'"

With this she swung her rifle over her shoulder and retired, according to orders.

"Now, lads, away!"

Bob took the lead.

The town was now one mass of fire, and rapidly were the shanties disappearing from the ground.

On the brow of a gentle hill Bob saw that Pluto had secured his position.

"We will rout him out. I will charge with the centre line; you, Ironfist, the right wing, and the king with the left."

The lines were formed, and Bob gave the caution not to charge until he gave the signal to do so.

"And whatever you do, Ironfist, keep back your darkies until the signal is given. They are impetuous, and nothing but coolness will enable us to win the battle, for our numbers are small."

"Right, sir."

"Now then, lads, ready; open fire."

A shower of arrows was first sent at the enemy.

Then the rifles played pretty heavily upon them.

Bob saw that he could dislodge Pluto from his position by rockets, so the doctor threw a number of shells into their midst, which, when they burst, caused indescribable confusion and alarm, not only to the enemy, but also to the friendly darkies.

They could not make it out to see fire balls mount to the skies, and then explode with such force.

This served to strengthen King Aga's confidence in our hero.

King Pluto's position was critical.

He resolved to continue the attack on the enemy at all hazards.

So Bob saw him start with a wild roar down the hill, followed by his troops, thirsting for blood.

"Now then!" cried Bob; "they are upon us."

The main body charged first, and then the left and right wings.

A terrific hand-to-hand fight ensued, for both sides were like demons in the fray.

Bob did not spare himself.

He singled out Pluto.

The stalwart king fought as if possessed by a devil.

Bob faced him.

"Come on, demon!" he cried. "You shall not have another chance, if I can help it."

The king was armed with his heavy sword, but our hero also was well armed.

They fought desperately for a time, when there was a cry behind him—

"Ah, look out, sir! Fire!"

A shot was discharged over Bob's shoulder, and he saw a foe fall.

"Thank you, Buttons," said Bob, for he saw the man had been in the act of striking him with his sword.

Buttons had saved his life.

King Pluto was in a very critical situation.

Inch by inch Bob fought his way, until they gained the brow of the hill.

Then Pluto made a last desperate stand for his life.

Bob cheered on his men.

King Aga now joined him.

On seeing Pluto before him, his rage knew no bounds.

He rushed at him.

But twenty of Pluto's followers rushed between them, and though Bob fought with desperate fury, they managed to carry Pluto off.

King Aga fell back with blood flowing, but Bob, hoping to make Pluto a prisoner, followed up the retreating enemy.

He got nearer to Pluto.

Taking his revolver for the first time from his belt, he fired six shots in quick succession.

To each of his shots a man fell.

The others, speechless with terror, took to their heels.

King Pluto was about to do the same, when Bob called on him to stay, or he would fire.

They were now on the brow of the hill, and on the one side was a ravine nearly hidden by thick shrubs and creeping plants.

Bob could hear the waters rushing beneath him.

King Pluto, seeing that our hero's followers had branched off to the left in hot pursuit of his flying warriors, looked about for a place of escape.

But Bob stood in his way.

"Hold, mad demon; now I have you," cried Bob, seizing his enemy by the throat.

The fierce eyes of the king nearly darted out of his head as Bob seized him.

His sword dropped.

Bob did not relax his hold, but called loudly on his followers to assist him in securing the king alive.

But no one was near.

Pluto—by far the stronger of the two in a prolonged struggle—saw that he might yet kill Bob.

And releasing himself by a dexterous movement, he struck our hero in the breast, who rolled backwards.

Pluto stooped down to recover his sword, to strike our hero, when to his astonishment he could not see him.

He looked around.

"Gone!" he cried, "magic is around me."

Turning up his eyes with horror, he turned away, and fled as hard as he could down the hill.

CHAPTER LIL

THE PYTHON.

ONE horrified looker-on had seen our hero fall through the thicket, and disappear into the ravine.

This was Buttons.

He was just coming towards our hero when he fell.

He had heard his cry for help, and then, when he beheld his fall, rushed forward.

He knelt down, but could see nothing of his master.

"Oh, he is killed! I have lost him!" cried Buttons, wringing his hands.

He was peering over the brushwood, when his foot slipped, and he fell head foremost through the opening.

Buttons, in a moment of agony, thought it was all up with him, when, to his surprise, he found himself in a cave, the opening of which looked down into the ravine.

When he had somewhat recovered his sudden shock, he laughed.

"Hurrah! we're safe. Mr. Blunt, sir! are you here?"

Buttons looked round.

It was a lofty cave, with a sanded bottom.

"Very dry this; let me see whether I can find any trace of my master."

Sure enough he found the imprint of a recent footstep.

"That's the ticket; now Buttons the traveller is himself again."

Buttons followed the footsteps as long as he could see.

The cave grew darker as he proceeded.

Innumerable bats flitted about overhead, and startled Buttons until he discovered the cause.

He had not proceeded far before he was suddenly seized by the arms.

"Stand!"

"Oh, Lor'!" said Buttons, gasping and thinking it was a nigger who had got hold of him; "let me go."

"Why, Buttons, my boy, I am Bob Blunt."

"Hurrah, sir! I'm glad I found you."

They passed on until they came to a small stream running through the cave.

This they crossed.

Buttons had just landed on the opposite side of the cave, when Bob saw two shining spots, that glistened like diamonds.

"Stop; we must see what this is."

Bob struck a light, and ignited the end of a wax candle which he carried in his tinder-box.

The small flame would hardly have afforded them means of seeing, had it not been for the many stalactites that frosted the sides and roof of the cavern.

But when he had advanced a few steps into the cave, he suddenly started back.

"Fly, Buttons, fly! It's a python curled up there, and the brute is slowly uncoiling itself."

Buttons stood spellbound.

"Keep steady," cried Bob; "do not move."

He then drew his revolver, and fired at the serpent.

Never would he forget as long as he lived the echoes that rang through the cavern on the report.

The bats, dislodged from their haunts, fluttered about, and heightened Buttons' terror.

And the python was slowly coming towards him, with his gleaming eyes.

"Run, Buttons!" cried Bob again. "Run for your life! my shot has not harmed the brute."

"I'm off, sir," said Buttons.

And away he went.

Bob fired again at the serpent, and this time he struck it in its mighty coils.

But he knew he had only wounded it, and not broken the vertebræ.

Bob then had to run for his life after Buttons.

But owing to the darkness, he could not go far before he stumbled and fell to the ground, right on the top of poor Buttons.

"Oh! he's got me!" groaned Buttons. "I know he has got me; I can feel his bite!"

"No it's me, Bob Blunt. Up and away again or it will be all over with us."

They started on again with greater difficulty than ever.

The serpent had now nearly extended the length of his coils.

They could hear its hisses behind them.

"Oh, we shall never find our way out of these caves—never see the daylight again; and to think that I'm going to die here, and never see the glorious halls of Blunt Castle again! Oh, sir, what shall we do? It's coming upon us."

"Quick," cried Bob. "I see a spot where we can creep to; don't hang fire. Buttons, my boy, be as brave as you were in the fight; don't shirk; remember we are brave sons of Old England, and duty and action are the words. Come on!"

Bob pulled Buttons along.

Of a sudden a gleam of light penetrated the cavern.

It was another bend of the small stream, and the light shone from a crevice in the rocks.

Bob quickly crossed it, dragging Buttons with him.

And no sooner had they reached the other side, than they beheld the serpent with its ghastly head erect, and protruding its forked tongue, dragging its now unfolded coils across the narrow stream. Bob drew his revolver.

Taking careful aim, he again fired.

This time the ball penetrated its extended jaws, and it fell dead.

Buttons sank down on his knees when he beheld the monster fall, with its head smashed, and lying a few yards from him.

But still the huge coil rose and fell, and quivered as in life.

"It's all right, Buttons," said Bob, "we are saved. That is about the best shot I ever made. I never saw such a brute before, and if I can manage to entice the doctor into this place, I'll make him skin that snake ; I rather fancy it will look well in the museum of Blunt Castle."

"Oh !" cried Buttons ; "I have had enough of serpents to last me a life time."

"Now," cried Bob, smiling at Buttons, "we will try and find an exit from these caves."

Bob and Buttons carefully reloaded the empty chambers of their revolvers, and then pushed on again.

The caves appeared to be illimitable.

Bob was very weary.

Not one of the caves led into the open, and the prospect before them began to look very dismal.

"Buttons, I don't half like it," said Bob at last.

"Neither do I, sir ; and we may run over some more snakes. I'm ready to drop."

"So am I."

They stood looking at each other in silence, when Bob handed his faithful retainer his brandy flask.

Each took a sip.

This revived them somewhat.

They had now travelled a long way from the serpent.

Bob sat down on a piece of rock lying at the side of the cave.

All at once he started up, and stood in a listening attitude.

"What is it, sir?" whispered Buttons.

"Hush ! did you not hear something ?" said Bob.

Buttons listened.

A low and indistinct murmur came from the distance.

"Buttons," said Bob, "that sound tells me we are not far from the presence of human beings, and I hope our voices have not travelled as distinctly as those we hear, for we might meet with enemies."

"Oh, dear, sir, this is very dreadful," said Buttons.

"It is life or death with us now, but we will follow that sound."

Without saying more, Bob led the way softly through the many winding caves.

"Don't speak to me," he said at length to Buttons ; "but do as I do."

Buttons nodded assent.

The sound of voices arose at last with greater clearness.

Bob, following the sound, crept slowly on.

At last he could hear two persons distinctly in what he supposed to be a neighbouring cave, and so creeping up to an opening between them, he lay down with Buttons, and looked over the edge of the rock.

Two persons were seated here before a fire and lying on their rugs.

"Silence," whispered Bob. "We have stumbled upon Master Dick Howard and his crony, Lame-legged Bill."

CHAPTER LIII.

BOB HEARS SOMETHING THAT MIGHT BE USEFUL TO HIM IN THE FUTURE—THE BURIAL PLACE OF KINGS.

BOB and Buttons crouched down and listened attentively to what was passing between the two worthies upon whom he had so unexpectedly stumbled.

"How's your knee now, Bill?" asked Howard, looking at his wounded companion, who was stretched at his length before the fire.

"It's a little better, but I shall walk

lame for life. Curse that cousin of yours! he has done it," growled Bill, savagely, shaking his fist.

"Never mind him now, we shall settle him in due time; but one thing I want now, and that's money."

"Well?"

"And we can get it—it's within our reach; we can get it."

Howard stretched out his hand as if already grasping the treasure.

"Where can we get it?" growled Bill. "I ain't seen much of it yet, though you did lure me over to this country with fine promises, yet not a brass farden have I seen; it's all gammon."

"No, it is not. Listen, we are within a dozen yards of King Pluto's burial ground, where his ancestors have all been buried. You must know it is the custom here to bury all the treasure with the king when he dies. Now why should we not have this treasure?"

"But we don't know where it is."

"We can soon find out."

"How?"

"There is only one priest that keeps watch over the mouldy remains of the kings. We will force him to tell us and——"

"And kill him when he has done so. No tales, you know."

"That's the ticket. I see you tumble to it now. Are you game?"

"I am."

"Then we'll do it."

"Now?"

"Now."

"I'll try to walk," said Bill, rising.

Howard assisted Bill to rise.

"Stay, we must be sure that Pluto has not returned, although I don't think it, for he is too busy in collecting his scattered forces, in order to make one last grand effort to vanquish his foes, in which I hope and trust he may be successful."

"I hope he will; but let us go and see what the swag is like."

Bill walked along pretty easily, after making a start, and soon disappeared with Howard from the cave.

The two watchers breathed hard.

"My eye! this is a caution," whispered Buttons. "Lord, what villains! Take care, sir, how you proceed."

"You watch me, and all will be well; but don't speak," said Bob.

The two crept on stealthily, passing the fire where Bill and Howard had formed their camp, and then entered a long, vaulted passage, at the bottom of which they beheld the two schemers disappearing.

Bob followed rapidly upon their footsteps; and at the end of the passage was what appeared to be a door, but on examination proved to be a large bamboo square, spliced together with the fibres of the cocoa-nut, and placed so as to block up the entrance.

Through the crevices of the bamboo, our hero and Buttons had a good sight of what was taking place within; and, as this place of mystery and death deserves describing, we will introduce the reader into its awful and dark interior.

It was a long and lofty hall, evidently a cave, but draped from top to bottom with numerous silk hangings of every glaring colour, and, to Bob's horror, many thousand human heads, festering and bloody, were placed around the sides of this charnel-house of King Pluto's.

In the centre was a large cauldron of brass filled with the blood of numerous victims, shed in order to propitiate the deities in favour of the deceased monarchs

Into this the priests dipped their hands when performing the human sacrifices, which were pretty frequent.

In many parts of the place were mounds of earth, all surrounded by human heads, and these, Bob thought, denoted the graves of the kings.

To complete the horrors of this ghastly place, some hundreds of ugly and shapeless idols lined the corners of the place, and all were smeared with blood, which, indeed, was the principal colour here, and the light from a lamp showed it up flaringly to the spectators.

Added to these outer horrors, the effluvium arising from the decaying human remains was sickening in the extreme.

Buttons and Bob were forced to revive themselves from their flask of brandy ere they could venture to look again at this horrible spectacle.

Howard and Bill fared no better.

They entered the place with evident trepidation, and looked around with anything but a confident mien.

At the end of the hall Bob saw an aged feticheer, almost bent double with his years, seated within a circle of skulls.

He was clad and adorned with all the horrible paraphernalia of his calling, and appeared quite at home amongst the glassy eyes of the dead around him.

Howard advanced towards this feticheer, and addressed some words to him, the purport of which the watchers could not hear, but could pretty well guess by the surprise depicted in the feticheer's countenance.

"I'll have your life if you don't !" cried Howard, so loud that Bob could hear him.

The old man arose in visible alarm.

He appeared to point to the seat beneath him as he arose.

"That's the place, Bill ; now for it," cried Howard to his confederate.

"I daren't," replied Bill, looking shudderingly around him.

"What! it must be done. It is within our grasp ; these dead heads won't eat us. Would you let such a prize escape you, coward ? We shall gain that which will make us rich for life."

"I dare not. Let's cut it," growled Bill

"Never !" hissed Howard. "I'm ready to do anything, and I shan't hesitate ; 'tis a case of fortune at a grasp. Now for the old man."

Before Bill could reply, Howard drew his revolver, and shot the aged feticheer through the heart.

The deed was done.

The echoes resounded through the caves for full five minutes, and were again and again repeated, and during that time Bob and Buttons took the opportunity to slip into the hall, and glide behind the hangings on the wall.

Through a slight rent in one of them they could still see what passed between Howard and Bill.

When the smoke had cleared away, Bill, with chattering teeth, said—

"You've done it now. Oh, it's awful, to do murder in this den of dead men's bones ; and if Pluto should come suddenly, and surprise us in the act of rifling his gold, eh, guv'nor, it would be all up with us."

"Curse you, he won't come ; here, help me to throw this body aside."

With heightened terror, Bill assisted Howard to drag the body to a distant part of the hall.

This done, they returned with a couple of rudely-fashioned spades, and began to dig at the spot the feticheer had indicated.

They soon turned the ground up, for it was soft sand.

After about half-an-hour's labour, Howard cried out exultingly—

"I told you so ; see here, gold, diamonds ! we have 'em."

"Fill yer pockets, guv'nor ; I'm all right now. Hurrah, won't I be a rich man when I get back to London !"

Bill scrambled a good deal of gold and a few diamonds into his pockets, and Howard did the same.

"We must have the lot," said Howard, eyeing the treasure greedily.

At this moment a hollow groan startled them, and made them pause in their efforts to secure the treasure.

"What was that ?" gasped Howard.

Bow-legged Bill looked around, and shook in every limb.

"Psha !" said Howard, it's only fancy ; go on, we must take all we can."

"I don't like it," said Bill, looking round at the skulls.

"Fool ! Come, pick up the gold."

Bill's avarice got the better of his fears.

He was in the act of stooping down, to assist Howard, when a second groan, more awful than the previous one, deprived him of all power.

"Oh, Lor' ! I thought I saw some of the heads move !" he gasped. "I can't stand this, it's awful ; come on, let's go ; his ghost there is speaking to us. "I'm off, guv'nor. Look at it."

He pointed to the body of the feticheer.

Even Howard was not proof against the ominous sound.

"BOB RESCUES NAHITA,'

"Stay, Bill. What is it?" he gasped.

"It ain't right—it——

A third groan came, deeper than before.

This was enough.

With a loud shout Bill dropped his gold and fairly took to his heels.

Howard was forced to follow ; and as soon as they were out of the charnel-house, Bob stepped from behind the hangings.

"Run, Buttons, follow them ; give them another groan," he whispered.

Buttons did run ; and, to his surprise, a narrow passage brought him at once into the open air.

He saw Howard and Bill running away as fast as they could.

He returned and informed Bob.

"We've done 'em, Buttons—we've done 'em. Lor'! and how frightened they were, the curs ; but let us hasten away from the tomb—faugh! I'm nearly dead with the stench. I think that Europeans should civilize this country—for this is a sight that even Dante could not have pictured in his vision."*

They hastened away into the open air, and inhaled it with such gusto, after the foul vapours, that Bob vowed it was the sweetest draught he had ever tasted in his life.

* Alluding to the "Inferno," which Dante beheld in a vision—and described, with Virgil as his guide.

CHAPTER LIV.

TWO WARRIORS—JOY IN THE CAMP—MAKING A NIGHT OF IT.

HA, HA,! that groan was as good as a fight, for it answered the same purpose, Buttons," said Bob, as soon as they were well away from King Pluto's family vault, as our hero aptly styled it.

"I should think so—just ; but had we not better go in search of our friends at once, sir?"

"Yes ; come on, Butt. I feel a new man. I am certain Howard and Bill took the opposite direction to that which we are about to take."

"As certain, sir, as that I have still got my old noddle on my shoulders ; which is a wonder, for on several memorable occasions I thought I had lost it for good."

"Well, you have got it still, so don't grumble ; we will be all right soon ; no doubt our friends will look out for us. But let us see where we are."

Bob took out his pocket compass.

He took the degrees, and then they continued their journey, keeping a keen look-out for any ambuscade that King Pluto might have laid in their way.

But they passed on without any molestation from either man or beast.

They travelled on in the direction of the camp for a couple of hours, and hoped to reach it before sunset.

As they passed on, Bob's attention was suddenly attracted by hearing a couple of voices exchanging high and angry words.

"Halt!" he whispered to Buttons ; "what is up here? Let us creep up to these fellows."

"I'm on, sir."

Bob made his way through the bushes, and then, when near enough, he discovered, to his surprise, the owners of the voices to be none other than Jingo Johnson and the redoubtable General Orlando Bombast.

But what could they be doing here all by themselves?

This query very naturally presented itself to Bob's mind.

His curiosity was soon set at rest, for there was no doubt but that the two niggers had come to an open rupture.

But for what reason?

Bob wondered greatly, but resolved to listen and watch their proceedings.

Accordingly he and Buttons lay snugly hid so that they could observe every movement of the two darkies without being seen themselves.

"Jingo," said the general, drawing his cavalry sword, " dis am de weepon ob de bravest warrior bold dat eber draw a African breff. Yah, yah! dat's as true as dat I have killed fifty lions and one hundred tigers. Yes, Jingo, it am true. I scorn to tell a lie."

Jingo eyed his opponent with great coolness, and then slowly walked round the clearing and measured it with his feet.

When he had performed this curious action, he turned upon Bombast.

"Gen'ral, I find room in dis yere cle'ring yere for yer body—twelve fut by futeen, dat's plenty big—you shall sleep wid de turf for yer nightshirt ; you shall neber interfere wid a gem'mun 'gin, and I shall run you trough de body twenty times and kill you—yah !"

Jingo paused, and tried to look fierce.

He then took up his sword, which had evidently been broken in half some years before, and fitted into a wooden handle, some two feet in length.

"Here am my weepon," he exclaimed.

"And here am mine, which will make you weep," responded the general.

Both began to sharpen their rusty "weepons," as they styled them, upon two oblong pieces of stone.

Then when this operation had been performed, they poised them with much elegance and saluted each other.

"Now, Massa Jingo, de cause ob de quarrel am dis, you am de 'griebed party."

"Me am ?"

"Cos Massa Blunt make you carry de gree-gree, Stumps, and me get off ; cos de lubly Nosie lub me better than you ; cos de bunderful head dat spoke de oracle said de best man ob us two should win de day wid Nosie ; cos we make up our minds to settle it on de fly—in quiet— by our two selbes, and nodin' besides but the buzzin' bees, de gollopshus monkeys, and de pratin' cockatoo—and dat's agreed ?"

"It am ; but dis I denies, de statement you made regarding the lubly Nosie ; for she lub me de best. I carry her fust in my arms to dese bressed shores. I kiss her little futs. I make de lump ob de lub to her fust, and I'm de bery 'dentical 'dividual wot means to stick by her too -—to de deaf !"

"You do, yar, do you—de droof is de droof—me am de man she lubs, and I scorn to tell a lie ; so come on."

And the general with three tremendous strides brought himself up to within an inch of Jingo's face, and raising himself on tip-toe, threw back his head with an ejaculation—

"Dare, me am to do battle on de man dat's dog's meat to gemblemen !"

Jingo raised himself still, and there they stood looking at each other steadfastly for a few minutes.

Bob had to smother his laughter as best he could, so greatly did the ludicrous actions of the darkies tickle him.

At last Jingo drew back.

"Come on," he cried, " to de deaf, to de deaf ; me not afraid."

"To de deaf," echoed the general ; " me not afraid neither."

Their swords crossed.

They were both in a lamentable state of ignorance in regard to fencing.

The general, in fact, more so than Jingo, for he could not wield the cavalry sabre half so well as his opponent could the sword-blade with the wooden handle, but it was evident to the on-lookers that each was afraid of the other.

Although there had been a good many feints, still neither took advantage of the other, but they kicked up the turf, they shouted and made most preposterous lunges, but never approached nearer than within about eight feet of each other.

At length, by accident, Jingo's sword struck his foe's with such terrific force on the hilt that the general dropped it as he would have done a red-hot coal, and putting his hands between his thighs for a second, he then thrust his fingers into his mouth.

"Oh, golly !" he cried ; " now, massa, dat am not fair ; you hit too hard."

Jingo gave a terrific roar.

He seized the general's sword, and thus doubly armed, he came on to the attack.

"Ha, ha!" he cried ; "I'm coming at you. Dead mans tell no tales, so down you goes, my frien'—down you go ; you neber see de lubly Stinger no more."

The general, seeing that Jingo was in earnest, took to his heels.

He ran round and round the circle, Jingo after him.

He dodged, then suddenly falling on his hands and knees before Jingo, the latter, before he saw the movement, came to the ground, the two swords burying themselves in the grass.

The general quickly drew his body away from Jingo, and falling on the latter's back, his sinewy fingers were soon twined round the nape of poor Jingo's neck.

"You 'fernal nig, now who am got de best ob de two? Who am de one de lubly Nosie lub de best? Speak, or by de bery bones ob de debil, you neber more see de glorious light of de sun !"

Poor Jingo groaned.

"You are de best, jin'ral."

"Me am? You tell the Stinger so."

"Yes."

"Me bery proud ; fine nigger."

"Yes ; you am de biggest nig dis side Cape Coast ; de strongest and de bravest."

"Enuf ; git up. I will let you libe little time longer."

The general released Jingo.

No sooner had he done so than Jingo arose with a bound, threw away the sword, and, clenching his fist, he dealt the general such a stinging blow on the nose that he measured his length on the ground, bleeding profusely.

"Now you am de smallest and de ugliest nigger, and I am de bery man of anybody."

"Oh, Jingo, to hit de best frien' you eber had like dat! Oh, Jingo, you know we're brudders—beloved ones! Oh, Jingo, it am too bad, to knock my nose nearly off."

Jingo looked mollified.

"Get up, jin'ral, me got an idear."

"Where?"

"In here."

Jingo tapped his forehead.

"Wall, now, what is it?"

"You cover yourself wid de blood, and we make believe dat we had terrible duel ; eh ?" said Jingo, with a leer.

"Tell Missie Stinger we fight wid swords, and lose all our blood."

"Yes."

"And Massa Blunt? Yah, yah !"

"Yes."

"And you mus' hab blood on you nose as well."

Jingo did not seem to see this.

"No ; me's de wictor."

"Pooh! no matter ; let me gib you a light tap on de sniffer."

"Don't hit hard, now."

"No."

"'Pon honour, as gembleman ?"

"Oh, me hit you soft ; me scorn to tell a lie."

"Hit, den, but soft."

"Bery good ; stand straight."

The general put on a very solemn face, and as he wiped the blood away with one hand, he went up to Jingo.

"Now, look, me hit softie ; dat don't hurt, do it ?"

He gave Jingo a gentle tap.

"No," responded Jingo.

"Dat very softie."

"Yes."

"And dat !"

The general suddenly lunged out, and hit Jingo on the nose with great force, so that he knocked him down flat on his back.

"Now, dare now, Jingo, why don't you stand up ?" said the general. "What for you fall down ?"

"Oh! you hab done it now," said Jingo, still on his back.

In fact the blood was flowing plentifully, and soon Jingo was as bad as the general, with face and chest as if they had been in the wars all day.

"Now it am right," said the general, consolingly ; "you hit me, I hit you ; your nose look big like mine now."

"Dat ain't kind, brudder."

"It am ; here, let me rub you blood over um little chest and belly."

The general sat down by his side, and rubbed the blood well over his face and stomach.

"Now we are brudders indeed, but de blood must be on de weepons."

"Course it must."

They picked up their swords and allowed the blood from their noses to drop on their blades.

It was a sublime sight to see them shoulder their weapons and then walk off arm-in-arm.

"Now we hab done it, Jingo; we're friends for life."

"We am."

"Now we'll go and tell de white folks a wonderful bundle of white lies, eh, Jing?"

"We will. Hurrah! hoop!"

And away they went arm-in-arm, with their swords across their shoulders.

As soon as they were out of sight, Bob and Buttons stepped forth.

"Well, I never saw anything to beat that; did you Buttons?"

"Never, upon my word, sir."

"It's as good as a pantomime. Up, Buttons: let's after them; we'll have some fun."

Laughingly they went in pursuit of the two darkeys.

They soon sighted them.

Arm-in-arm as before.

"Halloa!" cried Bob.

The niggers paused, and looked round.

At first they did not recognise Bob, but as soon as he came in sight, they set up a joyous shout.

"Hurrah! help! Massa Blunt am alibe!"

"How are you, niggers? Here we are, safe and sound. Holloa! have you been fighting?" asked Bob, as if surprised.

"We hab."

"Who with?"

"Duel," responded Jingo.

"Between you two?" asked Bob.

"Yes."

"What for?"

"Nosie," they replied.

"Hum! you are wounded."

"Drefful, Massa Blunt," they replied.

"Where?"

"Face, head and heart."

"Well, let us hasten on. The doctor will soon bind up your wounds."

Bob and Buttons managed to get a deal of amusement out of the niggers on their way, and they had a hard matter to restrain their mirth.

At last they reached the camp.

On their arrival Bob set up a wild holloa, and this brought everyone to the front.

The Stinger, Stumps, Ironfist, the rescued Longsight, the doctor, King Aga, and last and not least, his beautiful daughter, Nahita.

King Aga's heart was light, and as he wrung Bob's hands, and thanked him again and again, our hero knew that he had made a firm and fast friend.

"Now let us spend the evening pleasantly," said Bob, after shaking hands with all his old friends.

"We will!" they cried.

"What have you got for supper?—for I'm as hungry as a wolf."

"Baked elephant's foot; it's been in the embers these eight hours, and must be nearly done," said the Stinger.

"That's the ticket; it's a supper fit for a prince; let us have it soon."

"Right, Mr. Blunt, sir," said Old Tom, coming forward. "I've been attending to it. Happy to see you back again well and hearty, sir."

"Thank you, Tom, never better in my life; up with the supper."

The supper was served.

Fires were ignited all round the camp, and every preparation was made for thorough enjoyment.

That same evening our hero was seated in his tent, posting up his accounts, or, in other words, compiling from his pocket-book a complete list of the wild animals he had slain during his African travels.

Buttons was in attendance, packing up his master's portmanteau, and otherwise preparing for the return journey to the coast.

"Two lions, three elephants, one gorilla, two serpents, one hippopotamus," said Bob, reading from the note-book.

"Why, master, that's a good list."

"Yes, and there's a good list against your name, too, Buttons, though it does not quite come up to mine."

Now this speech considerably roused the ambition of Buttons, and he resolved to do something to distinguish himself before returning to the coast.

He could hear various wild animals howling round the camp, and when he had done all his master required of him, he resolved to go out and kill something.

He did not care to go alone, but chancing to see General Bombast strolling about the camp, he enlisted the services of that distinguished officer as a companion in his hunting expedition.

And off they started.

But it so chanced that Ironfist saw them depart.

"The idiots! They'll get into some fix if they are not careful, so I'll just watch," said the amateur boxer.

And catching up his rifle, he followed them.

Buttons and the general made their way towards some rocky ground a little distance from the camp.

"Golly! what's dat?" exclaimed the general suddenly.

A scream of harsh, discordant laughter was heard, and then another.

"It's that 'ere villain Howard," said Buttons. "I know there are none of our party out of the camp. Look out, general."

And the valorous Buttons thought that if he could kill or capture his master's scoundrel relative, it would be a fine addition to his game list.

Followed by the general, he climbed up a rock and peeped over a ledge.

He then found that the laughter came not from Howard or his bow-legged companion in iniquity, but from some hyenas that had crept out of a cave in the rocks, and were now howling, snarling, and laughing over some human bones that lay in front of the cave.

"I'll have one of them," said Buttons, as he prepared to fire.

But at that moment, Ironfist, creeping up softly behind, laid his hand on the general, who was waiting the signal to commence the attack.

This upset all their plans, as well as the chief actors in the scene.

The general, startled out of his wits, jumped forward against Buttons, who dropped his weapon and rolled over the rocks, the general following head foremost.

The hyenas were at first startled by this sudden descent of the foe; but they very soon set up their bristles, and showed every disposition to devour both Buttons and his friend.

The shouts of Buttons and the general were loud enough to alarm the distant camp, and Bob Blunt, with some of his friends, came out of their tents to see what was the matter.

Ironfist, however, was at hand, and seeing the danger they were in, raised his rifle. It was unloaded.

But without a moment's hesitation, the brave fellow jumped down and fell upon the beasts with the butt-end of his weapon.

One of the brutes had its thick skull crushed at the first blow.

Another sweep of the gun sent the second brute on its back kicking.

The third gave him some little trouble, but at length Ironfist quieted it.

"I've killed this one," said Buttons, in triumphant tones.

Ironfist looked round and laughed loudly.

Buttons had caught up the general's sabre, and had thrust it through the body of the second hyena.

"That's one to me!" he exclaimed, putting his foot on the body of the beast as it gave its expiring kick.

"Well, I'll admit you killed that one, Buttons," said Ironfist. "Get up, general."

General Bombast was raised to his feet, and seeing that the beasts were all slain, regained his valour.

"Now you had better come back to the camp," said Ironfist.

"All right, old pal." said Buttons. "Here, general, lend me a hand to carry this brute."

"What are you going to do with it?" asked Ironfist.

"Skin it and put it in my museum," replied Buttons, gravely.

Ironfist laughed as loudly as even the hyena had done, though in a more jovial manner.

"Well, Mr. Blunt is going to make a museum of the beasts he has killed, why shouldn't I?"

And accordingly the hyena was conveyed back to the camp, and its skin stripped off to dry before being stuffed.

That done, the trio sought their couches

CHAPTER LV.

KING AGA RECEIVES A FRIENDLY VISITOR—BOB BLUNT DELIGHTED—THEIR NEW
ALLY—THE GREAT HUNTING EXPEDITION ORGANISED—THE LAND OF THE WHITE
BULLS, AND OTHER MATTERS OF INTEREST.

ON the morning after the safe return of Bob Blunt, Buttons could not sleep very well, so he arose early and amused himself by giving his livery hat and coat a good brush.

When he had done this, and had a good wash, he resolved according to his usual custom, to take a stroll round the camp.

He did so, and was soon joined by Stumps, who appeared to have something upon his mind.

"Well, Stumps, how are you?" inquired Buttons.

"Queer, Buttons."

"How is that?"

"Well, I've had nasty thoughts entering my head about our dear master."

"What are they?"

"I fancy that something is about to happen to him that will not tend to our future comfort," said, Stumps solemnly.

"Bosh! If it's only fancy, I'm not afraid. I believe in the reality of everything. What is the use of fancies?"

"Oh, yes, it's all very well for you to talk; but I'm not so straight in body as you are, and, therefore, I am presumedly somewhat crooked in mind. And that makes me fancy things, you know, my friend."

Stumps looked sadly at his deformed shape; Buttons was silent.

In spite of his levity, Buttons respected the dwarf, and would not on any account hurt his feelings.

"Never mind, old friend Stumps," he said; "we are as God made us; therefore cheer up and keep your pecker up to the mark."

"I will, Buttons. But it's not for myself I care; it's for my master."

"So do I. But trust in Providence, Stumps. Holloa! what was that!"

They paused.

By this time they had walked some dozen lengths beyond the camp.

A slight rustling in the trees had attracted their attention,

In another second Buttons had caught sight of a tall chief, with a number of warriors at his back.

"The enemy!" cried Buttons.

"Can't be!"

"It is though," said Buttons. "Just look."

The boy pointed out what he had seen, and the dwarf was convinced.

Buttons and he set off for the camp at a great rate.

"The enemy, the enemy!" they cried.

The alarm at once spread.

Everyone rushed out armed and prepared for combat

"Where are they?" asked Bob.

"There," said Buttons, pointing in the direction of the forest.

"How many were there?"

"Thousands!" replied Bottons, whose terror had magnified them.

"Impossible! Pluto never could have collected his forces so rapidly."

"He has, though," said Buttons.

The whole camp had fled to the palisading ready to defend it to the death.

Bob Blunt and King Aga went to the entrance of the camp, each armed with his rifle.

Presently the sound of a horn was heard, then the form of a warrior familiar to both the chiefs appeared before them.

"No enemy," whispered King Aga to Bob as soon as he beheld them.

"I know him; it is, let me see, the chief we first met on our arrival in Africa," said Bob.

Such was the fact.

It was King Kalu.

Bob was delighted.

"He has come as a friend; I feel it," he cried.

With lowered spears the warriors advanced, and King Aga, with Bob, stepped forth to meet them.

Bob and his friends drew up in array, to meet the African monarch.

"King Aga," said King Kalu, advancing, "I hear thou art in sore need of help; I am come to offer thee all the assistance I can render thee."

"How, great king?"

"Listen. King Pluto has threatened me that if I move hand or foot in your behalf, he will burn my town and murder my people. Now, I don't fear his threats, and to prove that, I come and bid them defiance by offering to fight your battles with our great white chief."

"Hurrah!" cried Bob; "shout, boys, for the noble King Kalu."

"Hurrah!" they cried, with one voice.

King Kalu, with some twenty of his warriors, for he had left the main body of his warriors behind him, were invited to enter the camp.

King Aga ordered the best of everything to be placed before his guest.

King Kalu was placed in Aga's chair of state, and the time passed in mirth and feasting.

Stumps appeared to possess a great attraction for King Kalu.

The dwarf, according to our hero's request, performed many tricks, which had a marvellous effect upon the king.

His good humour was increased in consequence, and all good feeling and fellowship reigned between them.

* * * * *

Two days did King Kalu remain with his new allies.

On the third day, Bob Blunt and King Aga organised a great hunting expedition in honour of their guest.

Up they all got with great rejoicings, for now they did not fear Pluto.

Numerous beaters were sent out in advance.

When all was ready, King Kalu took Bob aside.

"You have not been to the black hill," he said; "if you wish to have good sport, let us thither."

"I'm agreeable."

"Then let us push on; I have my canoes with me—for you will have to go by river—and also to pass through some of my own and Pluto's territory.'

"We may have to fight, then?"

"No; we shall only cut off his hunting ground at a corner."

"So much the better; but I hope it will not be necessary for us to take all our men with us?"

"No, white chief; twenty will be sufficient," replied the king.

Bob was pleased at this, for he hoped to keep the camp as it was.

"But you'll take me with you, sir," said Buttons, gazing wistfully at Bob.

"Yes, you may come."

"And old E. A. S., the pride of Africa, the sunflower of your existence, is she not to go?"

"Of course; the more the merrier," said Bob, giving the Stinger a hearty shake of the hand.

Jingo and the general procured extra ammunition for the party, and away they started.

It was a bright and beautiful summer morning, as they wended their way from the camp towards the river.

Here several canoes were in waiting, by which King Kalu had arrived.

They entered them, and were soon speeding away down the river.

For some hours they continued their course without pausing, save when the overarching trees caused them to duck their heads to avoid knocking them.

At last they reached a lovely tract of country, with wide plains—green as English meadow land.

"This is the place for me," said Bob. "I like this; it's something like a place. Give me this for a hunting ground, and I'll rest perfectly satisfied. What game abounds here?"

"Game!" said King Kalu. "It abounds—lions, tigers, antelopes, monkeys, and last, not least, the lovely white bulls; they come down to these plains by thousands, as my mighty friend King Aga well knows."

"True," said Aga.

"Now, then; let us await the beaters. They must be here soon."

"They are here," said King Kalu, quietly; "they run as fast as we can row in the canoes."

"That'll do; then—ho—away!"

Bob gave the tally-ho in fine style,

much to the astonishment of the natives, and then the hunters set upon the game.

The first thing they started was a large lion.

The number of the enemy made him turn tail.

Our intrepid sportsmen gave chase.

Shot after shot was fired at the brute, till Bob had the good fortune to strike him in the head.

The lion rolled over.

Buttons and the Stinger rushed on ahead.

"Catch hold of his tail, Betsy. Hurrah!" cried Buttons.

Suddenly the brute arose to his feet with a loud roar.

"Lor'-a-mercy-me! he's alive," said E. A. S., falling back, and her umbrella being in the way, she measured her length on the ground,

"Oh! Mr. Blunt, sir, the lion; he's got hold of the Stinger!"

Bob dashed forward.

Before, however, he could reach the scene of action, the lion had placed his two paws upon the Stinger's chest.

It was a perilous position for the poor Stinger to be in.

The natives looked on terrified, expecting every moment she would be torn to pieces.

"Take courage, old lady!" said Bob, and rushing forward, he fired.

The shot was fatal.

The lion fell dead upon the Stinger.

They dragged her away from beneath the huge brute.

"My bottle!" she gasped, "my bottle."

Buttons searched for it, and finding it, he applied it to her lips.

"Oh, don't she like it?" cried Buttons. She soon rallied.

"Oh, I'm a poor lone woman. I'm always catching it hot. I think I had better go back to London," she moaned.

"Never mind, Betsy; better luck next time—halloa!" said Bob.

This last exclamation of Bob's was caused by the sudden appearance of a drove of bulls.

They came on in a compact mass, some hundred or so.

"Stand away, or they will be upon us."

The doctor knew the nature of the animals well.

"They are pursued by some lions, if I mistake not."

The doctor was right.

The bulls, splendid animals, came on at a terrific pace.

The hunters hid themselves behind hillocks and trees as well as they were able.

But the shelter was hardly enough to cover them well.

The native kings formed their men into a line, to frighten away the animals; but in vain.

The herd of bulls came on like a charge of cavalry.

"Be ready to fire!" said Bob.

"Right!" was the reply.

It was a magnificent sight to see these powerful animals coming along, their heads low down, the fore feet thrown out, and their nostrils extended and discharging their breath. With their eyeballs glowing, their tails erect, they came on.

Bob and his friends discharged their volleys at them.

The sudden stampede that followed is indescribable.

In all directions they fled, some of them falling mortally wounded, and others fleeing again.

The doctor's surmise proved to be correct; three lions were in their midst, and began at once to devour those bulls that had fallen to the rifles of the hunters.

Our hero watched them attentively for a moment, then he cried out— "Fire!"

At once a volley was poured into the lions; two were mortally wounded, the third escaped.

"This is grand; this is something like! Talk about fox-hunting in England; why, the excitement is three times as great. Hurrah for hunting like this, my lads!"

Bob was delighted.

"This is a wonderful land—glorious! always something new. Now, boys, skin the lions."

When Bob saw that this was accomplished, he sat down with his followers to some dinner, and heartily enjoyed some steaks from the bulls.

Then the expedition was continued.

Many heads of game fell to their lot, and they returned, and having enjoyed their sport immensely, and in celebration of their success, and in honour of their quest, a merry evening was passed by all in the camp.

CHAPTER LVI.

THE MERRY-MAKING—A DISASTER—SAD FOREBODINGS.

THE following night King Kalu, as usual, was an honoured guest, and occupied King Aga's chair of state.

What with Stumps's trombone and the horns of the natives, the music had sufficient charms to sooth and allay all war-like feelings for the time.

At last, the camp and its inmates were at rest.

King Kalu was escorted with great ceremony to King Aga's state room.

There he was left to his repose, and now all retired to rest.

The Stinger was very elevated; Buttons likewise, and most of the others had imbibed pretty freely.

When our hero had retired, he too felt the influence of the excitement through which he had lately passed.

He could not sleep.

He lay awake for a long time in the dark, until at last he fell into an uneasy slumber.

How long he slept he knew not, but he awoke suddenly.

Hark! what was that?

A cry had startled him.

Wide awake, he arose in his bed or hammock, and listened.

The sound was not repeated.

Again he went to sleep; again the cry startled him.

He listened, and not hearing a repetition of the sound, he fancied he must have been dreaming.

But no: his imagination could not throw off the cry he had heard.

He got up quickly, and dressed.

Groping his way out of the tent, he entered that of Ironfist.

Shaking the sleeper, he cried—

"Awake, Ironfist; awake. Heard you that groan?"

"Not I," replied Ironfist.

"Then I must have been dreaming; but still, I will go and inquire whether anything has occurred from the sentinels."

He left the tent.

At the door he met Stumps.

"Well, Stumps, have you had any bad dreams?" he asked.

"Master," replied the dwarf, "something has happened."

"What, have you heard a cry, as it were of death?"

"No."

"What, then?"

"I feel it is not all right."

"Speak. What is the matter?"

"As I came from my tent, I thought I beheld a dusky form drop over the palisades," said the dwarf.

"Let us search."

The two made the best of their way round the camp.

All was quiet.

No signs of disturbance were to be seen in the camp.

But as they passed King Kalu's tent, they beheld the matting open.

"What can this mean?" said Bob.

"We had better see," replied Stumps, with pale lips.

The day was breaking then.

Already the sun could be seen gleaming through the forest trees.

Stumps entered the tent, Bob followed more slowly; but on entering the tent both started back with a cry of horror.

King Kalu was lying on his side, in King Aga's state bed, pierced to the heart with a knife.

"Murder has been done," they cried, retreating.

In a very short time the camp was alarmed by them.

All rushed forward.

"King Kalu is murdered!" cried Bob. "Look, he has been killed in his sleep."

Horror was depicted on every countenance present.

"Who can have done this?" asked Bob. "Who could have entered the place without meeting the sentinels?"

These latter were questioned.

Not a soul had passed them.

Then Stumps approached the corpse of the murdered king.

He drew forth the dagger from his heart, and then discovered a small piece of the dried palm-tree leaf around the handle.

He untied this and handed it to the doctor to read.

The latter did so.

"It is thus King Pluto pays the traitors who side with his enemies. Traitors, beware of King Pluto!" read the doctor.

The mystery was explained.

"King Pluto is the assassin; there is not a doubt of it," cried Bob.

"Let us search for him," said Ironfist.

"No; it is useless," said Bob, sadly.

"You see," he continued, turning to King Kalu's followers, "how your king has lost his life."

"We do," replied the chief of the dead king's followers; "and he must be revenged fully. We beg leave of you, great white king, to remove the body to King Kalu's town, where the tears of his people may mourn for him."

"Let it be so," said Bob.

The deed was done, and the murderer was beyond the reach of vengeance for the present.

Before the sun had gone far in the heavens, King Kalu's followers had departed from the camp with their master's lifeless body.

The black deed had made a deep impression upon our hero.

"Doctor," he said, "I feel unwell; this climate is telling greatly upon my health."

"I think so too; I fear you have an illness coming on. I must ask you to keep quiet in bed," replied the doctor.

He was compelled to obey the doctor's orders, and accordingly retired to bed.

King Aga came to see him.

"Chief of the white men," he said, "you have proved a true friend to me, and I am grateful; but I have to tell you the rainy season is coming on, and I should advise that you returned to my town until it is over."

"Good; I think it best," said Bob, in a weak voice.

The doctor shook his head.

"Doctor I'm going to get up now."

Bob was as good as his word.

He did get up, and busied himself about the camp, not without dire misgivings as to the future.

He retired to rest early.

So did Buttons, Stinger, Ironfist, and Stumps, for the climate was telling on all of them.

"I dread the morrow," said the doctor to Ironfist, "for I feel that we shall have a lot of illness to contend with; but at any rate we must make our way to Aga's town, and then I can nurse you all, if I myself escape free of the—

"What?" asked Ironfist, anxiously.

"Fever, my boy, I'm afraid of it; but let us wait till tomorrow. I fear the worst," replied the doctor.

CHAPTER LVII.

ILL TIDINGS—A SORROWFUL JOURNEY—KING AGA'S VILLAGE—THE RETURN TO CAPE COAST.

THE next morning, when Bob Blunt attempted to move, he found that his head ached violently, his limbs were stiff in the joints, his tongue parched, and in fact his whole system seemed out of order.

Bob sent for the doctor.

"Just as I expected," said the medical man. "Fever sooner or later ; this part of the country too watery. There's poor Buttons down with it, and Longsight, and Stinger, poor old girl ; in fact I don't know whether I shall not be laid up myself ; I feel remarkably like it."

Bob looked very grave.

"You don't think it's as bad as all that, doctor ?"

"I do though, it's no joking ; and neither is it any use mincing the matter," replied the doctor.

"Send for King Aga."

The king came.

"My friend, it appears we shall all be very ill ; will you have us removed to your town ?"

"Willingly."

"Then we will have the arrangements made at once. Doctor and you, Ironfist, I leave myself in your hands."

They gazed sadly on him.

The doctor gave him some medicine, and then left him to make the necessary arrangements.

*   *   *   *   *

In two hours' time the entire camp was moving to King Aga's town.

Bob Blunt, the Stinger, Buttons, and Longsight were in litters carried on the backs of the natives.

Jingo and the general were quite broken-hearted about the sad mishap that had occurred to their friends and protectors.

The doctor, too, was unwell.

"I'm afraid, Mr. Blunt, I shall not be able to keep up," he said to our hero ;

"but I will leave instructions as to the requisite medicine with Ironfist. He will not be knocked down easily."

"That will do," said Bob faintly ; "only let us get on."

After two days' travelling, they at length neared King Aga's town.

They stood on the brow of the hill where poor Strongback slept his last.

Suddenly King Aga gave a cry of pain and spoke to Bob.

"What is it ?" asked our hero, feebly, for he was very ill.

"My town is a mass of smouldering ruins. The villains have been here before us."

Bob's illness left him in that moment of excitement.

But the news was too true.

King Pluto had burnt it to the ground.

Not a hut was left standing.

Words cannot describe King Aga's rage and despair.

He vowed vengeance dire against his foe.

When the stragglers came into camp, they reported all.

King Pluto had been there with two white men, burned the town, and put to the sword all who were unfortunate enough not to effect their escape.

"There is no help for it," groaned Bob. "We cannot take vengeance on them now. Oh, that I were not lying down ill, I would make them repent their work ; but enough, there is no help for it. Ironfist, push on for Cape Coast. King Aga, my friend, you will come with me with your men. When I am better, we will weave plans to revenge ourselves."

"I go," replied the king, sternly.

"I am content."

Bob rested back in his litter.

The doctor also had to be placed in

one, and thus the weary travellers returned to Cape Coast.

*   *   *   *   *

We will not pause to tell the many adventures that befell them on their return journey.

Enough, Ironfist more than did his duty in guarding his master against the attacks of all his enemies, even King Pluto, who, on several occasions, had followed the cortége up.

But he was driven back.

At length, one fine morning, Ironfist and his tried little army sighted the white tower of Cape Coast Castle once more.

"Thank God, we are safe!" he cried· "Now, Mr. Blunt, all will be well."

Bob smiled feebly.

"Rest, rest," he murmured.

"You shall have it. Hurrah! there's plenty of life in us yet, and at the best hotel in the place, we shall not only bring round our fair Stinger, Buttons, Longsight, and the doctor, but also our brave and gallant leader, Bob Blunt, the Traveller."

And Ironfist kept his word.

Before night all the patients were in comfortable beds, and receiving the best attendance the place afforded ; and all were eager to administer to the wants of the brave and adventurous explorers of mysterious Africa.

Bob soon recovered from his attack of fever, in the glorious sea breezes from the mighty Atlantic, and he was quickly on his legs again.

The worthy Doctor Know-all was unremitting in his attention to his other patients, who were longer in recovering.

But the patients were anything but patient under his treatment.

"Oh, doctor," moaned Elizabeth Ann, as she held her hands to her aching forehead, " prove yourself worthy of your name, and give me something to stop this dreadful throbbing."

"My dear madam, I assure you I am doing all I can," replied the doctor soothingly.

"That isn't enough," returned the invalid impatiently ; "oh, do pray administer some powerful remedy that will cure me at once, and enable me to stand up again as the vindicator of woman's rights."

Buttons' request was much the same.

"Get us round, ole son, as quick as you can," he cried, entreatingly ; "my head feels like a baked tater, all hot, and then there's my 'Tropical Adventures,' that's going to make my fortune when I get back to England, at a dead standstill. Why can't you cure us offhand ?"

Dr. Know-all mildly replied that it was simply impossible, and suggested quinine and patience.

"Quinine and patience be blowed!" returned the fretful Buttons, desperately. "Who can be patient under such excruciating circumstances ? I can't."

And in despair he buried his face in his pillow and kicked wildly.

One of the first things Bob Blunt did was to ask about news from England.

He was told many a tale of war and peace, fearful accidents, and political convulsions ; but nothing that concerned himself.

But happening to be in the smoking-room of the hotel, looking over the last batch of papers from England, he saw the following advertisement.

" R. B——, Esq., a minor, who recently inherited a splendid estate in Kent, and then left England to carry out an exploring expedition in Africa, is requested to communicate at once with his solicitor. Title to estate disputed. A relative of R. B.'s has gone to Africa, as is supposed, with some evil design. Letters explanatory have been sent to R. B., care of Mr. Sledge, Merchant and Shipowner, Cape Coast Castle."

Bob dashed down the paper, caught up his hat, and proceeded at once to the factory or warehouse of Mr. Sledge, one of the most prosperous traders in the settlement.

"Ha! Mr. Blunt, I am glad to see you," said the merchant, as our hero entered the office.

"The pleasure is mutual, Mr. Sledge," responded our hero ; "though I am puzzled to understand how you can know me without an introduction."

"Why, Mr. Sawyer, your agent, had the forethought to send me your portrait and also a letter bearing your signature, so that his letters might not fall into the hands of the wrong person."

"He is a careful man."

"Yes ; luckily, for I have had a gentleman here asking for those very letters."

"You don't mean it !"

"I do indeed," said the merchant, who then described the person.

"Howard, by all that is unholy !" exclaimed Bob.

"I have not seen him since I refused to give him the letters, though he made some big threats then."

Bob thanked the merchant for his kindness and care, then began to read Mr. Sawyer's long letter.

It was to the effect that he had received notice from a firm of solicitors that Howard disputed Bob's title to the estate, that the tenants had been served with notice not to pay any rent to Mr. Blunt or his agent, and finally he had heard that Howard himself had gone to the African coast in the company of a desperate ruffian, and had been heard to utter some diabolical threats before leaving.

The letter concluded by entreating our hero to come back to England—not so much because the estate was threatened, for the writer could defend that—but lest Howard should carry out his threat and assassinate the heir to Blunt Castle.

Bob considered for a few minutes, then requested Mr. Sledge to favour him with pen, ink and paper.

It was a short reply he made to Mr. Sawyer the worthy lawyer, and wound up with these words—

"*I authorise you to defend my title to the estate. If defeated in one court, appeal to another. As for me, I shall not run home to avoid that cowardly hound Howard.*"

He sealed the letter and placed it with the merchant's correspondence for the next homeward mail.

"And now, Mr. Sledge, I may draw what cash I require."

"I am instructed by Mr. Sawyer to honour your cheque."

"Then I shall want a thousand pounds in cash ; and you deal in all kinds of ammunition ?"

"Yes, both for rifles and smooth bores."

Bob then made out a hasty list of what he should require in the way of cartridges, which the merchant engaged should be ready in twenty-four hours.

"And now, Mr. Sledge," said our hero, "allow me to thank you for the care you have taken of my correspondence."

"You will act on Mr. Sawyer's advice and go home, Mr. Blunt ?"

"No."

Mr. Sledge looked surprised.

"I shall not go home yet. But I have had almost enough of Western Africa, so by the first ship I sail for the east coast, to see how far I can penetrate in that direction."

And he went back to his temporary home.

An hour later, Bob Blunt and his comrades were assembled together in the dining-room of a house he had hired for a term.

It had formerly belonged to a great slave-dealer and stood facing the sea, and still bore the remains of its ancient splendour, although these marks were fast disappearing.

Our hero was just about to explain his future plans, when Doctor Know-all entered.

"Well, doctor," he asked, "how are your patients ?"

"I think I may pronounce them to be progressing favourably. The feverish symptoms have abated, but they are still very low, and I may add very restless."

"Poor Stinger, poor Buttons !" said Bob Blunt, commiseratingly ; "they are beginning to find that the tropics have their bitters as well as their sweets,"

"I think, Mr. Blunt, we have all made that discovery by this time," returned the doctor, with a smile.

"Well, yes," admitted our hero ; "at this moment it strikes me we've none of us much to boast of."

"The climate is certainly deadly."

"Undoubtedly ; and it is my earnest

wish that we should reach our native shores. If we are spared to return in health and strength, I have determined upon a step which I believe will have the effect of recruiting us all."

"What is it, captain?" asked everyone, eagerly.

"A sea voyage," Bob answered.

The languid eyes of the adventurers brightened and their cheeks flushed hopefully at this.

"That's yer sort, captain," exclaimed old Tom, joyfully; "a good sniff of the briny'll set us all on our pins in no time."

The conversation was here interrupted by the appearance of Jingo Johnson, who announced—

"Massa Blunt, here's a dam black nigger wantee see you."

"Who is it, Jingo?"

"Dunno, massa."

"Send him in, then."

And next moment there entered as black a nigger as ever walked.

He gravely bowed, but as it was soon evident that he could not speak English, Jingo was recalled, and made interpreter.

The man proved to be one of King Aga's tribe.

He had been taken prisoner in one of the many skirmishes that enlivened the journey, but had escaped a day since, and now had very important news to tell.

He had heard King Pluto swear before his fetiche man to be avenged on our hero for the maiming his hand had suffered ; and moreover he had heard that the alliance between Pluto and Howard was confirmed.

They would follow our hero on sea or on land for the sake of vengeance, and were even now within a day's march of Cape Coast.

"We must be careful," said our hero, who then rewarded the black man, and had him informed where he could find his tribe.

A few minutes later, King Aga himself entered, accompanied by his daughter Nahita.

The sable monarch had become so attached to his white friend that he could not bear the idea of parting ; and Nahita, too—well, she had fallen deeply in love with our hero.

Bob explained to him that they had just been discussing the proposed sea voyage, and Aga made reply—

"I will go with you. I owe you my life and my daughter's ; we will be your slaves if you will not have us else. And I have not yet avenged my injuries on King Pluto's head."

END OF VOL I.

"THE LION, WITH A LOUD ROAR, LEAPED UPON THE BACK OF HIS FOE."

BOB BLUNT, THE TRAVELLER.

PART II.—ABYSSINIA.

CHAPTER I.

PREPARING FOR THE VOYAGE.

IT being decided that Bob and his friends should make a voyage, the question was, in what vessel.

Our hero pointed to a smart American clipper that was lying in the bay.

The whole party hastened to the open windows to look at her.

"That is the barque that is to carry us."

"Why, captain," exclaimed his companions, "we were not aware you owned a vessel."

"Nor did I until yesterday," returned Bob, with a smile. "The fact is, I wished to give you an agreeable surprise, and so I sent General Bombast, who has a strong faculty for making bargains, to purchase any available craft he might be able to find for our use. There is a vessel !"

"And a lovely crittur she is and no mistake," exclaimed a tall, thin personage, in the lightest of suits, the broadest of hats, and speaking the most Yankee of twangs, who happened to be passing the window at the moment."

He stopped, and after puffing a long stream of smoke from between his lips he continued—

"I guess there ain't the equal of that there clipper for speed in the whole world; give her only half a capful of wind, and off she is like a flash of lightning. The brute that's bought her, wal, he's got a barguin if ever he had one."

"Oh, she's sold, is she?" said Bob, assuming ignorance of that fact.

"It's a fact, she is," responded the Yankee. "I've sold her to a rascally nigger in a cocked hat. The ugly beggar got her dirt cheap too."

"Might I ask the price she fetched ?"

"Twelve thousand dollars was the price, and she was honestly worth double the money—she was by Jingo."

The Yankee, having made this statement, thrust his hands in his pockets, and walked away, smoking like a steam engine.

It was just at this moment that the important individual who had made the purchase appeared in sight.

He was stalking along with as much self-complacency as though the whole of Africa belonged to him.

He was magnificently attired, that is, according to his own ideas of magnificence, which were peculiar.

He had contrived to possess himself of a new cocked hat about twice as large as that he usually wore, with a tall feather to match, which he had stuck jauntily on his head.

A scarlet military coat with faded epaulettes covered his body, whilst his feet were thrust into a pair of hessian boots.

To complete the picture, his long cavalry sword dangled from his waist, and dragged along the ground.

Onwards he came, holding between his

thumb and finger a white cambric handkerchief, with a lace edging.

A negro followed him at a respectful distance.

"Hilloa!" cried Bob, "look at the get-up of the general."

Waving his hand in a graceful and condescending manner to his European companions, he approached the window.

But before entering, he stopped and turned to the darkey behind him.

"Come heah, you niggar!" he exclaimed in an exquisitely affected tone; "gib me some smellum water on my hank'cher."

As he spoke he held out the cambric, which his attendant sprinkled with eau-de-Cologne from a bottle which he carried.

This operation over, the general wiped his black face, and fanned himself after the manner of a languid swell, and then entered the room.

He was greeted by a simultaneous roar of laughter.

Not in the least disconcerted, he drew himself up to his full height, and smiled blandly on the company.

"General," said Bob Blunt, seriously, but with a smile twinkling in the corner of his eyes, "it is customary for gentlemen, when they enter a room, to remove their hats."

"Iss, massa," replied the general, very composedly; "me puffec'ly aware ob dat fact, but dis heah hat got one piccalilli (he meant peculiarity); when me get him on my head, me not able to get him off ag'in bery easy."

"Oh, that's it, is it?" said our hero. "Stumps, assist the general."

The dwarf came behind and by a nimble spring up, knocked the cocked hat over the wearer's eyes.

"Me bery much 'bliged to you, Massa Stump," said the sable swell, as he caught his *chapeau* in his hands; "me happy to 'blige you in same manner some day."

The general accompanied this with a polite bow, which the dwarf returned, amidst the laughter of the lookers-on.

"Well," said Bob, "have you completed the purchase of the vessel?"

"Iss, Massa Blunt, me rader tink me hab," he replied, in an intensely chuckling tone; "de clipper's ours. Lubly vessel,

splendiferous sailer—can't match her nowheres."

"How much did you give for her?"

"Oh, Massa Blunt, de Yankee capt'n tink me know notink about trade, ask lot too much. I say—'No, no.'"

"How much did he ask?" said Bob.

"Twenty-four tousan dollar, only tink ob dat."

The general looked round upon his auditors to see the effect his words produced.

"A large sum, a very large sum; too much," they exclaimed.

"You did not give it, of course?" said Bob, inquiringly.

The general placed his finger perpendicularly alongside of his nose, and gave a wink that would have cracked a filbert if it had been between his eyelids as he replied—

"Not exactly; dis general know him way about lilly better dan dat."

"Well, what did you give?" asked our hero.

"Me get de clipper great barg'in, bery great barg'in, cheap as mud. No tanks to de capt'n though; him want——"

"Never mind what the captain wanted," interrupted Bob Blunt; "what did he get?"

The general took a long breath, and looking round once more at the company, exclaimed triumphantly—

"De sum was twelve tousan' five hundred dollars, exactly."

"Oh!" exclaimed Bob Blunt.

"Oh!" echoed everyone present.

General Bombast could see they were all astounded, and he said—

"Dere, now, what you tink ob dat? Ain't dat de way to trade, ain't dat great, big, woppin' bargain?"

His master made no reply for a moment, but fixed his eyes steadily upon him, and then said—

"I won't call it a bargain, but something else instead. A great, big, whopping——"

"What, Massa?"

"Lie!" exclaimed Bob, sternly.

"Oh, massa," gasped the general, his jaw dropping considerably, "me scorn to tell a lie."

"Ah, you may well look aghast," went

on our hero ; " you know well enough you gave twelve thousand dollars for the clipper, not a cent more."

" Twelve—five, sar. Take him oath him did," protested the general.

" Let me see the receipt, then ?" asked Bob.

" Cert'nly ; dis minnit," answered the mendacious negro readily.

General Bombast felt in all his pockets for the receipt, but failed to find it.

He took off his boots and searched there, but with no better result.

He examined the interior of his cocked hat.

It was all in vain.

The acute nigger scratched his woolly head in a profound and reflective manner, and finally supposed he must have lost it.

But this would not satisfy Bob Blunt, and rising from his seat, he approached the dandy nigger.

" I'm waiting for the balance of my cash," he said ; " hand it over."

The general glanced at his master, and knew by the compression of his lips, and the flash of his eyes, that he was in earnest.

Into his breast pocket went his hand, and out came a canvas bag.

" Dere dey am, massa ; me only make big mistake. Me scorn to tell a lie," he said ruefully, as he delivered up the balance.

The money being counted, it was found minus some twenty dollars, which the African dandy had expended in dress and perfumery ; but having got the bulk of the sum, his master overlooked this defalcation.

General Orlando Bombast was astonished that his master should be so intimately acquainted with the bargain he had made, and after a short time he said to our hero—

" Massa Blunt."

" Well ?"

" How you know de exact sum me gib for the clipper."

Bob looked at him scrutinisingly for an instant, and then, thinking that it would be a check upon his dishonest propensities in future, he said to him in a low earnest tone—

" You forget my good fetiche, who never allows me to be deceived."

" Ah, massa! an' so your fetiche tell you, eh ?"

" Yes."

The general said no more, but departed a sadder if not a wiser man.

" Why me no get fetiche tell me same as massa's fetiche ?" he muttered to himself, as he went along. " Black man's fetiche no good ; great big humbug ; eb'ry one of 'em humbug ; dirty humbug, too ; dere now !"

CHAPTER II.

ALL ON BOARD THE CLIPPER—CHRISTENING PERFORMED IN A NOVEL MANNER—AN UNEXPECTED CATASTROPHE.

THE vessel being purchased, there was a general desire to get on board as quickly as possible.

All were anxious to leave the arid shores where fever and death seemed hanging over them.

All longed to be once more bounding over the bosom of the ocean, with the fresh sea breezes playing upon their suntanned faces and debilitated frames.

But there was much luggage to be transferred from the shore to the vessel.

Fresh hands would be wanted to work her.

For this purpose our hero determined to engage some of the coast negroes—

Kroomen, or Kroo-boys, as they were called.

A find, stalwart set of fellows they were, too.

Of these, Bob Blunt selected twelve, whom, with his own followers, he considered would be sufficient.

The arrangement being concluded, the baggage was put on board as rapidly as possible.

The announcement of a sea voyage appeared to act beneficially upon the invalids.

The Stinger sat bolt upright in her bed with heartfelt expression of joy at the intelligence.

"Going to sea!" she exclaimed hysterically. "Oh, thank goodness, my precious life will be preserved, and woman's rights be vindicated on more congenial shores."

As for Buttons, he became slightly insane at the news, and made a desperate effort to express his rapture by standing on his head, and then walking on his hands round the Stinger.

It was quite as good as a play to witness the departure from the house of the illustrious Elizabeth Ann.

She was carried forth, reclining on a litter, borne by four stalwart negroes.

Jingo Johnson himself superintending her removal, lest they should incautiously shock his dear Nosie's unstrung nerves by the slightest jolt.

Propped up by pillows, and wearing her elaborately-frilled nightcap, she looked like—well, something between Queen Anne and Mrs. Gamp.

In spite of the weakness which fever had imparted to her usually indomitable spirit, her memory was still remarkably vivid, and she kept a sharp look-out after her goods and chattels.

"Are you sure there's nothing left behind, Jingo?" she inquired very emphatically, before the *cortege* moved on.

"Quite sure, missie," Jingo replied.

"Is my umbrella safe?"

"Iss, missie ; here it am."

"My pattens?"

"Here 'em are."

"And my teapot? Pray don't forget my teapot."

"De teapot under de pillar," replied Jingo, with an affectionate grin and wink ; "and de spout not fur off missie's lubly mouth."

"Faithful creature," murmured the enervated Stinger.

And forthwith the frilled nightcap descended, and the "lubly mouth" was applied to the before-mentioned spout, which operation comforted her greatly.

"Now I am ready," she cried, to the men ; "forward to the boat, and whatever you do, don't drop me."

"Me cut de bla'guards into mincemeat if they do," exclaimed Jingo.

They were about to start, when Buttons' voice was heard.

"Stop, stop!" he shrieked, in a shrill treble. "I've left my manuscrupt behind. 'Buttons' Tropical Adventures' is under the bed ; run and fetch it, someone."

The valuable document was quickly sought for and found, and Buttons' peace of mind being restored, he said cheerfully to his negroes—

"Now, then, darkeys, step out. Stinger, old gal," he added, "keep up your pecker; your Buttons is behind you."

They were soon on board the vessel, and before noon the anchor was weighed, and the clipper was standing out to sea.

The exhilarating effect of the fresh breeze was speedily felt by all.

The invalids insisted upon leaving their pallets.

And now Bob Blunt, partly to cheer his companions, and partly as a necessary duty, proposed christening the vessel, and also the new hands he had taken aboard.

The proposal was received with universal acclamations.

The first portion of the ceremony was performed by the Stinger, with immense dignity and effect.

It was simple enough.

She broke a bottle of wine, and pouring it on the deck, exclaimed—

"I christen thee, thou gallant craft, by the name of the 'Adventurer.'"

Next came the darkeys engaged.

The task of giving them appropriate names fell to Bob Blunt and his friends, and the manner in which their new cognomens were impressed on their memories was at once novel and amusing.

The men being assembled on deck, he said to one whom he selected—

"Stand forward."

The Kroo-boy advanced, grinning all over his black face.

"Look up there," said Bob, pointing to the maintop.

The darkey looked up.

"You can climb, of course?" asked our hero.

"Iss, massa," answered the negro, 'like monkey."

"Then just mount aloft, and when you reach the top, stand on your head an instant, and come down again."

The man run up the shrouds with the agility of a monkey.

The next moment a pair of dark legs were seen stuck up in the air at the masthead.

"Oh, good gracious! he'll fall," shrieked the Stinger, nervously.

"Not he," said Bob.

He had hardly said the words when down came the negro again like lightning to the deck, having descended by a single rope.

"Very good," said our hero to him; "you will remember that your name henceforth is Maintop."

"Yah, yah!" grinned the newly-christened party, "Paintpot very good name."

"No, no," corrected Bob, laughing in concert with the rest; "not Paintpot, Maintop."

"Ah, iss, Maintop. Yah! fine name, sah."

"Now then, doctor," said our hero, as he summoned a second forward, "you will be good enough to christen this one."

"Very well," the doctor replied.

He looked about him for an instant, and at length his eyes rested on a marlingspike.

"The very thing," he said to himself, as he picked it up. "Now then," he cried to the man, "off with you."

Away ran the darkey, and the doctor after him, giving him an occasional dig with the implement he carried.

The worthy surgeon was a nimble man for his years, and the pursuit and the dodging up and down the deck was sufficiently amusing, and caused shouts of merriment.

"You will answer to the name of Marlingspike," he said to the man, as the chase came to an end.

A third now stood forward.

"Ironfist, it is your turn now," said Bob Blunt.

Ironfist, required no weapon but his own broad palm, and advancing, he took the unsuspecting nigger across his knee, and in spite of the darkey's struggles and ejaculations, gave him a sound spanking on the spot.

"That will do for to-day," he said, as he set him on his legs again. "Your name's Spanker; mind you don't forget it."

"Ugh! dere not much fear of dat," responded the Kroo-boy, as he rubbed his tingling posterior; "him felt spanker all over."

Our hero now turned to Swiftfoot.

"You will christen the next," he said to him.

A fourth man advanced.

Swiftfoot looked at him reflectively for a moment.

Under ordinary circumstances, he would have given him half an hour's run.

But the climate had, for the present, taken all his running out of him, and he sought for some easier ceremony.

A rope, hanging from one of the yards, attracted his attention.

"Just make a hitch at the end, will you?" he said to old Tom, as he pointed to it.

The hitch was quickly made.

"Thank you," said Swiftfoot. "Now then darkey," he cried to his man, "step this way."

The negro came to him.

In an instant the noose was thrown over his head and body, and drawn tight under the arms.

"Now then, hitch him up!" called out Swiftfoot

Half a dozen hands seized the rope.

Up in the air went the Kroo-boy, who spun round as if he had been fastened to a roasting jack.

"Enough! Let him down."

The negro was lowered once more to the deck, and Swiftfoot said to him—

"Now, when you're asked your name, remember it's Hitch."

The darkey rejoined his comrades, shrugging his shoulders, and murmuring to himself—

"Hitch—Hitch! Me not much like that name."

But whether he liked it or not, it stuck to him.

Bob Blunt now looked round upon his companions for a new deputy.

He espied Buttons, who was lying on his pallet quietly enjoying the proceedings.

His pocket-book and pencil were in his hand, and he might be supposed to be taking notes for his wonderful "Tropical Adventures."

"Well, my boy," said our hero to him, "do you feel equal to the task of christening number five?"

Buttons smiled rather languidly, as he replied—

"I ain't up to much, guv'nor, just at present; but I'll do my best."

"The best can do no more," rejoined his master.

Buttons beckoned old Tom to him, and whispered a few words in his ear.

"All right," said the old salt, with a grin, and immediately disappeared through the hatchway.

Very shortly he returned, bringing with him a half-gallon can of some smoking hot compound, that had the appearance of hasty pudding.

In his hand he carried a large wooden spoon.

"What is that?" asked the Stinger, who reclined near him. "Gruel?"

"No, Betsy, dearest, it isn't," Buttons replied.

"What is it then? I feel curious to know."

"It's burgoo."

"Burgoo? Never heard of it," murmured Elizabeth Ann, reflecting to herself.

"Now, then, number five," called Buttons, "come this way."

Number five advanced, casting his eyes longingly on the can.

"Kneel down," was the order he received, which he at once obeyed.

"Spoon, Tom," said Buttons.

Tom handed it to him.

"Open your mouth," cried the page.

The kneeling darkey extended his jaws, revealing a cavity of vast extent.

Buttons, having stirred up the burgoo, gave him a couple of spoonfuls.

It was not hot enough to scald, but quite sufficient to bring the water into the Kroo-boy's eyes, and to cause him to make some extraordinary grimaces.

"Very good, ain't it?" asked Buttons, with a grin.

"Yes, massa, bery good, and bery dam hot as well," answered the darkey.

"Then you can take the can, and finish the rest when it gets cooled, and mind in future your name is Burgoo."

"Burgoo! all right, massa."

And the negro rejoined his companions in high glee, being the happy possessor of half a gallon of soup and a wooden spoon.

"I think I should like to nominate one of these poor heathens," said the Stinger rather faintly.

"With much pleasure," replied Bob Blunt. "Stand out, number six."

Number six approached the couch of the invalid lady.

Elizabeth Ann made a mysterious dive under her pillow, and presently reappeared, grasping her never-to-be-forgotten teapot.

"Down on your marrow-bones," she said to the darkey; "shut your eyes and open your mouth, and take what I'm going to give you; but mind one thing——"

"What dat, missee?"

"Don't swallow the pot!"

With this, the worthy lady placed the spout between his eager lips.

The darkey sucked away with evident delight, and would doubtless have kept on sucking till this present moment had he been permitted.

But the Stinger knew when he had had enough.

"There, that will do," she exclaimed, after a moment, as she withdrew the spout from his lips, which exhaled ambrosial odours.

"And now, in remembrance that you have sipped tea from the hands of Elizabeth Ann Stinger, consider yourself henceforth christened Teapot."

"Ee, ee!" grinned the nigger, as he went back to his place; "Teapot! Oughter been Rumpot."

Longsight was then summoned to christen one.

He did this by making the man climb along the bowsprit, descend by the chain, and climb up again.

After which he named him Bobstay.

The next in rotation was a burly negro.

A giant in size, and apparently one in strength, and with a countenance anything but agreeable to look upon, its expression being extremely savage and repulsive.

In additon to the usual ugliness of the African native, there was a gleam in his eyes, and a frequent display of his white teeth, that undoubtedly betokened much cruelty of disposition.

This was further manifested by the request he made to Bob.

Advancing to him with a sardonic grin on his features, he said.—

'Massa, dese here niggers bad lot, all of 'em. Give me de job to keep 'em in order. Me strong; me break 'em in— yah, yah!"

The eager manner in which he pointed to his comrades, and the deep guttural chuckle that accompanied his words, convinced our hero that he was a brute who required to be taught a lesson.

But he made no reply at the moment, simply ordering the giant to fall back, whilst he whispered a few words to Stumps.

Stumps gave a scrutinising glance at the burly negro from under his thick eyebrows, and hurried below with a grim smile on his face.

In a few moments, he reappeard, holding something up his sleeve.

"There is one more yet to christen," said our hero, as he advanced towards him; "I leave him to you, Stumps."

As he spoke, he pointed to the evil-minded negro.

"Last, but certainly not least," muttered Stumps.

Then he called aloud—

"Step forward, Goliah."

"Dat not my name," said the African, in a low, growling tone.

"I'm aware of that," returned Stumps; "but it will do till I give you a better. Off with your shirt."

The command was sullenly complied with.

With a motion of his head, Stumps then beckoned to several of the Kroo-boys, who advanced at once.

"Fasten his hands to that grating." he said to them.

In an instant, Goliah was seized and his wrists fastened securely together with rope.

"That will do," said Stumps.

He then drew from his sleeve the "something" it concealed.

This was a cat-with-nine-tails, used for flogging refractory sailors.

This he placed in the hand of Kroo-boy No. 1, and cried—

"Lay on, Maintop; let us see how he likes it."

The negroes, who had heard the very kind opinion the giant had expressed of them, exulted, and cried unanimously—

"Lay on, Maintop; gib him pepper."

It is needless to say these injunctions were heartily obeyed; so heartily, that the giant writhed and growled, and finally began to yell lustily.

"That will do for you, Maintop. Now, Marlingspike, relieve your comrade."

Marlingspike, grinning all over his black face, took the cat.

But what he did was anything but in the way of relief to the man at the grating, for he laid it on with increased energy.

In this way the cat was passed from hand to hand until the giant had shouted himself hoarse.

"That will do," said the dwarf, complacently, as he received the cat from Bobstay.

Then approaching the subject of their operations, he said to him—

"You have now had a pretty good taste of the physic you wished to administer to your comrades, and know what it's like. And in order to impress it still further on your memory, I christen you 'Rope's End;' loose him!"

The giant was set free.

And, cowed by the sharp whipping he had received, he skulked away aft, and sat down in the scuppers, muttering curses, not loud, but deep, upon his comrades and the dwarf, who had authorised the stinging ceremony of christening in which he had been an unwilling participator.

The gigantic nigger might have been heard (if anyone had listened) to say—

"Dese here ships sinks sometimes. Dey catches fire sometimes : and sometimes de white folks dies. Dere will be fire or death on board this craft, *if she doesn't sink on the voyage!*"

The black giant, Rope's End, walked moodily below deck.

General Orlando, who had been for some time silently watching the proceedings, uttered an impatient ejaculation.

"Ugh !" he grunted. "Why me not axed to chizzle (he meant christen) one ob dem niggars ?"

"'Cos you only niggar yourself," scornfully replied Jingo Johnson, who stood at his side ; "dat's why."

Between Jingo and the dandy general there was arising a kind of vendetta.

In reply to Jingo, he simply sneered, and waving his cambric, that was saturated with *eau de Cologne*, he sauntered forward, his cocked hat on his head, and his customary sword trailing along on the deck.

"How now, Signor Orlando ?" exclaimed Bob Blunt, "what is it, eh ?"

"Dis is what it am, Massa Blunt," replied the general ; "me tink me jas as well able to chisel one ob dem darkies as anybody else."

There was a general laugh at the unintentional candour of this remark, and our hero answered dryly—

"I have no doubt whatever, general, as to your chiselling capabilities, but as I object to any of my servants being chiselled by another, I shall not require your assistance. Stand aside."

The sable swell was considerably taken aback ; but quickly recovering his usual *sang froid*, he muttered to himself—

"Him not a-goin' to stand aside. Him goin' to sit down by de lubly Stinger."

With these words, he flopped himself down at the side of the couch of that fascinating female.

"You black beast, mind my teapot !" shrieked Elizabeth Ann.

But General Orlando had something else to mind at that moment, for the indignant Jingo, unable to repress his jealous wrath, sprang forward, and seizing the general by his woolly locks, shook him till he turned almost white.

"You ugly 'tinking bla'guard !" he shouted, "you dare set yourself down side ob my lubly Nosie ? Eh, what you mean ?"

"Murdah ! Let go my hair, you temptible niggar."

"What you mean, eh ? What you mean ?" cried Jingo continuing to shake.

"Dat what I mean !" yelled the general, as he swung his hand up and gave his rival a tremendous slap across his nose.

Jingo fell back with a bundle of wool in each of his clenched fists ; and the dandy, springing up, fell upon him.

Rolling over and over on the deck, they continued the battle, mauling one another like a couple of angry dogs.

"Enough, enough !" cried Bob Blunt, advancing towards them ; "let me have no more of this."

The combatants, at the sound of their master's voice, released each other, and got up wiping their noses, from which the blood was flowing.

Elizabeth Ann once more sank upon her pallet, and calmed her agitated nerves by placing the spout of her teapot to her mouth.

The day passed away.

Night overspread the ocean.

All had retired to rest save our hero and a few of his companions, who remained on deck.

King Aga and his daughter Nahita were below.

Old Tom was at the helm.

For some time past the vessel, which had previously careered rapidly through the waves, had slackened her speed.

"Can't make it out quite," said the old tar.

"She don't seem to answer her helm as she did a bit ago."

It was strange, especially as there seemed no sufficient cause for the change.

Old Tom was evidently perplexed.

The vessel seemed to labour more and more every moment.

" Old Scratch has got his hands on the craft, I think," muttered Tom, as he scratched his grey head in perplexity.

No one answered, and a dead silence fell on all.

Suddenly it was broken by a wild shriek from below.

In awful accents it rose to the deck— " Fire ! fire ! The ship's on fire !"

CHAPTER III.

THE STINGER'S MISTAKE—SPRUNG A LEAK—A NOVEL METHOD OF STOPPING HOLES—THE VESSEL SAVED—THE RETURN TO THE COAST—JINGO JOHNSON MISSING.

IT was the voice of the Stinger.

" Good Heaven preserve us !" exclaimed our hero, in a tone of horror; " can it be possible ?"

Hardly had he uttered these words, when the Stinger shouted again—

" I don't mean fire—I made a mistake; I mean water. Help ! help ! it's coming in."

" I see what's the matter now," said old Tom ; " the ship's sprung a leak."

" Well, that's better than fire, anyhow," said Bob in a tone of relief ; " let's go below and see."

The whole party hurried down the hatchway.

To their surprise and dismay, on reaching the bottom, they stepped into a pool of water.

" This is serious," cried our hero ; " a lantern, quick !"

A lantern was speedily procured, and it was then clear enough that the mischief had been going on some time.

The voice of the Stinger was heard again.

She seemed in great consternation.

" Oh, Mr. Blunt, I dreamt the ship was on fire," she cried excitedly, " and on getting out of bed to see, I stepped into water. Oh, dear ! oh, dear ! I shall catch my death of cold, and woman's rights——"

" We must waive them for the present, my good woman," interrupted our hero, ' if we wish to save the ship and our lives. She has sprung a leak."

The Stinger uttered a shriek and dropped the lantern, which went out with a sharp hiss.

" Follow me to the hold ; we must set the pumps at work," shouted Bob to his companions, as he hurried away.

The next moment Buttons appeared at the door in his nightshirt.

" Sprung what ?" he asked, anxiously.

" A leak, and we shall all be drowned," cried the Stinger.

" Oh, Lor' !" gasped Buttons, " and my book that I'm writing of ' Tropical Adventures'——"

" Will go to the bottom of the briny deep. But never mind them, come and help me."

" I ain't in a fit state," groaned the page ; " and, besides, I must look after my manuscript."

" Dress yourself, my dear Buttons," entreated the Stinger ; " if we must die, at least go to the bottom respectable."

With a groan Buttons disappeared, and hurriedly dragged on his clothes, and collected his MS. and notes.

" Buttons, Buttons !" screamed the Stinger, " I can't find my teapot ; come here !"

" Bother your teapot. I'm coming," cried the page, as he stepped out of his cabin into a pool of water.

The shock startled him extremely, and made him shudder from head to foot.

But in order to reach his estimable friend he went splashing through it, till at length he plunged head first over the ridge of the door into her arms.

"Oh, Betsy," he gasped, "here's a pretty go!"

"Pretty go!" moaned the lady; "I call it an awful go. Thank goodness, I've found my umbrella and my teapot."

With these words, the advocate of woman's rights took a resigned suck at the spout of the latter article.

"I could do with a drop, Betsy," said Buttons wistfully.

"It isn't good for boys, as a rule," replied the Stinger; "however, under present circumstances——"

She handed him the teapot.

"Ah, that comforts a fellow," he said, after taking a good pull; "and now what's the matter?"

"I told you the ship's sprung a leak."

"A leek's an onion, ain't it?" asked Buttons.

"Onion? No, you silly young noodle; it's a hole, and the water's pouring in in gallons a minute."

"Oh, Lor', who's to stop it?" inquired Buttons.

"Who? Who but Elizabeth Ann Stinger?" was the sublime reply. "I'll stop it."

Having thrust her pattens firmly on her feet, she said, in a deep, low voice—

"Give me the teapot.

"Here you are."

"And my umbrella."

"There it is."

"And now follow me."

Without another word, E. A. S. stepped forth from her cabin and went bravely through the water.

Buttons followed.

*   *   *   *   *

On descending to the hold, it was found to be full of water, and the sea was making fresh inroads every moment.

In a very short time, unless prompt and energetic measures were taken, the vessel would be completely water-logged.

"Depend upon it, sir," said the old tar, "there's an ugly hole somewhere in the bottom of this here ship, and unless that can be found and stopped—mark you—from the outside, we're booked for Davy Jones, as sure as my name's Tom."

Our hero looked serious.

"Stopped from the outside!" he echoed. "That's a difficult task, and would require a skilful diver."

"Well," returned the steersman, "where are you likely to find better swimmers and divers than amongst your Kroo hands?"

"Ah, true!" exclaimed Bob. "I forgot. I will put the matter to to them."

In a few words, he explained the cause of the disaster and the remedy.

He had hardly finished when Bobstay cried out—

"We know what do massa; we been in this pickle afore—know how get out of it."

"You can stop the leak, then, you think?" said our hero.

"Iss! let me hab sack stuff wid something soft; me stop him."

In a very short time this was procured.

And Bobstay, a rope having been fastened round his waist, grasping the sack in his hand, plunged overboard.

In intense anxiety, Bob Blunt, holding the rope, waited the result.

In vain he strained his eyes down into the dark waters.

He could see nothing.

After a lapse of time, and just as he was beginning to think that the negro had perished in his bold attempt, the rope was jerked, and a voice sounded in his ears—

"All right, massa, me fix him," he cried.

The next moment the darkey was hauling himself up the ship's side, and quickly gained the deck, dripping like a waterspout.

The success of his venture was soon manifest.

The vigorous working of the pumps quickly dislodged the water in the hold, and the sack preventing any more from intruding, in a short time it was quite clear.

Bob and his companions then descended.

The cause of all the mischief was at once perceptible.

A yawning rent was discovered in the ship's bottom, through which the sack bulged, kept firmly in its position by the upward pressure of the body of water.

This must have existed, and have been known to exist before the clipper changed hands.

But at any rate the peril was averted for the time at least.

And a grateful exclamation at their preservation rose to their lips.

But there was one voice silent.

It was that of Rope's End.

The sullen giant felt no gratitude.

He was smarting still from the effects of his christening, and would have rejoiced to see the ship founder, and all on board with her, trusting to his skill as a swimmer to reach the shore in safety.

With moody brow he stood skulking in the shadow.

His eyes fixed with an intensely evil expression on the hole which the sack stopped.

It was just then the Stinger's well-known voice came travelling down into the hold. It cried—

"Where are you all? Show a light, somebody; Elizabeth Ann is coming to sacrifice herself and save you all!"

"Ha! dat my beau'ful Nosie's voice!" cried Jingo Johnson; "me coming, missie, help you down."

In an instant he had clambered up the ladder, and as quickly reappeared, bearing his lovely burden on his brawny shoulders.

The equanimity of the heroic lady was slightly disturbed as she descended into the depths.

"Be careful, Jingo! pray be careful, my good man. I'm heavy, you know. Buttons, mind you don't drop the teapot!"

Buttons followed, but being somewhat excited, he missed the first step of the ladder, and came down with a run, head first!

Luckily Stumps caught him, and thus preserved the brains of the aspiring young page from being shattered on the floor.

There was some little excitement caused by these unexpected arrivals.

Nor was it lessened when Elizabeth Ann, drawing herself up, exclaimed—

"Where's the leak?"

"There it is," replied Bob Blunt, as he pointed to it.

"Well, I've come to stop it."

"You're very kind indeed, Stinger, but I'm happy to say it's stopped already."

"Stopped!" almost shrieked Elizabeth Ann. "Why, the briny element is rushing in as fast as it can."

Bob looked, and uttered a cry of dismay, in which all joined. It was too true.

The sack had become displaced, and the peril was now returning with all its former violence.

But no one dreamt that the cause of this calamity was the malignant Rope's End.

Yet it was he.

In the momentary confusion he had, with his strong arm, thrust the sack from its position.

Destruction once more threatened the vessel and all on board.

"Not a moment must be lost!" cried our hero; "where's Bobstay?"

"Here, massa," replied the negro, readily stepping forward.

"You will have to take your dive again, my brave fellow," said Bob to him; "but I'll reward you handsomely. Another sack, quick!"

There was quite a rush to the steps to obey this demand.

When suddenly the sonorous voice of the Stinger arrested the progress of the eager throng.

"Stop!" she cried; "there's no need either of divers or sacks. Elizabeth Ann is here, and she flatters herself she is quite equal to this tremendous emergency. Behold!"

With these words, and flourishing her umbrella, she went clattering along the uneven flooring of the hold in her pattens.

Till having reached the cavity, through which the water was pouring, she paused, and having taken a good aim, turned round and dropped herself down upon it with a tremendous splash.

Whatever the Stinger's sensations might have been at this awful moment, it is certain she never disclosed them.

All the heroic female did, was to clutch her umbrella with remarkable tenacity, and smile—or rather try to smile.

But her teeth chattered audibly.

She was getting rather wet.

And presently she said, in a low tone slightly shaky—

" Buttons, the water's cold—th-th-the t-t-t-t-tea-p-p-pot."

Buttons rushed forward.

And after a prolonged sip, she was quite herself again.

The plan the philanthropic Betsy had adopted was entirely successful.

No sack could have more effectually shut out the water.

But not to impose too much on her generous self-denial, Bobstay was once more launched overboard with another sack, which he placed as before.

And Stinger was released from her particularly cold position, and escorted to her cabin amidst the cheers and congratulations of her admiring friends.

A glass of hot rum and water completely restored the circulation of the gallant Stinger, and she slept and snored peacefully.

Finding it impossible to continue the voyage under the present circumstances, the clipper put back to Cape Coast Castle for repairs.

At the end of a week, all was ready for departure.

When, at the last minute, Jingo Johnson was found to be missing.

CHAPTER IV.

A SEARCH DETERMINED ON—THE STINGER RESOLVES TO MAKE ONE OF THE PARTY —BUTTONS ALSO—THE START—STUMPS'S SUGGESTION—ELIZABETH ANN HAS A PRESENTIMENT—THE CRY OF AGONY.

HIS disappearance created some surprise. And Bob Blunt felt some annoyance, since he wished to take advantage of a fair wind that was blowing.

But he was unwilling to leave Jingo behind.

Therefore our hero awaited his return as patiently as he could.

But when the day waned and the night drew on, and no signs of Jingo Johnson, he began to grow uneasy about him.

So also did Elizabeth Ann.

" He was a very ugly nigger, certainly, was Jingo," she remarked ; " but, then, he was strong and active, and very devoted to my interests. Heigho! I wonder where he can have got to? I hope he hasn't been devoured by a lion."

The Stinger's anxiety increased as the night wore on.

And she found it necessary to apply frequently to her teapot for support.

The next morning, Jingo still being absent, a general council was called, and the result was that it was determined to go in search of him.

This displeased General Orlando extremely, who was congratulating himself of being well rid of his rival.

" Don' see why dere need be all dis bobbery made 'bout dat ugly nigger Jingo," he said, in an affected tone of disgust, " 'specially when you got me."

" You! you contemptible Jack-a-dandy, you ugly scarecrow!" retorted the Stinger, indignantly ; " what are you compared with my Jingo? Get out of my sight !"

She enforced this last injunction with her umbrella, which she laid across the head and shoulders of the dandy general with such telling effect, that he was glad to run for it.

" Take it cool, Betsy, dear," said Buttons, soothingly ; " don't excite yourself, or you'll be bringing back the fever."

"How can I help exciting myself, boy?" replied Elizabeth Ann, sharply. "I—I feel as if I—I should—but no, I won't. Pass the teapot, Buttons."

The page did as he was ordered.

"For my part," said Buttons, "I've made up my mind to take everything as cool as I can in these parts."

"So have I. But these harrowing circumstances——"

"Well, since I turned author, I looks on 'em as nothink more than interesting incidents. I shall have 'em all down in my 'Tropical Adventures.'"

"But poor Jingo, who used to worship the very ground I walked on, and call me his beautiful Buster and his lubly Nosie! and to think I may perhaps never see him again. Oh, dear!"

"Well, never mind, old gal; if you don't, what's the odds? You've got your Buttons left, ain't yer?"

"Oh, yes; that's true," sighed the afflicted Stinger; "but then you're such a little whipper-snapper, you know."

"Whipper-snapper!" echoed Buttons, indignantly; "come, I say, Elizabeth Ann, draw it mild, will yer?"

"Well, you can't carry me, can you?"

"I'm not up to carrying elephants, certainly," returned Buttons.

"Do you dare to call me an elephant?" exclaimed the Stinger, becoming very angry all of a sudden.

"Well, why do you call me a whipper-snapper?"

The aggrieved lady made no reply beyond a hysterical sob, which she gulped down with a sip of rum from her teapot.

Buttons melted a little at her grief, and said, soothingly—

"Mr. Blunt, Stumps, Ironfist, and a lot more are going in search of him."

"And so am I," cried the Stinger. "Give me my umbrella."

"My dear Miss Stinger," exclaimed Bob Blunt, as he caught sight of her portly figure on the beach, "what brings you on land again?"

"The same purpose that brings you, Mr. Blunt. I'm here to join in the search after that unfortunate Jingo."

Our hero looked a little annoyed at this information.

"But you are still somewhat of an invalid, and your strength might hardly be equal——"

"Allow me to remark, Mr. Blunt, as I have done more than once, that the strength of E. A. Stinger will be found equal to every demand that may be made upon it."

"Then you really are resolved?"

"Quite. Nothing can turn me; therefore, don't attempt it. I'll find Jingo, or perish in the attempt."

And the Stinger looked very resolute indeed.

Finding all argument entirely thrown away, our hero was compelled to submit.

He merely said—

"Buttons, you will look after Miss Stinger."

"All right, guv'nor," was the cheerful reply. "Buttons & Co. will look after each other."

From inquiries made in the neighbourhood, it appeared that the missing Jingo had been seen on shore after the rest had embarked.

But that was all the intelligence they could glean respecting him.

"At all events," said Bob, "no efforts shall he spared to find him if alive."

The lively but reckless Buttons chuckled secretly.

Anyhow, whether dead or alive, the mystery of Jingo Johnson would form another powerful incident for his "Tropical Adventures."

The party, having made their start, pursued the same route as they had done when they commenced their explorations.

All were well armed.

The Stinger for the time being, had exchanged her umbrella for a rifle, and her teapot for a flask, which hung by a strap across her shoulders.

Buttons bristled with formidable weapons; a breech-loading rifle in his hand and two six-barrelled revolvers in his belt, and his manuscript buttoned up securely under his jacket.

After proceeding several miles without meeting a living soul, or discovering any traces of the object of their search, they came to a halt.

"I'm afraid," said our hero, as they

sat beneath the shade of the trees for rest and refreshment, " we're engaged on a wild-goose chase."

"The faithful creature," said the Stinger, " knew I wanted a feather for my bonnet. Might he not have wandered away for the purpose of shooting tropical birds with gorgeous tails, and——"

She was interrupted by the report of a gun at some distance.

The Stinger sprang to her feet like a suddenly emancipated Jack-in-the-box.

"Ha, ha, ha! Hark!" she cried, hysterically. " 'Tis he! I'm sure it is; p-p-popping away at parrots and macaws, and all for me."

"We had better not lose any time," said our hero, hastily, "but hasten forward at once."

"Excuse me, captain," suggested Stumps, "but I think——"

"What?"

"That if we were to divide ourselves into three parties, and make a slight circuit, gradually approaching to a centre, some of us must come in sight of him."

"A very good idea indeed, Stumps," Bob replied.

The party was soon divided according to the dwarf's suggestion.

"Now, then, forward!" said the Stinger. "Something like a presentiment strikes me that the honour of finding Jingo is reserved for me."

Shouldering her rifle, the strong-minded woman strode briskly along with all the energy of a British volunteer.

Suddenly there arose on the air a hoarse cry—a cry of mortal agony.

All those who heard it halted, for it was a strange, deathly cry, weird enough to chill the blood of the hearers.

CHAPTER V.

THE TWO NEGROES—A WONDERFUL VOLLEY—LONGSIGHT GIVES AN OPINION, AND ENTERS THE JUNGLE IN PURSUIT—BUTTONS AND THE STINGER ENCOUNTER A TERRIBLE MONSTER, WHICH THEY BRING DOWN WITH THEIR RIFLES.

HARK! That's Jingo's voice," shrieked Elizabeth Ann Stinger, coming to a dead stop.

"By Jingo! I think it is," exclaimed Buttons, suddenly halting also and clutching his rifle.

"What can be the matter with him? Where is he? Jingo, where are you?" called out Elizabeth Ann.

"Jingo, ahoy!" shouted Buttons.

It was just then two dark forms burst from the covert of the wood at about two hundred yards distant from the spot where they were standing.

"Heigh! you niggers, stop, stop!" shouted the Stinger, at the top of her voice; " I command you."

The men turned and looked towards her, but instead of obeying her order ran on more swiftly than before.

"I must teach these disrespectful heathens a lesson," muttered the indignant lady, as she cocked her rifle.

Then turning to her companions, she cried—

"Take aim—fire!"

A tremendous report rang through the air as the weapons were discharged.

When the smoke cleared away the men were nowhere to be seen.

"We've blown them to smash, that's certain," exclaimed Buttons; " poor buffers."

"They ought to have stopped, then, when I ordered them," remarked the Stinger, in a sternly grand tone; " let us advance and search for their remains."

"What an incident for my 'Tropical Adventures,'" thought Buttons, as he made a note of it in his pocket-book.

"THE SERPENT'S FOLDS WERE QUICKLY WOUND ROUND THE GORILLA'S BODY."

They hurried forward, but on reaching the spot not a vestige of a human body—not a fragment of a limb—not even a tooth or a toenail could be found.

The Stinger drew a long breath, and remarked proudly—

"Our volley was tremendously effective, my friends. The black rebels are utterly annihilated."

The party stood now between two enclosures, the vast forest on the left hand, and a kind of jungle of high, reedy grass on the right; and Longsight, after contemplating their position for a moment, took upon himself to offer his opinion.

"It strikes me," he said quietly, to the Stinger, "that these blacks have not undergone the annihilation you seem to imagine; they will yet live to do us harm."

Elizabeth Ann opened her eyes, and glared at the author of such a daring remark.

"Not dead!" she almost gasped.

"No, madam; in fact, I don't think our bullets have touched them."

The Stinger frowned sternly.

"I believe I command this expedition, Mr. Longsight," she said; "and when I give my deliberate opinion upon any subject, it's your duty to coincide in it."

Longsight shrugged his shoulders.

"What reason have you for thinking these niggers have escaped?" asked the female leader, after a moment.

"Well, madam, first because we can't find the bodies."

"Not a bad reason either," said Buttons; "a feller couldn't very well cut and run after he was dead."

"Silence, Buttons!" cried the Stinger, sternly. Then addressing herself once more to Longsight, she continued—

"What else?"

"Why, madam, at the moment we fired I saw—you know my sight's pretty clear——"

"Yes, I know that."

"Well, I saw distinctly the two men throw themselves flat on the ground."

"Dead! didn't I say so?"

"No, madam, not dead; for as the smoke was clearing away, I observed them crawling towards the long grass, in which they disappeared."

The Stinger looked thoughtful.

Buttons made a note of this last circumstance on the spot.

"Well, then," said Elizabeth Ann after a moment, "if that really is the case, these two niggers are alive at this moment?"

"That is my opinion."

"Concealed in this jungle."

"Yes."

"Precisely what I thought myself," cried the Stinger, altering her opinion with wonderful facility; "I feel sure they've fled."

"What's to be done then?" asked Buttons.

The Stinger moistened her throat from her bottle, and then answered—

"They must be pursued."

At this crisis a strange, unearthly groan reached their ears.

"Good Heaven!" exclaimed Elizabeth Ann, impatiently. "What is it? Who is it? Where is it?"

"Not far off, my sweet Betsy, I think," whispered Buttons.

"Whoever it is, I wish they'd speak out, and let us know what ails them," Betsy replied, in a fretful tone.

"The jungle must be searched," said Longsight.

"Of course it must; I was just going to propose it," snapped the Stinger; "you, Mr. Longsight, and your comrades, will conduct the search."

In an instant the gallant Longsight and his companions had plunged into the jungle, and were out of sight.

Buttons and the Stinger were left alone.

She then took a refresher from her flask and offered it to her companion, who accepted it readily.

Buttons had only time to smack his lips in admiration at the draught, when a low growl caught his ear.

"Oh, Lor', Stinger!" he exclaimed, "what's that?"

"Oh, dear, I'm sure I don't know," returned the Stinger, who had also heard the sound. "Be firm, Buttons. Look at me."

"Who's afraid?" cried the page

clutching his rifle and looking round. "Come on, who or whatever you are—lion, leopard, elephant or boa-constrictor; Buttons defies yer!"

Nothing appeared in answer to this friendly invitation, and again the roar was heard louder than before.

There was also a crackling sound in the jungle, as though something living were forcing its way through the tall, thick reeds.

At this critical moment, the Stinger was a sight to see.

Her cheeks were flushed; her nose rosy as a ripe cherry; her eyes very wide open, and apparently about to start from their sockets.

But this was probably caused by the desperate effort she made to look six ways at once.

"Whatever can it be, Buttons?" she murmured, excitedly. "Is it a man, or a—a—monkey? Oh! if it should be a gorilla, Buttons, I am lost."

"Blest if I know what it is," returned the youth; "I'm ready for either."

Again the awful howl rose upon the air.

It was too much for the over-wrought nerves of Elizabeth Ann, and she cried with a nervous burst—

"Buttons, dear, do come here. If it should be a gorilla, I would rather he ran away with you than me. Oh, dear!"

Buttons flew to her side.

"Keep close to me; don't leave me again," she murmured.

"I won't. I'll stick to you like cobbler's wax, Betsy."

The crackling in the jungle now became more audible.

The tall, reedy grass was violently agitated.

The roaring previously heard grew louder than ever.

Buttons and the Stinger, back to back, and looking as if they were propping up each other, waited for what was to come.

The next moment it did come.

An awful-looking head, armed with tremendous horns, and ornamented with dreadful shaggy black hair, appeared towering over the top of the reeds.

"Boo—oo! Boo—oo!" roared the terrible-looking monster.

"Goodness gracious me!" gasped Elizabeth Ann, as she gazed in horror "is it a b—b—buffalo or a b—b—bison?"

"Blest if I don't think it's the d—d—devil come for you, Stinger," muttered Buttons, whose nerves were unusually shaken at the sight.

The strange animal continued its discordant noise, but, strange to say, made no attempt to burst from its covert to attack the adventurers, although it seemed evident to them its black, glassy eyes were fixed upon them.

This gave Buttons and the Stinger time to recover their self-possession to some extent, and it suddenly occurred to them that they had loaded rifles in their hands.

"I really think," said the Stinger, in a low and confidential tone, "it would be as well to fire at that horrid beast."

"I was just thinking so myself, Betsy," returned Buttons; "take a good aim, and have a pop at him."

"Oh, dear! Suppose we both fire together."

"Oh, yes, and we'll fire both barrels at once. Now then, are you ready?"

"Ye—e—e—es."

Bang!

There was a tremendous report from the rifle barrels.

It almost seemed as if the shooters had shot themselves.

Both measured their length on the ground; whilst, singular to relate, the monster bull, or bison—or whatever the strange animal might be—only tossed his head, as if in defiance, and began to move off.

"Where are you, Buttons?" inquired Elizabeth Ann, in a faint voice.

"On my back, my Buster," replied the page, ruefully.

"Help me up!" she entreated.

Buttons rose from the ground, and with some difficulty succeeded in getting his companion on to her feet again.

"Look!" he cried, suddenly, "the what-you-may-call-it's escaping."

"It musn't!" exclaimed the Stinger, recovering much of her usual boldness; "I must have the skin of that brute. Load your rifle, quick!"

"Now, then," said the page, as they came up with the monster, "better luck this time."

"Shut one eye, and take good aim," called out Elizabeth Ann. "Fire!"

Bang! bang! bang! bang!

"Bravo, it's hit!" shouted Buttons, as the animal threw up its shaggy head, as if in its last agony, and disappeared, making a tremendous crashing among the reeds.

At this moment Bob Blunt and his followers emerged from the wood near to where they were standing.

CHAPTER VI.

A STARTLING DISCOVERY—THE RETURN

WHAT have you shot?" our hero asked, eagerly, as he ran towards them.

"A monster, Mr. Blunt, an awful monster!" replied Elizabeth Ann. "He has taken no end of bullets to bring down."

"Let's go and look for him," said our hero; "come on, some of you."

Stumps, Ironfist, and the doctor hurried forward, and were just about to plunge into the jungle, when the Stinger placed herself before them.

"Let no one stir," she exclaimed, "but me and Buttons."

Without the slightest hesitation, the dauntless Elizabeth Ann rushed at the reeds, and forced a passage through them, Buttons keeping close at her heels.

They pressed forward for some distance.

"I say, old gal," suggested her companion, "don't be too venturesome. P'r'aps it mightn't be quite dead, yer know."

"It must be dead," insisted the Stinger; "nothing could stand four bullets in its head."

"All right, my queen," responded Buttons. "You go first, and I'll keep close behind you."

They searched for some little time without success.

At length the Stinger uttered a shriek.

"There it is, there, there!" she cried.

And there it was, sure enough, its awful head drooping and laid low—all its roaring taken out of it—motionless—dead.

As for the body, that was invisible, being concealed by the dense grass in which its ponderous weight had fallen.

The heroic pair stood gazing at the result of their efforts for several moments in silent astonishment.

"It's perfectly wonderful how we did it, Betsy; but it's a moral we've settled him," said Buttons, at length.

Suddenly the Stinger grasped her young companion by his hand.

"Buttons," she said, "I'm inspired."

"The rum's got into your head, old gal, that's what it is," grinned the page.

"No, no, it isn't that; but I've a strong conviction."

"What is it?"

The E. A. S. lowered her voice to a deep whisper, and continued in a freezing tone—

"That we shall find poor Jingo Johnson inside the body of this ferocious monster."

"Good 'Evvin!" gasped Buttons; "if we do, what a stunnin' incident for my 'Tropical Adventures.' But how are we to move this whopping big animal?"

As Buttons spoke, he grasped one of the terrible horns.

Elizabeth Ann grasped the other.

"Now then," he cried, "a strong pull and a long pull, and a yoy-hoy-hoy! Oh!"

"Oh, Lor'!"

There was a yell and a shriek, and Buttons and the Stinger fell crashing amongst the reeds with a horn apiece in their hands.

A burst of laughter rang in their ears,

and looking up, they saw Bob Blunt and his comrades, who had come in search of them.

It took but a few seconds to set the prostrate hunters on their legs again.

" How precious strong I'm getting," said Buttons, as he recovered his perpendicular ; " I've pulled the animal's horns right out by the roots."

" Wonderful !" said Bob Blunt, with a wink at his comrades.

" What an awful head !" joined in Stumps.

" What a mane !" said Ironfist. " Let's see if we can move him."

" No,' cried the Stinger, firmly ; " I object. Let Buttons and myself make another attempt. Now, then, Buttons."

Buttons grasped the long hair that covered the head, and in concert with his companion, tugged at it with all his might.

" Hooray ! it's a-comin'! I feels it move," shouted the page, black in the face with his exertions. " Tug away, Betsy."

No more was said, for at that moment off came the head, and the persevering pair once more fell backwards, with the shaggy object in their hands.

The trick was now discovered.

The monster had no body, but simply a piece of loose skin that hung down from the root of the neck.

Buttons and the Stinger looked somewhat astonished.

" What a swindle !" growled the former.

" Capital incident, though, for your ' Tropical Adventures,' " suggested Stumps, drily.

Buttons glared at the dwarf as though he could have annihilated him.

" We're the victims of some heathenish joke," said the Stinger, in a spiteful tone. " What do you think, Mr. Blunt ?"

" That this has been a decoy to lure us away from this spot," our hero replied, " but by whom employed, I cannot tell."

" I think I can, Mr. Blunt," replied Longsight, who, with his companions, had just returned, and came pushing through the reeds.

" Let us hear."

" Two negroes, I suspect, whom we startled from their place of concealment in this jungle."

" Ha ! and did you capture them ?" inquired Bob, eagerly.

" I'm sorry to say we did not," returned Longsight ; " they were more accustomed to jungle travelling than we are, and contrived to elude us and escape."

" One thing I know," said Longsight ; " they came from the forest yonder."

Bob Blunt remained silent.

" Perhaps Jingo is in yonder forest," said Stumps.

" I've heard cries and groans to-day that augur the commission of some deed of blood, and, depend upon it, that deed is connected with the missing Jingo Johnson."

" Well, let us search, at least," urged our hero.

The party at once forced their way out of the jungle, and, guided by Longsight, bent their steps towards the wood.

Here a diligent search was commenced.

The Stinger had now recovered all her native grandeur and self-possession.

She paused at the entrance of the forest and took a long draught from her flask.

" Now, then, to find my Jingo," exclaimed Stinger.

Then, grasping her rifle, she hastened forward on her errand.

For some time the search continued unsuccessfully.

At length a piercing cry was heard from the Stinger.

" Here he is ! here's poor Jingo !" she screamed. " Help, help, for the noble black Roman."

All heard her voice, and came hurrying towards her.

There lay the body of the unfortunate Jingo, motionless, and bleeding from several wounds, to all appearance dead.

" Oh ! my Jingo, my precious Jingo !" wailed the Stinger, wringing her hands ; " you'll never have the pleasure of carrying me on your back any more. Oh, oh, oh !"

Dr. Knowall examined the wounds of the black man.

" He has lost much blood," he said, " but he still lives. With care he may recover."

A litter was formed, and Jingo was lifted into it, after his wounds had been bound up.

CHAPTER VII.

ON BOARD AGAIN—THE GUN IN THE DISTANCE—AN ENGLISH SHIP—HURRAH!

OUR hero deemed it prudent, on more accounts than one, not to linger on shore.

Accordingly, his ship being ready for sea, they went on board at once, taking with them the wounded Jingo Johnson.

For some time he remained perfectly unconscious, but this was rather an advantage than not, since it enabled Dr. Knowall to extract two bullets from his body.

Gradually his senses returned to him, and on the third day, although very weak from loss of blood, he was sufficiently recovered to be moved on to the deck, where he lay upon a bed, with the fresh sea air blowing over him.

Bob Blunt now felt that he might speak to him.

"Ah, Massa Blunt, dat you?" said Jingo as our hero approached.

"Yes," returned his master, kindly, as he took his outstretched hand in his.

"That lubly missie, too?" continued the wounded negro, as he caught sight of the portly form of the Stinger.

"Yes, it's me, Jingo," returned the latter, reproachfully; "and a pretty dance you led us, going away as you did."

"Me not dance, missie," echoed Jingo, ruefully; "me hab to run for life."

"There, there; don't excite yourself, my good fellow," exclaimed the Stinger; "but get well as fast as you can."

Our hero, having seated himself by the side of the couch, said to Jingo—

"How was it that you came to stay behind? You have caused us all great delay and anxiety."

"Me not stay behind on my own account, massa."

"Not?" echoed Bob.

"No, massa; me hab oder reasons."

"I shall be glad to hear them when you're stronger."

"Me strong enough to tell you now."

"If so, go on then."

"Well, massa, while we stood on de shore waitin' for de boat, me see two men watching us."

"Watching us?"

"Yes, massa."

"Were they black?"

"Yes, massa; black as Ole Scratch."

"What made you think they were watching us?"

"'Cos dey point to de ship so, good many time."

"Well?"

"Well, massa, me not like de look ob dese two men; and me say to myself, me jess keep my eye on 'em."

"You were quite right there; and so——"

"So me walk up towards 'em."

"And what did they do?"

"As soon as dey see me coming along, one jog de oder and point to me, and den dey sneak away. 'Ho, ho,!' me say to myself agin, 'dat's it, is it? Me jes find out whar you going.'"

"So, I suppose, you followed them?"

"Yes, massa, till dey reach the forest."

"What did they do then?"

"Dey make great bolt among de trees, and get out ob sight."

"And you?"

"Me scratch my head a minnit to tink what best to do."

"Prudent Jingo," muttered Elizabeth Ann.

"And den me make up my mind to go slap into de wood after 'em."

"Heroic nigger!" again exclaimed E. A. S.

"Bah! fiddle-um-dee. Pooh!" growled General Orlando, in a tone of disgust, as he stood leaning against the ship's side.

Fortunately for the general's well-being, his indignant ejaculations did not reach the Stinger's ears, or it might have gone hard with him.

"Go on," said Bob Blunt to Jingo;

"you were just going into the wood after the men, you said."

"Yes, massa, but me didn't go; at least, not den."

"Why not?"

"Cos jes den me see wonderful strange animal come out from twixt de trees."

"Was it a tall animal with horns?" asked Elizabeth Ann, eagerly.

"Yes, missee, great long horn."

"And a mane like a bison's?" added Buttons.

"Yes."

"It must have been the identical monster we attacked," cried the Stinger.

"Well," continued Jingo, "this monster jump along into de jungle near de forest, and me follow. Den me creep forward till me come upon lot of niggers sitting round a fire—some ob King Pluto's lot, me sure."

"Why so?"

"Cos de three-fingered rascal, King Pluto, wor sit down in de midst; and dat not all. Dere wor two white men among dem."

"You mean Howard and Bow-legged Bill, don't you?" asked our hero, excitedly.

"Yes, massa, dat's dem."

"By Heaven! that accounts for the ill-treatment you have received. Well, what then? Let us hear quickly."

"Well, massa; I tink den me better go back let you know what me see. But as me creep away, dey ketch sight ob me."

"Poor Jingo!" murmured Elizabeth Ann.

"Bang go rifle."

"Did it hit you?"

"No; but de nex' minnit bang go 'noder one, an' dat did. Den dey bang all togeder. Me don't remember more arter dat."

"The whole affair is explicit to me now," said Bob. "Our arrival startled these murderers, who used every effort to throw us off the scent, and that they are still on our track."

"Well, if they follow us, captain, they'll have to come by water, anyhow," said Stumps, with a smile.

"But ours is not the only vessel in the world," replied Bob Blunt; "and it is possible that some fine morning we might descry them bearing down upon us."

"Well, captain, if we did, I dare say we should know how to stand to our guns," said Ironfist, boldly.

Boom, boom!

The report of a gun came booming across the water, whilst the man at the mast head sang out—

"Ship in the distance!"

All eyes were instantly turned seaward.

A vessel was distinctly visible.

Our hero's telescope was instantly brought into requisition.

"Can you make her out, captain?" asked Stumps.

"Pretty clearly."

"What flag?"

"English."

"Hurrah for old England!"

CHAPTER VIII.

INFORMATION CONCERNING THE SLAVE TRADE.

THE fact that a British vessel was so near was like good news from home.

There was not one of our travellers whose heart did not thrill within him at the welcome fact.

The Stinger was compelled to apply to her tea-pot for support.

Buttons having made a hasty note of the joyous incident, took a walk on his hands for several seconds as the shortest way of calming his excitement.

Rapidly the vessel approached, and she was then found to be an English cruiser.

Having cast anchor, a boat was seen approaching the clipper.

"Who commands this vessel?" demanded the lieutenant, as soon as he approached within hail.

"I do," replied Bob Blunt.

"Where from?"

"Cape Coast."

"Whither bound?"

"Anywhere," answered our hero, with a smile.

"Your course is not very definite," said the lieutenant, smiling in his turn.

"You are right; it is not."

"You are American?"

"No, English."

"But the vessel is American built."

"True; but the owner is English."

"Why, then, do you not display the English flag?"

"Simply because we don't happen to have one on board," Bob answered.

The lieutenant looked a little puzzled.

"What is the nature of your traffic?" he continued, after a moment.

"We are not engaged in any trade."

"The deuce!" muttered the officer to himself.

"The fact is, my dear sir," explained our hero, "we are simply a company of English explorers, here for scientific purposes, and whose only object in coming to Africa is to make such discoveries as may enlarge our own minds and benefit our country."

This reply satisfied the officer entirely.

"I thank you, sir," he said to Bob Blunt, "and beg to apologise if my numerous questions seemed to suggest suspicion."

"If you will favour me by coming on board, you will soon discover that you are among friends," replied our hero.

The lieutenant, attracted by the hearty manner and genial tone in which the invitation was given, at once accepted it.

He, too, as an Englishman, felt a pleasure at the prospect of meeting a body of his fellow-countrymen, and in a few moments he was standing on the deck.

The sight of so many dark faces on board seemed at first to perplex him, but a few words of explanation from our hero, and the warm welcome he received on all sides, removed every lingering doubt from the mind of Lieutenant Calder.

Himself a young man, he was at once attracted to Bob Blunt, and there was soon a perfect understanding between them.

"You were kind enough to question us as to the nature of our traffic," said our hero to him, in the course of conversation; "may I return the compliment, and ask yours?"

"Oh, certainly! But we are here to hinder traffic, rather than encourage it. I mean the traffic in human flesh."

"You allude to the detestable slave trade?"

"Yes."

"Its profits, I suppose, are great?"

"Yes; so great that those who practise it are willing to run every risk, rather than forego the unholy barter."

"The slave dealers are principally to be found amongst the Brazilians and the Portuguese, are they not?" asked Bob.

"Yes; but there are some of negro blood, who prey upon their own countrymen."

"Indeed?"

"Yes. We are on the look-out now for a Congo slaver, of which the captain and crew as well as the living freight she carries are all Africans. Perhaps in your cruisings you may meet her."

"I hope we may," exclaimed Bob, fervently; "for if we do, for the honour of Old England and freedom, we'll have a slap at her."

"You'll know her by her dark hull, and by her lying very low in the water."

"I'm glad of your description, since it strikes me this African slaver would not be so ready to answer questions as we were," said Bob, with a laugh.

"Oh, you need not stand on any ceremony with such; and as to the questions, we have only one medium through which we put them," said Lieutenant Calder.

"And that is?"

"The guns of a British ship, and the brave hearts of our British Tars.

"Will you kindly let me know the plan of proceeding?" asked Bob.

The lieutenant explained very distinctly what he meant to do, and after sitting down to lunch with our hero and his companions, departed in the boat with a mutual interchange of good wishes.

The Stinger had been very much impressed by the young officer.

"Farewell, gallant sailor," sobbed the subdued, but heroic female. "My heart's in the Highlands wherever I go! The anchor's weighed! and—oh, dear—I'm too overpowered to say more. Adieu! Remember me!"

There was something slightly rambling in this her farewell address, as the reader will probably observe.

Lieutenant Calder promised faithfully never to forget her, which promise he doubtless kept.

In course of time the boat returned to the clipper, with a present from the English captain.

A Union Jack, which our hero received with much pleasure and many thanks.

"Now," he cried, with enthusiasm, as he unfurled it, "under the shadow of England's flag, let our foes beware of us."

A loud hurrah from all on board echoed his defiance.

And as if the very elements answered in sympathy, the breeze freshened.

The clipper weighed anchor and stood out to sea, the Union Jack flying at the fore.

The day declined, and the moon rose, bathing the ocean in her silver light.

Our hero stood on the deck alone, looking thoughtfully out across the glittering waves.

Suddenly a soft hand was placed upon his.

He turned and found Nahita at his side.

"I am so glad to see you," she murmured, softly; "are you glad to see Nahita?"

"I am always glad to see my friends," replied Bob, but with some little reserve in his tone.

Nahita seemed disappointed.

"Ah!" she said, reproachfully, "but you are not more glad to see me than you are to see any of the rest; you do not find the time pass heavily in my absence; you do not watch for my coming, and count the moments till we meet. I do."

There was much in the tone and manner in which these words were uttered, that proved to our hero what he had often suspected, that the young African girl loved him.

But he would not encourage this feeling in her breast, knowing that the semi-barbarous life she had led would preclude the possibility of his making her his wife, and he said to her, in a gentle manner—

"It is very well for you, Nahita, who have nothing else to do, to amuse yourself with watching and counting the minutes as they fly, but if I were to indulge in such dreamy pastimes, what would become of us all?"

Nahita made no reply.

"You have yourself been witness to some of the perils we have passed through."

"Yes," she replied, in a low tone. "I am always ready to listen to you."

"I know it," replied our hero, warmly; "no master ever had a more obedient pupil."

Nahita smiled, and her dark eyes flashed with pleasure at these praises.

"I will not complain any more," she said, as she once more took Bob's hand and pressed it to her lips. "I do not ask you to love me; only let me love you, and I shall be content. May I?"

"Certainly, if you think me worth it," replied our hero, cheerfully.

This assurance satisfied her, and releasing his hand, she was about to retire to her cabin.

At the top of the companion ladder was General Orlando.

His attitude was imposing, and had been carefully studied in order to produce an effect—a striking effect.

He had been smitten by Nahita's beauty.

"Notink like habing two strings to de bow," he argued. "Nahita king's daughter; me marry her, me be king some day, p'raps."

With this idea in his mind, he waited till Nahita approached, and then stepping forward, threw himself on his knees before her.

"What do you seek?" she asked, recoiling a step.

"Me not seek notink but you, lubly Nahita," answered the general.

The eyes of the African beauty flashed scornfully.

"I am a king's daughter," she said, in a proud tone.

"Dere no doubt 'bout dat," returned Orlando; "dat de reason why me tink so much ob you. Me offer you my hand an' heart, an' dis here cocked hat."

As he spoke, he took off the ornament alluded to and laid it at her feet.

"And do you suppose I should degrade myself by mingling my race with such as you?" she exclaimed, drawing herself up haughtily.

"My race bery good race," explained the general. "Me got relatives 'mongst de roy'l family som'eres. Say you gib me your hand, an' dat all I ask."

Nahita instantly gave him her hand, and boxed his ears soundly.

"Let me pass," she cried, indignantly, "and never dare to speak to me again."

Then giving his cocked hat a contemptuous kick, with her small foot, she darted down the cabin stairs.

The general was furious.

Not so much at having his ears warmed as at the assault upon his hat.

"Dere's a cantank'rus wermin," he muttered, as he carefully picked up the dishonoured article; "de idea ob treatin' gen'l'man in dat ar way, jes' as if he was a pig."

He arranged the feather, which had been ruffled.

"Nebber mind," he said, at length; "me not take no more notice of Nahita. She impudent, ugly minx. Me pay my 'dresses to Missie Stinger, an' if dat 'ere Jingo Johnson poke himself in de way, me pull him nose, dat what me do."

And with this heroic determination, General Orlando prepared to descend the cabin steps, but his sword became entangled in his legs, and unable to recover himself, he pitched headlong down, falling upon Rope's End, who was just coming up.

There was a yell of rage, and a volley of growls, and finally a tremendous fight at the foot of the stairs between the angry negroes.

So great was the uproar that everyone was aroused from their sleep, and came forth to see what was the matter.

Then they found the general and the black boatswain rolling on the ground, tearing each other's wool off by handfuls, and biting, and snarling, and scratching like a couple of wild wolves.

Bob Blunt, hearing the tumult, hurried below.

"Stop! Let there be an end of this," he cried, in a tone of command.

But the belligerents fought on with undiminished fury.

At length a voice was heard amidst the throng.

"Where are they? Let me get at them," it cried.

It was the well-known tones of the Stinger.

The next moment the illustrious lady appeared in all the majesty of dressing-gown and night-cap, and armed with all the terrors of female authority, in the shape of her umbrella.

Buttons was at her heels, with his note-book in his hands.

"More incidents," he chuckled. "Go it, Betsy; let 'em have it."

"They shall have it—as we say in the tropics—hot. Stand aside, everyone," she cried.

All made way for her.

Bang!—swish!—swash! went the ponderous domestic article on the backs and heads of the combatants, with an energy of which none but herself would have been capable.

"Golly! Missee Stinger, dat you?" was the remark of General Orlando, who was the first to turn his head and look towards her.

"Yes, you heathen, it is me; get up this moment."

The general gave his opponent a parting punch on his nose, and rose to his feet.

"Now then, you!" said E. A. S. to the herculean boatswain, who was growling and rubbing his nasal organ.

She accompanied this injunction with a dig in the ribs with the point of her umbrella, which caused him to spring to his feet at once.

The two negroes stood eyeing one

another fiercely, as if half inclined to begin again.

Seeing this, Bob Blunt stepped forward.

"You two fellows are a couple of mutinous rascals, and I order you both under arrest. Let them be put in irons," he cried, in a stern and imperative tone.

The general gave an imploring and penitential look at this sentence.

Not so his countryman, whose eyes, always evil in their expression, glared like live coals, whilst his teeth, gleaming from betwixt his protruding lips, gave him the expression of an incarnate fiend.

"No man put me in irons; me no slave," he growled.

Ironfist went quietly up to him.

"No," he said, in a calm tone, "you're only a big bully; but we have our own way of dealing with such."

Rope's End looked scornfully down upon Ironfist, and drew up his arm as if about to give him a back-handed blow and sweep him away.

But Ironfist anticipated him.

Swift as an arrow from a bow, his powerful arm shot forth upwards, catching the rebel boatswain clean under his chin.

Never in his life before had the giant received such a blow.

His jaws shut with a sudden snap, and big as he was, he was hoisted clean off his legs.

In falling, his head came in contact with the last step of the cabin stairs, with a violence that would have crushed the skull of anyone but a negro; but as it was, it completely stunned him.

His giant bulk lay motionless on the ground.

"Away with him!" cried our hero, as he pointed to the prostrate form. "Let him be handcuffed until the rebel spirit in him is tamed."

Rope's End was instantly hoisted up, and conveyed to the hold, Ironfist superintending the operation of handcuffing.

Bob Blunt then turned to the general, whose sable features, swollen from his recent encounter, looked ludicrously mournful.

"You will be placed under restraint," he said to him, "until you learn obedience to the rules of discipline."

It was just then the man on the lookout called—

"Ship in the distance!"

Our hero and his comrades hastened on deck.

The day was only just breaking, and it was impossible to discern in the dim light what the vessel was.

In fact, at present nothing could be seen of her but the tops of her masts.

Many were the opinions hazarded by those who stood watching her.

Some supposed her an American; some a Frenchman.

The Stinger, who had a small field glass to her eye, boldly declared it was an English man-of-war; whilst Buttons, who had rolled up his manuscript, and looked through it, sagely pronounced it to be a coal barge.

The day grew apace, and before long it was quite light.

Still the vessel was at a great distance.

"Can you make her out?" called Bob Blunt to the man aloft.

"Yes, sir; pretty well," was the reply.

"Any colours?"

"No, sir."

"Anything strange about her?"

"Dark hull; sits deep in the water."

Our hero's cheek flushed at this description, and he exclaimed aloud—

"The African slaver, by Heaven!"

CHAPTER IX.

THE SLAVER—BUTTONS' OPINION.

"A SLAVE SHIP!"

The freedom-loving hearts of the Englishmen at once began to throb with indignation.

"You'll give chase, won't you?" Iron-fist demanded, eagerly.

"More willingly than I ever gave anything in my life," was our hero's hearty reply.

"Nobly spoken, Mr. Blunt," exclaimed the Stinger, in a tone of strong approval; "yours are the words of a true Boy of England."

"Hooray!" shouted Buttons; "Britons never will be slaves."

Again the cheer was taken up vociferously.

The "Adventurer" was then put under an extra press of canvas, and her course was altered so as to intercept that of the suspected vessel.

Like a bird she bounded over the waters.

Everyone kept their eyes in the direction of the strange craft.

In the meantime, our hero made preparations for an attack.

The large guns were sponged out.

The rifles and revolvers were loaded; and weapons and cartridges were served out to the Kroomen who evinced a disposition to be faithful to their new master.

After an hour's rapid sailing, they had made so much head-way that they were able to distinguish the vessel more distinctly.

Bob Blunt by means of his glass could now form a better opinion as to her distinctive character.

One thing was especially observable.

Scarcely any of her hull was visible above her water line, and what could be seen was of a dead black, unenlivened by any other colour.

These peculiarities, so particularly mentioned by Lieutenant Calder, seemed to point to her without any doubt as the slaver which the English cruiser was in search of.

Our hero stood watching her as she ploughed the waves, looking more like a long raft rather than a ship capable of holding several hundred human beings stowed away under the dark noisome hatches.

Maintop, one of his Kroo sailors, volunteered some information respecting the vessel.

"Massa look arter dat 'ere dhow?"* he said, as he quietly placed himself at his captain's elbow.

"Yes," replied Bob; "do you know anything of her?"

"Well, massa, me tink she come from up yonder."

He pointed landward as he spoke.

"And have you any idea what her cargo may consist of?"

"If she got any cargo at all, it sure to be all same kind," returned Maintop, his eyebrows contracting as he shrugged his shoulders.

"What kind is that?"

"Niggers."

"Why, that craft does not seem large enough for such a freight," said Bob.

"Oh, yes, she am, massa," returned the Krooman, nodding his woolly head significantly; "de ship body down underneath the water, long way, where massa can't see."

"And her hold perhaps filled with helpless slaves?"

"Dat very like, massa," assented the negro.

Our hero compressed his lips as he muttered—

"With Heaven's help, I'll make the wretches give up their miserable victims?"

"Dat right, massa, do," said the Krooman, earnestly. "We niggers all help you fight."

---

* An African slave ship.

At this juncture, Stumps and several of his companions gathered round.

"You've quite decided upon overhauling this black-looking craft?" inquired the dwarf of his commander.

"Quite," returned our hero.

"Bravo, captain ; we'll stand by you."

"To the death !" joined in Ironfist and Longsight.

The Stinger and Buttons, with a noble indifference to such a fate, expressed themselves in the same manner.

"I tell you what it is, Betsy," he said to her, confidently. "We shall blow that black object to smithereens at the first fire."

"I have not the least doubt of it," replied Elizabeth Ann.

"Just stick to me, my dear, and we'll work one of the big guns between us, eh?"

"So we will, Buttons."

"You shall load and ram down, and I'll fire."

"No, you had better do the loading, and leave the firing to me," suggested the Stinger.

"Well, as you like ; only, mind, it is rather startling to the nerves."

"My nerves are iron."

It suddenly struck the page that he had left his note book below, and together he and his staunch companion left the deck.

"What a lot of first-rate incidents I shall get for my 'Tropical Adventures' out of this," he chuckled to himself, as he descended.

But little did he dream then how nearly one of these was to concern himself.

They were now within a mile of the slaver.

Not a soul appeared to be on her deck, and yet she was kept in her right course by a masterly hand, although an invisible one.

"They work under a mask," said Bob Blunt to Stumps.

"We'll soon have the mask off, captain," laughed the dwarf.

The dhow had evidently sighted the clipper, and was doing its best to avoid it and get towards the shore.

"It's a pity we've lost two of our hands," remarked our hero, after a moment.

"You mean Rope's End and the general, don't you, sir?"

"Yes. I've half a mind to release them. In an affair of this kind we can't afford to spare one of our number."

"You can do as you please, of course, sir," repeated Stumps, respectfully ; "but I'm inclined to think they're better out of the way than in it. Not that I apprehend any danger from the general. I think he's harmless enough. But the other——"

"You mistrust Rope's End?"

"I do, indeed, sir. If ever the fiend had lodgings in a human breast, he has taken up his abode in that black boatswain."

"Oh! I think we may be able to keep the fiend down," said Bob. "And besides, he's a powerful fellow——"

"Who will betray you at the first opportunity."

"He'd better not attempt it if he values his life," exclaimed our hero, sternly. "At the first sign of treachery, I'll blow the rascal's brains out."

"In my humble opinion, captain, you couldn't do a better thing. He's one of those sullen brutes that nothing but shooting will take any effect upon."

"I should think the lesson Ironfist gave him will——"

Our hero's remarks were abruptly interrupted by loud yells from Buttons, accompanied by shrieks from the Stinger, who were below.

"Halloa!" cried our hero ; "something unusual must be the matter."

Before they could reach the hatchway, Elizabeth Ann herself made her appearance, her face flushed, her dress ribboned, and in a state of the highest excitement.

"Murder—murder—help! Oh, Mr. Blunt! that heathen wretch! Mur—ur—der !"

"What do you mean?" inquired Bob.

"Poor Buttons!" gasped the Stinger, as her legs gave way under her and she sat down abruptly on the deck ; "he'll be killed !"

"Who's killing him?"

"That black giant."

"Rope's End?"

"Yes! I had—a—a—tussle with him, but he was too much for me. Oh, dear!"

"Follow me!" cried Bob Blunt, as he rushed to the companion ladder.

His companions were close to his heels, but their further progress was arrested by a loud splash in the water, and again the voice of Buttons was heard in a loud tone—

"Oh, help—help—somebody!" he cried.

"By Heaven, he's overboard!" exclaimed our hero.

All rushed to the ship's side, and there sure enough was the page struggling in the waves.

CHAPTER X.

BUTTONS' RESCUE—THE WARNING.

WITHOUT pausing to remove a particle of his dress, Bob Blunt sprang up on to the bulwarks and plunged into the sea.

The luckless Buttons had disappeared; but the next moment he rose again to the surface.

Our hero at once caught him by the neck.

Ironfist, Stumps and Bobstay had followed their captain's example in leaping into the waves; so that there were plenty to assist the page.

A rope was quickly thrown, and in a few seconds the whole party were once more safely on deck.

Buttons, having recovered his breath and emptied himself of about a gallon of salt water, which laid heavy on his chest, gave a hurried account of the catastrophe that had befallen him.

He had gone downstairs for his note book, he said.

While seeking for it in his cabin, he heard a strange noise beneath the flooring.

Suddenly, as he was looking to ascertain the cause, two planks started up with a crash, and a hideous black head appeared.

It was the head of Rope's End who had been confined in the hold beneath.

With a second crash two more planks gave way, and the brawny shoulders of the boatswain rose up to view.

His first act was to seize Buttons by the leg and hold him whilst he drew himself up out of his prison house.

"I ordered him to let go my leg and go back to prison directly," said Buttons, "but he grinned like a tiger cat, and said he'd strangle me if I made the least noise."

"And you?"

"Not wishing to be scragged by a nigger, I assumed the defensive," exclaimed the page.

"What do you mean?"

"Gave him a oner in his ribs," was the plucky reply.

"And he?"

"Didn't like it; for he let go of my leg directly."

"Good!"

"No, it wasn't; for he caught me directly after by my arm and began shaking me."

"And then you called out——"

"'Murder' like a good un. The dear old Stinger heard me, and came to the rescue, like a brick as she is, with her umbrella."

"Did she attack the ruffian?"

"Rather! She let him have it hot over his head and shoulders, till at last he caught hold of her, and almost turned the beautiful Buster inside out."

"And what then?"

"Why, then, with a horrid demoniac grin, like Mephistoffles, the atroshus nigger hoisted me up and sent me flyin', head fust, out of the cabin winder into the briny deep."

"You don't know, I suppose, what became of him?" asked Bob Blunt.

"No, that I don't," answered Buttons. "I was only thinking what was to become of my precious self."

"I'm not surprised at that," returned our hero.

Then turning to those around him, he said—

"Let us search below"

Down they went into the hold.

It was empty.

But they discovered that the negro, with his knife, had cut into the flooring of the cabin above, and by dint of his enormous height and strength, had forced up the planks, as Buttons had explained.

The question then arose, where had he concealed himself?

Every hole and corner of the vessel was explored, but the giant was not to be found.

There was only one way of accounting for his disappearance.

He must have thrown himself overboard.

"These black fellows can swim like fishes," said Bob Blunt; "water is with them almost a native element, and my opinion is that he is at this moment making for the shore."

"Bring the glasses to bear. Let's see," cried Bob Blunt, as he hurried up on to the deck.

Bobstay, the Krooman, at this moment advanced, and said to him in an undertone—

"Rope's End good swimmer, massa. He dive much; go 'long under water long time."

"Ah! I forgot that," exclaimed our hero, to himself.

And again he looked through his glass.

But to no purpose.

Maintop stood by, watching him for a few moments.

At length he said to him—

"Massa quite sure Rope's End go towards de shore?"

"Why, where else could he go?" asked our hero.

"Massa forget dere ship yonder."

As he spoke the Kroo boy pointed to the slaver.

"Is it possible he would have sought refuge there?" asked Bob.

"Tink it bery possarble, massa," returned Maintop.

"What! where they would take him and sell him as a slave?"

"Not so sure 'bout dat, capt'n," replied Maintop and Bobstay. "Rope's End sell oders, but he no slave himself."

Bob Blunt waited to hear no more, but at once, by means of his telescope, scanned the waters in the direction of the slaver.

At first he could discern nothing, but gradually, as he looked, he fancied he could descry an unusual commotion beneath the waves.

He pointed this out to his companions.

"What should you take that to be?" he asked them.

"It might be the track of a shark," said some.

"Or a sea serpent," remarked the Stinger, who had now recovered herself, and was taking part in the general outlook, and a hearty pull at her teapot.

"Or a man," said Bob Blunt.

"You see presently, massa," said Bobstay; "he come up get bref of air."

A very few seconds elapsed, and the dark head and brawny shoulders of the boatswain became visible.

"It is the rascal!" cried Longsight, whose visual organs were alone able to distinguish him clearly; "he's looking round at us."

"He deserves a shot, captain," said Ironfist, as he half raised his rifle.

"Perhaps he does," replied Bob Blunt; "but let him go for the present; to fire at him now would only be wasting powder and bullet."

As if to prove the truth of this fact, the dark form again disappeared; and did not again show itself for several minutes.

When it was seen again, it was like a mere speck.

And almost under the bows of the slaver.

*   *   *   *   *

Let as now take a peep on board the slave ship, and see what was going on there.

"THEY FOUND THE GENERAL AND THE BLACK BOATSWAIN ON THE FLOOR, FIGHTING LIKE WOLVES."

In her dark hull were packed some hundred and fifty negroes, who were being drafted from one part of the coast to another, to be sold as slaves.

We will not pause to describe the foul prison-house in which these hapless beings were crammed.

Enough to state that it was all that the base cupidity of man or the infernal malice of fiends could have devised of torture and discomfort.

The poor victims were tightly battened down in the depths of the vessel, where little light could penetrate and less air.

The deck was low, so that those on board, even when standing erect, could be scarcely visible from the deck of another vessel.

Yet concealed behind the bulwarks of this floating mass were the captain and crew who guided her in her infamous traffic.

All were black, although the captain, from certain modifications of feature, might have been suspected of being of a mixed race.

It was evident that they were extremely apprehensive of the clipper.

By means of glasses which they possessed, they had sighted her long since.

They had made strenuous efforts to get away from her.

It was therefore with no little dismay they found the latter cleverly drawing nearer and nearer, coming athwart their track.

They could see the Union Jack at the fore, and the white faces on her deck.

And they recognised these as English, and knew what they had to expect, unless they could either evade the clipper, or run ashore in defiance of her presence.

The captain, whose name was Charon, was smoking a cigar, and looking through a loophole in the ship's side, with a moody frown upon his brow.

"What fetiche devil has sent these English here?" he growled at length. "In two hours, with this wind, we might have reached the bay and landed the whole cargo."

"Well, captain," replied one who seemed to be second in command; "devil or no devil, there she is, and the question is how are we to get away from her?"

"Yes, that is the question. Curse them; curse every white man among them!" cried the captain, clenching his hands fiercely; "but they shan't ruin me."

"They'll rescue your cargo and scuttle your vessel, and I call that ruin," said the black mate.

The only answer to this was a low growl, like that of an enraged lion, that rolled forth from the capacious chest of Charon.

And again Charon fixed his eyes upon the clipper that was steadily advancing.

It was just then a splashing sound was heard over the starboard side, and a voice cried—

"Throw rope dar, will yar?"

The tones seemed familiar.

For the captain at once turned across the deck and looked down into the waves.

"Karfa!" he cried in surprise; "is it you?"

"Yas, it's me. Whar de rope!"

"Here!"

Instantly the rope was thrown.

And Bob's black boatswain, whose rightful appellation was Karfa, clambering up, rolled himself over the low bulwark and quickly stood upright on the deck, and his first demand was for a drop of rum.

This luxury having been supplied, the captain of the slaver said to him—

"And now tell me what wind has blown you here?"

"Same wind dat blow dat ar clipper, me tink," grinned Karfa, nodding his head in the direction of the vessel.

The dark fierce eyes of Charon opened eagerly at this reply; and he said, quickly—

"Have you been aboard her?"

"Yes; me jess leave her."

"Good! then you can tell me what I want to know."

"Me tell you, capt'n. In de first place dese English am debbils outright. But I will help you to destroy all of them."

"I know the English fight well," said the captain of the slaver.

"And they hate slavers."

"I know that too."

"An' last, dey arter you; cos dey tink you got slaves aboard."

"I thought so," muttered Charon, half to himself; "and these English fight like lions."

"Golly, yes!" exclaimed Rope's End rubbing his jaws, that were puffed and swollen; "an' dey hit like thunderbolts."

"They have guns on board?"

"Yes, big guns—big ball—and much powder."

"Are you sure they are in pursuit of me?" asked the African captain.

"Sartin."

Charon's countenance fell.

Rope's End observed it, and said to him—

"You got lot ob niggers stowed below—eh?"

Charon nodded, as he replied, bitterly—

"The finest cargo I've had for many a day."

"Then, by golly, you hab to look sharp," said Rope's End, "for dat English ship after you."

"I'll do one of two things," said the captain, in a tone of terrible determination.

"What's dat?"

"I'll either land them or sink them."

"There may be one way still of baffling these English," said Poonah, who had been silently listening to the foregoing conversation.

"Let me hear!"

"To run up another sail and make a dash for the shore. If we can reach land first, all may yet be well."

"It shall be tried," replied Charon.

An extra sail was quickly hoisted.

Already the slaver felt the additional impetus to her motion.

The eyes of the captain flashed with satisfaction, but it quickly changed to a dark frown.

Boom!

The report of a gun from the clipper came booming across the sea.

"They think to frighten us," said Charon, scornfully. "That was only a blank discharge."

"To make us heave to," added Poonah.

"You no do dat?" asked Rope's End.

"They shall blow us out of the water first," responded the captain, sternly.

The boatswain grinned at this, as he said—

"You soon hear someting more from de clipper."

They had not long to wait before the gun belched forth again, and there was a dull splash on the starboard side of the slaver.

"Sometink in de gun dat time, captain," remarked Rope's End, with a shrug.

Charon bit his lips with sudden vehemence till the blood almost started forth.

Then, dashing down his cigar, he hastily gave some directions to his crew.

It was evident enough his passions were aroused.

The desire to retain his property and to avenge himself upon his pursuers made his features terrible to behold.

At this juncture a ringing shout from the clipper came floating to his ear.

He answered it with a bitter malediction, and a dark frown.

CHAPTER XI.

"JUMP FOR YOUR LIVES!"—THE EXPLOSION.

IN opening fire, in order to arrest the attention of the slaver, our hero had followed the instructions of Lieutenant Calder to the letter.

But when neither of the discharges seemed to produce any effect, save that of inducing her to hoist more sail and quicken her speed, he thought it time to take more decided measures.

Out of pity to the poor wretches imprisoned within her, he forbore bringing his loaded cannon to bear upon her; since, by so doing, he might have destroyed the lives he so earnestly desired to save.

He therefore briefly addressed his devoted followers.

"My gallant friends," he said, "you see how yonder craft, whose traffic I believe to be as dark as her colour, seems stricken dumb at our summons and makes no response. She evidently intends to elude us if she can. But it is not my intention to allow her to escape; and since we cannot bring her to by fair means, I have made up my mind to board her!"

A hearty British cheer burst from every breast at these words.

It was this cheer that had sounded so ominously in the ears of the captain of the slaver.

It seemed to ring the death-knell of his hopes.

In a very short time the boats were lowered.

Bob Blunt commanded one, Stumps the other; whilst the Kroomen—strong, active, and capital sailors—took the oars.

All the Englishmen were thoroughly armed with cutlasses and revolvers.

The boats, impelled by such willing hands, made rapid progress.

Whilst the dark, mysterious craft ploughed her way through the billows, as some prowling thief, conscious of guilt, skulks away from his pursuers.

There was something weird and unnatural in the sight of her, since not a living soul appeared on deck.

She might have been a phantom vessel, manned by a phantom crew.

As our hero approached her he shouted—

"Are you alive, there, or dead?"

His question was immediately answered by the captain himself, who started up and exclaimed hoarsely—

"We are alive!"

There was something indescribably ferocious in the aspect of Charon, as he uttered these words.

A tiger at bay is but a faint illustration of the deadly ferocity expressed in his flashing orbs and clenched teeth.

"From good authority," said Bob, "we suspect you of having slaves on board; and therefore, in the name of the Queen of England, we demand assurance on this point, and for that purpose intend to overhaul your vessel."

He was answered by a demoniac laugh.

"You are welcome," he cried, ironically; "come if you dare! Death is around!"

And with this defiance he disappeared.

The men bent to their oars with redoubled energy, and it was not long before they had reached the slaver.

The grappling-irons were thrown out, and in a few seconds our hero and his comrades trod the slaver's deck.

Surprise again seized them. It was perfectly deserted.

"What does this mean?" exclaimed Bob Blunt, as he looked around him.

A hand was laid sharply and suddenly upon his arm. He turned and encountered the anxious face of his Krooman, Maintop.

"Me tell you what it mean," he said, in a low, earnest tone; "if massa an' his friends stop here anoder minnit, it mean death to all."

"Death!" echoed our hero, with an incredulous smile. "Why, who's to kill us? There is no one here."

"No, dere no one here," returned Maintop. "Dat true 'nough; but look dere."

As he spoke he pointed to where a thin, bluish smoke came streaming up through a crack in the deck. At the same moment a strong smell of something burning became perceptible.

A cry of horror burst from Bob's lips.

"They have set the ship on fire!" he exclaimed, in a voice hoarse with indignation, "and the poor wretches below are suffocating. Quick! wrench open the hatches," he shouted.

In an instant everyone was at work with knives and axes, and any weapon that came first to hand.

As soon as the first plank was torn up, a thick cloud of sulphurous smoke poured forth from the opening.

But no imploring cries came from below.

The poisonous vapour had, most probably, already done its work and hushed the voices of the victims for ever.

Before any stroke could be made, Maintop yelled out loudly—

"Massa, massa, get 'way! Down dere full ob gunpowder!"

At this fearful intimation the boldest paused, whilst again the Krooman's voice was heard in a wild, panic-stricken tone as he sprang upon the bulwarks—

"Quick, mass! jump; jump, all, for your lives!" and then sprang off into the sea.

But not an Englishman stirred.

All remained calmly at their posts, looking inquiringly at their captain, and waiting for his orders.

"We can do no good here," said Bob, after a moment, as the smoke rushed up in a thick, dense column, "and may only sacrifice ourselves to no purpose. Let each one leave the ship at once. Now, lads, into the sea for safety."

The next moment the whole party had plunged into the waves and were making their way as rapidly as possible from the scene of danger.

Not a moment too soon had they taken the Krooman's advice.

They were hardly thirty yards from the slaver when a bright flash, a tremendous shock, and a deafening report was heard.

The vessel had blown up.

For one instant the air was dark with fragments of timber and mangled human limbs, borne upwards to a great height by the violence of the explosion; the next the sea had covered the victims, nothing remaining but a few timbers and spars that still floated on the surface.

Our hero and his followers had all felt the concussion caused by the sudden expansion of the air at the moment of the explosion.

The sea was violently agitated and seemed to threaten the destruction of the boats, but fortunately they were preserved.

It was just as they had contrived to clamber into them that they perceived a small dark object struggling in the waves.

It was soon found to be a negro boy.

"Thank Heaven! there's one of the poor fellows escaped at least," cried Bob Blunt, fervently.

The young negro, seeing the occupants of the boat were white men, swam towards them.

He was quickly grasped by the strong hand of Ironfist, and hoisted on board, and in a short time the whole party were standing once more high and dry upon the clipper's deck.

The Stinger's attire—to say nothing of her nerves—having been considerably disarranged by the rough treatment she had received at the hands of Rope's End, she had not accompanied the boarding expedition.

Buttons, for the same reason, remained behind, and both had watched the proceedings at a safe distance.

He and the strong-minded Elizabeth Ann warmly greeted their companions on their return, and all gathered round the African boy who had been preserved so wonderfully from the general wreck.

"And now tell us, my lad," said our hero, kindly, to him, "how it was you contrived to escape?"

The dusky youth glanced round at the eager eyes that were fixed on him for an instant, and then said, as he shook his woolly head—

"Me hardly know, massa. Me fastened down tight in dark hole wid de rest."

"You must have found it very close," remarked the Stinger, with a shudder.

"Yes, missee; drefful close—drefful hot—drefful stench; eb'ryting dere drefful!"

"There were a great number of you altogether, I suppose?" said Bob Blunt.

"Yes, massa," returned the boy; "dere great big lot black mans and womans. Place quite cram full."

"Poor wretches!" exclaimed the listeners, in a tone of sympathy.

"Ah, yes!" continued the boy; "dey much cry, dey much groan, but none take no notice."

"And what then?"

"Dis go on long time, till by an' by dere strong smell ob fire an' de smoke begin make chokee chokee. Great many begin struggle and fight like mad—get out; but no good. Some dey drop down, lie quite still; not move any more."

"Suffocated—dead!"

"Yes, massa; tink so."

"And how was it you managed to get

out of the way of the 'chokee chokee?'" demanded Buttons.

"Dere chink in de boards, an' me put my mouf dere, an' de air come in."

"Lucky chink for you, old fellow," remarked the page.

"But you could not have existed long under such circumstances," said our hero.

"No, massa, not long," repeated the boy, making a grimace indicative of suffering; "me jess beginning to gasp when me hear drefful loud bang."

"And what did you do then?"

"Notink, massa. Me feel like me shot up eber so high in de air."

"As you undoubtedly were," said Bob Blunt, with a smile.

"Yes, massa. Den see de daylight agin; an' me fly up—up—up—till me tink me going bang into de clouds. Den me stop all of a sudden, turn over heels, an' come down quicker dan me go up, till me fall splash into de sea."

"And then we picked you up after your aërial voyage, perfectly sound and unhurt," said our hero, cheerily, as he patted the young darkey on his shoulder.

"Yas, massa," returned the latter; "me not hurt bit."

"Wonderful!"

And Buttons recorded the hair-breadth escape in his note-book.

"Well, my lad," said Bob Blunt, to the boy, "we are Englishmen, and will neither ill-treat you nor sell you into slavery. Only be faithful to us."

"Me be faithful, massa."

"That's right. And now I must christen you. What shall your name be?"

"I think, guv'nor," said Buttons, "for a young nigger that's been shot up sky-high as he has been, you couldn't choose a better name than Sky-rocket."

"I agree with you, Buttons," replied his master; "Sky-rocket be it then."

He turned to the young African, and laying his hand upon his head, said to him—

"Henceforth your name is Sky-rocket."

The boy grinned all over his dark features.

"Me Sky-rocket!" he exclaimed, as he capered about the deck with delight;

"dat bery good name. Yah, hah; Sky-rocket."

Our hero having settled this point, looked out towards the spot where the explosion had taken place.

It was quite clear.

The *débris* of the wreck had floated away, and none could have dreamt that more than a hundred souls had been engulfed beneath the surface of the sun-lit waves; but suddenly a thought suggested itself to our hero.

The slaver had been destroyed, and with her the hapless victims she carried; but her owner and his crew where were they? Had they also perished?

During the intense excitement and confusion that had prevailed, self-preservation and anxiety for the lives of others had been the absorbing thoughts of every breast; but now that reason and reflection had resumed their sway, Bob Blunt found that he was asking himself this last question over and over again.

At length he called his followers round him, and suggested the inquiry to them.

It was one not easily answered.

Stumps was the first to offer a suggestion.

"We can all understand," he said, "these slave-dealers who traffic in human flesh blowing up a vessel, with its living cargo, rather than let it be taken from them, but at the same time, we may also suppose that these same dealers would have a very great objection to blow up themselves."

"Well, if they have got away, they must have gone in the boats," said Stumps.

"Undoubtedly," said Longsight, as he raised his glass, and scanned the ocean round.

To the naked eye nothing could be seen floating on the vast expanse of water.

But after a few moments he uttered an ejaculation.

"I think I have them," he cried; "but the distance is too great to define anything accurately, but I am just able to discern a small dark object, which I take to be a boat."

Every square inch of canvas that she could carry was at once put upon the clipper, till she literally flew through the waters like a race-horse on the course.

But still the small dark spot in the distance seemed to progress with equal speed.

It was only as the day was drawing to a close that the clipper gave evidence of her superior swiftness.

The dark spot was discerned in the waning light to be two boats.

But the sudden darkness of the tropics fell upon them, and all was shrouded in the veil of night.

And when morning dawned, every vestige of the boats had disappeared.

CHAPTER XII.

THE CLIPPER FINDS SAFE ANCHORAGE.

THERE was much disappointment felt by our English adventurers that the murderous slave-dealers had slipped through their fingers.

The weather was lovely.

The heat of the tropical climate, allayed by the fresh sea-breezes, was no longer oppressive.

And now their health and spirits were all that they could wish.

Feeling this, Bob Blunt, summoning his companions around him, said to them—

"My friends, it has just struck me that the fact of our having a vessel is no reason why we should keep continually out at sea. And therefore, bearing in mind that our object is to learn as much as possible of the resources of the vast African continent, I propose that we run in ro the shore for a time."

"Hurrah!" cried the men.

"I have no doubt," continued our hero, "that we shall be able to light upon some snug creek in which our ship will find safe anchorage ; and, having moored her, then we can take our rambles, so far as we desire, into the interior, making the clipper our central station, our rendezvous —in fact—our home, in case of danger."

A loud cheer having died away, orders were given to old Tom to steer for the shore.

Accordingly he quickly put the clipper about, and soon the eager cry of "Land ho!" resounded from her deck.

Fortune and nature seemed to have united in selecting a favourable spot for her anchorage.

A beautiful bay, sheltered by cliffs from the shore, whose sides were covered with variegated mosses, which gave them a rural aspect, delightful to the eye.

In this earthly paradise, then, our adventurers settled down for a time.

Nahita especially was charmed when our hero brought her on deck, and pointed out the coast, which he told her much resembled that she had left.

"You were a wild huntress, wandering through the woods then," said he, "but now you must try and become civilised."

Nahita resolved that she would do anything our hero wished.

Our hero, anxious to keep up his *prestige* as an English gentleman, and the heir to an English estate, determined to inaugurate their safe arrival at this beautiful bay in a special manner.

This was a grand banquet.

"I'll make a speech after dinner that will astonish everybody, see if I don't," cried Buttons. "I'll give the guv'nor a lift ; an', when my 'Tropical Adventures' comes out, I'll let the world know what he is."

This point being settled, the Stinger proposed a stroll on the beach.

For some distance they rambled along, the Stinger drinking in the fresh air from the sea, and occasionally imbibing a little something of a warmer description from her teapot, whilst Buttons took notes of everything.

"It's nice walking on the sand," said Elizabeth Ann, after a time ; "only it's very hot to one's feet, especially when you have corns."

"Well, I ain't troubled with any sech things myself," responded Buttons, "but if I was, I know what I should do."

"What would you do ?"

"Put my feet into one of them nice little pools of water and cool 'em."

It was a tempting idea, and the Stinger approved it.

"I think I'll take your advice, my dear boy," she said.

The Stinger laid down her umbrella and teapot, and divested herself of her pattens, and got on a sand heap.

The Stinger pulled herself together for her jump. |

"Now, then, go it ; dance away," grinned Buttons. "One—two—three—and——"

He was startled by a sudden shriek from the portly lady.

"What's up now ?" he asked.

"Oh ! it's moving," she cried.

"What's moving ?"

"The sand heap."

"Oh, gammon, Betsy."

"But I tell you it is. Oh, Lor' ha' mercy on me ! I'm sure it is !"

And sure enough the hillock on which she stood at once started off at a rapid pace in a slanting direction.

Buttons looked after it with eyes and mouth open.

Finding the Stinger still continued to glide along briskly towards the sea, he bawled out—

"Where the dooce are yer going to, yer old treat ?"

"I don't know," wailed Elizabeth Ann back in reply. "Come and stop me."

"I'll come," cried Buttons.

"Oh, Lor' ! oh ! I can't !" he shrieked suddenly.

"Why can't you ?"

"'Cos I'm a-moving like wildfire myself."

And as he spoke, away went his sand heap, with him on the top of it, just as the Stinger's had previously done.

"Oh, murder ! help !" he yelled. "We've got into enchanted regions ! Elizabeth Ann, you old humbug, help your Buttons, can't you ?"

Alas !

That worthy female had lost her equilibrium, and now lay on her back on the sand.

"Stinger, here, you——"

Buttons could say no more, for at that precise instant he overbalanced and went down himself in a soft bed of seaweed, whilst the sand hillock continued its cheerful but slow career towards the sea.

Buttons was not hurt, although considerably startled.

And having quickly picked himself up, he hastened after the moving mound, which he regarded as a wonderful natural curiosity.

When, however, he reached it, the mystery was explained.

"Why, it's a giant of a turtle !" he exclaimed. "Lor', Stinger ! what a monster it is."

Buttons hurried towards Stinger, and placed the worthy lady on her feet.

But it required a long application to the teapot to restore her to herself.

But in a few moments she was braced up.

She hastened, arm-in-arm with Buttons, to inspect the crustaceous specimen.

But when they reached the spot where Buttons had left it, the animal had disappeared.

They had gone into the water.

"Come along, or you'll ketch yer death of cold," grinned the page. "I'm sure yer will, and then—oh, Lor' ! something's got hold of me !" he shrieked suddenly.

He had stepped into a pool up to his knees himself.

"Oh, oh, oh ! my good gracious !" the Stinger gasped. "Something's catching hold of my toe."

"Oh, oh !" yelled Buttons. "Murder ! Help !"

"Help me, Buttons !"

"Help me, Betsy !"

Thus they stood shrieking together till the shore rang with their outcries.

It was just then a loud voice rang out in answer—

"It is my love that calls. Belinda Jane, I'm coming!"

The next moment a most extraordinary long individual, with extraordinary long legs and an extraordinary long, lantern-jawed face, in an extraordinary light suit and an extraordinary broad-brimmed straw hat, came bounding towards them.

CHAPTER XIII.

MAD MANGLES ASTONISHES THE STINGER.

HAVING reached the spot from whence the cries proceeded, he stooped, and snatching off his hat, he threw back the straggling elf locks from his forehead, and pressing his hand to his brow as if to assist his memory, gazed intently at the Stinger.

"Ha! ha!" he burst out at length, "I know you now, though you have grown fat and ugly, and dyed your hair."

These accusations were an addition to the other painful circumstances of which the illustrious lady was at that moment the victim, and she could not forbear an additional shriek of indignation.

"Fat and ugly—dyed my hair!" she cried. "Oh, you vile slanderer—oh, oh!"

"Don't stand there 'oh oh-ing,' but look at me, Belinda Jane," said the stranger.

"I'm not Belinda Jane; I'm Elizabeth Ann," returned the Stinger.

"Don't contradict. I tell you you're Belinda Jane—my Belinda, and thus I snatch you from your impending fate."

With these words he sprang towards her, and throwing his arms around her portly form, hoisted her out of the pool.

The Stinger was heavy, but something that was tightly clinging to her foot made her heavier still.

This something being an enormous crab.

"Ha!" cried the stranger, as he stamped his foot on it and caused it to let go its hold; "lobsters, avaunt."

Elizabeth Ann, what with the nipping her toes had received, and what with the sudden and startling aspect of her tall preserver, felt it necessary to sit down at once on a rock and take a long sip from her teapot.

The unknown watched her as she performed the operation with a melancholy smile in his dark, fierce eyes.

As soon as the spout was removed from her lips, he pounced upon it.

"Belinda Jane was always fond of tea," he exclaimed, "and I take after her. Good health."

He placed the pot to his lips, but almost instantly removed it.

"Tea!" he then shouted; "no, rum, by jingo!"

Dropping the precious article unceremoniously on the sand, he turned towards the horror-stricken Buttons, whose face expressed the most intense suffering.

"Ha! Popkins, there you are," he cried, with a cheerful grin and nod.

"I ain't Popkins; I'm Buttons," said the page.

"What are you doing there then, eh?" he cried.

"I c-c-c-can't get out."

"Pooh! bosh! bah!" roared the tall man.

With this he gripped Buttons by the arm, and jerked him clean from the pool.

He, too, had a gigantic animal with formidable claws attached to his boot.

"Ha!" shouted the stranger, as he caught sight of it, "more lobsters."

And then he gave the second crab a crunch with his foot as he had done the first.

Buttons was released, much to his satisfaction, although he evidently regarded his deliverer as a suspicious and singular character.

But he had little time for reflection, for the stranger exclaimed, in a sudden and startling manner—

"Where do you hang out, you two, eh? Answer me—quick."

"W-w-we live o-o-out there," gasped Buttons, who was almost scared out of his wits.

"Where's ' out there?' " demanded the stranger, who was gazing intently up at the clouds.

"Not in the sky," said Buttons; "but yonder."

He pointed as he spoke towards the spot where the "Adventurer" lay moored.

"Ha! I see. What's your captain's name?" asked the stranger.

"Captain Blunt, A Number 1 clipper," returned Buttons.

"Very good; I'll give you a call some day. You won't forget me? I'm Mangles—Professor Mangles, of the Royal Botanical Soiety. Some call me Mad Mangles, but that's absurd, of course—anyone can see I'm not mad. Ah! whoo-oo-oop!—well, good-bye, Braces; good-bye, Belinda Jane."

He threw his arms round the Stinger's neck.

"Oh! you little duck!" he exclaimed, as he gave her a hearty kiss, crushing her bonnet at the same time in a most reckless manner.

"Oh, you brute!" she growled, as she snatched up her gingham, in a paroxysm of indignation, and made a desperate lunge at Mr. Mangles' ribs with the point.

The attempt was utterly vain.

The professor caught it in some miraculous manner, and quietly took it out of her hand.

"Ha! what's this?" he cried, as he opened it, and spun it round; "an umbrella, I declare. The very thing I wanted; thanks, my Belinda, for your gift."

"Gift!" shrieked the Stinger, in a tone of desperation; "it isn't a gift—drop it this moment. Buttons make him drop it."

"Drop it, long un," cried Buttons—but rather dolefully.

"Ha, ha! ho, ho!" grinned the "long un," derisively.

And instead of dropping the treasure, he took Buttons by the scruff of his neck, and dropped him instead into the pool again.

Then hoisting the gingham over his head, he darted off as fast as his lengthy legs could carry him.

"Stop thief!—give me back my umbrella," bawled the Stinger.

"Send it back by Parcels Delivery," shouted the strange man in reply.

In a few moments he was out of sight.

The Stinger stood aghast like a statue of horror.

"I've lost my umbrella, my precious umbrella," she exclaimed, despairingly. "Buttons, where are you, Buttons?"

Buttons, who had only just managed to crawl out of the water, and was wiping the sand out of his eyes, gasped dolefully—

"Here I am."

"That long-legged villain has stolen my umbrella; run after him and get it back."

"Blow yer umbrella; go and get it yerself," growled the irreverent youth. "I don't like that wild fellow."

"Oh, B-b-b-buttons!" she sobbed—"oh, Buttons!"

This recalled Buttons to himself.

He was not made of iron, and his heart was touched.

Flopping himself down on the sand by the side of the weeping Stinger, he began to blubber vociferously himself.

"Oh, Betsy! my precious Betsy!" he cried. "Don't give way—don't, that's a good creature!"

And then the pair wept upon each other's shoulders.

After a time they felt better and rose to their feet.

"Never mind, old gal," said Buttons, soothingly. "If you've lost your umbrella, consider what incidents we've got for the ' Tropical Adventures,' to say nothing of these two splendid crawfish."

"Ah! they'll come in nicely for the forthcoming dinner, won't they?" remarked the Stinger, somewhat consoled at the prospect.

"Splendid, my dearest Elizabeth," returned Buttons.

With these comforting remarks, he tied the two shellfish together with a piece of string, and dragging them after him, they retraced their steps to the beach.

* * * * *

In a wood not two miles distant from the beautiful bay where our hero and his followers had taken up their position another party had located themselves.

A glance at the latter would have been sufficient to settle the point that they were Africans ; not only Africans, but the living captain and crew of the demolished slaver.

That Charon, the slave captain, should still be in existence might appear at first sight little short of miraculous, but, like many other marvellous events, his escape when explained, becomes the simplest and most commonplace of incidents.

At the first gun fired from the clipper Charon fully comprehended what the English intended.

At the second shot, he had quite made up his mind what to do.

As the British cheer came borne upon the wind to his ears, he at once commenced the carrying out of his deadly purpose.

This was to knock out the head of one of the powder barrels in the hold ; and then, having carefully laid a train, he ordered the boats to be lowered and the crew to get into them.

As soon as the English boarding party were at a certain distance, he applied a light to the end of a coil of match, and dropping into his boat, ordered his men to pull away with all speed.

He had calculated the time with much accuracy.

Had not the black sailor detected the smoke curling up through the crevices in the deck, all on board must inevitably have been sacrificed.

During the general excitement, none noticed the departure of the boats from the slaver until they had got so far ahead as to render capture impossible.

"Those English — those cursed English !" he muttered, bitterly ; "they have ruined me. I will have revenge."

"Well, captain," said Poonah, "the day may come, perhaps, when you will be able to ruin them."

"I hope it may—I hope it may !" exclaimed Charon, with fierce intensity. "I'll cut their hearts from out of their living bodies, and offer them a bleeding sacrifice to the god who gives them into my hand. I will—I swear it !"

"Den, by golly, captain, you hab de chance now," cried a hoarse, eager voice.

Charon and Poonah looked up.

The gigantic boatswain stood before them, his broad chest heaving breathlessly, and his eyes gleaming with malignant joy.

"What mean you, Karfa ?" demanded Charon.

"Me mean de English ship cast anchor in de bay yonder."

Charon sprang to his feet with a bound.

"Are you sure of this ?" he asked.

"Quite sure, captain ; me see her myself. You got chance to cut out de hearts and eyes too of all on board if you like."

"I swear by all the gods I will," cried Charon, with terrible emphasis, "come, come, let me see the ship."

His informant was perfectly willing, and with a wolfish eagerness, the vindictive pair hurried forward together.

Their road lay through a rocky ravine, and half-way through they were suddenly startled by a wild, unearthly yell.

So strange and unnatural was it that, in spite of their excitement, the two Africans stopped at once and looked around them.

"What cry dat ?" asked Rope's End.

"It was not the roar of an elephant," answered his companion.

"No ; nor de cry of a gorilla ; what war it ?" murmured the boatswain in a perplexed tone.

"Hark ! there it is again," exclaimed Charon, hastily ; "let us hurry away."

Rope's End made no objection, and they continued their course till they reached the cliffs.

Here throwing themselves full length on the ground, they approached the extreme edge, where they could distinguish the ship and the crew on her decks.

The eyes of Charon glistened at the

sight, and he hissed between his clenched teeth—

"That ship and every white man on board her are doomed."

"Ho, ho, ho!" came floating faintly from the distance, as though a spectre had heard and answered him.

"Tink de white fetich mock us. I tell you it bellows like a gorilla, and goes about like large white horse on dis coast, captain," remarked Rope's End with a scared look in his face.

Charon turned his stern dark eyes upon him, as he replied, scornfully—

"Let the white fetich mock! it will be more than he can accomplish to save that vessel and her crew."

"What do you mean to do, captain?" inquired Rope's End.

"Serve these English as they compelled me to serve my vessel," returned Charon.

"Blow 'em up?"

"Yes; with their own powder. I will kill them all—all!"

CHAPTER XIV.

THE NIGHT SHRIEK—MYSTERIOUS APPEARANCE OF A HORSEMAN.

THE preparations for the dinner party on board the clipper went on in a most energetic manner.

Everyone did what he could to contribute something towards the entertainment.

From stem to stern, from deck to topmast, she was a mass of foliage.

From the cook's cabin, savoury odours ascended to the upper air.

"They seem to live well here," said the slave captain.

"Yes; and they keep good watch," said Rope's End.

Hour after hour did they stand under cover of the darkness, watching the lanterns as they flitted to and fro upon the deck, and never seemed to be extinguished.

The boatswain grew irritable at the delay.

"What dey want kept watch for so much?" said Rope's End, sharply.

"For the approach of foes," replied the captain.

Rope's End shook his woolly head in dissent.

"Don't tink dat's it at all," he said after a moment.

"Why not?"

"'Cos dey neber 'spect us to be alive. Dey tink we blow up wid de ship."

"You cannot be certain of that."

Rope's End lost all patience.

"If dey expec' foes, dey not cover de ship all ober green boughs an flowers, would dey?"

Charon made no reply.

"It seems to me more like as if dey expec' frien's."

Hardly had he said this when the sound of of approaching footsteps caught his ear.

"Hush! someone comes," he whispered, hastily.

It was a dark, moonless night, and they had little fear of being seen.

But presently the glimmering light of a lantern appeared coming towards them.

Stepping behind one of the rocks that rose on every side, they awaited its approach.

The light was found to be carried by a negro, who, with his companion, was proceeding very leisurely towards the ravine.

Rope's End recognised them at once, as they passed, as two of his Kroomen.

"Ha, ha!" he chuckled to himself, with a hideous grin, "dere go Hitch an' Burgoo. We larn someting from dem, captain."

The two men, little suspecting they were watched, proceeded up the ravine.

Rope's End and Charon followed at a little distance.

Having reached a clump of trees, the men hung the lantern on a branch and began to work with their axes at one of the smaller stems which they intended to cut down and chop into logs.

Chip, chip—chop, chop—went the axes.

The horror of the Kroo boys may be imagined, when a gigantic dark form rose up and stretching forth its hand, grasped the lantern and held it up so that the light fell upon his features.

At once they recognised the face of their comrade Rope's End.

Rope's End, who they knew had jumped overboard and been drowned.

The negro is essentially superstitious, and the two men, believing they gazed upon the spirit of their dead companion, closed their eyes and fell on their knees, before the supposed spectre, and their teeth chattering audibly.

Rope's End then spoke.

" Hitch—Burgoo !" he said, in an awful and impressive tone ; " me come up from de bottom ob de deep to ax you question."

" It—w—w—what a—a am it ?" they inquired, tremulously.

" We want to know why de clipper am covered all ober wid green, lamps and flowers ?"

" 'Cos de captain gib gran' dinner party on board to-morrow ; dat why," they answered, rattling their teeth together.

" You quite sure dat de reason ?"

" Quite."

" Dey hab plenty nice t'ings to eat—eh ?"

" Iss, much plenty."

" And lot ob wine to drink ?"

" Iss, big lot."

This was all that Rope's End desired to learn, and having gained his intelligence, he said to his dupes—

" You two no go back again to de clipper."

The men looked considerably dismayed at this.

" Why not ?" they asked.

" 'Cos de great fetich say you not go ; if you do you die."

" Where we go den ?"

" Me show you."

With these words, Rope's End stepped forth from the clump of trees, lantern in hand.

" Follow me !" he said to his dupes, as he began to move slowly away.

At the same time, Charon, who had hitherto remained aloof, picked up the axes and stood thus armed behind the two Kroomen.

Just at that moment, and before another word could be uttered, an unearthly cry—half halloo, half shriek—burst upon the silent night.

The negroes heard it, and already under the influence of superstitious fear, they trembled with terror.

Nor was Rope's End unmoved.

He recognised the sound as one he had heard before, and he also trembled, though less palpably than his countrymen ; but he resolved to turn this unearthly incident to his own advantage, and he said in an ominous tone—

" Dat de great white fetich ; keep your eye on de lantern, an' follow me quick, 'fore he catch you."

With these words he started away at a rapid pace, with the two terrified Kroomen at his heels.

Charon, calm and unmoved, holding an axe in his hand, brought up the rear, looking, with his compressed lips and stern eyes, as though, if the great white fetich had attacked him, he would certainly have cut him down with his axe.

Let us leave them to pursue their journey, whilst we return to the clipper, on the deck of which our hero and his followers were standing.

All had heard the wild night cry, and though superstition had no share in the feelings it produced, it had not been without its effect upon them, so unnaturally shrill and startling was it.

" What is your opinion, Miss Stinger, of this strange shriek ?" asked Bob Blunt.

" I have no decided opinion," she replied ; " I can only suppose it was—something."

" That's jest what I think it was," wound up Buttons ; " something uncom——"

The word was still lingering on the lips of the page when the wild, harrowing shriek was repeated.

A bright clear light streamed forth suddenly from the summit of the cliff, and in its clear blaze there appeared, dashing along the extreme edge of the precipice, a colossal figure, white as marble.

The half-horse, half-man, as it appeared, galloped along until the light faded away in the distance.

CHAPTER XV.

THE BANQUET ON BOARD THE CLIPPER.

IT may be as well to remark that neither Buttons, nor the Stinger had made any mention of their meeting with the cracked-brained professor Mat Mangles.

And now the great day of the banquet had arrived.

It was extremely jolly, and the excitement only added to the festivity of the moment.

Everything turned out well.

But while festivity reigned in the cabin, no one on board was forgotten.

Every darkey had his share, and under the management of old Tom, they were soon as merry as grigs.

There was no moon on this particular night, but the absence of the luminary was not missed in the cabin, and the deck was lighted by lamps intermingled with the green foliage.

Still, everything surrounding the vessel was shrouded in deep gloom.

It was under cover of this that Charon and the giant Rope's End were enabled to approach without any fear of detection.

The ridges of coral rock which, when the tide was low, were out of the water, formed an easy means of access from the beach.

Having reached the hull of the clipper, they contrived by means of a rope to clamber up her sides and peer furtively in through the cabin windows at the merry guests.

None suspected the presence of an enemy, and after feasting their eyes upon their intended victims for a moment, they descended and withdrew to a little distance.

"They cannot escape us," said Charon, in a low tone of exultation.

"No, dat certain," rejoined his companion.

"All you have to do," continued the slaver captain, "as soon as all is quiet, is to get on board and make your way to where the powder is kept, and then lay the train."

Rope's End made no response to this.

Charon observed his silence, and said to him—

"You do not answer."

"No me don't," was the boatswain's somewhat sullen reply.

"You are not afraid?"

"Afraid! No."

"Why are you silent, then?"

"Me tink ob somet'ing."

"What?"

"You no keep your word to de gods."

"Not keep my word?" echoed Charon, in surprise.

"No. Did you not swear you cut de hearts out ob de living bodies of dese English, and offer dem sacrifice to de gods who gib dem into your hands?"

"Well?"

"Well, now dey am got into your hands, and you not do so."

It was now Charon's turn to be silent.

At length he said—

"At least they will be sacrificed."

"But not de way you promise," returned Rope's End.

"What matters that?"

"It must matter," insisted the boatswain, who was suddenly seized with a great tenderness of conscience on this point. "How can you cut de hearts out ob dere bodies if dey all blowed up—eh?"

This was an unanswerable argument.

At length, after a long pause, Charon said—

"In order to keep my oath strictly, I must have my foes in my power."

"And so you may," returned Rope's End, his eyes and teeth gleaming even through the gloom.

"No; I have not men enough to secure them all."

"P'raps not all, captain; but you got 'nough to carry 'way some."

The boatswain's doggedness had entirely passed away, and he was now full of intense eagerness.

"Let me hear your plan, then," said Charon, moodily,

"It jess so, captain. All in de ship much eat, much drink, an' by-an-bye, dey much sleep."

"Ha! yes."

"Well, den, we an' our niggers climb up de ship side, take 'em up, make dere limbs fast, an' carry dem off to de forest."

"But if they wake?"

"Dey not wake," said Rope's End; "'specially if we let dem sniff de sleep juice."*

"Have you any of this?" eagerly asked Charon.

"Iss, captain, me got lot," the latter replied, with a grin; "'nough send de whole lot ob 'em 'sleep."

"And how many would you carry away?"

Rope's End considered for a moment, and then said, deliberately—

"Four."

"Name them."

"Fust dere's the captain, Massa Blunt. Ha, ha! He look sharp if he 'scape us dis time."

"Who next?"

* A strong and deadly aromatic extract, the smell of which produces insensibility and the taste death.

"Ironfist. He knock me down, de white debil."

"Go on."

"Den Longsight. He lock me up."

"Any other?"

"Yes. Dat dam white boy, Buttons. He try stop me when I try get away from de clipper. Me want his heart berry partic'lar."

"You forget it's already promised to the gods," said Charon sternly.

"Dat do jess as well," returned Rope's End, cheerfully. "Let de gods hab Buttons' heart, and welcome."

"Then these four you have named are to be removed," resumed the captain.

"Iss. Me know de exact spot whar dey sleep; all done quite easy."

"And the rest?"

"We blow dem up sky-high next night."

These arrangements were quite satisfactory to Charon, who thirsted keenly for revenge.

"Let us go and prepare our men," he said, after a moment; "I long to have these white men in my grasp."

"You hab 'em all right, captain, 'fore long," was Rope's End's soothing prediction.

And with this they stepped lightly over the coral reef, and made their way to the ravine, where the dusky crew of the slaver awaited them.

All unconscious of the deadly machinations on foot against them, our hero and his followers were at the very height of hilarity.

They had been drinking the health of friends far away, till the cabin rang again.

Bob Blunt had just concluded an animated speech relative to their own past and future prospects.

Suddenly the unearthly yell that had startled them on the previous night sounded again in their ears.

Coming at that moment, the effect was trebly impressive, and there was an immediate and profound silence.

Then everyone hurried to the windows, and looked forth.

The same bright light was visible, and as on the former occasion, a white statue-like figure, semi-horse, semi-man, was

"IT SEEMED AS IF THEY HAD SHOT THEMSELVES. THEY MEASURED THEIR LENGTH ON THE GROUND."

dashing along in the midst of the glare.

Not this time, however, on the summit of the cliffs, but at their base, and advancing at a rapid pace towards the vessel.

A thrill of something like horror at the strange and unnatural appearance of the apparition passed through every breast.

"Have we wandered into enchanted regions?" exclaimed Bob Blunt, in profound astonishment.

"Who—what can this be?"

"Blest if I don't think it's a new edition of the equestrian drammer of 'Mazeppa and the Wild 'Orse of Tartary,'" gasped the page.

Just at that moment the figure came to a sudden stop, and proved that he was not in any way part of the horse by dismounting and continuing his way on foot over the rocks towards the clipper.

"By all that's wonderful, he's coming here, I do believe," cried our hero.

There could be no possible doubt upon this point, and the stranger stepped along from rock to rock with great alacrity.

One circumstance was particularly remarkable respecting him.

The nearer he approached the more human and less spectral he appeared.

He carried in his hand a bright light which revealed his appearance distinctly.

Yes, the light suit, the broad-brimmed hat, the long legs certainly belonged to a man—a white man, too.

Buttons and the Stinger had already recognized their acquaintance of the beach.

Buttons felt his legs becoming slightly shaky as he crept towards his illustrious colleague, and whispered in her ear—

"It's that cranky professor, Betsy; he's coming here."

"I'm glad of it," she replied, firmly.

"Glad?"

"Yes, for I shall take particular care he doesn't go away again till he returns me my umbrella."

It was just at this juncture a loud voice was heard bawling—

"Ship ahoy!"

CHAPTER XVI.

PROFESSOR MANGLES JOINS THE FESTIVE PARTY.

BOB BLUNT and his companions hastened on deck and looked down over the ship's side.

There stood the mysterious, long-legged stranger on the coral reef, looking up at them.

"Anyone at home?" he inquired.

"Plenty," returned Bob, good-naturedly.

"I'm right, ain't I?" continued the stranger. "A 1 clipper, Captain Sharp?"

"Blunt, you mean."

"Oh, yes, Blunt—so it is. Said I'd give you a call, and here I am. Throw us a rope or a ladder, will you?"

Our hero at once ordered a ladder to be lowered.

The stranger scrambled up it with the agility of a monkey, and quickly reached the deck.

He was evidently pleased at the sight of his fellow-countrymen, and burst out at once in a declamatory and theatrical manner—

"My brave companions, partners of my toil, my feelings and my fame, can Rolla's words——"

He broke off suddenly.

"I forgot, I haven't introduced myself yet," he said. "Which is the captain?"

"I am," said Bob Blunt.

"And I'm Mangles," went on the other, with a bow and a flourish, "Professor Mangles of the Royal Botanical Society—heard of me, no doubt."

Everyone shook their head.

"No; that's strange—thought everyone had heard of Mat Mangles. Some people call me Mad Mangles—ha, ha! very absurd that of course. Well, and how are you all, eh?"

"I am happy to say we are all in possession of most excellent health," Bob Blunt replied; "in proof of which you have just found us in the midst of a little conviviality."

"Ha, ha, capital!" returned the professor, "just as I could have wished; nothing like conviviality to make your hair grow. I'll join you if you've no objection."

"Not the least in the world," replied our hero; "in fact, I was about to invite you to make one amongst us."

"You're a brick."

And with this expression of approval the professor shook hands with all within his reach.

"By-the bye!" he exclaimed suddenly, "where's Belinda Jane—my Belinda, you know?"

He accompanied this last with a confidential wink at Bob Blunt.

"We have no Belinda Janes here," Bob replied with a smile.

"Oh, come now, that won't do," said Mat, throwing a comical look into his face. "I'm sure my Belinda's here; I've seen her, lovely sylph-creature—that is, she was before she got fat and ugly, and dyed her hair."

The bystanders glanced at each other, and a pitying smile passed from face to face.

"Well, suppose we go below," said Bob, "and if your Belinda is here, she'll soon find you out, I'll warrant."

"Ah, yes; let's go below by all means," returned the tractable visitor.

And striking up the "Good Rhine Wine" at the top of his voice, he was escorted by Stumps and Ironfist to the banquet-room.

The first two living objects he caught sight of were the Stinger and Buttons.

His eyes opened very widely, and he drew himself up as he gazed at them.

"Who said she wasn't here?" he exclaimed. "There she is as large as life—how are you, Belinda?—and there's Popkins!—how are you, Popkins?"

This last playful remark was addressed to Buttons, who looked anything but happy in his mind.

But before anything else could take place, the Stinger, with an expression of determination in her features that would have done honour to Boadicea, advanced towards the new guest.

"I'll thank you, Mr. What's-your-name," she said in her sternest and most decided tones, "not to address me by a name that doesn't belong to me. I am not Belinda Jane, but Elizabeth Ann please to remember that."

Having concluded this preliminary harangue, the illustrious and strong-minded female made a sudden grasp at the professor's collar.

"And now!" she added with intense energy, "I demand my umbrella!"

"You shall have it, my queen of the pumpkins!" retorted Mat Mangles.

And thrusting his hand behind him, he brought forth from some mysterious receptacle beneath his coat the memorable gingham, which he courteously presented to the Stinger.

The latter pounced upon it at once with a burst of joy.

"My umbrella—my umbrella!" she cried, hysterically; "I've found my umbrella! Ha, ha, ha! ha, ha, ha! Buttons, let us be joyful."

In order to bring Buttons as quickly as possible up to the state of rapture she desired, the worthy lady gave him an excited bang on his cranium with her gingham.

The effect was rather too stimulating, and the page measured his length on the floor.

"Oh, oh! my skull's fractured!" he yelled. "Betsy, you've done for your Buttons now!" as he lay on his back.

"Pooh! nonsense!" cried Professor Mangles.

As he spoke he made a swoop upon Buttons, and catching hold of him by one of his boots, held him out at arm's length head downwards.

"That's the way to cure fractured skulls," he said with a laugh, as he swung him to and fro.

"Let me go, Mister Mangles; all the blood's a-running into my 'ead!" shrieked out the page.

"Ah! I see the healthy action of the brain is returning," remarked Mad Mat with a grin.

"Yes, I'm a good deal better; let me down."

The professor lowered Buttons till his palms rested on the floor and then released him.

The youth was quite at home in that position, and in order to obliterate from the memory of those present the absurdity of his recent position, he started off for a walk round the cabin on his hands.

Mat Mangles exhibited all the delight of a little child at this simple acrobatic feat.

"Bravo, Popkins; very good indeed! Very good. Hurrah for Popkins!" he shouted.

Buttons, having thus recovered himself, resumed his usual position; and taking an early opportunity of whispering confidentially into the professor's ear that his name was not Popkins, but Buttons, the whole party resumed their seats.

The social harmony which had been interrupted was again resumed.

"This is a delightful meeting," said the professor, looking round at the company with a beaming countenance, "very delightful; it does my heart good to meet so many of my fellow countrymen in these wild regions. But there's one question I should like to ask?"

"What is that?" said Bob Blunt.

"I should like to know what it is that brings you all here."

"That is easily answered," returned Bob, with a smile. "I am a young fellow with money, and our object is to explore the vast African continent."

"Oh, umph!"

"Yes; and I presume that is your motive also in coming hither?"

"Not a bit of it," replied the professor, shaking his head. "The vast African continent may go to Jericho for me."

"Why did you come then, Mr. Mangles?" inquired the Stinger, with evident curiosity.

"I had two motives," returned Mr. Mangles, rubbing his hair till it looked like an excited mop.

"Two?"

"Yes. One of these was to search for a particular vegetable."

"May I ask what vegetable?" said Bob.

"Beetroots and turnips," answered the professor, very seriously.

"Ho, ho!" laughed Buttons, somewhat derisively; "the idear of coming all the way out here after beetroots when yer can get cartloads of 'em at home."

Mr. Mangles contracted his brow and looked at the reckless youth.

"Not such beetroots as I want," he replied, after a moment.

"What kind do you want, my dear sir?" asked Bob.

"Pickled of course," was the sharp reply.

"Pickled!" echoed Bob, in amazement.

"Yes; in jars."

The company glanced significantly at each other.

"Strikes me, you'll have to look a long time before you find any ov that sort," remarked the page, struggling hard to suppress a grin.

"Nonsense, Popkins," cried the professor, irritably; "there are thousands, millions, billions, of pickled beetroots in Africa, if you only know where to find 'em."

"Ah, yes, if yer do," admitted Buttons; "that's the point."

"I shall discover them some day, and then my fortune will be made," said Mr. Mangles, confidently.

"I drink to the success of your search with all my heart, my dear sir," said Bob Blunt, in a hearty tone; "and I am sure our friends will do the same."

Every glass was instantly raised in assent.

"That's very kind indeed," returned the professor, evidently gratified.

"And now, my dear Mr. Mangles, may

I ask your second motive in coming here?" inquired the Stinger, in her most insinuating tone.

The eccentric guest fixed his eyes upon her.

"My second motive was to seek for my lost love—my Belinda Jane; but why should I think of her?

> "'They have given her to another,
> They have broken every vow;
> They have given her to another,
> And my heart is lonely now.'"

From the manner in which he chanted these lines, it seemed to all that the unfortunate gentleman had been crossed in love.

The Stinger became particularly sympathetic.

"Take comfort, Mr. Mangles," she said; "you'll be united to your Belinda one day."

But this, instead of consoling, seemed rather to excite him, for he sprang on to the table.

Then he went into a sudden and maniacal burst of laughter.

"Ha, ha, ha, ha! ho, ho, ho, ho!" he roared; "chi-ike! What's the use of fretting? Cock-a-doodle-doo!"

And having finished this frantic paroxysm, he sprang from the table, and, dropping down by the side of the Stinger, seized hold of her by the wrists.

"You're like my Belinda—very like," said Mad Mangles.

"I don't think I'm like your Belinda," simpered Elizabeth Ann.

The remark elicited another peal of hearty laughter.

"Like Belinda," he echoed; "no, by the gods! I am mistaken! She was young and lovely, you—bah! you're old, fat, and ugly."

The Stinger uttered an indignant shriek, and snatching away one of her hands, aimed a tremendous slap at her insulter.

But all in vain.

Quick as lightning he had disappeared under the table, leaving the luckless Buttons to catch the blow on his ear.

Having got out of sight, the professor commenced playfully pulling the legs of the Stinger and Buttons, who retorted by sundry kicks.

It was now past all doubt that their strange guest was a raving madman, and, in confirmation of this, the next moment he hoisted up the table from beneath.

Bottles, decanters, glasses, fruits, and cigars, descended to the ground with a terrible crash.

Having effected this destruction, he let the table down with a bang, and, darting from beneath it, sprang on to his feet.

"Whoo-op!" he yelled, as he strode to the door, "whoo-op! I'm off now. Good-bye, Belinda Jane; good-bye, Popkins; good-bye, everybody. Look in again and have another jolly evening before long. Ha, ha, ha!—ho, ho, ho!—whoo-op! Hurrah!"

And shrieking and hallooing at the top of his voice he rushed up the cabin stairs.

Having reached the deck, he threw himself over the ship's side, and was seen no more.

Only his wild cries came echoing through the darkness till they faded away in the distance.

CHAPTER XVII.

CHARON AND ROPE'S END COME ON BOARD.

CONVIVIAL parties, as a rule, have a tendency to make those who attend them sleep soundly.

It was so in the present instance.

No sooner had our explorers laid heads on their pillows than they fell asleep, and slept heavily.

Nor was this unusual somnolence confined to our hero and his friends.

Even old Tom, who on ordinary occasions slept with one eye open, on this particular night shut both eyes, and snored away in blissful unconsciousness.

The lights were extinguished on the deck, and all was shrouded in gloom and silence, unbroken save by the distant roar of some prowling lion.

Some time was allowed to pass, and then, gradually and cautiously, dark forms began to scale the side of the clipper's hull.

Like so many venomous spiders they crawled up till they reached the deck.

Having arrived thus far, they remained perfectly still, until they had arranged their ropes, to which a strip of canvas was attached for the purpose of lowering their prisoners.

This being done, Rope's End whispered to Charon—

" Now den, cap'n, de sooner we get 'em out de better."

" I'm ready," the latter replied ; " lead the way."

Having given the signal to two of their men to follow them, they glided down the hatchway with their bare feet.

As noiselessly as ghosts they went below.

Here they paused a moment, whilst Rope's End saturated a piece of cotton rag with the pungent fluid he designated " sleep juice."

As he did this, sundry nasal sounds, that travelled from the neighbouring berths, assured him satisfactorily that their occupants were not likely to give him much trouble.

" Ha, ha !" he chuckled under his breath ; " me tell you dey sleep well to-night."

" Whom will you remove first ?" asked Charon.

" Take Massa Blunt fust, 'cos he got most ob de debbil in him," responded the boatswain.

Knowing every inch of the ship, Rope's End approached the cabin which our hero occupied.

The door was not locked, and, opening it softly, he looked cautiously in.

A lamp burned dimly.

By its light Bob Blunt could be distinctly seen stretched in his berth in an attitude of profound repose.

His well shaped limbs covered only by a shirt and a pair of thin white trousers.

" Dey do for me arter he done wid 'em," muttered Rope's End, placing the sleep juice close to Bob's face.

He then bent down to assure himself that his victim really slept.

Being satisfied on this point, he proceeded at once to fetter his arms and ankles with pieces of rope which hung from his girdle.

Our hero seemed utterly unconscious of the treatment he was undergoing, until the two negroes whom Rope's End had beckoned in for the purpose raised him from his bed.

Then he made a sudden effort to resist.

Finding his limbs fettered, he struggled for freedom.

His eyes opened, and their quick, wild glance flashed upon the giant form of the boatswain.

But only for an instant.

The heavy hand, holding in its palm the deadly drug, was pressed upon his mouth and nostrils.

Then there was a sudden, smothered gasp, and the eyes closed heavily.

There was no more struggling.

The victim lay as still and unconscious as though death held him in his iron grasp.

" Ha, ha !" laughed Rope's End. " Sartin him no able stand dat ar."

He nodded to the two men, who, knowing what they had to do, moved with their burden towards the cabin door.

But they had scarcely taken two steps when, to their surprise and dismay, a female figure stepped in and confronted them.

Young, graceful, and extremely beautiful, clad in light, flowing robes.

It was Nahita.

She had not slept, and her quick ear, rendered trebly acute by the love she felt for our hero, had caught the cautious footfalls and the murmured whispers.

Accustomed to the secret attacks of midnight foes, she suspected danger, and had come to avert it if possible.

" What do you here ?" she demanded, sternly, as she closed the door and placed herself before it, her beautiful eyes flashing with fury. " Answer me !"

As she spoke she raised a bright, keen dagger.

There was no reply to her question.

The two men who bore the body of our hero remained as mute and motionless as if carved in stone.

But her eyes fastened upon the senseless form, and the sight roused her to desperation.

"Release him! He is not, shall not be your prisoner!" she exclaimed, in a low, intense tone.

"Release him, or——"

The dagger gleamed in the air.

Charon, who had never removed his eyes from her, sprang forward with a bound like a panther.

The weapon descended.

But he eluded its stroke, and in an instant wrenched it from the grasp of the beautiful half-caste girl.

At the same moment the strong arm of Rope's End encircled her.

His hand was pressed upon her face.

A convulsive shudder passed through her frame, and she fell powerless into the arms of Charon, who placed her on the ground.

The obstruction being thus removed the negroes hurried away with their prey.

Rope's End then proceeded to the cabin where Ironfist and Longsight reposed.

With them there was not much difficulty, they were so soundly asleep, but the drug was used to make all safe.

The last he secured was Buttons.

The page was discovered just as he had entered his berth.

He had evidently been making a note for his "Tropical Adventures," and been overtaken by slumber in the midst of it, since he was lying on his back on the floor in his usual costume, with his note-book in his hand.

"Ha, ha! Massa Buttons, you try stop me, did you, eh? Me try stop you dis time," grinned Rope's End.

Rapidly he tied up the limbs of the youthful author.

After which, he bade the negroes in attendance take him up.

Buttons seemed to resent this.

Something appeared suddenly to trouble him in his sleep.

"Betsy—Mangles," he murmured, incoherently, "ribs—umbrella."

A smile passed over his features, as he added—

"Beetroots."

The next moment he was hoisted up.

"Old 'ard, ole gal!" he exclaimed. "I say, Elizabeth Ann——"

Then he opened his eyes.

A doleful screech was about to proceed from his lips, when the useful "sleep juice" was rapidly brought into play.

Instead of screeching, he gave a kick and a gasp, and nothing more was heard of poor Buttons for several hours.

The plan had been entirely successful, and whilst the rest of the exploring party slumbered peacefully in their berths, their less unfortunate comrades were being hurried along through the darkness of that moonless night, to awake and find their fate staring them in the face, a fate at which humanity must shudder.

CHAPTER XVIII.

THE CALM DEFIANCE OF AN ENGLISHMAN.

THE grey light of morning was stealing through the forest boughs, when Ironfist awoke with an unpleasant sensation of headache and cramp in his limbs.

His thoughts were somewhat confused, too.

He opened his eyes and looked up, but saw nothing but trees over his head.

"Why, where the deuce am I?" he exclaimed, as he tried to get up and fell back.

He turned his head and glanced aside.

Longsight lay close to him, and like himself had just awakened from his slumber.

"I say, old fellow," he said to him; "I'm tied up hand and foot."

"Are you?"

"Yes."

"Very strange; so am I."

"Well, but what does it mean?"

"Hang me, if I know," said Longsight.

"Nor I either. I went to bed last night in my berth on board the clipper, and this morning I find myself in the woods unable to move," grumbled Ironfist.

"Someone must have been playing us a practical joke."

"Ah, yes; perhaps so. Stumps or the doctor."

"Any other victims besides ourselves?" asked Longsight.

Ironfist wriggled himself on to his side and looked around.

Suddenly he uttered an exclamation of astonishment.

"Why, this is strange!" he cried.

"What?"

"Unless I'm dreaming, there lie Buttons and—no—yes, it is—the captain."

"What, Captain Blunt?" asked Longsight, rolling himself over.

"Yes, as I live; and both bound hand and foot as we are."

"Well," returned Longsight, "this looks like treason."

Ironfist lay silent and thoughtful for several moments.

"I don't like this prospect at all," he said, at length. "I wish Mr. Blunt would awake."

"Suppose we rouse him," Longsight suggested.

"I will. Captain, captain," called Ironfist.

There was no answer.

The captain was still under the influence of the potent narcotic he had inhaled.

"He lies as still as if he were dead," murmured Ironfist, fretfully; "and I not able to help him."

"Not able," echoed his companion.

"Why, one wrench from those strong paws of yours would burst a band of steel, much less a rope of twigs. Try."

Ironfist did try, not only once, but again and again to set himself free from his shackles, but they were tied in such a peculiar manner that his strength took no effect upon them.

"Confound it all!" he cried, passionately, "there's something more than a joke in this. I begin to suspect some treachery, though where it comes from, hang me if I can even guess."

"Nor I. Our Kroomen are faithful."

"I believe so; but——"

The voice of Buttons interrupted the conversation at this moment.

"Water," he murmured, faintly, "Betsy, ole gal, give me some water."

Almost at the same instant our hero's voice was heard, and he too uttered the same request—

"Water, water!"

Ironfist could stand this no longer, and in stentorian tones he roared out—

"It's time to drop this tomfoolery, Stumps. Doctor, don't you hear the captain wants water?"

He was somewhat dismayed at hearing an ironical laugh in reply, and a hoarse voice exclaiming in a jeering tone—

"Call little louder, Mass'r Ironfist; den p'raps de doctor an' Stumps hear yer."

The voice seemed familiar; but before he had time to decide whose it might be the giant form of Rope's End came in sight.

Striding up to the spot where the prisoners were lying, the black boatswain stood with folded arms, regarding them with eyes full of malignant exultation.

"Alive, ruffian?" exclaimed Ironfist, in surprise, as he recognised him.

"Me nebber been dead yet," grinned Rope's End.

"Why are we here?" demanded Ironfist.

"You know why, all in good time," was the answer he received.

There was a significance in the tone and manner of the giant negro that aroused heavy suspicions in the mind of the Englishman, and he said after a moment—

"How is it we came hither—who brought us? I insist upon knowing how."

Rope's End, chuckling within himself at the recollection of his successful stratagem, replied—

"Well den, mass'r, dis is how. You come 'cos you not able to help it. Me carry you off in your sleep."

"I understand then that we owe our present position to your infernal malice?"

"Me rader tink me hab sometink to do with it," was the boatswain's cool rejoinder.

"And you have dared also to lay violent hands on our gallant captain?" said Longsight.

"Dared!" echoed Rope's End, with a contemptuous laugh, "me dare anyting. What your gallant capten to me more dan any oder white debil—eh?"

The indignation of Ironfist was greatly excited at this.

"You insulting beast," he burst out, fiercely, "you do well to boast, bound hand and foot as we are. Unfetter our limbs, and see what we will do then."

The boatswain screwed up his features into a curious sort of "Don't you wish you may get it?" expression, and shook his head, as he replied—

"No, no; me got you fast, and mean to hold you so, Mass'r Ironfist; no more knocks me down; so keep quiet, or me thrash you wid rope till de blood comes out ob you."

He to whom these words were addressed writhed under the bitter irritation he felt.

With desperate muscular efforts Ironfist strove once more to release himself, but his efforts were fruitless; and just at that moment his attention was directed from his own position to that of his leader, who again repeated his faint cry for water.

Rope's End turned his head towards the spot where our hero lay with a fiendish smile, but made not the slightest motion to comply with his request.

"Don't you hear the captain asks for water, you black beast?" exclaimed Ironfist, indignantly.

"Yes, me hear," was the dogged reply.

"Then why don't you fetch him some?"

"Me not slave to get water for de white man," returned Rope's End, drawing himself up proudly.

"You're an unfeeling brute," cried Ironfist; "your heart's as black as your face is ugly."

"Yah, yah!" returned the negro, with a diabolical grin, "can't all 'xpec' to be handsome like you."

And with these words, a kick, and a parting sneer of contempt, the giant slowly retired.

Bob Blunt was just recovering from the deleterious effects of the sleep juice.

His brain throbbed, his nerves were unstrung, and he was tormented with a raging thirst.

"Buttons," he cried, again, "Buttons, why don't you bring me some water?"

Buttons, usually the sharpest and most active of attendants, made no reply.

He had dozed off again.

Our hero, in an impatient paroxysm, essayed to stretch forth his hand to ring the bell that usually hung at the side of his berth.

It was then for the first time he discovered that his limbs were shackled.

"What is the meaning of this?" he murmured to himself, in a wandering manner.

His eyes opened heavily, and he caught sight of the boughs over his head.

"What has happened? Where am I?" were his next wondering exclamations.

"I can tell you, captain," called out Ironfist, who had been listening to the rambling remarks of his leader.

"Who speaks?" asked the latter, as he caught the tones of his follower's voice.

"Ironfist, captain."

"What! are you there?"

"Yes, and Longsight also."

Our hero recognised the familiar tones, and, after a moment, he asked, dreamily,

"What has happened? What does all this mean?"

"It means, captain, that treachery has proved too much for us, and that we are in the power of our foes."

"Foes !" echoed Bob Blunt, struck by the last words ; "foes. You mean Howard and—and Pluto ?"

"Oh, no. The author of our present capture is that infernal black villain, Rope's End."

"The boatswain ?"

"Yes, captain."

"He is not dead, then, after all ?"

"No ; worse luck."

By dint of a great effort, our hero's memory was becoming stronger, but still the recollection of the past was vague and indistinct.

"And so we are in his power, are we ?" he remarked, after a pause of silence.

"Yes."

"How many of us are there here ?"

"Four, so far as I can see at present."

"Who are they ?"

"You and I, captain, Longsight and Buttons."

"Oh, Buttons is here, then ?"

"Yes ; close to you."

Bob Blunt turned his head, and found his page lying on his back, with his mouth open, by his side.

As he looked, Buttons opened his eyes also.

He made several abortive efforts to rise, and at length gave up the attempt, and muttered—

"What the dooce is the matter with my arms and legs ?"

"You're tied up, my poor fellow," said Bob.

"What, captain," exclaimed the page, in profound astonishment, "is it really you ?"

"It is, indeed ; and in the same plight as yourself."

"Good gracious me ; so yer are," said Buttons. "'Ere's incidents for my 'Tropical Adventures.' "

"I sincerely hope they may not terminate tragically," said our hero, in a serious tone.

"Tragically, guv'nor ! Why, what's up ?"

"We are prisoners, in the power of that giant ruffian, Rope's End," said Bob.

Then turning to Ironfist, he cried—

"My throat is quite parched."

"So is mine," wailed Buttons ; "an'

my 'ead feels as if a steam ingin' was at work inside it."

"Does this vindictive African mean to kill us with thirst ?" cried our hero, with bitter indignation.

"No, capt'n," answered a voice.

It was the voice of the boatswain, and, looking round, there he stood, a short distance off, accompanied by his colleague, Charon.

"Dere oder ways of killin' better dan dat," he said, after a moment, with an evil smile on his dark features.

Bob Blunt heeded not its deadly expression, but said, desperately—

"Then bring us water."

"Bring dis har white gen'lman water, you nigger," called Rope's End, in a tone of mock politeness.

In an instant a negro advanced with a calabash, and, kneeling down, he held it to the parched lips of the fettered prisoners.

The draught greatly revived them ; and Bob Blunt's natural pluck and self-possession having returned to him, he said to Rope's End, as firmly as if he had been on the deck of his own vessel—

"And now, you ruffian, tell me what is your motive in bringing us hither ?"

"My motive, revenge," answered the giant, promptly ; "and my comrade's motive 'xac'ly the same—revenge."

As he spoke, he pointed to Charon, who stood by his side.

Bob looked at him ; but as he encountered the steady unblenching look of the slave captain's dark, stern eyes, he felt that little mercy was to be expected.

But he said to him—

"What wrong have we done you that you should seek to retaliate in this treacherous manner ?"

"You have frustrated my plans, and ruined me," Charon replied, fiercely.

"Ruined you ?" echoed Bob Blunt, in surprise. "I never saw you before ; I do not know you."

"I am the captain of the slaver you attacked. You will know me now."

Our hero, at these words, at once comprehended his perilous position.

"To save my prize from falling into your hands," continued Charon, "I was compelled to blow up my vessel. Two hundred and fifty slaves were sacrificed."

"Will our death bring them to life again?"

"No; but in return for their loss, I have sworn by my gods to sacrifice you all."

"Your gods," exclaimed Bob Blunt, indignantly; "what are they but stocks and stones? There is One above, mightier far than they, to whom I commit myself and my companions."

"Then let that One save you if he can," cried Charon, his eyes flashing with vindictive wrath; "if not, ere the sun casts his beams on yonder knotted trunk, I swear again this weapon shall be crimsoned with the heart's blood of you all."

These terrible words could not be misunderstood.

Buttons fainted on the spot.

His companions evinced no emotion.

Our hero simply fixed his eyes steadily on the slaver captain, and said in a firm tone—

"My intent in attacking you was to rescue your hapless victims from a fate accursed and abhorrent to every free born Englishman. You, in your blind folly, have destroyed them, and now you threaten us as though we were the cause of their destruction."

"You were the cause," hissed Charon from between his clenched teeth, "and you shall die for it."

"If Heaven permit, not else," interposed Bob Blunt, placidly. "In Heaven we trust, barbarian; and so trusting, we scorn your threats and defy your malice. Do your worst."

A grim smile of fiendish mockery played over the features of Charon and Rope's End, as talking together in a low tone, they turned away from the spot, leaving their prisoners to meditate upon the fate that awaited them.

CHAPTER XIX.

A WARNING DREAM RESPECTING BUTTONS.

LET us now return to the clipper.

Let us clamber up once more on to her evergreen deck and look around us.

All is still, dark and silent.

A few forms are curled up snugly here and there, under the thick masses of foliage, fast asleep.

It is evident they have no thoughts of waking for the present.

Let us go below.

What voice is that murmuring in broken and incoherent sentences?

It comes from the Stinger's cabin.

It is the Stinger herself, beyond doubt, who is speaking.

Let us approach cautiously and listen.

She is talking in her sleep.

What is she saying?

"You shan't take him, you black monster," she exclaims, excitedly; "let him go, I command you. Drop him this instant, I say, or—or——"

The voice dies away, and nothing is heard but indistinct murmurs about "vengeance," and an "umbrella," mingled with "pattens and a teapot."

Something troubles her.

What can it be?

Nightmare, possibly.

Let us venture—with the profoundest feelings of veneration and respect for the champion of "woman's rights"—to peep into her cabin.

What is that large yellow mass we see yonder, rising out of her berth?

It might be a sandbank, only sandbanks do not usually wear frilled nightcaps.

No, it is the portly form of the

Stinger herself, enveloped in the folds of her ample dressing-gown.

She is talking again.

It must be some very evil dream that troubles her slumbers.

"Spare him!" she cries. "Spare my B-B-Buttons—good boy—much attached —author—talent. Ha! would you, base nigger? Buttons, cling to me! Take that, black man! Ha, ha, ha!"

And with a hysterical laugh, the bonds of sleep were broken, and the Stinger sat up in her bed and looked around her.

She was excited by a terrible dream, which may be thus briefly described.

Some dark, ferocious negro had pounce upon Buttons, and was about to bear him off in triumph, when she interposed in his defence.

The dream had all the vividness of reality.

"It was but a dream," she argued with herself.

For some time she sat pondering upon the vision.

But the more she pondered, the more her anxiety increased, until at length, unable any longer to control her apprehensions, she rose from her couch.

"I feel confident something has happened to Buttons," she exclaimed, "and I shan't be able to rest until I know whether my fears are true or not."

There was only one way to do this, and that was by going to the cabin which the page occupied.

This she determined to do at once.

Accordingly, taking the lantern in her hand, she bent her steps to Buttons' sleeping apartment.

On reaching it, one circumstance struck her as suspicious.

The door was wide open.

No youthful form snored in the vacant berth.

Buttons was not there.

Nothing was visible but his notebook, which lay on the floor.

This was something, however, and she eagerly picked it up and put it into her pocket.

It then suddenly struck her that it was just possible that the page might be in attendance upon his master.

In order to assure herself upon that point, she at once proceeded to our hero's cabin.

Much to her surprise, the door of that was wide open, exactly as the other had been.

"Bless me!" exclaimed the worthy lady, with much emphasis; "all the doors seem to be open to-night."

She paused a moment.

"I think, in a case like this, I might venture to look in," she argued with herself. "Yes, I must—I will."

And accordingly she looked.

But, alas, neither Bob Blunt nor Buttons were there.

"Whatever does it mean?"

But almost immediately she started aback.

There, stretched upon the ground right before her, lay the beautiful Nahita apparently fast asleep.

The Stinger's sense of propriety was greatly shocked at this discovery.

"Whatever does this girl do here?" she exclaimed, indignantly. "It isn't right at all."

Stooping down, she shook her sharply by the shoulder.

"Get up directly, do you hear?" she cried in a loud tone.

But the sleeper took no notice whatever.

Nor could all the shaking administered by the Stinger's vigorous arms rouse her in the least.

Suddenly a glittering object caught the eyes of Elizabeth Ann.

It was the dagger Nahita had let fall.

She picked it up, and contemplated it with a look of horror in her face.

"Something dreadful has been going on, I'm sure," she murmured. "I must summon Ironfist."

Away she tramped to his cabin.

His door, like the others, was wide open, and his berth empty.

The Stinger was quite overcome.

"Everybody seems to have run away," she cried despairingly; "the ship's deserted, and I'm left alone."

What should she do—faint or go into hysterics, or call police and shriek murder?

She decided upon doing neither but

hurrying to where a gong was suspended she hammered away at it with all her might.

The deafening clang speedily had its effect upon the sleepers, and in a few minutes all were aroused and came hurrying to the spot.

"What's the matter?" exclaimed the doctor.

"Is the ship on fire?" inquired Stumps.

"Are we boarded by pirates?" asked old Tom, who was in a dreamy state.

The Stinger at the sight of so many of her comrades, recovered her self-possession at once.

"There's something wrong," she said.

"What is it?" demanded everyone.

The illustrious female threw an expression of profound mystery into her face, as she replied—

"Follow me!"

Leading the way, she conducted her companions to Bob Blunt's cabin.

"Look there!" she said, as she pointed at the prostrate form of the African princess.

"The beautiful Nahita!" exclaimed all present.

"Yes, Nahita."

"Is she dead?"

"She is not dead, but in a state of coma," said the Stinger. "I found her here quite unconscious, and with this weapon lying near her."

As she spoke she produced the dagger she had picked up.

"You found Nahita here, in the captain's cabin, you say?" asked Stumps, much astonished.

"Yes, I did."

"Where is the captain, or King Aga, her father?" was the next question asked by all, as they looked towards the vacant berth.

"Her father seems like a dead man in his cabin; but where is Mr. Blunt?" repeated Elizabeth Ann. "Where is Buttons—where is Ironfist? Echo answers—'Where?'"

"Can they not be found?" inquired her listeners, with a look of dismay.

The Stinger made no reply to the question; but drawing herself up, said in an authoritative tone—

"Find out how many of our number are missing, and let me know at once."

A rapid inquiry was made, when the list of absentees was discovered to comprise Bob Blunt, Buttons, Ironfist and Longsight.

Where they had disappeared to was indeed a mystery.

At length the day dawned, but it brought no signs of the missing ones.

"I am inclined to think there is treachery somewhere," said Stumps to Dr. Knowall.

It was just at this crisis that Nahita began to evince signs of returning consciousness.

The first name on her lips was that of him she loved.

"The captain—the dear captain!" she murmured. "Save him!"

But that was all she could utter.

But at length, as her senses became less under the power of the narcotic drug, she was able to throw more light upon what was yet a profound mystery.

From her the adventurers learnt that their leader had been carried off by the negro, Rope's End, and his confederate, and that being the case, it was not difficult to surmise that the other missing ones had shared a similar fate.

What was to be done?

The Stinger was ready with an immediate answer.

"These black wretches must be pursued without a moment's delay, and our gallant companions rescued from their power," cried the heroic female. "Let us start at once; I will lead you on."

"Nahita will go too," exclaimed the young African girl, endeavouring to shake off the remains of her lethargy.

But the Stinger objected to this.

"No," she replied, in a very grand, decided tone. "Nahita will not go. She is giddy and unable to walk, and must stay on board. Those who undertake warlike expeditions mustn't be weak on their legs."

The beautiful princess looked imploringly at the Stinger, but the latter would not yield in the slightest.

"It's no use your looking at me with those great eyes of yours," she said, sharply. "You will remain behind and look after the ship with old Tom and your father."

Poor Nahita's bright eyes filled with tears of disappointment, but only for a moment.

A sudden bright flash irradiated them, and, clasping her hands, she muttered something no one but herself understood.

In a very short space of time everything was prepared.

As for the Stinger, she fairly bristled with weapons, like a porcupine.

With several revolvers slung at her waist, a rifle at her back, her umbrella in hand, and her teapot under her arm, she looked a very formidable personage indeed.

"All ready?" she cried, as she surveyed her followers.

"All."

"Then forward to the rescue, brave hearts," she cried ; "and remember our war-cry is Old England, Elizabeth Ann, and Victory. Forward !"

CHAPTER XX.

HOW THE EXPEDITION PROGRESSED—ALTERATION OF THE COURSE—THE PROFESSOR AGAIN—ALARMING INTELLIGENCE.

THERE were two great difficulties under which our gallant friends laboured.

First, they were entirely ignorant of the surrounding country, and secondly they knew not in what direction their comrades had been carried.

A brief conference was held.

The Stinger, having taken a preliminary sip from her teapot, spoke.

"My friends," she said, in a cheerful tone, "I am sure we all share in each other's anxiety to rescue our beloved comrades from the grasp of their foes."

"We do ! we do !" was the fervent reply.

"Very well, then ; listen to me."

Every ear was eagerly attentive.

"Whenever I lose my way, and am at a loss how to proceed, I always make a point of keeping straight on. We will do the same."

"Agreed ; agreed !" cried the rest ; and on they went in a straight line.

They were barely out of sight when a slight, boyish figure appeared at the entrance of the ravine.

He was black, or his face was dyed, but his features were uncommonly beautiful.

For a moment he remained motionless, looking earnestly after the distant escort,

"I will find him," he murmured, fervently, "or die. Oh ! kind Heaven, give me power to save my dear captain, that he may know how much I love him."

Having said this, the youth adopted a plan very different from those who had gone before him.

He did not leave anything to chance, but, stooping down, examined the ground with the closest attention.

For some time he did not appear to make any satisfactory discovery, but, far from discontinuing his scrutiny, he moved hither and thither, making a tolerably wide circuit.

At length a joyful cry burst from his lips.

"I have found it—I have found the track !" he exclaimed. "Thank Heaven for that."

Keeping his eye upon the footprints, he continued on his way rapidly, pausing occasionally when the traces became indistinct, and then proceeding more carefully till he had found it again.

In this way he went on, regardless of the burning heat, till he reached the borders of a wood.

After carefully examining the grass, the smile returned to his face, and, plunging into the dense thicket, he disappeared.

* * * * *

In the meantime the other party had, after progressing a long and weary distance, come to a halt.

But they seemed as far from the object of their search as ever.

A general murmur of something like discontent broke forth.

"You mustn't be impatient," remarked the Stinger, whose face glowed like a red-hot furnace. "Depend upon it we shall in course of time—arrive—somewhere."

Still, as time passed on and no signs of any living thing appeared, the murmurs again broke forth, and Lightfoot said to the Stinger—

"I really think it would be as well to alter our course."

Elizabeth Ann gave him a withering look, but before she had time to reply, Maintop said, as he pointed towards the south-west—

"Tink, missee, if go dat way we more like find de captain."

The route was altered, and they went on until at length, in the distance, the dark outline of a forest appeared.

"Ha!" cried the doctor, "that looks more promising."

It was just at this crisis that a cloud of dust no bigger than a man's hand appeared far off across the plain.

Gradually it grew larger, and seemed to be coming towards them.

As it drew near it was seen to be a horse and it s rider, and presently Stumps exclaimed—

"Professor Mangles, as sure as I'm alive."

Sure enough it was that singularly eccentric individual, in his light suit and straw hat, mounted on his white horse.

He checked his steed abruptly as he reached them.

"Hollo!" he cried, "there you are again—all well? That's right; steady, Chalks."

This was to his horse, and having dismounted, the professor at once embraced the Stinger warmly.

"Glad to see you, Belinda," he said. "Where's the captain and Popkins, eh?"

"Alas!" returned Elizabeth Ann, "they've been carried off, and we know not where they are."

"Carried off!" echoed Mat Mangles, his eyes opening with a sudden glare. "By whom?"

"By black wretches—niggers."

"Niggers," shouted the professor, fiercely, "blackbeetles, vermin! I met a lot yonder in the forest; demanded my horse—told 'em to go to old Nick and get one. Ha, ha, ha! split one beggar's skull for him. And so the captain's carried off, is he?"

"Yes."

"And the tender Popkins?"

"Yes; did you see anything of them?"

The professor shook his head.

"You might perhaps have remarked amongst the black heathens you encountered in the woods one particularly gigantic——"

"And particularly ugly—eh?"

"That was him."

"Oh yes, I fired at his top knot, but missed—never mind, I've marked him; better luck next time."

The Stinger now stepped forward.

"Oh, Mr. Mangles," she said in her most pathetic tones, "will you aid us in preserving our hapless friends from death?"

"No!" roared the professor, with startling abruptness, "I've nothing to do with preserving; I'm in the pickle line."

"But in this distressing case, I'm sure you will——"

"Can't stop—off on important business; can't stop for anything!"

As he spoke he sprang on to his horse.

"Put off your business!" entreated Elizabeth Ann.

"Can't," shouted the crack-brained Mat; "got a large order—million jars of pickled beet-roots must be shipped to-morrow. Yo-icks, off we go, Chalks! Good-bye, charming Belinda!"

And, with a wild yell, off he darted with the speed of the wind.

Hardly had he gone when some horse-

"NAHITA IN HER FOREST HOME."

men appeared dashing along in the direction he was taking, as if in pursuit.

From their costumes and complexions they seemed to be English, but the speed at which they rode prevented them from noticing the explorers, and they were soon out of sight."

Altogether the party felt somewhat depressed.

The Stinger was first to recover herself, and in her usual lofty tone of confidence, said, as she pointed to the forest before them—

"My opinion is that our missing friends are in yonder leafy shades, held in the power of cruel foes."

"We quite agree with you on that point," replied Lightfoot and Stumps.

"I'm glad to hear it," returned the illustrious lady. "Forward then!"

The party resumed their march till they reached the confines of the forest.

Here they paused for a brief conference, the question discussed being whether they should separate or continue their search together.

Their numbers being few, the latter course was decided on.

It was just as they were about to enter the forest that a dark form burst from the thicket right before them.

To their surprise they recognized Burgoo.

The Kroo boy recognized them and bounded towards them.

"Oh, missee! oh, massas!" he exclaimed, excitedly, as he came up, "de poor captain!"

"What of him?" inquired the listeners eagerly.

"He caught—he an' de rest—all tie up tight—goin' be kill."

"Who's going to kill them?" asked everyone excitedly.

"Rope's End and de oder one."

"Never! that is, if our presence can avert his doom," cried Elizabeth Ann, with strong determination.

Then, addressing herself to the Kroo boy, she added—

"Do you know whereabouts the captain and our friends are?"

"Dey yonder in de woods," replied the negro indicating the direction with a nod of his woolly head.

"Lead us to the spot at once."

Burgoo shrugged his shoulder in a very rueful and hopeless manner.

"Oh lor, missee! great lot niggar all 'bout dere. Dey keep watch—see yah," he answered.

"Well, but you managed to get away yourself without being seen," said the Stinger; "can't you guide us by the same path?"

"Ah, missee," pleaded Burgoo, "me creep 'long de ground like snake, bery sly."

"Well, we'll be snakes 'bery sly,' for once," said Elizabeth Ann, "and creep along as you did. Now, then, start at once."

The Stinger, in addition to her determined tone, drew one of her revolvers, which she pointed at the negro.

The Kroo boy, having no resource but to obey, led the party cautiously by a narrow path into the wood, where the thick undergrowth closed around and concealed them from view.

CHAPTER XXI.

UNEXPECTED ARRIVALS.

THE sun was now rising high in the heavens.

Our hero and his three companions still lay stretched upon the ground, bound and helpless.

The quietude of the scene was broken at length by Ironfist.

"This is a melancholy termination to our expedition, captain," he said ruefully.

"Both melancholy and ignominious, if it is really about to terminate," replied our hero.

"I see no prospect of escape," remarked Lightfoot.

"No more do I," wailed Buttons, in the most desponding of tones.

"Well, there's one thing to be said, at least," said Bob Blunt; "the end has not come yet, and until it actually does come, I prefer clinging to the old proverb —'While there's life there's hope.'"

"Can't see where any hope comes, guv'nor," replied the page dolefully. "Oh lor'! oh lor! the idear of being slaughtered in cold blood by those ugly niggers."

"We must not despair," said his master.

"I shall never see my precious Betsy or dear ole England again," continued Buttons, the tears coming into his eyes.

"Well, my lad," replied Bob, kindly, "if even the worst should come you must remember you're a Boy of England, and prepare to meet your fate bravely."

"Oh, I dare say I shall be all the way there when it comes to the point; but that's not the wust. I'm a-thinking of all the startling incidents I've collected for my 'Tropical Adventuers,' and now they'll all be lost. It's reg'ler heartbreaking."

It was just as Buttons concluded this pathetic lament that the branches near at hand were slightly stirred, so slightly that it might have been caused by a bird or a gentle puff of wind, and awakened no attention.

But it was neither of these that caused the motion, and almost immediately after a young, handsome face peered forth from the surrounding foliage.

The eyes in that face flashed with delight as they rested on the English prisoners, but especially on the leader.

After gazing at them an instant their owner emerged from the leafy screen.

A slight, graceful, boyish figure.

It was the same whom we left on the track of Rope's End and his myrmidons.

He had succeeded in his enterprise, and now, with light step that scarcely ruffled the grass beneath his feet, he hastily approached our hero and knelt by his side.

"Dear captain," he murmured tenderly.

"Dear Nahita!" exclaimed Bob Blunt, a thrill of joyful surprise rushing through his breast, "is it indeed you?"

"It is."

"And that disguise, too—ah! but I guess its motive."

"It is to save you, dear."

"I felt sure of that. You knew, then, that we had been carried off?"

"Yes and tried to prevent it, but was overpowered by the same drug that robbed you of consciousness."

"Dear, brave girl," exclaimed Bob, gratefully; "you have indeed rendered myself and friends a signal service."

"Do not thank me yet, dear," replied Nahita; "you are yet surrounded by deadly peril."

"But your presence, dear girl, is an omen of safety."

The eyes of the young African flashed with mingled love and joy.

"I will save you if I can," she murmured, tenderly; "or die with you."

With these words she drew her dagger and severed the rope that bound our hero and his comrades.

Then from a flask she carried at her side, she gave them a draught of brandy, which put new life into their exhausted frames.

Buttons became so exhilarated that he was about to make an immediate stand on his head.

But his master checked him.

"Husband all your strength, my good fellow," he counselled; "you will doubtless want it presently."

As he said this a rustling was heard in the brambles close by.

The Englishmen sprang towards each other and stood side by side, waiting for the coming foe.

But no foe appeared, although to their surprise, the next moment the woolly head of a friend, Burgoo, popped out from the bushes in front of them.

"Oh, golla! massa, massa, frien's near," he exclaimed, with breathless eagerness.

"Ha!" returned Bob, excitedly; "where are they?"

"Dey come 'long yonder," replied the Kroo boy, pointing behind him.

"Thank Heaven!" said our hero and his comrades, fervently.

Buttons uttered a stifled "hooray," which he could not suppress.

A crackling in the brushwood followed, and presently the well-known voice of the Stinger reached their ears, speaking in jerky, breathless sentences.

"How much further is it? Where are they? Oh, my poor feet!" she gasped, as she struggled along through the thicket.

"That's Betsy," cried Buttons in an ecstasy; "I can hear the precious Buster."

"Here dey are, missee," called out Burgoo, in a subdued, but eager tone.

"Yes; here we are, old gal. Come on," joined in Buttons.

"I am here," responded Elizabeth Ann, grandly.

The next moment her portly form burst through the foliage, her face crimson with heat and exertion.

"Found at last," she exclaimed, as she waved her umbrella triumphantly. "Oh my dear Mr. Blunt, how glad I am to see you! Oh my poor Buttons, how glad I am to see you, too!"

With these words she rushed to the page, and fairly hugged him in a transport.

They were almost immediately joined by Lightfoot, Stumps, the doctor, and their black followers.

The greetings on both sides were hearty and sincere.

After the first excitement had passed the Stinger said—

"We've arrived here with much difficulty, and now the question arises how are we to get away?"

"There will not be much difficulty about that, I imagine, now we are together again," Bob Blunt replied.

"I must differ with you, my dear captain," said Elizabeth Ann, shaking her head.

"Why, what is to hinder our departure?"

"Our foes," said the Stinger.

"Well, they cannot be so very numerous?"

"Yes they are," exclaimed the Stinger. "We're surrounded at all points."

"I really do not think so," said Bob. "There will be that rascal Rope's End and the slaver-captain, with, say, twenty of his crew, at the outside. Surely, after the odds we have encountered, we are a match for them."

"I hope we are," replied Elizabeth Ann; "but from what Burgoo said as we came along, it seemed to me that there must be black men lurking in every hole and corner of the wood."

"If so, how was it you were able to penetrate thus far?"

"Burgoo guided us to this spot, and we crept through the long grass on our hands and knees like so many lizards. There's only one way of progression possible in that horrible brushwood, and that is, to wriggle oneself through it like a worm."

"Well, then, however abasing it may be to our pride," said Bob, with a smile, "our best policy will be to become worms at once."

Our hero said a few words to his comrades, whom he summoned round him.

The close of day was the time arranged for their death, and they were now anxiously watching the sunbeams, which had almost reached the fatal trunk.

Ironfist had explained to them the approaching doom of which the setting sun was the indicator, and they were all eager to depart at once.

"Let us, if possible, get clear of this wood," counselled Bob; "then, if attacked, we shall be more likely to discover the number of the foes we have to contend with, although, in this instance, as we are short of weapons and ammunition, I should prefer avoiding an encounter."

His companions agreed with their leader.

All being ready to start, Burgoo, who was to act as guide, was ordered to lead the way.

The Kroo boy was about to plunge into the thicket, when suddenly a terrific yell rose upon the silent air.

Not from one or two throats, but, apparently, from a multitude.

The sounds fell like a thunderclap upon the ears of our adventurers.

Burgoo paused in dismay, and turned instinctively to his master, uttering not a word, but gazing at him inquiringly from out his keen, dark eyes.

It was a terrible moment, one in which the lives of all present, with their bright aspirations, their future joys and sorrows, seemed to hang upon a thread.

It remained for our hero to decide what step to take.

The word "forward" trembled on his lips, when, at the very moment, the voice of Rope's End was heard.

"De time has come for de sacrifice," he bawled, in his usual hoarse, guttural tones.

These words induced Bob Blunt to change his tactics instantly.

"Flight is worse than useless now," he said, hurriedly; "the wretches are coming here."

"What shall we do?" exclaimed his comrades.

"Remain where we are."

And Bob drew Nahita close to his side.

CHAPTER XXII.

THE PRISONERS ASTONISH THEIR CAPTORS.

THE unexpected order Bob Blunt had given had appeared somewhat strange to his companions, but no one stirred to disobey it.

Ironfist alone said respectfully—

"To remain here, captain, is certain death."

"To attempt flight would be also," was Bob's quick reply.

"But our position is desperate, hopeless, my dear sir," said the doctor.

"Desperate, I admit, but not hopeless altogether," Bob answered coolly.

"How so?"

"Our foes are now approaching," exclaimed our hero, rapidly.

"Me hear 'em on de move now," exclaimed Burgoo, who had been listening intently under his breath.

"Were we to fly," continued Bob, "they would at once pursue and overtake us in the thicket, where we should be at their mercy."

"What do you propose then, captain?" asked the rest.

"A *ruse de guerre.*"

"Let us hear."

"It is simple enough," said our hero, as he threw himself on the ground. "Now then, Ironfist, Longsight, and Buttons, follow my example."

This they did instantly.

"Now, Nahita, bind our arms and legs as before, only arrange the ropes so that a slight effort will unloose them."

The young princess, with a quick appreciation of what was required, performed her task with wonderful skill and celerity.

Then Bob Blunt directed the rest of his colleagues to conceal themselves in the adjacent bushes until he called on them to advance.

In a few seconds the prisoners were lying bound, and apparently as helpless as ever, on the ground.

Not a soul besides was visible.

"Now, my dear fellows," said our hero to them, "our only chance lies in a sudden and vigorous onslaught at the proper moment."

"Will you give the signal, captain?" asked Ironfist.

"Yes. Be sure you remain perfectly quiet till I cry out, 'strike!' then each must do the best he can; and Heaven prosper us all in our efforts!"

Hardly had these directions been given, when murmuring voices were heard approaching.

As Bob listened, he detected tones familiar to him—the language of his own countrymen, but not the tones of friends.

Nor was he mistaken.

The next moment the branches crackled, and Rope's End and Charon appeared.

Not alone.

At their heels were two white men.

Those two were Richard Howard and his ruffianly colleague, Bow-legged Bill.

They had evidently been drinking, for their eyes were bleared and blood-shot, and their gait was unsteady.

But, from the expression of their features, their old hate had lost none of its deadly quality.

Rope's End strode forward to our hero, and it was evident that he, too, had been indulging in copious applications to the rum-bottle.

"Wal, you brave cap'n, how you get on by dis time, eh?" he said, in an ironically insulting tone, as he looked down upon his prisoner.

Bob Blunt condescended no answer.

"Ha, ha! you look so bery grand on you back, cap'n; me bring frien's of yours look too."

As he spoke he beckoned with a hideous grimace and a wink to the Englishmen behind him.

They advanced at once, and their eyes encountered those of our hero.

For a moment they continued to gaze without speaking.

At length Howard said, in a sarcastic, jeering tone—

"Well, and how do I find Robert Blunt, Esq., of Blunt Hall, by this time, eh?"

"As well as ever he was, and still able to congratulate himself that he is not Richard Howard," was Bob's calm retort.

"Umph! you still keep up your bravado—your pluck, as you're pleased to call it."

"On the contrary, it's my pluck that keeps me up," returned our hero, coolly.

"What a blessing it must be to possess such indomitable resolution!" remarked Howard, sneeringly.

He glanced round at the rest, and continued—

"And our friends here, Ironfist and—no! yes! Buttons!—so it is, I declare! Do they, too, belong to the plucky breed?"

"Of course we does!" answered the page, with a sudden flash of heroism;

"you ought to know that by this time!"

Richard Howard laughed a low, evil laugh, as he replied—

"I'm glad to hear it—you'll soon have an opportunity of proving your words."

"Yah, yah!" grinned Rope's End, who had been an interested listener to the preceding conversation, "dat true, massa, dat bery much true. You soon hear 'em screechin' out to us hab mercy on 'em."

Having said this the giant pointed to the trunk, about which the sunbeams were hovering, and with fiendish glee amused Richard Howard with the complete details of the torture about to be shortly inflicted.

The latter listened complacently, without the slightest shudder of horror or regret.

After exchanging a few words with his confederate, Bow-legged Bill, he once more approached our hero, and, seating himself by his side, fixed his eyes steadfastly upon him.

"Cousin," he said, seriously.

"Don't 'cousin' me!" exclaimed Bob Blunt, in a sharp contemptuous tone. "I disown the relationship."

"As you please," returned Richard, shrugging his shoulders. "Well, then, I'll call you captain, if you like it better."

"Call me nothing, but be silent. I shall like that the best of all," said our hero, sternly.

"I must speak," went on Howard, "if only for your own sake."

"Very kind and considerate indeed," interposed Bob, with a sarcastic laugh. "Well, what is it you have to say?"

His cousin looked at him with a well-assumed mixture of horror and commiseration in his eyes, as he said—

"Are you aware of the punishment in store for you?"

"Perfectly," returned our hero, coolly. "It has been all thoroughly explained to us some hours since."

"Were you informed of the particular kind of torture to which you are just about to be subjected?"

"I told you so just now," returned Bob, with perfect placidity. "Our hearts are to be cut from our bodies."

"And do you mean to tell me that you can contemplate such a terrible death without a shudder?" demanded Richard Howard, almost passionately.

"Yes, I can," was the firm and courageous answer of our hero.

For a few moments Howard remained silent and thoughtful.

At length he said to our hero, in a husky, spiteful tone—

"You can't impose upon me by this wonderful show of equanimity. You are overacting your part; notwithstanding your outward firmness, your heart shrinks within you at your approaching fate."

"If you think so," replied Bob, "place your hand upon that heart, and see whether it beats less firmly or more rapidly than usual."

"Psha! yours is simply idiotic insensibility, not courage!" exclaimed Howard, in bitter wrath. "Had you been reasonable, I might, perhaps, for a consideration, have been able to avert your fate; but, as it is——"

Our hero interrupted him with the question—

"On what terms will you give us our lives?"

"My terms are a clear half of your property—nothing less," said Howard.

"Only half?" exclaimed Bob, with an ironical laugh.

"Better lose half than all, as you will do!" hissed Richard Howard from between his clenched teeth.

"Even if I agree to your terms I doubt your power to render us assistance," said Bob. "What can you do with a handful of followers?"

"I have more than you know of," growled Richard. "My friend, King Pluto, is upon me, so you see, our protection is worth something."

"No," cried Bob; "the protection of false-hearted traitors is worth nothing."

"Do you call us traitors?" almost yelled Richard Howard.

"Yes, from the crowns of your head to the soles of your feet."

The baffled villain sprang to his feet, and, glaring down upon his cousin, shouted—

"Then you shall all die cruel and violent deaths, without hope of mercy."

"Well," said Bob, "we can die like Englishmen."

"Hooray, Mr. Blunt!" sang out Buttons.

But he felt inclined to change his tune as the stern voice of Charon fell upon his ears, exclaiming—

"The sunbeams give the signal—it is time for the sacrifice."

Rope's End burst into a discordant laugh, and, beckoning to some of the slaver-crew they approached the prisoners.

He himself with two of their number, advanced to where our hero lay.

"Now, den, massa cap'n," he said to him, "you bery much brave. Me cut your heart out fust—see how you likee."

With these words he drew from his girdle a terrible looking curved knife, which he placed between his teeth, motioning to his myrmidons to seize our hero and hold him fast, little dreaming that at that moment two wild beautiful eyes, flashing like those of a tigress, watched him.

The fate of the prisoners seemed sealed when suddenly Nahita's hand, from behind, clutched the handle of the formidable weapon, and snatched it from the giant's mouth, inflicting a terrible gash.

At the same moment Bob Blunt burst from the fetters and sprang to his feet.

"Strike!" he shouted.

The effect was electrical.

Up started the rest of the prisoners, free as the air, and their fists went to work at once.

Our hero, with a powerful, right-handed blow, stretched Rope's End on his back.

His companions followed his example.

Buttons flew about here, there and everywhere, like a parched pea in a frying-pan.

In a few seconds the grass was strewn with prostrate niggers.

Charon, with a savage bound, sprang forward, weapon in hand to strike down Bob.

It was the last step he ever took.

Nahita intercepted him.

Bang!

He fell to the ground, dead, from a shot fired by the brave Nahita, ere his body reached the turf.

Then came our hero's signal to his followers—

"Advance !"

There was a shout and a crackling of branches, and then the foliage poured forth its contents.

The reserved force led by Stumps and backed by the Stinger, burst from their covert and joined their companions.

Together they formed into a compact body, with the heroic Elizabeth Ann in the midst, her round face glowing like a furnace.

"Hooray ! Long live the Queen !" shouted Buttons.

"Victory !" joined in the Stinger, triumphantly as she put up her immortal gingham and completed the picture.

CHAPTER XXIII.

REAPPEARANCE OF FOES—THE SAVAGE HORDE.

"THAT will do," said Bob ; " so far so good, but perhaps it will be as well not to halloo too loudly till we're out of the wood."

"Where are our foes ?" asked Ironfist.

Strange to say none were to be seen.

Richard Howard and Bow-legged Bill had conveyed themselves off during the brief *melée*.

Rope's End and his fellows had taken a similar advantage.

Save the dead body of the slave-captain not a single enemy was in sight when, after their mutual congratulations, our brave friends looked round.

"They evidently overrate our numbers," exclaimed our hero.

"All the better for us, captain," said Ironfist, significantly.

"Decidedly. Now let us at once enter upon the secret trail that leads from the forest," said Bob.

"Me quite ready start, massa," said Burgoo."

"Start then."

The Kroo-boy plunged at once into the narrow path and the rest followed.

Very secretly they proceeded.

It was terribly hot and suffocating in that dense thicket, and the Stinger, who had already crawled through it once, found it terribly hard work.

But she had Buttons by her side now to cheer her.

"Come on, my ole teapot !" he whispered ; "pull yourself together, and, never mind the prickles ; it's a good deal better to be scratched than killed."

Elizabeth Ann quite agreed with Buttons on this point.

After an hour's travelling a slight breeze became perceptible, and Burgoo informed them that they were approaching the end of their uncomfortable passage.

The good news stimulated all to increased exertions, and in a short time they emerged from the covert into the open plain.

To their great joy no one appeared.

"We go on, I suppose, captain ?" asked Stumps and Ironfist.

"Yes, at once," answered their leader, "I long to find ourselves once more safely on board the clipper. Forward !"

Hark !

At that instant the hoarse blare of an African trumpet made of a buffalo-horn was heard.

"That is a signal from our foes !" cried Bob Blunt. "Quick, lads, get in order."

He placed his small force in single ranks, so as to offer as thin an edge as possible to the weapons of the foe.

It was just as he had completed this brief arrangement that Richard Howard and Bow-legged Bill stepped forth from the covert.

With them was the giant, Rope's End. The wide mouth of the latter was dripping with blood.

This feature of his ugly face had always been sufficiently capacious, now it had been extended by the gash he had received almost from ear to ear, and he was furious with rage and pain.

"Shoot de cussed white debils! shoot 'em! hack off dere limbs! burn 'em ober slow fire!" he howled. "Ugh! me like see 'em frizzle—hear dere bones crackle!"

Richard Howard would have had no objection to the application of this torture, but he was anxious to get a share of his cousin's property—some written note of hand, signed by our hero, that would have given him a legal claim to some of the wealth he coveted.

This he knew he could never procure from a dead man, and, until he had this, his cousin's life was of some consequence to him.

But that once secured, he would have doomed him to a lingering death.

"How infernally impatient you are?" he said to Rope's End.

"Me want revenge," exclaimed the giant, hoarsely; "blood for blood. Me will hab it."

"And you shall, if you will wait a little."

"Bah! dey run away; you lose 'em all."

"You black idiot! you don't know what you're talking of," returned Howard, irritably; "do you suppose I intend to let them slip through my fingers?"

"Seems like it," muttered Rope's End, sullenly.

"Then learn from me that their lives are as securely in my hand as though their corpses were already stretched yonder upon the plain."

Rope's End looked at him.

"Me don't see how, massa," he said, after a moment.

"You will if you listen."

With these words Richard Howard, holding his rifle in his hand, and accompanied by Bow-legged Bill, advanced towards the English party.

Having reached sufficiently near he stopped and cried—

"Now, my worthy cousin, you see you have run the full length of your tether."

"According to your measurement, villain, I have," was Bob Blunt's scornful answer.

"Measure your present position how you please," continued Richard, "you'll find that you must make terms with me or perish, every one of you."

"I will make no terms with you save such as our weapons shall dictate," returned our hero, proudly.

"Ha, ha! your weapons," laughed Howard, derisively; "what have you—none!"

"I have six loaded barrels here, and one shall be for you," replied Bob, as he held up his revolver.

"Ditto," echoed the Stinger.

"Ditto, ditto," joined in Buttons; "and take pertikler notice, I'm a dead shot—when I hit."

They each held up their revolvers as they spoke.

Richard Howard only laughed again; but our hero stopped him by remarking, drily—

"A few weapons in a good cause are sometimes better than many in a bad one."

"That inveterate pluck of yours is leading you astray again, cousin," sneered Richard. "What can you and your handful of followers do against me and mine?"

"We shall do our best, as you yourself have seen us do many times before; so beware, Richard Howard," returned Bob, calmly.

Howard made no reply for a moment, but stood silently gazing at his cousin.

"Come now, be reasonable," continued Howard, hoarsely. "Remember, I have only to give the word and your fate is sealed. For the last time, will you come to terms?"

"No."

"Half your property?"

"Not a single farthing."

"Then, by Heaven! you shall pay for your sordid avarice with your life."

As he spoke he placed a whistle to his lips, and blew a sharp, shrill note.

In an instant there started up from a

hollow, about a hundred yards distant, a horde of wild, savage forms, armed with bows and arrows.

With loud, fierce yells they spread themselves out upon the plain, whilst their leader, ascending a small hillock in advance of the rest, stood, spear in hand, gazing at the small body of explorers, who were now hemmed in on all sides.

It needed but one glance at the single chief to recognise him as the formidable Three-fingered Pluto.

CHAPTER XXIV.

THE DESPERATION OF DESPAIR.

THE African king's first act proved that he had not forgotten his old animosity to the English.

He held up his mutilated left hand, and shouted, exultingly—

"For every finger, five English lives."

Again his followers yelled furiously, and their outcries being taken up by the other party, the din was something awful.

"Oh, Lor'! Betsy," murmured Buttons to the Stinger, "do you see a ghost of a chance of the 'Tropical Adventures' ever being published by me?"

"Well, my dear boy," returned Elizabeth Ann, "just at this moment matters seem to me to have taken what I might call a doubtful turn, but I beg to say that I don't intend to be quietly settled; if any of those black fellows, or white ones either, think so, let 'em try, that's all."

And as she spoke the strong-minded lady clenched her umbrella and looked sternly towards King Pluto.

"I think we may call this the ultimatum of all our past experiences," observed Doctor Knowall.

"And, therefore," exclaimed the Stinger, "never so splendidly provided with an opportunity of distinguishing ourselves."

"Well said, my brave heroine," cried Bob Blunt; "you have put new life into this jaded frame of mine. Courage, my dear friends; we are Englishmen; let us never forget that. Three cheers for our country."

"Hurrah! hurrah! hurrah!" burst from the lips of the small band.

Richard Howard and King Pluto, who were speaking together, turned and looked towards them.

"Use your voices while you can," shouted the latter; "they will soon be silent."

"Yes, bawl away," growled Rope's End, savagely; "you soon hab de death-rattle in you throats."

The Stinger compressed her lips, and, after taking a suck at her teapot, was quite herself again.

"Now, comrades," continued Bob Blunt, "at this crisis I have no commands to issue, only this—Fight to the last, and fight as Englishmen alone can."

"We will, we will!" shouted his comrades.

The British lion was fairly roused in our adventurers, and they were ready for anything.

It was just then that Richard Howard's voice was heard.

"Resistance is hopeless; be wise, and yield yourselves prisoners."

"We would as soon think of yielding ourselves prisoners to the devil and his legions," shouted Bob Blunt, excitedly. "No, coward, we defy you and all your savage crew; do your worst."

"Come and take us if you can," bawled Ironfist.

"Yes, come on, all at once," joined in Buttons, whose pluck had returned, and who was now perfectly reckless. "I'm on full cock, and ready for yer."

The stern tones of King Pluto now came floating towards them.

"When my warriors advance," he cried, "you will hear your death-knell."

"And yours also," retorted Bob Blunt, scornfully. "I have not forgotten your threat, dark heathen—for every one of your fingers, five lives."

"I'll keep that threat," returned Pluto.

"Then hear mine," cried Bob, "For every English life, ten Africans, beginning with yourself."

As he spoke he levelled his revolver and fired.

The aim was true, and Pluto recoiled from the force of the bullet, which struck him on his broad chest.

Had it taken effect it would have killed him on the spot, fortunately for him, the bullet came in contact with one of the large metal ornaments that hung suspended from his neck and formed a kind of breastplate.

Instead of piercing his heart, the leaden pellet fell partially flattened into a skull which dangled at his belt.

The African monarch paused, and, picking out the bullet, held it up between his thumb and finger.

"Ha, ha!" he laughed to our hero, scornfully; "you shall have this back again."

Then, turning to his followers, he said to them—

"Let not one of these white men escape."

"Cut up de cussed debils; hack off dere flesh; spike out dere eyes; drink dere blood!" yelled Rope's End, as he flung his arms in the air with all the wild gesticulations of a raving maniac.

The voice of Three-fingered Pluto checked him.

"Listen to my commands," he exclaimed, sternly; "you are not to slay my foes, but take them alive—mark me, alive. Their doom is lingering torture. Now advance and take them."

With fierce yells the savage horde rushed, like a torrent set loose, upon the devoted band.

Without moving from their position our hero and his gallant comrades waited their approach with calm intrepidity, determined to meet the fate which now appeared inevitable, as brave men should meet it.

It was not until their enemies were close upon them that Bob Blunt gave the word—

"Now, then, fire!"

Then the revolvers belched forth their deadly contents with a sharp cracking sound.

Almost every shot told, and the ground was strewn with dark forms that would never rise again.

But there was no time to reload before the living swarm of savages was upon them.

Hemmed in on every side the Englishmen defended themselves with desperate energy.

Bob Blunt, with only the butt-end of his empty revolver, fought like a lion.

Beneath the scientific blows of Ironfist many stalwart Africans went down like reeds.

The Stinger laid about her with her gingham in a way that astonished her friends as much as her foes, being quite as perilous to the one as to the other; whilst Buttons administered many heavy blows to his sable adversaries.

But it was impossible for the most determined courage to withstand the overwhelming numerical superiority of the assailants.

At length the English party were completely borne down by the sheer weight of numbers.

It was just as the act of pinioning the arms of the prisoners had been completed that King Pluto and Richard Howard approached.

The latter glanced towards his cousin.

"Don't you wish you had accepted my offer?"

Bob Blunt made no reply, either by word or look.

He permitted himself to be dragged into the hut, which was now King Pluto's palace.

As the African monarch looked at his captives his eyes gleamed with a deadly light.

Presently they fell upon pretty Nahita,

who had stationed herself close to our hero's side.

All thoughts of her own danger seemed to have been absorbed in the peril of him she loved better than herself.

Her eyes never left him.

The grim Pluto was not slow in comprehending the cause of this devotion.

After a moment he said to her, sarcastically—

"You love the handsome white captain, Nahita—you love him very much?"

The young princess threw a hasty glance at her questioner, as she replied in a low, fervent tone—

"Yes, I do love him very much."

"Better that you love me, eh?"

"I hate you! but I love my dear captain more than all the world beside."

A hideous grin overspread the face of the three-fingered chief as he said to Nahita—

"'Tis well. You shall see him die."

He then turned to some of his followers, and ordered them to kindle three fires upon the ground.

In a very short time logs and brambles were collected, and soon blazed with a fierce flame.

Three-fingered Pluto watched the conflagration with evident satisfaction.

At length the flames had died out, and nothing but the red-hot embers remained.

Then, pointing to our hero, Stumps and Ironfist, he exclaimed—

"Bring the white men forward!"

CHAPTER XXV.

A GENERAL PANIC.

THE order was at once obeyed, and the Englishmen were placed side by side.

Then said Pluto to his myrmidons—

"Put a rope round the young white captain's neck."

This being done, he fixed his eyes upon his three captives, and said to them, with a malignant smile—

"Can you guess your fate?"

There was no reply.

Pluto continued—

"I am going to have you placed over those glowing ashes. There two of you shall lie till your flesh drops from your bones."

Then, addressing himself especially to Bob Blunt, he went on—

"There is something more in store for you. When you have been well warmed by the fire you will be hung up by the neck to yonder branch, and I shall then finish you by a shot from my rifle."

As he spoke he took from the skull at his side the piece of flattened lead which our hero had fired at him, and held it up exultingly.

"This is the bullet—yours—I shall use," he said, with a significant grin.

He then gave the signal to his slaves by clapping his hands.

A dozen brawny negroes advanced.

But ere they could carry their orders into effect Nahita sprang forward with a cry of horror and despair.

"You must not do this—you shall not!" she exclaimed, desperately. "If you do, the God of the white man will mark you for destruction."

Pluto burst into a hideously scornful laugh.

"The God of the white man!" he echoed mockingly. "Where is He?"

"He may be nearer than you dream of, heathen," said Bob Blunt, calmly.

"No, no," cried Pluto; "it is all lies!"

"Yes, yes, all lies!" joined in Rope's End, who had been indulging in more rum, and was mad drunk; "all big lies! White mans got no one to help 'em; roast 'em all, eb'ry one!"

The negroes at once seized the victims, and were about to drag them to their fate when a shrill cry from Nahita caused them to pause.

"See! see there!" she exclaimed, as she extended her arm towards the north.

"What see you?" demanded Pluto, hoarsely.

"The Spirit of the Wind is advancing," she replied as she stood erect and rigid as a prophetess.

"Who de debil him? Neber hear ob dat sperrit," muttered Rope's End.

"Hear him now then," said Nahita.

At the same moment a wild, unearthly shriek was borne upon the air from the distance, and a cloud of dust came rolling onwards.

At that awful moment it seemed as if Heaven itself had interposed for the preservation of our explorers.

Bob Blunt regarded the interposition in this light, and he cried with sudden exultation—

"It is the great white spirit, who comes to save us and annihilate our foes! Look, where he comes!"

"Ah, whoo-oo-oo-oo-ooo!" was yelled out upon the air, as if in reply, and dimly amidst the cloud the form of the white horse and its rider became visible.

King Pluto and Rope's End stood glaring at it in a kind of bewilderment.

Their followers evidently regarded it with superstitious dread.

Again the wild yells were shrieked forth.

Rope's End, brutal as he was, was full of superstition.

He reeled against King Pluto at the harrowing sounds.

"Oh, golly, it de great white debil!" he gasped.

"He comes! he comes to heap destruction on our enemies!" shouted our hero, at the top of his voice.

His companions joined in the cry, and it struck terror to the hearts of the ignorant negroes.

"Tink we better shoot de pris'ners at once, an' den run away, Massa Pluto," counselled the boatswain.

The African king, whose teeth already began to chatter, glanced hurriedly towards his men.

But they seemed half paralysed with fate

His own rifle was empty, and his trembling hands refused to load it.

Richard Howard hastily approached at this moment.

"Look at your wretched men, how they tremble with fear; they will not fight now. Our best plan will be to retire with the prisoners into the wood," he said to him.

Pluto, recovering himself a little at these words, gave the order to remove them.

But it was given in vain.

The scared negroes could scarcely support themselves.

"'Sdeath!" growled Howard, "are you children to be scared by a man on a white horse?"

"It is no man, but a spirit," returned Pluto, glancing apprehensively across the plain.

"Humbug!" replied his English friend; "but even if it were, are you to be cheated of your revenge—or at least your reward? For Blunt must sign his property over to me before he dies."

These suggestions roused the monarch.

"I do not care about your property. I'll slay the captain!" he cried as he began to load his rifle.

But the captain was the precise one whom Richard Howard just then wished to live.

He was not without hopes that he might yet bring him to make over his wealth to him.

"Slay no one now, you have no time!" he said, hurriedly. "Let us retreat into the wood; see, the spirit or devil, or whatever he is, is coming upon us!"

This was quite true, and the trampling of the steed's hoofs could be heard.

"To the forest, all of you!" shouted Richard; "take the prisoners to the forest, quick!"

In order to enforce this command he presented his rifle at them.

Neither blacks nor whites moved an inch.

The former were too terrified, the latter had too much contempt for the threat.

"To the forest, ye white dogs!" cried

King Pluto, as he raised his rifle and fired full at our hero.

Nahita was just in time to knock up the barrel, and the ball whizzed harmlessly over the head of the intended victim.

There was no opportunity for any further attempts, for at that moment Mat Mangles, mounted on Chalks, came flying up to the spot, whooping, hallooing and shrieking at the top of his voice, his lank wiry hair streaming in the wind, and brandishing a long branch which he had torn from a tree.

He was greeted with a unanimous cheer from the English.

"Hooray! Mangles for ever!" burst out Buttons.

The Stinger rushed forward with clasped hands.

"Mr. Mangles—oh, Mr. Mangles!" she exclaimed, imploringly, "preserve us from this dreadful pickle!"

The Stinger's last word roused the professor at once to action.

Urging on Chalks, he dashed in amongst the negroes.

"Pickles—beetroots, you black beggars—beetroots!" he yelled, as he laid about him right and left with his branch. "I'll pickle you! I'll have your topknots! Whoo-oo-oo!"

The horror-stricken darkies, thinking the Great White Fiend had come to carry them off on his white horse to receive the reward of their misdeeds, fled howling to the wood.

Pluto and Rope's End, who were similarly oppressed by their superstitious fears, beat a hasty retreat in the same direction.

Richard Howard, though much chagrined at the turn events had taken, had also deemed it prudent to slink away with his bow-legged associate.

Within three minutes after the arrival of the professor our English Adventurers stood once more free and unfettered on the plain.

Mat Mangles seemed thoroughly to have enjoyed his pastime.

Loud and long he laughed, after his own wild fashion, as the enemy fled before him.

His onslaught being over, he threw himself from his saddle and strode towards his countrymen, holding his staff on his shoulder.

"Capital fun—capital!" he said, in a tone of strong hilarity. "How the blackbeetles ran! didn't they? Ha, ha! see how they run!"

"Your sudden appearance, my dear sir, has been of signal service to us," remarked our hero, gratefully.

"Has it though, really?" returned the professor, pushing back his long hair. "Glad to hear it. Didn't know I'd done anything particular."

"You've saved all our lives, Mr. Mangles, that's what you've done!" exclaimed the Stinger, with deep emotion.

Mat glanced towards her, and made a somewhat strange grimace.

"Who are you?" he asked, abruptly, after a moment.

"Don't you remember me? I'm Elizabeth Ann Stinger," she answered.

"Gammon! you're not. You're my Belinda Jane Jumper—my Belinda Jane Jumper."

"Well, whatever I am," returned the lady, in a grateful tone, "you've saved me from being roasted alive."

"What, you?"

"Yes, me."

"Roasted alive?"

"Yes."

"The black rascals! the atrocious cannibals!" exclaimed the professor, fiercely, flourishing his staff in the air, and looking wildly around him. "Where are they? Let them come on, and we'll show them some fun, for we live on a tight little island."

"You've frightened them away. They are all gone now," returned our hero, "and I think the sooner we make a start ourselves the better."

"Mr. Mangles will no doubt accompany us," said the Stinger.

"Mr. Mangles won't do anything of the kind; oh, dear, no—not for Mangles," was the abrupt answer she received.

"We shall be most happy of your company," interposed Bob Blunt, "if you feel disposed to join us."

"But I don't feel disposed. I'm off."

"Perhaps we shall see you on board the clipper?"

"Ah, perhaps you may—when the moon changes, but not now. No, no; I'm off while I'm safe."

"While you're safe?" echoed our hero.

"Yes ; he, he! they're all after me."

"Who, may I ask ?"

"Harrowly, Pockersgill, Jefferson, Bryant, Stickler, and the whole lot," returned Mat.

"Englishmen, eh ?"

"Of course. 'Fa, fe, fi, fo, fum ! I smell the blood of—you know all about it. You'll find the rest in 'Jack the Giant-killer.' Whoo-up—off and away."

Mat Mangles at the end of this rambling speech, hurried to his horse and sprang into the saddle.

"Ha, ha, ha !" he shouted, "let 'em catch me if they can. I'll give 'em a dance. Yo-oicks ! good-bye. If I'm inquired for, say I'm gone."

"Where ?" cried Buttons.

"To Jericho, to hunt for pickles and beetroots !"

And with a farewell shriek, Mad Mangles galloped off at full speed.

The brief conference between the English party and the Great White Fiend had not been unmarked by the foe.

And now that the White Fiend had taken his departure the courage of Pluto and his tribe began to return.

Before the retreating form of the professor had faded in the distance a discharge of rifles was heard, and several bullets whizzed past the group of Englishmen.

Almost immediately after a swarm of dusky figures emerged through the wood, bent on recapturing our hero and his friends.

<hr/>

CHAPTER XXVI.

FRIENDS AND FELLOW-COUNTRYMEN.

BUT just at that moment, before the blacks could make an attack, shouts were heard in the distance.

A troop of horsemen was seen rapidly advancing.

"Pray Heaven they may prove friends!" murmured our hero, fervently.

"They are—they are, captain !" cried Longsight. "They are white men."

"Hurrah !" shouted the whole body, at this welcome intelligence.

Their negro pursuers, who had caught sight of the approaching escort and heard the shouts, once more took to their heels.

In a few moments a band of twenty Englishmen came up to the spot where Bob and his comrades stood.

The horsemen halted at the sight of Bob and his little band, and the foremost of the party said, courteously—

"Am I right in supposing I address a body of my fellow-countrymen ?"

"Quite right," returned our hero, with a smile. "We are all true Britons here."

"I rejoice to hear it," said the first speaker.

"Come, gentlemen," he added, turning to his comrades, "let us dismount."

In a moment all had left their saddles, and were shaking hands with each other with that heartfelt warmth which only those who meet suddenly thousands of miles from home can thoroughly understand.

"You are explorers, I presume ?" continued the leader of the newly-arrived party, after the first greetings were over.

"We are," returned Bob Blunt ; "and you, gentlemen ?"

"Undoubtedly," returned the other ; "we are here for scientific purposes."

"Oh, indeed ? May I ask your name ?"

"Harrowly."

"THEY BELIEVED IT WAS A SPIRIT, AND FELL ON THEIR KNEES.

"Harrowly?" echoed our hero, in some surprise.

"Yes; Doctor Harrowly, of the Royal Botanical and Geological Society. My name seems known to you."

"I have heard it before."

"Allow me to introduce you to my brother professors; but first let me know whom I have the pleasure of addressing."

"My name is Robert Blunt."

"Of Blunt Castle, Rochester, England?"

"The same."

"I know your place well, and rejoice to meet you."

The ceremony of introduction was speedily performed.

"And how have you progressed in your explorations?" asked the doctor, at length.

"We have encountered many deadly perils and vicissitudes," answered our hero; "but I think I may say the results of our efforts have been up to this time fairly satisfactory."

"I am happy to hear it; penetrating into the heart of Equatorial Africa is no child's play," returned the doctor.

"Have you been successful in your scientific pursuits?" asked Bob, in his turn.

"Very much so," answered Dr. Harrowly; "but we have been somewhat hampered by one of our party."

An idea flashed across our hero's mind with reference to this one, and he said—

"Is his name Mangles?"

"Yes," exclaimed the doctor, eagerly; "do you know anything of him?"

"We have encountered him accidentally at several different times," Bob replied; "in fact, he was with us here, fortunately, not half an hour since."

"Yes, indeed, gentlemen," burst out the Stinger; "but for the gallant but somewhat eccentric Mangles, we should all have been roasted alive."

"Is it possible?" exclaimed the professors in a breath.

"I can vouch for that," said our hero; "we owe our present safety entirely to him. He is a most extraordinary man."

"Ye—es, he is," returned the doctor; "but alas! poor fellow!"

He shook his head sorrowfully as he spoke, and Bob said—

"His mind appears somewhat distraught."

"Very much so, I am sorry to say. An unfortunate love affair changed him from a cheerful, jovial companion into a moody misanthrope."

"Poor dear man!" murmured the Stinger, in a tone of deep sympathy. "That accounts for his addressing me as Belinda Jane."

"That was the name of his inamorata. Ah! it was a sad thing; and, in order to rouse him from his melancholy, we brought him out with us to Africa; but you say he has been here?" inquired the professors.

"Yes. He heard you coming and galloped off."

"Which direction did he take?"

"Almost due south," said Bob; "but I was going to request you to cover our retreat—at least, during a portion of our journey—towards the sea-coast."

"Have you enemies, then, still on your track?" asked the doctor.

"Indeed we have, and unpleasantly close upon it, too," answered our hero, pointing as he spoke to the wood; "and your company would be an effectual check to their approach."

"Then you shall have it, my dear Mr. Blunt," said the professor, warmly; "fifteen lives are of more consequence than one; and besides, our friend Mat has, in spite of his wandering proclivities, a wonderful knack of turning up safely."

"Oh, he's safe enough, sir," observed Buttons. "All the niggers are frightened to death at the very sight of him; they think he's the devil."

"That's a comfort," laughed the doctor; "and now, if you are ready, let us proceed."

"We are extremely willing, my dear sir, to start at once," was our hero's reply.

And with this the whole party commenced their march.

The lurkers in the wood, both black and white, remained looking moodily after them; but not a negro dared to venture forth in pursuit.

The scientific body were well armed,

wore light suits and broad-brimmed hats, and presented altogether such an alarming similarity to their terrible companion, Mat Mangles, that the superstitious darkies regarded them as a troop of equally potent fiends, sent expressly to rescue the Englishmen.

The sun was declining in the west, and the twilight was setting in, as the sea, bathed in glowing crimson, once more greeted the sight of our explorers.

"I think we may venture to leave you now," said Dr. Harrowly to our hero, as they came to a halt.

"You may doctor, and many thanks for your welcome company," returned Bob Blunt; "all I hope is that you may find your comrade, and that we may meet again one day."

"I hope both your prayers may be heard, with all my heart," replied the professor, in a fervent tone; "and as we shall remain on these shores for some time yet, I do not think it impossible that we may meet again."

"Till then, farewell," cried our hero.

The escort rode rapidly away, and our explorers pressed forward towards Beautiful Bay, which they were not long in reaching.

Old Tom and King Agra were looking out for them anxiously, and received them with a royal salute.

Before the darkness set in they were all safely on board the clipper.

The tide came in rapidly, and the vessel soon floated.

By the time the moon had risen she had made her way out of the bay, and lay about half a mile from the shore.

It was while she was dropping her anchors that a number of dusky forms might have been seen cautiously creeping along through the ravine.

By degrees they emerged from its dark shadow on to the beach.

Foremost among these were Richard Howard, Bow-legged Bill, King Pluto and the ruffian Rope's End.

The last plan they had determined on was to inflict some injury upon the vessel.

To burn her if possible.

Great was their rage and disappointment when they found the clipper far beyond their reach.

King Pluto looked out moodily across the waters, and muttered darkly to himself.

Richard Howard stood with folded arms in silence, his lips compressed, his teeth clenched, watching the distant vessel.

"Me hab de cussed white debils!" Rope's End raved furiously, as he shook his clenched fist towards the clipper. "Me hab 'em yet! me blow up de ship! kill 'em all, eb'y one! Ugh! me swear me will!"

Suddenly a strong hand gripped his arm, like a vice.

The giant turned, and found Three-fingered Pluto glaring at him.

"You threaten like a woman. Dare you carry out your threats like a man?" hissed the latter in his ear.

"Iss, me dare," growled Rope's End in a sullen surly tone.

The lips of the king curled scornfully.

"You talk of blowing up yonder ship and killing all on board. How can you do that when both are far from land?"

"Me swim like fish, me climb like monkey, me cunning as de snake; what me make up my mind to do me do," was the self-conceited reply of Rope's End.

"Umph!" returned Pluto, "you speak big words, but let us see big acts. Do as you say and I will reward you and make you a great chief."

"Den me will, me swear," said the boatswain; "you see."

CHAPTER XXVII.

ROPE'S END STARTS ON HIS MISSION.

ROPE'S END, urged on by three very potent stimulants—rum, revenge and the hope of rewards —lost no time in making preparations for his enterprise.

These were simple enough, and consisted merely of a piece of rope made of a cocoa nut fibre, to one end of which a hook was fastened, and a long curved knife.

The first of these he wore coiled round his body, the knife he stuck in his belt.

Being ready, he said in a low tone to Pluto, to whom alone he confided his intentions—

"Now me goin' to start; you keep watch, by-an'-by you see bright light; dat ar clipper blow up in de air bang! an' all de cussed white debils blow up wid her."

The three-fingered king replied grimly—

"I'll watch."

Rope's End hurried away, and in a few seconds had plunged into the sea.

The salt water made his gashed mouth smart terribly.

But he consoled himself for the pain he suffered with the thought of the vengeance he was going to inflict.

He approached the ship very cautiously, propelling himself along beneath the waves as he drew near, and coming to the surface when close under the hull of the clipper.

Rope's End remained floating like a dark log in the water listening intently.

No sound met his ears, and he already chuckled inwardly at the prospect of success.

"White debils all sleep—hear notink," he muttered to himself; "me climb up bery quiet on to de deck, creep down below like snake into cabin, den lay train to de powder-barrels an' set um light. Bang! flash!—yah, yah, yah! how dey fly up in de air!"

Having thus arranged his diabolical programme, the chuckling scoundrel, as he floated, uncoiled the rope from his body and threw it up to where some of the clipper's tackle hung down loosely over her bulwarks.

The hook caught, and all was ready for his ascent.

Rather more ready than he suspected.

Old Tom the helmsman, the boy Skyrocket, and Jingo were awake and on deck, and, having nothing to do but to keep watch, had determined to enliven their vigil with a little fishing.

A stray shark might be hovering near, and to catch one of the voracious monsters would be a feat worth performing, they thought.

It was just then that Rope's End's muttered soliloquy caught their ears, and Skyrocket exclaimed, in a whisper, as he pointed over his shoulder—

"Some un dere, Massa Tom."

The old sailor placed his finger to his lips to enjoin silence whilst they listened.

As soon as the voice ceased he motioned with his head to Jingo Johnson to reconnoitre the intruder.

This Jingo did effectually.

"It's Rope's End," he said, after a moment, under his breath.

"The devil it is!" muttered old Tom. "Anyone with him?"

"No one."

"Splice my old shoes if we won't give him a taste of his own name if we can only lay him by the heels, the overgrown lubberly son of Beelzebub!" growled the tar, as he rose to his feet and seized a rope.

In the meantime the boatswain had pulled himself up.

His nose was now on a level with the piece of salt pork—the bait for the shark—which dangled just in front of that organ.

It was not a very fragrant piece of

pork, but it seemed to have a peculiar charm for Rope's End's nose.

He stopped in his ascent and sniffed eagerly.

"Golly!" he muttered to himself; "what lubly smell dat?"

His eyes fell upon the tempting luxury.

In spite of his peculiar position the giant's mouth fairly watered.

Skyrocket was cautiously peeping down upon him, and he whispered suddenly, with much glee—

"He found de pork! he found de pork!"

"I hope he may swaller it hook and all," returned old Tom, fervently.

Rope's End's desires were in perfect harmony with those of the helmsman, so far, at least, as the pork was concerned.

To the hook he might have objected.

"Muss hab bit ob dat lubly chow-chow," he said to himself, as he smacked his thick lips.

With this he held on by one hand, and with the other drew his knife, cut off a trifle, which might have weighed half a pound or so, and thrust it into his mouth.

"Oh, golly, golly! dis am proper kind of chow-chow," he murmured to himself.

Having commenced he found it impossible to leave off, and, making a hitch in the rope in which to rest his foot, he hacked away at the pork in good earnest.

"Yah, yah!" grinned Skyrocket, as he watched him from above, "he eat it all; shark get none."

"Yah! the greedy cannibal," muttered old Tom, in disgust.

But the ancient tar was not idle all this time.

He had fully resolved to capture the treacherous giant, if possible; and for that purpose, whilst he was feeding, he fastened a strong rope, with a noose at the end, to a windlass, and having summoned General Orlando to assist, waited quietly for his opportunity.

Rope's End went on cutting and chewing, till at length he came to the hook.

"What de debil dis har?" he exclaimed to himself, as he felt the point. "Golly, von iron hook. Bery good job me no swaller him."

"Now, den," he said, "me get on board."

He listened an instant.

"All quiet," he thought.

And with this he pulled himself up, and, resting both his hands on the bulwarks, looked around him.

"All safe; no one 'bout," he muttered, as his eyes roamed up and down the apparently deserted deck.

The words were scarcely out of his mouth than up sprang Skyrocket.

Over the giant's head and shoulders went the noose.

A tremendous jerk followed, tightening the noose and holding him fast.

A loud "Yo-hoy-hoy-hoy!" from old Tom and his mates rang out cheerily as he worked at the windlass, and up in the air flew Rope's End, startled almost out of his senses, struggling and roaring like a trapped elephant.

"Let me down, you cussed debils! you cussed ugly white-black debils!" he raved, as he kicked furiously. "Me tear you to bits for dis har."

"Strikes me you've done tearin', yar wenomus, murderous warmint, for this time," cried old Tom. "It's no use yar tryin' to dance. We've got yar, an' we means to hold yar tight."

This explanation drove the prisoner mad with rage, and he roared louder than ever, so much so that all on board were roused from their slumbers.

In a few moments our hero and his companions, hardly knowing what new disaster to expect, came hurrying upon deck.

To their profound astonishment, by the light of the ship's lanterns they recognised the gigantic form as it dangled in the air.

"Rope's End!" they exclaimed, with one voice.

"Yes, there he is," said old Tom. "The atroshus wag'bond swum from the shore wi' th' idear o' sneakin' aboard as he did afore, an' then blowin' up the wessel. Yer knows ye did, ye ugly black son o' Satan. I heerd ye say so."

A shudder ran through the breasts of all at this terrible statement, and our hero said, sternly—

"Then, by Heaven! if this be the case, he shall die the murderer's death."

"No, no; it lie, it big lie!" raved the suspended boatswain.

Rope's End, finding that his protestations were unheeded, changed his tune.

"You no right keep poor Krooman hang up here," he moaned. "De rope cut me right in half. Why you not let me down?"

There was some truth and reason in these appeals; for the weight of the giant negro increased the pain of his position; and had he been kept hanging as he was, the rope would in a short time have buried itself in his flesh.

Bob Blunt could see this.

"Let him down," he said; "but secure his limbs so as to remove every possibility of escape."

"Aye, aye, captain," returned old Tom; "I'll fix the warmint. If he can untie my knots I'll forgive him."

With this the boatswain was lowered until his feet almost touched the deck.

His lower extremities were then bound with strong lashings of rope.

Skyrocket, with great alacrity and much dexterity, next clambered up and pinioned his arms firmly.

These operations performed, Rope's End was allowed to descend by easy stages until his bulk rested on the deck.

Here he was secured by additional ropes passed through iron rings, so that if he had had the strength of twenty men he could not have moved an inch.

"Leave him there," said our hero, as he looked down upon his prisoner: "he is safe now. To-morrow morning I will deal with him in strict justice."

"Tank'ee, capt'n," whined Rope's End, hypocritically, with a rueful grin on his disfigured face; "dat all me want. De English bery good to poor nigger; allers gib 'em justice."

"You shall have justice!" said Bob Blunt, emphatically; "justice to the full!"

With these words he turned away.

But in the glance of his eye at that moment there was more justice than mercy.

CHAPTER XXVIII.

ROPE'S END UNDERGOES A TRIAL BY JURY.

THE morning dawned bright and beautiful.

Buttons, considerably refreshed by his night's repose, left his cabin and came on deck.

The first person he encountered there was Skyrocket.

"Ah, Massa Buttons, dere you am!" said the Kroo-boy, heartily.

"Yes; here I am, Skyrocket!" responded the page, in a tone equally cheerful.

"You glad get back to de ship, eh?"

"Rather! I never expected to see her again."

Skyrocket grinned all over his face as he remarked—

"Dat jolly lark last night!"

"What was?" asked Buttons.

"Dat big nigger comin' aboard."

"To cut our throats and blow us all to smash!" said the page; "I don't see where the lark comes in."

"Me don't mean 'bout dat," said Skyrocket.

"What do you mean, then?"

"Me mean 'bout him eatin' de lump ob salt pork. About eight pounds of bad pork."

"Ha! let's go and look at the cannibal brute."

Together they advanced to the spot where Rope's End lay bound hand and foot.

The boatswain's eyes were closed, and he appeared to be asleep.

But presently one eye opened, and fixed itself upon the page.

"Well, ugly mug! how does the pork agree with you, eh?" the latter asked.

"Bery bad, Massa Buttons," Rope's End answered, screwing up his features into a hideous contortion. "Got drefful pain in him tummick."

"Serve you right, you greedy rascal," said Buttons.

"Eee, ee!" grinned Skyrocket; "um ought to hab swallered de shark-hook well as de pork; no hab pain den."

Rope's End ground his teeth for an instant, and glared savagely at his facetious countryman.

But, realizing how useless it was to put himself in a passion, he calmed down and said, in his former whining tone—

"Massa Buttons."

"Well," said the page.

"'Spose dere no chance ob gettin' lilly drop ob rum, am dere?"

"Not the least in the world."

The giant groaned, and muttered—

"Tink me die outright if me don't hab some rum."

"I think it's very likely you will die," replied Buttons.

All the ship was now astir; and, breakfast being over, our hero and his followers came on deck.

"Let all hands be summoned," he said.

In a few seconds the entire crew had assembled and ranged themselves in rank on each side of the deck.

This being done our hero fixed his eyes sternly upon Rope's End.

"It is now my duty to deal with you," he said; "but I shall endeavour to deal justly."

"Tankee, capt'n," replied the prisoner, in a doubtful tone.

"You are accused of a terrible crime," Bob continued. "No less than the murder in cold blood of all on board this vessel!"

"Dat not true, capt'n! Dat Massa Tom tell big lies!" protested Rope's End, grinding his teeth at the helmsman. "He know it big lies."

"I know it's as true as gospel!" ex-

claimed the old tar. "I'll take my davy on it!"

"I quite believe you," said our hero.

Then, turning once more to the prisoner, he continued—

"If you had no evil intent, what was your motive in swimming so far from the shore and seeking to get on board the clipper in the dead of night?"

"'Cos me bery sorry for what me done; want to ax come back agin," replied Rope's End, in a whimpering tone.

"No, no; that won't do," said Bob Blunt. "You have not acted in any way like one who was sorry. Had you done so I might perhaps be induced to pardon you. But I can see no redeeming point in your conduct to justify me in pardoning you."

"None! none!" echoed those around.

"Better let me off dis time," murmured the giant.

"To set a treacherous, ungrateful, cold-blooded miscreant like yourself at large would be simply to deserve the fate that you intended should be ours," replied our hero.

"Most decidedly it would, Mr. Blunt," said the Stinger; "and my advice, now you have caught this very large and ugly specimen of African inhumanity, is, don't let him go again."

"It is not my intention to do so," returned Bob.

The negro clenched his teeth and uttered a subdued growl.

"You say you let me hab justice!" he muttered, hoarsely.

"You're a-having it as fast as you can," exclaimed Buttons. "Don't be in a hurry."

"How me hab justice if me no let go?" demanded Rope's End.

"Freedom does not always follow the administration of the law," said our hero to him; "all depends upon the verdict."

"Who de debil him? You not kill me?" cried the giant, making a sudden effort to burst the ropes that bound him.

"That will be as the jury shall decide," returned Bob, calmly.

Then turning to his comrades, he continued—

"Gentlemen! you are all well acquainted with the character and disposition of the prisoner. You know the deadly nature of the plots he has contrived against us, and which, had not Providence interfered in our behalf, would have led to our destruction. He is now in our hands, and it is for you to decide upon his fate. Do you find him guilty or not guilty?"

"Guilty!" responded every voice.

"And his punishment?"

"Death!"

"Prisoner," said our hero, solemnly, "you are found guilty, and your doom is to be hanged from the yard-arm of this vessel!"

There was a dead silence.

Rope's End glared around him with wild eyes, that seemed ready to start from their sockets.

"You no kill me, you English debils!" he burst out at length, in a paroxysm of rage. "If you do de Great Fetiche come down eat you all! De three-finger king hab revenge too!—all de——"

He broke off suddenly, as his eyes caught a glimpse of a dark face peering down upon him from aloft.

Some of the branches—relics of the grand banquet—still remained fastened to the mast; and they concealed that mysterious form from all but himself.

The giant at once recognised the figure as that of a friend come to help him in his distress.

Nor was he mistaken.

It was Poonah, the lieutenant of the slave-ship.

King Pluto had waited on the beach all night, looking out anxiously for the bright flash, and listening intently for the big bang which was to announce the demolition of the clipper.

But when neither of these events happened, and his confederate did not return, he became uneasy as to his fate.

It was then that Poonah volunteered to swim to the vessel and endeavour to learn what had happened to him.

The interest of all on board being absorbed in the prisoner, no one had noticed his approach.

The same cause enabled him to climb up the ship's side, and glide nimbly into the rigging, without his presence being observed or even suspected.

Rope's End was far too cunning to allow any sign of recognition to appear in his face.

And in his heart he felt pretty certain that he was not going to die just yet; but that by means of his accomplice up in the shrouds, he should baffle his executioners and escape.

In the meantime the preparations for carrying out the extreme sentence were rapidly performed.

The burly giant being already pinioned, all that was necessary was to fasten a block to the extreme end of the yard-arm, and to pass a rope through it.

This being done, and a noose made, old Tom and four of the Kroomen approached the negro.

"Your time's come!" said the old tar.

"Oh, am it?" replied Rope's End, with much *sang froid*. "Berry well; me quite ready!"

The contrast between his recent excitement and his present indifference was so great that everyone noticed it.

Old Tom could not help remarking—

"You takes hangin' pretty cool, mister blackee."

"Iss—me rader like it," was the somewhat startling rejoinder.

"Let's hope you will," said the tar significantly.

Rope's End had now been raised to his feet, and stood with the noose round his brawny throat.

A dozen Kroomen grasped the other end, waiting for the signal to run him up.

"Have you anything to say before you die?" asked our hero.

"No, me habn't! me say what me got to say afterwards!" was his reply uttered with a grin.

"I would rather have heard some expression of regret from your lips than such reckless words as these," said Bob.

"Oh, well, den, me bery sorry me bin so wicked, but me never do um ag'in neber!—not till de nex time—yah, yah, yah!"

And again a hoarse laugh burst from his lips.

Our hero turned away in disgust.

Old Tom made a signal to the Kroomen, who tightened the rope.

Then one of the guns of the clipper sent forth its deafening report.

At the same moment the executioners ran forward, and the burly form of the giant was hoisted up and dangled in the air.

But ere he had time to give one convulsive struggle, the dark form of Poonah glided rapidly down and ran along the yard-arm as nimbly as a monkey.

Through the misty cloud of smoke a knife flashed—a wild shout was heard—and the suspended body dropped like a plummet into the waves beneath, accompanied by Poonah.

All this was accomplished with such extreme rapidity that it seemed to be the work of some enchanter.

"What can this mean?" exclaimed the doctor, breathless with amazement.

The twelve Kroomen, from the sudden removal of the counterpoise at the other end of the rope, had fallen in a heap on the deck, and for a few moments everything was confusion and dismay.

"My opinion is that the prisoner has been rescued by some confederate," our hero answered after a moment.

Hardly had he said this when a hoarse cry was heard.

All eyes turned in the direction of the sound.

Two dark spots could be seen at some short distance from the vessel, rising and falling with the waves.

"See!" cried the doctor; "one of them is waving his arm!"

"It's Rope's End," said Longsight.

The next moment the voice of the giant came floating across the sea—

"Yah! yah!—good-bye, English debils! —yah! yah! yah!" he shouted mockingly.

"We'll stop your mouth yet, you black rascal!" muttered Bob. "Your rifles all of you! quick."

There was a general rush for the weapons, and in a few seconds everyone had his loaded rifle in his hand.

"Now, then, altogether; it will be hard if we can't settle him amongst us. Fire!"

As our hero gave the word of command there was a general volley.

A loud yell and a splash of water in the distance.

The dark forms were seen no more.

"I think our lead has proved more effectual than our rope," said our hero.

"Hooray!" said Buttons.

Nahita alone looked doubtful, and kept her eyes fixed upon the waters.

"You are less sanguine, dear Nahita?" said Bob Blunt to her, as he watched her.

"I know the habits of the African better than you do, dear captain," she replied, placing her hand fondly on his shoulder.

After several moments had elapsed the two dark spots appeared again—but more indistinctly now than before; and the mocking voice of Rope's End was faintly heard as he yelled out—

"Yah! yah! yah!"

The next moment he and is confederate dived again under the surface, and were seen no more.

Rope's End had escaped after all.

CHAPTER XXIX.

A SEA MONSTER.

THE ruffian was not deemed worthy of pursuit.

But our hero determined to give his enemies a wide berth by standing out to sea for the present.

All hands at once went to work.

The branches and flowers that still hung to the masts and rigging were taken down, the ropes underwent a thorough supervision, the sails were unfurled, the anchor was weighed, and the clipper, under the influence of a favourable wind, sped merrily onwards.

Bob Blunt and his companions stood on the deck smoking their cigars, enjoying the bright sunshine and fresh breeze, and the sense of security which the wide ocean gave them.

Here there were no dense jungles or shadowy coverts for foes to hide in.

The only enemies they had to look for were the winds and storms, which now, happily, seemed far distant.

"What course do you intend to take, captain?" asked Stumps after a time.

"You mentioned your desire to visit Abyssinia," said Dr. Knowall; "you have not, I suppose, altered your intention?"

"Not at all," answered Bob. "I am most desirous of exploring that land of giant mountains and yawning ravines."

Buttons seemed particularly delighted at the idea of visiting Abyssinia.

"Of course we shall get any amount of incidents in the mountains," he said to the Stinger, "to say nothing of the 'yawnin' ravens.'"

"Yawning ravens?" echoed Elizabeth Ann.

"Yes! didn't you hear the guv'nor say that yawnin' ravens was plentiful in Abyssinia? I means to ketch one and tame it."

"You silly young donkey!" exclaimed E. A. S.; "he said 'yawning ravines.'"

"What are they?"

"Why narrow passages, with high rocks on each side, you ignoramus," explained the Stinger.

"Oh! I thought they were birds," said Buttons. "Well, never mind! Anyhow I like the idea of Abyssinia. I fancy it must be a jolly place; it sounds like it."

The time came when the youthful speaker had occasion to alter his opinion and to come to the conclusion that the jollity of this portion of African territory was of an extremely awful description.

The weather was fair, and the clipper continued her course calmly and pleasantly.

Early in the fourth week they sighted a vessel.

She proved to be a Dutch schooner bound for the Gambia.

Our hero hailed her, and the ships having been brought to, the commanders were able to communicate with each other.

The Dutch captain fortunately spoke English fairly well, which greatly assisted the conference, which consisted principally of questions put by Bob Blunt, and answered by the other.

"And now farewell, mein friend," said the Dutchman, as the colloquy drew to an end; "but pefore ve parts, let me prepare you for sometink."

"What?"

"Ah, vot? dat is der question."

"Is it of some peril you would warn me?"

"Yah!"

"From slavers or pirates?"

"*Nein, nein*—no, no."

"What then?"

"Vell," replied the Dutchman, scratching his head, and screwing up his features in a perplexed manner, "I hardly know vot to call him."

"Perhaps you can describe it in some way," said Bob.

"Vell den, it was someting very pig and large vot appear rising out of der vorters."

"Had it the form of a fish?"

"No; it was more like von snake."

"Indeed?"

"Yah, yos, inteed! Foorst it lay on de top of de vaves—very long—terrible long."

"Yes. And then?"

"Den on de sudden he rear his pig head up aloft higher dan de ship topmast, an' open his big jaws. *Teufels!* I tink he go to svaller us all."

"What next?" asked Bob.

"Vell, joss at dat moment he catch sight of von shark dat swim by."

"Did he attack it?"

"*Teufels!* yes; he duck his pig head down like lightning, an' snap ope der shark as if he vos noting at all, after vich he disappear."

"And you saw no more of him?"

"No; noting more."

"And where was it you encountered this monster?"

"Joss after ve had rounded de Cape."

"We are sailing in that direction; possibly he may pay us a similar visit."

"Ah! yes; dat is vy I give you varnin'."

"I thank you," said our hero, "and wish you a prosperous voyage."

"Same to you, mein friend."

With these words the grapnels were unfastened, and the vessels procceded on their different courses.

The Dutch captain's account had been listened to with much interest by all on board.

"Have yer ever heerd o' the great sea sarpent, captain?" asked old Tom.

"I have, certainly," replied our hero;

"but always regarded it as as fabulous an invention as the dragon slain by St. George."

"Ah!" returned Tom; "then that's where we don't agree, captain."

"You believe in its existence then?" returned Bob Blunt.

"Yes, I do, captain," the old tar replied, earnestly; "an' I tell yer what, I believes that 'ere monster the Dutchman spoke of was that identical sarpent; an' more than that, I've got a strong present'ment that we shall see him too."

The old helmsman's tone and manner were almost solemn.

CHAPTER XXX.

THE GREAT SEA SERPENT AT LAST.

THE wind and weather had been hitherto all that could be wished, but as they approached the Cape —which has been well-named the Cape of Storms—it began to change.

The "Skipper" no longer danced merrily over the waves under sunny skies.

The heavens were now dark with drifting clouds, and the wind blew in fierce, angry gusts, almost lifting the light craft out of the water.

Old Tom maintained his silence, and a certain moody rigidity in his face that seemed to imply all was not quite right.

Skyrocket had been rather astonished at the rough sea and the boisterous wind that had been lately prevailing, and Buttons took upon himself to explain the cause.

"I can tell you," he said to his sable comrade, as they were struggling with the gale in a heavy sea, "wot's the cause of all this."

"Can you, Massa Buttons?" the other replied. "Me like to know."

"Open all the ears you've got, and I'll tell yer then," said Buttons.

Skyrocket opened all his ears as he was directed—they only amounted to two—and the page then commenced, impressively—

"I 'spose yer never 'eard o' the 'Phantom Ship,' did yer?"

"Neber," responded the negro, shaking his head. "Wat dat?"

"Well, it's a ship that ain't a ship at all—only a shadder."

"What dat?" asked Skyrocket, looking particularly mystified.

"Why, somethink yer can see but can't touch. Like the reflection o' yer nose on the wall when there's a light behind it, d'yer see?"

"Ah, iss, iss; me umblecomstand now."

"Well then," continued Buttons, "it's this phantom ship a-comin' near us that brings this 'ere squally weather."

"Tink she better keep 'way den," remarked Skyrocket.

"Ah! that's just the pint," exclaimed Buttons, in a mysterious tone; "she can't keep away."

"Why not?"

"'Cause she's under a dreadful spell."

"What she smell off?"

"I didn't say smell, I said spell," exclaimed Buttons, sharply.

"Oh, what you mean by spell?"

"What a donkey you are! it means a—a—a somethink as makes yer move on whether yer likes it or not."

"Ah, iss, iss; whip, whip, me know now."

Buttons groaned inwardly at his comrade's ignorance, but he went on—

"Well, this phantom ship is commanded by a man named Vanderdecken."

"Who Vanderpeckin?"

"He's the 'Flying Dutchman.'"

"Golly! me like see Dutchman fly. Me went flying up out of ship once. And what de Dutchman do?"

"Well, a great many years ago, he was a-trying to get inside Table Bay in the midst of a storm."

"Iss."

"Well, the more he tried the more he couldn't, and so, in a rage, he swore an orful oath that he'd make the bay though he beat about till the day of judgment."

"Dat bery long time, me tink; ain't it?"

"Rather."

"And what he do den?"

"There was a dreadful clap of thunder and tremendous flashes of lightning, and a terrible voice cried 'For ever.'"

"Iss. Wot den?"

"Why, then the ship and the captain and crew was turned into phantoms on the spot."

"Dey keep sail 'bout still?"

"Yes; they're always sailing, and always a-trying to reach Table Bay, and never able to get near it."

At this moment the wind gave a dreadful howl, and the clipper such a tremendous lurch, that Buttons and his chum were shot violently into the scuppers.

"Oh, lor! he's a-coming," muttered the page.

"Who coming?" asked Skyrocket.

"The 'Flying Dutchman.'"

Before another word could be said, the man at the look-out called—

"Something ahead!"

In a few seconds everyone had hurried on deck.

The Stinger, enveloped in her flannel dressing-gown, for the wind was cold.

All eyes were strained across the foaming waters.

It was true there was something ahead, though what that something was, no one could yet discover.

It was not a vessel, but a dark ridge that lay upon the surface of the waves, and rose and fell with them.

"What can it be?" asked Elizabeth Ann, breaking in upon the silence.

"A mass of floating seaweed, I opine," said Dr. Knowall, after a moment's consideration.

The voice of old Tom was now heard.

"No, no, it ain't seaweed."

"It looks not unlike it," remarked Bob Blunt.

"Ah, captain!" exclaimed the tar, "there's life in that dark object as I expect you'll all find out afore long."

The tone of the helmsman was so strangely ominous that it recalled to our hero the warning of the Dutch captain, and he said—

"You don't think it possible that it might be that—"

He paused, and old Tom taking up his words, continued—

"That monster, Mr. Blunt. Well, I do think it's possible. In fact, it is my firm conviction as that there long dark line yonder is neither more nor less than the great sea serpent."

The words produced some sensation amongst the listeners.

At length the dark motionless mass began to stir as if awaking from sleep.

Its size could scarcely be calculated, as only a portion of it could be seen, but, judging from what was visible, its bulk was enormous.

The feelings of our adventurers rapidly underwent a change.

Not exactly to fear; they were too inured to perils for that.

"I think you're right, old fellow," said our hero to the helmsman.

"Aye, aye, sir; I'm right enough," was the latter's reply; "but there's the sweet little cherub that sits up aloft," added the old man, turning his eyes to the dark clouds, "an' he'll look arter us."

This trusting speech was instantly

followed by a startled exclamation from the Stinger.

"Oh! good gracious! see! the brute's rising up!" she almost shrieked.

An involuntary thrill passed through every breast, as a terrible head, bearing a strong resemblance to that of a serpent, rose up with slow and stately motion from out of the depths.

Having reared itself to a height of some thirty feet, it remained poised in that position, its neck arched, and slowly inclining from side to side, as though reconnoitring the surrounding expanse of ocean.

Suddenly it plunged down again, and began to move forward through the water with great velocity.

Not one of the gazers uttered a word.

The monster was evidently coming in the direction of the vessel.

The sea serpent was now rapidly drawing near.

At length Bob cried, in his usual firm tone—

"Let the guns be loaded—quick!"

This order had the effect of arousing his comrades, and there was an instantaneous rush below.

In a few seconds all returned, bringing with them rifles, revolvers and cutlasses.

The monster had now reached to within forty yards of the vessel.

Again it reared itself aloft as it had done before.

Its gigantic proportions could now be distinctly seen.

It was covered with small scales of a dusky brown colour, and the expression of its countenance and the fixed glare of its eyes were terrible in the extreme.

Its neck for several yards downwards was covered with a kind of mane—if such an expression may be used in reference to an inhabitant of the sea—whilst its mouth was full of long, sharp fangs.

Its gaze was riveted upon the vessel.

"Now, lads," shouted Bob, "fire!"

The order was at once obeyed.

A volley of bullets was discharged at the monster.

But they took no more effect than a handful of pebbles might have done in the way of injury.

If they did anything, it was rather to irritate or startle it.

The next moment it lowered its head, and launched itself at the clipper's hull with the swiftness of a battering ram.

Providentially, its intent was frustrated.

A rising wave lifted the vessel, and the serpent passed under instead of striking her.

But all could feel the shock as the mighty bulk ground itself against the keel.

Suddenly the hideous form rose up as before on the other side, and again fixed his cruel, unwavering eyes upon the vessel.

"The ugly brute don't seem to have any feelings," whispered Buttons to the Stinger.

"Oh, Lor'! I don't know anything about his feelings," returned Elizabeth Ann, nervously, "but I fancy he's taking particular notice of me."

"Me get up aloft; get better look at him dere," said Skyrocket, as he glided to the shrouds and ascended as nimbly as a monkey.

"I must go below," the Stinger exclaimed suddenly; "I don't feel safe here."

As she spoke, she made a hasty advance towards the hatchway.

But she had hardly taken half a dozen steps when the gigantic serpent, attracted probably by her light wrapper, swooped down upon her like a hawk.

The next moment the Stinger was unceremoniously hoisted off her legs over the ship's side, and found herself, to her horror, suspended over the boiling waters in the fangs of the monster.

Consternation seized upon the gazers at the terrible fate that seemed to threaten the Stinger, and they uttered a cry of dismay.

"Oh, murder! Help! help!" cried the Stinger.

"Stand back, men!" cried Bob.

Bang!

At that moment Bob Blunt discharged one of the large guns.

The fastenings of the Stinger's wrapper gave way suddenly, and she fell out of it into the sea with a tremendous splash.

When the smoke from the cannon cleared away, Elizabeth Ann was dis-

covered floundering in the waves, with
Skyrocket at her side doing his best to
support her.

The leviathan serpent was seen sailing
away majestically with the flannel dressing-gown in his jaws.*

A rope was instantly lowered, and the
immersed parties were quickly hauled up
on to the deck, to the great joy of all.

* The London papers of May 1 publish an extract
from the *Glasgow News* giving an account of the
killing of a Sea Serpent at Oban, in Argyllshire.
The animal having appeared in the bay, its retreat
was cut off by boats, while a number of volunteers

Soon the weather changed for the
better.

The wind moderated, the clouds dis-
persed, and the sun shone forth again,
and they went round the Cape in gallant
style, and having passed through the
channel of Mozambique, anchored in a
small bay that seemed to afford a safe
protection from winds and storms.

on shore fired at it with their rifles till it was killed.
The dimensions given are—length 101 feet; circumference at the thickest part, 11 feet. The account
has since been proved to be a hoax.

CHAPTER XXXI.

AN IMPORTANT INCIDENT OCCURS TO BUTTONS.

SO snug and secluded was the spot
that our hero determined to leave
the clipper there in harbour, whilst
he and his comrades pressed forward into the interior.

Accordingly, the operation of unload-
ing the vessel was at once commenced.

The wheels and axletrees they had
brought with them were drawn up from
the hold, and the kroomen were set to
work to chop down timber.

With this they fashioned rude waggons,
fit to transport baggage.

On these vehicles the cargo Bob Blunt
had brought with him was packed.

The waggons being loaded, a difficulty
started up at once.

How were they to be drawn?

They had no horses, or any other beasts
of burden.

King Aga suggested to our hero that a
small detachment should proceed inland
and endeavour to procure mules or oxen
from the natives.

Jingo Johnson at once volunteered.

" Me go, capt'n," he said, eagerly ; " an'
if der any animal to be got, me get 'em."

" Me go too," joined in General Orlando
grandly ; " when dey see dis hyar cocked
hat, dey not dare refuse notink."

Accordingly, they started off with

several of the kroomen, who carried with
them a bale of goods to be used in lieu of
coin in effecting their purchases.

They were wonderfully successful, and
in two days returned in triumph, bringing with them a dozen mules and two
elephants.

And not only these, but a number of
the Shoho Galla tribe, whose confidence
Jingo Johnson had contrived to gain.

The savage, gipsy-like beings would be
invaluable, not only in managing the
elephants, but in guiding them over the
rocky steeps, and through the deep ravines
they would have to pass.

Our hero received them with much
kindness ; and all being ready, they bade
adieu once more to the trim clipper,
which they left in charge of old Tom, and
set forward.

We pass over the long and toilsome
journey across the arid sandy plains, until
the Abyssinian frontiers were reached.

We catch up our brave adventurers
once more in a deep gorge of the stupen-
dous mountains of that rock-bound country.

*　*　*　*　*

The sun was setting as our hero, sur
rounded by his followers, sat looking upon

the scene of solitary grandeur that met their gaze on every side.

" What do yer think of Abyssinia, ole buster?" asked Buttons of the Stinger, after a long pause of silence.

" I think it's very fine indeed," the latter replied ; " but the precipices are so awfully deep they make me shudder."

" I don't think it 'ud be good for a feller's health to drop down one of 'em," responded Buttons.

" Golly, no," remarked Jingo Johnson with a grin ; " take all de shine out of dat nigger 'Lando's big cocked hat if he fall down dere."

The general heard this remark, and groaned as he replied grandly—

" Dis chil' not in de habit of falling down precipikes."

" I've had enough of the precipikes," grinned Buttons ; " it's the yawnin' ravens I want to see."

" You'll have the pleasure of making their acquaintance before very long," observed Dr. Knowall with a smile.

Gradually the sun sank behind the giant mountains, and darkness rapidly threw a veil over the prospect.

Having a long march before them on the morrow, the travellers sought their resting places for the night.

Soon all were stretched upon their grassy couches, fast asleep ; and profound silence reigned around.

*　　*　　*　　*　　*

It was early dawn on the following morning when our hero was roused from his slumbers by loud wailing cries of grief.

Springing from his bed, he left his tent, and hastened towards the spot from whence the lamentations proceeded.

On reaching it, he found his troupe of Gallas wringing their hands over the body of one of their comrades, with all the vehemence of intense grief.

" Dead ! dead !" they cried wildly to him.

" Dead !" echoed Bob Blunt, in surprise.

" He kill ! he kill !" was their answer, given with much excitement.

" Who can have killed him ?" said our hero, as he knelt down and examined the body.

" Some from mountain dere," exclaimed the indignant Shohos, as they pointed along the rocky chain.

But their was no wound, not even a scratch, upon the corpse ; until at length Bob Blunt looked at the throat, on which the prints of fingers could be distinctly seen.

It was then pretty evident the unfortunate savage had been strangled.

Whilst our hero was perplexing himself with thoughts as to who the murderer could be, he heard a fresh outcry, and several of the kroomen, with Jingo Johnson at their head, came hurrying forward.

" Oh, massa ! oh, captain !" they exclaimed, tumultuously.

" What now ?" demanded our hero, in a voice hasty from apprehension.

" De baggage waggins, massa, de baggage waggins !" cried Jingo, in an excited tone.

" What of them ?"

" Someone been in de night—steal, rob."

Bob Blunt sprang to his feet.

" Stolen the waggons, do you mean ?" he asked.

" No, massa, not de waggins, but de goods dat war on 'em."

" Confusion !" muttered Bob, fiercely, through his clenched teeth ; " let us see."

He strode forward to the spot where the waggons stood, with eager steps.

The report was too true.

The merchandise which he had collected with so much pains and care, and which he regarded as his passport through Abyssinia, was gone.

A cry of mingled wrath and dismay at his irreparable loss burst from our hero.

" Let all our native followers be summoned at once," he cried.

In a few moments they were all drawn up together on the spot.

Bob Blunt questioned them closely as to the act of spoliation ; but he could extract nothing that afforded the slightest clue to it.

The only probable explanation he could arrive at was that given by the Shoho guides.

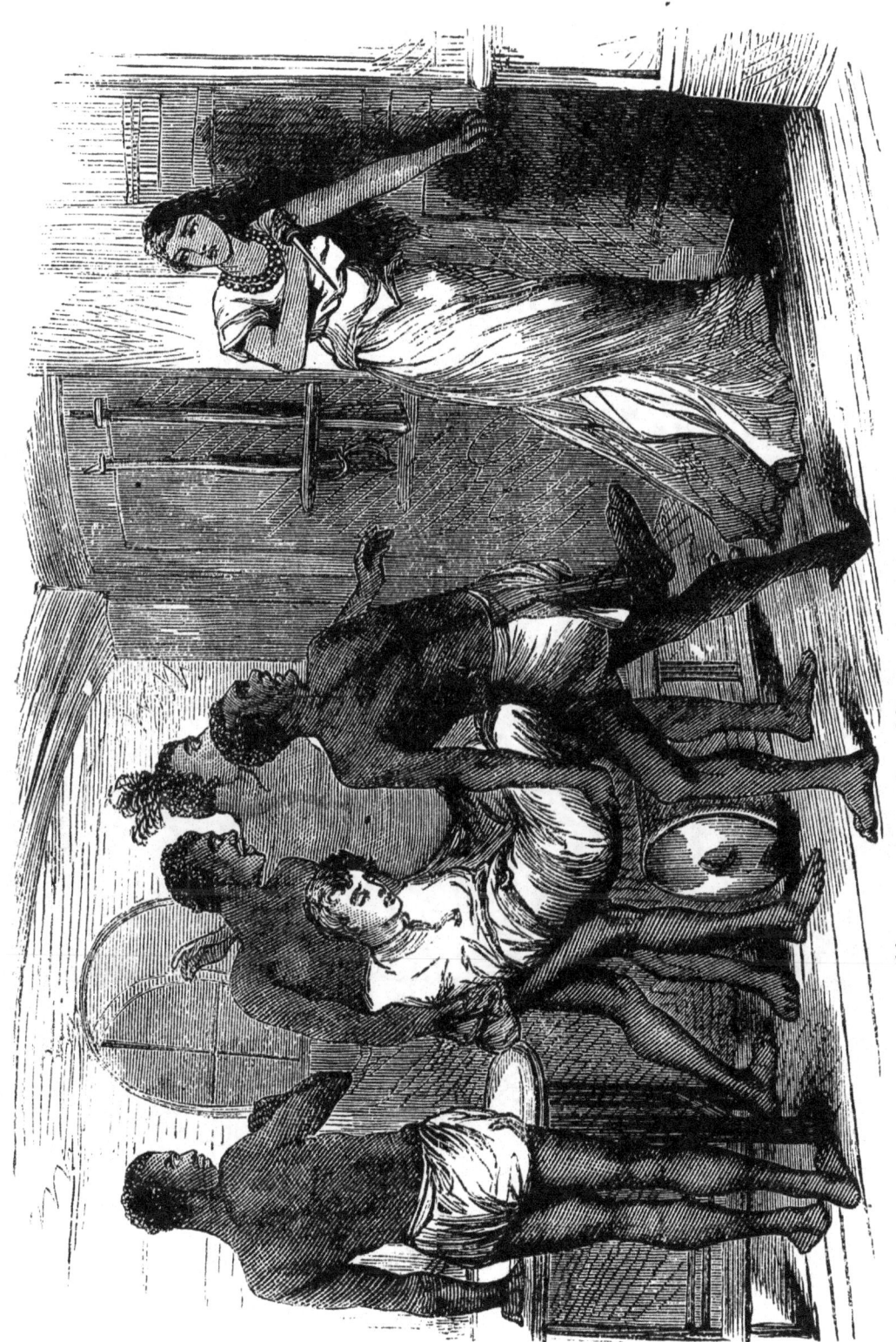

"'WHAT DO YOU HERE?' SHE DEMANDED, 'ANSWER ME!'"

"Robbers come right 'long mountains when sleep, carry tings away," they said.

"The infernal marauders!" cried Bob Blunt fiercely. "But they cannot have got far."

"Ah, massa, the mountaineer run 'long like goat—quick," said his dark followers shrugging their shoulders.

"Quick or slow, we must overtake them!" exclaimed Bob. "Let the signal for marching be given instantly."

Buttons had been aroused by the sound of the horn.

Springing to his feet he peeped out of his tent.

He could see the whole camp was in motion, and on the very point of moving onwards.

"They're a-goin' forward," he said to himself; "it won't do to be left behind in these 'ere regions. I must slip into my togs quick."

But on his looking for these useful articles, he found they had vanished, and he had no "togs" to put on.

CHAPTER XXXII.

BUTTONS IN A FIX.

HERE'S a pretty go!" he exclaimed ruefully; "wherever are the blessed things gone to? I'm certain I put 'em in the corner yonder when I took 'em off last night."

It was very mysterious their disappearance, and extremely awkward to Buttons.

"It's a moral certainty I cannot go out of the tent without my clothes on. Wherever can they be?" he muttered.

As he spoke, he peered cautiously through his leafy chamber.

The start had already commenced, and there was he a prisoner, with nothing on him but his shirt.

"What a 'cussed noosance!" he groaned.

Suddenly he started, as he caught sight of what seemed to him to be the very garments he had lost.

They were on the back of a human being, there was no doubt of that.

The human being—whoever he was—was walking on his hands, with his heels in the air, very complacently, in the midst of the brushwood.

Every portion of this person was visible but his head, which the bush concealed; but Buttons could see

quite enough to enable him to identify his clothes.

There were the stripes down the legs, and the rows of bright buttons on the jacket.

The page's eyes fairly rolled round in his head at the sight.

"Good gracious!" he exclaimed, at length, in a paroxysm of bewilderment; "is it my own ghost I'm a-lookin' at; or am I turned into somebody else?"

This question was answered by the individual he was inspecting suddenly dropping on to his feet, and standing right side uppermost.

Buttons then discovered that he had a black face.

"I see who it is now; it's that humbugging Skyrocket."

Having thus expressed himself, he ran out of the tent, as far as a clump of bushes, and shouted—

"Heigh! you nigger!"

The kroo-boy, who was strutting about in evident delight, stopped and looked towards the tent.

"What de matter, Massa Buttons?" he asked innocently.

"You've prigged my clothes, my only

clothes ; that's what the matter !" Massa Buttons answered, wrathfully.

"No, me not prig notink," grinned Skyrocket, shaking his woolly head, and his face beaming with pleasure.

"Why, yer know you've got my togs on yer back."

"Well, me only change my tog for your tog. You say 'change am not bobbery."

"There'll be bobbery next time I ketch yer, I know !" growled Buttons, waxing very furious ; "give me my jacket an' trousers, d'yer hear ?"

"No, tankee, Massa Buttons ; dey suit me bery well ; me look better in dem dan you—me keep 'em," was the cool reply.

"But you can't keep 'em ! you shan't, you ugly black pig !" yelled the enraged page. "How can I come out before company without anything to cover my mortal outline ?"

"You got something."

"No, I haven't !"

"Yes, you hab. Me leave you my what you call little bit ob rag in the tent."

"Your bit of rag won't do for me, I tell yer," yelled Buttons.

"Your tog do for me den, anyhow," returned Skyrocket ; "me always keep dem, me look nice. You put on mine, do bery well for ugly white boy like you."

And with these parting words, he started off and disappeared up a narrow rocky path.

Buttons was in despair.

"The villain ! the pilferin' varmint !" he exclaimed, "a-goin' an' runnin' off with my close, an' leavin' me nothing but——"

He broke off suddenly, and picked up something from off the ground.

It was what Skyrocket was pleased to call his tog.

It is needless to state that the wardrobe of the kroo-boy was of the most limited description, consisting simply of a thin strip of linen which he wore round his waist.

But this scanty attire did not at all suit Buttons' English ideas of propriety.

He fastened it round him, just to see how it looked, but immediately threw it off again in disgust.

"Sooner than go out in sech a state as this I'd stop here for ever !" moaned the unfortunate Buttons.

In the meantime, while Buttons remained without clothing, the shouts of his master and his companions became fainter and fainter, until at last they died away altogether in the distance.

The robbery of the previous night had been so daringly committed that it engrossed the minds of the explorers.

Buttons was not missed in the general excitement.

And there he sat, alternately lamenting his fate and execrating the purloiner of his garments.

"I shall be starved, that's what it'll end in," he whimpered ; "an' when they come back—if ever they does—they'll find nothing but my skelington an' my shirt."

This thought affected him.

Suddenly, however, he cried—

"I ain't a-goin' to be starved if I can help it. I've a brilliant idea."

This he at once commenced carrying out.

He first manufactured a kind of framework of twigs, in shape strongly suggesting a jack-in-the-green.

This he covered entirely with leaves, twisting their stems in between the interstices of the branches, until he had constructed as efficient and respectable a covering as youth could desire in a hot climate.

"It's first rate !" he exclaimed to himself admiringly ; "anyone meetin' me now might take me for a jack-in-the-green."

And so Buttons, congratulating himself, started off after his companions.

At length, after many weary miles had been got over without seeing them, it occurred to him that he had taken a wrong path.

He was getting awfully hungry, too, having had no breakfast.

It was just as he was beginning to feel himself quite done up that the sound of voices reached his ear.

"Thank goodness !" he said within himself. "Here they are at last."

In the joy of having once more caught up his comrades, he was about to utter as cheery a " Halloo " as his empty stomach would permit.

But experience in the wilderness had taught him caution, and he thought he would approach a little nearer and reconnoitre in silence.

Suddenly an outburst of hoarse laughter made him start as if a peal of thunder had rattled in his ears.

He had recognized the tones of the ruffian negro Rope's End.

The shock was so great that Buttons almost dropped out of his green covering.

But after a moment he recovered himself, and his natural pluck having returned to him, he felt a strange curiosity to see who the parties encamped behind the trees were.

Forward he crept, looking more like some strange species of vegetable endowed with motion than a human being.

At length he had approached near enough to peep through the interlacing branches and gaze upon the scene beyond.

CHAPTER XXXIII.

BUTTONS MAKES SOME IMPORTANT DISCOVERIES.

IT was a plateau of considerable extent covered with furze bushes, and bounded by trees and rocks.

A large fire was blazing on the ground, around which were seated no less important personages than Richard Howard and Bow-legged Bill, King Pluto and Rope's End.

Buttons, with his eyes almost starting out of his head with excitement, remained gazing at the scene.

At a short distance were a number of large packages.

Some of these had been opened, and the ground was strewn with their contents.

Bright-coloured cloths, gaudy printed calicoes, pieces of stuff of crimson, blue, and yellow, gilt ornaments, chains, buttons, and small looking-glasses, were scattered about in reckless confusion.

Rope's End had evidently taken care to help himself.

On his head he wore a scarlet turban, a gorgeous stripe scarf encircled his waist, whilst his brawny neck, wrists and ankles were loaded with gilt chains and ornaments.

King Pluto had also made a selection according to his own taste, being decked out in all the colours of the rainbow.

The more Buttons looked, the more confident be became that all these treasures belonged to his master, Robert Blunt, Esq.

Rope's End's voice recalled his distracted faculties.

The giant and his three fingered majesty were drinking rum and smoking tobacco, both being far advanced towards intoxication.

" Yah, yah, yah !" roared the former, " dis bery good—bery much good ! Dere nebber better game dan take away dem English debils' tings. Yah, yah !"

King Pluto grimly smiled his assent.

Richard Howard, who was sitting moodily with his chin resting on his hand, was annoyed at the clamorous outburst, and looking across towards the boatswain, said sternly to him—

" Keep your tongue between your teeth, you son of Satan ; you talk too much."

" Can't help it, massa ; muss talk when de rum in him," was the other's reply.

" I'll stop your rum and your tongue too before long, you overgrown brute !" muttered the Englishman to himself.

Pluto, having taken a draught of liquor, whispered a few words to Rope's End, and then turning to Richard Howard, said—

"Our prisoners—what do you mean to do with them?"

"I haven't made up my mind," returned Richard, sharply.

"No matter," Pluto continued; "do as you like with the men—I think only of the girl."

"The girl?" echoed Howard, with a half start of surprise, a heavy frown darkening his features.

"Yes. Nahita was fair, but she hated me; this English maiden we have captured is fairer—she shall love me."

A sarcastic smile, which he could not suppress, flashed across the pale face of Richard Howard at these words.

"Love you!" he exclaimed. "You must be mad to think it."

"Why mad?" demanded the African potentate, his dark eyes flashing indignantly. "Am I not a king, great and powerful?"

"Psha!" returned Richard, scornfully. "This young lady despises men of your colour."

"By the gods! I will teach her who I am!" cried Pluto, fiercely. "I love her, and she must return my love!"

"No, no, no," burst out Rope's End; "dat not do at all! Me lub de white girl, and me mean to hab her—ugh!"

"My claim before yours," remarked Pluto sternly to him.

"And mine before either," joined in Richard Howard, speaking in a very stern and determined manner.

Rope's End, whose brains were excited by drink, started up.

"De English girl mine!" he raved—"my wife! Me be king some day, den she be queen! Who dare say not—who dare?"

"I dare!" answered Richard Howard, who, though a villain at heart, yet was no coward.

With a fierce execration, Rope's End sprang towards him.

But the Englishman received him with a well-delivered blow between the eyes, which stretched him on his back, stunned and senseless.

"Lie there, you African hog, and learn better manners," he muttered between his clenched teeth.

King Pluto looked moodily from under his hanging brows at the striker, but said nothing.

Richard Howard looked angrily at him.

For a moment there was a pause.

"There'll be a fight presently, I think," muttered Buttons to himself; "an' p'rhaps that bad lot'll kill one another. Good job if they do."

From the brief conversation he had heard the page could only conclude that there were some white prisoners near at hand.

And, while Richard Howard and his sable colleagues were settling their dispute, he thought it would afford him an opportunity to make a few cautious observations.

Perhaps even to set the captives—especially the beautiful young English girl—free.

With this idea in his mind, Buttons, in his extinguisher, glided round behind the bushes until he reached the piles of bales.

But just as he was reflecting what he should do he heard the sound of voices—not the hoarse voices of negroes, but deep, manly English tones, mingled with the pleadings of a girl.

"It's the beautiful young lady!" he muttered to himself, all his chivalry reviving. "Buttons, old boy, don't be afraid," he cried; "you must see what's a-goin' on."

He was about to leave the spot, when he paused abruptly.

"I couldn't do much to assist a lovely young creature in this 'ere jack-in-the-green apparatus."

He cast his eyes upon the goods that strewed the ground.

Presently they lighted upon two articles that looked promising—a striped woollen shirt and a pair of scarlet pantaloons.

"They'll do!" he cried.

In his eagerness he popped out of his covering and pounced upon the treasures.

Having quickly put them on, he crept again under his extinguisher, and, under its cover, hastened back to his former post of observation.

When he arrived there he beheld a handsome Englishman of middle age and a younger one bound with ropes; and a young girl, not more than sixteen years of age, the most beautiful creature he had ever seen.

The men were pale, as if with fatigue and anxiety, but calm and self-possessed; and carried themselves with the dignified bearing which proved that, although captives, they yet defied their captors.

The blue eyes of the young lady were filled with tears.

It was evident she thought more of the safety of her relatives than her own.

"Oh, go, my dear father and brother! accept the offer of these barbarous men!" she urged, eagerly.

"And leave you at their mercy, Elinor?" returned the elder of the gentlemen.

"I shall be safe," she replied, "until you can send the ransom they demand, and then I shall be restored to you."

"I dare not leave you," said her parent.

"But has not your own countryman pledged his word for my safety?" argued the young girl.

She pointed as she spoke to Richard Howard.

Richard, hearing the young lady's allusions to himself, turned and approached.

"You may safely trust your daughter to my care, Colonel Cleveland," he said, in a low persuasive tone; "and, if you will be guided by me, you will embrace the opportunity of escape."

"Oh, yes, do, dear father! do!" earnestly entreated Elinor.

"Oh, that you could be permitted to accompany us!" said the colonel sadly to her, without replying to Richard Howard.

"It is impossible," said the latter. "I have had a hard battle to secure permission for your departure. Your daughter must remain as a hostage."

Colonel Cleveland remained silent a moment, in deep thought.

Then, turning to Howard, he said to him—

"You solemnly promise to preserve my beloved child from all harm until I send the ransom that is demanded of me?"

"I promise," replied Richard, without a blush on his sallow cheek.

"Then I trust you," returned the officer. "Leave us alone to exchange a few parting words."

Richard Howard bowed and turned away.

Buttons could see the sardonic smile that flitted over his features as he did so.

There was "traitor" written in every lineament; and the page felt strongly tempted to call out—

"Don't believe the lying humbug!" but stern necessity closed his lips.

The parting was soon over, and the Englishmen were then unbound.

"Which route do we take?" they asked.

"Straight across the plateau and up the narrow path you see before you," answered Richard Howard. "Farewell! and a safe journey to the nearest station."

"Farewell for a time," said the Englishman, "and remember your promise to protect my child till my return."

The gentlemen after a tearful, lingering glance at the loved one left behind, started forward.

Pluto and Rope's End, like two dark fiends, had retreated into the shadow of the trees.

There they stood, each grasping a rifle.

Onwards went the Englishmen, suspecting no injury.

Elinor Cleveland standing fixed as a statue, with her eyes steadily fixed upon their retreating forms.

Buttons' attention was quite absorbed by the fair form before him.

But he was suddenly aroused by hearing the voice of Richard Howard exclaim in a low, hissing, snake-like tone—

"Make ready!"

For an instant the page could hardly make up his mind what it meant.

But at that moment he heard two sharp clicks like the cocking of guns.

And just then, the gentlemen, who had reached the end of the plateau, turned for the last time to wave their hands.

"Now!" said the hissing voice, hastily. "Fire!"

In reply to this, two thin blue puffs of smoke appeared amongst the bushes.

Two sharp reports were heard, and the unfortunate victims were seen to spring up wildly in the air and then fall lifeless on the ground.

A piercing, heart-rending shriek burst from the horror-stricken girl.

For an instant she stood as if rooted to the spot, and then rushed madly forward.

But her strength failed her, and after running a few yards she sank down fainting and insensible.

Pluto and Rope's End now advanced with their smoking rifles in their hands.

"Yah, yah, yah!" chuckled the latter, with demoniac glee; "dat good shot, Massa Howard; dat very much good shot, eh?"

"Yes; it wasn't bad," was the traitor's cold reply; "there are two obstacles out of the way."

Every drop of blood in Buttons' veins was boiling at what he had seen and heard.

Crouching down into the depths of his extinguisher, he put his hands to his mouth and called in a deep and hollow tone—

"Richard Howard! Murderer! Beware!"

The effect was electric.

All heard the strange and awful warning.

All started and looked round.

"T'ink 'dere some un callin' yar, Massa Howard," whispered Rope's End, softly, looking frightened after a moment.

"Nonsense, it was fancy, merely," returned the Englishman.

But his face was pale, and his lips quivered with conscious guilt.

Again the hollow voice was heard.

"Bow-legged Bill, beware!" it said.

"Dat not fancy, anyhow!" muttered Rope's End to Bow-legged Bill; "it you dis time."

The individual addressed turned as white as a sheet, and began to tremble visibly at his knee-joints.

But the mysterious voice had no regard to the sensations it produced, and continued, from a greater distance.

"Pluto! you three-fingered vag'bon! an' you, Rope's End, you half-hanged villain! Look out for yourselves; death is near you all!"

The two Africans started as though stung by snakes, and glared round them with evident apprehension.

But they saw nothing.

"Whar de woice come from? who de debil am it?" gasped the giant, at length, hoarsely.

"The sperrits of yer dead victims!" returned the solemn voice, sounding now in another direction; "tremble, sanguinary murderers! Blood will have blood! Ye're all doomed! Beware!"

Those mysterious and awful communications, following as they did close upon their crime, strongly impressed the hearers.

The sounds seemed so strange and unearthly that the guilty murderers were completely scared.

Richard Howard alone struggled to combat with his superstitious fears, and at length he cried—

"Come, let us bury those bodies yonder out of our sight."

Glad to get away from the haunted spot, the four colleagues walked across the plateau.

Elinor Cleveland had revived, was before them, and was endeavouring vainly to recall her beloved parent and brother to life.

Buttons was left alone at the bottom of his leafy extinguisher.

He felt dreadfully famished.

On the ground in the vicinity of the fire were the remains of their repast.

A loaf of bread and a bottle of rum.

Buttons' mouth watered at the sight.

"I'll have 'em at any price," he said to himself.

But in order to secure the luxuries he coveted he was obliged to leave his extinguisher for a moment.

But in doing so he forgot that there were a number of dark-skinned followers lying about who might observe him.

He was recalled to a sense of his imprudence by a tremendous yell, and a score of savage forms started up with their spears in their hands.

Buttons, grasping the loaf and the rum bottle with desperate tenacity, dived once more under his extinguisher, and at once commenced his retreat.

The ignorant savages, seeing the leafy object moving along the ground, were struck with surprise and terror, and remained fixed as statues staring at it, but not venturing to follow.

Richard Howard and his companions, startled by their wild outcry, left the bodies on the ground and came hurrying back.

"What has happened?" demanded the former, sharply.

"Oh, massa, massa! de debil in de bush!—him move!" they cried, excitedly extending their arms towards the strange object.

All this time Buttons was making his way back to his covert.

Richard fixed his haggard eyes upon the leafy machine for an instant, and speedily divined the truth.

"You set of idiots," he shouted to the negroes; "if the devil's in the tree now's your time to trap him. Advance at once and never let him leave his covering alive."

The savages, thus encouraged, uttering a second discordant yell, rushed forward.

The extinguisher had reached the trees and come to a halt.

In an instant the dark troop had approached, and a score of spears went whizzing through it, pinning it to the ground.

Richard Howard and his confederates could not forbear a triumphant laugh at this feat.

Rope's End and Bow-legged Bill roared again.

"Yah, yah, yah!" cried the giant, "if de debil be inside dere he get more den he can swaller."

"Draw out the spears and let us see," ordered Richard.

The weapons were withdrawn and the extinguisher turned over.

A general murmur of disappointment burst forth.

It was perfectly empty.

The devil had not remained to be speared.

He knew a trick worth two of that.

Buttons had slipped out of it, and with his loaf and rum-bottle had effected a triumphant retreat.

Richard Howard did not like this incident.

But it was quickly followed up by another, which he liked still less.

Whilst his attention had been absorbed in the contemplation of the moving bush the young English girl, dreading the fate that awaited her, had fled.

CHAPTER XXXIV.

THE STINGER ANNOUNCES THAT BUTTONS IS MISSING.

WE come up with our explorers again some miles from the spot at which we left them.

It is needless to say no traces of the stolen property or the robbers had been found.

They were on the wrong track.

The loss had thrown a greater damp on the spirits of our explorers than anything that had yet occurred, and a general gloom prevailed.

"I know not what to think of our expedition now," said Bob Blunt; "this loss will make it a difficult matter."

"We must take a hopeful view of it," remarked Dr. Knowall, trying to speak cheerfully.

"It isn't the value of the goods I regret," continued Bob, "but the impossibility of replacing them. I had looked upon these stores as a sure passport through Abyssinia, a certain means of making friends wherever we went. Now we have nothing but ourselves to depend upon."

"Well, captain, we have had to do that before now," joined in Ironfist.

"And can do it again," added Stumps.

"So," said Bob, "I am determined at all risks to push on."

"And then, dear captain," whispered Nahita, who sat nestled by his side, "perchance your goods may be recovered."

Our hero gave her an incredulous smile and shook his head as he replied—

"I hardly hope it. But what says our worthy Stinger? I should like her opinion on this knotty subject."

He looked round, for just at that moment her voice was heard speaking in tones of lamentation.

She was evidently labouring under some unusual excitement.

"Oh, captain! Oh, Mr. Blunt!" she gasped. "Oh, poor, dear Buttons!"

"What is the matter with him?"

"The matter!" almost shrieked the Stinger, "he's not to be found."

"Good Heaven! you don't say that?" cried our hero; "but he came along with us, did he not?"

"I'm sure I don't know," whimpered Elizabeth Ann; "I only know he's not with us now."

Bob Blunt sprang to his feet.

"Has anyone seen anything of Buttons?" he asked.

No one had seen anything of him.

"The dear boy was always venturesome," wailed the Stinger; "he's been wandering away after the 'yawnin' ravens,' and has fallen down a precipice, I know he has. Oh, dear! Oh, dear!"

"If him fall down de precipikas, no good to cry; won't fetch him up 'gin," remarked General Orlando.

The Stinger looked at him like a tigress, and then gave him a tremendous bang on his ear with her umbrella.

"Take that, you unfeeling brute!" she exclaimed.

It was just then that a confused sound of voices was heard.

And Jingo Johnson appeared hurrying along the path with a human being, kicking and struggling, under his arm.

Nothing could be seen of the latter but his legs.

But everyone recognised them as Buttons' legs, from the stripes down the trousers.

There was a general cry—

"He's found; he's found; hurrah!"

But on Jingo's reaching the spot, and setting the individual he carried on his feet, the mistake was discovered.

It was not Buttons after all, but Skyrocket, in Buttons' clothes.

"Me find dis hyar young niggar hid away up in hole in rock yonder with a bit of looking-glass in his hand, looking and admiring of himself," explained Jingo.

For a moment there was a dead silence.

And then, Bob Blunt, addressing the kroo-boy, said to him sternly—

"Where is Buttons?"

"Dunno!"

"How came you with his clothes?"

"Dunno!"

"Don't know, sirrah!" cried the Stinger indignantly; "how could you have his things on yer back without knowing how you came by them—eh?"

Skyrocket winced at this, and replied, after a moment—

"Massa Buttons give me him toggem."

"When?"

"Dis mornin', 'fore start 'cross mountains."

"I doubt that," said Bob Blunt,

"So do I!" echoed the Stinger, with a very flushed and angry face; "it's the most unlikely thing in the world, especially when he has only one suit to his back."

But Skyrocket declared that it was so.

Our hero fixed his eyes upon the kroo-boy, and said—

"Did you not steal the clothes?"

"No, no! me sure me didn't. Buttons say to me, 'Skyrocket, me lub you—me gib you my toggems!'" the latter replied.

"Who knows whether this benighted heathen may not have m—m—murdered poor dear Buttons for the sake of the buttons on his jacket!" exclaimed E. A. S.

The matter was becoming serious.

"Now listen," continued Bob Blunt; "the law of our country is life for life, and if you cannot give some more satisfactory explanation of your comrade's disappearance you will be regarded as his murderer and be hung."

This terrible sentence was more than Skyrocket could bear; and, uttering a piercing yell, he fell on his knees.

"No hang me! no hang!" he cried, "den me tell reel trufe."

"That is all we require," said his master.

"Well den, massa, me creep inside hut an' steal Massa Buttons' toggems while him sleep, dat all."

"He must be sent for instantly!" cried Bob Blunt. "Who will go back in search of Buttons?"

A score of voices, both from white men and black, replied eagerly—

"We will!"

"And I'll conduct the expedition myself!" exclaimed the heroic Stinger.

She stopped short as a faint "halloa" in the distance came floating to the spot.

"My good gracious alive! I really think that's his voice!" she exclaimed.

"It is," said our hero.

And suddenly a strange figure appeared at a turning in the winding path.

Its body was striped and its legs bright scarlet.

Its gait was particularly straggling and unsteady.

It carried a bottle under its arm.

"Is it our Buttons, or isn't it?" murmured the Stinger, perplexed at his eccentric costume.

All doubts were quickly set at rest on this point as he drew nearer.

"Hurrah! it is himself. Three cheers for Buttons!"

"Hurrah, hurrah, hurrah!" they all shouted with one voice.

Buttons evidently heard the enlivening sounds, and, as he came onward in a very zigzag and peculiar manner, it was pretty evident he had something on his mind that burdened him.

"Oh, guvnor!" he exclaimed, as he staggered up to his master, "oh, guv'nor, something the matter with——

He stopped and stood swaying to and fro.

"My dear fellow, what's the matter?" asked Bob Blunt, in surprise at his appearance and dress.

"Robb'ry! Murder! ev'rything that's —hic— horr'ble!" replied the page, rolling his eyes vaguely.

"The poor boy's very ill, going out of his mind!" exclaimed the Stinger, in a tone of alarm.

"No," responded Buttons, "it's not that. I'm all—hic——"

He left the sentence unfinished and reeled slightly.

"He's dying, I'm sure he is!" continued Elizabeth Ann, in much anxiety; "his nose is turning blue."

"Blow my—hic—nose!" exclaimed the strange, eccentric youth, staggering back but recovering himself.

"He's exhausted with his journey and long fasting," remarked Bob Blunt.

"Oh, yes, I'm quite sure he is," said the Stinger assentingly; "he's tired to death."

"Right you are, old gal," returned Buttons; "and besides that I'm very——"

"Hungry, of course," said Elizabeth Ann.

"No, very—hic—tight."

And having delivered this confession, his legs gave way under him, and he dropped into the arms of the Stinger.

He was instantly fast asleep, snoring furiously, and was therefore put to bed at once.

CHAPTER XXXV.

OUR HERO DISCOVERS A FAIR FUGITIVE.

IT was not until late the next morning that Buttons awoke.

It is needless to say that our hero was intensely excited at Buttons' story.

So much so, that he had hardly patience to listen to the end.

Then, starting up, he summoned his companions, and, having hurriedly explained to them what he had just heard, he ordered preparations to be made for marching at once.

Without pausing even for refreshment they pressed onwards until, as the day was drawing to a close, they reached the plateau.

Buttons recognized it at once as the scene of his previous day's experiences.

There were the burnt out ashes of the wood fire.

But the living actors in the tragedy had taken their departure.

At the end of the plateau a ghastly sight presented itself.

The dead bodies of the unfortunate Colonel Cleveland, and his son still laid there unburied.

A burst of indignation came from the swelling breasts of the explorers as they gazed on the sad spectacle.

"They shall be avenged if I live!" exclaimed our hero, solemnly; "and now let us give them decent interment."

The mournful ceremony was soon performed; but, before committing the bodies to the dust, our hero took from the pocket of the colonel's coat a miniature portrait of his daughter.

They then resumed their journey by a path which their native guides pointed out to have been recently travelled by human footsteps.

They had proceeded several miles when it became necessary to halt for refreshment.

Our hero, having despatched a hasty meal, strolled away a short distance from his companions along the road.

He came shortly to a spot where diverging paths descended into a ravine.

Here he halted, wondering which would be the right one to take.

Suddenly he heard a faint moan.

He listened intently and the mysterious sound was repeated.

"A woman's voice," he thought within himself.

He had not gone many paces farther when in a small recess, formed by nature in the rocks, he perceived a female form stretched upon the ground.

Bob wondered for a moment who this strangely-discovered female could be, especially as her skin was white. But he lost no time in entering the cavern and raising her.

She seemed to revive somewhat at his touch, and our hero could feel her shudder at the contact.

"Leave me!" she murmured in a faint horror-stricken tone. "You have destroyed those I loved; leave me here to die that I may rejoin them."

Bob Blunt almost started at these words.

For he felt that he had providentially alighted upon the person he was most anxious to discover, the orphan daughter of the unfortunate Colonel Cleveland.

In order to correct her mistake, he said soothingly to her—

"Fear not. You are in the hands of a friend, not an enemy."

At the sound of the kind voice, the young girl looked up.

One glance at our hero's handsome face, with its pitying eyes looking down upon her, was enough to dispel her fears, and to assure her that he spoke the truth.

"Oh, forgive me, sir," she faltered, the colour rising in her fair face. "I am so distracted, I knew not what I said. I—

I thought—I feared those wretches had discovered me, and I wished to—to die here alone."

Our hero's heart thrilled within him as it had never thrilled before.

There was no doubt that he held in his arms the original of the portrait, and, after a moment, he replied, encouragingly—

"You shall not die, my dear young lady, either alone or in company, if I can help it. You will not be afraid to trust me, will you?"

She turned her sad, dark eyes up to his, and answered earnestly—

"Oh, no. You do not look like a traitor. I feel I may trust you. But I have no wish to live."

"I'm scarcely surprised to hear you say so," returned Bob, kindly, "after the cruel bereavements you have so lately suffered."

"You know my loss, then?" exclaimed the young girl, with a look of wonder in her face.

"I know every particular," replied our hero. "Nay, more ; I know too well the villains who inflicted it."

After a long pause she said, in a low, tremulous voice—

"The remains of my poor father and brother yet lie unburied."

"My dear lady," interposed Bob, gently, "we have consigned them to their kindred dust, and moistened the earth that covers them with our tears."

"God bless you for that," murmured Elinor, fervently ; "God bless you !"

In her gratitude the poor girl clasped our hero's hand and pressed it unconsciously to her lips.

After a few moments Bob Blunt led his fair charge to his companions, who received her joyfully.

There was only one of the number who looked gloomily at the young English girl.

This was Nahita.

Up to that moment she had clung to the hope that our hero might return the passionate love she felt towards him.

Now this hope was dashed to the ground, and as she gazed at the sweet face and dark loving eyes of Elinor Cleveland, she almost groaned in bitterness of spirit.

She felt that the man she loved was lost to her for ever.

CHAPTER XXXVI.

HOWARD PLAYS A DESPERATE GAME.

RICHARD HOWARD, although greatly chagrined at the flight of Elinor Cleveland, did not lose much time in looking after her.

At present he had other views, other schemes in his brain, which must first be carried out.

The principal of these was nothing less than to establish himself as a prince in some Abyssinian territory.

The booty he had so dishonestly obtained gave him an immense power, and with that and his own tact he trusted to be able to accomplish his desires.

With all possible expedition he had continued his course towards the south, and descended to more tropical and fertile regions.

Fate seemed to favour his aspiring projects.

On his arrival at a town called Kwara, he at once proceeded with his retinue to the palace of the reigning prince, taking care to make as much display as possible in his approach.

Here he gave himself out as a special ambassador from the Queen of England, who had sent him to solicit an alliance with the Abyssinian prince.

The Dejaj Maro, as the prince was

called, flattered at the honour done him, received the supposed delegate with much kindness.

The prince trusted him implicitly ; the ministers of state and the officers bowed down before the representative of the throne of Great Britain, and in a short time the Englishman was second in importance only to the prince himself.

It was then, when Richard Howard had skilfully paved his way, and all his plans were ripe for execution, that the Dejaj Maro died.

His death was mysterious and sudden, he being found dead on his couch.

There were no marks of violence upon his person.

Not a tongue raised even a murmur of suspicion against Richard Howard.

He was the friend and constant companion of the deceased prince, and of course could have had no hand in hastening his decease.

Such was the general opinion, although there was one, who, had he spoken out, might have thrown a ghastly light upon the truth.

But he was silent ; and whilst the dead was yet green in earth, preparations were on foot for proclaiming his successor.

*　　　*　　　*　　　*　　　*

The coronation morning had arrived.

The plain that lay outstretched before the city was crowded with dark forms.

Soon the sound of trumpets, gongs and cymbals were heard, and forth from the gates issued a large body of officials and troops, the ministers and grandees of the kingdom, accompanied by the high priest.

In the midst, mounted upon a white horse, was Richard Howard.

Next to him was his satellite, Bow-legged Bill, riding on a mule, and carrying in his hand the sword of state—an enormous scimitar, that seemed expressly made for cutting off heads wholesale.

The friends of the late prince surrounded him, whilst his former colleagues King Pluto and Rope's End, followed last of all in the procession, the moody expression of their countenances indicating much chagrin at being placed in the background.

In this order, and greeted by the shouts of the multitude, they advanced till they reached a spot where a gorgeous canopy of crimson and yellow silk had been erected.

Beneath this, placed on rich carpets, was the royal couch.

To this Richard Howard, after dismounting from his steed, was conducted with much ceremony.

A great change had taken place in his appearance.

His European garb had been thrown aside, and he now wore the costume of the country.

As for Bow-legged Bill he was so transmogrified that, to use his own words, " his own blessed mother wouldn't have knowed him."

The trumpets blared and the cymbals crashed, and wild shouts rent the air, as the new monarch stood upon his throne.

" People of Abyssinia, hear me!" he commenced, as he stretched forth his arm to enforce attention.

In an instant a dead silence prevailed, and he continued—

" It has pleased the great powers to remove to Paradise the prince who ruled over you. But they have not left you alone. In compassion for your loss they have sent you a white king to take his place."

These consoling words were answered by a burst of acclamations, and the speaker went on—

" In me, the representative of the great English Queen beyond the sea, you have one who will govern you in peace, and in war lead you on to victory over your foes."

Again shouts of approval rang through the air.

" All I require is devotion to my person and obedience to my commands. Are you prepared to render these ?"

" We are ! we are !" shouted the great multitude.

" Then we shall go on and prosper," said Richard ; " but should anyone dispute my authority, let him remember I am a powerful king, and have the means of punishing rebels !"

The royal speech being ended, Richard Howard seated himself, and the high priest approaching placed the royal coronet upon his head.

Then Bow-legged Bill, who acted as crier on the occasion, put his hand to his mouth, and bawled in a voice that would have warmed the heart of a coster-monger—

"Long live 'is royal majesty the Dejaj Richard Howard, Hemp'ror of Habyssiniar!"

To which the vast assembly responded—

"Long live the Dejaj Richard!"

This ceremony performed, the newly elected prince shook hands with his ministers.

These proceedings did not cause general satisfaction.

King Pluto and his companion Rope's End were full of discontent.

"I am a king," muttered Pluto, his chest heaving and his dark eyes darting baleful flashes, "and am I to be treated by this white man like a slave?"

"It big dam imperence! dat what it ar," growled Rope's End, as he glanced enviously at the presents in the hands of the chiefs.

"I shall speak," cried the former.

Together they advanced towards the throne.

But on their approach, Bow-legged Bill with his scimitar objected to them coming nearer.

"No admittance on the carpet for niggers," he said, as he extended his weapon.

It is probable the Whitechapel official might have received personal chastisement on the spot, had not his glittering weapon, flashing before the eyes of the negroes, restrained them.

"What is all this?" said Richard Howard, in a grand and lofty tone.

"You break your word with your friend," repeated King Pluto sternly.

"In what have I broken my word?"

"You said when you were king we should rule together," returned Pluto.

A cold, sneering smile passed over the face of the Englishman as he replied—

"I have altered my mind. I have now determined to rule alone."

The heavy brow of the African darkened like a thunder cloud.

"Beware how you treat me," muttered Pluto, "or I may tell something you would rather have untold."

There was something terribly vindictive in the look of the speaker as he uttered these threatening words.

But Richard Howard would not allow them to seem to trouble him.

He only said in a coldly indifferent tone—

"I shall treat you as I treat the rest of my subjects. If you are obedient, you are safe; if rebellious, count upon the rebel's doom."

"What is that?" hissed Pluto in his ear, quickly. "Poison?"

The white king started in spite of himself at the last word.

But recovering himself instantly, he replied with wonderful self-possession—

"That entirely depends upon the position of the offender and the nature of his treason."

With these words he turned away.

But from that moment Richard Howard resolved to get rid of King Pluto.

A grand banquet, given in the native style, followed the coronation.

In the midst of the feast some scouts brought intelligence.

A company of Englishmen had been seen descending the mountains.

Howard knew well enough of whom the company consisted, and he muttered to himself, with grim exultation—

"Only let Robert Blunt and his party fall into my hands, I'll teach them a lesson that shall last them their lives!"

In order to increase the chances of such an event, he described them to the chiefs who were his guests.

They all pledged themselves to render their assistance.

One giant chieftain, Nootka, who had been drinking freely, swore that he would never rest until he had seized the foes of his white sovereign and brought them bound into his presence.

With such a formidable array against them, the doom of the gallant explorers seemed now all but inevitable.

Time will show how these plots succeeded.

CHAPTER XXXVII.

BUTTONS INSULTS THE IDOL TCHUM-TCHUM MEE.

TWO months had elapsed since our hero landed on the Abyssinian coast.

They had wandered from spot to spot without finding those of whom they were in search—namely Howard, and his black friend Pluto ; nor had they heard of his elevation to the throne.

It was now at the expiration of this period they were retracing their steps, and descending to the plains of Amhara.

The keen but invigorating air of the mountains had strung up their nerves, and banished all the lassitude caused by the enervating climate of Western Africa.

And they were now as strong and hearty as when they first left the shores of good old England.

It was as he stood looking down from the heights, he descried a large well-built town, in the midst of a fertile tract of country, where here and there men might be seen ploughing the soil with bullocks fastened to branches of trees.

Towering above the town, on a rocky eminence, was a strong fortress.

"What place is that ?" he asked of one of the guides.

"Dat castle of Dejaj Djalma ; he great prince," the man replied.

"Would he be willing to traffic with us on friendly terms, do you think ?" continued our hero.

The guide nodded.

"Most like ; he good prince."

This was encouraging to Bob.

He made as much of his escort as possible, and advanced with banners flying and Stumps played on his trombone with all his might.

The prince on learning that the visitors were English, came out to meet them, accompanied by his chiefs and all the heads of his tribe.

The meeting was cordial in the extreme

and the prince willingly promised them as much provisions as they could conveniently carry away with them.

"The English are a great nation," he said, in flattering terms ; "their queen is a great queen, whom I long to cross the seas and visit."

Bob Blunt politely assured him that he would be hospitably received if ever he should travel so far.

Djalma was so pleased with our hero's manner and address that he took quite a fancy to him, and requested him to make his town a home as long as he pleased.

Bob accepted the hospitable offer, and spent a week very pleasantly.

At the end of that time our hero expressed his intention of resuming his journey.

The regrets at parting were mutual and sincere.

"You will not fail to visit me, if you should again pass through my territories ?" said the kindly Abyssinian.

Bob Blunt assured him that he should not be so ungrateful.

"In which direction do you shape your course ?"

"Towards the south," Bob replied.

The prince looked pleased, and said—

"You will reach Kwara then. My brother, the Dejaj Maro, is the prince of that district. On reaching his territory proceed at once to his palace ; give him this ; tell him you are his brother's friends, and rely upon it he will receive you kindly."

With these words he presented our hero with a massive gold ring : but he knew not then that his brother no longer lived to receive it.

After the prince's departure the explorers continued their course alone.

It was towards the end of the day's march they came upon what seemed to be a village.

"'I WILL RESCUE YOU, OR DIE WITH YOU,' SAID NAHITA."

But it presented an entirely different appearance from the town they had recently left behind them.

Rows of wretched mud huts alone met the eye, whilst dark, gaunt, half naked forms sat staring at the travellers in mute astonishment.

One peculiarity was observable ; in various spots hideous images—some carved out of wood, some made of clay —were erected.

"These are the first signs of superstition I have looked upon in this country," remarked our hero to Dr. Knowall. "I thought the Christian religion prevailed here."

"It does so," the doctor replied ; "but not universally. This village is an exception, and is evidently a village of idolaters."

"It looks like it," returned Bob.

At this moment a wild kind of chorus rose in the air.

Buttons was furious.

"Shut up, yer howlin' donkeys!" he bawled indignantly.

But the noise only grew louder.

And presently a troupe of men appeared, walking in procession, and singing —or rather, as Buttons justly put it, howling—as they went along.

One peculiarity in this was very remarkable ; and that was the number of children that accompanied it, and the strange way in which they were carried.

The leader of the procession bore upon his head a kind of framework of iron, on the top of which was a little black infant, quite naked, and secured by a band round its waist ; whilst in a kind of scarf fastened round his shoulder, there was slung another child of tender years.

Both seemed very uncomfortable, and both did their best to add to the general harmony by shrieking lustily.

Next came one carrying on his head a wicker basket, and leading a child by its hand.

Behind him walked a ferocious-looking being, with a heavy club upon his shoulder.

And he was followed by others who either held in their arms, or had slung at their backs, luckless specimens of infantile humanity of all sorts and sizes.

As they reached the spot where our explorers stood, the procession halted.

It could then be seen that there was in all their features an expression of brutal ignorance.

The chorus of singers had ceased, and nothing was heard but the wailings and cries of the unfortunate children.

Our hero stepped forward, and, addressing the leader of the procession, said in an imperative tone—

"What ceremony is this you are performing ?"

The dark individual addressed only muttered some uncouth words in reply and shook his head.

"He don't understand yer, guv'nor," whispered Buttons.

"So it seems," said Bob ; "but I'll try and let him know what I mean before I've done with him."

"Perhaps some of the others may be acquainted with our language," suggested the Stinger.

"I'll see," said Buttons.

And then raising his voice, he bawled—

"Is there any one among this dirty lot of ugly screamers as understands plain Henglish ?"

There was a pause, and presently a strange-looking being, wearing an extraordinary head-dress, and with the skin of some wild animal wrapped round his waist, advanced.

"English ?"

"Yes," he replied.

"We wish to know the meaning of this assembly," said our hero to him.

"We go make worship our gods," was the reply.

"And what do you want with all these children ?"

"We offer them sacrifice to our gods," responded the dark man in the skins.

At this confession there was one intense burst of indignation from the English.

"We are Englishmen," said Bob Blunt, "and we are determined to put a stop to such barbarities. Therefore at once set those poor infants free, or we will compel you."

The priest rolled his haggard eyes in all directions, but did not obey the injunction he had received.

Our hero, therefore, drew his revolver.

"Now," he said, as he cocked it, "do you mean to release the children?"

The priest still hesitated.

Bang! went the revolver, and off flew the priest's headgear with a bullet in it.

The report so scared the holy man that he fell on his knees in terror.

The rest of the procession followed his example, and Bob and his companions quickly unbound the unfortunate little objects, and restored them to their wretched-looking mothers, who came creeping forward, and carried them off in their arms rejoicing.

Having effected this deliverance, our hero warned the priest and his followers to abstain in future from such practices, and continue his course.

They had not gone far, when they came to a miserable-looking kind of shed covered with thatch, beneath which was a hideous nondescript object carved in wood, in a sitting position.

"An' I s'pose that's what they calls a hidol," said Buttons. "Ugh! what a guy!"

In his disgust the youth could not refrain from stopping behind to pelt the hideous monstrosity with stones, after which he put both his fingers to his nose at it, in order to express his profound contempt.

"There, take that, you ugly pot-bellied, wooden-'eaded, 'umbugging lump o' nothing!" he cried.

It was whilst thus engaged he heard a hideous yell, and suddenly the priest in his skin garment, who had been watching his proceedings, sprang forward, clenching his fists and foaming at the mouth with fanatical fury.

"You insult great Tchum Tchummee!" he raved, fiercely. "Tchum Tchummee kill! kill!"

"Chum Chummy be blowed!" cried Buttons boldly.

And as the priest advanced to seize him, he gave that holy personage a punch in the ribs that sent him reeling on the ground at the feet of the idol.

"Lie there, old bogey!" he said; "there's a pair of yer."

But the enraged fanatic was up again in an instant, and sprang upon Buttons with the ferocity of a tiger.

Luckily, the Stinger, who had come back to look after her young colleague was close at hand, and she settled the matter by knocking down the priest once more with her umbrella.

Before he could recover himself sufficiently to rise, Buttons and E. A. S. had rejoined their companions.

CHAPTER XXXVIII.

BUTTONS ASTONISHES THE IDOLS.

IT was in a beautiful and romantic retreat our explorers encamped at the close of the day's march.

Behind them was a wood, interspersed with tropical plants and flowers of gorgeous hue; before them a wide river, on the opposite bank of which could be seen the huts of a village, and a smiling landscape dotted with stately palms.

The canoes which our hero had brought with him from England were unpacked and put together.

When their evening meal had been discussed, Bob and three of his band paddled up the stream to reconnoitre.

He wished to see what other villages were in the vicinity, and to learn if any other white people had been seen in the neighbourhood.

After paddling a short distance the river narrowed considerably, and both banks were clothed with thick woods.

"Best be prepared for a possible attack," said Bob.

He had scarcely spoken the words, when a party of Abyssinians, who were concealed near a fallen tree, sent a flight of arrows and javelins at the occupants of the canoe.

"By Jove! that was a narrow escape," exclaimed Bob, as his hat went flying away to the other shore on the point of a spear. "Up with your rifles and give them a volley. Fire, lads!"

The bullets went rattling among the branches, and several black forms could be dimly seen hurrying away.

Bob and his friends landed at the point towards which they had aimed their bullets.

All was quiet—quiet as death.

And death was there; for stretched across the branches of the dead tree were the bodies of two African savages, who had fallen from the fire of the English rifles.

Bob could not recognise them (although in fact, they were two of King Pluto's warriors), so he returned to the canoe.

"We will get back to camp now," he said. "It would not be safe to go higher up the river till daylight."

But when they got back to the camp they found Buttons and the Stinger missing.

The loving couple had, it appeared, taken a canoe soon after the departure of our hero, and had gone down the stream.

The page exerted himself so vigorously with his paddles that he soon left the camp behind them.

"I say, ole gal, this is jolly, ain't it?" exclaimed Buttons, as he lifted his paddles out of the water and paused to wipe the drops off his face.

"Delightful," returned the Stinger, as she took a sip from her teapot, which she had stowed away under the seat; "quite reviving, I declare."

"So I think," said Buttons, "an' I'll trouble you for the teapot when you've done with it."

The Stinger handed it to him.

"It is prime," he said with a grin, after taking a tolerable pull; "your tea always is."

Elizabeth Ann smiled graciously.

"Where are we?" she asked, after a moment's pause.

"On the water, Stinger," answered her facetious companion.

"I'm aware of that, but ain't we getting a long way from the shore?" she said a little apprehensively, for the river was widening out into a lake.

"What's the odds if we are?" returned Buttons, in an indifferent tone; "there's no crocodiles to gobble us up; we're all right."

"It seems so," said the Stinger; "but still, we've come a long distance; I can hardly see the spot we started from."

"Very likely," replied Buttons; "but we can see the spot we're a goin' to."

"Why, where are you going to?" inquired Elizabeth Ann, in surprise.

"Over yonder."

And with these words, in spite of the scared look on the Stinger's face, the reckless youth once more dipped his paddles in the water.

The canoe shot over the surface with wonderful rapidity.

In vain Elizabeth Ann called to him to stop.

The paddles moved faster than ever, and before long the canoe glided to the shore, where it lay snugly concealed behind a clump of reeds.

"That'll do first rate!" said Buttons, as he sprang on to the bank.

"You're not going to get out, are you?" asked the Stinger.

"I am out," grinned Buttons in reply, "and so you'll be in a minnit; come on!"

"Not if I know it!" she answered, stubbornly.

"Oh, yes, you will!"

"I tell you I won't!" said Elizabeth Ann firmly.

But Buttons would take no refusal.

Extending his hand, he landed his portly companion in safety.

"That's all right!" he said; "and now we can take a stroll and make our observations, Elizabeth Ann."

"I hope none of the natives will make observations upon us," said the Stinger ruefully.

"Don't be nervous, Stinger, but let's come on."

"Let me get my teapot and umbrella

out of the canoe first," said Elizabeth Ann.

These necessaries being secured, the two companions commenced their stroll.

Not a soul appeared in sight, and the evening was lovely.

They wandered along through some beautiful tracts of country, till at length the Stinger evinced symptoms of fatigue, and called upon Buttons to halt.

"I've had enough of pedestrian exercise," she said ; "let's go back."

The twilight had been falling for some time, and almost as quickly as she spoke it grew quite dark.

"Oh, lor' 'ere's a nice go! Blest if we ain't lost ourselves !" murmured Buttons as he found himself benighted.

"It's all your fault ; you would be so venturesome !" exclaimed the Stinger, ruefully ; "whatever shall we do now ?"

Buttons, however, could not answer that question.

"Where are we ?"

"Blest if I know," was the unsatisfactory reply of the page.

"We're lost !" she cried, dolefully, "lost in these pathless wilds ! oh, dear ! oh, dear !"

"Well, it's no good hollerin' about it ; let's persevere," counselled Buttons.

Accordingly they persevered.

But the further they went the more they seemed to wander out of the right track.

The aspect of the surrounding country seemed to have changed too in a remarkable manner.

"Where the dooce have we got to ?" said Buttons, at length, suddenly coming to a standstill.

"I'm sure I don't know !" moaned Elizabeth Ann. "What's that place yonder ?"

She pointed as she spoke to a curious-looking building.

Buttons strained his eyes in the direction she indicated.

An exclamation of surprise burst from his lips.

It was the identical idol-temple they had passed that morning.

They had wandered back again to the village of idolaters.

There was the idol, Tchum Tchummee, staring them in the face.

For a moment Buttons remained rooted to the spot, with his eyes intently fixed upon the ugly effigy.

Suddenly a flash of inspiration passed over him.

"I see it all now," he exclaimed, in a profound tone ; "fate's done it. Come on ; don't be afraid."

"What has fate done now ?" asked the Stinger, in considerable astonishment.

"Why, made us lose our way on purpose that we should come here again."

"And what are we to do now we are here ?"

"Smash that grinning idol, of course," replied Buttons.

And, without further pause, he began to pick up stones and pelt the wooden deity.

The Stinger, anxious to expedite so good a work, assisted.

The great Tchum Tchummee had never been so battered and bumped in his life before.

At length a large stone, well aimed, struck the luckless image full in the face and knocked off its head.

Buttons picked it up by its nose, which formed a convenient handle.

"This goes along of me, as a trophy," he cried triumphantly, as he waved it in the air.

"And now let's see about returning," suggested the Stinger, in an anxious tone,

"No," returned Buttons, determinedly. "I don't go back till I've smashed ev'ry idol in this dirty place."

"Take care you don't get smashed yourself," said Elizabeth Ann, nervously.

"No fear ! Come on !"

Together they proceeded ; and every clay image Buttons came to he knocked off its legs without the least ceremony.

It was as he was performing this operation on the sixth of Tchum Tchummee's relatives he was startled by a roar, hoarse and loud as that of a tiger, and up started from the ground the dark priest in his skin robe, and sprang upon him.

A dozen more quaint, dusky figures rushed forward, and, before Buttons had time to strike a blow or utter an objection, he and his companion were captives.

The wooden trophy was found in his possession and taken from him, and terrible was the outcry when it was recognised.

"You break idol!" yelled the frantic priest; "you knock off great Tchum Tchummee head!"

"Yes! and I'd knock off yours as well if I could, yer 'owlin' 'umbug!" muttered Buttons, desperately.

And, amidst the wailings and ravings of the idolaters, he and the Stinger were dragged away.

They were hurried along till they reached the dwelling of the chief, a mud building like the rest, but larger, and ornamented with grinning skulls.

The chief had not retired to rest, but sat in his mud palace, drinking himself drunk with arrack.

When he heard from the frenzied lips of the priest the outrage that had been committed he also became furious.

"Bring dem before me!" he shouted.

Buttons and the Stinger were hauled into his presence very unceremoniously.

It was the giant chieftain, Nootka, on whose domain they had unconsciously trespassed, and in consequence of the orders he had received from Richard Howard, he would not be likely to show any white prisoners mercy.

"So!" he shouted, "you insult—break my idol?"

"How did I know what it was?" returned Buttons, determined to put on as bold a face as possible.

"Yes, indeed," joined in the Stinger, grandly; "how should we know? We are natives of England."

"You not in England now," remarked the chief, with a grim scowl, "you in my territory."

"And a filthy place it is," remarked the undaunted Elizabeth Ann.

"Only fit for pigs," added Buttons.

"We kill pig when we catch him," rejoined Nootka, with ominous significance.

"Sucking pigs, I think," retorted Buttons, in allusion to the infant sacrifice.

"You see to-morrow—you know your fate," replied the chief coldly. "Begone!"

And not caring to prolong the interview, which interrupted his drinking, he dismissed them with an angry wave of his hand.

The prisoners were immediately hurried out, and dragged away to a miserable hovel.

Into this they were thrust and the door made fast.

The hut was surrounded by the priest and his ministers, who shouted at the top of their voices throughout the night, till Buttons and the Stinger were driven nearly mad.

It was not until near daybreak they ceased, when the weary captives instantly fell asleep.

CHAPTER XXXIX.

A TERRIBLE CRISIS AND JOYFUL DELIVERANCE.

THEIR brief slumbers were broken by renewed howlings.

But the prisoners had hardly time to utter a complaint, for the door of the hut was suddenly opened and a ferocious-looking black entered.

He wore a number of thick metal rings on his bare arms and ear-rings in his ears. a formidable weapon, with a particularly awful-looking blade, hung at his side, and he was altogether a terrible object to look upon.

Both Buttons and the Stinger thought nim so.

But, if they shuddered inwardly, they evinced no outward signs of fear.

And Buttons, in a semi-playful tone, said to him—

"Well, ugly mug, what do you want?"

The dark man turned his large, fierce eyes down upon the speaker, and replied hoarsely—

"Me want you; one—two," pointing to each as he enumerated them.

"Well, yer ain't got to go far to find us," said Buttons, cheerfully.

The dark, semi-naked figure made no reply, save by pointing to the door.

"Are we to go out?" asked Buttons.

The black nodded.

"Come on, ole gal," said the page in an undertone, to his companion.

The Stinger having hastily picked up her teapot and umbrella, they walked forth from the hovel.

Outside, ranged in two rows, were dark, savage figures, who surrounded the prisoners as they emerged, and marched along with them.

They stopped at the chief's palace with the skulls on the front door-posts, and presently Nootka himself made his appearance—a tall, burly Abyssinian, naked to the waist, from whence a drapery descended to his feet.

For a moment he stood regarding his captives attentively.

Then, as if possessed by a sudden freak, he approached Buttons, and snatching off his hat, put it on his own head.

Possibly it was the first time he had ever assumed an European article of dress, and it did not seem to please him.

"No good!" he grunted, shaking his head impatiently.

"No wonder," grinned Buttons, derisively, "when you've got it on the wrong way."

The chief scowled, but took the hint.

And the hat, fitting him better, he appropriated it without further comment.

A large open umbrella, covered with gaudy feathers, was then brought him, and the order was given to proceed.

In the same manner as before they went on till they came to a miserable-looking building, which had only a door, and a few narrow openings like pigeon-holes in the upper portion of the walls.

Buttons glanced around him.

Right and left, before and behind, were dark stern faces, looking as though they were chiselled out of black rock and could never smile.

Apart from the rest the chief strode along in Buttons' hat, with his umbrella over his head.

And he, too, looked—if possible—more sternly forbidding than all his slaves put together.

Buttons noticed, also, that the black with the formidable-looking sword and the rings on his arms walked by the side of another dark figure of smaller dimensions but equally hideous aspect.

This last carried in his hand a kind of round wicker dish somewhat resembling a sieve, and Buttons could not help remarking that it was stained and clotted with—blood.

Buttons began to feel **very** uncomfortable.

"I say," he said, in a half-whisper, "I begin to wish we was well out er this."

"I've been wishing so a long time," returned the Stinger, fervently.

"Well, keep up your spirits, ole gal," said Buttons, encouragingly. "We'll die game if they kills us."

The day was hot, and the captives, who had had nothing since the previous night, were both hungry and thirsty.

At length Buttons, looking towards the man with the sword, said—

"I say, rings, when are we goin' to have breakfast?"

The dark individual only shook his head and answered, curtly—

"No eat!"

"It's a thundering shame, then," replied Buttons, indignantly. "We shall be starved."

"No, no, no," returned the other, with a ghastly grin; "you no live long 'nough for dat."

It was the first attempt at pleasantry the page had experienced, and it struck him as awful in the extreme.

"Yer don't mean to say yer a-goin' to—to k—k—kill us?" he gasped out.

"Me not. Big broder he kill!" The speaker pointed his thumb, as he spoke, towards the burly black with the sword at his side.

"Oh!" gurgled Buttons, faintly; "an' what do you do?"

"Me ketch head, when dey cut off, in dis."

As he spoke he held up the blood-stained dish.

Buttons groaned.

"It's all up with us, my precious Betsy,' he said, in a horror-stricken tone; "we're a-goin' to be decapitulated."

He meant decapitated; but his mistake, under the intense anguish he felt, is pardonable.

In a short time they arrived at the widespread sheet of water.

Moored to the bank was a large raft, and on this the whole party stationed themselves.

The raft, paddled by the black attendants, glided out from the shore.

Nootka was an epicure—a kind of Abyssinian Nero—in cruelty.

He liked to witness the torments of his victims, and to know that they felt afraid of the shadow of death.

And he sat glancing from time to time at his white prisoners from under his heavy brows, gloating over their pale faces and anxious looks.

Suddenly Buttons whispered to his partner in affliction—

"Betsy, ole gal!"

"What?" she replied.

"Do yer know it strikes me we're on the very identical lake as we come across last night?"

"I was just thinking so myself," returned the Stinger.

"I'm sure it is."

"Possibly, then, our friends on the other side may observe us."

At that moment, at a sign from Nootka, the raft stopped, and the chief, looking towards his captives, said to them, sternly—

"You know why you're brought here?"

"N—n—no!" they gasped.

"See pig kill," Nootka explained.

"I d—d—don't see any p—p—pigs!" murmured Buttons, faintly.

"You soon see," returned the chief.

He gave a sign to the man with the basket.

In an instant he placed it on the raft: and, seizing an emaciated black wretch who had been taken from the prison-house, forced him on his knees.

Then strode forth the burly black with the formidable sword.

Drawing it from his side, and measuring his distance, he raised it aloft.

Flashing through the air, it fell with a sharp whizz, and a black head fell in the wicker basket.

The horror of the unfortunate white prisoners may be imagined.

It took but an instant to roll the bleeding corpse over the side of the raft, and everything was ready for the next victim.

This was Buttons.

But he did not submit to his fate as placidly as victim number one.

He kicked and struggled; and finally pitched the individual with the basket into the water.

But he could swim like a fish, and was soon on the raft again, as lively as if nothing had happened.

But, as Buttons insisted upon kicking and punching, his arms were tied behind him, and he, too, was compelled to kneel.

The Stinger, at this dreadful crisis, grew perfectly desperate.

"You murderous wretches!" she cried, as she rushed forward, umbrella in hand. "If you dare to deprive that dear and interesting youth of his head, which is his lawful property, I'll—I'll——"

Here her feelings rose to boiling-point, and flourishing her gingham, she rushed in madly upon the dark throng.

Regardless of the consequences she banged the executioner, poked Nootka in the ribs till he roared again, knocked the dish-carrier into his own vessel, and threw the entire escort into dire confusion.

But the excitement was too much for her; and after a moment her legs gave way under her, and she fell exhausted into the arms of one of the slaves.

Buttons' last chance was gone, and the chief cried sternly—

"Kill white pig!"

Once more the executioner raised his awful sword ; but it did not fall—at least not on Buttons' neck.

A sharp report was heard, and the dark form, recoiling, dropped his weapon and himself into the waters of the lake, with a bullet from Bob Blunt's rifle in his brain.

At the same moment a cheering shout from friendly voices rang out upon the air, and a canoe, containing our hero and his followers, came gliding with the swiftness of an arrow up to the raft.

In an instant the English sprang upon the raft, headed by their captain.

But the Abyssinian chief and his followers did not wait to give them battle.

With a loud splash they plunged helter-skelter into the lake, and dived beneath the surface.

It was not until they had almost reached the shore that they showed their heads again.

A volley of shots was fired, but few took effect.

By far the largest proportion got safely to land.

Amongst them the chief, Nootka.

Buttons was unbound, and the Stinger, with tears in her eyes, declared she had never been so scared in her life.

Buttons promised never to stray away again, and the whole party returned rejoicing.

CHAPTER XL.

KING PLUTO THREATENS TO REVEAL THE SECRET.

RICHARD HOWARD had gained the position for which he had plotted.

But at present he did not feel himself as secure upon the throne as he could have wished.

That one startling word, hissed into his ear with such intensity by the African Pluto, troubled him ; and he sat in his palace moodily pondering over it.

" Does he suspect me ?" he continually asked himself, and as often as he put the question his guilty conscience answered, " Yes."

It was while he was in this unsettled state of mind that his lord chamberlain, Bow-legged Bill, entered his presence.

The rough was attired in regular Abyssinian costume, which did not seem to sit at all comfortable upon him.

This was especially the case with the turban, which was continually falling off.

But it was necessary to wear it for the sake of appearances, although it was a sore trial to the temper of Bow-legged Bill.

" Ye're wornted, yer rile 'ighness," he said, as he made an awkward attempt at a salaam, and shot off his turban at the same time.

" Who wants me ?" demanded Richard.

Bow-legged Bill, having vented an angry oath on his unmanageable headgear, answered—

" That there three-fingered bloke an' 'is pal, Rope's End,"

" What is their business ?"

" Blest if I knows, yer majesty," responded the rough ; " but they don't look partickler good-tempered either on 'em, 'specially Pluto."

Richard Howard frowned and bit his lips.

" I won't see them," he muttered to himself.

But a thought suddenly crossed him that caused him to change his mind, and he said aloud—

" Conduct them hither."

Bow-legged Bill vanished.

After a few moments' delay the drapery at the end of the apartment was drawn aside, and Pluto and his companion were introduced.

The rough, having performed this duty, retired modestly out of sight.

The negroes strode proudly forward, making no obeisance, by which they would have acknowledged themselves in the presence of a superior.

Richard Howard fixed his eyes upon them with stern scrutiny for a moment, and then said—

"Now then, what is your business with me?"

"I wish to know when you mean to keep your promise with me," replied Pluto, in an imperative tone.

"Me want know same ting, Massa Howard," joined in Rope's End.

"Hold your tongue, dog!" exclaimed Richard, sharply, to the latter.

Then, turning to Pluto, he said, coldly—

"What promise do you speak of?"

"My half share of the kingdom."

Richard Howard's sallow features flushed with wrath, as he exclaimed, passionately—

"Your half share? Curse your impudence!"

"Yes, my half share; my fair half, according to our agreement," reiterated the African, firmly.

"Psha! fool!"

Three-fingered Pluto drew himself up proudly.

"Call me what you please, white prince," he said; "but you shall still keep your promise to me. If not——"

"Well, if not?"

"I shall tell what I know."

"What do you know?"

"That you destroyed the life of the lawful prince."

"Destroyed his life?"

"Yes, by poison."

Richard Howard started from his seat.

"Do you dare accuse me of such a crime?" he cried, hoarsely.

"Yes, I dare," returned Pluto, "for I saw you give your victim the death-draught."

Richard Howard turned lividly pale at these words.

"There are many around you who loved the dead prince better than the living one," continued Pluto, "and who, were I to accuse you, would——"

The guilty man held up his finger.

"Sh! sh!" he cried, in a hasty, subdued tone; "not so loud."

"The only way to stop my voice is to deal truly with me," said Pluto.

"Iss, an' mine, too," joined in Rope's End; "if not me kick up awful bobbery 'fore long."

Richard Howard ground his teeth with rage, but, dissembling, he said to Pluto—

"Your accusation takes me by surprise. You must allow me time for reflection."

"How long?"

"An hour."

"Goou. I will give you an hour," said Pluto, magnanimously.

"An' mind not anoder single minnit," joined in Rope's End, in a consequential tone, puffing out his burly chest.

"At the end of that time you can return, and you shall have your answer," Richard replied.

Holding up his hand, his factotum behind the curtain stepped forth.

"Our interview is ended for the present," said Richard Howard; "but our friends will return in an hour. You will then conduct them to me."

"Yes, yer serene 'ighness," said the Whitechapel chamberlain.

As he was escorting the visitors to the door, he caught his master's eye, and hastened back to him.

"The executioner and a guard," whispered the latter, quickly.

"All right, guv'nor," returned the Bow-legs, as he hurried after the visitors.

"What Massa Howard say to you jess now when he call you back, eh, bandy-shanks?" asked Rope's End a little suspiciously, as he joined them.

"Oh, nothink partic'ler, old son," the rough answered, in the cheerfullest manner possible.

"Tink he gib some order," continued the speaker, whose ears were remarkably acute.

"Oh, ah, er course 'e did," replied Bill, as if he had just recollected. "He did give an order."

"What for?"

"Rum and pipes to be ready ag'in yer comes back."

"Ah, dat war it, eh?"

"Yes that was it. 'Is rile 'ighness is a-going to give yer a reg'ler blow out."

"Ah, dat bery good," chuckled Rope's End.

But his exultation was merely assumed, and when they had got outside the gates, he said to his companion—

"You mean go back?"

"Go back! Yes; and you, too," returned Pluto, sharply.

"Well, me not quite sure 'bout dat," said the boatswain, scratching his woolly head in a doubtful manner.

"Why not?"

"Dunno wedder it quite safe."

"Safe!" echoed Pluto, in surprise. "What is there to fear?"

"Me tink me hear Massa Howard tell Bow-legs call de guard."

"Psha! he dares not harm us," cried the African king, impetuously. "He's afraid."

"Well p'r'aps you better go fust by yourself," said Rope's End, after a moment's consideration; "den if it all right me come arter."

Pluto did not seek to persuade his colleague, but, drawing himself up proudly, he said to him—

"Come or stay away, as you please. I shall go, and this white prince shall either keep his word with me or lose his throne."

He said no more, and the hour having expired, he repaired once more to the palace.

But he went alone.

Rope's End, not feeling inclined to put his head into the lion's jaws, did not accompany him, but prudently kept himself aloof out of harm's reach.

Pluto was at once conducted to his prince's presence.

"Well," said he confidently, to Richard Howard, as he entered, "have you reflected?"

"I have," was the cold reply.

"And what is your answer?"

The white prince made no answer, but simply held up his hand.

Instantly four dark stalwart guards sprang forward and seized the African, and a rope was thrown over his shoulders pinioning his arms firmly.

Then forth from the shadow of the throne there stepped a hideous, deformed figure.

It was the executioner.

Pluto knew then that he had been trapped.

His dark eyes glared wildly round with a fierce startled look in them till they lighted upon Richard Howard.

"Lying white dog!" he cried, furiously, to him.

These were the last words he was ever able to speak.

For the guards who held him dragged him back over their knees; and the executioner, approaching, gripped his throat with his enormous hand.

So terrible was the pressure that the African king gasped for breath, and his tongue protruded from his mouth.

This was what the executioner desired.

And quickly drawing from his girdle a small, narrow bladed, curved knife, he thrust it between the open jaws of his victim.

A single turn of his wrist, a fierce, guttural howl of pain, and the dreadful operation was over.

Three fingered Pluto had no longer the power to reveal secrets.

His tongue had been cut out at the roots.

He was silenced; but where was his colleague, Rope's End?

To all inquiries respecting the burly boatswain, the only answer was—

"Not to be found."

"Let search be made after him," cried Richard Howard, and then he issued fresh orders to the unsightly executioner, which the next chapter will see carried out.

CHAPTER XLI.

BOW-LEGGED BILL ATTEMPTS A CAPTURE.

WITHOUT the least ceremony the wretched African king was dragged from the apartment by his custodians, and out by a door in the rear of the palace gardens.

The executioner accompanied them.

Richard Howard and Bow-legged Bill followed leisurely.

It was evident that the absence of Rope's End made the white monarch uneasy.

"He must be found," he said at length, to his chamberlain ; "I am not safe while he remains at large."

"I allus had my doubts erbout that theer p'isonin' bisness, guv'nor ; I told yer so," said the rough, shaking his head ominously.

"Well, it's done now, and can't be undone," was Richard's irritable reply ; "I've stopped the mouth of one, and "I'll stop the mouth of the other as soon as I can lay hands on him."

"It's yer only chance, guv'nor, I think," returned Bow-legs.

They went on till they reached a wood at some distance.

There they found the executioner, and his prisoner, surrounded by the guards.

Pluto with the blood streaming from his mouth, was fastened by strong ropes to the trunk of a tree.

The final deed of torment was yet to be performed.

The misshapen administrator of a tyrant's decree stood mute and motionless, with his hand resting on the haft of his curved knife, awaiting further orders.

These quickly came, in the shape of a nod from his white master.

Then forth flashed the knife.

And stepping towards the prisoner, he grasped Pluto's right hand.

The African monarch divined his intent.

But he was powerless to escape, and too proud to exhibit fear.

With professional coolness the executioner examined the wrist he held for an instant.

And then placing the knife upon it as unerringly as a surgeon, he made a circular incision by one sweep of his blade.

This done, he gave the half-severed hand a wrench, and with a second stroke of his knife severed the wrist-joint.

The hand fell to the ground.

The executioner then, without any pause, performed a similar operation upon the prisoner's left foot.

The dire and brutal work was finished.

And the victim now was to be left to bleed and languish, till death terminated his sufferings.

Despite the cruel anguish he had endured Pluto neither winced nor uttered a moan, but suffered in dogged silence, keeping his haggard eyes rivetted upon his betrayer with an expression of undying hate in them.

Richard Howard paid little heed to this ; he was quite satisfied with his atrocious act, and after repeating his injunctions that Rope's End should be captured, left the spot with his followers.

Hardly had they gone, when the dark face of the boatswain peered forth from a clump of foilage and looked after them.

"Ha, ha !" he grinned, "you tink ketch me, eh ? No, no ! me go long way off, to de mountains. He, he ! no ketchee no habee !"

But before he started he could not resist the desire that seized him to take a parting look at his comrade.

He accordingly advanced cautiously till he stood right before him.

The tortured victim, now that he thought himself alone, uttered low sounds of agony.

As soon as he caught sight of Rope's End his moans ceased and his eyes flashed with hope.

"You no good to me now," said Rope's

End, with a brutal grin ; "you on'y got one foot an' t'ree fingers and no tongue, so I leaves you here."

The brute put out his tongue derisively at his tortured colleague.

Suddenly he felt his arms gripped from behind.

Looking over his shoulder, he found he was in the grasp of Bow-legged Bill.

"You're wanted, blackee," grinned the rough ; "the rum an' pipes is waiting for yer. Come on !"

The Bow-legs was wiry and tough, and calculated upon being able to capture the burly boatswain.

But the latter was as strong as a horse, and when he found that Bow-legged Bill was intent on dragging him backwards, he quietly ducked down and sent him flying over his head.

Before Bow-legged Bill recovered himself sufficiently to rise, Rope's End had plunged into the thicket and disappeared.

"Cuss it all !" growled the rough, as he dragged himself to his feet ; "I thought to grab him, an' he's gorn now for good."

He was in the midst of a volley of execrations when suddenly the martial sounds of a bugle, mingled with shouts, interrupted him.

"That ain't a Habyssinian hinstrament, I'll swear ; no more's the woices," he said to himself, as he listened. The sounds were approaching, and, creeping into the thicket, he waited to see what was coming.

Presently the tramp of feet became audible, and in a few moments the party of English explorers, with colours flying, appeared, marching along in full feather.

"Well, I'm blest !" exclaimed Bow-legged Bill ; "if this ain't a slice er luck nothink ain't."

He remained quite quiet in the bushes watching their approach.

They continued to advance until they reached the tree where the mutilated form of their old foe hung and bound helpless.

His features, distorted with agony and ashen grey with the hue of death, might have prevented recognition ; but the three fingers on his left hand served to identify him.

"Three-fingered Pluto!" they cried, in a tone of horror.

"Release him !" cried our hero.

In a moment the cords were cut and the victim set free. But too late to save him.

For as they laid him on the grass, one last groan came quivering from his blood-stained lips, and his spirit fled.

"Whose bloodthirsty deed was this ?" exclaimed Bob Blunt. "Surely not that of the Dejaj Maro, whom we are about to visit."

"Oh, impossible, captain," replied Doctor Knowall, "for did not the Prince Djalma describe his brother as a kind and generous man ?"

"Truly, he did," said Bob, "and as we can do him no good by remaining, I propose that we continue our course."

"To the palace of the Dejaj ?" asked his companions.

"Yes. Forward !"

Again the bugle sounded, and the flags waved, and the shouts were resumed.

Bow-legged Bill, having heard every word that had been spoken, crept from his concealment.

Into his master's presence he rushed.

"Oh, guv'nor, what d'yer think ?" he cried excitedly. "Bob Blunt's a-comin' !"

"Then at last fate has given him into my hand. Call Nootka and his executioner to me."

"But there's all the blessed lot comin', guv'nor," said Bow-legged Bill.

"So much the better for me, then," responded Howard, "for I can be happy, perhaps, if I have all my foes in my power. But are you certain ?"

"Yes, guv'nor ; I've seen 'em. They're a-comin' to the palace."

"How the devil did they know I was here ?"

"I don't think they does know, guv'-nor," said Bill.

"What are they coming for, then ?" asked Richard.

"I thinks they're a-comin' to see the Dejaj Maro."

"Who is dead !"

"Yes. But they don't seem to know that."

"You seem very well informed," remarked Richard to his factotum.

"Yes, guv'nor. I was stowed away behind a bush, and heerd all as wos said," grinned the Bow-legs.

"Tell me every particular," said his master.

Bill recapitulated everything.

Richard Howard listened attentively, and remained thoughtfully silent for some moments.

At length he muttered to himself—

"Let them come! I am prepared to receive them now. Ha, ha!" he laughed, grimly; "if they're fond of surprises, I think I can give them one."

Hardly had he uttered these words, when the sound of a bugle reached him, accompanied by loud shouts.

"That's them, guv'nor," exclaimed Bow-legged Bill. "They're a kicking up a nice rumpus, ain't they? Wot they calls doing the grand."

"It's the usual bounce my plucky cousin is so fond of displaying," returned Richard, contemptuously.

At this moment the shouts ceased, and a dark-skinned slave entered.

Having salaamed with most profound respect, he said—

"An armed force is approaching the palace, O Prince. There are white men among them."

Richard Howard beckoned his chamberlain to his side, and gave him some whispered directions.

Bow-legged Bill, who perfectly comprehended what he had to do, grinned, bowed, dropped his turban, picked it up again, and disappeared, accompanied by the slave.

CHAPTER XLII.

A STARTLING DISCOVERY.

BY the time our hero and his comrades reached the palace gates, preparations had been made within for their reception.

The messenger sent to receive the travellers was a mute, who could give no information whatever.

Like a black statue he stood evincing no surprise, but listening with Oriental gravity to our hero's words.

"We would see the Dejaj Maro," said Bob Blunt to him.

He simply bowed his head in reply, and Bob continued—

"You will tell his highness that we are English explorers, and that we come from his royal brother, Prince Djalma, who assured us of welcome and friendly treatment at his hands."

Having thus spoken, our hero drew from his finger the ring he had received, and gave it to the statuesque personage he was addressing.

The latter took it, and, bowing again, retired, still leaving our hero and his friends at the gates.

Bow-legged Bill was waiting for the mute, and, having received the ring, hurried with it to Richard Howard.

"'Ere's another keepsake, guv'nor," he grinned as he handed him the ornament.

Richard coolly took it and put it on his finger, and then said to his chamberlain—

"You have placed the guard as I ordered?"

"Yes, guv'nor."

"That will do," said Richard, approvingly; "you can admit our dear friends now."

A sarcastic smile flitted over his face as he added, significantly—

"The Dejaj Maro is ready to receive them."

Bow-legged Bill was not long in giving his master's orders to his satellites.

And very shortly the gates were opened and our hero and his party invited to enter.

On entering the vestibule, or outer court, they were required to deliver up their weapons.

"We come here as friends," said Bob Blunt, "and it is an unusual thing for us to relinquish our arms."

"It is the custom of the country," explained one of the swarthy attendants.

At length it was decided that they should yield obedience to the etiquette of royalty.

And accordingly they resigned their weapons without further argument.

No sooner was this effected than a file of guards, armed with scimitars and spears, marched in in solemn silence, and ranged themselves in two lines on either side of the vestibule.

"Is it the custom of the country to receive visitors in this way, Mr. Blunt?" asked the Stinger.

"I suppose so," returned Bob, looking at the dark, savage forms in some surprise.

"If it is, then I think it's a very ugly fashion," replied Elizabeth Ann, in a tone of disgust, "and the sooner it's altered the better. I shall tell the Dejaj so."

She had scarcely uttered these words when one who appeared to be the leader of the troop approached her, and, pointing to her umbrella, which she still held in her hand, said—

"Your weapon—give up."

The Stinger flushed crimson at this preposterous demand.

"What!" she cried, indignantly, "give up my gingham? I shall do nothing of the sort, you ignorant heathen. It isn't a weapon."

"The Dejaj command!" returned the soldier sternly.

"There! you've got it now," returned the Stinger, as she swished it across his ears with startling energy.

The soldier would, doubtless, have resented the assault had not a messenger appeared to conduct them to the presence of the Dejaj.

As they went along, our hero could but remark the long rows of grim, dark figures, bristling with spear and dagger, that hemmed them in on every side.

A slight doubt flashed across his mind as to whether he had acted quite prudently in consenting to lay down his weapons.

They presently found themselves in an apartment covered with rich carpets, and furnished with Oriental magnificence.

At one end was a couch, slightly raised, and on it reclined a figure attired in rich robes.

Doubtless the Dejaj Maro.

But at present they could not see his face.

Having stationed themselves at a respectful distance, a figure emerged from the shadow of the drapery that overhung the throne, and advanced a little towards them.

A strange figure this.

And the turban he wore had tilted down over his eyes and nose, so that his face could only be partially seen.

"Now, then," he said, in the most approved tone of cockney slang, "wot's yer business?"

Buttons exclaimed instantly—

"Blest if it ain't Bow-legged Bill!"

These words seemed to produce quite an electric thrill amongst the explorers.

"Oh, yes, it's me right enough," he said, as he set his turban straight and grinned at the visitors. "Look away as long as yer likes; I shan't charge nothink."

"What imposture is this?" said Bob Blunt. "What are you doing here, fellow?"

"That's no odds wot I'm doin'," returned the other, insolently. "The p'int is, what's your business 'ere?"

"My business is with the Prince of Kivara," answered Bob sharply; "and I'm not to be questioned by a scoundrel like you."

"Thankee fur nothink," said the Bowlegs; "but you'd best be civil, 'cos I'm somebody 'ere. I'm the prince's pertickler friend and adviser. In fact I'm lord 'igh heverythink."

"Well, then, perhaps without any further loss of time you'll inform his majesty we are waiting his pleasure," said our hero in a tone of disgust.

"'I'LL PICKLE YOU!' HE SHOUTED, AS HE LAID ABOUT HIM WITH HIS BRANCH OF A TREE."

Approaching the couch, Bow-legged Bill exclaimed, in a very hoarse and foggy voice—

"The Henglish visitors, yer rile 'ighness."

Slowly the form attired in gorgeous robes raised itself.

Slowly he turned his head, and looked full at our hero.

For a moment, as the well known features were recognized, there was a dead silence, and then every tongue exclaimed with one accord—

"Richard Howard!"

"Yes! Richard Howard, at your service," was the cool reply, accompanied by a bitterly sarcastic smile.

"It is not you I seek," returned Bob Blunt, "but your master!"

"There is only one master here—that is myself, cousin," said the usurper, with peculiar emphasis.

The supercilious tone and manner of the speaker almost drove our hero mad.

"My business is with the Dejaj Maro," he cried, passionately; "let me see him!"

"You'll have to dig deep to find him," Richard answered.

"What am I to understand by that?"

"That the Dejaj Maro has been in his grave a month, and that I reign here in his stead."

At these ominous words, delivered in a tone of suppressed triumph, a chill fell upon the hearts of all.

And the speaker continued—

"Whatever business you have to transact will be not with the Dejaj Maro, but the Dejaj Howard!"

"I have nothing to say to you, you murderous remorseless villain!" cried Bob Blunt, in a paroxysm of indignation he found it impossible to repress. You are beneath contempt!"

"Oh, indeed! Am I?" returned his cousin, two bright scarlet spots flushing into his sallow cheeks.

"Yes!" shouted Bob, fiercely.

Then turning to his companions, he continued—

"Come, friends, let us leave this place; I feel contaminated by remaining within its walls."

Our hero and his party were about to leave the chamber without further ceremony, when the voice of Howard fell on their ears.

"Stop!" he cried, imperatively; "having entered these walls, you will stay here until I give you permission to depart."

"You—you give permission?" returned Bob Blunt, hoarse with rage.

"Yes, I; you are my prisoners—all!"

This last was like the spark to the train of powder, and with an uncontrollable execration our hero rushed forward.

Bow-legged Bill made an attempt to arrest his progress, but he received such an awfully stinging blow on his nose that his turban flew one way and he another.

Before Richard Howard could stir a step he was in the grasp of his infuriated cousin.

"Wretch! murderer! fiend!" shouted Bob, as he dragged him from his seat, and rained a shower of blows upon his face.

It seemed more than possible that the white Dejaj would be beaten into a mummy.

"Help! help!" he cried.

Upon this, the inner chamber poured forth its contents in the shape of an armed guard.

Bob Blunt was seized by four stalwart Abyssinians, whilst the rest surrounded his companions.

The blows Howard had received had only deepened the deadly animosity he felt towards him who had dealt them.

Bob Blunt, writhing under the grasp of his captors, struggled desperately for a time, but finding himself overpowered by numbers, he subsided into dogged quiescence, but he could not forget Elinor, who was a prisoner like himself.

He glanced sadly towards her.

She was looking towards him, and their eyes met.

In that brief look, what a world of meaning there was!

Richard Howard noticed the glance, and composing his puffy features as best he could, he approached Elinor.

"You withdrew your charming society rather suddenly when we first met, fair Elinor," he said to her in a sarcastic semi-polite tone. "I rejoice to renew our acquaintance under more favourable auspices."

The young girl looked at him with mingled horror and loathing, and turned away with a shudder.

Our hero bit his lips till the blood almost started from them. And then he spoke.

"If you dare to offer insult to that young lady, whom you have already made fatherless, look to yourself," he cried with terrible intensity.

Richard Howard turned ghastly pale, but raised his eyebrows with assumed surprise.

"I don't know what you mean," he replied, after a moment, hoarsely.

"Liar and coward ! you do !" continued Bob, fiercely ; "your guilty conscience thunders your vile deed in your ears at this moment. But mark me ! that dear girl is dear to me as my life, precious as an angel in my eyes. If you injure her Heaven's direst vengeance will fall upon your recreant head !"

Howard only answered by a sarcastic smile, and then gave a signal.

The explorers were at once hurried away by the guards.

Their clothes were searched, and every thing found upon them seized.

Buttons lost his note-book, and was broken-hearted in consequence.

But neither expostulations nor complaints were heeded in the slightest.

And the spoliation being completed, the prisoners were immured in a building in the palace gardens, with a band of fifty armed men surrounding it day and night.

CHAPTER XLIII.

ROPE'S END TAKES A HASTY DEPARTURE.

THE fate of the unfortunate King Pluto set Rope's End thinking rather more seriously than he was usually wont to do.

Not that his ignorant brutal nature in the least regretted the loss of his confederate.

But the burly boatswain had a strong propensity to look after what is known as number one.

His own safety must be provided for.

Accordingly, as soon as he had got rid of Bow-legged Bill by pitching him over his head, he commenced his flight in earnest.

Through woods, across plains, the giant African pursued his way, till he once more found himself in the vast mountains.

It was at the close of a long day's march that he threw himself down on a slab of rock.

He was famished and parched with hunger and thirst, and exhausted with fatigue.

Suddenly, as he lay there, he fancied he heard the sound of voices in the distance.

He started up, with his ears tingling, and listened.

He was not deceived.

They were voices—human voices.

All his weariness vanished in an instant, and, rising once more to his feet, he hastened forward in the direction from whence the sounds proceeded.

Presently his nostrils caught the fragrant scent of a peculiar wood that was burning.

"Ha, ha !" he chuckled to himself ravenously ; "me find 'em now."

Creeping forward through the brushwood, he pushed along, till at length large round space, like a natural amphitheatre, burst upon his sight.

To his surprise this was alive with men.

Wild, savage-looking forms, black as jet, clad in short white skirts, with hanging mantles of tiger, lion, or leopard skins, and wearing metal rings upon their arms and ancles.

Rope's End remained peering from his covert at this strange assembly.

But, so far from being cowed or intimidated at the sight, his eyes brightened with hope; he looked as if he had fallen amongst kindred spirits.

As indeed he had; for in that horde of heathen desperadoes he recognised a gang of Dahomey pirates.

With them he felt himself safe.

In the centre of the rocky hollow was a blazing fire, and the bright glare falling upon the dark bodies, with their white skirts and glittering ornaments, gave a weird and demoniac aspect to the whole scene.

Round the fire numbers were stretched.

Some were smoking their reed pipes and drinking strong liquor from gourds, others devouring strips of raw meat, which they cut from the carcass of an animal which had been recently killed.

At length, having made up his mind what to do, Rope's End burst from his concealment and advanced boldly into their very midst.

At the sight of his gigantic bulk a furious yell arose on every side.

Fifty of the dark forms sprang up and surrounded him in an instant.

Fifty glittering weapons, flashing in the fire's rays, were pointed at his breast.

The intruder winced not in the slightest at these hostile preparations.

He simply extended his hands in appeal, and exclaimed—

" Me broder !"

Strange that that name should have had power over those lawless spirits !

Yet no sooner was it uttered than every weapon was lowered.

After a moment, one who had hitherto remained reclining on the ground, on a lion-skin, rose and advanced.

The superior number and size of the rings he wore, and the metal band that encircled his head, proclaimed him the captain of the band.

The rest made way for him as he came forward till he reached Rope's End.

" You call yourself a brother," he then said to him ; " whence come you ?"

" Long way 'cross de mountain," Rope's End replied, as he pointed in the direction he had been traversing.

" Is that your home ?" continued the inquirer.

" No ; me goin' dere now."

" Where is your home ?"

" On de west coast."

" You have travelled far ?"

" Iss ; many long miles," said Rope's End, ruefully. " No food, no drink ; me empty as bag ; me dry as sand."

" Eat and drink, then," said the captain, " before you talk."

The famished boatswain needed no second invitation.

Throwing himself on the ground, he seized a calabash, and emptied it at a draught.

Then, picking up a knife, he attacked the food, cutting off huge strips and devouring them with all the eager haste which his intense cravings demanded.

His meal ended, the captain again approached him.

" What have you been doing ?" he asked, as he eyed him closely. " You seem to be running away."

Rope's End refreshed by his meal, and stimulated powerfully by the liquor he had swallowed, drew himself up.

" Me not do notink," he said grandly. " Me great chief. Me come look for men."

" Slaves ?" asked the captain, eagerly. " You would buy ?"

" No, no, no ! not buy at all," returned Rope's End, shaking his head in utter contempt at the idea. " Me neber buy notink."

The countenance of the captain fell.

He was evidently disappointed.

" How, then, do you get men ?" he asked, after a moment.

" Me get 'em same way you get 'em ; me steal," grinned Rope's End.

The dark face of the captain grew

darker still in the heavy frown that over-shadowed it.

"You cannot steal alone," he said at length in a scornful tone.

"Me know dat well as you, massa captain."

"My name is Kassa Kobo," interrupted the other proudly.

"My name Karfa!" returned the boatswain, with true African bombast.

"I do not know that name," was the cutting reply.

"Got 'noder name as well—Rope's End."

"Nor that either."

"Tell you me great chief," exclaimed the boatswain, impatiently. "You come 'long wid me—serve me—be good for yar."

A withering look of scorn flashed from Kassa's eyes, as he replied—

"No; you will come with me, and serve me, or I shall cut you up, joint by joint, and hang your limbs to dry on yonder rocks."

But even this dire threat did not at that moment arouse the boatswain to a sense of his rashness.

"Oh, bery well," he cried in a drunken reckless manner. "Cut me up. Me not care. Only mind, if yar do, yar lose all de gold—all de fine tings—all de rich white slaves me meant to gib yar."

These words impressed the pirate-captain.

Gold, fine things, and rich white slaves—or black ones—were the precise objects he coveted, and he said to Rope's End, after a slight pause—

"Have you the power of gaining these treasures you speak of?"

"Ob course," promptly returned the boatswain.

"If I go with you, then, and help you to secure these treasures, what do you offer?" he asked, after a moment.

"We broders," replied Rope's End, in a cajoling tone. "We share, go half in eberytink, eh?"

The pirate considered a little, and then said—

"I agree to that; equal shares."

"Iss, ekal shares."

"But mark me," added Kassa; "if I find you have deceived me you die without mercy."

"Me neber deceive no un; me allus 'peak trufe," affirmed Rope's End, with drunken solemnity.

This singular compact being completed, the burly giant staggered back to the fire, and after eating some more strips of raw meat, and emptying all the calabashes he could lay hands on, he fell back on the ground utterly unconscious.

CHAPTER XLIV.

THE PARTING TAUNT, AND WHAT IT LED TO.

SEVERAL days had passed. Richard Howard sat alone one evening in his private chamber in the palace.

Before him was a packet of letters, which had been rifled from the pockets of his prisoners.

But one alone interested him.

This was a letter which Bob Blunt had written to Mr. Sawyer, his Rochester lawyer, intending to forward it to England at the first opportunity.

As he read this the voice of the fiend seemed speaking to him.

Now was his chance to make his own terms with his cousin, and secure the rich possessions.

"I'll have the property—by Heaven, I will!" he exclaimed, as he finished the letter. "I have the power, and I'll put on the screw hard enough this time."

But he knew well enough the temper and disposition of his cousin.

He knew that he was not one to be intimidated by threats, or the prospect of death itself.

Howard lit a cigar, poured out a glass of sherbet, which he fortified with brandy, and meditated.

Suddenly a bright idea darted through his evil, plotting brain.

Elinor Cleveland, he thought.

"I will make her 'the screw,'" he muttered to himself, with a grim smile of triumph. "In order to secure her safety he will assent to whatever I demand."

With this project full in his mind he summoned Bow-legged Bill.

The "lord high everything" imagined his official duties were over for the day, and was now smoking a quiet pipe, moistened with Jamaica rum from the royal cellars, a certain dark-skinned Abyssinian, who answered to the name of Jumbo, being his pal for the time being.

Bill was in a state of comfortable *deshabille*, which means that he had thrown off his official robes and tucked up his shirt-sleeves in regular Whitechapel fashion.

On receiving the summons to attend his royal master he made use of very strong expressions.

But, as he dared not refuse obedience, he dragged on his state apparel in a very hasty manner, and presented himself, with his turban on his head, wrong end uppermost.

On his entering, Richard Howard looked up from the letter, and said to him—

"You are quite sure the prisoners are secure, and the guard placed?"

"Yer means Mr. Bob Blunt an' 'is gal, I s'pose?"

Richard Howard did not like Bill's insolent mention of Elinor, and he cried sharply—

"More respectful terms when you speak of Miss Cleveland; remember she is a lady."

"All right, guv'nor; begs your parding, I'm sure," replied Bow-legged Bill humbly.

"Well, what of them?"

"They're locked up in separate cells."

"You did not neglect to secure Mr. Blunt?"

"Not I, guv'nor; I slipped the heaviest chain I could find round 'is waist and fastened it by a staple to the floor."

"So that he can't move far, eh?"

"Not a hinch, if it was to save his precious life," grinned the rough.

This piece of information evidently gratified his master, for his features relaxed, and he exclaimed—

"Good! then give me the keys of those two cells."

Bow-legged Bill fumbled for some time, having got on his robes hind-side before, which made his pockets difficult to arrive at.

At length he produced the keys.

"'Ere they are, guv'nor," he said, as he laid them on the table.

"That will do: and now——"

"Yes, guv'nor."

"Get out!"

The chamberlain vanished like a flash of lightning.

As soon as he was alone, Richard Howard lighted a small lantern; then thrusting the keys into his girdle, walked quietly out by the arched window, into the garden, and bent his steps towards the cell where our hero was confined.

"Does he sleep?" was his thought as he thrust the key into the lock.

He looked in cautiously.

The prisoner was seated on the ground with his back against the wall.

An iron band encircled his waist, to which was attached a heavy chain, fastened to a strong iron ring in the floor.

He was not asleep, but very wide awake.

Richard Howard was rather disconcerted at finding his cousin's clear bright eyes fixed steadily upon his.

Not a word, however, did the latter speak.

The Dejaj entered, closed the door, and stood gazing at him.

"I have come to talk to you," he said, after a long pause.

Bob Blunt returned no answer.

"I dare say you are surprised at my

condescension after your treatment of me ?" continued Richard, loftily.

" I'm surprised at nothing you can do," was the scornful reply.

Howard bit his lips. and the scarlet spots appeared again on his cheeks.

But, suppressing his inward rage, he went on—

" If you realised your position at this moment——"

" I do realise it," burst out Bob, bitterly, " I am a fettered prisoner, or you would not dare to stand where you now do."

" Yes, you are in my power," said Richard, exultingly, " and I am determined to use it to the full. Those estates of yours must be mine."

" Never !" cried our hero, vehemently. " As I told you often before, so I tell you again, you shall never possess them— never !"

" I'm afraid then, your obstinacy will cost you your life."

" I care not if it cost me twenty lives !"

" Ah ! but there is something more even than that."

" What more ? You can but kill me."

" You forget Elinor Cleveland."

This was true.

In his excitement he had forgotten her, but only for a moment.

At the mention of her name his eyes flashed and the blood rushed crimson into his face.

" What do you mean ?" he exclaimed.

" Simply that she is also in my power," returned Richard Howard, coolly.

" But, lost as you are to the better feelings of humanity, you would not surely take advantage of that power to——"

He was interrupted by a bitter oath from his listener.

" You talk like an idiot !" he cried. " We are in Abyssinia, where I shall not allow any conscientious scruples to stand between my will and the accomplishment of my designs."

" You are a remorseless villain, who has no conscience at all," was Bob's reply.

" You are right," shouted Richard Howard, furiously, no longer attempting to conceal the bitter rage he felt. " I have

no pangs of conscience. Blunt Castle and Elinor Cleveland shall be mine—both mine !"

Bob Blunt sprang up and made a fierce dash towards him ; but, alas ! the heavy chain held him fast.

" Insulting, cowardly villain !" he cried, breathlessly, as he struggled vainly to burst his bonds.

Richard Howard mocked his efforts with derisive laughter.

" I will leave you now," he said sneeringly, " for more congenial society. I am going to pay a visit to sweet Elinor— make love to her."

" She will not listen," gasped our hero tugging, like a raging lion at his chain ; " she scorns and despises you as bitterly as I do !"

" Let her scorn and despise me as much as she pleases ; she is in my hands and will be mine !"

" Never, never, wretch !"

" She must ! she shall ! if not by fair means, by foul ! Go to sleep and dream of that, Robert Blunt, of Blunt Castle !"

And, with this final taunt, Richard Howard left the cell and closed the door.

With one mighty effort our hero sprang forward. So intense was the sudden tension upon the chain that one of the links snapped close to the waist-band.

So far he was free.

But, alas ! the key had turned in the lock, and he was still a prisoner within the four walls of his cell.

In his rage and despair he was about to dash himself against the door ; but suddenly, prudence came to his aid.

His mad fit passed off, and he grew strangely calm.

He knew that his ruthless cousin was about to intrude his hateful company upon the girl he loved.

He fell on his knees and prayed earnestly that Heaven would avert the peril that threatened his beloved Elinor.

There let us leave him while we follow the ruthless Richard Howard.

As that villain walked back to his apartments he muttered to himself—

" Elinor shall be mine ; Blunt Castle shall be mine ; and when my cousin has lost both his sweetheart and his possessions he shall die."

CHAPTER XLV.

THE UNSEEN FIGURE.

ELINOR CLEVELAND, in her solitary prison chamber, had fallen into a light slumber.

When her visitor, who had for a time resumed his European clothing, entered softly she did not hear him, and he stood for some time watching her.

Very lovely she looked in that attitude of unconscious grace—her white arm fully displayed in all its exquisite proportions, and her dark hair escaped from its bonds, falling in rich luxuriance down to her shoulders ; whilst the dark fringes of her eyelashes rested on the pale cheeks that looked like marble from the contrast.

"Umph !" thought Richard Howard ; " she is very handsome, and will suit me exactly. She shall be my queen, and, as for love—pshaw !—let that pass. I will compel her to obey me at least."

Having said this, he advanced a little nearer.

The light roused her and she opened her eyes.

"What do you want ?" she asked in a startled tone.

"I have come to have a chat with you, sweet Elinor," answered Richard, suavely.

"You have no right to intrude yourself upon me ! Begone !" she cried indignantly.

"It is not for you to command," returned her visitor, coolly, "and be good enough to remember that I am master here."

"Not my master."

"Yes, yours, as you will find. Therefore, prepare to obey me."

"Never !" returned the young girl, turning away her face in loathing.

Richard Howard was already irritated by his interview with his cousin, and the disgust evinced at his presence by Elinor Cleveland increased his spleen still further.

But, conscious that the game was in his own hands, he determined to hurry it on regardless of consequences.

Setting down the lantern, he approached to where Elinor was sitting.

"Look here, girl," he said, dropping at once his tone of assumed respect and speaking coarsely, " I've taken a great fancy to you. Do you hear ?"

The young lady took no notice—made no reply, but sat still, with her face averted.

"It's no use you sulking with me," continued Richard, taking her by the arm and pulling her round.

But he was almost startled at the stern gaze he encountered from her flashing eyes.

"Murderer of my father and brother, avaunt !" she cried, fiercely, her lips quivering with strong emotion.

"I did not kill your father and brother," returned Richard, hoarsely. "Who dares to say I did ?"

"If you killed them not with your own hand you gave the order for their death."

"Well, never mind them ; they are gone, and let them rest. My business is with you—I love you."

Elinor shuddered and buried her face in her hands.

"I love you, and intend to marry you," continued Richard.

"I would rather die !" was the firm reply of the fair prisoner.

"If you refuse it will cost a certain dear friend of yours his head. I speak of Mr. Robert Blunt, of Blunt Castle, Rochester."

"You would never dare to harm him—your own relative."

"You'll see what I dare !" cried Richard Howard, savagely : "and, I swear, unless you promise to become my wife without any further bother, I'll sweep off his head and the heads of his followers without the least compunction."

A cry of anguish burst from Elinor's lips.

"You are merciless—remorseless," she wailed.

"I am in this case. Will you be mine?"

"How can I break my plighted vows to dear Robert?" cried the poor girl bursting into tears.

"Oh, don't let that trouble you," sneered her hateful suitor. "Dear Robert is perfectly willing to give you up in order to secure his own safety."

"Did he say that?" asked Elinor, quickly.

"To be sure he did."

"I don't believe you; it is not like him—he is too generous and true!" exclaimed the young girl, warmly.

"You will not consent then? You would rather see him perish," said the ruthless Howard.

"Oh, no! no! If I consent, will you pledge yourself to save his life and the lives of his friends?"

"Well, on that condition, perhaps, I might," drawled Richard.

"Nay, you must swear it—swear it solemnly!"

"Well, then, I swear."

"Keep your word, Richard Howard; set Robert Blunt and his friends at liberty, and, as the price of that deliverance, I will consent," said Elinor in a low, but firm voice.

"That's much better," returned Richard, rubbing his hands triumphantly. "Our nuptials shall take place to-night."

"To-night!" echoed Elinor, with a visible shudder.

"Yes, darling," replied her exulting suitor, with a sinister smile; "you might change your mind to-morrow."

The hapless girl uttered a groan of despair.

"I'll go for the priest at once," he said; "nothing like striking while the iron is hot."

Elinor sank in her seat and buried her face in her hands.

At the same moment a figure slipped in at the half-open door.

Richard Howard did not observe this, and, having cast a sardonic grin at his victim, he went out, locking the door after him.

"It is to save you, my beloved! only to save you I make this terrible sacrifice!" cried Elinor in a voice of anguish, as soon as the key was turned.

The sound of a light footstep caused her to look up.

Could she believe her eyes?

There, before her, stood the object of all her anxiety.

For an instant she remained gazing at him in speechless astonishment—almost terror.

But her fears were soon dispelled when he advanced and clasped her in his arms.

"Elinor, my beloved, don't you know me?" he said.

"Oh, yes!" she faltered; "but your sudden appearance—I—I thought——"

"I was a ghost, eh?" interrupted Bob, with a half smile.

"I hardly know what," she answered; "I am almost distracted. Oh, Robert! that cruel wretch!"

"Hush, my love! I know all he said."

"You know?"

"Yes; I had been listening some time before I entered."

"And how were you able to escape from your cell?"

"Providence, I think, gave me the strength of Samson, first to break my chain, and then to dash out one of the planks of my prison walls with my foot."

"And you are with me once more! Oh, thank Heaven for that!"

"Yes, darling, I am here to save or die with you!" cried our hero, as he pressed his betrothed fondly to his heart.

But it was by no means the intention of Bob Blunt to perish in that magnanimous manner, if human wit or energy could avert the catastrophe.

To accomplish this no time must be lost, and taking the lantern, he examined the door and walls minutely.

He found that the key had been left in the lock, but, unfortunately, it was on the outside.

Nothing daunted, he continued his observations.

He noticed that in the wood that formed the door there were several large knots, one of these not far from the lock.

This removed, there would be no difficulty in reaching the key.

He pressed his hand and heel against it, but it resisted all his efforts to push it through.

"Oh, if I had but a chisel, or even a nail!" he cried, in a paroxysm of nervous impatience.

Again Providence came to his assistance.

In one of his pockets he felt a hard substance.

Joy! it was a knife, which had escaped the general search.

It was quickly in use working its way round the knot.

The wood was of a resinous quality, and he soon began to feel it yield under his efforts.

Before long he had dug it completely out with the point of his blade.

The hole was large enough to admit his wrist and he was able to secure the key.

In a transport of joy he thrust it into the lock.

The door was open.

Having proceeded thus far our hero carefully replaced the knot, and, leading Elinor out, closed the door, locked it, and threw away the key.

All was quiet, and not a soul was in sight.

The murky gleam of a few torches could be seen in the distance, but nothing more.

"Now, darling," he said, "this way."

The next moment he and his fair betrothed vanished into the mass of shrubbery that grew thickly in the garden.

The first part of their escape was accomplished.

But how was it to end?

Heaven alone knew that!

CHAPTER XLVI.

THE DRUNKEN CHAMBERLAIN.

NEITHER our hero nor Elinor Cleveland were selfish; and although they had broken from their own cells, they could not forget that their companions in misfortune were still prisoners.

"We ought not to depart, even if we could, and leave them to perish," said Elinor, generously.

"I should never forgive myself if I did, love," said Bob, warmly, in reply. "They must be saved if possible. But how?"

That was a question most difficult to answer.

Our hero remained silent and thoughtful as he pushed forward under cover of the shrubs, till at length he could hear the voices of the guards that surrounded the prison that held their comrades.

A few steps further, and he could see from his covert the dark building looming through the smoke of the torches, with here and there the glimmer of spears.

He almost fancied he could detect the sharp tones of Buttons and the plaintive wail of the Stinger.

"How can we get them out?" he said, after a moment, in a perplexed tone.

"Could we employ any stratagem?" asked Elinor.

"If there were only one or two sentinels we might, perhaps," returned Bob; "but, unfortunately, the place seems to be completely beleaguered."

It was just at this moment that a voice caught his ears.

The voice was at some distance and was singing.

What the song was Bob could not yet discover, only it seemed that the tones were English.

Gradually the sounds came nearer, and presently a shuffling of feet on the path announced that the singer was approaching.

The words and melody were now distinctly audible.

There was nothing at all Abyssinian about the song, which was decidedly cockney.

It went thus—

"I'm a chickaleary cove, with my—hic—one, two, three,
    Whitechapel is the—hic—willage I wos born in ;
If ye'd ketch me on the—hic—'op -—"

The vocalist came in sight just as he was singing this interesting refrain.

He had a long pipe in his hand and a large key at his girdle, and staggered considerably as he walked.

"Blow these 'ere petticoats !" Bob heard him say, in a drunken, growling tone, as he caught his foot in his drapery, and nearly pitched on his nose ; "theer's no getting along in 'em at all."

Having recovered himself he approached the prison.

"Now then, you Ab'ssinian pigs, stand out er the way an' make room for a—hic—gen'lman, will yer ?" he cried to the guards, as he reached the door.

The "pigs" bowed themselves humbly to the chamberlain, and opened a passage for him.

Bow-legged Bill with some difficulty found the keyhole, thrust in the key and opened the door.

Then from within there burst forth a torrent of indignant voices, amongst which the most distinct were those of the Stinger and Buttons.

"The idea of shutting up human beings like cattle, in a horrid, close den like this ! it's abominable !" cried the former, with vehement emphasis.

"Never mind, Betsy ! I'll let the world know all about it ! I'll expose the villany in my 'Tropical Adventures,' " joined in Buttons.

Bow-legged Bill did not appear to trouble himself about the feelings of the prisoners.

He only grunted to them to " shut up an' not make such a row."

And, having performed his duty of seeing that they were all fast bound for the night, he came out, and, locking the door after him, commenced his return by the way he had come.

Bob Blunt, whose thoughts had not been idle all this time, suddenly conceived an idea, somewhat desperate, perhaps, but one which the urgency of the situation demanded, and which might be successful.

"Follow me, darling," he said to his betrothed, as he retraced his steps through the shrubbery on the track of the Bow-legs.

Bill was staggering along at all sorts of angles, growling at the unevenness of the path and swearing at his petticoats, when suddenly he felt a violent blow between the eyes.

Fire-sparks flashed in them, and he had a sort of dim idea that he had run his head against a tree.

But it was not so.

Bob Blunt had simply knocked him down with one of his very best " right-handers."

And the " chickaleary cove " now lay on his back in a state of collapse, feeling nothing—utterly insensible.

Having accomplished this necessary feat, our hero stripped off the official's robes, very unceremoniously, and arrayed himself in them.

He then fastened the girdle, to which the key was suspended, round his waist, and placed the turban on his head.

And, lastly, pitched the rough headlong into the bushes to recover his senses, or not, as fate might decree.

"Now then, love, for a bold move," he said to Elinor, "and may Heaven give me success !"

"I pray that it may !" was the fervent reply.

Once more they returned through the shrubbery until they reached a spot not far from the prison.

Here Bob paused and said to his betrothed—

"You must not accompany me, darling, but remain here till I join you."

Elinor knew that this was necessary, and offered no objection.

There was one fond embrace—one

earnest, loving kiss, and our hero stepped from the foliage on to the path.

Taking the precaution to pull the turban well down over his face, and holding the pipe in his mouth, he advanced, imitating very accurately the drunken, staggering gait of the Bow-legs.

It must have been a very keen observer who could have detected the difference.

Our hero had made up his mind how to act, and he went forward without hesitation.

The guards saw him coming, but evinced no surprise that the white minister should return.

They simply fell back as they had done before, bowing to the ground as he passed them.

Bob, reeling and swaying to and fro, approached the door and inserted the key in the keyhole.

Then, turning round, he exclaimed in Bow-legged Bill's drunken tone and manner—

"Now then—hic—pigs! put down yer spears an'—hic—go to bed."

The effect of this injunction was increased by a peremptory wave of his hand.

The guard understood him, and, not at all sorry to be released from duty, laid down their weapons and departed.

The instant they were out of sight Bob Blunt turned the key in the lock, opened the door and entered.

CHAPTER XLVII.

OUR HERO RELEASES HIS FRIENDS.

THE moonlight peered dimly through some narrow chinks in the upper portion of the walls.

But it was sufficient to show that the prisoners were bound with ropes to the upright beams that supported the roof.

Some had fallen asleep.

The Stinger unclosed her eyes at the opening of the door.

"I think it's like your impudence, you vulgar bow-legged brute, to intrude at this unseasonable hour!" she exclaimed, sharply, not recognising the visitor.

Bob took off his turban, and she knew him at once.

"What! Mr. Blunt! is it really you?" she cried, in a tone of joyful surprise.

"Yes; it's myself, Miss Stinger," returned our hero; "but don't make a noise."

But his voice had already aroused Buttons and Stumps, and quickly Ironfist, and the doctor, and the rest awoke.

"It's the captain!" passed quickly from mouth to mouth.

"'Ooray!" exclaimed Buttons, in an ecstasy, under his breath; "we're all right now."

In a few minutes they had all recovered the free use of their limbs.

They then crowded round and grasped their leader's hands with affectionate warmth, inquiring how he had effected his deliverance.

But he checked them at once.

"Every second now is precious," he said. "All depends upon our being able to get outside the palace walls."

"If we only had our weapons," exclaimed Ironfist, regretfully.

"There are spears outside," said Bob; "you must make use of them for want of better."

In an instant all had armed themselves except the Stinger, who had her umbrella.

All being ready, Bob Blunt led them out.

His first act was to go for Elinor, whom he found anxiously waiting for him.

"Is all well?" she asked, eagerly, as he rejoined her.

"Yes, love, thus far," he answered, cheeringly, "and I trust fortune will continue to favour us."

But this seemed doubtful, for at that moment a confused sound of voices was heard in another part of the garden.

"Our escape is discovered," said our hero. "But," he added, with his usual determination, "let the worst come, we must hold together and fight our way through it!"

"Bravo, captain!" cried Ironfist, enthusiastically; "we shan't flinch."

"I'm sure of that," returned Bob.

The shouts were now louder.

Lights were seen flashing hither and thither between the trees.

Our hero led his followers into the shrubbery with the intention of making for the outer wall; but, it being night, and he ignorant of the garden paths, the progress they made was uncertain.

But our hero quickly settled this difficulty in his usual prompt manner.

He led Elinor, Nahita, and Miss Stinger to the shrubbery, bidding them remain there until he came for them.

Then, with the wild yells resounding in their ears, and the flashing torches dancing before their eyes, they once more sallied forward.

The garden was of large extent; and its paths, being constructed to secure privacy, were deceptive, and, after progressing some time—as they supposed—in the direction of the walls, the explorers emerged suddenly almost close to the large prison.

At the same moment a bright light blazed up, and they found themselves opposed by a body of fifty armed blacks, with Richard Howard at their head.

"Upon them! seize them!" shouted Howard. "You shall answer for every one that escapes with your own lives!"

Bob Blunt had just time to lead his party under the prison walls, which protected them in the rear.

And then, with a fierce, savage yell, the Abyssinian soldiers rushed forward to the attack.

A number of javelins came whizzing from their hands, burying their points—

not in the bodies of the Englishmen—but only in the prison walls.

Our hero and his comrades had, at the moment of the discharge, suddenly opened their ranks and wheeled round under the shadow of the side walls.

Their adversaries, yelling and shouting in a frenzied manner as they advanced, did not perceive this till they found themselves attacked in the rear.

Then the fight began in earnest.

It was a hand-to-hand fight, in which fists were more useful than weapons.

Bob Blunt, Ironfist and Stumps led the van, and being all splendid boxers, did tremendous execution.

The Abyssinian guards were completely staggered by the force and rapidity of their blows, which they could neither parry nor return.

Longsight, Buttons and Dr. Knowall, assisted by Jingo Johnson and General Orlando, did good service with their spears.

Nahita, at the sight of our hero's peril, rushed from her concealment, and fought like an Amazon by his side.

The Abyssinians were getting much more from the white prisoners than they had bargained for.

Many had fallen, and those who remained wavered, and struck only random and unavailing blows.

It was evident that they had had enough of it, and, after a few more faint, feeble efforts, they turned and fled.

A loud cheer from our hero and his friends announced their victory.

Richard Howard, chagrined and furious at the unexpected turn events had taken, found it necessary to look after his own safety.

This he did by plunging into the shrubbery; but he was not quick enough to escape the quick eye of Bob Blunt, who sprang in after him, with Stinger and Ironfist at his heels.

In a few moments the Dejaj Howard was dragged forth from his covert, ghastly pale and abject, and looking considerably more contemptible than princely.

Bow-legged Bill had recovered from his knock-down blow, and, hearing an un usual tumult, now came staggering to the spot to see what was the matter.

He was seized the instant he appeared, and master and man were pinioned together ignominiously, arm to arm.

"Now, villain!" cried Bob Blunt to his cousin; "after your base conduct to me and mine, what treatment ought you to expect at my hands?"

Richard Howard made no reply; but, if his thoughts could have been translated into words, they would have said—

"Death without mercy."

"You have outraged the laws," went on Bob Blunt, sternly; "the guilt of blood is on your soul, and I should be justified in taking the life you have forfeited."

Richard Howard shuddered, as the prospect of a halter flashed before him.

Bow-legged Bill gave vent to his feelings in a loud hiccup, and our hero, continuing, said—

"But I am not a judge, and, therefore, I shall content myself with making you and your accomplice my prisoners, and carrying you with me until I can hand you both over to the strong hand of the law, to be dealt with as you deserve."

Richard Howard still maintained a dogged, sullen silence.

He was to be spared for the present, and might find an opportunity to escape, he thought.

It was our hero's wish to get free from the palace-grounds as rapidly as possible, and he said to his cousin, in an imperative tone—

"You will conduct us at once to the gate in the rear of the palace."

"Anything else?" asked Richard Howard sulkily.

"Yes; you will then send an order that our weapons shall be brought to us."

Richard's moody face grew darker still at this, but he dared not refuse, and, being ordered to go forward, and stimulated by a smart whack on the back—which the Stinger gave him with her gingham, in mistake for Bow-legged Bill—he advanced, dragging his drunken prime minister along with him.

Bob Blunt, having given a few directions to Stumps and ascertained the direction in which the gate lay, went for Elinor.

He reached the spot where he had left her, but she was not there.

He called her by name, but there was no answer.

"Good Heaven!" he murmured to himself; "what can have happened to her? Can that villain have——"

He broke off suddenly at the horrible suspicion that crossed him, and a cold sweat bedewed his limbs.

After a moment he recovered himself.

"I must search for her!" he said, as he hurried forward through the shrubbery.

He had not gone far when he heard a footstep approaching.

"Is that you, love?" he asked.

"Yes, Robert," was the cheering answer.

The next moment they met, and his protecting arm once more encircled his betrothed.

"I feared you were lost, darling," he said to her. "Why did you leave the spot at which I left you?"

"Because I saw Richard Howard approaching, and I feared the worst from his malice."

"You did quite right to avoid him," said Bob, approvingly; "but I think I have put a check upon his career this time."

"Have you caught him?" asked Elinor.

"Yes; he is my prisoner at this moment, and I intend to keep him so if possible. And now, love, let us rejoin our friends."

Our hero, leading his betrothed, was about to step once more into the path, when a sudden and terrible sound burst upon the silent night, and made him pause.

It was like the roar of a thousand wolves, and yet hardly that, for there was something human in it.

"What can that be?" he exclaimed, as the yell died away.

"Is it some new foe?" asked Elinor, apprehensively, clinging closer to the arm that guarded her.

"I know not, love; but it scarcely appears to me as the voices of friends."

Hardly had he uttered the words than

again the wild fierce yell burst forth with increased intensity, and a light almost meteor-like in its brilliancy lit up the surrounding scene.

"Something more than common must have taken place," murmured Bob, in a perplexed tone.

He was right.

The palace was completely surrounded by the DAHOMEY SLAVERS.

CHAPTER XLVIII.

BURNING OF THE PALACE.

OUR hero hesitated what course to take.

Had he been alone he would at once have hastened to assure himself as to what had occurred, but his anxiety on account of the fair girl whose only protector he was, chained him to the spot.

But he was not long left in ignorance, for, as the bright glare spread itself over the garden, the hurried tread of many feet became audible, mingled with the hoarse murmur of voices; and presently a tumultuous crowd of wild savage-looking forms came hurrying forward.

All were armed with short, stout scimitars, and most of them carried torches of a peculiar resinous wood, which burnt with a bright flare and emitted a potent odour.

Whooping and yelling like fiends, the dark stream poured in.

Bob Blunt stood in his place of concealment, gazing at the strange scene like one in a dream, wondering who those dark strangers might be and what brought them there.

It was not until he beheld his comrades, in company with Richard Howard and Bow-legged Bill, marched along between a file of dark savages, armed with glittering, formidable weapons, that the truth flashed upon him.

But when he observed that the arms of all were pinioned with iron links, and that the negro, Rope's End—his face full of malignant glee—walked at their side, he knew the worst.

They were prisoners in the power of a relentless foe.

Having reached the prison they stopped, and many voices shouted—

"Where is Kassa Kobo? Where is our captain?"

And many dark, fierce eyes peered anxiously along the garden, evidently in search of their leader.

But he did not appear.

Rope's End, observing this, strode forward.

He had already adopted the dress of his new colleagues, and his gigantic limbs glittered with metal rings.

"Neber mind 'bout de capt'n!" he exclaimed, in an arrogant, imperious tone; "yar mind me!"

His enormous bulk and bombastic manner had their effect upon his uncouth hearers; but still some cried, discontentedly—

"Where is Kassa Kobo?"

"Kassa Kobo come presently?" growled Rope's End, irritably.

This silenced the speakers.

"You know me an' Kassa frien's an' broders," continued Rope's End; "you know we make compact togeder, an' he say to me, when me away you take my place. He away now, an' me take him place."

This seemed sufficiently comprehensive to the listeners, who shouted their assent; and the boatswain went on—

"All you got to do's to 'bey my orders, den we git on like notink. If any ob you

"UP IN THE AIR FLEW ROPE'S END."

say 'no' to dat, me knock him brains out."

As he uttered this threat he clenched his sledge-hammer fist and rolled his eyes like two enormous saucers at the throng before him.

The semi-brutal beings felt that it would be tempting fate to provoke one so formidable, and yielded passively under superior force.

Rope's End saw that he had got the mastery, and he chuckled over his success ; and then, turning to the English party, he said—

" Now den, you white people, yar better mind what yar 'bout. Me great pirate chief now, an' if yar not bery civil me chop you up to mince-meat."

To this threatening speech the party addressed returned only scornful silence.

Suddenly he paused, as though he missed some one, and presently he said—

" Whar de brave Massa Blunt an' de white gal ?"

No one answered.

But our hero heard the question asked with a strange thrill at his heart.

" Whar de white captain an' de lady ?" repeated Rope's End, fiercely.

" They're not far off," replied Richard Howard. " Concealed somewhere in this garden."

" That is false," cried Ironfist, emphatically, " our captain and his fair betrothed are beyond your power ! The Great White Spirit has removed them from your power."

Rope's End muttered an oath and asked no further questions, but turning to some of his men, he said to them—

" Now den, you come 'long wid me."

About fifty accompanied him to the palace, and a work of spoliation then commenced in earnest.

Everything was seized and carried out, till the building was completely sacked, after which Rope's End ordered it to be fired in several places.

The royal residence in a few minutes was wrapped in flames, and during all this time Kassa Kobo remained mysteriously absent.

The plunder, being packed up, was placed on the backs of mules, and, the destruction having been completely accomplished, the deputy-captain gave the order to his wild followers to march.

Our hero, from his post, beheld them and their prisoners depart, the red glare of the burning palace lighting up the sky with an angry crimson glow.

It was with feelings amounting to agony that Bob saw his comrades disappear in the midst of their fierce captors.

Could he have rescued them by sacrificing his own life he would willingly have done so ; but this was impossible.

And to have shown himself would have been only to ensure his own capture and that of his betrothed, without in the least benefiting his companions, whereas, being free, he might still be able to accomplish their deliverance.

And so he remained shrouded in the dense shrubbery, listening to the hoarse shouts and the tramp of feet till they died away in the distance, and all was once more calm and still as death itself.

Then, in the overpowering sense of loneliness that came over him, he buried his face in his hands and shed bitter tears for the fate of his brave comrades.

CHAPTER XLIX.

A MYSTERY EXPLAINED.

BUT Bob Blunt was not long allowed to remain in this desponding state.

The soft pressure of Elinor's hand upon his arm and her gentle voice aroused him.

" Don't droop, dear Robert," she said, " our position might be worse."

He looked up at once.

"You are right, love!" he replied, as he dashed away his tears; "we are at liberty—still spared to each other—that surely is something to be grateful for."

"Oh, yes! and for our unfortunate friends we must hope for the best."

"I will try to, Nell; and, not only that, I will endeavour, Heaven helping me, to rescue them yet."

As our hero spoke thus hopefully the cloud vanished from his face and he smiled.

"My principal difficulty is your own dear self," he continued, in a tone of fond anxiety, to his betrothed.

"Oh, dear! and I was just flattering myself that I was your principal consolation," she returned, with prettily assumed chagrin in her looks.

"And so you are, darling," replied Bob, warmly; "but you know what I mean. Of course I must not imperil you."

"I have no fear, dear, while you are by my side," was Elinor's flattering response.

Our hero pressed the arm he held and remained silent.

"I was just thinking——" he exclaimed, suddenly, after a moment.

"What dear?"

"Whether I might venture to leave you for a time under the care of Prince Djalma?"

"Oh, no! no!" cried Elinor determinedly. "I would a thousand times sooner remain with you."

Bob Blunt glanced down in admiration at the fair face upturned to his.

"You shall remain then," he replied, "and we will share all dangers together."

"That is all I wish."

"But, at least, we might procure the prince's aid in rescuing our comrades," suggested Bob.

"Ah, yes, we might do that certainly; but then while we are travelling back to his territory we may lose altogether the route our friends are pursuing."

"We shall find it hard though, if not impossible, to travel through this country without horses or provisions," said Bob, after a moment.

"Might we not possibly find some stores in the palace?" said Elinor, suggestively, to her betrothed.

"A capital idea, love!" he exclaimed, cheerfully; "let us see."

Together they made their way to the spot where the palace had stood; but, alas! nothing now remained of the royal abode but charred and blackened beams and smoking ashes.

"Ruthless miscreants!" cried Bob, indignantly, "they might have been content with plunder."

But still he did not give up the hope of finding something that might assist them on their journey.

Passing by the heated ruins he and his fair companion continued their explorations.

Before long they came upon some detached buildings which the pirates had not noticed.

In these were found the very necessaries our hero required.

One of these buildings was a stable, containing several horses in excellent condition.

Another was a storehouse, containing provisions; and the third led, by steps, to the royal cellars under ground.

Our hero's heart bounded with grateful joy at these discoveries.

But that which afforded him the greatest delight was the discovery of the firearms and ammunition which had been taken from himself and his comrades.

These were piled together in a corner of the stable and covered with dried grass.

He called Elinor to look at them, and, although they appeared to her as somewhat ominous of what they might have to encounter, she could but acknowledge they were invaluable assistants.

"I must teach you to use both rifle and revolver," said Bob to her.

"I am willing to learn," was her brave reply.

Our hero determined to take three horses, the third being to carry such baggage as they must else have left behind.

Elinor Cleveland was an excellent horsewoman, and Bob, having made one of the saddles suitable for a lady, assisted his betrothed to mount; then, springing on the back of his own steed and leading the third by a halter attached to its head, they took their way towards the gates in the rear of the garden.

Not a soul interrupted them.

Our hero on emerging into the open space, looked cautiously on every side, but saw nothing save the plain, bounded by the dark wood before him.

Neither did any sound reach him save the gentle rustling of the night wind amongst the distant branches.

"Our start is propitious, darling," he said.

"Pray Heaven our journey may be prosperous and our efforts successful!" replied Elinor, fervently.

"Amen to that!" was our hero's solemn reply.

And then they went forward.

Ere long they had entered the forest and were soon shut in its pathless confines.

Ever and anon was heard the distant roar of some wild beast, but they saw none, though Bob held his rifle in his hand, as they rode, to be ready for any sudden emergency.

They had travelled for several hours when, Elinor feeling fatigued, he proposed halting until daybreak.

His companion gladly assented.

Quickly Bob lifted her from her saddle, and, having unpacked some provisions and tethered the horses' legs to prevent them straying away, they sat down on the thick soft grass.

So far as they could, under the circumstances in which they were placed, they made a comfortable meal.

That over, Bob lit a cigar from the lantern which he had brought with him, and, leaning his back against the massive trunk of the tree under which they sat, with his arm encircling his beloved, whose fair head rested on his breast, he fell into deep thought.

Suddenly he was startled by a faint, muffled groan.

The sound at once dispelled his reverie and brought him back from dreamland into the regions of stern reality.

"Was it fancy?" he asked, as he listened. "No."

Again the groan was repeated, and it came evidently from some human being in dire extremity.

Elinor had fallen asleep and had not heard it.

Bob gently aroused her.

"Don't be alarmed, love," he said, quietly, "but I fancy there is some one needs our help."

This was quite sufficient to banish the drowsiness from her eyes.

"Where?" she asked.

"I know not yet," Bob replied; "but I heard a groan and——"

"Hark!" exclaimed Elinor, as the sound of pain was repeated; "let us see what it is."

In a moment they had risen to their feet and were searching by the light of the lantern.

They had not far to go, for within a few yards of the spot where they had been seated they espied the body of a man black as ebony, wearing the short white skirt and the skin mantle of the Dahomey pirates, with metal rings encircling his arms and ankles and a coronet of the same round his forehead.

His eyes were closed and he was apparently sinking.

Our hero, kneeling down, proceeded to examine into the cause of his distress.

It soon revealed itself, for the mantle he wore was dyed with blood, and a gaping wound revealed itself under the right shoulder, from which the thick drops oozed slowly.

"He has been evidently wounded," said Bob, pityingly, "and from the position of the wound I am inclined to think it has been dealt by the hand of treachery."

"Likely enough," assented Elinor; "there seems nothing else in these wild regions. Poor fellow, we must do what we can for him."

As she spoke she rose, and, going to one of the saddle bags, brought forth a bottle of rum and a cup.

Bob forced a little of the spirit between the lips of the sufferer, and the effect was quickly perceptible.

He breathed heavily and opened his eyes.

"So far so good," said our hero, hopefully. "Now then, to stop the hemorrhage if possible."

This was not so easy, since he had neither lint nor plaister.

What was to be done?

Suddenly his eyes fell upon the ground, which was thickly strewn with leaves.

"I have it!" he thought.

And at once he began to collect them.

As he picked them up he could feel that they were of a glutinous, gummy nature, and this was an additional advantage.

He had soon gathered enough to make a compress or pad.

This he placed upon the wound, after carefully closing its edges, and bound his handkerchief tightly round it.

He then gave the stranger, who seemed to have recovered consciousness, a second drink of rum.

He was soon sufficiently revived to be able to speak.

The first words he uttered were English words, spoken in a grateful tone—

"Thank you! Kassa Kobo thanks you."

The name struck Bob Blunt as familiar.

"Kassa Kobo!" he murmured to himself; "where have I heard that?"

"In the palace garden," said Elinor.

Our hero then remembered.

It was the name by which the Dahomey pirates had called their missing captain.

"You have been badly wounded."

"Yes," was the curt reply.

"By the hand of an assassin it seems."

Kassa made no answer for a moment, but the contraction of his brows proved that the thought was as painful as the wound itself.

At length he said—

"Yes, by the hand of an assassin."

"Do you know his name?"

"I do, the treacherous dog!"

"Will you tell it me?"

"Karfa!"

"Karfa!" echoed our hero, eagerly; "has he not another name besides that?"

"He has—Rope's End!"

All was now clear enough.

The villainous boatswain had stabbed his colleague on the march in order to obtain the sole command.

"I know the scoundrel," said Bob. "You had better sleep now."

The pirate-captain inclined his head and closed his eyes, and soon fell into a doze.

Our hero and Elinor, weary with the day's excitement, followed his example.

CHAPTER L.

A TERRIBLE PROSPECT.

THE next day it was evident enough that the wounded man was not in a fitting state to be removed, and Bob Blunt felt it his duty to remain with him.

It was a sore trial to his patience to be thus delayed, but his generous nature could not endure the thought of leaving even a pirate to perish helplessly in that lonely region.

So he remained tending him, contenting himself with occasionally taking flying rambles through the woods in the hope of coming upon the track of his countrymen; but these hopes were doomed to disappointment.

But in the course of a week a marked change for the better took place in Kassa.

His wound was healing, and he was strong enough to bestride a horse.

But their progess was necessarily slow, and it was some days before they reached the confines of the forest.

At last, however, they emerged on to the open plain.

An hour had scarcely elapsed when, as they were riding very leisurely across the sandy waste, a cloud of dust appeared in the distance.

At first Bob thought it was the pirate-horde returning but, as the cloud came rolling on nearer and nearer towards them it proved to be an Arab tribe.

It might have proved a fatal meeting to our hero and his betrothed had they been alone, but fortunately Kassa was well known to these wandering sons of the desert, and on this account they were treated with kindness and respect.

The Arabs were going to encamp for a time, waiting for some of their tribe to join them, and it struck our hero, who was anxious to push on, that it would be as well to leave Kassa to their care till his wound should be sufficiently healed to enable him to follow.

The pirate-captain was perfectly satisfied with this arrangement, although sorry to part company.

Bold and lawless as his life was, he was not deficient in gratitude.

The unvarying kindness and attention he had received from his preservers had touched his heart, and he took leave of his English friends with many grateful acknowledgments and an oath, sworn upon a relic he carried round his neck, that he would repay the debt he owed them if ever he had the opportunity.

And so they separated.

Once more Bob and his betrothed were pursuing their weary journey alone.

Day after day passed, and still they came upon no traces of those they wished so earnestly to overtake.

At length they reached the mountains over which they must pass, and all this time their provisions were becoming less and less.

At length their store was entirely exhausted.

Gaunt famine stared them in the face, and they were hemmed in on every side by giant rocks, every echo of which seemed to speak of death in its most painful shape.

One of the horses had died long since, and the other two, famine stricken, wandered away in the night in search of pasture, and were seen no more.

The travellers had eaten nothing for three days, and it was on the morning of the fourth day that they sat looking mournfully at each other, each seeming to know too well the thoughts they shrunk from putting into words.

At length Elinor said, despairingly—

"Oh, dear Robert! this cannot last much longer. I feel so terribly weak. There is no hope!—none!"

"Nay, love," returned Bob, gently, trying to cheer her, "there is hope so long as life lasts."

"It will not last long," was her desponding answer. "Hark! what voices are those?" she asked, suddenly.

"I hear nothing," answered her lover.

"I do! sweet voices singing."

Her manner, as she spoke, was strange, and her eyes dreaming and wandering in their gaze.

"Merciful Heaven! her brain is turning!" murmured our hero in a voice of anguish.

Elinor only answered by a vacant laugh far more terrible than tears would have been.

Bob Blunt looked up and around in despair.

"The end has come at last," he thought; "it is impossible to avert it."

As he uttered these words a hat fell at his feet.

He looked at it without motion, and merely said in a listless tone—

"It must have dropped from the clouds."

He then took it up, and turned it over in his hands.

It was a straw hat, very broad in the brim—one which he fancied he had seen before.

"But where?—where?" he asked himself.

At that moment, as if in answer to his thought, a shrill "whoo-oop" rang in his ears.

"I know now," he cried, as he sprang to his feet; "that hat belongs to Mat Mangles."

Memory had returned, and he shouted wildly—

"Where are you? Speak! speak!"

"Here I am, and I'll trouble you for my tile," responded the voice.

And at the same moment the form of the professor appeared scrambling down a rocky path with perilous haste.

He recognised our hero at once, as he reached the end of the declivity.

"Ah, Mr. Sharp, is it you?" he exclaimed as he took his hat.

"No," returned Bob, "it's Mr. Blunt—Blunt enough now I'm afraid."

"Well, Sharp or Blunt, I'm glad to see you, my dear sir," returned Mat heartily, as he shook him by the hand.

"And what are you doing here?" asked Bob, eagerly.

"Oh, same old game—exploring," was the cheerful answer.

"And your friends, where are they?"

"Not far off. I'll give them a call."

And raising his voice, he uttered a prolonged shriek that rang through the rocks, awaking a thousand echoes.

The cry was answered by voices at no great distance, and presently a body of travellers appeared descending the narrow path.

In a few moments Bob Blunt was surrounded by the party of scientific gentlemen who had rendered him and his followers such signal service a few months before.

It was a fortunate meeting for our hero and his fair companion—their lives were saved.

The professors had a good stock of provisions which quickly recruited their strength, and it was arranged that they should all travel together to the coast.

CHAPTER LI.

ON BOARD THE CLIPPER ONCE MORE.

SOME weeks have passed.

The clipper has once more stood out to sea, and is careering gallantly on her way.

Bob Blunt stands on her deck—old Tom is at the helm, and Elinor is at our hero's side, whilst his new friends surround him; but his old colleagues whom he had seen carried away prisoners—where were they?

During the march to the coast he had not overtaken them, or come upon any sign to indicate the route they had travelled.

Our hero felt naturally much depressed.

"You seem dull, dear," said Elinor to him, as she marked the sadness in his features.

"I am, love," he replied, with a sigh; "I am thinking of our brave companions."

"Ah!" returned his betrothed mournfully echoing his sigh, "what can have become of them?"

"I almost shudder to put that question even to myself," continued Bob.

"Did you not say they had been seized by a gang of Dahomey pirates?" joined in Doctor Harrowby.

"Yes."

"If you were asked to give an opinion, where should you say your comrades were at this moment?" asked Doctor Harrowby.

"Jericho, no doubt!" cried Mat Mangles, whose head at that moment popped up from the hatchway; "I've a strong notion they've gone to Jericho."

"I haven't," replied Bob, curtly.

"Where, then, Mr. Sharp—I mean Blunt?"

"My impression is that they reached the coast before us and are now at sea in the slaver's vessel, on the way to Dahomey."

"Well, all the better if they are," said Mat cheerily; "we may come across them, don't you see?"

"I wish I did."

"So do I," cried the crack-brained professor; "nothing in the world I should like better than a sea-fight. Whoo-oop! I would give the rascally pirates a broadside of pickled beetroot."

The tone and manner of the speaker were so ludicrous that every one laughed, but their transient mirth was checked by the voice of the man on the look-out.

"Ship ahead!" he cried.

In an instant the telescopes were brought forth, and all eyes were intently scanning the distance, where a small dark object was hardly visible between them and the horizon.

"It is a vessel, no doubt," said our hero, after a careful examination.

"Pirates, do you think?" asked Professor Jefferson, anxiously.

"Bogies!" exclaimed Mat, confidently; "black bogies! I'll be after 'em presently."

The craft was too far off to be able to pronounce then what she was; but the very sight of a vessel that might possibly contain his comrades sent the blood coursing like lightning through the veins of Bob Blunt.

"Hoist every inch of canvas we can carry!" he cried, excitedly.

The order was at once obeyed, and the clipper flew over the waves like a sea-gull.

Night fell whilst they were yet far distant, but, when the morning broke, they were near enough to be able to remark the peculiarities of the vessel they pursued.

She was a dark-hulled, heavy, lubberly-looking hulk; and the cut of her sails and the make of her masts had a very suspicious appearance.

Our hero stood looking at her through his glass for a time, and at length he burst out—

"I'll stake my life that that is the pirate vessel!"

"That contains our friends?" asked Elinor.

"Yes!" and then he shouted, "Hoist more sail! we must overtake her at any risk."

The captain's confident assertion inoculated all on board.

Mat Mangles was particularly excited, rushing hither and thither collecting arms, and mopping out the cannons with an energy worthy of a man-o'-war's man.

The day wore on, and every moment it was evident they were gaining on the strange vessel.

At length they were near enough to take notes of her appearance.

They could see distinctly dark forms, wearing short white shirts, and rings on their arms, moving to and fro on the deck.

Our hero was certain now that he was not mistaken.

And presently he cried aloud—

"Ha! see! here's that black scoundrel, Rope's End!"

There were but few on board besides Bob Blunt and his betrothed who knew the boatswain.

But there he was distinctly enough, watching the clipper with evident interest.

The sight of him inspired Bob with intense bitterness and loathing, and he shouted—

"Let the guns be loaded!"

As they were short of hands on board, he himself assisted in performing this operation.

As soon as this was done, he fired one loaded with powder only, as a signal to the pirate to heave-to; but no notice was taken of the summons.

Rope's End had a pretty correct notion of the power of English artillery, and he was equally well informed as to the value of the prizes he had captured; and, not being willing to disgorge them, he made every effort to keep as far ahead of the clipper as possible.

But it was very evident the latter was gaining upon him.

The pirate-vessel was a large, unwieldy craft, old and leaky, and could make but little way, whilst the clipper went along like a racehorse.

It was with a wild feeling of exultation that our hero found himself, at the close of the day, drawing nearer and nearer to the object of his pursuit.

At length the vessels were within speaking distance of each other.

Rope's End, who had assumed the

leadership of the pirates, stood moodily watching the clipper.

Bob Blunt shouted to him—

"You have English prisoners on board your vessel?"

To which Rope's End growled politely—

"It big lie! me habn't got no pris'-ners."

"Liar, in your teeth! scoundrel!" exclaimed our hero, fiercely. "I saw my friends carried off under my very eyes, and I am certain they are on board your vessel."

"Know notink about dem," replied Rope's End, shaking his head vacantly; "some un else got 'em—not me."

But, as if in direct contradiction to his barefaced assertion, just at that moment, from a porthole between decks, their protruded an article which Bob Blunt recognised at once.

It was the handle of the Stinger's umbrella.

How the worthy lady contrived, under the most distressful circumstances, to retain possession of her gingham, was a mystery.

But there it was plain enough, and our hero took it—as it actually was—for a signal of distress.

His comrades were battened down in the stifling depths of the pirate-vessel.

Bob Blunt, with his blood boiling, turned his flashing eyes upon the villanous face of the boatswain.

"You infernal wretch!" he cried, "if you don't instantly liberate my comrades, I'll blow you and your black-hole of a craft to atoms."

"Yah, yah! you know better dan dat!" grinned Rope's End, not at all moved by the threat.

"I will, I swear!" repeated Bob intensely irritated.

"You forgit; if you blow me up you blow up yar frien's same time."

Our hero in his excitement, had forgotten this, and now he could but acknowledge to himself that his guns were silenced.

He could not fire upon his foes, for fear of destroying his friends.

The giant boatswain could guess what was passing in his mind, and he chuckled over the trap in which his pursuer was caught.

Bob Blunt ran his eyes wistfully over the deck of the pirate-ship, crowded as it was with dark, savage-looking forms.

And then he looked at his own small crew, so reduced as to be scarcely sufficient to work the vessel.

The idea of attempting to board the pirate against such formidable odds seemed madness, and yet to give up the hope of saving his colleagues seemed worse than death itself.

As he was thus reflecting, Doctor Harrowby, one of Mat Mangles' friends, advanced to him, and said boldly—

"My dear Mr. Blunt, I wish you to understand that you may rely upon the assistance of myself and party in any plan you think proper to adopt for the rescue of your friends."

Bob thanked him heartily, and replied—

"There is but one way."

"What is that?" asked the doctor.

"A hand-to-hand struggle with these desperadoes."

"Would there be a chance of succeeding?"

"Barely, on account of the superiority of their number," said our hero, "yet I feel strongly inclined to risk it."

"We'll stand by you!" exclaimed the scientific gentlemen, warmly.

"Of course," joined in Mat Mangles; "we'll physic the black rascals! Ah, whoo-oop!"

With a yell, the frantic professor rushed away.

The next moment his voice was heard again, shouting—

"Now then; one—two, and pop goes the weasel."

Then followed a flash of light, and something more than a pop.

A tremendous boom, that shook the clipper to her centre.

"Good Heavens! he has discharged one of the cannons," exclaimed Bob Blunt as he rushed aft.

This was perfectly true, and our hero was only just in time to prevent Mat Mangles firing the second.

"Hold, hold!" he exclaimed, as he caught his arm.

"I won't be held!" shouted Mat, excitedly, as he whirled the lighted port-fire over his head; "death to the pirates!"

"Madman, you forget that was is death to them is also death to our friends."

"Ah, yes, so it is; I forgot that," admitted Mat, calming down; "it might knock Belinda Jane's eye out, so it might."

So, out of consideration for his dearly-beloved, Mat Mangles refrained from firing the second gun, otherwise he might have done more damage than could easily be repaired.

Bob Blunt turned once more towards the pirate-vessel.

The ball from the cannon had swept her deck, and, from its crowded state, done fearful execution.

Rope's End was untouched, but all around him lay bodies crushed and mangled by the terrible missile.

"Now's the time," cried Bob Blunt, determined to take advantage of the confusion; "lower the boats!"

But even as the order was given the waning daylight departed and a sudden darkness came upon the face of the water.

"Too late!" said one.

"No!" exclaimed our hero. "It is never too late to rescue those who are in distress. Lower away there, and be sharp about it!"

The boats were lowered, and sped away over the water.

"We must rescue our friends, no matter what are the odds against us," said Bob Blunt, the traveller.

CHAPTER LII.

OUR HERO'S DESPERATE PLAN.

IN the close, stifling space where Bob's friends were confined on board the pirate-vessel intense excitement prevailed.

In the midst of their despair they had, from their gloomy prison, caught the sound of a friendly voice.

"I'm sure it was the captain's," cried the Stinger, vehemently.

"So am I," joined in Buttons; "the clipper's overtook us, an' you'll see the guv'nor 'll soon have us out er this 'orrid 'ole. As soon as he caught sight on it, he let fly one of 'is cannons. Didn't you 'ear?"

"I fancied I heard something," responded the doctor, mildly.

"There is no doubt about the discharge of the cannon," joined in Ironfist; "but I hardly think the captain would have fired had he known we were here."

"Why not?"

"What do you think would be the consequence if a cannon-ball was to come crashing in amongst us through the side of this old hulk?"

"The guv'nor wouldn't be sich a fool as to fire low," Buttons replied, indignantly; "'e'd let 'em have it amongst the masts an' riggin'. The capt'n never'll let us come to grief if he knows it."

"Never," joined in Stumps, speaking for the first time.

"But don't you see it has grown pitch dark?" growled Ironfist.

"Wot of that?" returned Buttons.

"Why, that the captain can't see the foe in the dark."

"Well, if 'e can't see in the dark, the foe can't see 'im. I think that's a chalk to me," grinned Buttons, cheerfully.

Stumps echoed his laugh, and the Stinger said, approvingly—

"A very sensible remark, my dear boy; depend upon it, he'll do all that living man can to rescue us."

Hardly had she said the word, when a scraping sound was heard at the porthole.

"Hark!" cried Buttons, as he sprang up and staggered forward, stumbling over his companions; "there's somethink going on at the cabin winder."

"What is it?" asked Stumps, eagerly.

Buttons looked out.

All was darkness, but on placing his hands on the ledge, he felt some iron hooks.

"Grapplin' irons, by jingo!" he exclaimed.

"Then you may be certain there's a boat alongside," cried Stumps.

The dwarf was right.

Our hero had lowered the boats, and rowed under the bows of the vessel, determined to save his comrades at any risk.

It was a desperate resource, but it was the only one.

Life or death!

The next moment a sharp whisper was heard.

"Hist! hist!"

Buttons recognised his master's voice instantly.

"It's the blessed gov'nor 'isself!" he exclaimed, in an ecstasy; "I'm 'ere, capt'n."

"Are you all there?"

"Yes, guv'nor."

"Alive?"

"Yes, an' kick——"

He checked himself, and added—

"No, there's no room for kickin'."

"And Miss Stinger—is she——"

Elizabeth Ann answered for herself—

"She is as well as possible, Mr. Blunt, under existing circumstances."

"Can you get out of the porthole by any means?" he asked.

"No, guv'nor, theer's iron bars across it," explained Buttons, wistfully.

"Well, then, listen. I have brought a cargo of revolvers and ammunition with me in the boat."

"Bravo!"

"Stretch forth your hands."

Buttons did as he was told, and our hero placed in them the weapons.

The bars were wide enough to allow them to pass through.

"They all are loaded and capped," said Bob.

In a few seconds every one of the prisoners had a revolver in his grasp.

"Anything else?" asked Buttons, through the bars.

"Yes, some cutlasses."

"Hand 'em up, please."

"Is that Ironfist, who spoke?" asked our hero, as he passed the cutlasses through the porthole.

"Yes, captain."

"Good; our attack must be made simultaneously."

"How is it to be arranged?"

"Thus; as soon as the other boat from the clipper joins me and all is ready, I will give you a signal."

"What is it to be, captain?"

"A watchword—'Liberty.'"

"And what then?"

"You will then shout, all of you together, as loudly as you can. The uproar will cause some one to descend to know the cause. As soon as the trap is raised for that purpose, shoot whoever appears, and then rush up in a body to the deck."

"Yes, captain; and you?"

"We shall have clambered up the ship's side in the meantime, and will be there to meet you. In the confusion and panic which will ensue, we may hope to overpower the pirate-crew, or at least to be able to regain our own vessel."

These directions having been given, our hero said no more, but remained listening intently for the approach of the boat he was expecting.

The hope of liberty inspired even the weakest among them with enthusiasm.

Every trace of depression vanished, and they determined to fight for their freedom to the last gasp.

Presently the second boat came silently under the side of the pirate-vessel.

It had not arrived too soon, for Rope's End, furious at the discharge which had killed and maimed so many of his crew, had determined to revenge his loss upon his unfortunate prisoners.

"Me sarve out dese English debbils," he growled, savagely; "chop 'em up, ebery one!"

Our hero fortunately heard these words, and at one gave the signal—

"Liberty!"

Then from below there issued a wild burst of discordant sounds.

"What debbil dat 'ar?" demanded the boatswain.

"It de pris'n'rs down below," answered one of the crew.

"Ha, ha! Me soon stop dat," chuckled the giant, with a hideous grin. "Git me rope an' de sword wid the big blade!"

These articles being brought to him, he said to several of the men—

"Now, den, go down an' bring up de white pris'n'rs one by one. Bring 'em to me."

The captives in the meantime were all ready and waiting.

Bob Blunt and his men were also ready.

Their hands on the ropes which they had fastened by grapnels to the shrouds waiting for the moment to mount.

The giant boatswain stood on the deck, grasping his formidable sword and licking his thick lips like a savage tiger thirsting for blood.

Presently there was a sound of chains being removed, followed by the sharp report of two revolvers.

Then burst forth a ringing cry—

"Old England and liberty;"

And then the prisoners poured forth from their dungeon.

By the light of a flickering torch Rope's End caught sight of the white men.

A fierce execration burst from his lips.

"Ha! dey 'scape! de pris'n'rs 'scape! cut 'em down!" he yelled.

A second shout rang in his ears from behind him.

And he very narrowly escaped being cut down by Bob Blunt, who sprang from the ship's side on to the deck at that moment, cutlass in hand, followed by his companions.

Rope's End, who held our hero's prowess in considerable respect, beat a hasty retreat aft, shouting to his crew to annihilate "de English debbils!"

But the pirates, scared by the sudden attack, seemed to have lost their usual ferocity, and hurried hither and thither, their eyes glaring timorously, like so many wild beasts caught in a snare.

A few, however, fought desperately, but were soon overpowered.

Some leapt overboard into the sea.

Their new captain disappeared as mysteriously as their old one had done.

Nothing could be seen of him.

Bob Blunt and his comrades, having cut down all who opposed them, dropped into the boats as quickly as possible.

In half an hour every one of their party was safely on board the clipper.

"We'll give this hulk her quietus to-morrow," said our hero, after he had joyfully welcomed his friends and they him.

But during the night a violent storm arose, and, when the daylight broke, leaden and gloomy, the sea was running mountains high, and the wind blowing a hurricane.

The pirate-ship was not to be seen.

"She must have gone down with all hands!" said Bob.

"Good riddance too!" remarked Buttons.

But Richard Howard and his friend, Bow-legged Bill, who had been forgotten in the confusion of the night-attack— where were they?

Had they gone down like the rest into the watery depths?

If so the storm had proved a friend indeed.

PART III.—DAHOMEY.

CHAPTER I.

OUR HERO RECEIVES A WARNING.

AFTER another lapse of time we find our hero and his companions in the kingdom of Dahomey.

They had not landed there from choice, but a succession of storms had so damaged the clipper that they had no resource but to run her ashore.

Their botanical friends had parted from them for a time, for the purpose of prosecuting their scientific researches in the interior; and Bob Blunt and his party had now established themselves in a forest some miles distant from the city.

It was a lovely tropical morning as our hero reclined upon the verdant carpet of grass with Elinor Cleveland at his side, and his companions around him.

They had just finished their morning meal, and most of them were indulging in their after breakfast cigar.

"What say you, friends, to a ramble through the forest, with our guns?" said Bob as he finished his weed.

The proposal was eagerly seconded by Stumps.

"I'm quite willing, captain," he said.

"And I," joined in Ironfist.

There was not a dissenting voice, and in a short time they were all ready to start, with their rifles slung over their shoulders.

Elinor Cleveland was not to accompany the expedition, but to remain in the encampment with the Stinger, under the care of Jingo Johnson and Buttons.

"Wish us success, love," said our hero to his betrothed before they started.

Elinor looked at him anxiously.

"I wish you success," she replied with a forced smile, "but I am somewhat apprehensive."

"Of what?"

"I don't know; nothing particular.

I suppose I am not in very good spirits this morning."

"Oh! there's nothing to fear, darling," said Bob, cheerily; "remember we're old hunters."

"Of course they is," joined in Buttons, sarcastically, feeling awfully annoyed at having to stay behind. "What's a few elephants or a dozen lions to old 'unters?—flea-bites!"

"Are you likely to meet any of these fierce animals?" asked Elinor, in an anxious tone.

"No love," answered our hero, assuringly; "I think our sport this morning will be confined to——"

He was not allowed to finish his speech, for at that moment a loud fierce bark rose on the air and then died away into a deep roll, like distant thunder.

"Goodness gracious! what's that?" exclaimed the Stinger, after a moment.

"It was not the cry of an elephant," said Dr. Knowall.

"P'r'aps it was the sneeze of a rhinoc'res," sneered Buttons, with a facetious grin at his own joke.

"Or the braying of a young donkey," said our hero, as he boxed his ears to teach him better manners.

Buttons rubbed the side of his cheek and looked rather surprised.

And Jingo Johnson said—

"De roar ob de wild man ob de woods, dat's what it am."

"Ah! you mean——"

"De gorilla!"

"Ah, we've seen some of those animals before," said our hero. "Well, gentlemen, shall we have another interview with the 'monarch of the woods,' as some people call the gorilla?"

"Agreed!" said everyone.

A few moments after the hunters were making their way through the forest.

For some time they went on, but without encountering anything in the shape of a gorilla.

"I'm afraid we shall be doomed to disappointment after all," said our hero.

"We won't give up yet, captain," replied Stumps and Ironfist.

"Oh no," returned Bob; "these gigantic wild men are shy, and require a good deal of hunting up."

"I fancy we shan't have to hunt long," said Dr. Knowall, coming to a stop.

"What makes you think so?"

"I observe," replied the doctor, "a peculiar kind of sugar-cane very prevalent in this part of the forest. The gorilla is remarkable for its fondness for this particular plant."

The hopes of the hunters revived at once.

A sharp, angry bark was heard close at hand.

"By Jove! there it is again," cried the doctor.

Loud, shrill, and brute-like, but yet with something terribly human in it, the fierce yell swelled and died into a deep, low growl, like thunder.

"Where the deuce are they?" said our hero, his eyes flashing with intense eagerness as he looked on all sides but saw nothing.

"Come out and show yourselves," shouted Stumps.

"We only jass want shake han's, ax how you do, dat all," grinned General Orlando politely raising his cocked hat to an imaginary gorilla.

Suddenly he clapped it on his head, uttered a cry, and pointed.

"Ah, see! dere! dere!"

"Where? what?" cried the rest simultaneously.

"De wild man! de gorilla! One, two, three, four of dem!" he almost gasped.

All eyes followed the direction of his extended finger, and there, at about fifty yards' distance, could be seen, between the trunks, that number of these animals, dark, hairy, unsightly looking monsters, whose hoarse barkings again burst forth upon the air.

Nothing daunted, our hero shouted—

"Forward!"

And at once the whole party were advancing towards them.

At the approach of the hunters they started off at full speed, running in an upright position, like human beings.

To overtake them was impossible, and Bob Blunt called to his comrades—

"Fire!"

The report of their rifles rang through the woods, but the shots took no effect, and by the time they had reached the spot not a single gorilla was in sight.

Only their sharp, barking cries were heard in the distance.

"Dey notink," said General Orlando, somewhat contemptuously, after a pause; "dey only young ones."

He had hardly said this when an awfully devilish yell thundered through the forest.

"Do you call that nothing?" asked Bob Blunt.

"No! dat sometink!" returned the general; "dat de roar ob de ole gorilla!"

"By Jupiter, you're right, and here he comes!" cried our hero, as a violent crashing was heard amongst the canes.

The next moment his wish was gratified.

An enormous full-grown gorilla, six feet in height, burst forth.

A terrible monster, with immense hairy body, huge chest, and long muscular arms, large, deep grey eyes, glaring fiercely, and a face whose hellish expression could never be forgotten.

He was not afraid, but stood beating his breasts with his huge fists, till it resounded like an immense bass drum whilst at the same time he uttered roar after roar.

"Dat mean to say he not care button for us," whispered General Orlando to his master.

"Perhaps he'll care for this," quietly returned Bob, as he cocked his rifle.

But at this moment the sharp bark of a young one was heard, and the old one, at the sound, turned and plunged into the thicket, and was gone ere anyone could raise his weapon to his shoulder.

It was a disappointment to lose so splendid a specimen, and the hunters gave vent to their feelings in vain regrets.

Their annoyance was increased, too, by an ironical laugh behind them.

Turning round, they saw, to their surprise, a group of dark figures, who had been watching them for some time.

"You tink kill gorilla," said the blacks in a mocking tone to the English as they approached.

"I am sure I shall the first time I get near enough to him," was Bob's confident reply.

The dark faces wreathed themselves into a smile, half scornful, half pitying at this.

"You neber kill gorilla," they said shaking their heads.

"Why not?"

"'Cause de spirit ob de great Bomeranga lib in him."

"I doubt whether the great Bomeranga or any other spirit would be able to stand the contents of this," laughed Bob, holding up his rifle.

"Take care what you do," replied the Dahomites, warningly; "you try kill gorilla, gorilla kill you."

"Pshaw!" returned our hero, in an irritable tone; "it will take more than an ape to do that. Come, friends, forward in pursuit."

With these words he plunged into the thicket at the point where the gorilla had disappeared, and his companions followed.

CHAPTER II.

A HARROWING ADVENTURE WITH TWO GORILLAS.

I SAY, Elizabeth Ann," said Buttons, as with that lady he came to a halt in a thick part of the forest.

"Well?"

"Where are we?"

"Don't ask such ridiculous questions. You know we're in the forest, and I wish I was back at the encampment," continued Elizabeth Ann, fretfully; "it was very foolish of me to leave it."

"Why did you then?" demanded Buttons, in a savage tone.

"It was entirely your fault. Didn't you say, 'Let's come out in search of gorillas?'"

"No, I didn't," snapped Buttons; "it was you."

"Oh, you wicked, mendacious boy!"

"So it was. You says, 'Let's go an' ketch a gorilla,' an' I says, 'All right,' an' 'ere we are."

"Yes, here we are, lost in the wood, and instead of catching the gorillas, perhaps the gorillas will catch us."

The Stinger uttered a faint wail of despair, but her companion, utterly unmoved, continued—

"There's one comfort; if one er these wild men er the woods comes, 'e's sure to collar you fust. That one in Ashantee, yer know, was werry fond of yer."

"Oh, you insulting young villain!" almost shrieked the indignant lady, shaking her umbrella at him.

The page by this time had exhausted his spleen, and he said—

"Well, never mind, I was only in fun; 'ere, 'ave a sip."

As he spoke, he drew a small flask from his pocket, and held it up before her.

"What is it, sir?" she asked grandly.

"Rum, Betsy."

The sternness passed out of the Stinger's round features, and she said—

"I think I'll take a sip."

"Don't drink it all, my precious Betsy," returned Buttons.

And in order to put such an act out of her power, he half emptied the flask himself before handing it to her.

"'HERE! GIVE ME BACK MY CLOTHES,' CRIED BUTTONS."

Elizabeth Ann finished the other half.

" I feel better now," she said, her good humour returning.

" So do I," responded Buttons.

" And now, let's try and get back to the encampment."

At this instant a most fearful howl almost startled the two speakers out of their boots.

" Oh ! good gracious !" cried the Stinger, tremulously, " isn't that one of the horrid monsters ?"

" Y—e—es, I—I— rather th—think it's a g—g—g—gorilla !" gasped Buttons, his knees knocking together.

Again the dreadful roar burst forth ; and it seemed almost close to them.

" Whatever will become of us ?" wailed Elizabeth Ann, wringing her hands.

" I think we'd better get into th' nearest 'oller tree as we comes to," suggested Buttons.

" Oh, yes, let's go somewhere as soon as possible."

Hardly had she spoken when from the thick boughs over her head there descended two enormous hairy legs, the feet of which caught her round the neck like a pair of nippers.

She shrieked as she found herself being drawn up—

" Oh, help ! help ! I'm going I don't know where !"

Buttons, with his eyes almost out of his head with horror, staggered forward, and grasped the Stinger by her boots.

Alas ! they came off in his hands, and he fell on his back.

By the time he picked himself up the unfortunate advocate of woman's rights had disappeared, and, as he was looking up, vacantly, to see what had become of her, a second pair of gaunt, hairy legs descended and gripped him round the neck in the same manner.

In vain he yelled and struggled ; he was held as firmly as if a noose had encircled his throat and hoisted him off the ground.

He heard a faint cry from above—

" Oh ! Buttons dear, help me ! I'm up in the branches !"

" I'm a-comin' arter yer !" was all the half-strangled youth could gasp out as

he was hoisted into the leafy regions overhead.

As soon as he was fairly landed on a branch the full horror of his situation revealed itself.

He found himself clasped in the hairy arms of a monster gorilla.

A few yards from him was the Stinger, being nursed in the same manner.

Terror had paralysed the strongminded Elizabeth, and she lay in a state of unconsciousness.

But just at that moment a loud shout startled them.

Buttons recognised the voices of his friends at once, and shouted lustily in reply.

For a moment the monsters sat listening, their deep-set, malignant eyes glaring, and the wrinkled skin on their foreheads twitching backwards and forwards with anger.

Then pealed forth their hideous, thundering roar.

The terrible sounds brought the Stinger to her senses, and she shrieked loudly.

Buttons was already in the full possession of his, and he bawled " Murder " at the top of his voice.

This combination of cries above and below was rather too much for the gorillas, and, having secured their prisoners in a very peculiar fashion, they descended to the ground.

*　　*　　*　　*　　*

" I'm sure it was their voices !" said Bob Blunt.

" Whose ?" asked the doctor.

" The Stinger's and Buttons'."

" It sounded like theirs, certainly."

" Hark ! again !"

" Cries of ' Murder !' Good Heaven ! what can have happened ? Let us push on !"

These rapid remarks were spoken by Bob Blunt and his companions.

They had been following on the track of the gorilla that had escaped them, and had arrived, providentially, at the very spot where the wild brutes had caught up their victims.

It was the piteous cry of the Stinger and Buttons that had first aroused the hunters, whilst the awful roar of the gorillas had led them to suspect the truth.

They hurried forward with nervous haste, not knowing what horrible catastrophe had happened, guided only by the sound of their comrades' doleful voices.

At present they had not espied the gorillas; but suddenly, at an opening in the wood, the thundering roar broke forth again, and the two monsters, male and female, suddenly sprang from behind the trees.

Gnashing their formidable teeth and beating their huge breasts, like deep-sounding drums, they advanced.

It was an awful moment.

To have fired at them and missed would have been sure destruction to all.

Even General Orlando forgot his usual pompous affectation at this crisis, and whispered to our hero—

"Wait till dey come close, capt'n, 'fore you fire!"

"All right!" returned Bob.

And then, addressing his comrades, he said—

"Be steady, friends, and keep cool."

"As cucumbers, governor," returned Stumps.

"Stand well together, and don't fire till I give the word."

In the meantime the gorillas, uttering their terrible defiance, advanced.

As they stood they looked like two malignant, gigantic demons from the realms of darkness let loose upon the earth.

Twelve yards alone separated them from the explorers.

Still our hero did not give the signal and still the brutes continued to approach.

Ten—eight—seven—only seven yards between them now.

"Hadn't we better fire?" asked the doctor, a little nervously.

"Not yet!" was the decided reply he received.

On came the gorillas, roaring like demons.

Six—five—four.

"Fire!" cried Bob Blunt.

There was a tremendous volley, a fearful yell, and a dense cloud of smoke; but through all could be seen the gigantic forms writhing on the ground, looking awfully human in spite of their hideousness, as they struggled in their last agonies.

These were soon over, and the two monsters lay together on the grass lifeless.

For a few seconds the hunters stood around, gazing almost in wonder, when suddenly plaintive appeals were heard to proceed from some adjacent locality.

"Oh, mercy! help me! Captain! my dear captain! Somebody! anybody! everybody! oh, oh!"

It was the Stinger's voice, beyond a doubt; and it was instantly followed by another equally recognisable.

"Oh, Lor'! oh, crikey! murder! Capt'n, 'elp! my 'ead's a swimmin' round, an' my jacket's a-splittin' up the back! oh, murder!"

The precise spot from whence these lamentable exclamations proceeded was not at once perceptible.

But at length, guided by the sounds, it was discovered.

There were the two victims, suspended by their garments, from two sharp projecting branches, as though they had been hung up on pegs.

Elizabeth Ann was retained in that aerial but uncomfortable position by her ample petticoats, whilst Buttons was in danger of falling, as his jacket was rapidly giving way.

The position and the horror expressed on their countenances were such that at first the beholders felt strongly inclined to laugh; but they restrained their risible emotions.

General Orlando, having climbed up into the branches, detached them from their perilous perch and lowered them into the arms of their friends.

"Oh Lor', capt'n!" murmured Buttons as he reached the ground; "I thought I was a gone coon this time!"

"If ever I go hunting gorillas again," cried the Stinger, "I shall deserve to be eaten alive."

Luckily they had received no harm beyond a terrible fright.

"Now then, my friends," said Bob Blunt, cheerfully, "let us be getting back to the camp. Elinor will be anxious."

They gave one last look at the dead bodies of the slain gorillas, and were about to commence their return, when suddenly a wild, discordant blast of trumpets and a loud banging of drums aroused them.

Looking round they saw, to their astonishment, that they were in the presence of strangers—dark, fierce-looking men, with spears and weapons at their sides, and apparently every disposition to use them.

In front of all were a body of men, evidently of superior rank.

They advanced to where the explorers now stood.

One of them, who seemed to be the chief, said to our hero—

"You kill dem gorillas?"

He pointed to the lifeless bodies as he put the question.

"Yes," Bob replied, calmly.

"You not kill all yourself?" was the next question.

"Oh, no," returned our hero, smilingly ; "we all had a finger in the pie."

"Ah! iss! iss! all finger in de pie," echoed the questioner ; "you mean you all——"

"All had a pop at the monsters," interposed Dr. Knowall.

"All but me an' the. Stinger," joined in Buttons, remorsefully.

The chief glanced at him and the portly form of the Stinger, and then nodded significantly to a dark gentleman in striped drawers and a turban.

Bob Blunt, still anxious to get back to the encampment, said to the other official in a friendly tone—

"We must now be going. Good day !"

He was somewhat surprised at the reply he received—

"You not go ; you come with me ! Negomba great king. He say you come, and you must come."

"We have nothing to do with him," exclaimed our hero, haughtily ; "we are Englishmen, and subjects of Queen Victoria, and are not in the habit of being coerced, and I refuse to come."

This was very plain speaking, and the official seemed to regard it as such, for he gave a signal to his followers, and instantly the explorers were surrounded by a swarm of burly negro guards, all armed to the teeth.

CHAPTER III.

THE MURDER IN THE FOREST.

THERE is an old saying that "those who are born to be hung will never be drowned," and it seemed that the proverb would be verified in the case of Howard and Bow-legged Bill.

The pirate-vessel, tempest-tossed, was at length driven ashore on the western coast.

Many of her crew had, as we know, jumped overboard to avoid the attack of Bob and his friends, and now most of those who had remained were drowned, or dashed to death against the rocks by the violence of the waves.

Some, however, escaped with their lives.

Amongst these were Richard Howard and his satellite, Bow-legged Bill, and the giant boatswain, Rope's End.

Without weapons or food, and scantily clothed, the survivors stood now upon an equal footing.

Richard Howard was the first to recover the exercise of his faculties.

As he sat upon the beach, drying his

drenched garments in the sun, he said to Bill—

"I think, altogether, this is preferable to that infernal hole we were buried in on board the pirate-vessel."

"Well, pr'aps it is, guv'nor," replied the rough, doubtfully; "but it seems to me as we're in a pertick'ler fix, any'ow."

"No doubt of it," was his master's candid response.

"No grub, no togs, no rum, no 'bacca," went on Bill, dolefully; "what th' dooce is to become on us?"

"You don't suppose I intend to stay here and starve, do you?"

"Where are we to go, guv'nor?"

"Oh, we'll soon strike out a path and make off alone. There's only one little service you might perform upon that same black bullock yonder."

"Wot's that?"

"Knock his brains out!"

"Oh, Lor', guv'nor! I should want a good feed fust. I ain't got 'arf a knock in me just now."

"Well I confess I'm not much in knocking-down trim myself," said Richard Howard, regretfully, "so I suppose he must live. Yet it's a pity."

"I think it more than likely he'll be starved outright," remarked Bill.

Presently he looked up, and said—

"When are we goin' to make a start, guv'nor?"

"To-night."

Richard Howard adhered to his intention.

As soon as the sun set and the earth was shrouded in darkness, he and his comrade turned their backs on the sea, and commenced their journey inland.

When the sun rose over the sea-shore, the pirates and Rope's End were far behind them.

After many days' toilsome travel through a dreary wilderness where both food and drink were scarce, they came in sight of a comfortable-looking edifice.

It stood in a clearing that was perfectly solitary, no other house being near it for miles.

Richard Howard guessed by the look of the structure that it belonged to a Dutch settler, and his spirits rose at the prospect of obtaining food and shelter.

"That's our mark," he said as he pointed it out to his follower.

Bow-legged Bill gave a grunt of satisfaction.

Without any hesitation Richard Howard walked forward and approached the house.

Some dogs began to bark as he drew near, and presently a man, with a round good-natured face appeared at the door.

He stood gazing out of his somewhat sleepy eyes for a moment at the strangers, puffing at his pipe all the time.

"Vort you vornt?" he asked at length.

"Food and shelter, meinheer," was Richard Howard's answer, in that genial tone he knew so well how to assume.

The farmer looked puzzled.

"You nort Dutch—no?" he said thoughtfully.

"We're English, and have been ship-wrecked on the coast," explained Richard Howard.

"Ah! ah! I see! shipwrecked! dat is bad!" returned the kind-hearted farmer, in a voice of sympathy. "I haf peen shipwrec' vonce meinself, an' know vort it is."

With this he threw the door wide open, and said, warmly—

"Come in! I like der English; come in, and welcome."

The travellers did not require a second invitation, and soon they were seated before a well-spread table, eating and drinking to their hearts' content.

After dinner Dutch Hollands and pipes completed the comfort of the guests.

"You seem very comfortable here," said Richard Howard to his host, as they sat smoking together.

"Yah, tank Gott, I am," the latter replied. "I coom out here from Amsterdam, ten years aga, wit mein vrau an' mein son, an' I have prospered."

"And is your wife——" Richard was about to ask.

The old man shook his head mournfully.

"Nien," he said, "she died last year, poor ting!"

"And your son—he helps you in farming, I suppose?" continued Richard.

"Oh, yah, yah! he is a goot lad. I don't know vort I should do widout him."

After they had been thoroughly refreshed, the hospitable Dutchman conducted his visitors over the farm.

Peter Van Droonk was much taken with Richard Howard, as was also Jan his son, who came home in the course of the afternoon—a round good-humoured, Dutch-built young man of twenty-five, the image of his sire on a smaller scale.

It was at supper that Richard Howard said—

"I have often had a desire to try my hand at farming."

"It is hard vork, but very goot for health, mein friend," replied his host.

"Do you think you could find us something to do on your farm?" continued Richard, after a slight pause.

"Yah, I tink so," returned the Dutchman. "I haf often vish for more hands."

"Then engage us ; you will find us very useful."

"I b'lieve yer," joined in Bow-legged Bill ; "we're reg'lar demons to work."

"Ver' goot, den, I engage you," replied Peter Van Droonk, with a smile.

And from that hour Richard Howard and his confederate were domiciled at the farm.

Little did the worthy, unsuspicious owner dream what a pair of evil souls he had taken into his service.

Jan instructed them in their new duties, and all seemed to be [going on well.

So several weeks passed.

It was one morning they had gone out into the forest with the cart to chop wood.

Richard Howard presently ceased work, and with his axe in his hand, was looking back, lost in thought, towards the farm, that was just visible in the distance.

"Wot are yer a-thinkin' about, guv'nor?" asked his colleague at length.

"That it's the bounden duty of every man to take advantage of the opportunities that fortune places in his way," Richard replied.

"Yer means as a cove ought to look out always for number one, don't yer, guv'nor?"

"Precisely ! and that's what I intend to do."

These words were uttered in such a peculiarly significant tone that Bow-legged Bill looked up at the speaker.

"Wot's yer little game, guv'nor?" he said.

"That farm," returned Richard, with a deadly smile lurking in his evil eyes. "I mean it to be mine."

"Goin' to buy it, eh?"

Richard nodded, and laughed outright. So did Bow-legs.

"Ho, ho, ho!" he grinned ; "'ow much are yer goin' to give, guv'nor?"

"Not much. Only a few——"

"Poun's?"

"No, ounces—ounces of lead ; or, in other words—two bullets."

Bow-legged Bill expressed his full comprehension of the idea by a long whistle.

"Well, yer don't stick at trifles, guv'nor, blest if yer do," he said at length.

"I'm not one of that kind," was Richard's reply.

And with this he urged on the oxen that drew the cart.

* * * * *

A few more weeks had rolled by.

One morning Peter Van Droonk called out to his assistant—

"I say, mein friend !"

"What, meinheer ?"

"Me an' Jan must go some miles up der countree. You can manage der farm till ve came pack ?"

"Oh, yes," said Richard, assuringly ; "we can manage well enough."

In less than half an hour everything was ready for the start.

Richard Howard and Bow-legged Bill bade them "good-bye" at the gate, and wished them a pleasant journey.

But they had not gone five minutes, when Richard said to his confederate—

"Come in and load your gun quickly."

"Yer means bisness, eh, guv'nor?" the latter asked.

"Yes," was the abrupt reply.

Five minutes later the two traitors might have been seen skulking out of the gate in the rear of the farm.

They had their guns in their hands, and proceeded in the direction which the waggon had taken.

But they were particular to keep out of sight.

The Dutchman and his son kept steadily on till they reached the forest into which they turned.

It was necessary that they should cross a portion of it by a beaten track which was capable of being traversed by a waggon and horses.

Richard Howard and his accomplice took a short cut, and having reached a secluded spot, which they knew the lumbering equipage must pass, they waited, weapons in hand, for their victims.

Leisurely jogging along in the waggon, with their pipes in their mouths, came the Dutchman and his son.

They were talking about their English assistants, and evidently in terms of great satisfaction.

"Ve'll drink dere health!" exclaimed Peter Van Droonk, as he stopped the horses and drew a flask of Hollands from his capacious pocket.

He raised the flask to his lips.

Bang! bang! went a couple of guns.

There was a sharp cry of pain as the flask dropped from his nerveless hand, and the farmer fell back a corpse.

The son also, stricken by the bullet of Bow-legged Bill, dropped at the same time, and lay motionless by the side of his father.

"Well aimed!" exclaimed Richard Howard, as he sprang forth from his covert and clambered up into the waggon.

"Dead shots, I declare," he muttered, complacently, as he looked down upon his lifeless victims as they lay weltering in their blood.

"Never see a neater bit o' bisness in my life, guv'nor," joined in Bow-legs, who had climbed up after his master.

Richard Howard made no reply, but simply ordered him to help him lift the dead bodies out of the waggon.

"Are yer sure they are dead, guv'nor?" asked Bill.

"Oh, yes! they're dead enough," returned his master, after glancing at their pallid features.

"But this one's a-lookin' at me," gasped Bill, as he pointed to the ghastly face of Jan Van Droonk, whose round eyes were wide open and fixed on him in a glassy stare.

"There's no sight in them," said Richard, hoarsely; "let's put them away."

This was the easiest thing in the world to do, and, in a very short time, the murdered men were lying in the midst of a dense mass of weeds and brambles, where no human eye would ever discover them.

The remorseless deed performed, the murderers took a prolonged drink of the spirit; then, driving the waggon into the thicket, they cut the horses loose to roam whither they listed, and returned to the farm as cautiously as they had left it.

"Mine now! all mine!" cried Richard Howard, exultingly, as he looked round the comfortable domicile.

"All, guv'nor?" echoed Bow-legged Bill, in a disappointed tone. "It ought to be share an' share alike, oughtn't it?"

Howard was suddenly seized with deafness and did not hear him; or, if he did, he took no notice.

Richard Howard had long since made up his mind that he would never allow Bow-legged Bill to stand upon anything like an equal footing with himself.

So, therefore, he took not the slightest notice of Bill's proposition that they should "share and share alike."

CHAPTER IV.

LIFE FOR LIFE.

BOB BLUNT saw that he could not resist the crowd of angry negroes that surrounded him ; so, turning to the chief, he said, condescendingly—

" We will go with you, to oblige his majesty ; but he must regard it as a special act of favour. Come, friends !"

With these words the explorers submitted with as good a grace as possible to what it was impossible to avoid, and were marched off between a file of guards.

Buttons and the Stinger seemed to be forgotten, and were left behind.

Whilst their companions were being escorted to the royal presence with the hideous accompaniment of African drums and trumpets, they made the best of their way back to the encampment, to tell Elinor Cleveland what had happened.

His African majesty had decided on meeting the explorers in the open plain in front of his palace.

On the arrival of our hero and friends at that spot, they beheld the potentate, seated in his chair of state, under an awning.

He was surrounded by the various dignitaries of his kingdom.

The English were then ordered to advance.

They came forward boldly, walking upright, and looking the Dahomey monarch full in the face.

"You kneel down ! go on your all-fours!" suggested Nigdhiva, the chief who had brought them to the royal presence.

" Certainly not !" returned Bob Blunt, passionately ; " we are British subjects, not miserable slaves."

Holding their heads higher than before, the party of explorers drew near the throne.

Negomba, who was a very ugly specimen of a very savage negro, peered at them searchingly from under his contracted brows for several moments in silence.

Having finished his scrutiny he whispered something to an attendant, who made a signal to someone else.

Instantly the drums and gongs began to beat, and, amidst the din, appeared a body of negroes, carrying two figures, seated in chairs, which they brought forward and placed on the ground on the right of the throne.

These chairs contained two dead bodies, and the Englishmen could hardly believe their eyes when they recognised the gorillas which they had slain in the forest.

There they were, each wearing a gilt crown, and robed in a piece of tawdry drapery, looking hideously burlesque even in death.

The countenance of the king and his ministers were extremely solemn and serious, and, after the former had descended from his throne, and bowed himself before the dead brutes, and shaken them by the paws, he reseated himself, and, looking towards our hero, said to him, sternly—

" You kill dose gorillas ?"

" Yes !" Bob replied, boldly.

" Augh !" grunted the king again ; " you know what you do ?"

" Perfectly ; we have rid your territories of two of its most formidable inhabitants."

" But we ask no reward," joined in Dr. Knowall, innocently.

" Reward !" yelled the African monarch, whose countenance, distorted by fury, bore a strong resemblance to the dead brutes at his side ; " do you know who you have kill ?"

" I believe I told your majesty," coolly responded Bob Blunt ; " two gorillas."

" Augh ! baugh ! waugh !" barked Negomba, fiercely ; " you kill my fader an' moder !"

Our hero opened his eyes in astonishment at this extraordinary assertion, and the words of the dark natives in the wood at once recurred to his mind.

He saw at once that he had to deal with a grossly superstitious nation.

" Well, certainly," he admitted, as he glanced at the dead animals, " there is a very strong family likeness, though I can't quite understand how, in killing these gorillas, I have taken the lives of your majesty's worthy relatives."

" I tell you, den, you hab," returned the king, sternly ; " dis how—when my roy'l fader an' moder die dere sperrits go an' lib in de bodies ob dem gorillas—you see—eh ?"

Bob inclined his head to hide the smile that flitted across his face.

" You wicked white men drive dem out when you kill de gorillas. Now dey got no home ! You kill my roy'l fader, Bomeranga, an' my roy'l moder, Jamjaika, an' I kill you all ! all ! eb'ry one !"

The glaring eyes of the African despot rolled wildly in their sockets as he uttered these words.

Schava, the executioner, taking the hint, stepped forward with ominous celerity, grasping his terrible blade.

Our hero saw at once that the position of his comrades and himself was critical.

" We were not aware, your majesty," said he, " that we were offering violence to the spirits of your departed parents, or we should never have shot the gorillas."

" Don't talk lie, white man !" shouted Negomba. " I no hear lies ; you kill my fader an' moder, me kill you ! Schava !"

This was the signal.

In an instant Bob Blunt was seized and forced upon his knees.

" The Queen of England will demand the price of our blood at your hands, tyrant."

" De Queen of England nothing to me !" roared Negomba, with savage scorn. " Schava, off wid his white head !"

A burst of horror came from the very hearts of the explorers at this terrible sentence.

But it availed nothing to avert it.

The strong arm of the executioner was swung back.

The glittering blade flashed in the air.

Another moment and our gallant hero would be beyond the reach of human aid.

It was just then, when all hope seemed fled, a shrill cry, almost unearthly in its wildness, came floating from the neighbouring forest.

" Stay, oh, Negomba !" it said, in the African tongue.

The monarch, at this injunction, extended his hand to the executioner.

Schava at once lowered his weapon.

The king listened intently, and the voice was heard again.

" I am going, noble Bomeranga ! I am going, noble Jamjaika !" it cried, with wonderful distinctness, " I am going to tell your wishes to your royal son."

The next moment a graceful female form, of dusky hue, came flying from the wood with the swiftness of a deer, and paused not till she reached the very foot of the throne.

It was Nahita.

Her eyes were wild with intense excitement, and her bosom heaved tumultuously.

But one glance at our hero and she knew she was not too late to save him she loved, and she grew suddenly calm, and stood erect before the king, firm as a statue on a rock.

Negomba looked at her with a strange expression of something like awe.

" I bring a message to you, oh, king !" she said, after a moment.

" A message ?" echoed the monarch.

" Yes, from your royal father and mother."

Negomba half rose in his seat, and then sat down again, with his eyes and mouth very wide open.

" My fader an' moder ?" he echoed in a hollow tone.

" Yes."

" Where you see dem ?"

" Just now, in the forest yonder," returned Nahita, as she pointed behind her.

The king looked eagerly in that direction, but seeing nothing, he said—

" What dey say to you ?"

" He said that you were not to harm

a hair of the white man or his friends, because they have been good to them."

"Did dey say dat?"

"Yes."

Negomba was so impressed by this message that he sprang from his throne, kicking away the attendants that held our hero unceremoniously right and left.

Then, raising his prisoner, he embraced him cordially.

After this, he turned to Nahita, and said, with tears in his eyes—

"De spirits of my fader an' moder wander in de forest—eh?"

"No, your majesty, they have found a shelter."

"Ha, ha! good, good! where?" he demanded eagerly.

"In the bodies of two noble white people," replied the young girl.

"Let me see dem!" cried the king with intense excitement.

"They are coming now!" exclaimed Nahita.

As she spoke she again pointed in the direction of the forest, and cried aloud—

"Approach, royal Bomeranga and Jamjaika! Your son awaits you."

In response to this summons there approached from the wood Buttons and the Stinger.

Nahita, who had come from Abyssinia in the same vessel with our hero and friends, had remained behind with Elinor Cleveland when Buttons and the Stinger went forth gorilla hunting.

On their return her quick wit suggested the plan which the others consented to help carry out.

*   *   *   *   *

The white bodies in which the African spirits were supposed to dwell remained silent all the time they were in the presence of the King of Dahomey, who feasted his deceased relatives right royally.

They, however, soon signified by signs their desire to depart, and then moved off to the place where they had left Elinor Cleveland, where the rest of the party joined them an hour later, having parted in a most friendly manner from the King of Dahomey.

CHAPTER V.

THE STORE ON THE COAST.

DANIEL JEDDHA was well known at a certain town on the African coast, where he kept a store for general merchandise.

Though he had African blood in his veins on his mother's side, his father was a Jew, and with the peculiar tact of that nation he managed to keep on good terms with the traders on the coast and to make money.

He was regarded as a fair-dealing man as times went, and goods were often shipped from European and American ports and conveyed to his care.

It was one broiling hot afternoon that two men approached his store.

Both were habited in Dutch-looking garments, and one was particularly bow-legged.

"Any letter or parcel from England for Captain Robert Blunt?" asked the better looking of the two, as he looked in at the door of the store.

"No, dere's no ship arrived from dat part yet," was the reply he received from the proprietor.

"There is one expected shortly, is there not?"

"I should tink dere vould be von shortly," responded Daniel Jeddha, who was quietly smoking his pipe.

"Good."

"Are you Capitaine Robert Blunt?" inquired the Jew.

"Yes, and I am expecting some important consignments from England."

"I shall take great care of dem, capitaine, vhen dey come," said Daniel.

"Mind you do; you'll be paid handsomely."

"You may depend upon me, capitaine."

"I shall call again in a few days," said Richard Howard—for it was he—as he left the store.

"Well, guv'nor, you are a cool un, an' no mistake," remarked Bow-legged Bill as he waddled along at his master's side.

"What do you mean?"

"Why, the free-an'-easy way in which you does things. There's one thing puzzles me wery much."

"What's that?"

"Why, 'ow you knew there was anything expected to arrive for Captain Blunt."

Richard Howard burst into a laugh.

"I've a right to expect what I've written for, haven't I?" he said after a moment.

Bow-legged Bill gave a low whistle.

"Oh, you've written, 'ave yer, guv'nor?"

"Yes," laughed his master, "to James Sawyer, attorney of Rochester, and agent to the Blunt Castle Estate, to send me a remittance."

"Well, but won't Mr. Sawyer detect the difference in the 'andwritin'?" asked Bill, scratching his head in a doubtful manner.

"Not as I have written it," returned Richard, complacently; "my epistle is a *fac simile* imitation of my cousin's caligraphy. The devil himself couldn't discern the difference."

"You are a wonderful man, an' no flies about it," was Bow-legged Bill's emphatic answer.

They had reached their horses by this time, and mounting, continued their journey, till at length, after a long and toilsome ride, they arrived at a farm—which Richard Howard had obtained in exchange for that of the murdered Dutchman.

The next day he despatched his confederate to reconnoitre and make inquiries near the town.

It was towards evening when Bow-legged Bill returned in a state of considerable excitement.

"Wot d'yer think, guv'nor?" were his first eager words as he entered; "ye'll never guess."

"I'm not going to try," returned Richard, coolly; "tell me."

"The Henglish explorers is 'ere."

Richard Howard dropped the pipe he was smoking, and sprang to his feet.

"Do you mean Bob Blunt's party?" he asked eagerly.

"Yes, 'im an' the whole lot."

"The deuce they are!" ejaculated Richard Howard after a moment.

The instant following he had recovered his usual cool indifference, and asked—

"Where are they located?"

"Well, they're lodged in the town."

"Indeed!"

"Yes, an' in fust-rate quarters, too, I can tell you."

"Humph! Do you know if Elinor Cleveland is with them?"

"Oh, yes, she's there all right enough an' jest as good lookin' as ever."

The eyes of Richard Howard gleamed savagely for a moment, then he resumed—

"You say they're well lodged?"

"Yes, an' ev'rybody seems to think a lot of the noble white people, as they calls 'em."

"There must be some reason for this," muttered Richard, thoughtfully.

"Well, no doubt theer is," returned his colleague; "my erpinion is, they've been a-'umbuggin' the ole king."

"In what way?"

"Well, as far as I could make out theer's a sort o' cock-an'-bull story that the Henglish trav'llers 'as got possession of the sperrits of ole King Gumby's diseased parints."

"Ah, I see; my clever cousin and his clever associates are working upon the superstition of the ignorant African potentate for their own ends."

"Yes, that's it, I think, guv'nor."

"No doubt of it," said Richard, reflectively.

"Wot d'yer mean to do now?" asked the Bow-legs.

"Floor the lot with one good throw of the ball!" cried his master, with a sudden burst of vindictive exultation.

"Can yer, guv'nor?" said Bill.

"If I can't it's very strange to me; but I must first know a little more about their proceedings."

"How are yer goin' to get at this, guv'nor?"

"By making inquiries myself."

Richard Howard said no more, but the next day he took a great deal of trouble to inform himself of such facts as were publicly known at Dahomey.

The story of the gorillas was in everyone's mouth, and there was not a dark-skinned native who did not implicitly believe in the truth of the legend which Buttons and the Stinger had set on foot.

Richard Howard pondered on what he heard, and very speedily made up his mind how to act.

For some days he wandered in the forest, rifle in hand, very much to the surprise of his confederate Bow-legged Bill, whom he took with him.

At length the latter said—

"Wot's yer little game ere, guv'nor?"

"You'll know before long."

"If it's all the same to you, guv'nor, I should like to know now," urged Bill.

Richard Howard had come to a stop, and was examining some traces on the ground.

Presently he looked up, and replied—

"Since you're so anxious I'll tell you. My little game here is—gorillas."

"Gorillas!" echoed the Bow-legs; "d'yer mean yer wants to ketch one."

"No; I want to shoot one."

"They're rather scarce, ain't they?"

"Rather; but I think I am on the track of one of them."

Hardly had he said these words than a harsh bark was heard, gradually gliding into a deep bass roar, like thunder.

"Oh, Lor'! muttered Bow-legged Bill; "if that woice ain't enough to freeze the marrer in a cove's bones nothink ain't."

"Psha!" cried his master, hastily; "pull yourself together and look to your weapon; you'll want it in a minute or two."

The rough made an effort to overcome his nervousness, and cocking his rifle, looked anxiously on all sides.

Presently a loud crashing of branches was heard, and an enormous gorilla burst through the thicket at a few yards' distance from where he stood.

Bill's knees knocked together, and his short hair bristled like porcupine quills at the sight of the monster.

The gorilla roared and beat his breast with his tremendous hands.

"Steady!" whispered Richard Howard; "let us both fire together."

The brute advanced.

The report of the rifles echoed through the forest.

The gorilla fell dead with two bullets in his breast.

"Well aimed!" cried Richard, exultingly; "and now I see a way to upset all the plans of my clever cousin."

"Do yer see a way to upset him, guv'nor?" said his colleague, in a puzzled tone.

"Yes, and there it is," Richard replied as he pointed to the lifeless body of the gorilla.

"Blest if I can see 'ow that can be," returned Bill.

"You never can see anything an inch beyond your nose," was his master's contemptuous rejoinder; "but come, let's get home with our prize, and then for the palace of King Ne—— what's his name?"

"Gumby, I thinks."

"No! Gomba—King Negomba!"

*   *   *   *   *

Deep groans were heard to proceed from the royal chambers in the palace at Dahomey.

The king was suffering from an acute malady, which had kept him awake all night and was driving him frantic.

In plain English his majesty had the toothache.

"Oh! oh!" he groaned at length; "de gods am angry wid me, send me dis drefful ache. What me do?" he asked, as he rocked himself to and fro, holding his head in his hands.

Bunbaki, the officer in waiting on his majesty, suggested some slight sacrifice by way of propitiating the offended deities.

Negomba jumped eagerly at the idea.

"Yes! yes!" he cried; "me cut off two or tree dozen heads; dat please de gods. Send Schava here."

It was just as the executioner was about to be summoned that a message was brought to the king.

A white stranger wished to see him.

Negomba, if the truth must be told, was growing rather tired of white strangers, and he demanded, irritably, what he wanted.

"He brings presents for your majesty," was the answer returned.

The king groaned and grunted, but, not wishing to lose the presents, he said eventually—

"Bring de white stranger here."

In a few moments Richard Howard was introduced.

On entering Richard prostrated himself with becoming humility.

"Great king," he said, "I have ventured into your presence to bring you—"

"Stop!" roared Negomba, as a sudden twinge racked him; "hab you brought anytink dat can cure de toothache?"

"I have, your majesty. It is for that very purpose I am come."

"Oh, dat good! dat bery good!" exclaimed the king, eagerly. "Where is it?"

"Here, your majesty," replied Richard, as he went to the door and, extending his arm, led in a large gorilla, fastened by a chain.

Negomba uttered a cry of surprise and fell back in his seat.

"My fader! my roy'l fader!" he exclaimed.

"Yes, 'ere I am, ole son," said Bow-legged Bill, who, stitched up in the skin of the gigantic ape, looked wonderfully like the animal he represented; "'ow d'yer find yerself?"

"Me bery bad, fader," groaned Negomba.

"Your royal son has the toothache," explained Richard Howard to his gorilla confederate, "and wishes you to cure him."

"Ow the dooce can I cure him?"

growled the latter, inwardly; "I ain't a dentist."

Howard whispered something, and then Bow-legged Bill said to those in attendance—

"I'll want a lamp and a piece o' wire."

These being brought him, the king was placed in a chair in a convenient position.

"Open yer mouth," said Bill.

Negomba obeyed.

"Ah, I see! it's in the bottom jor; a werry bad tooth indeed; yer must be sufferin' orful wi' that tooth," remarked the gorilla-dentist, as he investigated the royal grinders.

"I am! I am!" wailed Negomba.

"All right! take it easy! I'll soon cure yer," grinned Bill.

It took but a moment to make the iron wire red hot in the flame of the lamp, and, all being ready, the operator said—

"Now then, ole son, open your 'tatur-trap once more."

Open went the huge mouth, in went the red-hot wire, hissing down into the hollow tooth even to the very root of the fang.

A wild roar, like that of a wounded tiger, burst from the monarch as he sprang to his feet under the startling agony of the operation, but almost instantly the pain ceased.

The nerve was destroyed, and the toothache was gone for ever.

"Your majesty is better?" said Richard Howard, who was watching him keenly.

"Oh, yas, yas! much berrer! yah, yah, yah!" grinned the monarch; "me quite well now."

"If you wish to keep well let me give you a piece of advice," Richard continued.

"What dat?"

"Get rid of all those white people. They make you ill by witchcraft."

"Me get rid ob de white strangers—cut off all dere heads. Order Schava cut off de heads of all de rest ob de white people."

"Yes, your majesty," said the officer to whom this command was addressed.

The negro official departed on his mission, but presently returned with a very rueful expression of countenance.

"Your majesty," he said, "none of the white people are to be found."

"Not found?" echoed the king.

"No, your majesty. They are all gone."

"And the English maiden?"

"She is gone with them."

"Go fetch 'em back!" roared Negomba fiercely; "if you not fetch 'em back, eb'ry one, me chop you up in pieces. Go!"

In much trepidation the luckless functionary hurried away, whilst Bow-legged Bill and the African monarch indulged in brandy until both were speechless and fell on the floor.

Richard Howard looked at them with disgust.

He was irritated also at the departure of his countrymen.

All his clever scheming had been again completely brought to nought.

CHAPTER VI.

DISCOVERY OF A FORGERY.

THE abrupt departure of our hero and his companions from their quarters was in no way connected with Richard Howard.

They knew nothing of the arrival of their enemy, nor how he was plotting to injure them.

The cause of their flight was owing to another circumstance; this was the evident admiration of King Negomba for Elinor Cleveland.

The African monarch had intimated his intention of adding her to his list of wives, which already amounted to more than two hundred.

This was quite sufficient to fill the heart of the beautiful English girl with apprehension, and to excite the intense indignation of Bob Blunt.

In his present position he felt that he was not sufficiently strong to resist the will of an ignorant, despotic tyrant, and therefore he determined at the first opportunity to seek safety by leaving the town, and moving off to the coast.

They were now many miles from the capital, encamped in the heart of a dense forest.

Active search was made after them, but their retreat remained undiscovered.

One morning Nahita approached Bob Blunt, and said to him, somewhat timidly—

"Dear captain, may I speak to you?"

"Certainly, my good girl," he replied kindly.

"Alone, if you please."

"If you wish it."

The young African led the way to a retired spot, whither our hero followed her.

She then stopped, and fixing her large dark, lustrous eyes upon him she loved, she said, mournfully—

"You are weary of Nahita—is it not so?"

"Weary of you? What should make you fancy that?" asked Bob.

"Oh! it is not fancy," interrupted Nahita, bitterly; "ever since the fair English girl crossed your path your heart has changed towards me. Once you might have loved, now you hate me!"

"Nahita, you are mistaken," said our hero, earnestly. "If it were possible that I could hate one who has done so much for me I should be the most ungrateful wretch on earth."

"I would as soon you hated me, if you do not love me," was Nahita's petulant reply.

Bob Blunt regarded her for a moment in some perplexity.

It grieved him to wound her feelings, yet he felt that it was best for him to speak the truth.

"Nahita," he said, after a pause, "if I say I love you as a brother, will not that content you?"

"No!" she exclaimed, smothering a sob, "that is not the love I covet."

"I regret that a brotherly affection is all the love I have to offer you."

"I have known this long ago," returned the young girl, "and it has made me very sad. I have seen your heart going from me day by day, till at last it is quite gone. Elinor Cleveland has stolen it from me!"

"Nahita!"

"Yes! I say stolen. She loves you, she will be your wife, whilst I——"

The young African stopped, overcome by emotion, her lips quivering, her bosom heaving like a troubled sea.

Suddenly she sprang towards our hero, and clasping his hands in hers, said—

"Elinor Cleveland will be your wife, will she not?"

"She will," replied Bob Blunt in a low tone.

"Then farewell hope and joy for ever! Henceforth Nahita's path will be darkness and despair."

With these words she released the hands she held, and rushed wildly away.

"Stay, Nahita!" cried our hero.

She paused not in her career, but hurried on until she was lost in the recesses of the forest.

With feelings of real regret for the suffering he had been compelled to inflict, Bob Blunt rejoined his companions; and after taking an affectionate farewell of Elinor and those who were to remain behind with her, he and his escort set forward on their journey.

It was towards the end of the first day that our hero and his friends were somewhat startled by loud outcries from the advanced guard.

This consisted of Jingo Johnson and several of the Kroomen, who still accompanied them.

They hastened forward, hardly knowing what to expect.

When they reached the spot from whence the sounds proceeded a strange sight presented itself.

Jingo Johnson was dancing, with the most extravagant demonstrations of joy, round a very singular-looking object, this being an old man, black as himself, with white hair, and attired in a faded military uniform and a cocked hat.

So excited was Jingo that he did not notice the arrival of his master and his friends, but continued to caper and shout at the top of his voice, every now and then stopping to embrace the aged negro in the uniform.

"Why, Jingo," asked Bob Blunt at length, "what is the matter? Who is this?"

"Oh, massa! massa!" Jingo replied, excitedly, "dis my fader! my ole fader! Yah, yah, yah, yah! golly! 'im find 'im fader!"

Our hero welcomed the old darkey, who joined the party and went along with them to the coast.

The English vessel lay at anchor.

Our explorers gave a hearty cheer at the sight of her.

"Let us go at once to the stores," said Bob Blunt.

They proceeded thither, and found the proprietor amongst his bales and merchandise.

"Any letter or package from England for Captain Robert Blunt?" asked our hero.

"Dere was a letter and a small box," replied Daniel Jeddha.

"Where are they then?" asked Bob.

"Why, Capitaine Blunt have got dem," the Jew answered.

"I beg your pardon," returned our hero, emphatically; "I have not got them."

"You are not Capitaine Blunt?" said Daniel Jeddha in surprise.

"Yes, I am."

"Well, den, dere's two Capitaine Blunts," returned the storekeeper.

"No, there are not," said Bob, irritably.

"I say yes," returned Daniel. "I gave de letter and de box to de oder Capitaine Robert Blunt two days ago."

"You did?"

"WITH A FIERCE EXECRATION, ROPE'S END SPRANG AT HOWARD."

"Yes, I did, upon my honour," the Jew replied; "here is his receipt."

As he spoke he produced the bill of consignment, with the signature "Robert Blunt," fixed at the bottom.

Our hero's eyes almost started from his head as he looked at the paper.

Not only was his name there, but it appeared written in his own hand.

Bob Blunt knew at once that it was a forgery, and he exclaimed—

"Some impostor has taken my name."

"It certainly seems like it," admitted Daniel Jeddha.

"What kind of a person was it to whom you delivered this box and letter?" our hero asked him, after a moment.

The storekeeper gave a tolerably correct description of Richard Howard.

"Had he a companion?"

"Yes; a thick-set man, vid a pair of legs you could roll a brandy-keg between without touching."

This description gave a clue to the listeners, and they exclaimed simultaneously—

"Bow-legged Bill!"

"If so," cried Bob Blunt, vehemently, "then the receiver of my property can, as I suspected, be no other than Richard Howard."

Daniel Jeddha shrugged his shoulders as he said—

"How vos I to know that?"

"You are not to blame," replied our hero; "still, this is a very serious matter to me."

In a very gloomy and disappointed state of mind, he left the stores.

A boat was just putting off from the beach for the ship.

A few words to the sailors, who were English, was sufficient.

"We'll take you on board, your honour, with pleasure," said the coxswain.

In a few moments Bob Blunt and his companions were on their way to the vessel.

The captain received them with genuine cordiality.

On learning what had occurred he expressed his regret, and generously supplied our hero with a loan from his own private purse, with such weapons and ammunition as he could spare, together with other necessaries.

It was with much unwillingness the explorers parted from their kind-hearted countryman.

But it was necessary that they should return to their companions as quickly as possible.

"I shall remain here for a few weeks," said Captain Allen at parting; "and, if you wish for a homeward passage in my vessel, I shall be happy to receive you."

Bob thanked him warmly for the offer, but, not being quite decided as to his future destination, he left it an open question.

"If we decide upon returning to England," he said, "you will see us within the time you mention."

With this understanding they separated.

On reaching the shore our hero and his comrades at once commenced their return journey.

They were proceeding along the beach when suddenly Buttons espied a piece of paper which the wind was driving over the shingles.

Without any particular object he picked it up.

An exclamation of surprise broke from his lips.

"What's the matter?" asked his master, aroused from his reverie by his voice.

"Why, captain, it's a letter addressed to you," he answered.

"To me?" exclaimed Bob, eagerly; "let me see."

Buttons handed him the letter.

He at once recognised the hand of his agent, Mr. Sawyer.

The contents ran thus—

"Rochester, England.

"DEAR SIR,—In accordance with the wish expressed in your letter from Cape Coast Castle, I beg to transmit the sum of one thousand pounds in gold. At the same time I rejoice to hear that you and your gallant companions are in health, and that the expedition so bravely undertaken is being carried out so thoroughly, and in a manner satisfactory to yourself.

Wishing you a continuation of your success, I beg to remain,

"Yours, very respectfully,

"JAMES SAWYER.

"To Robert Blunt, Esq.

"P.S.—I address the case containing the gold, as you desire, to you, at Daniel Jeddha's Stores, Cape Coast Castle."

Our hero looked up with a strange expression in his face.

"The whole thing is a vile forgery, perpetrated, I believe, by my recreant cousin!" he said at length, indignantly.

"What can be done?" asked Stumps and Ironfist.

"Nothing!" returned Bob. "Even if I could bring home the crime to him there is neither law nor justice here."

"What, then, is he to collar the thousand, and get clear off?" asked Buttons, looking particularly vicious.

"Oh, he may escape for a time, as many other scoundrels do," returned his master; "but there'll come a day of reckoning yet, when all accounts will be settled in full. Come, let us continue our journey."

CHAPTER VII.

BOB BLUNT'S FATAL DISCOVERY.

NAHITA, in the wild frenzy of her excitement, sped onwards, utterly heedless of the course she was pursuing.

At length she sank down, breathless and exhausted, but more from emotion than fatigue.

"Oh, he is cruel! cruel!" she moaned, as she lay prostrate on the ground; "after all my love to renounce me for another—for this English girl—this Elinor Cleveland! Can she love the captain as I love him? Would she give her life for him as I would? Oh, no, no! Oh, wretch that I am! What shall I do?"

"I can tell you!" answered a voice.

Starting up from her prostrate position she beheld a man standing before her.

It was Richard Howard.

Her first impulse was to fly, but a second thought kept her still where she was.

"You seem in trouble, Nahita," said Richard, after a moment, in a sympathetic tone.

"What has my trouble to do with you?" she replied, sharply, as she fixed her dark eyes upon him.

"Oh, nothing. But, being naturally tender hearted, I thought I might be able to give you good counsel."

"How can you give any good advice?"

"You shall judge of that yourself," said Richard, quietly.

"I see you are breaking your heart about that ungrateful cousin of mine."

"He is not ungrateful!"

"Yes, he is; and cruel into the bargain! I heard you call him so just now."

"That was in anger."

"Perhaps so; but it is perfectly true, for all that. He must be, indeed, to give you up for a pale-faced girl like Elinor Cleveland."

This shaft went home, and the African girl clenched her hands with all the intensity of jealous rage.

"I don't see at all that you need despair, Nahita," continued Richard Howard, after a moment. "If your white rival were out of the way, Captain Blunt would soon forget her, and you would occupy her place in his affections."

"Do you think so?" exclaimed Nahita eagerly, springing to her feet.

"I am sure so!" returned the tempter.

"But how can she be got rid of? I could not kill her!"

"I would not advise you to do so."

"What than?"

"Lure her away from her companions, that is all."

"She would not trust herself with me, I think."

"I will guarantee that she will."

"Have you some charm to compel her?"

"Yes; it is here!"

As Richard spoke he placed in her hand a scrap of paper, on which were a few words written in pencil.

"It is my dear captain's hand," exclaimed Nahita, as her eyes fell on the familiar characters.

"No; it is only a good imitation," laughed Richard. "But it will have the effect desired, I am certain."

The dark orbs of the young African flashed exultingly.

"Yes, yes!" she cried, "I will give her this; but where am I to lead her?"

"To this spot."

"And what then?" asked Nahita.

"Leave the rest to me," Howard answered.

The maiden looked around her scrutinisingly for a moment; then taking a ribbon from her hair she fastened it to a branch.

"Now I cannot mistake," she said. "You will see me here again before long."

"With Elinor Cleveland?"

"Yes, with Elinor Cleveland!"

The next instant she was gone.

*   *   *   *   *

It was about an hour after the departure of our hero that Nahita glided up to Elinor and placed in her hand a scrap of paper.

It was folded and addressed to her.

"From Robert!" she murmured to herself, a bright flush irradiating her fair face.

Hastily opening the note, she read—

"MY DEAREST,—I have just remembered something most important which I ought to have confided to you before leaving. It is not, however, too late. On receipt of this come to me at once.

Nahita will guide you to the spot where you will find me waiting for you.

"Yours till death,
"ROBERT.

"P.S.—Do not mention your intention to anyone, what I have to say being secret."

Without the least hesitation Elinor Cleveland obeyed the injunctions thus conveyed; never for a moment suspecting that the note was a forgery.

She stole away so secretly that no one was aware of her departure.

She walked along in silence by the side of her guide, until at length she said—

"Have we much further to go?"

"Not much, lady," returned Nahita.

A few steps more brought her to the appointed spot, where the bright-coloured ribbon hung fluttering from the branch.

"This is the place," said the young African, as she came to a stop.

"I do not see Captain Blunt," remarked Elinor, looking round.

"You must accept his deputy instead!" exclaimed a voice.

And, at the same moment, the hateful form of Richard Howard stepped from behind a tree and confronted her.

With a startled cry of horror Elinor turned to flee; but her progress was interrupted by Howard, who grasped her by the wrist.

"Wretches! what would you?" she demanded, in a voice hoarse with terror.

"Don't be alarmed, sweetheart," said Richard, soothingly, "no harm is intended you."

"Murderer! perjurer!" exclaimed Elinor, indignantly, as she struggled to get free. "Nahita, help me," she cried.

"Call not upon me for help," replied Nahita, with bitter vehemence; "I hate you! Help yourself, if you can!"

And, with these harsh words, she turned away and hurried from the spot.

"Stay!" called Richard Howard, after her.

But the African girl paid no heed to his voice.

"She must not be allowed to go," he muttered to himself, as he unslung his rifle from his shoulder, and fired.

A sharp report rang through the forest, followed by a cry of pain.

Nahita's fleet footsteps had been suddenly arrested, and she now lay prostrate on the ground, bleeding and motionless.

Elinor Cleveland uttered a shriek of horror and despair.

But a handkerchief, bound tightly over her mouth, stifled her cries.

Her eyes were then bandaged, and she felt herself lifted into a vehicle, which rolled along at a tolerably rapid pace through the forest.

But only for a brief space did she feel the rude jolting of the waggon. A deadly faintness seized her, and she lay utterly unconscious.

*   *   *   *   *

The first disastrous intelligence that reached our hero on his return to the encampment was the disappearance of Elinor Cleveland.

The news fell upon his ears like a knell of death.

In vain he sought for some explanation amongst those he had left with her.

Neither the Stinger nor any one else could afford the slightest clue.

"Oh, this is terrible!" cried Bob Blunt, as he pressed his hands despairingly to his forehead. "I could have borne anything but this!"

"It's very dreadful," said Elizabeth Ann; "but you haven't heard all yet. Nahita has gone, too."

"Nahita gone!" echoed our hero, his dismay increasing; "what does it mean?"

"It's a mystery," returned the Stinger, solemnly, "a profound mystery; and that's all that can be said about it."

"P'r'aps they've strolled into the forest, an' lost theirselves," suggested Buttons.

"It's not impossible," returned his master; "and yet, if they were together, it is hardly likely that Nahita would have missed the path. At all events, we must search."

Forgetting all the weariness of the journey, our hero and his comrades at once set off to explore the wood.

For several hours they wandered through the dense thicket, till at length they reached the spot where the scarlet ribbon hung suspended.

"See!" cried Bob Blunt; "this belonged to Nahita."

The clue, slight as it was, inspired the seekers with some hope.

"Let us divide our numbers and start from this as a central point," counselled our hero. "If they are any way near we cannot fail to find them."

This advice was taken.

A very short time had elapsed when a loud shout rang through the woods, and the cry—"Found! found!" echoed in the ears of Bob Blunt.

He hurried forward, and soon reached the spot where his companions had already congregated.

A piteous sight presented itself—the dead body of the hapless Nahita.

For a moment all were silent.

Then our hero, bending down, gently raised the lifeless form.

The cause of her death was then at once perceptible.

She had been shot in the back, and the bullet had severed the spine.

In solemn silence they dug a grave, and the remains were placed beneath the greensward.

And then came the thought—where was Elinor Cleveland.

Had she shared the fate of her hapless companion.

Suddenly our hero threw off the gloom that seemed almost to overpower him.

"Elinor, my beloved!" he cried, with intense and passionate emotion, "if you are yet upon the face of the earth I'll find you; if you are dead I swear to avenge you and poor Nahita! Now, friends, let us search, and Heaven guide us!"

All day they searched until night fell, and still Elinor Cleveland was undiscovered.

CHAPTER VIII.

SUDDEN ARRIVAL OF A LOST FRIEND.

KING NEGOMBA was in a very irritable state of mind.

He was annoyed at the escape of the English maiden ; and, still more, that Kassa Kobo had not returned.

The slave-captain was a highly important personage at Dahomey, the king holding him in great estimation, for the simple reason that he sold his subjects into slavery and brought him cash in exchange.

The time when he usually made his appearance was long passed, and he still remained unaccountably absent.

Negomba, who wanted his treasury replenished, began to wax furious.

It was just at this critical period, when the native courtiers scarce dared approach their royal master, that Richard Howard was announced.

He entered, leading his confederate—who was once more stitched up in the gorilla's skin—by a chain, and, hearing the king's words, he said, cheerfully—

"I bring you good news, your majesty. The white travellers are hiding in the forest."

"An' the English gal El'nor wid dem ?" inquired Negomba, eagerly.

"Yes, your majesty ; you have only to send a strong guard to capture them all."

"Dat good ; you bery clever man," cried the king, in a satisfied tone.

"I owe my knowledge entirely to my faithful gorilla," said Richard, looking gratefully at his bow-legged accomplice. "It was he that whispered it to me."

"Ah, my dear fader !" exclaimed the Negomba, as he embraced the rough warmly ; "you bery kind to your son."

"I'll take a drain o' brandy then, if it's all th' same to you, Gumby, my boy," returned Bow-legged Bill, with amiable familiarity.

The brandy was brought, and, after drinking, a messenger entered.

"The white strangers wish to see your majesty," he said, as he prostrated himself before the king.

Negomba sprang up with a savage yell of delight.

Richard Howard and Bow-legged Bill fairly started with surprise.

Never did it enter into their minds that the English party would dare voluntarily to approach the African despot.

Yet there they were.

"Bring dem in," cried the king, with a chuckle ; "me bery glad to see dem."

Richard Howard felt anything but comfortable in his mind at the idea of confronting his cousin.

It was the very last thing he would have expected.

And he said—

"I think, your majesty, we had better retire."

"I think so, too," joined in Bow-legged Bill.

"No, no ; why you want go away ? Stay where you am," replied the king.

There was no escape.

At that moment the door opened, and the explorers, headed by Bob Blunt, entered in a body, with their revolvers in their belts, their cutlasses at their sides, and their rifles in their hands, presenting altogether a very determined appearance.

Richard Howard and his confederate, compelled to remain very much against their inclination, retired into the shadow of the drapery that overhung the throne and kept out of sight.

The king peered curiously at the English party from under his thick heavy brows, a gleam of ironical exultation imparting an ominously savage expression to his dark features.

The king was in fact as savage as he could be, and as our hero and his friends were well armed and resolute, a desperate fight was certain.

Negomba, however, resolved to try a little palaver before using force.

"Why you go 'way widout axin' ?"

asked the King of Dahomey, scowling on the English explorers.

"We are not in the habit of asking permission either to run or walk, your majesty," returned our hero, proudly.

"Aug'i !" grunted Negomba, his eyes flashing; "you hab to ask my permission !"

"We are not prisoners," said Bob Blunt.

"Ah, yes; an' now you come back 'gain."

"Yes, we have !" replied Bob Blunt, in a voice so sternly emphatic that the king opened his eyes widely.

Our hero's look was as fixed and determined as his voice, as he repeated—

"We have come back—to demand justice."

"Justice !" echoed his companions.

This word was uttered with such a burst of heartfelt intensity that it almost startled the monarch.

"Justice 'bout what ?" he inquired, after a moment.

Bob Blunt, with all his former sternness of look and tone, continued—

"One of our party has been foully murdered and another carried off, whither I know not."

"Who have been murdered ?" asked the king, indifferently.

"A young girl who had attached herself to us, called Nahita."

Negomba did not appear to be in the least moved.

"And who de oder ?" he said, listlessly.

"A young English lady, whom your majesty will, doubtless, remember, named Elinor Cleveland."

"Ha ! de English maiden !" exclaimed the king, becoming more interested; "yes, yes ! me remember her. And she carried off, eh ?"

"Yes, by some vile treachery !" continued Bob, fiercely. "I am here in the name of the Queen of England to demand your help in seeking her out !"

"How me know whar de English gal am ?" cried the king; "me told you got her."

"She was here with us, but she is not now," explained our hero; "and her disappearance fills me with apprehension for her safety."

Negomba scowled.

"What you mean tell me lies, eh ?" he exclaimed in a rage, looking round for Richard Howard and his confederate, but they kept back out of sight.

The king grew furious.

"Sperrit of my fader an' de oder one, where are you ?" he shouted.

As he spoke he dashed aside the throne drapery with his hand and revealed their skulking forms.

"Why you tell me lies, eh ?" demanded Negomba, in a harsh, angry tone, of them.

"I told your majesty what I thought was the truth," replied Richard Howard, sullenly.

As he spoke, he glanced towards the English party, and his eyes encountered those of his cousin fixed sternly upon him.

"Your majesty must never believe that man," said our hero; "he knows not what truth is."

"Me tink you right dere," growled the king.

"He is a perjured liar, a robber and murderer !" continued Bob Blunt, with vehement emphasis, "and I believe the unfortunate Nahita died by his hand. His companion is a vile impostor."

With these words he sprang forward, and seizing Bow-legged Bill, he tore off the gorilla mask from his head, and the skin from his limbs.

Bow-legged Bill, shorn of his disguise, presented a ludicrously doleful spectacle, having nothing on but a dingy shirt and a pair of cotton pantaloons, which displayed the malformation of his lower limbs with painful distinctness.

"Now, your majesty, you can look upon the scoundrel as he is !" cried our hero.

The king was highly indignant, and roared lustily for the guard, who came tramping hastily in.

"Take dese two imperent 'posters an' chain dem togeder !" he cried.

This operation was instantly performed.

The two confederates were more firmly attached to each other than they had ever been before; but ere any further orders could be given loud shouts were heard outside the palace.

Trumpets were blown loudly, and voices became audible, crying—

"Kassa Kobo! Kassa Kobo!"

The king started from his seat in a paroxysm of delight.

"Kassa come! Kassa come!" he exclaimed with frantic exultation; "bring him here quick! quick!"

The guard flew to obey the orders of their despotic master.

The shouts increased.

The trumpets blew more vehemently than before.

Amidst the din the sound of footsteps was heard, and presently a crowd of dark forms poured in.

Foremost amongst them was one wearing a skin mantle and metal rings on his arms and legs.

This one strode forward with immense assurance, till he stood before the throne.

The king, who had risen to greet him, fell back in surprise and disappointment.

He was gazing upon a face and form entirely strange to him.

Nor were our hero and his comrades less astonished, when, in the burly form of the supposed captain, they recognised the boatswain, Rope's End.

CHAPTER IX.

A TERRIBLE RETRIBUTION.

FOR a moment there was a profound silence, during which the king looked at his visitor and the visitor looked at him.

At length Negomba said, angrily—

"You say you Kassa Kobo?"

"No, your majesty," returned the giant, with perfect self-complacency, "me Kassa Kobo's broder."

"Augh!" grunted the king; "me not want you. Why you come?"

"'Cause Kassa send me."

"Why he not come himself?"

"'Cause he not able."

"Why? why?" demanded the king, impatiently.

"'Cause he dead!"

"Dead!" echoed Negomba, his jaw dropping and his countenance expressing intense regret; "Kassa dead?"

"Yes; but before he die he tell me to come to your maj'sty. He say to me, 'Karfa'—my name Karfa——"

"Boder your name! Go on, sar!" growled the king, irritably.

"He say, 'When me dead, go to de king and say, I send you take my place to sell slave, get gold for your maj'sty.'"

"Hab you got any slave?"

"No, yar maj'sty," returned the boatswain, rolling his eyes furtively at the white men, whom he had recognised from the first moment of his entrance.

"How dat?" exclaimed the king, his features growing hard and stern with anger.

"De white men dat kill Kassa Kobo sink de ship wid all de slaves on board," replied Rope's End, with deliberate emphasis.

Negomba uttered a perfect howl of dismay.

"What!" he almost gasped, his lips turning ashy white in his fury; "de white men kill Kassa Kobo—sink de ship—what white men?"

The boatswain pointed towards Richard Howard, and continued, coolly—

"Dat de man dat p'ison poor broder Kassa."

Then turning to our hero and his comrades, he added, in the same tone—

"And dem are de ones dat sink de ship an' lose all de gold."

The consummate impudence with which these statements were made for a moment deprived those accused of the power of speech, and when they at length vociferously denied them, the king, embittered at his loss, would not listen.

"You shall die, all ob you!" he roared, fiercely, "wedder you hold de sperrits ob my fader an' moder or not."

The spirit of our hero, depressed as it was by the loss of his beloved Elinor, had not greatly asserted itself during this interview; but now his English blood was roused.

"Stay, King Negomba!" he cried, sternly; "neither myself nor my friends are responsible for the loss of your treasures; and if, on the word of that unprincipled scoundrel yonder, you regard us as guilty, be assured that we shall defend ourselves against you!"

Having spoken these words, he gave a signal to his comrades.

Instantly they formed themselves into a compact body, from which bristled ominously a score of rifle-muzzles.

"Now," he continued, "if our progress be interrupted, we fire."

The king foamed with fury at this defiance; but he knew the terrible power of English firearms, and he hesitated to give the word that might have sacrificed many lives, his own included, since Buttons had pointed his rifle in a direct line with the monarch's right eye.

He paused in mingled rage and embarrassment, till at length he glanced towards the portal, which was completely blockaded by dark forms, armed with spears and darts.

This reassured him, and he shouted—

"Cut down dem white men!"

"Fire!" cried Bob Blunt.

Every rifle was at once discharged, but ere our hero and his followers had time to reload, they were surrounded by a crowd of burly negroes.

In an instant they were seized and their weapons snatched from their hands.

Negomba, who had rolled from off his throne at the deafening report of the volley, sprang up exultingly.

"Yah, yah, yah!" he yelled. "Now, you cussed English, you die; eb'ry one!"

As he uttered these words there slowly entered the hideous executioner, holding the terrible weapon of his office in his hand.

"You see dat, you Massa Blunt, eh?" demanded Negomba, as he pointed to it.

"Yes, I see," replied our hero, coolly.

"Well, den, you feel presently. You rescue my prisoners; you kill Kassa Kobo——"

"False!" cried Bob. "I did not kill him!"

"It big lie!" shouted Rope's End, his eyes gleaming vindictively. "He did kill him!"

"He shall die the fust!"

As Negomba spoke, he made a motion with his hand.

Our hero was forced upon his knees.

With a shudder of intense horror his comrades beheld the hideous Schava raise the fatal blade aloft, but they did not observe a figure shrouded from head to foot in a white mantle, who had entered during the confusion and stood listening to all that passed.

Now this figure strode forward.

"Hold!" it cried.

At the sound of the voice the king started; the weapon of the executioner remained poised in the air.

All present stood as if spellbound.

"Who spoke?" asked Negomba, in a tone of apprehension, after a moment.

"I did," returned the figure. "Captain Blunt is innocent of the death of Kassa Kobo."

"No, no!" yelled Rope's End. "He kill him! Me take my oath he killed him!"

"Liar!" thundered the shrouded man. "Kassa Kobo lives! Behold him!"

As he spoke he cast aside his white garment and the form of the pirate-captain stood revealed.

"That is the man who stabbed me, coward-like, in the back," he continued, as he pointed to Rope's End; "Karfa the Krooman."

The guilty man, thus brought to bay, glared wildly round for an instant, and then, drawing himself up, he made a spring forward, as if to escape; but all in vain, for even as he sprang, Kassa, the pirate-captain, snatched the sword of the executioner from his grasp.

Brightly it flashed in the air as it

descended, cleaving the boatswain's head in twain.

Then, with another wave of the weapon, he swept the divided skull clean from the neck.

The two halves had fallen ere the giant corpse reached the ground.

Negomba was perfectly delighted at this latter feat.

The return of Kassa Kobo pleased him ; but the skill he had shown in the art of decapitation pleased him still more, and he embraced him warmly.

As soon as the pirate could extricate himself from his clasp he approached our hero.

With much respect he raised him from his humiliating position, and knelt at his feet, kissing his hands with warm affection.

This done he presented him to the king.

"This noble Englishman and the dear young English lady saved my life," he said, gratefully ; "but for them I should not now be here."

This changed the aspect of affairs at once.

The turn events had taken had restored the African monarch to perfect good humour, and once more Bob Blunt and his party were restored to liberty and favour ; but the fate of Elinor Cleveland was still a secret.

Negomba affirmed, and with truth, that she was not within the precincts of his palace.

There were only two who could have given any information respecting her.

These were Richard Howard and his confederate ; but they were the very last persons in the world to criminate themselves by confessing anything ; and they remained doggedly silent.

Bob Blunt spoke a few words to Kassa Kobo, and Kassa whispered to the king.

The result of this was that Negomba ordered Richard Howard and Bow-legged Bill to be detained as prisoners and carefully looked after.

As they were being removed a dark figure fixed his eyes very earnestly on the rough and made him a peculiar sign.

Bill recognised him after an instant and made him a sign in return.

"Jumbo," he muttered to himself, thoughtfully, as he went along ; "he means somethink. Wot, I wonder?"

CHAPTER X.

BOB BLUNT PAYS THE PRISONERS A VISIT.

RICHARD HOWARD and his companion were confined in a building sufficiently strong to render all hope of escape without assistance impossible.

Then their irons were removed.

"'Ere's a poorty kettle er fish," grumbled Bill, as the daylight through the bars of their prison began to wane ; "we're done now to a certainty."

"Psha!" growled Richard ; "we've been in worse straits than this."

"I don't see it. I think this is a settler."

"Nonsense."

"Well, I thinks it is," Bill insisted ; "we've lost the game, and Mr. Bob Blunt's got it all in his own hands."

"You forget there's one thing he hasn't got," remarked Richard Howard, triumphantly.

"Wot's that?"

"Elinor Cleveland."

"Umph!" growled Bill ; "I don't see as she's much good to any one, and one thing's sartin, if we're kept shut up here, she'll be starved, and then there'll be no more bother about her."

A serious expression stole over the features of Richard Howard at these words.

He knew they were true, and bad as he was he shuddered inwardly as he thought of the poor girl—barred and bolted in one of the upper rooms of the farm, without the means of procuring food or drink.

Something between a groan and an oath burst from his lips.

His confederate did not seem to be much more resigned than himself.

"This is all come about from putting on the skin er that beastly griller," he growled. "I knew we should be bowled out."

"We should have been all right enough but for that clever cousin of mine," returned Richard, bitterly; "but no matter, it only adds to the debt of vengeance I owe him."

This was rather too much for the Bowlegs, who was rapidly losing every vestige of respect for his master, and he said, scornfully—

"Wot's the good er your talking erbout paying debts er wengince when ye're locked up in this 'ere hole?"

"We shan't be confined here for ever, idiot!" retorted Richard.

"'Oo said we should? We shall only stop 'ere till we're taken out to be hoperated on by that ugly cove with the large carving-knife. Ugh!"

Bow-legged Bill fairly shuddered at the fate he had pictured to himself.

At this moment the bolt was drawn, the door opened, and Bob Blunt entered.

The latter gazed at his cousin in silence for a moment, and then he said—

"Are you aware that your life is in my hands?"

"I was not aware of it," was the sullen reply.

"Believe me, then, it is so. I have only to speak the word, and the executioner would at once appear, and strike off your head."

A ghastly smile flitted over the sallow face of the prisoner as he said, coolly—

"Did you come here expressly to tell me this?"

"No; I came to offer you life and liberty."

"Indeed!" exclaimed Richard Howard, startled out of his assumed indifference at these prospects.

"On certain conditions," added his cousin.

"We accept 'em," cried Bow-legged Bill.

Richard Howard turned and glared at his confederate like a fiend; then, looking once more towards his cousin, he said, inquiringly—

"What are these conditions?"

"First, that you reveal the place where you have concealed Miss Cleveland," replied Bob Blunt, eyeing him sternly.

"I know nothing of Miss Cleveland," he answered, doggedly.

"You do," returned our hero. "A portion of her dress has been found in the forest, and near to it a hat such as you have worn."

Richard Howard bit his lips, but still denied all knowledge of her.

"What else?" he asked.

"Next that you restore the thousand pounds in gold of which you robbed me by means of a forged letter to Mr. James Sawyer, my agent in England."

"Thousand pounds—forged letter—James Sawyer—agent," repeated Richard, in an innocently dreamy manner. "Are you going out of your senses, cousin?"

"Not at all," returned Bob; "but I am inclined to think that is your condition. But, mark me well, I believe you to be guilty on both the points I have mentioned. If you make reparation by confession your life will be spared; if not, as surely as you are now before me so surely will you die to-morrow. I leave you to reflect, and will visit you again in the evening."

With this warning our hero took his departure.

"I tell yer wot it is, pardner," said Bow-legged Bill, as soon as he was gone; "yer'll have to give up the gal an' hand over the coin."

"Curse me if I do!" cried Richard, his eyes flashing wrathfully.

"If yer don't I'll split on yer, as sure as my name's Bill."

"You will?"

"I will. Wot's a bit of a gal and a few yeller boys compared with life an' liberty?" argued the rough, very sensibly.

"Nothing, perhaps. But revenge is worth everything!" hissed his master, through his set teeth. "To gain that I'd even part with life."

"I wouldn't."

"Bah! You're a soulless idiot."

"That may be your opinion, Mister 'Oward; but it strikes me as theer's another idiot, not fur orff, a sight bigger than me."

Richard gave a sharp growl, and looked as if he could have murdered his soulless comrade.

Just at that moment a shuffling of feet was heard beneath the window outside, and a voice called, in a cautious tone—

"Massa Bow-legs, you dere?"

"Yes, I'm here," returned Bill, springing up and approaching the grating. "Who is it?"

"Jumbo," returned the voice.

The rough glanced down through the bars and could just catch sight of his Abyssinian friend.

"Wot's your little game, Jum?" he asked.

"You like get out whar you am?" Jumbo inquired.

"Shouldn't I?" returned Bill.

"Bery well. Den me try git yar out."

"You're a brick, Jum; a reg'ler brick. 'Ow are yer goin' to manage it?"

"Guard ask me watch prison while he go see 'im sweetheart to-night. And den me unlock de door and let you out."

"Yer worth yer weight in pig-iron, Jum, ole son," exclaimed the Bow-legs, enthusiastically. "An' wheer's the guard now?"

"Talkee to gal ober yonder," returned Jumbo. "Sh! Here him come."

The sentinel approached, little suspecting the plot that had been hatched in his absence.

The sun set, and, as soon as it was dark, Jumbo repaired to the prison.

He found the guard anxiously waiting to be released from duty.

It took but a few moments to make an exchange of certain of their garments, in order to avoid suspicion.

This done, Jumbo said—

"Now, den, for de key."

The guard shook his head.

"No, no," he said. "Me not gib up dat."

"S'pose any one want get inside de prison while you away, what den?" asked Jumbo. "What me say if dey ask me for de key?"

The sentinel was impressed by this question.

"If I leabe de key, you be bery careful not open door let out de white prisoners, eh?"

"Oh, no."

"Dere it am, den."

With these words the guard handed over the key to Jumbo, and hastened off on the wings of love to his sable mistress.

In less than ten minutes after his departure Jumbo forgot his promise and opened the door.

Richard Howard and Bow-legged Bill were once more at liberty.

"Me come 'long wid you, Massa Bow-legs," said Jumbo.

The rough did not at all object to this. He believed in Jumbo very much more than he did in his master, and he said—

"Come on, if you like, Jum. But mind, yer'll have to make yourself useful, an' work."

Richard Howard was about to upset this arrangement, which had been made entirely without his permission; but on second thoughts he determined not to interfere, and together they hurried away to the forest.

When Bob Blunt visited the prison in the evening he found the guard absent, the door locked, but no prisoners inside.

It was with intense chagrin he made this discovery.

His chance of recovering his beloved Elinor seemed fainter now than ever.

CHAPTER XI.

THE CRY IN THE DISTANCE.

IT was on a sultry afternoon a few days after the foregoing events that Buttons and Skyrocket found themselves in the heart of the wood.

They had been away from the encampment for some hours, and had halted for rest and refreshment.

Buttons was ventilating a grand scheme he had formed in his own mind to his sable companion.

"The fact is, Sykhigh," he said, "I feel I was born to be hero. I've made up my mind to find out what has become of Miss Cleveland."

"Ah; de pretty young English lady?"

"Yes. The captain's almost off 'is nut about 'er, and if I could only discover 'er my fortin' 'ud be made."

"Whar you tink she am?" asked Skyrocket.

"'Ow do I know? That's just what I've got to find out."

"'Ow you mean to find out?"

"By searchin' er course."

"Whar you goin' to search?"

"Everywhere."

"Golly! dat take long time."

"The sooner we begin, then, the better," said Buttons, grandly; "and first we'll explore this forest."

In pursuance of this magnificent but impossible idea the page rose and started off at a good pace.

They went on till they came to a spot where there was a kind of roadway. The marks of heavy wheels being perceptible, Buttons paused and examined them.

The spot looked wild and unusually lonely. Suddenly Skyrocket uttered an exclamation, and pointed.

"See, see! Dere man," he cried.

"Where?" demanded Buttons, looking with all his eyes.

"Dere, in de bushes."

Buttons could barely discern something that looked like a human form.

"Jest go an' see what it is," he said, in a light tone to his companion.

"No, tankee, Massa Buttons; you go fuss."

"Well, I'll go myself!" exclaimed Buttons.

With a burst of determination he pushed through the bushes till he reached the object.

"Oh—oh Lor'!" he bawled; "it's a corpse!"

Skyrocket ran towards him.

There, in a sitting posture in the bushes, was the ghastly frame of the unfortunate farmer, Peter Van Droonk.

Every particle of flesh had disappeared, and nothing remained but his skeleton, on which his garments hung.

Buttons and his comrade remained gazing at the terrible sight in horror.

"Him bery much dead," remarked the negro boy, at length.

"Very much indeed," returned the page, "considerin' there's nothink left of 'im but 'is bones."

"'Ow he come dere? He no walk."

"No; people don't walk after they're dead, as a rule."

"He put dere, den, eh?"

"Yes. I tell you what I think."

"What you tink?"

Buttons lowered his voice to its most awful depths and whispered—

"'E's been murdered!"

"Oh, golly!" ejaculated Skyrocket. "Who murder him?"

"That's more than I can tell yer,' returned Buttons, solemnly. "It's a awful mystery!"

"P'r'aps de young English lady murdered too," suggested his companion.

"What, Miss Cleveland?" exclaimed Buttons, indignantly. "No, no; it isn't possible. Who'd murder her?"

"Whar she gone, den?"

"That we have got to discover, and, as

we can do no good to this unfort'nate skelington, let's continue our search."

Buttons took particular note of the surroundings, and carved a rude cross on the bark of a tree close by in order to identify the spot, after which the adventurers resumed their march.

They encountered nothing, either living or dead, save a few monkeys and macaws, which were too insignificant to arrest their attention.

The sun was setting when they came to the borders of the wood.

Before them was a vast plain glowing with the crimson and purple rays of the departing luminary.

Once more they sat down to rest and refresh.

"It strikes me," said Buttons, as he puffed a cigarette, "we shan't get 'ome to-night!"

"Dat no matter much," grinned the negro; "we sleep here bery good."

"Yes, but how about supper? The grub's all gone, and it's not 'bery good' to go to bed fasting."

"P'r'aps we find some village whar we sleep—get chow-chow."

"Come on, then. Wouldn't it be glorious if we could light upon Miss Elinor? We'd carry 'er 'ome in triumph, wouldn't we?" cried Buttons.

"Iss, iss; we carry 'er."

"Ooray!" shouted the page, with a burst of enthusiasm.

"'Ooray! 'oo——"

The negro's cheer was cut short by Buttons laying his hand warningly on his arm.

"Hush!" he whispered. "Look yonder."

He pointed as he spoke to two figures who were standing about a hundred yards off.

"Who dem?" asked Skyrocket.

The setting sun lighted upon them very vividly, and Buttons answered, after a moment—

"One of 'em's Bow-legged Bill, but who the other is I don't know, only that he's a darky."

The appearance of these two in such a spot struck Buttons as strange and mysterious.

A moment before the plain had been perfectly clear.

It seemed as if the parties must have suddenly risen from the bowels of the earth or else dropped from the clouds.

But they had done neither. The Bow-legs and his pet Jumbo had been lying down on the grass, which concealed them, and only became visible upon their rising to their feet.

They had evidently been startled by the shouts that had reached their ears, and were now straining their eyes in all directions in search of the shouters; but the latter stood in the deep shadow of the trees, where the rapidly deepening gloom rendered them perfectly secure from observation.

After a little further scrutiny the two men walked away across the plain. Buttons remained watching them for a few moments.

Suddenly he exclaimed, with eager intensity—

"We must follow that Bow-legged rough and the darky. We may get some intelligence."

"'Bout de young lady?"

"Yes."

"We go den."

With rapid steps Buttons and his comrade hurried along in the track of Bow-legged Bill and Jumbo; but, to their great disappointment, they saw no more of them.

It had now grown quite dark, and they were brought to a stand, knowing not in which direction to turn their steps.

"What a cussed noosance!" muttered Buttons, fretfully; "we've lost 'em now."

"Better stop whar we am till de moon rise," counselled Skyrocket. "Den we able see; find 'em p'raps."

"Not a bit of it," growled Buttons, intensely chagrined; "they'll be many miles off by that time."

But there being no better course to adopt, he and his comrade seated themselves until the moonbeams should throw a light upon their path.

Buttons chafed greatly at the delay.

"I can't help thinkin' that if we could a-follered Bow-legs an' the other, we should a-learnt somethink worth knowin'," he said, discontentedly.

"Well, neber mind, Massa Buttons; moon soon be up, den we start," said Skyrocket, soothingly.

"It seems twice as long gettin' up as it is any other night," grumbled the page, as he peered up into the dark sky.

"It's no good goin' on widout light," suggested the negro; "not able see de young lady if she right before us."

"I don't think we shall ever see her again," returned Buttons, who had worked himself up into a thorough bad temper. "The best thing we can do's to——"

The speaker broke off suddenly, for, at that moment a faint cry reached him from the distance.

"You hear dat, Massa Buttons?" exclaimed Skyrocket, eagerly.

"I did," returned Buttons, excitedly. "That was a woman's voice, I'm certain."

Buttons and his black friend listened eagerly and again heard the cry.

"Tink it Miss El'nor's woice?" asked the negro, in an eager tone.

"Can't say for cert'n, it's too fur off; but there's somethink in it, I feel sure," Buttons replied, hurriedly. "I can't stop 'ere a minnit longer arter that. On we goes to the rescue—victory or death—'ooray!"

The dauntless youth, carried away by his excitement, rushed wildly forward, followed by Skyrocket.

They had travelled some distance, and now stopped to reconnoitre and see where they had got to.

In one direction there was nothing but a dark mass of trees; but in another a large building loomed forth in the moonlight.

It was a farmhouse built entirely of logs.

It stood on a considerable space of ground, being only one storey high.

The adventurers stole cautiously forward till they stood close under the side of the building.

The door and windows were closed, the latter being strongly secured by shutters.

"It looks a tough sort er place, don't it?" whispered Buttons, as he glanced up at the massive jambs and beams.

"Iss; bery strong," admitted Skyrocket. "How you get in, eh?"

"There's only one way, it seems to me."

"What dat?"

"By knocking at the door."

With these words he approached the porch.

Skyrocket followed close at his heels.

He was about to knock, when a faint, moaning sound arrested his intention.

"Did you hear anything?" he asked his companion.

"Iss; me tink me hear someun say 'Oo-oo-oo.'"

"Some one in pain, it seems to me," said Buttons. "We'll put off knockin' for a minnit, and see if we can find out what that groaning means."

They stepped out from under the porch, and, keeping close to the wall where the shadow was deep, they commenced making a circuit of the building.

They had got round to the rear, when the moans, which had ceased for a few moments, broke forth again.

The sounds were muffled and indistinct, and Buttons gave it as his opinion that they came from some subterranean cellar, and that the voice was a woman's.

"P'raps it de young English lady," suggested Skyrocket.

"That's 'xac'ly my opinion, Blacky-top," returned Buttons, emphatically. "I believes we've got the end er the clue at last, and that Miss El'nor's 'ere."

"'Ow we get to her?"

"Ah! that's the question. We must see."

"It too dark see much, Massa Button."

They looked about them eagerly in search of some trap or grating in the ground, but could find nothing.

It was in the midst of their search that they were interrupted by the sound of voices.

"Someun comin'!" whispered Skyrocket, hastily.

"Get out of sight, quick!" said Buttons, in reply, as he sprang into the shadow and crouched down.

His comrade instantly followed him.

They were only just in time to accom-

"BUTTONS FIRST OF ALL SEIZED THE BOX.'

plish this when two figures came in sight.

These were Bow-legged Bill and Jumbo.

They walked arm-in-arm, and seemed to be on the most amicable terms.

As they came along they rolled from side to side in a manner that proved they had indulged pretty freely in powerful potations.

"Jum, ole feller, I respecs yer," hiccoughed the Bow-legs, as he clung to his black friend's arm.

"Me suspecs yar, too, bery much," was Jumbo's reply.

"We'll stick together, ole son—like—hic—bricks an' mortar," continued the rough.

"Me 'tick to yar."

"Yer know, Jum, I've got a fust-rate idear."

"Whar dat?"

"My pardner's got a heap er coin."

"Massa Howard?"

"Yes."

"He go 'long wud us to Inglan'?"

"No. We don't wornt him. All we wornts is 'is money."

"'Ow you git dat?"

"Well," explained the rough, "he keeps it in a snug corner in the cupboard, an' my game'll be to get the key and nick the lot."

"Dat bery good."

"Fust-rate. We can't do without the needful."

"When you git key?" asked Jumbo.

"The wery first minnit as I gets the chance. Then as soon as we've got th' thousan' poun's we'll take our 'ook; an' jolly glad I shall be to get away. I've 'ad too much of 'im."

"S'pose he not let you hab de money, what den?"

"He can't 'elp 'isself," returned Bill. "If he makes any bother erbout it I've made up my mind wot to do."

"What you do?"

"Knock 'is brains out."

"Bery good knock dat," grinned Jumbo. After a moment he continued—

"What you do 'bout de white gal?"

"Miss Cleveland?"

"Iss."

"Well, I shouldn't mind takin' 'er with us. She'd soot me wery well for a wife."

"She not like yar bery much, eh?" said Jumbo, doubtfully.

"P'r'aps not," returned Bill; "but theer's ways er breakin' in obstrop'lus gals jest as theer's ways er breakin' in 'osses. She'd like me well enough arter a few good wollopins."

With these words he led his pal round the building till they reached the door. Then, by some peculiar pressure, applied to a particular spot, the latch went up.

The door swung open on its hinges, and they entered, after which the door swung to and closed upon them. Buttons and Skyrocket, who had followed pretty closely on their track, were left standing outside.

"Well," exclaimed the former, after a moment, "if this 'ere discov'ry ain't a merrikle, nothink ain't."

"You find what you want, eh, Massa Button?" remarked his comrade.

"Everythink. The thousand poun's, Miss El'nor, and the scamps as have carried 'em off. We've got the 'ole affair in a nutshell."

"What you do now?"

"Don't bother!" cried the page, sharply. "It's a noosance to be asked what yer a-goin' to do when yer don't know yerself."

"S'pose we break open the door and get de money," suggested Skyrocket.

"Yer talks like a idiot!" snapped Buttons, irritably. "Do yer want yer brains knocked out? Our plan 'll be to get back to the encampment as soon as we can."

"Ah, iss; tell de capt'n?"

"Yes, and return in a body and storm the crib and collar the vagabonds in it."

"We got long way to go, Massa Button," remarked Skyrocket.

"I know's that."

"We hab no supper eider," continued the negro, wistfully.

"I knows that, too," returned Buttons, pressing his hands together upon his stomach. "I'm as 'ungry as a hostrich."

Just at that moment a savoury odour was wafted to their nostrils.

"There's a jolly feed a-goin' on inside, I know," muttered the page.

With this remark he slowly walked away from the door until he reached the window. Here he stopped, as a crackling sound as of something frying caught his ear from within.

"I should like to see what's agoin' on inside," continued the page, after listening a little.

"We able to see if de shutters not dere."

"P'r'aps there's a crack we can peep through," said Buttons. "Jest give us a back, Skyhigh."

Skyrocket bent his body, and his comrade quickly scrambled up, holding on by the crossbeam of the shutter to steady himself. To his dismay it suddenly swung open.

Had he not grasped it he would certainly have fallen.

"We're bowled out now to a certainty," he muttered.

But, to his great satisfaction, those within took no notice of the open shutter, being too much engrossed in cooking some buffalo-steaks.

Very much relieved in his mind, Buttons gently closed the shutter again, leaving just sufficient space for peeping through.

He could see Richard Howard stretched placidly on a mat near the fire, smoking his pipe. His brows were knitted and stern as he lay watching his two assistants.

In a short time the meal was ready.

Richard did not join in it, but kept his position on the mat; but Bow-legged Bill and Jumbo did full justice to the food, which they moistened with copious draughts from a bottle which stood on the table.

It was terribly painful to the famished Buttons to see the juicy steaks disappearing, and he not able to get the smallest morsel, but he consoled himself with the idea of making up for lost time at the first opportunity.

At length the meal was finished.

Bow-legs and his comrade then lit their pipes and threw themselves on the ground, where, after a few puffs, they fell fast asleep and snored like a couple of wild hogs.

Richard Howard regarded them for some time with an expression of profound contempt.

At length, their stertorous breathing assuring him that they were sound in their slumbers, he rose, and, taking the lamp in his hand, approached and scanned their faces intently, then murmuring to himself, "They're certainly safe enough now," went straight to the cupboard.

Having unlocked it he brought forth a small wooden box, which he placed on the table.

Touching a spring, he opened this and showered its glittering contents on the table.

"There's a power in money!" he exclaimed, exultingly. "Ha, ha! how cleverly I managed to secure this thousand!"

Richard, having gloated over his ill-gotten gains for some time, counted the gold pieces, and, putting them into a bag, restored them to the box.

He then lit his pipe, and, producing a blotting-case and some pens and ink, sat for a few moments apparently wrapped in thought.

"The girl's safe enough in my power," he soliloquised, after a little time, "and the sooner I leave this infernal dust-dried country the better; and Elinor must go with me."

"Oh, ha!" chuckled Buttons, quietly, "wouldn't yer like it?"

"But," continued Richard, "before I start there is one whose life I must take, or all that I have risked and endured will be but lost labour. Yes, my plucky cousin, I know you are lurking in the woods, and it shall go hard if a bullet from my rifle does not find its way to your heart."

"Murderous viper!" ejaculated Buttons, breaking out into a cold sweat at the terrible idea.

Then, spreading his paper before him with the letter which had been taken from Bob Blunt's pocket, as a copy, Howard commenced, speaking the words aloud as he wrote them, Buttons listening the while with great interest.

The epistle ran thus—

"MY DEAR SAWYER,—The remittance arrived safely, and was duly handed over to me by Daniel Jeddha. I am happy to say our party still continues in excellent health and spirits. You will be glad to hear that I am reconciled to my cousin, Richard Howard. We came across one another in these wild regions, and we have experienced some hair-breadth escapes together. I find him a capital fellow, and he has twice risked his own life to save mine. On this account I feel I owe him a large debt of gratitude, which I am anxious to repay. I may tell you in confidence I intend to appoint him as my successor to the Blunt estates. If, therefore, anything should happen to me, you will take this as an expression of my kind intentions towards him. With best wishes,

"I am——"

At this moment a knocking at the door in the rear of the premises interrupted him.

"Who the devil's that?" he growled to himself, as he started up, turning a shade paler than usual. "I expect no one."

The knocker was Skyrocket, who was acting under the directions of Buttons.

A brilliant idea had flashed across the mind of the youthful page.

He had rapidly concocted a little plot, which was now being carried out.

Richard Howard remained hesitating.

He glanced at his sleeping satellites, and appeared half-inclined to rouse them.

Had he done so, the scheme of the heroic Buttons would have been nipped in the bud ; but, on the knocking being repeated, Howard seized the lamp, and went to the door.

As soon as he was gone Buttons flung back the shutter, softly opened the window, and stepped inside.

His proceedings were rapid in the extreme.

First of all he pounced upon the box of gold.

"'Ere, ketch 'old," he exclaimed hurriedly, as he handed it to his comrade, who had by this time returned to the window.

"Me got him all right, Massa Button!" grinned Skyrocket, as he received it.

Then Buttons seized the pen, and, dipping it in the ink, performed certain operations upon the forged letter, adding a few remarks of his own.

He next thrust his master's letter into his pocket, and finally made a swoop upon the remains of a buffalo-steak and a bottle of rum.

"Grub!" he said, as he handed them to his confederate, and immediately followed himself, closing the window softly and the shutters after him.

The next moment they were skudding along at full speed with their treasures.

Richard Howard, in the interim, had unbarred the back-door and looked out.

No one was there.

He called, but no one answered.

"It must have been fancy!" he muttered to himself, at length, as he closed the door.

When he returned to the room his satellites were snoring as harmoniously as when he left them, and everything apparently was as it was before.

He went to the table.

The first thing he missed was the box of gold.

It had been there a few moments before.

He knew he had not moved it himself, yet now it was gone.

An execration of mingled horror and surprise burst from his lips.

"What, in the fiend's name, does this mean?" he almost gasped.

His eyes rolled wildly round until they lighted on the sleepers ; but they were so thoroughly unconscious that even he could not suspect them.

"Have I been robbed by some invisible agent?" he continued.

He glanced towards the table.

The letter of his cousin, which served as his model for his forgeries, had disappeared.

His own letter next caught his sight.

He had left it incomplete—now it was finished.

Buttons had kindly taken it up where he left off, and finished it for him, and the termination now read thus—

"With best wishes, I am ever,

"A lyin', swindlin' 'umbug,

"RICHARD HOWARD."

"Witness —Thomas Buttons."

A bitter yell of rage burst from the lips of the baffled forger as he read these words, and he gnashed his teeth in impotent rage.

"How, in the fiend's name, could this whelp have come here?" he cried, hoarsely.

Suddenly his eye fastened on the window. The shutter had again swung open, revealing the bright moonlight without.

This gave a clue.

"He must have entered by the window, the young thief!" he exclaimed, bitterly; "but I shall lay hands on the pitiful wretch yet, and when I do he shall have cause to remember his night's work!"

He strode fiercely up and down the apartment for some moments, until at length, in a fit of uncontrollable rage, he rushed towards his sleeping confederates, and vented his spleen by kicking them violently in their ribs.

With loud yells they awoke.

"What're yer up to?" growled Bow-legged Bill.

"Rouse yourselves, you sluggards!" shouted Richard, fiercely. "I've been robbed!"

"Eh—what—robbed?" echoed the rough, rubbing his ribs and his eyes at the same time.

"Yes, of a thousand pounds. Get up and prepare to accompany me in pursuit of the thief."

The loss of the money the Bow-legs had marked out as his own prey completely restored his faculties.

"Get up, Jum! We're robbed!" he cried, as he sprang to his feet. "The thousand pounds is nicked!"

Jumbo, half asleep, struggled from his mat, and in a few moments they were ready to start.

CHAPTER XII.

FOES CONVERTED INTO FRIENDS.

GREAT was the joy at the encampment when Buttons and his comrade returned; but the joy was greatly increased when he handed the gold to his master and related all that he had seen and heard and done.

It was perfectly clear now to our hero that his beautiful betrothed was in the power of his remorseless relative, and he resolved to proceed at once to the farmhouse and demand his beloved girl from her abductor.

It took but little time to prepare for departure, and soon the small camp was broken up and in motion.

They were entirely dependent upon the memory of Buttons and Skyrocket to guide them to the spot they sought, and, the journey of the page and his comrade having been made in the night, the task of retracing their path was difficult; but they set to work in earnest, and, though their progress was somewhat slow, it was tolerably sure, and the course they took correct.

It was on the second day they halted in the forest, and, while they were taking their meal in silence, they were suddenly aroused by the murmuring of voices— voices, too, that seemed familiar.

Bob Blunt sprang up, and laying his finger on his lips to enjoin perfect stillness, he motioned his comrades into the bushes.

This was at once obeyed.

The voices grew more and more distinct; the speakers were evidently approaching, and presently Bow-legged Bill and Jumbo appeared, making their way through the brushwood.

The countenance of the rough was anything but pleasing in its expression at that moment, having a strong resemblance to an ill-tempered bull-dog.

"I ain't a goin' to stand any more er Mister Richard 'Oward's bounce," he growled; "I've had enough on it."

"What you mean to do?" asked his comrade.

"I means to give him two ounces er lead in 'is nob, that's wot I means to do," answered Bill, very defiantly.

"Den he be kill, eh?" said Jumbo.

"Yes; and about time he was," returned Bow-legs.

By this time they had reached the spot where the explorers had been seated a short time before.

In the hasty retreat of the latter a bottle of brandy had been left behind.

The eyes of the rough at once fastened on this.

"Coniyac!" he exclaimed, after picking it up and tasting it.

He took a prolonged draught and handed it to Jumbo, who followed his example.

The spirit seemed to have a happy effect upon the temperament of Bow-legged Bill; the scowl departed from his face, and he again put the bottle to his lips; the attitude was favourable, and at a signal from Bob Blunt the English party sprang from their concealment.

The next moment Bow-legged Bill and Jumbo were on their backs, with a dozen revolvers pointed at them.

"Now, scoundrel," cried our hero, sternly, to the rough, "if you know a prayer, breathe it, for you have only a few moments to live!"

Bill glanced up ruefully at the muzzles of the revolvers; they looked particularly terrible and deadly.

He scanned the countenances of those who grasped them, and could read in them only stern determination.

The prospect was very depressing, and the fear of death began to chill the heart of the Bow-legs.

Jumbo seemed perfectly indifferent.

"Wot's the good er killin' me?" said Bill, at length, in a hoarse, faltering voice.

"Wag'bons like you are better out er th' world than in it," Buttons replied.

"You've got th' best on me this time," continued the rough, his face twitching nervously; "but I don't know as yer couldn't get more out of me alive than dead."

"What do you mean?" asked Bob Blunt.

"Well, I means that if yer was to spare my life I might be able to do yer a good turn, capt'in."

"Spare you in order that you may return to Richard Howard and plot more evil against us, eh?" said our hero.

"I don't want to return to Richard 'Oward," protested Bill; "I 'ates im' as I 'ates th' devil!"

"I can't trust you," said Bob, shaking his head.

"Yer may then, capt'in; an' I tell yer wot, I think yer'd better, if ever yer want to see a cert'in young lady ag'in. I don't know whether you're aware on it, but she's in 'is power."

"I am aware of it," answered Bob; "but I have the means now of compelling him to deliver her up to me."

"P'raps yer 'ave," said the rough; "but remember, there's two ways er givin' a woman up. I know summat er Mister 'Oward's ways, and I'm sartin if he found things goin' agin 'im, sooner than you should 'ave the young lady 'e'd blow 'er brains out 'fore yer eyes, that's wot 'e'd do!"

"Merciless wretch!" murmured our hero, in a tone of indignant horror; "she must be preserved at any cost!"

"Well, an' if yer spares my life and trusts to me so she may be," said Bill. "I swear by all that's good in this world an' the next I means yer fair; if I don't I wish I may die like a dawg!"

"Enough! I trust you," said our hero; "but remember, if you act treacherously you die without mercy."

"I won't capt'in! I swear I won't! I'll stick to yer now through thick and thin."

"Release him!" said Bob.

Bow-legged Bill was unbound and allowed to stand up.

"You will answer for your companion?" asked our hero.

"Oh, yes, capt'in, I'll answer for Jum; 'es' a pal er mine."

"And now, what of Miss Cleveland? Let me hear," continued Bob, anxiously.

"Well, capt'in, she's a prisoner up at the farm."

"Let us all proceed in a body to the farm and take it by storm," cried Ironfist.

"That wouldn't do," said Bill; "if Richard 'Oward was to be brought to bay he'd do wot a tiger does, and then, woe to those as is in reach of 'im. We must go to work on the quiet—do the artful dodge and not startle 'im."

"Let me hear your plan if you have one."

"Well, then, I think you'd better leave it to me, capt'in."

"Well?"

"Well, then, at the very first opportunity I'll unlock Miss El'nor's prison doors an' bring 'er out to yer. As soon as sh²'s all right yer can do whatever yer likes."

Bob Blunt and his comrades approved of this plan.

"When shall you be able to effect Miss Cleveland's deliverance?" asked our hero, eagerly.

"To-night!"

"You are sure?"

"Sartin! I'll give Mister 'Oward sometink strong in his rum as shall knock 'im right orff 'is legs, and then I'll release th' prisoner."

"I depend on you."

"So yer may; Master Buttons there'll guide yer to the farm, 'cos 'e's bin there, I know."

"At what hour shall we come?"

"Two 'ours arter th' moon rises."

"We'll be there."

"An' if I don't bring yer out th' young lady safe an' sound say I'm a duffer, that's all."

With these words Bow-legged Bill and his companion were permitted to depart.

Congratulating himself that his life was spared, and that he would have an opportunity of paying off his grudge against the master he had learnt to hate, the rough strode along through the forest; but he knew not that death lurked behind him.

He saw not a ghastly white face that rose up like a spectre from out a clump of bushes, nor the pair of evil eyes full of fiendish hate that followed his retreating form.

Yet there was such a figure.

Richard Howard had been concealed in a thick bush within a few yards of his confederate during his conference with Bob Blunt.

He had heard all that had passed, and was fully upon his guard; with an awfully bitter oath, he doomed Bow-legged Bill to destruction, and vowed with equal depth and vehemence that sooner than yield up Elinor Cleveland to his rival he would stab her to the heart with his own hand.

CHAPTER XIII.

THE RETURN OF THE EXPLORERS TO ENGLAND.

BOW-LEGGED BILL and Jumbo made their way back to the farm with all expedition.

Richard Howard was still absent, at which Bill congratulated himself, for he had been away for some time, and did not wish to excite his master's suspicion.

All things considered, he was rather glad that he had been dropped upon by our hero, for he had a kind of floating idea on his mind that this circumstance would turn out to his advantage.

"Now, Jum," he said to his pal, as soon as he got inside, "we've dropped in for a very good thing."

"Iss," ejaculated Jum.

"I sees my way clear now back to Whitechapel," continued Bill; "but we must be werry pertickler, 'cos we've got a tickerlish job to do in gettin' th' young lady wit'out Mister 'Oward knowin' anythink erbout it."

Jum promised to be cautious, and produced a small bottle full of a dark-coloured liquid.

"Dis do de trick ; dis am poison," he chuckled.

"The very thing," responded Bill. "I shall want yer to lend me that."

Jumbo hesitated a moment.

"It bery good stuff ; gib deal trouble to make," he said, as if he hardly liked to part with it.

"What er that ? Jest consider what a deal er good you're a-goin' to get by it," suggested the Bow-legs.

"Ah, iss. Den dere am de bottle ; dere 'nough dere p'ison eber so many."

Bow-legged Bill eagerly clutched the vial.

From the moment his fingers clasped it he felt himself secure.

"Better do the job quiet in this 'ere way," he said, in a complacent, satisfied tone. "P'ison makes no noise—guns does. Don't you see that ?"

Jumbo nodded expressively.

"Now, mind," said Bill, as a final exhortation, "yer must be pertickler in yer conduc'. Yer must seem to be as jolly as a sandboy, so as Mr. 'Oward don't suspec' nothink. Mind an' be outer-the-common jolly."

"Iss, me be bery jolly," grinned Jumbo, and commenced chanting at once an Abyssinian comic song.

In the midst of it Richard Howard entered.

No one, to look at him, would have guessed the deadly thoughts that were in his heart at that moment.

If his followers were wearing a mask, so also was their master.

"You're merry to-day, my boys," he said, good-humouredly ; muttering, however, to himself—"Treacherous vipers."

"Yes, guv'nor," returned Bill in the most genial of tones ; "our sperrits is up wonderful. It's all right," he thought ; "he don't suspec' nothink."

Dinner passed over in a jovial manner. Richard Howard even indulged his colleagues with several bottles of African port.

He himself, too, drank more than he was accustomed to do ; perhaps, to nerve himself for the work that lay before him.

Bow-legged Bill, though he strove hard to conceal his feelings by an assumption of extra jollity, was beginning to feel extremely anxious.

Moment after moment was flitting by, and he saw no chance of mixing the poison with the wine.

Richard Howard, who divined exactly what was passing in his mind, gloated over the anxiety he knew him to be suffering.

He had already determined on his own course, and was perfectly calm and self-possessed.

Suddenly Howard exclaimed—

"Come, boys, our spirits are flagging, and no wonder, for, see ! the source that supplies them is dried up."

He turned the bottle upside down as spoke. Bow-legged Bill breathed again. His chance had come at the eleventh hour.

"Will it run to another bottle, guv'nor ?" he asked.

"Of course it will," returned his master, cheerfully. "Go to the cellar and fetch one."

Bill was on his legs in an instant.

"Like a blessed shot," he cried. "Come along, Jum, ole son, and 'old th' light."

As their footsteps died away, Richard Howard rose and approached a small closet in the room.

This he opened, and, taking thence a small axe, thrust it into his belt underneath his coat, which concealed it.

Having secured his weapon, he returned leisurely to his seat.

Bow-legged Bill was holding a brief conference with his confederate in the cellar.

"The bis'ness is a-goin' on now as right as th' bank," he said, with a beaming countenance, as he uncorked the bottle he held and poured half the contents of the poison-vial into it.

"Yah, yah, yah !" grinned Jumbo.

"Now, mind," continued Bill to him,

"be sure and don't taste this on no account."

When they returned to the room they found Richard Howard calmly smoking his pipe.

"Ha, there you are," he said. "Now, fill me a bumper, and yourselves too."

Bill filled his master's glass, but said he would have a little brandy himself.

"Good 'ealth, guv'nor," he cried, ironically. "May yer live till yer dies, an' I bury yer."

"Thank you," returned Richard Howard, in thick, muffled tone. "I—why, who—what's the—the matter with me?"

His eyes closed, and he nodded drowsily.

"The matter is that ye're a gone coon, Mister Richard 'Oward!" shouted Bow-legged Bill. "Th' matter is yer've took poison, an' in two minutes yer'll be orff to sleep, an' never wake agin."

Howard uttered a cry of assumed despair.

"Oh, villain!" he gasped; "trai——"

His voice died away, and he fell back in his chair, thrusting his hand into his vest convulsively, as if struggling for breath, but really to grasp the handle of the keen axe he had concealed. The next moment he lay motionless.

"That job's finished," said Bill, with intense satisfaction. "Mr. 'Oward will never trouble any one agin."

"You go fetch de young lady now?" asked Jumbo.

"Yes. Wait 'ere till I calls yer."

With these words Bow-legged Bill departed on his errand.

Jumbo turned away, and went to the cupboard for some tobacco.

The supposed victim of poison instantly rose, and with noiseless steps followed close behind him, and as he opened the door, Richard Howard drew forth his weapon.

"Die, black dog!" he hissed from between his teeth as he struck him.

The blow was delivered with such energy that the unfortunate Jumbo fell forward a lifeless, huddled-up heap.

"Number one," said Howard, coolly, as he closed the door; "and now for number two."

Bow-legged Bill, to whom this remark referred, was just at that moment, with a lighted brand in his hand, drawing the bolt of Elinor Cleveland's prison.

"Don't be afraid, miss," he said, as he entered her apartment; "it's only me."

"What do you want?" she asked after a moment.

"I'm come to take yer to yer friends, miss," responded Bill, respectfully.

"My friends?" echoed Elinor, mournfully; "alas! I have no friends now. Of whom do you speak?"

"Why, of Captain Blunt, miss, and the 'ole lot."

"And are they really near at hand?" asked Elinor, eagerly, her pale face flushing with hope.

"It's a moral they is, miss," Bill assured her; "yer've only got to come along er me, and I'll take yer to 'em."

But the young girl had no confidence in the speaker, and she hesitated.

"Where is your base employer?" she said presently.

Bill grinned as he replied—

"Oh, 'e's all right, miss."

"What do you mean?" asked Elinor.

"Why, I mean 'e's asleep," chuckled Bill. "Yer needn't fear erbout him troublin' yer, so come on, I'll take care on yer."

The young lady shrank from accepting the invitation of the rough.

Bow-legged Bill pretty well understood her thoughts; and in order to assure her he quickly said—

"I've took my solemn oath to Mr. Robert Blunt as I'd get you safe out o' this 'ere crib, and I means to keep my word. If yer'll jest come erlong er me yer'll see I'm a-speaking true. Do come."

Elinor still hung back; yet the tone and manner of her rough visitor were earnest.

She could scarcely be worse off than she was, whilst there seemed to be a glimpse of escape before her.

These reflections influenced her, and after a moment, and a brief prayer to Heaven for protection, she said—

"I'll come with you."

"That's right, miss," returned Bill, as he opened the door.

He went out carrying the torch, and led the way to the farm kitchen.

Elinor followed.

On entering, Richard Howard was found motionless in his chair; she shuddered at the sight.

"Are you sure he sleeps?" she whispered.

"Sartin, miss," returned Bill, with a grin and a wink; "so sound as no-think'll ever wake 'im up."

"Is he dead?" exclaimed Elinor, with a look of horror in her face.

The rough nodded.

"That's it, miss," he replied; "Jum an' me settled 'im. 'Ere Jum! Jum! where are yer?"

Jum not appearing in answer to this response, he looked round about for him.

Suddenly his eye was attracted by a thin, dark stream which trickled from under the cupboard door.

"Wh—what th' dooce is that 'ere?" he muttered, with a half start.

"Do you not see?" Elinor Cleveland answered; "it is blood."

"B—blood!" almost gasped Bow-legged Bill; "'ow should there be any blood there?"

As he said this he opened the door, and the mangled corpse of his Abyssinian comrade fell forward with a heavy thud at his feet.

Elinor uttered a cry of horror at the terrible sight; the lower jaw of the rough dropped.

"There's somethink wrong some'eres," he growled to himself; "wot is it?"

As if a sudden thought struck him he turned towards the chair where he had last seen his master.

"Empty!"

Ere he had time to frame this word Richard Howard sprang forward with a bound.

The Bow-legs had only time to turn his head when the weapon descended with terrific force.

A hoarse, stifled cry gurgled in his throat for an instant, and he fell to rise no more.

"Now, madam," said the murderer; "I am at your service."

Scared, and almost stricken into stone with horror, Elinor Cleveland could only gaze in silence at the speaker.

He approached to take her hand.

The dread of contact with him loosed her tongue.

"Fiend!" she cried, "touch me not."

Richard Howard smiled grimly as he grasped her wrist.

"It is time to end this fooling, Elinor Cleveland," he said, insolently; "you are in my power now, and you know it."

"No," returned the young girl firmly; "that you are the stronger I admit, but I trust to Heaven to protect me from your brutality, and I do not fear you now."

With these words she threw him from her, and at the same moment a hoarse shout reached the interior from without.

Elinor uttered an exclamation of joy.

Richard Howard rushed to the window.

The fierce voices burst forth again.

"Death to der murderer! death to der murderer, Richard Howard."

"By Heaven!" muttered the guilty man, turning pale; "it's a body of Dutch boors—I know them by their jargon. What proof can they have against me? and where can they have come from?"

Elinor Cleveland heard the voices, and she shrieked for help.

Richard Howard sprang upon her like a tiger and pressed his hand upon her mouth.

"Hark ye, girl!" he said, in a hurried, desperate tone, "whatever happens I am resolved not to part with you. If I leave this place you go with me. If I must perish we die together!"

Again the hoarse cries for vengeance rose upon the air.

"Death to der murderer of Peter Van Droonk!" cried the voices outside.

In that terrible crisis Richard Howard had determined what to do.

He rushed to the fireplace and snatched a blazing brand from the hearth; then, dragging with him the fragile form of Elinor, he hurried from the room.

Presently he returned.

"Ha, ha!" he laughed, recklessly, as the cries without increased; "roar your lungs hoarse, you Dutch brutes! you'll hear a louder roar presently to keep you company."

At this juncture there was a loud battering heard at the front-door, and a strong smell of burning wood came floating into the chamber.

Bang! bang! fell the blows upon the door; but the beams were thick and massive, and resisted the efforts.

The smoke of the flames, which were now laying hold of the dry wood, began to fill the house.

"The subterranean passage," muttered Richard, as he hurried below with his victim.

Onward he groped his way in the dark till he reached the end.

Here there was a strong door secured by bolts, which led into the air.

This he hastily opened; then, tightening his grip upon the wrist of his fair prisoner, he sprang out.

To his dismay he heard a shout, and found himself seized by the collar.

"Coward! wretch! release her!" cried a voice.

It was the voice of Bob Blunt.

This unexpected meeting checked him suddenly.

His guilty spirit sank within him, and, relinquishing his hold of Elinor, he tore himself free from our hero's grasp, who was occupied with the poor girl who clung to him.

"Seize the villain!" shouted Bob.

His comrades rushed forward, but too late.

Richard Howard had sprung back into the secret entrance and closed and bolted the door.

Hurrying along the passage, he regained the room.

The house was now filled with stifling smoke.

He glanced from the holes in the shutters.

He could see by the moonlight that the farm was surrounded by sternly-resolved faces; amongst them one he had never expected to see again—the face of young Jan Van Droonk.

His bullet had failed to reach a vital part, and, after a long illness, Jan had recovered and come to seek retribution for his father's murder.

A thrill of horror passed through the frame of Richard Howard at the sight of him and his companions.

"No mercy there!" he thought.

Rushing from the apartment, he made his way up the stairs; but here the fumes were denser still.

His position was growing more desperate every moment.

"Curses on this infernal smoke!" he gasped. "I shall suffocate!"

Hurrying to the window, he threw it open. Those without caught sight of him.

A volley of bullets was instantly discharged.

One struck him and shattered the bone of his arm.

A yell of rage and pain burst from him, but it was drowned in the roar of the flames that came rushing up the staircase, urged by the draught.

Faint, sick, and bleeding, the wretched man staggered from the window.

"One effort more!" he muttered, as he hurried up a narrow ladder to a loft.

But in vain he tried to escape.

The fiery element his own hands had kindled pursued him.

He could neither advance nor retreat.

"Mercy! help!" he screamed. "Cousin, save me! I am burning to death!"

His awful shrieks were heard by those without, but none could help him, and his cries were echoed by the stern reply—

"Death to the murderer!"

Then, in one vast sheet of flame, the fire shot up towards the placid, star-lit sky.

The cries ceased.

Richard Howard's turbulent spirit had been burnt out of him at last.

The farm was a heap of glowing ashes, of which his own body formed a part.

*   *   *   *   *

Little more remains to be told.

Elinor Cleveland was restored to our hero, and quickly recovered from the rough treatment she had received.

Our party of explorers returned to the

coast, where they found the English vessel still at anchor.

Captain Allen welcomed them warmly, and on board the "Victoria" they were transported to their native country.

Bob Blunt married the fair girl he loved and settled down on his estate.

For many years he lived the life of an English country gentleman, beloved and respected by all who knew him.

He never forgot his old friends, the companions of his adventures.

His house and heart and purse were ever open to them and annually at the festive Christmas season they assembled together, and, with the yule log on the hearth, and the holly-berries on the wall, once more recalled the stirring incidents in which they had engaged under the burning sun of Tropical Africa.

FINIS.

On Friday, October 13th,

WILL BE PUBLISHED

Nos. 1 and 2 of

JACK & HIS SEVEN FOES.

Beautifully Illustrated.   16 Large Pages Weekly.

No. 2 and a Coloured Picture

FOR BINDING WITH THE WORK,

Given Away with No. 1.

Orders should be given at once to your Bookseller.

"BOYS OF ENGLAND" OFFICE, 173, FLEET STREET, E.C.